Praise for *Legends of the Dragonrealm*

"It's always fun to go back and see where an author started—the raw work, full of energy and with hints of the good things to come. Such is the case with Richard Knaak's *Legends of the Dragonrealm*. All of the ingredients—great world building, memorable characters—that have marked Richard's long and successful career are there, and in reading it, it's easy to see why Richard has enjoyed so much success."

—R. A. Salvatore, *New York Times* bestselling author of
The DemonWars Saga, Forgotten Realms®, and more

"Richard's novels are well-written, adventure-filled, action-packed!"

—Margaret Weis, *New York Times* bestselling author of
Dragonlance Chronicles, Legends, and more

"Richard Knaak's fiction has the magic touch of making obviously fantastic characters and places come alive, seem real, and matter to the reader. That's the essential magic of all storytelling, and Richard does it deftly, making his stories always engaging and worth picking up and reading. And then re-reading."

—Ed Greenwood, creator of the *Forgotten Realms*®

"Endlessly inventive. Knaak's ideas just keep on coming!"

—Glen Cook, author of *Chronicles of the Black Company*

LEGENDS

—+ OF THE +—

DRAGONREALM

VOLUME II

RICHARD A. KNAAK

GALLERY BOOKS

New York   London   Toronto   Sydney

Gallery Books
A Division of Simon & Schuster, Inc.
1230 Avenue of the Americas
New York, NY 10020

First Gallery Books trade paperback edition October 2010

GALLERY BOOKS and colophon are trademarks of Simon & Schuster, Inc.

For information about special discounts for bulk purchases, please contact Simon & Schuster Special Sales at 1-866-506-1949 or business@simonandschuster.com.

The Simon & Schuster Speakers Bureau can bring authors to your live event. For more information or to book an event contact the Simon & Schuster Speakers Bureau at 1-866-248-3049 or visit our website at www.simonspeakers.com.

Manufactured in the United States of America

10 9 8 7 6 5 4 3

ISBN 978-1-4391-9679-3
ISBN 978-1-4391-9860-5 (ebook)

This one's for one great editor, Jaime,
who helped make these collections fantastic!
Thank you!

CONTENTS

N
W   E
S

Sea of Andramacus

Land of the
Hill Dwarves

Gordag-Ai

Elven
Settlements

DAGORA
FOREST

ESEDI

ZUU

LAND OF
QUEL

Legar
Peninsula

THE BARREN

The Dragon Kings and Their Domains

Ice Dragon - The Northern Wastes
Red - The Hell Plains
Blue - Irillian by the Sea
Storm - Wenslis
Black - Lochivar
Crystal - Legar Peninsula
Green - Dagora Forest
Gold - Tyber Mountains

Brown - The Barren Lands
Iron - Unnamed area in the Northwest
      that includes the Hill Dwarves
Bronze - Region that includes Gordag-Ai
Silver - Land that exists below the Tyber Mountains
Talak is bound to Gold's Domain and is just
  south of the Tybers
Penacles is ruled by the Gryphon

The Northern Wastes

Ice Passage

Kivan
Grath

Ruined
City

TYBER MOUNTAINS

IRILLIAN
BY THE SEA

THE HELL
PLAINS

AZRAN'S
CASTLE

TALAK

WENSLIS

Marshland

To the Empire of
the Wolf Raiders

The Lady of
the Amber

MITO
PICA

PENACLES

LOCHIVAR

Serkadian River

LANDS

Eastern Seas

0   200 miles

0   300 kilometers

A JOURNEY AROUND
THE DRAGONREALM

THE DRAGONREALM IS a place of myriad domains and fantastic creatures, and a careful traveler should know much of the land if he wishes to travel it safely. Here, then, are some of the places that you will come across. . . .

The Legar Peninsula thrusts out of the southwest edge of the continent. This is where the burrowing Quel—once masters of the Dragonrealm—live. This mountainous domain is inundated with gleaming crystal formations. Here is the domain of the most reclusive of the Dragon Kings, the Crystal Dragon.

The Sea of Andramacus: The violent waters west of the Dragonrealm. Little is known of them, but legend has it that they were named for a demon. . . .

Land of the Hill Dwarves: There is no true name for this region, but the hill dwarves are said to live in the eastern part of the region and the ambitious Iron Dragon rules without mercy.

Esedi lies southwest of the Iron Dragon's realm. This is where the Bronze Dragon holds sway and the human kingdom of Gordag-Ai is situated.

The Kingdom of Zuu: This other human kingdom is located southwest of Esedi and deep in a valley that is bound to the edge of the vast, magical Dagora Forest, situated in the center of the continent. The people of Zuu are famed for their horses. . . .

The Dagora Forest: This far-stretching forest is where most elves are said to live and where the more benevolent Green Dragon rules.

Mito Pica: A human kingdom lying east of the Dagora Forest and at the edge of the Hell Plains, Mito Pica holds a secret that will change the history of the Dragonrealm. . . .

The Hell Plains: To the northeast lies the volcanic Hell Plains, ruled by the Red Dragon. Here, it is rumored, also lies the castle of the foul sorcerer Azran Bedlam. It is guarded by the Seekers, an avian race once masters, but now slaves.

The Silver Dragon rules the unnamed land to the north of the Dagora Forest. He serves also as confidant of the Dragon Emperor, but covets his position.

The Tyber Mountains are situated north of that and include the mountain citadel of the Gold Dragon, also known as the Dragon Emperor. The mountains are riddled with deep caverns.

The Kingdom of Talak lies at the base of the Tyber Mountains. Though somewhat independent, it is supposed to show fealty to the Gold Dragon. Its ruler is Rennek IV, but his son, Melicard, is already taking much of the reins.

The Northern Wastes may be found far north of the Tyber Mountains. They are home to many great burrowing creatures and are the domain of the Ice Dragon.

The Barren Lands lie south and southeast of the Dagora Forest. Once lush, they were destroyed in a magical upheaval during the Turning War. What remains is ruled by the bitter Brown Dragon.

The Kingdom of Penacles, east of the Barren Lands, is no longer ruled by a Dragon King. Instead, during the Turning War, it was liberated by forces led by the Gryphon, a unique creature who resembles the mythic beast. He now rules, but must constantly be on guard against the Dragon Kings. The Serkadian River runs north to south next to Penacles.

The mist-enshrouded land of Lochivar, east of Penacles, is ruled by the Black Dragon. It is said he has dealings with the Wolf Raiders, who come from a land across the eastern sea.

Wenslis is a rain-drenched kingdom under the rule of the Storm Dragon, whose domain is north of both Penacles and Lochivar. The most vain of the Dragon Kings, the Storm Dragon thinks himself a god.

Irillian by the Sea, ruled by the Blue Dragon, is northeast of the Storm Dragon's lands. An aquatic being, the Blue Dragon is not as benevolent as his counterpart in the Dagora Forest, but sees use in humans and has allowed them to be an almost-equal part of his kingdom. He has, of recent times, had dealings with the Gryphon, much to the frustration of many of his kind.

These are but some of the fantastic places a traveler will discover. The Dragonrealm is a place in flux, and new and ancient wonders are revealing themselves. . . .

INTRODUCTION

WHEN SIMON & Schuster published the first three novels of the Dragonrealm series as the trade omnibus *Legends of the Dragonrealm*, I naturally hoped there would be enough interest from the readers for a second volume. Little could I imagine how much interest! The first volume quickly went into a second, third, then fourth printing. People began contacting me on my website looking for information on the stories that followed and asking if they would be included in another collection.

I'm happy the wait was not a long one. It's been a tremendous pleasure to return to these stories and visit again with some of my favorite creations: Cabe Bedlam, the heir to a legacy of magic with both its bright and dark sides; Gwen, the Lady of the Amber and Cabe's wife; Gryphon, part man, part avian, part leonine; and the unique figures of Darkhorse and Shade.

It's Darkhorse and Shade who truly bind the stories in this omnibus together. Not only because they are present throughout but because of what we learn about two of the most powerful—not to mention nigh immortal—beings in all the Dragonrealm.

Those awaiting their return after their abrupt departure in *Firedrake* should enjoy their equally abrupt return in *Shadow Steed*. However, this is no happy homecoming. Not only does the shadowy stallion become embroiled in the machinations of a bitter king but he must also deal with Shade, whose personality has become more erratic than ever. Add to this the plotting of a Dragon King and the inner struggle of a princess who may be Darkhorse's only hope and we have quite a story, indeed.

The next two tales take a very different turn from those presented before. In the world's distant past—and, in fact, beginning beyond that world in *The Shrouded Realm*, we meet the progenitors of the humans living in the Dragonrealm, the powerful Vraad. However, the Vraad suffer a great hubris that is about to meet with a new reality. Their legacy will touch the future of the

Dragonrealm in more ways than one, especially the choices of Dru Zeree and the unfortunate Gerrod Tezerenee.

And then there's what Dru discovers in the empty realm beyond his world and the Dragonrealm . . .

And in *Children of the Drake*, we discover the ultimate truth behind the rise of the Dragon Kings and how the world of the Dragonrealm has, in many ways, come full circle.

Also included in this volume is the novella *Skins*, previously available only as an eBook. Fans of *Wolfhelm* will recognize its protagonist, Morgis, son of the Blue Dragon. I had always wanted to return to this character and give some hint of what happened after the novel, and now I'm very happy to share it with readers as a bonus tale!

Lest the reader think these stories merely background, be assured that what happens affects this world long, long after in Cabe's time. I hope to return again to write about those stories. . . .

Welcome back to the Dragonrealm!
Richard A. Knaak

SHADOW STEED

I

Y OU WILL RAISE me a demon.

The words were seared into Drayfitt's mind. The chilling visage of his monarch haunted him still. There had never been any doubt that the king had been serious. He was a humorless, bitter man who had, over the last nine years since his horrible disfigurement, become everything that he had at one time despised. The palace reflected that change; where once it had been a bright, proud structure, it was now a dark, seemingly unoccupied shell.

Yet, this was Drayfitt's ruler, the man who represented what he had sworn his loyalty to more than a century before. Thus, the gaunt, elderly man had simply bowed and said, "Yes, King Melicard."

Ahh, Ishmir, Ishmir, he brooded. *Why could you not have waited until my training was complete before you flew off to die with the other Dragon Masters? Better yet, why did you have to train me at all?*

The chamber he occupied was one of the deepest beneath the palace and the only one suited to the task at hand. The seal on the door had been that of Rennek II, Melicard's great-great-grandfather and a man known for dark tastes. The chamber had been cleaned so that Drayfitt could make his marks, etch the lines of the barrier into the floor. The cage, a thing of enchantment, not iron, filled much of the room. He was uncertain as to what dimensions a demon might possess, and much of what he did was guesswork, even with the aid of the book Quorin had located for the king. Still, Drayfitt had not outlived most of his contemporaries by leaping blindly into things.

The room was dark, save for a single torch and two dim candles, the latter necessary for reading the pages of the tome. The flickering torch raised demons of its own, dancing shadows that celebrated the coming spell with gleeful movements. Drayfitt would have preferred the place brilliantly lit, if only for his own nerves, but Melicard had decided to watch, and darkness preceded and followed the king wherever he stalked. Shifting, the ancient sorcerer could feel the strength of Melicard's presence behind him. His lord and master was obsessed—obsessed with the destruction of the Dragon Kings and their ilk.

"How much longer?" Melicard's voice throbbed with anticipation, like a child about to receive a favorite candy.

Drayfitt glanced up. He did not turn to his ruler, but rather studied the design in the floor. "I am ready to begin, your majesty."

The voice of Quorin, the king's counselor, abruptly cut through the sorcerer's thoughts like a well-honed knife. Mal Quorin was the closest thing Talak had to a prime minister since the demise of old Hazar Aran, the last man to hold the position, two years ago. The king had never replaced him, though Quorin did nearly everything the prime minister was supposed to do. Drayfitt hated the counselor; it was the short, catlike man who had first reported to Melicard that there was a spellcaster in the city—and one sworn to the king. If there was any justice, any demon he succeeded in summoning up would demand the counselor as a sacrifice—if a demon could stomach such a foul morsel.

"One was beginning to wonder, Drayfitt, if your heart was in this. Your loyalty has been . . . cool."

"If you would like to take my place, Counselor Quorin, I will be happy to let you. I certainly would not want to stand in the way of someone obviously more well-versed in sorcery than myself."

Quorin would have replied, always seeking the last word, but Melicard cut him off. "Leave Drayfitt to his task. Successful results are all that matter."

The king supported Drayfitt—for now. The old man wondered how long that support would last if he failed to produce the creature his liege desired. He would be lucky to keep his head much less his quiet, simple position as Master of Appointments. Now, the latter was probably lost to Drayfitt, success or not; why waste a man of his power on a minor political post even if it was all Drayfitt had ever wanted?

Enough dreaming of things lost! he reprimanded himself. The time had come to summon the demon, if only to tweak the well-groomed mustache of Quorin.

Neither the king nor his counselor understood how simple the summoning itself actually was. There had been times when he had been tempted to tell them, to see the disbelief on their faces, but his brother had at least taught him that the secrets of sorcery were the most precious things a mage owned. To maintain his position and to counterbalance those like Quorin, Drayfitt had to build himself up as much as possible. It would have been laughable if it had not been so tragic. There was a chance that success might get them all killed. The barrier might *not* hold whatever it was, if anything, he summoned.

Raising one hand in a theatrical manner he had practiced long and hard to perfect, Drayfitt touched the fields of power with his mind's eye.

The summoning was simplicity itself; surviving the encounter with whatever happened to be snared was another matter.

"Drazeree's ghost!" Quorin blurted in growing fear.

Drayfitt would have smiled, had he heard the outburst, but his mind was on the link he had created. There was only the link—no chamber, no king, not even his own body. He was invisible—no—formless. It was an experience that he had never before achieved and the wonder of it almost proved fatal, for in maintaining his link with the spell, he nearly broke the one binding him to his mortal form. When the sorcerer realized his error, he immediately corrected it. A lesson learned, Drayfitt realized . . . almost too late.

Before him, the stream of light that was the mental representation of his bond disappeared into a gleaming tear in reality. He knew that the tear was visible to the king and Counselor Quorin, a sign of success for them to mull over while he moved up. If failure greeted him at any point onward, he hoped that Melicard would realize that he had tried his best, that he had proved his loyalty.

A cold presence with a feel of great age grazed the outer boundaries of his seeking mind. Ancient was not a satisfactory description for such a creature. A desire to abandon the summoning washed over Drayfitt, but he fought it, understanding that it was a ploy by the creature he had snared. The analogy of a fisherman who has caught the grandfather of all sea monsters did not escape him. What he had snared was powerful—and very reluctant to the notion of being forcibly brought to Drayfitt's world. It was ready to fight him with all weapons available to it.

Some would have fought the demon here, in this place with no name, but Drayfitt knew that he could only bind his catch if he battled it from the physical as well as the spiritual planes. The earth, whose existence was interwoven with both the fields of power and his own life, was his anchor.

As he retreated toward his body, the sorcerer was amazed at the ease with which he drew the demon after him. The struggle was far less than he expected, almost as if the demon had some strong bond of its own with his world, a bond it could not deny. That a thing spawned out *there* could have any tie with the mortal plane disturbed him. The thought of a trap occurred to him, but it was a brief notion. Such a trap was too daring; the closer they moved back to Drayfitt's domain, the more difficult it would be for the demon to free itself.

The sorcerer felt the creature's growing frustration. It *was* fighting him—constantly—but like someone forced to do battle on a number of fronts. Had they met on equal terms, both with their respective abilities intact, the elderly sorcerer knew that he would have been no more than a breath to his adversary. Here, the battle was in Drayfitt's favor.

The return seemed endless, far longer than when he had departed his body.

As he finally neared his goal, he was struck by a great wave of panic emanating from the demon. The link stretched as he had not known it could and, for a moment, it felt as if part of the demon had *broken away.*

Nonetheless, his prey was with him. Body and mind began to meld. Other things—sounds, pressures, odors—demanded a measure of his attention.

"He's *stirring* again!"

"You see, Quorin? I told you he had not failed. Drayfitt is loyal to me."

"Forgive me, my liege. Three hours we've stood here, waiting. You said he'd dare not die and, as usual, you were correct."

The voices echoed from a vast distance, as if the spellcaster were hearing them through a long, hollow tube . . . yet, both men surely stood nearby. Drayfitt allowed his senses time to recover and then, still facing the magical cage he had created, opened his eyes.

At first glance he was disappointed. The rip in the middle of empty space still remained and nothing stood within the confines of the barrier. Around him, the shadows still danced merrily, among them the two distended forms of his companions. The shadows of the king and the counselor loomed over his head while his own seemed to crawl across the floor and up a good piece of the far wall. Most of the pattern that he had drawn on the floor was smothered in darkness as well.

"Well?" Quorin asked testily.

The link still remained, but it no longer extended beyond the tear, instead twisting uselessly back into the shadowy regions within the boundaries of the magical cage. The rip was already closing. Drayfitt, confused, stared at the empty scene for several seconds. He *had* succeeded—at least all indications pointed to that. Why, then, did he have *nothing* to show for his efforts?

It was then he noticed the difference between the flickering dancers on the walls and the stillness of the inky darkness within the barrier. The shadows did not move when they should and even appeared to have depth. Drayfitt had the unnerving sensation that to stare too long was to fall into those shadows—and never stop falling.

"Drayfitt?" The king's confidence was turning to uncertainty tinged with burgeoning anger. He had not yet noticed the difference in the shadows.

The gaunt sorcerer slowly rose, a wave of his hand indicating that silence was needed. With one negligible thought, he broke the link. If he was mistaken and there was no demon, Melicard would soon have his hide.

Stepping nearer—though not so near that he was in danger of accidently crossing the barrier—Drayfitt examined the magical cage with a thoroughness that left the king and counselor fidgeting. When Drayfitt saw the shadows twist away, he knew he had succeeded.

There *was* something in his trap.

"Do not try to play me for a fool," he whispered defiantly. "I know you are there. Show yourself—but beware of trying any tricks! This cage has *surprises* designed just for your kind, demon!"

"What's that you're doing?" Quorin demanded, starting to step forward. It was clear he still assumed that Drayfitt had failed and that the sorcerer was now stalling in the hopes of saving his neck.

"*Stay where you are!*" Drayfitt commanded without looking.

The counselor froze, stunned by the sheer intensity of the spellcaster's tone.

Turning his attention back to the barrier, the elderly man repeated his earlier command, this time for the other two to hear. "I said show yourself! You will obey!"

He waved a hand in the air, using it to guide the lines of power to the results he wanted. He was not disappointed.

It *howled!* The noise was so horrifying that Drayfitt's concentration all but broke. Behind him, Quorin swore and stumbled back. Whether Melicard was also shaken, the sorcerer could not say. Even the king had his limits. As the ringing in his ears died down, Drayfitt wondered if everyone in the palace—everyone in *Talak*—had heard the demon's howl of pain. He almost regretted what he had done . . . but he had to show the creature who was master. So it had always been written.

At first, he did not notice the darkness draw inward, thicken even, if such a thing was possible. Only when the first limbs became recognizable—and then the fact that there were *four* of them, all legs—did he fully appreciate his success. The demon had finally, completely, bowed to his will.

The three men stood mesmerized by the transformation occurring before them. Forgetting their uncertainty, the king and counselor joined Drayfitt near the outer edge of the barrier and watched as a trunk joined the legs, and a long, thick neck stretched forth from one end, while a sleek, black tail sprouted from the other.

A *steed!* Some sort of ghostly steed! The head coalesced into a distinct shape, and Drayfitt amended his opinion. It was more like the *shadow* of some great horse. The body and limbs were distended, changing as the demon moved, and the torso . . . The spellcaster again had the uneasy feeling that if he stared too long he would fall *into* the demon and keep falling forever and ever. Anxious to rid himself of the idea, he turned his head, only to find the face of the king.

Unaware of the sorcerer's nervous gaze, the disfigured king giggled at the sight of his new prize. "You have done me a *wondrous* service, Drayfitt! This is all I asked for and more! I have my demon!"

With a smooth, swift motion, the huge head of the dark steed turned to face the trio. For the first time, the ice-blue eyes became noticeable. Drayfitt returned his gaze to his prisoner. He shivered, but not nearly so much as he did when the demon arrogantly shouted, "You mortal fools! You *children!* How *dare* you pull me back into this world! Don't you realize the havoc you've brought forth?"

Drayfitt heard a sharp intake of breath from beside him and knew immediately that Melicard was mere moments from one of his fits of rage. Not wanting the king to do something foolish—something that might release the demon in the process—the spellcaster shouted back, "Silence, monster! You have no rights here! By the spells I have performed, you are my servant and will do my bidding!"

The black horse roared with mocking laughter. "I am not quite the demon you originally sought, little mortal! I am more and I am less! You caught me because my link to this world is stronger than that of any creature of the Void!" The steed's head pressed against the unseen walls of his cage, eyes seeking to burn through Drayfitt's own. "I am the one called *Darkhorse*, mage! Think hard, for it is a name you surely must know!"

"What is he talking about?" Quorin dared to mutter. He had one hand pressed against his chest, as if his heart were seeking escape.

In the dim torchlight, neither of his companions could see Drayfitt's face grow ash white. He knew of Darkhorse and suspected the king did as well. There were legends, some only a decade old, about the demon steed, a creature whose former companions included the warlock Cabe Bedlam, the legendary Gryphon, and, most frightening of all, the enigmatic, cursed immortal who called himself Shade.

"Darkhorse!" the sorcerer finally succeeded in uttering, as a whisper.

Darkhorse reared high, seemingly ready to burst through the ceiling. In a mixture of regret and anger, the demon steed retorted, "Aye! Darkhorse! Exiled by choice to the Void in the hopes of saving this mortal plane from the horror of a friend who is also my worst enemy! This world's worst nightmare!"

"Silence him, Drayfitt! I want no more of this babbling!" Melicard's voice had a dangerous edge to it that the spellcaster had come to recognize. He feared it almost as much as he feared what now struggled within the barrier.

"Babbling? If only it were so!" Darkhorse shifted so that it was now the king who faced his inhuman glare. "Don't you listen? Can't you understand? In summoning me back, you've pulled him along, for I was *his* prison! Now he roams free to do whatever ill he so desires!"

"Who?" Drayfitt dared to ask, despite the growing rage of his liege at the lack of obedience. "Who is it that I have accidently released?" It was the thing he had feared all during the preparations, that he would accidently loose some demon on the Dragonrealm.

Darkhorse turned his massive head back to the sorcerer and, oddly, there was a sadness inherent in both the chilling eyes and the unholy stentorian voice. "The most tragic being I have ever known! A friend who would give his life and a friend who would take yours without a second's care! A demon and a hero, yet both are the same man!" The spectral horse hesitated and quietly concluded, "*The warlock Shade!*"

II

So *DIFFERENT FROM Gordag-Ai. So big!*

Erini Suun-Ai peered through the curtain of her coach window, ignoring the worried looks of her two ladies-in-waiting. A light wind sent her long, blond tresses fluttering. The breeze was pleasantly cool against her pale, soft skin and she leaned into it, directing the delicate, perfect features of her oval face so that the wind stroked every inch. Her dress, wide, colorful, and flowing, made it impossible to sit directly next to the window, and Erini would have preferred to take it off, hating it the way it ballooned her slim figure.

Her ladies-in-waiting whispered to one another, making disparaging remarks. They did not care to see their new home, the huge, overwhelming city-state of Talak. Only duty to their mistress made them come. A princess, especially one destined to be a queen, did not travel alone. The driver and the cavalry unit escorting her did not count; they were men. A woman of substance travelled with companions or, at the very least, servants. Such was the way of things in Gordag-Ai, in the lands once ruled by the Bronze Dragon.

Erini's mind was unconcerned with things of her former homeland. Talak, with its massive ziggurats and countless proud banners flying in the wind, was her new home, her kingdom. Here, after a suitable courtship, she would marry King Melicard I and assume her duties as wife and co-monarch. The future held infinite possibilities and Erini wondered which ones awaited her. Not all of them would be pleasant.

The coach hit a bump, sending the princess back against her seat, her companions squealing with ladylike distaste at the rough road. Erini grimaced at their actions. They represented her father, who had made the marriage pact with the late, unfortunate King Rennek IV almost eighteen years ago. Melicard had been a young boy just growing into manhood and she a newborn babe. Erini had met Melicard only once, when she had been perhaps five, so she doubted his impression of her had been very favorable.

What made all three of them nervous were the rumors that floated about the Dragonrealm as to the nature of Melicard. There were those who called him a fanatical tyrant, though none of his own people ever talked that way. There were rumors that he trafficked with necromancers, and that he was a cold, lifeless master. Most widespread of all were the horrible tales of his appearance.

"He has only one true arm," Galea, the stouter of the two companions, had whispered at one point. "They say that he cut it off himself, so as to wear that elfwood one he now sports."

"He has a lust for the worst aspects of sorcery," Magda, plain but domineering, uttered sagely at another time. "A demon it was that is said to have stolen his face so that the king must always hide in shadow!"

After such horrible statements as these, the two ladies would eye one another with their perfectly matching *Poor Princess Erini!* expressions. At times, they somehow succeeded in looking like twins.

The princess did not know how to take the rumors. She knew it was true that Melicard sported an arm carved of rare elfwood, a magical wood, but not why. Erini also knew that Melicard had suffered some catastrophe almost a decade before that had left him bereft of that original arm and disfigured as well. Even magical healing had its limits at times, and something involved with the incident made it impossible to repair the damage to any great extent. Erini knew she was marrying a crippled and possibly horrifying man, but her brief memories of gazing up fondly at the tall, handsome boy had combined with her sense of duty to her parents to form a determination matched by few.

That did not mean she did not wonder—and worry.

Returning her gaze to the spectacle outside, she studied the great walls. They were gigantic, though the arrogant ziggurats within thrust higher. Against any normal invader, these walls would be unbreachable. Talak, however, had always been in the shadow of the Tyber Mountains, lair of the true master of the city, the late and unlamented Gold Dragon, Emperor of the Dragon Kings. Drakes had little problem with walls, whether in their birthforms or the humanoid ones they wore more often.

Things have altered so much. She had, as a child, understood that, as queen, she would rule beside Melicard but that, at any time, the Gold Dragon might come and make demands of the city. Now, the Dragon Kings were in a disarray; with no heir to take the place of the Dragon Emperor—though there were rumors about something in the Dagora Forest far to the south—Talak was, for the first time, independent.

An army of majestic trumpets sounded, giving Erini a start. The coach made no move to slow, which meant the gates had been opened and they would proceed straight through. The sides of the road began to fill with the locals, the farmers and villagers, some clad in their holiday best, others looking as if they had just come from the fields. They were cheering, but she expected that.

Melicard's advisors would have arranged such a showing. Yet, Erini was somewhat skilled at reading faces and emotions, and in the dirty, worn features of the people cheering her she did see honest hope, honest acceptance. They *wanted* a queen, welcomed the change.

The rumors about Melicard whispered mockingly in the back of her mind. She forced herself to ignore them and waved to the people.

At that moment, the coach passed through the gates of Talak and the rumors were once again buried as Erini devoured the wonders of the inner city with her eyes.

This was the market district. Bright, clashing tents and wagons competed with decorated buildings, many of them tiny, multileveled ziggurats, exact copies of the titans looming over all else. The more permanent structures appeared to be inns and taverns, a cunning move to snare the unwary traveler who might, merely because it was so convenient, end up buying a few extra things from the bazaar. Even *more* banners flew within the walls, most bearing the patriotic symbol of Talak these past nine years: a sword crossing a stylized drake head. Melicard's warning to the remaining drake clans, including the Silver Dragon's, to whose domain the city was now geographically annexed.

Galea and Madga were oohing and aahing over everything, having finally given in to growing curiosity and forgetting that they did not want to be here. Erini smiled slightly at that and returned her attention to her new kingdom.

Clothing styles differed little here, she noted abstractly, though they tended to be even brighter, yet more comfortable in appearance than the bedsheet she was wearing. There was also a propensity toward military uniforms, a confirmation of one rumor that Melicard was still expanding his army. A troop of footsoldiers saluted smartly as she passed, as alike as a row of eggs—with shells of iron. The precision pleased her, though she hoped that there would be no need for all this training. *The best armies are those that never have to fight,* her father had once said.

The coach continued on its way through the city. The market district gave way to more stately structures, obviously the homes of an upper class, either merchants or low-level functionaries. There was a market here as well, but this district was subdued in comparison to that of the more common folk. Erini found this section pleasant to view, but rather lacking in true life. Here, the shadowy masks of politics were first worn. She knew that from this point on reality would be slightly askew. Without hardly being aware of it, her posture stiffened and her smile grew empty. It was time to play the part she had been trained for, even though she had not yet met her betrothed. For the lowest courtiers on up, the princess had to wear a mask of strength. Their loyalty to her depended on their belief in her power.

Power. Her fingers twitched, but she forced them still. In the excitement and then the uneasiness of finally arriving in Talak, she had almost dropped her guard. Erini glanced at her ladies. Magda and Galea were staring at the palace, awed by what was the greatest edifice in the city, and had not noticed the involuntary movements. The princess took a deep breath and tried to steady herself. She dared not trust them with her problem.

What would she do about Melicard, though?

By the time the coach reached the outskirts of the royal palace, she felt she was ready. The turbulence of her tired mind had been forced down again. Now, her only concern was making the proper impression when Melicard came to meet her at the bottom of the palace steps, as was custom.

"Don't these people know anything about protocol?" Magda sniffed imperiously. "The royal steps are all but bare of the members of the court. The entire aristocracy should be here to meet their new queen."

Erini, who had been straightening her clothing out of nervousness, looked up. Pulling aside the curtain of her window, the princess saw what, in her anxiety, she had not noticed before. It was true; there were no more than a handful of people awaiting her arrival and even at a distance the princess could see that none of them matched Melicard's description in the slightest.

The coachman reined the horses to a halt, and one of Erini's footmen jumped down and opened the door for her. As the princess descended, she caught sight of a short, graceful man with odd eyes and stylish mustache who reminded her of nothing less than a pet panther her mother had once bought from a merchant of Zuu. Erini felt an almost instant dislike for the newcomer despite the toothy smile he gave her. This could only be Melicard's counselor, Mal Quorin, a man obviously ambitious. What was *he* doing here instead of Melicard?

"Your majesty." Quorin took the tiny hand that the princess forced herself to thrust out and kissed it in a manner that suggested he was tasting her as a predator might taste its prey before devouring it.

She gave him her most courteous smile and withdrew her hand as soon as he released it. *You will not make a puppet out of me, grimalkin.* His nostrils flared momentarily, but he remained outwardly pleasant.

"Is my Melicard ill? I had hoped he would be here to greet me." She fought hard to keep emotion of any sort out of her words.

Quorin straightened his jacket. His pompous, gray military outfit made him look like a parody of some great general and Erini hoped he was not actually commander of the king's armies. "His majesty begs your forgiveness, princess, and asks that you indulge him in this. I trust you were informed as to his appearance."

"Surely my betrothed would not hide from me?"

The counselor gave her the ghost of a smile. "Until word arrived that you had reached the age of consent set down by your father, Melicard had completely forgotten about the pact. Please don't take it as any offense, lady, but you will find he is still trying to cope with it. His physical . . . detriments . . . only add to the difficulty. He tries to see as few people as possible, you understand."

"I understand far better than you think, counselor. You will take me to King Melicard now. I will not shun him because of his past misfortune. We have been paired almost since my birth; his life, his existence, is my tantamount concern."

Quorin bowed. "Then, if you will follow me, I will escort you to him. The two of you will have a private audience . . . fitting, I should think, for the beginning of your courtship."

Erini noted the hint of sarcasm but said nothing. Mal Quorin summoned an aide who was to assist the princess's people with settling down. Her ladies-in-waiting prepared to follow her but she ordered them to go with the others.

"This is not proper," Magda intoned. "One of us should be with you."

"I think I will be safe in the palace of my husband-to-be, Magda." Erini gave the counselor a pointed glance. "Especially with Counselor Quorin as company."

"Your parents ordered—"

"Their authority ended when we entered Talak. Captain!" The cavalry officer rode up to her and saluted. She could not recall his name, but knew he was inherently obedient to her from past experience. "Please help escort my companions to our rooms. I will also want to see you before you return to Gordag-Ai."

The captain, a thin, middle-aged man with narrow eyes and a hungry look, cleared his throat. "Yes . . . your highness."

Erini pondered briefly his hesitation but knew now was not the time to ask about it. She turned back to Quorin, who was waiting with slight impatience. "Lead on."

Offering his hand, the counselor led her up the long set of steps into the towering palace. As they walked, Quorin pointed out this object and that, relating their histories like a hired tour guide to Erini, who pretended to listen for the sake of appearance. Several aides and minor functionaries fell in behind them, as did a silent honor guard. All very out of place, but the princess had been warned that things had taken a strange turn in the years of Melicard's rule. So far, only Mal Quorin and the king's absence disturbed her.

The palace was spacious to say the least, but much of it had an unused look, as if only a few people actually lived or worked within its walls. It was true that Melicard was the last of his line now, but most rulers still surrounded themselves with a gaggle of fawning courtiers and endless numbers of servants. Melicard, it seemed, maintained only what was necessary.

Has he secluded himself that much? the princess worried. His state of mind concerned her far more than whatever scars he bore physically. On that rested the fate of his kingdom.

"Your majesty?"

Counselor Quorin was studying her curiously and Erini realized they had finally come to a stop at a massive set of doors. Two fearsome guards, hooded, kept a grim watch, armed with axes that stood taller than she did. Erini wondered if they were human.

"I shall be leaving you alone now, Princess Erini. I'm certain you and the king will want your privacy."

She almost wanted him to stay. Now that the princess stood within mere seconds of meeting her betrothed, the potential ramifications of her reaction to Melicard's features struck her dumb. Would hate or pity be the only bond tying the two of them together? She prayed it would not be, yet . . .

Quorin snapped his fingers. The two gargantuan sentinels stepped aside and the massive doors slowly swung inward. Within the chamber was only darkness. Not even a single candle glimmered in invitation.

The counselor turned back to her and his catlike face wore a matching feline smile. "He awaits within, your majesty. You have only to enter."

Those words, coming from him, strengthened Erini as nothing else could have. With a regal nod of her head to Counselor Quorin and the two guards, she walked calmly into the pitch-black room.

Her eyes sought vainly to compensate for the utter lack of light, as the doors slowly closed behind her. Erini fought hard not to turn back to the comfort of the light. She was a princess of Gordag-Ai and soon would be queen of Talak. It would be a disgrace to her ancestors and her future subjects if she showed her growing fear.

Not until the doors had closed completely did she hear the breathing of another within the chamber. Heavy footsteps echoed as somebody slowly walked toward her. Erini's heart pounded and her breathing quickened. She heard the other fiddle with something and then a single match burst into brilliant life, blinding her briefly.

"Forgive me," a deep, smooth voice whispered. "I sometimes grow so accustomed to the shadows that I forget how lost others can be. I shall light us some candles."

Erini's eyes adjusted as the burning match lit a candle sitting on a hitherto unseen table. The match died before she could study the hand that held it, but the one that reached for the candlestick, the left hand, gave her a start. It was silver and moved like the hand of a puppet. Neither it nor the arm it was attached to was made of flesh, but rather some other, stiffer substance that played at life.

Elfwood. The tale was *true!*

Then, the hand was forgotten as the candle was lifted into the air and Princess Erini caught her first glimpse of the man she was to marry.

The gasp that escaped her echoed harshly in the dark chamber.

THE INNKEEPER OF the Huntsman Tavern was a bear of a man named Cyrus who had once had the misfortune of owning a similar establishment called the Wyvern's Head some years ago. The hordes of the drake Lord Toma had ravaged it with the rest of the countryside, concentrating especially on the grand city of Mito Pica, where the powerful warlock Cabe Bedlam had been brought up in secret. Toma had not expected to find Bedlam there and was making the region an example to any who would dare protect, even unknowingly, a potential enemy of the Dragon Kings. Cyrus, along with many other survivors, had taken what he could salvage and made his way to Talak. The people of Mito Pica were welcome in Talak, for Melicard shared their hatred for the drakes. For a brief time, Cyrus had even been one of the raiders the king had supplied in secret, raiders who harassed and killed drakes with the help of old magic. The innkeeper found that he missed his former calling. A good thing, too. It was the raid on the home of Bedlam and his bride that had led to the king's maiming. The objects of the raid, the late Dragon Emperor's hatchlings, had completely escaped Melicard's grasp.

In all that time and the time that passed after, Cyrus had never told a soul that the warlock Bedlam had once been a serving man in his inn. The beginning of the end of his first inn was etched in his mind. It had started with a vague image. The image of a cloaked and hooded man sitting in the shadows, waiting silently for service . . .

Like the man who sat in the corner booth now.

Had his hair not gone gray long ago; Cyrus felt it would have done so now. He looked around quickly, but no one seemed to notice anything out of the ordinary and there was not a blessed soul to wait on the mysterious personage.

Just when I've set me roots down. Wringing his hands, the innkeeper made his way through the crowds and over to the dark table. He squinted, wondering why it was so dark even though there were candles nearby. It was as if the shadows had come with the stranger.

"What can I get ya?" *Make it something quick and easy!* he begged silently. *Then leave, by Hirack, while I've still got a place!*

The left hand, gloved, emerged from the enveloping cloak. A single coin clattered against the wooden table. "An ale. No food."

"Right away!" Thanking Hirack, a minor god of merchants, Cyrus retrieved the coin and hustled back to the counter, where he swiftly overfilled a mug. He would give the warlock the ale, the fellow would drink it, and the innkeeper would bid him a fond farewell. In his haste, Cyrus bumped several customers and spilled ale on a few more, but he did not notice. Nothing mattered but to serve his unwanted guest and get as far away as possible.

"Here ya go!" He slammed the ale down right in front of the figure and made to leave, but the hand, with astonishing speed and bone-crushing strength, caught his own and trapped him there.

"Sit down a moment." The slight amusement in the hooded one's tone made Cyrus go pale. He sat down with a heavy thud. The warlock released his hand, almost as if daring the innkeeper to run away.

"What city is this?"

It was an odd question, seeing as how a spellcaster of all people should know such a simple thing. Despite that thought, however, Cyrus could not stop himself from responding immediately. "Talak."

"Hmmm. I noticed a commotion earlier. What was the cause?"

Cyrus blinked in a mixture of fear and shock as his mouth formed the answers without his aid. "King Melicard's betrothed, the Princess Erini of Gordag-Ai, arrived only today."

For the first time, the figure in the dusky hood reacted. Cyrus was certain it was confusion despite being unable to make out the warlock's features. He had been trying to see the man's face for several seconds, but there was something wrong with his eyes, for the other's visage never seemed in focus.

"'King Melicard'? What's happened to Rennek IV?"

"Rennek died some time back. He spent the last part of his life mad as a sprite." *Where had this man been that he didn't know something common knowledge to everyone else?*

"I've been far, much too far away, innkeeper."

Cyrus shook as it hit him that he had not asked the question out loud.

The warlock reached over and touched Cyrus on the forehead with one gloved finger of his right hand. "There are people of importance that I would know more about. You know their names. Tell me and I will let you return to your business."

It was impossible *not* to tell the hooded figure what he knew. The names that flashed through Cyrus's unwilling mind frightened him, so powerful and deadly the bearer of each one was. His mouth babbled tale after tale about each, mostly from things he had heard from patrons, much of it forgotten until now.

Finally, it ended. Cyrus fearfully felt himself black out.

* * *

THE WARLOCK WATCHED with little interest as the innkeeper, his mind fogged, rose from the table and returned to his duties. The mortal would remember nothing. No one would recall that he had been here. He could even stay long enough to finish the ale, something he had not had in ten years. The long lapse made the drink even sweeter.

Ten years, Shade thought as he stared into his mug. *Only ten years have passed. I would've thought it longer.*

Memories of endless struggling in the nothingness that had been his prison, the prison that was a part of his enemy and his friend, flashed through his mind. He had thought he would never touch the earth again.

Ten years. He took another sip of ale and could not help but smile again at circumstances. *A small price to pay, actually, for what I've gained. A very small price to pay.*

Shade put a hand to his head as a sharp pain lanced through his mind. It was as short-lived as the others he had experienced since his return, and he ignored it once it had passed. The warlock took another sip. Nothing would mar his moment of triumph, especially an insignificant little pain.

III

THE SINGLE TORCH, left by the mortals, had long ago burned itself out, but Darkhorse had no need of such things, anyway. He did not even notice when the light sputtered and died, so deeply was his mind buried in a mire of concerns, fears, and angers—none of which he had come to terms with yet. What distressed him most was that Shade roamed the Dragonrealm untouched, free to spread his madness across an unsuspecting and, in some ways, uncaring land.

And here I lay, helpless as a newborn, trapped by a mortal fool who shouldn't have the knowledge to do what he's done! Darkhorse laughed low, a mocking laugh aimed at himself. How he continually underestimated human ingenuity—and stupidity.

His pleas of freedom fell on deaf ears and mad minds. Nothing mattered more to Melicard than his quest to rid the realms of the drake clans, whether those drakes were enemies or not. That Shade had the potential to bring the lands down upon them all—human, drake, elf, and the rest—meant nothing to the disfigured monarch.

"What threat is a warlock compared to the bloody fury of the Dragon Kings?" Melicard had asked.

"Have you forgotten Azran Bedlam so soon?" Darkhorse had bellowed. "With his unholy blade, the Nameless, he slew a legion of drakes, including the Red Dragon himself!"

The king had smiled coldly at that. "For that, he had my admiration and thanks."

"They might've easily been humans, mortal! Azran was no less dangerous to his own kind!"

"The creature you call Shade has existed for as long as recorded memory, yet the world remains. If you wish, you may deal with him *after* you have served me. That seems fair."

It was futile to try and explain that always there had been someone to keep Shade in check and that *someone* had more often than not been Darkhorse. Other spellcasters had fought and beaten the warlock, true, but always the shadow steed had been, at the very least, in the background. Now, he was helpless.

"Well, demon?"

In pent-up anger, Darkhorse had reared and kicked at the unbreakable, invisible wall, screaming, "Madman! Can you not hear me? Does your mind refuse to understand reality? Your damnable little obsession will never be fulfilled, and while you muster your fanatics Shade will bring both drake and human down! I know this!"

At that point, King Melicard had turned to the sorcerer beside him and said, "Teach him."

For his refusal to obey, Darkhorse had suffered. The old sorcerer Drayfitt had surprised him again, intertwining a number of painful subspells into the structure of the magical cage. The pain had not stopped until the jet-black stallion had been no more than a mass of shadow huddled on the floor. Finally, Melicard had simply turned and departed, pausing at the doorway only long enough to give some instructions to the spellcaster. With the king had gone the devious one, the mortal who was known as Counselor Quorin.

Alone with the elderly sorcerer, Darkhorse had pleaded his cause once more. Fruitlessly. Drayfitt was one of those men who embodied the worst and best trait of his race: blind loyalty.

And so here I remain, the spectral horse snorted in frustration. *Here I remain.*

"I once suffered a fate similar to the one facing you now," a familiar voice mocked. "Trapped with seemingly no way out. I think you can imagine how I felt."

Darkhorse rapidly drew himself together, all his power preparing for the worst.

The torch was suddenly ablaze again, but its flame was a deep red that bespoke of blood. Amidst the crimson shadows, a cloaked and hooded figure detached itself.

"Shade . . . or Madrac . . ." Darkhorse rumbled. "Come to mock only when you know for certain your hide is safe from harm."

The warlock bowed like a minstrel after a successful command performance. "Call me Madrac, if you will—or any other name, for that matter. I don't care. I've come to tell you something. I sat quietly drinking in a tavern, absorbing life itself for once. I remember, you see. I remember everything from every life. I recall the fatal day, the agony of being torn apart and restored to existence again and again and again! I recall more than I could ever recount to you!"

As long as he had known the human, Darkhorse had known a man condemned. Forever resurrected after each death, whether his body was whole or not, Shade was cursed to live lives alternately devoted to the dark and light sides of his nature. Each was only a shadow of the original spellcaster, however. Memories were so incomplete as to sometimes be nonexistent. Abilities altered. In desperation to be whole, each new personality even took on a secondary name of its own, such as Madrac, hoping that somehow *he* would be the final, immortal Shade. Now, after millennia, something had changed to make that possible. Understanding this, hope briefly spurred Darkhorse. "Then your curse is lifted; you can live in peace."

Shade chuckled bitterly and stepped forward. Raising his hood, he let the shadow steed stare into his face, or rather, the blurry mask that passed for it. "*Not yet*, my dear friend, not yet, but—Madrac is fading and I cannot be certain what sort of persona will replace him. A different one from those past, that much is evident. I felt the need to speak to you, though, to tell you, but . . ."

"If you can free me, I will do what I can for you, Shade."

"Free you? Don't be *absurd*! I rather enjoy the irony of this!"

The tone of the warlock's voice stirred the eternal's misgivings far more than the actual words did. *Has the curse given way to something darker, something much more sinister?* Darkhorse wondered. Shade's personality seemed to be swinging back and forth unpredictably. If the warlock had not been mad before, he soon would be under the pressure of this new torture.

Putting a hand to his forehead as if trying to relieve pain, Shade continued, "I also came to tell you this: I know where my mistake was made—where my spell went awry. I know why the 'immortality' I *did* receive turned out to be a never-ending agony. That can be rectified—this time."

He took a step closer to the magical cage. "You—you can do nothing to deter me. Not while you are trapped here. The spellcaster responsible for your pleasant little domain has touched upon Vraad sorcery to create the cage. Do you know what *that* means?"

Darkhorse did not respond at first, stunned as he was by the warlock's words, especially the last. "I know of Vraad sorcery. It no longer exists in this reality! The Vraad only live on in the seeds of their descendents; their magic has given way to the magic of this world!"

Shade inclined his head in a brief nod. "As you wish. Test the spell your-self—oh"—the spellcaster may have smiled; it was difficult for anyone other than him to know for certain—"that's right. You can't. You're inside, of course, and the patterns are outside, surrounding the barrier."

"Why did you come here, Shade? Merely to talk?"

"I came against my better judgment—but—I felt an overwhelming urge. Call it a whim."

"Call it conscience." Darkhorse retorted quietly.

"Conscience? I no longer have such a wasteful thing!" The hooded warlock stepped back, growing more indistinct with each step. There was always some-thing not quite right, not quite normal, about Shade's magic, but Darkhorse could not say what.

"Enjoy your vast domain while you can, *friend*. When you see me next, if you ever do, I will at last be master of my fate—and so much more."

"Shade—" It was too late; the warlock dwindled away into nothing. The torch died the moment he was gone, plunging Darkhorse into the blackness again. It was the least of his concerns, though. The brief, puzzling visitation by him who was both enemy and friend interested him much, much more.

To say that Shade's return to him was contradictory to what the spellcaster should have done was putting it so mildly that Darkhorse had to laugh. Shade did nothing without reason, even if Shade might not know the reason himself. To simply come to mock Darkhorse was not enough; it was not the warlock's way in any of his countless lives, at least, the ones that the shadow steed knew about.

How old are you really? It was a question he had asked Shade time and again and it blossomed unbidden now, but there was no answer. The spellcaster could never recall. He only remembered a few vague things; that he, an ambitious sorcerer, had tried to gain mastery over powers that were, at the time, known simply as good and evil, dark and light. Perhaps colored by such primitive perceptions, Shade had made some fatal error in the final steps of his master spell. The powers were not his to command; he was theirs to play with. Perhaps the enchantment had even succeeded, but not the way the spellcaster had sup-posed. That still did not answer the question that always bothered the jet-black stallion. *How old was Shade before we first encountered one another? Old enough to recall the Vraad? Old enough to—be one?*

The thought was so insane, he cast it from his mind. Generations upon gen-erations of Dragon Kings had come and gone since the brief, fiery appearance of the Vraad in this world. Humans were their descendants, yes, but nothing more.

All plans of immortality eventually fail. Even for the Vraad they did.

Darkhorse knew he was wandering away from the subject. He returned to the reason behind Shade's brief and mysterious visit. If not to mock his helplessness, then what explanation was there for the warlock's return? A warning? Perhaps. Possibly that and more. Darkhorse laughed low as another choice suggested itself. *Could it be . . . ?*

His thoughts were interrupted by the sound of a key unlocking the chamber door. *This is a busy day! I always thought prison was a lonely place!*

The door swung open with a protesting squeal and torchlight flooded into the room. A guard stepped in and, his eyes focused on any spot *other* than the captive, lit the wall torch. As the human departed hastily, a second figure, tall and familiar, entered the chamber in a much more sedate manner. The gaunt, ancient form waited quietly while another guard, as anxious as the first to be gone, placed a stool midway between the door and the edge of the barrier.

When they were finally alone, Drayfitt spoke. His eyes drifted to a spot to the right of Darkhorse. He seemed a bit preoccupied, as if he could sense that someone else had been in the room. "So . . . demon. Have you reconsidered what my liege has requested of you?"

The shadow steed shifted to his left, trying without success to meet the gaze of the sorcerer. "*That* was a request? Do as he commands—without question— and he *may* free me some day to chase after Shade?"

"He is king and must be obeyed."

"You are well housebroken, spelltosser."

Drayfitt flinched, but he did not shift his gaze. It was apparent he knew what might happen if his eyes locked onto Darkhorse's. "I swore an oath long ago to protect this city. It is my home. Melicard is my lord and master."

"As I said, 'well housebroken'! Every king should have such a loyal pup for a sorcerer!"

"Would that I had never needed to make use of these powers!" Drayfitt's gaze turned upward, toward some memory. Darkhorse cursed silently.

"Why, then, did you?"

"The king needed a sorcerer. Counselor Quorin sought me out, knowing from his spies that I had held one minor political post or another for more than a century, something beyond the lifespan of a normal human, of course. Always before I was able to bury myself in the shuffle of bureaucracy, claim I was my own son or some such lie, and utilize just enough power to make men believe it. I have no desire to follow in my brother Ishmir's footsteps and die fighting the Dragon Kings. I also have no desire to see Talak destroyed, which is a very real threat should the Silver Dragon ever succeed in his claim to the Dragon Emperor's throne."

So many things had happened during the years of Darkhorse's absence that it was difficult for him to say what was the most astounding. That Cabe Bedlam, grandson of the greatest of the Dragon Masters, had bested the Dragon Emperor and fought his own father, mad Azran, to the death cheered the shadow steed, for he had met the young mortal and even travelled with him for a time. The death of the Gold Dragon had broken the drakes; who now could claim the throne of the highest of the Kings was arguable. Cabe Bedlam and his bride, the Lady of the Amber, had been raising the hatchlings of the Dragon Emperor alongside their own children, trying to teach the two races to coexist. Whether the drakes would accept the eldest royal male as their ruler when he finally came of age—whatever age was to a drake—was a question bandied about with no answer as of yet. Meanwhile, at least two of the remaining Dragon Kings had sought the throne of their "brother" on the basis that to wait for the young to mature was too risky, too speculative. Neither of the two could gain sufficient support among their kind, but the Silver Dragon was growing stronger every day. Drayfitt knew that the first step toward reunifying the lands would be to stamp out Talak, the enemy now within Silver's own domain. Having just gained its true independence only a few years ago, the city-state was not going to give in, not while Melicard was king.

"Mal Quorin whispers in his ear at every opportunity, urging him to reckless crusades. Survivors of Mito Pica, the city ravaged by the drake Toma, still call for the blood of the reptiles and their voices are strong. Melicard himself is obsessed with the Dragon Kings. Once discovered, I came to realize that the only way to bring some sense to this chaos was to become an integral part of my liege's court, a voice of reason."

"And so you summoned a *demon*?" Darkhorse responded with false innocence. "Truly you are a master of logic! What genius! Never would *I* have thought of so cunning a plan!"

The sorcerer rose, his brief reverie broken by the stinging words. Almost, he glared at his captive. Almost.

"Mal Quorin would have found another to translate the damnable book! One more flexible to his will! Now, at least, I can control the situation, keep it from growing unchecked!"

"Is this what Ishmir would've done?"

The question was Drayfitt's undoing. Mention of his brother's name gave birth to a rapidly growing rage, a rage coupled with carelessness. He whirled on Darkhorse, intending to punish him for bringing to the surface the thoughts that had been wracking the old man's mind since agreeing to this insane plane. *Would Ishmir have gone through this*; Drayfitt knew the answer and did not like it. He glared at the shadow steed, his gaze making contact with the cold, blue eyes.

Darkhorse froze the sorcerer where he was, seizing control of his unprotected mind. The phantom stallion laughed quietly at the success of his plan, but it was a hollow laugh. Drayfitt was a good, if naive, mortal. Using his brother's name so pained Darkhorse, who had known most of the long-dead Dragon Masters, including Ishmir the Bird Master.

"Forgive me for this, both of you," he muttered, "but I had no choice."

All emotion fell from the spellcaster's face. His arms hung limply. He looked more than ever like a dead man; Darkhorse, who did not want to hurt him, moved cautiously.

"Your mind is mine, mortal! Your soul is mine! I could hurry you along the Path Which Men May Travel Only Once, but I will not! Not if you obey!"

Drayfitt remained motionless, but Darkhorse knew, as only he could know, that, deep within, the sorcerer's subconscious understood.

"You will remove the barrier, and open a gate in this Void-forsaken cage, and let me out! Do so and I will leave you untouched!"

Though his voice boomed, the shadow steed had no fear that the guards outside would give warning. Melicard had ordered Drayfitt to enshroud the chamber in a blanket of silence, meaning that all sounds would pass no further than the walls. A very important guest had arrived and the king, oddly subdued, did not want knowledge of his activities to reach that unknown personage.

The masks of royalty are many, Darkhorse thought snidely. *Who could it be who would make "handsome" King Melicard so nervous?*

Drayfitt worked smoothly, methodically, going through the motions of the spell. Though he no longer had the book, the memory of his first attempt still remained and Darkhorse had drawn that out. Had there been time, he would have had the mortal repeat the steps out loud so that he could study the makings of the spell. Vraad sorcery it was and the black steed was disturbed he had not seen it sooner. Again, had there been time, Darkhorse would have sought out the book—and the one who had discovered it. Vraad sorcery was dangerous, although on the surface it seemed amazingly simple at times.

With a stiff gesture, Darkhorse reversed the outcome of the spell. Instead of creating yet another cage around the first, he tore the present one apart.

The elderly sorcerer lowered his hands and resumed his deathlike stance. Darkhorse took a hesitant step toward the edge of his prison. One limb, stretched to needle-thin, touched the barrier—and passed beyond it. Jubilant, Darkhorse leaped free, not trusting his luck to hold long.

"Freedom! Ahhh, sweet-tasting freedom! Excellent work, my mortal puppet! Most excellent work!" He gazed down almost fondly at the spellcaster. "For that, you deserve a reward of great value, something I think you've lacked these past days! Sleep! Deep, restful sleep! A *long,* restful nap will do you wonders!

When you wake, I want you to do one more thing for me; seek out the source of your Vraad sorcery, this book, and *destroy* it! Rest now!"

Drayfitt slumped to the floor.

With one last, contemptuous scan of the chamber that had been his prison, Darkhorse reared, opened a path to the beyond, and vanished through it.

AS NIGHT PREPARED to give way to day, the object of Darkhorse's desperate quest materialized in the middle of a chamber that was quite a contrast to the one recently forced upon the shadow steed. Though a bit more austere than the personal quarters of King Melicard, they were elegant and, indeed, also fit for a king.

Shade reached out a hand and ran a finger along the edge of a massive, golden couch. A thick layer of dust flew off. The warlock may have smiled. No one had made use of this room in quite some time, years perhaps.

The rumors were true, then. These chambers had once belonged to the Lord Gryphon, inhuman but just ruler of Penacles; the legendary City of Knowledge. Once, the Gryphon had been a comrade, sometimes a friend, but only at those times when Shade could be trusted. The Gryphon had understood him better than most, save Darkhorse. As Shade wiped the dust from his fingertip, he found the almost missed his sometime adversary. The Gryphon was rumored to be somewhere across the Eastern Seas, fighting some war that seemed unwilling to completely finish itself. Despite numerous pleas by various city functionaries, the man he had left in charge, a minor spellcaster of masterful strategy, General Toos, refused to take on the mantle of king. Instead, the general had chosen to become regent, with powers equal to those of the monarch with the unique option of retiring in favor of the Gryphon if and when he returned.

So much the better, Shade decided. He turned in a slow circle, observing each and every object, whether it stood on the floor, was pinned to the wall, or hung from the ceiling. Most things were as he remembered them, even down to the two lifelike metal statues standing on each side of the door. They were iron golems, animated creatures of cold metal created by the former lord of Penacles to guard his personal chambers. Surprisingly swift, the creatures should have been on top of the warlock the moment he materialized. Unlike most intruders, however, Shade had the key to their control.

There were words, implanted deep in their very beings, that, when acknowledged by the golems, made them no more than fanciful statues. Words that Shade had silently flung at them before completely materializing. There were advantages to having once been privy to the secrets of the Gryphon.

The warlock chuckled quietly, then turned to one of the far walls, where the object of his search, a great, intricately woven tapestry of the entire city of Penacles, hung.

That the tapestry hung here, unwanted by the regent, said many things. The artifact was ancient, even older than Shade. He touched it delicately. General Toos had never hidden his dislike for talismans of power, though he tolerated them. The tapestry itself was only a link to another greater wonder, though. Leaning as close as he dared, the warlock slowly studied the pattern. Each and every street, every building, was represented. Despite having been originally weaved during the initial construction of Penacles, the tapestry revealed structures that were no more than a year or two old.

"Even after all this time, you still work flawlessly," Shade whispered. The creator had been a perfectionist and even Shade acknowledged the superiority of this artifact.

For several minutes he scanned the tapestry, seeking a masking that he could not even be certain he would recognize. Like the city, the mark he sought changed over the years. Sometimes, it was a stylized picture of a book. Other times, it had been a single letter. There had been many symbols over the centuries, a number of them highly obscure.

I need your fantastic eyes, Lord Gryphon! You were always able to spot the mark with little more than a glance!

Then, his eyes fell on a tiny, twisted banner, one familiar to him as it would be to no other creature living today. Shade smiled his hidden smile and the blur of face seemed to swirl with emotion. He memorized the location and briefly looked up at the tapestry in open admiration. "One would think you were living, old thing, and, if so, you have a wicked sense of humor! My—my *father*— might even have been amused!"

Father. The warlock shivered. Not all the memories that returned were particularly pleasant ones. He quickly buried himself in his task.

Locating the mark again, Shade rubbed the banner with one finger, and as he did, the room around him began to fade. Shade may have smiled. He continued to rub the mark as the Gryphon's chambers gave way to *another* room of sorts, a corridor. The tapestry, still whole, remained until the living quarters had completely dissipated. Then, it, too, faded away. The warlock was left standing in a corridor whose walls were lined with endless shelves of massive, bound tomes, all identical, even in color. *The tapestry still worked.*

He stood in the legendary libraries of Penacles.

The libraries had been standing long before the city. His memories returning, Shade recalled some of the truth about the odd structure, a building beneath the earth, beneath Penacles, that was larger on the inside than the outside and never to be found in the same location. Its true origins were unknown even to him, but he suspected that, as with the spell that Melicard's sorcerer had used to make Darkhorse's cage, this was Vraad work.

Other than the countless volumes stored here, there was not much to see. The floor was polished marble. The corridor he stood in and those he could see were all illuminated by the same unseen source. The shelves themselves might have been brand new, though Shade knew otherwise. Time seemed not to matter in the libraries.

"You have returned after all this time."

The matter-of-fact statement proved to be issued by a small, egg-headed figure clad in simple cloth garments. His arms almost reached the ground, due in great part to his uncommonly short legs. There was not so much as a strand of hair on his head.

One of the gnomes—or perhaps the *only* gnome—who acted as librarians here. As far as Shade could recall, the libraries had always had gnomes and all of them had been identical in appearance.

"Ten years is not so long to the two of us," the spellcaster mocked, recalling his final visit here with the Lord Gryphon.

The gnome seemed oblivious to the tone of mockery, replying simply, "Ten years, no. A *thousand* years, yes. Even to the two of us."

Though his face was unreadable, Shade's body was not. He stiffened and tried to speak, but was uneasy about his choice of words. The gnome chose to fill the silence.

"What you seek is not here. It is, perhaps, the one piece of knowledge the libraries refuse to contain."

Speaking of the libraries in terms of a thinking creature irritated the warlock. He had no desire to feel as if he were in the belly of a beast. "Then where is it? It exists!"

The librarian shrugged and slowly turned away, a book in one hand. The book had not been there before. "Seek the caverns, perhaps."

"Caverns?"

"Caverns." The gnome turned back to Shade, eyeing him as one might an inept young apprentice. "The caverns of the Dragon Emperor. What is left of the place where it all began for you."

The place where it all began for you. Shade may have smiled, but, if so, it was a grim smile. He had forgotten that. It was a memory only now restored to him and it was, quite possibly, the one he would have most preferred never to recall—even at the cost of his own existence.

IV

ERINI WOKE TO the light of midmorning intruding in her room, her thoughts and feelings a tangled web of half-remembered images and a full gamut of emotions ranging from joy to fear.

The bed was huge and so very soft. She tried to bury herself in it, both physically *and* mentally. Her old bed back home—*no, former home!*—was little more than a piece of wood and a blanket compared to this. The entire room was overwhelming, as vast as any chamber she had seen other than the main hall. Multicolored marble tiles made up the floor, partially obscured by the great fur rugs running to and from the various doorways. Columns thrust upward in each corner, festively decorated with golden flowers. Gay tapestries covered the walls. The furniture, including the bedframe, was carved from the finest northern oak, rare after the destruction of so much forest nine years ago during that horrible, unseasonable winter.

To her dismay, Erini found herself remembering how whole herds of giant diggers, great creatures of fur and claw, had torn their way south, leaving little more than churned earth. The princess shuddered, for they had been no more than a day from her city when a disease or something had killed off all of them within hours. Oddly, that was about the same time that Melicard—

Melicard.

Erini's eyes opened wide as she surrendered to the inevitable and turned her thoughts back to the night before. The princess had expected so many things when she had entered his darkened chamber, the elfwood arm being the *least* of those. Despite its graceful appearance—thanks to some skilled craftsman, no doubt—the arm moved with an awkwardness that would forever remind one it was not real. Even had it been painted so perfectly as to match the king's skin, Erini would have recognized it for what it was.

First seeing that arm in the dim light, however, had subconsciously made her anticipate the worst. That was why, when Melicard had held the light close to his face, Erini had let out a gasp without even actually seeing his features. When her eyes had at last rested on her betrothed and the images had sunk deep enough into her shocked mind, that shock had turned to confusion and, gradually, joy.

Melicard I, king of Talak and once the handsomest of men in her young eyes, had a visage that, Erini at last admitted to herself, was everything she had ever hoped for as a girl growing up. Strong, angular features, athletic, and with a commanding presence befitting his rank. It was a wondrous thing to behold, and the princess was so relieved she almost flew into his arms, barely missing knocking the candlestick from his hand.

Only then, when they were so near to one another, did the unholy nature of his face become evident. If there was a graphic indication of her own reaction to this sudden turn, it was the tightening of his mouth and the narrowing of his eye—*one* eye—when he saw her stumble and pause.

The "accident" that had claimed his arm had claimed much of his face as well, even as rumors had foretold. Because of the ancient magic said to be involved, that face would not heal. Whole sections of skin had been torn away and Melicard had even lost his left eye. When all else failed with his arm, the king had turned to elfwood, rare wood that, legend had it, was cut from a tree blessed by the spirit of a dying elf, and had his artisans carve him a new limb.

He had done the same thing with his face.

Erini, remembering what had followed, pulled the sheets around her. Tears streaked her own features and she whispered, "I'm *sorry!*"

While his bride-to-be stood where she was in what he could only believe to be disgust and horror, Melicard coldly lit other candles from the first. It was evidently his intention to give her the full effect, so positive was he that she loathed him.

"You certainly must have heard enough gabbers' tales about my—difficulties—before making your way here! Is it so much *worse* than even the stories?"

How could she tell him? Erini could not keep her eyes off his face. It *was* the face of Melicard, every curve and angle exactly as it should have been—save that most of the left side was masterfully carved from the same wood that his arm had been, even down to the cheekbone and lower jaw. A third of the nose had been replaced; the elfwood spread as high as the middle of his forehead and as far back as his ear. She was certain that unbuttoning the collar of his dark shirt would reveal more of the same.

The damage had not been confined to the left side, either. His right side was streaked by what almost looked like roots spreading from the left. Three major branches split across his cheek and each had one or two minor appendages as well. So contrasting was the enchanted wood to his own pale skin that the entire patchwork face looked like nothing less than that of a man dying of plague.

"You are free to depart any time, Princess Erini," he said after a time.

She shook her head, unwilling to trust her mouth. Melicard, carefully skirting her, came around and offered her a chair. Erini had been so engrossed in his appearance that she had not even noticed there was furniture, or anything, for that matter, in the room. "If you plan to stay, then please be seated. This should be more comfortable than those coach benches, even a royal coach."

With a whispered "thank you," Erini adjusted her ungainly dress and sat down. The king, moving swift and silent, suddenly leaned before her, a goblet of red wine in each hand. She took the proffered goblet and waited until he was seated in another chair directly across from her before sipping. The wine succeeded very little in steadying Erini's nerves, for her eyes could not leave his face even when she drank.

They sat like that for several minutes. Melicard, whose manner had been as politely cold as his words, drank from his own goblet in silence. With each sip, he seemed to draw deeper into his own mind. The princess wanted to say something, *anything*, to ease his pain and her own guilt, but the words would not come out. She grew angry at herself for becoming one of those helpless, useless maidens the storytellers often created for their fables. Until now, Erini had secretly mocked those pitiful women.

At last, the king set his goblet down and rose. The princess straightened, expecting some announcement, some word from her betrothed as to their future—or even lack of it if that was his desire. To her surprise, Melicard turned and walked to the far end of the chamber, where another door stood. Melicard opened it and, without looking back or even saying a word, stepped out of the room.

Erini stared at the door as it closed behind him, not comprehending immediately what had happened. Only when a liveried servant stepped in from the first doorway did realization sink in.

"If you will come with me, your majesty, I have been commanded to show you to your quarters." Through his manner, the servant verified her fears; Melicard was not returning. The king had read her disgust and pity and had been able to stomach it no longer.

She saw no one other than the servants who fed and cared for her and her two ladies-in-waiting. Galea and Madga pressed her for snippets of information about the king, but Erini would have none of that. After dismissing them politely, she had retired early, the combination of the journey and her trial here too much to bear.

Letting the sun now bathe her, heal her mental wounds, she silently swore an oath. *I must make it up to him somehow! I must show I can care without pitying! Small wonder he acts the way he does if everyone reacts as I did!* Melicard could not be faulted for his efforts, the princess decided guiltily. If his own flesh would not grow back, what was he *supposed* to do? Wear a mask of gold and silver? Leave his own, mangled features visible? In many ways, the elfwood face was the best solution, unnerving as it as. Even the king's sorcerer had come up with nothing better after failing to heal his master's wounds.

Her own fingers began to twitch at the thought and she clasped both hands together in order to fight the urge down. She would *not* succumb. There was nothing the princess could do that others more skilled, others who were *trained*, could not do better.

Erini repeated what had become a chant to her—she was a princess of Gordag-Ai and could never be a sorceress or witch. Never. She was destined to be a queen. No king would trust a witch for a wife. Her own people would not have.

Though she fought it down successfully, Erini shook so badly after that, that she rose and dressed herself, not daring to have Galea or Magda or any of Melicard's people wonder what made her shake. By the time the princess was finished, the danger was past. Erini inspected herself in the vast mirror that overwhelmed the wall opposite her bed and, satisfied, dared to summon a servant. If she succeeded in nothing more today, she would at least eat a decent meal.

NEITHER MELICARD NOR the unsavory Counselor Quorin met her at break-fast. Galea and Magda joined her, but she made some pretext and left them as soon as she was finished. When none of the palace servants seemed to object, the princess began exploring, trying to understand more about Talak and its monarch through the vast building itself. Erini already knew much of the city-state's "official" history, having been educated about her future kingdom most of her life, but there was more, so much more, beneath the surface of the facts that tutors had poured into her. All she had learned about her betrothed had availed her nothing in his actual presence. It was a mistake she did not intend to make a second time.

As lavishly decorated as the palace was, she soon discovered two things. One was that the vast majority of items had been gathered during the reigns of past kings, to the extent that whole wings had been built to house them. The second and more interesting point concerned those few treasures gathered or created during the years of Melicard's rule. Most of the pieces were dark in nature and not a few of them dealt with the death and destruction of foes, especially drag-ons. Faces in portraits were always shadowed or, if they *were* fully revealed, were sinister and even hideous. It did not paint a pretty picture of her betrothed. Erini began to have doubts.

At a window overlooking an interior garden filled with hanging plants and blossoming flowers of all colors, she paused to relax. A noise at the far end of the garden made her look there. Her eyes narrowed at an curious sight. Far below, two guards were carrying a third man between them. As opposed to the tall, muscular soldiers, the unconscious figure in the middle was thin to the point of emaciation and as old as any soul the princess had ever seen. He wore a dark robe with a cowl on it, identifying him from Erini's teachings as

Melicard's sorcerer Drayfitt. The history that the ancient spellcaster had lived through had always fascinated her, but not nearly so much as why Drayfitt now needed to be carried anywhere. She leaned closer.

Erini glanced back at the direction the trio had come from and noticed the small doorway buried beneath the vines of the far wall. The way to the sorcerer's inner sanctum? Possibly, and, if so, it was also possible that his present condition was due to some spell gone awry.

"What's going on here?" a voice that grated on her nerves snarled.

The two sentries paused and, readjusting their unconscious package, saluted Mal Quorin. He ignored protocol and repeated his question in the same vicious tone as before.

One of the guards, his face no longer visible to Erini, nervously replied, "His majesty gave us orders to seek out the sorcerer Drayfitt and find out why he had not reported to the king this morning. When we arrived, the guards on duty let us in, reporting that no one had entered or left since they had been stationed there." The man hesitated before concluding quickly, "He was lying on the floor! We tried to wake him, but nothing worked, my lord!"

Quorin looked at both of them, evidently not satisfied. "There's *more*, isn't there?"

"The *demon* is loose, my lord!" the other guard finally blurted. "Or, at least, it's no longer in the chamber!"

Erini, listening intently and growing more shocked with each word, fully expected the counselor to vent his rage and power on the two hapless soldiers. Instead, he simply stood where he was, staring. Whether he stared at the sentries or into open space, the princess had no way of knowing. At last, the counselor reached forward and, in a move that stunned not only Erini but the soldiers as well, slapped Drayfitt sharply across the face. The elderly spellcaster's head snapped to one side, but he did not wake. Quorin rubbed his hand.

"Be on your way, then. I want to know when he wakes."

"My lord."

Quorin watched calmly until the trio was out of sight and then whirled back in the direction of the vine-covered door. With tremendous, catlike strides, he covered the distance to his objective in mere seconds. The counselor put one hand on the handle and then, as if sensing he were being watched, turned around and glanced upward. Erini, however, anticipating such a move, was already flattened against a wall.

She counted more than twenty breaths before she dared to look. Mal Quorin was gone, evidently having decided he did not have the time to search for shadows. The princess debated going down to the mysterious door or following the guards and their package. Knowing that the counselor might be waiting for her,

Erini chose the latter and tried to guess where the two men might enter. They
had mentioned Melicard and his interest in the workings of the sorcerer. If
nothing else, they would eventually return to their monarch with some type of
report and that report would include Drayfitt's odd condition.

A demon, by my ancestors! Do all the rumors about Melicard have some basis in fact? Am I
engaged to a human monster? Have I been so wrong about him?

Drayfitt and the guards. They had to be inside by now. Where might they
go? The chamber in which she had confronted Melicard? It was her only real
choice. Taking a deep breath, the princess made her way to the central staircase
and started down, walking with the air of one who is inspecting her new domain. Erini did not know what might happen if she actually stumbled across
the trio, but that was a risk she was willing to take. Her only fear was running
into Quorin or the king himself. The counselor was an annoyance; her betrothed . . . Erini was not quite ready to deal with him. There were things she
wanted to think about before the two of them spoke again, especially if she had
properly understood the conversation between Quorin and the two guards.

At the foot of the stairs, she confronted four sentries, who saluted in simultaneous fashion. Erini nodded imperiously and continued on. No one made a
move to stop her wanderings. Once she was far enough away, the princess exhaled deeply, wondering if her heart would ever slow to normal again.

She was turning down the main hall when she spotted the two soldiers from
the garden. Drayfitt was nowhere to be seen. The guards themselves were just
marching up to the doorway of the chamber she had entered last night. The
same sentries stood watch. After a brief consultation, the soldiers who had discovered Drayfitt were ushered inside.

Disappointment washed over Erini. There was no way she could eavesdrop
on Melicard and his men. Barging in was also too risky, considering that she
might at any minute discover she was no longer to be his bride. Erini began to
wonder what room Drayfitt might have been deposited in by the guards. If she
could find some way to wake him . . .

"Your *majesty* is awake. Did you sleep well?"

The princess trembled in surprise. Her left hand made an automatic sweep
across her midsection and suddenly began to glow, but she reversed the motion,
thereby countermanding the spell. By the time the princess turned around, her
hand was back to normal.

Mal Quorin was standing behind her, his feline features enhanced by the
predatory smile spreading across his face. The counselor was all politeness as
he spoke. "My deepest sympathies for yesterday, princess. The king is—overwhelming—at times."

"And I was not understanding, Counselor Quorin. I have every intention of atoning for my lapse. The king has nothing to regret." She glanced down the hall at the guarded doorway with a majestically indifferent eye. "I thought I might speak to him now."

Rubbing his chin, Quorin diplomatically hesitated before replying, "I regret to say, your majesty, that now would not be a good time to disturb the king. He has thrown himself into his work, something he does when his mood grows dark, and I think it might be best to wait until this evening, when it is time to sup. I assure you that the evening meal would be a much better time to mend any rift between the two of you."

The false face of courtesy that the counselor wore for her irritated Erini and she was tempted to tell him so. The real Mal Quorin was the man who had been shouting in the garden, an ambitious, hot-tempered plotter in her opinion. To speak the truth would avail her nothing, however, and would probably make matters worse since this man had the ear of Melicard.

"As you say, Counselor Quorin. You will arrange, I trust, that the meal is a private one. The king and myself. I have much to make up for."

"I shall do my utmost." He gave one of his sweeping bows. "If you like, since the king is unavailable. I can have someone escort you through the city, show you all Talak has to offer its new queen. Would you like that?"

His tone was that of an adult asking a child if she wanted a piece of candy. Erini struggled to keep her temper. If there ever *was* a reason to let her powers loose, it was the counselor. She wondered what he would say if he knew how dangerous his position actually was at present.

"I think not, counselor. Not today, anyway. There is still so much to see and learn about in the palace itself. I should get to know Melicard's heritage, for it will be mine as well."

His eyes spoke otherwise in response to her quiet challenge, although Quorin's words themselves were nothing less than admiration and the desire to assist. "You are to be recommended, your majesty. If you will retire to your chambers, I will send a member of the royal archives who will be able to answer all of your questions for you. There are also a vast number of books, some in the handwriting of the king's illustrious ancestors, that I will have pulled from the archives."

Erini smiled so very sweetly. "You must be a godsend to your lord, counselor. There is no reason to do that as yet. I find I learn so much more just walking these exquisite halls. If you will excuse me now. . . ."

With Quorin watching her back, the princess walked sedately down the opposite hall, visibly admiring the treasures around her. After a few moments, she heard the scuffle of his boots as he turned away. Erini paused, pretending to study a statuette, and looked back out of the corner of her eye just in time to see the man barge into the same chamber that the two soldiers had passed through only a short time before.

More and more, Mal Quorin bothered her. There were times when he moved much like the creature he resembled and others when he made more noise than a full honor guard. He was also her enemy, that much was now completely evident, and she did not doubt that he might even turn to violence. The counselor had no desire for the king to marry, likely because he feared Erini's influence might some day overshadow his own.

Despite her lapses, the princess had no intention of folding up like the heroines of the storytellers. Come an endless army of demons and Mal Quorins, she would still mend the rift between Melicard and herself and, in the process, find out what had truly happened behind that garden door.

If it also meant giving in to her own curse, so be it.

IN THE ETERNAL darkness of what had once been the throne room of the Dragon Emperor, a searing light burst into life, flooding the entire chamber in its bloodred brilliance. Things that were not entirely of this world, things that had once obeyed the will of the Gold Dragon, scurried back into the safety of cracks and fissures where the light did not reach.

Like a wisp of smoke, Shade uncurled out of nothing and stepped forth into the ruins of the Dragon King's lair.

This had once been the chamber in which the Dragon Kings met in council. There had been thirteen of them until the end of the Turning War, when Nathan Bedlam had succeeded in destroying the regal Purple Dragon who had ruled Penacles before the Gryphon. The council—and the unity of the drakes—had broken up for the final time with the madness caused by the discovery of Cabe Bedlam, Nathan's grandson and successor, who carried a part of the spirit of the great Dragon Master within him. In this chamber, where some of the huge effigies of creatures long dead still stood despite all the violence that had passed through here, two drake lords, the battle-hungry Iron and his ever-present shadow Bronze, had paid for their rebellion against Gold. In this chamber, Shade had learned, Cabe Bedlam had defeated the Dragon Emperor, tearing his mind apart. Here also, it was said, Cabe and the Lord Gryphon had battled young Bedlam's mad father, the sinister Azran.

Death is so very much a part of this place still, Shade thought uneasily. If there was a place that could unnerve him, it was here. As Madrac, he had forgotten that fear briefly, coming here and using the Dragon Kings themselves to further that incarnation's goals.

Shade stood and scanned the cathedral-high ruins about him, marveling at the carnage for several seconds before finally deciding that enough time had been wasted. The warlock took two tentative steps toward what had once been the throne itself—

—and paused.

Though no one but the warlock himself would have been able to tell, Shade blinked. He studied the cavern again—and then for a third time. When that no longer seemed to satisfy him, he sought around for a safe place to sit. There, he stared into the darkness of an adjoining cavern and wondered . . .

. . . wondered why he had come here and why he had suddenly forgotten that reason.

V

DARKHORSE BURST FROM the portal at full gallop, all defenses ready. He did not stop until he was certain that Shade was nowhere near. It never paid to be too confident in the Dragonrealm, especially with the warlock, but still, he could sense nothing hostile within immediate range and decided it was safe to come to a halt.

A wave of sulfur drifted past his muzzle. Had he been less than he was, the treacherous smoke would have left him choking on the ground. Being Dark-horse, he noted it only for its pungent scent.

"The Hell Plains! How aptly titled!" the shadow steed muttered. It was ac-tually more of a shout than a mutter, for even he found it difficult to hear his normally stentorian voice in a land where few minutes went by without some sort of volcanic eruption. All around him, the ground shook. Hills formed, burst open as molten rock was spewed forth, and then collapsed as some new crater redirected the flow. The very earth beneath the eternal's hooves cracked wide and lava began to rise to the surface.

Darkhorse glanced down at the burning, liquefied rock and laughed. The lava licked at his forelegs, but it might as well have been the touch of a blade of grass. Mocking the power of the land with a swish of his thick tail, the phan-tom horse trotted to stable ground, the better to think.

He had been over a hundred places that Shade might choose to visit and none of those had been sought out by the mad warlock despite more than a day passing. More than a dozen times, Darkhorse had found himself tricked by false or old trails. Darkhorse did not feel defeated yet, but his options were diminishing.

The earth shook, alerting him to yet another crater forming beneath his hooves. Annoyed, the shadow steed began trotting north, toward the more stable regions of the Hell Plains. There was yet one place nearby that Shade might deem to visit. A place hidden from all during its master's reign, but likely to be unprotected now.

Darkhorse kicked up the ash in frustration. He was running blind. He had no idea what Shade planned, where the warlock was, or if the spellcaster had already struck. His only hope was to come across his former comrade in a place of power such as the one he neared even now. *Perhaps this time . . .* he dreamed.

The birdlike skull of a Seeker went bounding into the air, kicked high along with the soot it had been buried under. Startled, Darkhorse came to a halt—but not before kicking up a mangled pile of bones that had come from more than one creature and more than one race.

The bones were jumbled together, the result of continual tremors and eruptions. Treading softly, the shadow steed discovered that they literally covered the earth, hidden from view only by a blanket of ash that had accumulated over the years. Memories of the past stirred. He recalled bits of news picked up concerning the fates of his friends and foes. It was as if time had not passed, for he had been battling the new, deadly incarnation called Madrac when these creatures had died fighting one another. Drake bones mixed freely with Seeker bones. The Seekers, the ancient avian masters of this land, had fought, not for themselves, but for the lord forced upon them, Azran Bedlam. They had died defending his citadel and, when even that was not enough to keep the hordes of the Red Dragon from his walls, Azran had destroyed the fiery legions and the Dragon King with his accursed demon blade. Darkhorse eyed the remains with clinical interest. This, then, was part of the battle site. He was closer than he had thought. The shadow steed puzzled over the remains and then looked up, openly curious.

This had to be the region where Azran's sanctum was located—yet—it was *nowhere* to be found.

He stirred up more ash and bone as he searched the ground. There were a number of jagged hills and craters, but none massive enough to be what Darkhorse sought, unless . . . unless all that remained of the tower was—its *foundation*. The ancient structure, supposedly built by the Seekers to withstand time and the Hell Plains had to be no more than a ruin. It was the only answer and, if true, yet another failure on his part. Shade would never come here.

"Darkhorse, you are a vain, unmitigated fool!" He brought a hoof down on some unidentifiable bone, sending fragments and dust flying. He had been determined to do this alone because he felt the responsibility his. Shade was—had been—his friend. Shade's exile had been the eternal's doing and the warlock's escape had been Darkhorse's failure. Pride ruled the shadow steed as much as, if not more than, it ruled humanity.

A touch of latent power disturbed the edges of his mind.

"What have we here?" he rumbled. That which touched his thoughts was not living, not by any stretch of the imagination. It had the stink of death—no, it *was* death!—and it lay not too far from where he stood. Darkhorse, having few options of his own, followed the chilling trail.

Soon, Darkhorse found himself standing before a long, wide mound some two or three times the height of a normal man. The jet-black horse stepped up to the front edge of the mound and dug away at it with his hoof, not daring to unleash a spell in the vicinity of such a dark power. Darkhorse had no fear for himself, but he knew that careless action might very well rob him of his only possible chance to find and stop Shade. That, of course, depended on what had sought him out. There were things in the Dragonrealm that even he hoped never to meet.

After a few moments, he uncovered the edge of a wall. It was true, then. Something, perhaps Azran himself, had stripped the ancient castle of its preservative spells. Age and the primitive fury of this cursed region had caught up to the citadel. From what he could see, Darkhorse guessed that an eruption had taken place not too far from the once magically protected grounds. In a few more decades, there would be little or nothing remaining of the lair of Azran.

Somehow, Darkhorse could not bring himself to weep for the loss of such a place. If the Hell Plains buried the evil memory of Nathan Bedlam's treacherous foal, so much the better.

The touch of death returned. Shaking his head to remove the foul feeling, the stallion followed the trail left by the magical contact. Ash, mortar, and yet more bones flew as Darkhorse used the slightest touch of his own power to clear a path. One never knew what might be lurking beneath. The ground rumbled ominously; perhaps decades was too long an estimate. There might be nothing remaining in mere minutes.

He came across what had once been stairs leading down to a room, a room *still* protected by sorcery though the physical structure itself was no more than half a wall and several loose stones. Darkhorse paused only for a moment; then, spelling the ash away, he descended. The protective measures here were bound together with the same unearthly power that had reached out to him, which was why they still remained. Even if the entire region exploded in one massive eruption, this spot would go untouched. Darkhorse laughed, his challenge to what awaited him. He knew with what he dealt now.

His form passed through a spell that would have killed any mortal creature and several entities of lesser ability than he. As the tip of his tail passed beyond the deadly trap, the violent land of the Hell Plains ceased to be.

"I am unimpressed," was his first comment as he surveyed the chamber he now stood in. "Typical of your masters, who have no imagination!"

How the room had looked before Azran's death was questionable, though, knowing the necromancer's madness, it had probably been much the same. Without Azran's physical influence, however, control of this place had slipped back to the oppressive rulers of the Final Path, the beings known to men as the Lords of the Dead and other, in the eternal's estimation, overly pretentious titles.

I wonder what humans would think if they knew that even these Lords *must die at some time!*

The odor of rotting flesh filled the chamber. Decaying forms, human and otherwise, littered the place. A pool of some brackish liquid—definitely not water—bubbled ominously. Darkhorse laughed again.

"Save your show for those who *believe* in it, Lords of the Overacting! You know that I have no fear of you! If I should ever perish, my ultimate destiny lies elsewhere, not in your slime-crusted fingers! If you have something to say to me, then do so! One who has cheated you over and over for millennia threatens the mortals—mortals who have not yet lived the lives that are their due! Well? Do I need to start dumping this refuse into your little puddle?" He prodded an unidentifiable mass covered with black flies toward the pool.

The bubbling grew violent, creating a green froth that swelled high. The pool became more agitated, waves lapping the floor. Something long, large, and blacker than Darkhorse briefly broke the muck-covered surface before disappearing again. The shadow steed watched all in total disinterest.

In the center of the pool, a new form slowly rose. Accurate description failed, save that it was a hodgepodge of rotting limbs, torsos, and heads combined in impossible ways. Eyes dotted its form, all of them staring at the phantom horse with more than a touch of fury. Several limbs pointed in Darkhorse's direction.

"I feel no more pleasure in seeing your lovely face—*faces, I suppose I should say!*—than you feel in seeing mine! Come! Speak and we can be done with this—or are you going to pass along some unmanageable riddle like those you foist upon mortals who seek your—fools that they are!—*guidance!*"

"Child of the Void." The voice grated, scratched, pierced—it did *everything* as far as Darkhorse was concerned. Despite the irritation it caused him, however, outwardly he revealed nothing. Let them play their little games out as long as they told him something of importance.

"Dweller Without."

The shadow steed kicked the fly-covered corpse into the pool, which caused a flurry of bubbling as the scavengers sought unsuccessfully to escape their sinking home. Darkhorse focused an ice-blue eye on the guardian of the pool.

"Yesss, I have earned my share of pretentious titles as well! Second move to you, my pretty friend! Now, unless you concede this idiotic game and tell me what is so important, I will depart this godforsaken hole forever—but not before *sealing* it so that no one else has to put up with your stench!"

"Kivan Grath." The guardian of the pool spit the name out, along with a number of tiny, vague pieces of matter that Darkhorse did not bother to try to identify.

"Kivan Grath?"

"The Seeker of Gods, demon horse." It was the first understandable reply the thing had given him.

"I know what it is, but why—"

"Kivan Grath. Now." Each of the numerous mouths formed into what Darkhorse could only vaguely accept as a smile. A smile of triumph. "Do not lose him again, unwanted one."

The jet-black stallion met the guardian's multiple gaze. "And *how* many times has Shade departed your domain without more than a nod of his head?"

The guardian did not respond to his retort, instead choosing that moment to sink back into the mire. Up to the very moment its head submerged, all eyes remained fixed on Darkhorse.

He bid the guardian, who may or may not have been little more than a puppet through which his masters had spoken, farewell with a mocking laugh that echoed throughout the chamber. Turning, the shadow steed kicked yet another moldering form into the grisly pool as he burst back through the magical veil and out into the Hell Plains.

Ascending to the surface, Darkhorse scanned the area with renewed interest. "Not so bad a place after all! Almost pleasant!"

His gaze returned to the stairway and the ruins of the chamber. Azran's pool lay in some space between the mortal plane and the lands of the dead, a brilliant piece of sorcery. Almost indestructible, too.

Almost.

"Some doors are too dangerous to leave opened," he finally decided.

The black emptiness that was his form melted, changed. Like the molten rock flowing from the craters, the inky darkness streamed down the broken steps, pressing with purpose toward the magical doorway. As it enveloped the physical portal, a brief touch, a brief moment of protest, tapped at the edges of Darkhorse's consciousness. He ignored it and, as the magic which had created the portal was absorbed within him, the protest faded.

The shadow steed re-formed himself at the top of the stairs. At the base of those stairs was now a clean, flat surface. Other than the steps, there was no sign that there had ever been a portal. Indeed, there was not even a trace of the room remaining.

Kivan Grath. Most majestic of the Tyber Mountains. The name was familiar to Darkhorse and he cursed himself for not having searched there earlier. Lair of the Gold Dragon, long dead. The caverns within Kivan Grath were endless and they predated even the Seekers. Was it possible that one of Shade's redis-covered memories had sent him searching in those caverns?

Darkhorse paused. The rot-riddled masters of human mortality had given him a clue, but did he dare trust it? They cared nothing for him and *that* feel-ing was returned to them twofold. Why, then, were they aiding him? Was there something greater they feared, should the warlock remain free?

Again, he contemplated seeking out Cabe Bedlam, the one mortal who might be of help, and again the painful belief, that he was responsible for Shade, kept him from doing so.

The guardian had indicated that speed was of the essence and Darkhorse, knowing he had already stalled longer than he dared, opened a path through reality. This time, he would find Shade. This time, there would be no exile.

ONLY ONE SENTRY guarded the room where Erini guessed Drayfitt had been deposited. He stood at the doorway, a bored look on his rough features, his hand on the pommel of his sword. In the palace royal of the king of Talak, no one expected trouble. That, despite what had happened to the old sorcerer.

What exactly she planned to do, the princess could not say. Her ideas had gone no farther than locating Drayfitt and she was chagrined to realize she had no notion as to how to proceed now. Of what use would sneaking past the sentry be, always assuming that Erini could do even *that*, if success only meant confronting the unconscious spellcaster?

She was turning away, defeated for the moment, when she heard the sound of a door opening and the voice of the guard raised high in surprise. Erini, po-sitioned down a side corridor, glanced back in time to see the sentry's face glaze over as a determined Drayfitt stared into his eyes. The sorcerer had an odd look in his own eyes, a fanatical gaze that somehow did not fit the elderly man's ap-pearance. It was almost as if he, like the soldier, were under a spell.

Drayfitt wasted no time. Like a man possessed, he hurried down the hall— toward the corridor where Erini still stood. Quickly, she looked around for some place to hide, not wanting to chance the same fate as the hapless sentry. Sighting a stairway leading downward, the princess scurried over to it. She rushed halfway down and paused, hoping to hear the sorcerer as he passed.

A horrible thought occurred to her. If Drayfitt was returning to the garden, his quickest way to reach it was the very stairway she was standing on. Erini took several steps down and then paused. By now, Drayfitt should have been descending behind her, yet, his footsteps were growing *fainter*. She waited a moment longer and then slowly made her way back up. No sorcerer barred her way. The princess reached the top of the stairs and looked around. The elderly man was gone.

Holding her breath, she listened for some sound. Nothing. Drayfitt had continued down one of the two hallways, but she could not say which. The ancient sorcerer was much sprier than the princess could have believed possible. Now, there was no way she could follow him.

Voices and heavy footsteps down the original corridor made her turn. Quorin was one of them. The two soldiers who had carried Drayfitt to the room were likely with him. The other voice . . .

Melicard!

Erini cursed her luck. If she went down either corridor, they would see her. If she descended the stairs, they might notice her as she hurried across the garden. Either way, things would look suspicious. With her future already in a fragile state, this might be more than it could stand.

Strengthening her resolve, Erini did the only thing she could. It was time to rely on hope and her own ability to act as a princess acted. Smoothing her gown, she strode down the hallway and entered the corridor by Drayfitt's former resting place just as Melicard, Quorin, and at least *six* guards came into sight from her right.

She pretended to notice the stunned guard for the first time. Shock was not a difficult emotion to play; the sentry's slack features and blank eyes were a frightening sight. Without realizing it, she put a hand to her mouth to stifle a gasp.

"Princess Erini! Your majesty!" Quorin's voice. She refused to acknowledge it, instead shaking her head as if ready to break down at the sight of the unfortunate victim of Drayfitt's power.

"Erini."

The new voice was Melicard's and the soft tone of it turned her uneasiness to wonder. She gratefully tore her eyes from the sentry, fixing them instead upon Melicard's face. This time, the princess felt no uneasiness, only uncertainty. Would they suspect why she was here?

"Melicard, I—"

Quorin stepped forward to intercept her as she moved toward the king. "Your majesty, if you will permit me, I will have two of these men escort you to your chambers. There has been some unpleasantness here, as you can see, and we would not want you endangered."

She purposely sidestepped him. "If there is some danger to Melicard, I will certainly not abandon him for my own sake! If there is some danger to me, I will feel safer with my betrothed!" Erini looked up at the king. Melicard met her gaze momentarily, then looked down. "Unless, of course, he does not wish me here."

The king lifted his head and studied her. Erini kept her gaze on his eyes. Her own played tricks; she almost came to believe that both his eyes were real. Would he respond to her bald statement? Did Melicard understand that she would leave Talak now if he so desired it?

Beside her, Mal Quorin grew anxious. He put a hand on her arm, intending to lead her away from both the king and the present, dire situation. It proved to be a mistake. Life seemed to suddenly illuminate Melicard's visage, even that carved of elfwood. He looked from the counselor to Erini and back again.

"It's all right, Quorin. She will be fine with me."

The faces of Erini and Mal Quorin were a study in opposites. More pleased than she had thought she could possibly be, the princess barely noticed the scowling features of the counselor.

"My liege, I don't think—"

"We'll speak of the other matters later on. I know I can depend on you to deal with the present crisis as I would want it dealt with." The king's tone brooked no argument.

Defeated for the moment, Quorin obediently bowed. "As you wish, your majesty. I shall report to you as soon as we have the crisis under control."

Melicard absently touched one of the streaks of elfwood running across the right side of his face. "Unless you can't control it, I see no need why it can't wait until this evening. I leave it in your very capable hands."

"My liege." The counselor barked orders to the guards. Two of them took the stricken sentry away while the rest followed Quorin down the side corridor Erini had stepped out of before. The king by her side, Erini watched until the party was out of sight.

"Princess Erini," Melicard suddenly began, "I apologize to you for yesterday. You shouldn't have been expected to be at ease with something so . . . I sometimes try to provoke a response, I think."

"My conduct was reprehensible, my lord. I should apologize to you for that. As a princess of Gordag-Ai and your betrothed, I should behave better. It could not have been easy for you to accept the fact that you had a bride, not after all these years."

The thinnest shadow of a smile played briefly across the king's mouth. Through some trick of the light, Erini imagined that the elfwood portion of his face flexed and shifted as he talked, as if it believed it was flesh and blood. She wanted to reach up and touch it, just to be certain, but she doubted that Melicard would tolerate such a thing at this point—and she had no desire to do anything that might break anew the bond between them just as it was beginning to mend.

"It was a *bit* of a surprise," he responded. It was as if Erini had met twins, so different was this Melicard from the cold one she had encountered briefly yesterday. "I hadn't even planned on marriage for several years. I have so much to do."

The princess was careful not to press him on what sort of *projects* kept him so busy, instead saying, " 'The years pass as quickly as they once passed so slowly.' An old saying of Gordag-Ai. A king needs heirs if he wishes his legacy to live on. Where would Talak be if something happened to you and you had no heir? The city would fall."

From the look in his working eye, Erini knew she had struck one of his most sensitive points. Melicard's campaign would be all for nought if he died. There was no one with the drive, the determination, to take over. Mal Quorin had such dreams, but the princess knew that putting Talak in the counselor's hands like that would result in nothing less than civil war. The counselor was a madman and madmen made for short, brutal reigns.

Melicard reached out and took her hand. "Perhaps we can find a quiet place and talk for a little while."

Having no desire to destroy what she had so far wrought, Erini made no mention of the fact that, under these circumstances, it was proper for others, specifically her ladies-in-waiting, to also be in attendance. When it came to courtship, the king was a babe. Still, she understood that they could make no progress if he had to endure the stares of other, less flexible souls like Magda or Galea—besides, Erini had no desire for them to be in attendance, either.

Melicard led her down the hall, but not to the chamber they had met in the day before. Instead, the two of them walked toward the cathedral high doors of the main hall, where several startled guards quickly straightened. The king touched his face where elfwood and flesh met, hesitant. Then, with iron resolve, he took her arm and guided her forward. Two guards quickly opened the door for them and several others moved to fall in behind the royal couple.

The king turned and calmly said, "Return to your posts. We will be within the palace grounds and very safe. That is a *command*."

With some misgivings evident in their features, the guards stepped away.

"Such loyalty is commendable," Erini commented. "Where are we going?"

Melicard did not look directly at her, but she thought she detected a brief smile. *Twice in only a few minutes*, the princess marvelled. *There's hope.*

"If you'll permit, Princess Erini, I would like to show you my kingdom."

Her own smile was the only reply he received. Reddening slightly, Melicard escorted her outside and into the sunlight.

IN THE CAVERNS of Kivan Grath, a desperate Shade sat silently, his thoughts a raging fury in contrast to his still form. Try as he might, the warlock could make no sense of his memories; he barely even remembered the name by which he had gone for all these centuries. *Shade.* It was the only solid memory he had left. Somehow, he hoped, he would be able to build from it. Somehow.

From the darkened caverns beyond, a single, unseen watcher studied the human. When curiosity was satisfied, the watcher vanished into the darkness to tell the others.

VI

THE CRIMSON FIRE that illuminated the throne room of the Dragon Emperor was momentarily drowned out by the brilliant white glow of Darkhorse's gate as the shadow steed burst through. Chilling eyes quickly drank in the details of the massive cavern, from the few huge effigies still standing, to the flittering, frightened shapes seeking haven in the cracks and crevices. Darkhorse ignored the creatures, knowing them as useless servants of a long-dead Dragon King. There was only one thing, one creature who demanded his attention . . . and though he was nowhere to be seen, the ebony stallion could feel his nearby presence.

"Shaaade!"

The warlock's name echoed hauntingly through the endless labyrinth of caverns. It was said that here, if one dared, a way to the bottom of the world might be found. Darkhorse neither knew or cared. He wanted Shade and each passing second made that hope dwindle.

"Come, Shade! It is time to join the ghosts of our pasts! This poor world can ill afford our constant struggle! Let it end now!"

He waited, listening intently as the echoes of his challenge slowly died away. The things hiding in the cracks and crevices chittered in mad fear. More out of impatience than anything else, Darkhorse looked up in their general direction and laughed, sending them scattering to hiding places farther away from the phantom horse.

Still no one answered his challenge.

There was too much old magic here for him to pinpoint the spellcaster. Old spells abandoned, for the most part. There was also something else, something older *and* newer. Darkhorse sniffed.

Vraad sorcery.

Shade's words to him while the shadow steed had remained helpless in Drayfitt's cage resurfaced. The warlock had said that his elderly counterpart had used Vraad-style sorcery. Now, in this ancient place where Shade himself had come, there were again Vraad traces.

Darkhorse cursed silently. Now there was more than Shade to deal with. If he somehow survived his encounter with the warlock, there were still the legacies of the Vraad. Legacies that threatened more than a world.

Dru Zeree, the stallion thought, recalling the first being to befriend him. *I've need of your guidance. How do I fight what even the Vraad themselves could not?*

There was no answer, of course. It was a friendship of the far past. It was a reason that Darkhorse rarely sought the friendship of others, though he yearned for their trust. Everything passed beyond, save him.

And Shade.

If the spellcaster had come seeking the foul inheritance left by that ancient race of sorcerers, he would be deeper in the caverns, possibly miles below the surface. Though the Vraad were recent by this land's standards, they had been a jealous people and prone to secrets, especially from one another. If one of their number had left artifacts behind, those items would be buried deep—and well-protected.

Mystery upon mystery!

Darkhorse struck the floor furiously, leaving a gouge where his hoof had landed. It also worried him that generation upon generation of Dragon Emperor had made this mountain and its caverns the home of their clans—yet not one of them had ever been known to make use of whatever the Vraad had abandoned.

Scanning the chamber, he chose a likely side cavern. A gate would have been quicker, true, but only if he knew where Shade was. Besides, there was too much sorcery lingering in the air. There was no telling what effect it might have on his own abilities.

Darkhorse trotted cautiously toward the cavern entrance.

A sinewy, metallic appendage wrapped itself around his throat. Another trapped one foreleg and two more snared his hind legs. Momentarily disconcerted, the shadow steed struggled futilely, gouging the earth with the sharp hoof of his sole free limb, as his unseen attackers struggled to maintain their holds from their shadowy hiding places. Then, the true seriousness of his situation jarred him back to reality. No physical bond could hold a creature whose essence was part of the Void itself, not unless master sorcery was at work. Even then, he should have been able to free himself simply by truly becoming a shadow. To his dismay, however, Darkhorse found that the transformation was beyond him. The same sorcery that had been used to create his attackers' weapons also prevented him from utilizing his own abilities. Someone had planned well, though they could have hardly done so with him in mind. It was only unfortunate coincidence that he had fallen prey.

A final, jagged tentacle darted from one of the lesser caverns and snared his remaining leg. Each limb was pulled in a different direction, making movement impossible. The noose around his neck kept him from using more primitive methods to escape, such as biting his bonds in two.

"Hurry, you foolsssss! Bind him quickly!"

Slowly, so as not to lose the hold each had, the ebony stallion's attackers abandoned their hiding places and moved toward him. Their identities did not surprise him, not after hearing the hissing voice that commanded them. So engrossed had he become in his search that he had not noticed the spells that must have masked their presence, spells which he, more sensitive to sorcery than most, should have at least felt, regardless.

Despite his predicament, Darkhorse responded to his captors presence with disdain. *"Drakes!* I might have known your kind would be slithering about these holes in the ground!"

The crimson light poured over the newcomers, giving them the appearance of walking dead risen from some terrible battle. Each stood a little taller than a man and, outwardly, resembled savage warriors clad in masterly crafted scale armor that covered all but their heads. The heads themselves were mostly obscured by great dragonhelms that made the humanoid figures seem even taller. Within those helms, eyes the color of fire blazed and mouths full of sharp, predatory teeth opened wide in triumphant smiles. Their noses were little more than slits and, if one was so foolish as to get close enough to see, their skin was scaled, like a reptile.

Darkhorse knew far better than most that the armor was illusion. The scales were real, as real as those on the drakes' faces. It was not true clothing they wore, but their own skins *transformed* by the drakes' own innate sorcery. Even the mighty helms were false in nature, the intricate dragon crests being the true faces of the creature and not some craftsman's design. The shadow steed had seen drakes revert to their dragon forms, and watched as the fierce dragon head slid down and stretched, becoming animated with life. It was a sight none could ever forget—provided they survived the encounter.

Dragons who preferred the forms of men, that was the drake race. With each generation, there were more and more of those who could better copy the human form. The females were already adept—*too* adept, some human women said—but they sacrificed much of their power for that perfection.

The drake holding the noose wrapped around Darkhorse's neck gave it a tug. Pain burned the eternal where the metallic bonds touched his form, and all thought of drakes and their odd ways vanished as anger resurfaced stronger than ever before.

"Thisss isss our domain, demon," the apparent leader hissed with gusto. "To enter here meansss to sssacrifice your life!"

Darkhorse chuckled. "You sound like your cousin the serpent, reptile! Is proper speech beyond you?"

The leader hissed, revealing a long, forked tongue. A *throwback*, the shadow steed noted in one part of his mind. A drake whose ties to the dragon form of his birth were stronger than those of his brethren, those ties manifesting themselves in such things as the split tongue, jagged teeth designed to tear flesh, and a savage manner that made them the deadliest of their race.

"Your death will be mossst—most enjoyable, demon! Our lord will gain great pleasure from watching you perish slowly! Too many of our race have suffered the unspeakable at your hands!"

"Hooves, dear lizard, hooves! Those things at the end of your arms are hands—more or less! Tell me; can you really hold a sword with those gnarled appendages—or do you scratch and bite your opponents like a riding drake?"

Riding drakes were huge, swift, wingless dragons of an intelligence just below that of horses. That such mindless beasts were as much a part of the drake race as these warriors before him amused Darkhorse. It did *not* amuse the leader—as the ebony stallion had hoped. "It might prove interesting to see if a sword could cut you now that you are *forced* to remain in the form of a beast of burden, demon horse! I will have to make such a suggestion to our lord when we have dragged you before him!"

Darkhorse looked scandalized. "Drag me before him? Did I say that I would be party to such a thing?"

The drakes grew nervous. A few touched their swords, forgetting the type of creature they were dealing with. The sword was the most useless of their weapons.

"You have no say in the matter."

"Oh, my dear friend, but I *do*!" Darkhorse retorted. He began to laugh, taunting his captors with the very madness of his act. The sorcerous bonds burned into his solidified form, but he turned the agony, around, adding its strength to his mocking reply. In the vast maze of caverns, the sound of his voice echoed and echoed, but nowhere with more intensity than in the throne room. The more the pain sought to defeat him, the louder he roared.

One by one, his captors lost control as the laughter battered their ears. The drake keeping his right foreleg in check lost his grip on his weapon as he reached up and buried his head in his hands, trying without success to block out the noise. Darkhorse shook the coil loose and used the one leg to pull himself forward. The drakes behind him, barely able to even stand, could not maintain their grips. Freed, the shadow steed whirled and struck at the drake who controlled the coil around his left foreleg. The kick sent the warrior flying into one of the statues that still stood. Though he wrapped around it like a ribbon, the drake never felt his back break; Darkhorse's blow had killed him.

The noose around his throat still burned. Darkhorse, no longer laughing, turned to the source of his pain, the leader of his attackers. The drake was on one knee and slowly recovering as the agonizing sound died away. Throughout all of it, he had maintained a tight grip. One coil, however, was not enough to hold the shadow steed, not now. Darkhorse prodded two of the other coils before him and, as the drake rose, kicked them expertly toward his adversary. The reptilian warrior had just enough time to realize his danger when both deadly toys dropped on him.

He screamed—almost. The power needed to contain an eternal such as Darkhorse was more than enough to consume the drake completely. There was not even a trace of ash.

Desperate, one of the remaining attackers leaped at the shadow steed, beginning the transformation to dragon form midway through the air. Darkhorse made no move to stop him. To what would forever be his dismay, the drake found no solid flesh to rend. He did not land upon Darkhorse but rather *within* him. The now-completely transformed dragon sank into the emptiness that was the jet-black stallion. Smaller and smaller the unfortunate attacker became, dwindling the way a figure falling forever and ever gradually diminished—until there was nothing to see. He would continue falling in that abyss, as still did so many before him, until everything—the multiverse, chaos, and even the Void— ceased to be.

"I am the demon to demons. I am the traveller who defies the Final Path. I am the Void incarnate. *I* am *Darkhorse.*" The eternal fixed his chilling stare on the remaining drake warriors as he whispered.

The drakes fled, disappearing in all-out panic into one of the caverns. Darkhorse watched them escape, all the while chuckling in morbid amusement.

Lead me to your master, drakes! Though the cursed light that only Shade could have left behind colors you scarlet, I think that silver *is more to your lord's taste!* Darkhorse began trotting after the vanished drakes, his hooves making no sound despite seeming to strike the stone floor with enough strength to shatter it. This time, the advantage would be his.

Lead me to your master, brave ones, for I think that there might be a warlock I am seeking with him as well—and I will fight all the clans of your kind if that is what it takes to finally face him!

FACES VAGUELY RECALLED. Names only beginning to resurface. Images of the ancient dead walking the earth once more.

Shade could not say what urge had suddenly driven him to this subcavern far, far below the throne room. Not exactly a memory, but something more. Something to do with the insignia carved in raw marble and embedded in the wall he now stood before. An insignia he remembered seeing on the Gryphon's tapestry and which he now traced in an abstract manner with his left hand. A militaristic banner with the stylized image of a fighting dragon.

The banner of his clan. The banner of his *father*.

"What memories do you hold?" Shade whispered, not knowing whether he spoke to the relief on the wall or his own, murky mind. He still could neither recall what he had come to this mountain for nor why the image of a great black beast, a demonic horse, had burned itself a permanent place in his thoughts.

"What memories do you hold?" the warlock repeated. Unable as he was to see his own face—or lack thereof—Shade could not notice the brief clarity which played across it. The change came and went in less than a breath, but it left its mark, though the warlock could not know that.

"Give me your memories." The words were not the product of wishful thinking, but rather a command. The resistance was strong, but not enough, not to one who knew—now. Shade nodded. His own memories were returning again and now he would add new ones as well.

A pale, blue light formed in the center of the chamber and expanded. The warlock, his hand still on the ancient carving, turned to gaze on that light, seemingly fascinated by it as a moth to a flame. The light continued to expand and, as it did so, began to take on shapes. One after the other without stop. Tall. Short. Distant. Near. Simple. Unbelievable.

Memories of a long-forgotten time. Of a race of sorcerers called the Vraad. Of Shade's kind.

The images were indistinct at first. Shade put his other hand on the relief. The memories had been gathered over generations and from countless places. He could not say exactly when he recalled this information, but it was true, just as it was true that this carving had been set in the wall for just the reason he utilized it for now.

"Give them to me!" he swore between clenched teeth.

An image broke from the rest, solidified, and sharpened. Even though it was not yet distinct, Shade inhaled sharply, knowing already who it would be. It was not the one he had wanted—probably one of the *last* he had wanted—but it made sense, given the dragon banner on the wall.

Father . . . Shade raised his left hand to the top of the banner.

With a violent twist of that hand, he banished the image. It flared like a miniature sun—and was gone.

A new image separated from the jumble, grew, and defined itself. A tall figure, female and only recently into womanhood. Shade dismissed it as he had the first, though he briefly wondered why it bothered him almost as much as seeing his father had. There had been no name to put to the woman, but he knew her. He also knew that, whatever her connections to him, she was not part of what he now sought. Still . . .

Caught up in his thoughts, the warlock looked away for several seconds. When he returned his gaze to the blue light, he started in surprise, for another figure, tall and clad in armor, stood waiting patiently. Where the others had been bright, as if the sun of midday had shone overhead, this one stood with the light behind him, blocking the glow and creating a shadow.

A shadow?

Shade glanced down at the rocky surface, eyeing the shadow that stretched long and narrow. This was no memory of the past. What stood before him was very, very real.

"Warlock. Shade." The huge, armored newcomer took a few steps toward him. In the light, the scale armor glittered silver-blue. The voice was a quiet, soothing hiss. "I would have words with you, warlock. Words of things that concern both of us."

The distant sound of mocking laughter echoing through the caverns made both look in the direction of the sole entrance to the chamber. Images of a creature with ice-blue eyes once more demanded Shade's attention.

His new companion stirred visibly. Reptilian features partially masked by the massive dragonhelm were turned once more toward the warlock. Shade caught uncertainty tinged with greed—and fear.

The Silver Dragon spoke again, his words uttered a bit faster than the first time and his eyes continually darting toward the entrance. "I would have words with you, friend—and *quickly*, if you do not mind."

THE DRAKES WHO fled from Darkhorse led him deeper and deeper into the caverns. Even he, who had known that a fantastic system of chambers lay within and below Kivan Grath, was shocked at the complexity and extent of the labyrinth. Still, it did make sense, for this had been the home of the entire clan of Gold, the most royal of drake clans. In one hot, steamy chamber, a hatchery by the look of it, he had even come across the skeletal remains of a huge female dragon who obviously had been the guardian of the newly born drakes. Her death had been quiet if not peaceful from the look of it. Old age or lack of purpose, he judged. Darkhorse had also not missed the brittle fragments of the second skeleton in that area, a drake warrior who looked suspiciously as if he had been killed by the elderly dam herself.

So many things to wonder about, he thought as he turned down yet another corridor. Would he ever find out what had happened since his exile? There seemed to be so *much*. A sudden uneasy feeling filled him, but it had nothing to do with his unanswered question. Darkhorse paused. No, something else disturbed him. He sniffed the air.

Vraad sorcery—and close!

"Shade . . ." he whispered to himself. So close the shadow steed could almost see him. Darkhorse opened a path in reality and, without hesitation, stepped through.

The path itself was short, almost nothing, and the ebony stallion emerged from the other end of the portal in mere seconds. He found himself in the center of a chamber, bathed in a pale blue light and surrounded by phantom images that ignored him as they played out their brief lives.

"What manner of monstrosity is this?" the shadow steed bellowed without thinking. Had he fallen into some hell created by Shade?

Two figures whirled at the shout, both momentarily shadowed, Darkhorse stepped quickly from the light, shaking his body as if that would remove the thought of these disconcerting specters from it. They had about them the feel of Vraad sorcery, which made their existence all the more foul.

One of the two figures watching him stepped closer, as if taking a casual walk. "You . . . you're . . . Darkhorse . . . aren't you?"

"As much as you are the warlock Shade, my blurry friend! You know that very well! You remember *everything*—or have you *forgotten* that?"

Perhaps it was his eyes that played tricks on him, Darkhorse wondered, but he would have been willing to swear even to the Lords of the Dead that Shade was smiling just a little. Was it a trick or were those two dark spots his eyes?

Before the shadow steed could take it further, the warlock nodded and replied, "I remembered . . . but I forgot. I am remembering again . . . but not as Madrac. As myself, I think."

Darkhorse's eyes glittered. "Yourself?"

"I can't be certain yet." Shade indicated his companion. "The drake lord asked me the same question. He seemed disappointed. I think he wanted to make some sort of pact. I don't know."

"Thisss isss inssssanity!" The Silver Dragon raised a fist. Something crystalline glittered in its grip. "He isss our enemy!"

An oppressing weight crashed down on the black stallion. Darkhorse fell to his knees and grew distorted as the pressure on him increased and he was slowly flattened. The Silver Dragon took a step forward, the light of victory burning in his anxious eyes.

"It worksss! It worksss!"

Shade remained where he was, watching everything with clinical interest. "Of course it does. Vraad sorcery does not fade easily. Still, I doubt if it will be enough."

The drake cocked his head in sudden confusion. Victory had been replaced anxiety. "What'sss that? What do you *mean*, human?"

"He means," Darkhorse forced himself to his feet again, "that you'll need more than that pretty bauble to keep me kneeling before you, lizard!" The shadow steed chuckled. "Surprise was its only useful weapon—and you've used that up!"

The Dragon King cursed and shook the crystal, as if that would make it stronger. Shade shook his cowled head.

"He knows more about it than you do, it seems, drake. I would have to say he probably knows more than I remember, too."

Slowly, the Silver Dragon backed away. "I have my own power! I can deal with him!"

"Ha!" Darkhorse looked down at the reptilian monarch. "Power includes the confidence and will to back it up, my little friend! Do you have enough of either? Somehow, I doubt that!"

Shade crossed his arms and looked at both of them. "He may be right, Dragon King. He may be wrong as well."

"You! He is your enemy, too! If he defeats me, you will be next!"

"Possibly. Possibly not. I *could* just depart—but I suppose he would find me eventually."

Darkhorse moved cautiously. He was confident that the Dragon King would give him little trouble, being the most pathetic of his brethren that the horse could recall. *This is a drake lord? This one would be Emperor?* What worried him, however, was this *new* Shade, this indifferent, even possibly amoral creature who stood talking calmly while two powerful beings prepared to fight to the death—a fight that might very well include the warlock before long.

Desperation was written in every movement of the Silver Dragon. Darkhorse began to understand. This drake lord had lived under the favor of the Gold Dragon and had apparently drawn much of his strength from his emperor—who had been more than a little paranoid about his own position. That paranoia had evidently transferred itself to this Dragon King, who saw himself as the obvious successor to his former master.

The drake hissed and suddenly threw the crystal at Darkhorse.

"That was definitely foolish," Shade commented.

Knowing the artifact for what it was, the stallion stepped nimbly aside. A magical talisman could be deadlier when used in desperation than in planned combat. The Vraad device went flying past him, striking the cavern wall behind.

It bounced two or three times on the floor and then rolled to a stop—all without the slightest sign of danger.

Shade leaned over, clearly interested at the lack of reaction on the talisman's part.

The crystal split into two perfect pieces and a gray-green smoky substance began to rise from it, forming into a cloud that swelled with each passing second. The warlock straightened quickly with as much emotion as Darkhorse had seen him convey since his arrival here.

"I *warned* you that it was foolish. I think I may leave after all."

Darkhorse snorted and trotted a step closer to the cloaked figure. "None of us is leaving here, dear friend Shade, until—"

The shadowy warlock curled within himself and vanished with a slight *pop!* before the next word was even out of the eternal's mouth.

"No!" The Dragon King reached toward the spot where the spellcaster had stood, uselessly grasping at air.

"You!" Darkhorse turned on the drake. "Where has he gone, carrion eater? Where?" *Notagainnotagainnotagain!* the shadow steed mentally cursed.

Sizing up the chamber and knowing his chances against the creature before him, the Silver Dragon came to a rapid decision. He transformed.

The transformation was quick, almost unbelievably so. Wings burst from the drake's back and the creature hunched forward as his spine arced and his legs bent *backwards*. Taloned hands grew long and arms twisted, becoming more like the legs. The Dragon King's neck stretched high, an ungodly sight at first, what with the humanoid head, but then the dragon-crest slid down over the half-hidden face, slid down and lengthened. The jaws snapped and the eyes opened, the true visage of the Silver Dragon revealed at last. All the while, the form of the leviathan expanded, growing and growing until it threatened to fill the cavern and more.

All this in but a breath. Time enough for Darkhorse to have attacked—save that his limbs were suddenly heavy and the chamber was beginning to *fade*. He blinked, wondering if the ominous smoke cloud had affected his senses. His second thought was that Shade had made a fool of him, had returned somehow without Darkhorse sensing him and struck with some new spell. He struggled forward. The dragon, now whole, did nothing but stare. Stare and slowly smile that toothy smile that only his kind was capable of.

"The nag hasss been sssnared himsssself!" the Dragon King hissed jubilantly. He inhaled sharply and, as Darkhorse looked on in helpless frustration, bathed the shadow steed in white flame summoned up from his own magical essence. Darkhorse steadied himself, knowing that here was a fire whose burning touch even he might feel.

The flame passed through the trapped stallion without so much as a hint of its unbearable heat. The Silver Dragon roared angrily. Darkhorse laughed, covering his own surprise with bravado. What was happening?

You will come to me, demon! a familiar voice demanded. *Now!*

"Damn the Final Path, *no!*" Darkhorse renewed his struggles, fighting with such ferocity that that Dragon King backed away again. "No!"

The choice is not yours, demon! You will come!

He was wrenched from the cavern and the dragon with the ease that one might reach down and pick up a twig. The world—everything—twisted and faded. Darkhorse struggled, but he might as well have been trying to physically run the boundaries of the Void so futile was his attempt. He had underestimated an adversary again. His self-exile, he grimly decided, had warped his senses beyond help.

The world of the Dragonrealm returned then—and with it a place that he had thought he would never have to see again.

In the dim light of the torch, Drayfitt rose before him, exhausted but satisfied. The look in his eyes was unreadable, even to Darkhorse.

"He will not escape this time. We can stare in those dead eyes until the Dragon of the Depths comes to visit the king for lunch before the demon will be able to trick one of us again. His other abilities are stifled as well."

The markings around his magical cage had been altered slightly. Darkhorse tried to make them out but could not.

Mal Quorin joined his rival and eyed the shadow steed with a mix of fury and glee. "You've cost us much, demon! That book cannot be replaced! Rest assured, though, before long, you will have repaid us for it over and over again!"

"Mortal fools! I am not your fetching slave! Release me! Shade still wanders free and the danger may be greater than I supposed!"

The Silver Dragon was a bully, strong but with little true bravery to back it up. Yet, if he was allowed to study the Vraad for very long, he might become an even deadlier threat. Kivan Grath might again be home to an emperor, if it did not become the citadel of Shade first . . .

. . . and Darkhorse, trapped again through his own lack of forethought, would be unable to do anything about either peril.

VII

ERINI WOKE THE next day feeling as if the dreams of her childhood had become reality. Yesterday had turned the fears of the future back into hopes. Yesterday, she had met Melicard the man.

In the light of day, the magical aspects of his unique features had taken on a new quality. Erini had thought him handsome *in spite* of the coldness of his elfwood side; now, she saw that the elfwood could enhance as well. There was a beauty to the wood when it became one with the king's pale skin. The rare wood had always been beautiful by itself, but, as Melicard had seemed to draw from it, so, too, had it drawn from him. The two sides of his face had become one despite their differences.

Even the stiff, artificial arm had felt smoother, more supple than earlier.

Galea and Magda came and helped her this morning; a good thing, too, since she found she could not concentrate. Her thoughts continued to be of yesterday's journey out onto the palace grounds and the tower to which he had led her. It was part of the wall and there were three others identical to it spread equal distances apart. This was the best one, Melicard had informed her quietly, to view the city as a whole.

His manners were rusty, as would be reasonable after so many years with so little practice. Still, the more they walked together—*without* the ever-present shadow of Mal Quorin—the more a new man had emerged; a new man, or one who had been locked away for over a decade. More and more, Erini was discovering that the dark, moody ruler of Talak was a creation of Melicard's own fears and, though she dared not suggest it openly, the influence of men like the counselor. This was not to say that the drakes were innocent, not by far, but the princess knew that some, at least, were trying to make peace with humanity. The others . . . she could not entirely fault Melicard's crusade.

He had pointed to the north first. "There you see the old center. After the palace was built here, everything shifted. The buildings in the old center were torn down and new ones put up. Since there's a gate over there, merchants and travellers have taken it over much the way they have the other gates. Also out that way is the main garrison of the city. A remnant of the days when a drake ruled from the Tybers."

Sensing his mood changing at the mention of the Dragon Emperor, Erini had turned west and pointed at a number of fancier buildings. "What about those?"

"The wealthier families. Master merchants and the old blood make their homes there. You probably saw some of that since the gate you entered lies in that direction."

She smiled then, already knowing the effect a smile would have on him. Few women—few people—had smiled at him and meant it, possibly because the king never smiled himself.

In the tower, he had returned her smile. She wondered how she could have ever thought it would be a chilling sight. In reply to his comment, the princess said, "There was so much to see that I cannot recall half of what I passed. Besides, most of the time my thoughts were on meeting you."

Only one other thing disturbed the otherwise pleasant tour. Pointing to a large structure in the eastern side of Talak, the princess asked, "What is that? I saw a building like that in the west. Are they theatres? Arenas?"

"In a sense. You'll find similar buildings in the northern and southern parts of Talak as well. All together, they house a standing force at least five times the size of the armies of Penacles, Zuu, or Irillian by the Sea."

A standing army. The city of Zuu, though far to the southeast of Gordag-ai, was familiar to her by name at least. Though relatively small in comparison to giants like Penacles and the maritime Irillian, their armies were of similar strength—mainly because nearly every adult was willing to take on a foe and being a part of the army was considered an honor. Erini did not understand the ways of Zuu, but if Melicard had a force five times the population of that city-state . . .

THE REST OF the day went peacefully. She had eaten with the king for the first time and, during the course of the dinner, had carefully broached the subject of their courtship and impending marriage. Melicard's replies were short and vague, but more, she suspected, from shyness than reluctance. Realizing she was starting to push things too quickly, the princess turned to small talk.

Her betrothed had walked her to her room, where both ladies-in-waiting tried not to look disconcerted at the sight of their mistress and the king walking arm in arm. Melicard wished her a pleasant evening and departed. Erini could not recall when exactly she had finally gone to bed, only knowing that she had probably spent several hours either thinking or talking about the king—whether Galea and Magda wanted to hear it or not.

Now, at the beginning of what she hoped to be an even more promising day, the princess found she could not be satisfied with anything she wore. Magda tsked a lot, reminding her that it was Erini the king was to marry, not a particular dress. Erini grew flushed. Here she was acting like the mindless young things that had always surrounded her at the palace back in Gordag-Ai. Always they had spoken of this young duke or that in giddy terms, much to her annoyance. Now, she realized with a wry smile, she was acting every bit as empty-headed.

"Give me that one," she commanded with as much conviction as she could muster, pointing at a dress she had already tried on. Galea shook her head and picked it up again.

Some time later, as Erini studied her finished self in one of the mirrors, she discovered she was still dissatisfied with the dress.

Is this what love is? the princess wondered. *I hope not. I'll never be able to live with myself if I keep acting this way.*

A servant arrived just as she was about to leave her room and informed her that something had come up; Melicard was begging her forgiveness but he would not be joining her.

"What is it? Does Talak face an attack? Is Melicard injured or ill?"

"He did not say, milady. He seemed well, though, and there was no word of an encroaching army in the outlands. I know nothing more."

"Thank you." Erini ended up eating only with her ladies. All through her meal, a meal which proved that, if nothing else, Melicard had someone who could perform miracles with eggs and spices, she found herself returning to the mysterious actions of yesterday. The strange states of the sorcerer, Drayfitt. The anger and fear of Mal Quorin. The door in the garden wall.

The door in the garden wall?

After brunch, she insisted that her two companions learn more about the city so that they would feel more comfortable. With a start, she also realized that she had yet to speak to the captain of the troop that had accompanied her coach to Talak from Gordag-Ai. The hapless soldier had not disturbed her, obviously believing she was too busy adjusting to Melicard to speak to him. Surely, though, the captain and his men wanted to return home as soon as possible, didn't they?

"Magda, before the two of you depart, would you please ask someone to summon—oh, what is his name? The captain of the cavalry troop that my father had accompany us."

"Captain Iston?" Galea piped up quickly. "I'll do it for you, Madga. I know you have some things you want to take care of before we leave."

"Thank you, Galea. I'd appreciate that."

The princess, who felt she had missed something, looked at her other companion as soon as Galea was out of the room. Magda smiled briefly. "Little Galea and Captain Iston have known each other for several months. He is the third son of Duke Crombey and a career soldier himself. That his unit was given to you is a sign of favor on the part of your parents."

"*Gave* to me? Do you mean to tell me—"

"They're staying here, yes. Permanent attachment. Not one of those men has a family to return to. If I may be forward, I hope you'll encourage Galea. The captain is a bit older than her, but they are very serious and definitely a good match. She will bear him strong children."

Erini fought down a grimace. "Is that his main priority with her? Passing on his name to a new generation?"

"It has some importance." The taller woman looked at her curiously. "Your father, King Laris, and Melicard's father kept that in mind, I imagine. Most royal marriages are set up that way and quite a few more common ones as well—but, before you say what your face is already shouting, I think I speak truthfully when I say that Galea and her cavalry officer would marry even if children were out of the question."

The princess looked at her older lady with new respect. "You surprise me, Mag. The two of you aren't *that* much older than me—"

"Fourteen years is *not* that much older? You flatter me."

"As I was *saying*, sometimes I watch you and I see those creatures that my father insisted I associate with, those—those crystalline dolls of the court. Other times, you seem to be in command of the world."

Magda made some adjustments on Erini's dress. "No secret there. I'm a woman. If you want a puzzle to play with, try to figure out men. Now *there's* a mystery."

Erini thought of Melicard and nodded.

HER TALK WITH Captain Iston was short. Once she had gotten over the fact that her parents had turned an entire unit of Gordag-Ai's cavalry over to her—as a personal guard—the rest was simple. Captain Iston proved to be a competent soldier and one of the few who listened to her without trying to act parental.

"I have only one request, then, your majesty," he said at the conclusion of their talk.

"That is?"

"It makes little sense for your bodyguards to be so far away from you. True, we are cavalry, but any soldier of Gordag-Ai is also a master warrior on foot, too. We were given the honor of becoming yours. At the very least, let me set up a series of watches so that each man can perform his duties."

Erini thought it over and nodded. "I'll have to talk to King Melicard first, captain, but I don't think that *he* will object to my request." Counselor Quorin might, but his likes and dislikes meant little to the princess. "I think I'd also like you to have a permanent place in the palace itself, captain. There will be times when I'll need you and I want you to start developing ties with our new countrymen."

"Your majesty, I'm a *soldier!* I should be sleeping with my men!"

"You won't be far. Besides, an officer is allowed some privacy, I think. You've earned the right to live life a little, too."

Magda and Galea announced themselves almost as if on cue. Iston did his best to maintain a military appearance, though his eyes wandered to the shorter lady-in-waiting more than once.

"We were about to leave, as you suggested, when I thought that there might be something in particular you wanted us to look for. Good day, captain."

"Good day, my ladies."

Erini smiled while the officer's eyes were on other matters. "Nothing, thank you, but a thought occurred to me. Captain Iston, if it would not be inconvenient, I have one more request of you."

He bowed. "Name it."

"I am occupied with many things at the moment, but I want someone to get to know the city. Magda and Galea are performing that favor for me. I'd feel better, however, if they had someone trustworthy to protect them—just in case. Would you be so kind as to take a few of your men and escort them? It would give you a chance to study Talak for yourself, something you were undoubtedly planning, anyway."

Iston hesitated, then, with a glance at Galea, nodded. "A wise idea, your majesty. If the ladies will permit me a few minutes, I will have horses and half a dozen of my finest join us. Will that be acceptable, my ladies?"

Galea was silent with just the slightest crimson in her cheeks, but Magda took events in hand and gave her approval. "That will be fine, Captain Iston."

"Has the princess any other need for me?"

"None."

The cavalry officer extended his arms. "If the two of you will accompany me?"

Erini watched them depart, Galea's hold on Iston so tight, the princess wondered if it would be possible to separate them again.

Her feeling of joy increased tenfold. She was on her way to strengthening her relationship with Melicard and now her own people were beginning to adjust to their new home. She turned to the mirror for one last look, wanting to be her best when she found her betrothed, which she *would*. Now there was only—

Erini started.

A figure stood visible in the mirror. A hooded figure much like Drayfitt, only younger in stature, but clad in garments a bit archaic for the times. She could not make out his face; something about the angle seemed to make it indistinct, almost a blur. His cowled head had just turned in her direction . . .

She whirled instinctively. Her hands began to move of their own accord.

The room was empty.

Erini glanced back in the mirror, almost expecting to see the figure still standing there. Nothing. She turned and rushed to the spot where he had stood. Kneeling, the princess touched the floor.

There were bits of dirt in the vague shape of a heel.

A feeling of ancient, enduring power caught her by surprise and she fell backward, only barely managing to stifle a scream. It was the first time she had truly sensed another spellcaster and, though she did not understand exactly what she had done, Erini had a fair idea of what she had felt.

She debated for some time what to tell Melicard, if anything. All she had to prove her story was a tiny clump of dirt that even the princess had to admit could have come from her own shoes or, more likely, the shoes of some errant servant. Only because of her increasing sensitivity to the powers did she know for certain that what had been reflected in the mirror was no figment of her imaginative mind. Erini could visualize Mal Quorin's expression should she give in and tell Melicard or anyone else her secret. It would probably be the fatal blow to the betrothal.

Not now. Not yet. I have to wait. Her decision was far from strong and she wavered even as she chose. *Drayfitt! He might understand, but . . . won't he tell Melicard?* Erini knew that the sorcerer was extremely loyal to his liege and that such loyalty might demand he betray the princess. Erini muttered a curse her father did not know she had overheard countless times while growing up. She slowly rose, deciding that she would postpone telling anyone for the time being. Her only fear was that, by doing so, she might let some other danger grow unchecked.

Confused and no longer looking forward to the day, the princess left her chambers. Whatever else happened today, nothing matched the importance of strengthening her relationship with Melicard. Nothing save what might destroy that relationship before it matured.

Princess Erini found Melicard in the least likely of places in the palace. He was holding court—in a sense. What she actually discovered was a huge, nearly empty throne room in which the king sat on a simple chair—not even the throne, which stood empty at the top of a dais—and argued with four or five men whom Erini realized were emissaries from other city-states. Quorin, standing behind the king, looked on in a combination of barely contained anger and contempt.

". . . drake lovers, all of you. I should have guessed as much, especially from you, Zuuite. You've long lived under the *beneficial* rule of the Green Dragon, haven't you?"

The emissary from Zuu replaced his helm, which he had been holding in the fold of one arm. A bear in size, he looked more than ready to trade blows with Melicard. Instead, he retorted, "Tell that to Prince Blane and the others who died defending Penacles from the Lochivarites and the monstrous forces of the Black Dragon and the drake commander Kyrg! You recall the sadist Duke Kyrg, do you not, your majesty?"

It was a telling blow. Kyrg's name, Erini recalled, conjured images in

Melicard's mind of his father slowly losing control as the drake ate freely from the writhing bodies of still-living animals. Rennek IV had spent the next week babbling on and on about not wanting to be eaten alive, something he knew that Kyrg had been capable of doing. Those memories were only two of the many that haunted Melicard almost every night.

The king's face turned as pale as bone. The elfwood hand came down on the arm of the chair and broke it into splinters. Even Mal Quorin stepped back from the rising fury of his master.

"Get . . . them . . . out of . . . here, Quorin! Get them out before I forget treaties!"

As the counselor rushed around the chair to aid the emissaries in their hasty departure, Erini started forward. She had been waiting out of sight near one of the side doors to the massive room with the intention of joining her betrothed once the talks were finished. Now, the princess wanted nothing more than to soothe Melicard before his anger drove him to further destruction and possible injury.

A firm hand clamped itself on her shoulder. "Your majesty, I wouldn't recommend you speak to him at this time."

She turned on the sudden intruder, intending to give him a strong, royal reprimand, and met the sad gaze of the sorcerer Drayfitt.

"He is in a dangerous mood, milady, and neither of us should be nearby. Things have not gone well." The aged spellcaster shook his head slowly. "And I fear that I am the cause of much of it."

"So what have your problems to do with me?"

Drayfitt gave her a sour smile. "Counselor Quorin, in what may be his finest performance, has been trying to make your arrival and stay here a detriment to the king's crusade. He's already pointed out how you kept the king occupied while I destroyed Quorin's damnable book."

Erini blinked. "Book? What are you talking about, mage?"

"I speak too much. Suffice to say, milady, King Melicard is not quite certain about the courtship. We have to give him a little time to recall all you did for him yesterday—and it was significant, I can tell you. He was almost the Melicard of long ago."

"You ramble a bit, Master Drayfitt," the princess paused, "but I will stay clear of him for a short while—providing you give me some answers I seek."

Drayfitt closed his eyes in concentration. When he opened them, he quietly replied, "Don't ask me about yesterday. Even I don't know everything—as Quorin has reminded me again and again."

The spellcaster's muttered words did little to assuage Erini's curiosity, but she knew there were other ways to find out what she wanted to know. The princess was about to ask him a question that she was fairly certain he *would* answer, when the elderly man stumbled against the wall. Erini reached out and grabbed his hand to prevent him from sliding to the floor.

He regained his balance almost immediately, but the look on his face was the most tragic yet. "Forgive me, princess. My powers have been tested beyond their limits lately; I've made heavy use of them much too late in life. Had I continued to train, to practice, while I was still young . . ." Drayfitt's voice trailed off as he stared at Erini's hand, which he still held in his own. After several seconds, he looked up at the princess as if she had sprouted wings. All his grief, all his exhaustion, seemed to vanish as he said, "Step down the corridor with me, please. We need privacy. I think there is something we must talk about quickly."

Not knowing whether she was mad to trust him, Erini reluctantly followed. Drayfitt led her along for quite some time, refusing to release her hand from his own. She began to worry. What if the spellcaster cared as little for her as Mal Quorin did? Despite his polite, sometimes helpful attitude, he might object to the marriage as much as the counselor did. What did he see in her hand?

As if trying to relieve her fears, Drayfitt turned and smiled assurance. He led her around a corner and stopped. There were no guards in sight.

"I could've touched the minds of some of the sentries and had our talk in a more open place, but such flamboyancy always backfires. Knowing something as simple but important as that was one reason I lived peacefully most of my life. I dearly wish it was still true."

"What do you want with me?"

"You have a natural affinity like none that I have ever seen."

The sorcerer continued to hold her hand, studying it closely as if looking for some minuscule marking. Erini had a very uncomfortable idea that she knew what he was searching for. Nevertheless, she played innocent. "What sort of affinity? For excellent fingernails? For having the 'fair skin' of a *maiden* in the tales of the minstrels and players?"

His features grew grim. "Don't play games with me, your majesty! You know what sort of affinity I talk of. Have you felt the involuntary desire to test your skills? What do you see? Most burgeoning spellcasters see the lines and fields of power that crisscross the world. Others see the spectrum, the dark and the light, and choose what they need from that. Which are you, Princess Erini?"

He'll tell Melicard! The thought was an irrational outburst, but Erini did not care. She was not yet ready to face the king with her own curse, not until she was certain her relationship with him was stronger. The princess tried to pull away, pretending to be offended. "You're mad! I am a princess of Gordag-Ai and the betrothed of your own monarch! Release me at one and forget this nonsense!"

Drayfitt's other hand shot forward and Erini had momentary fear that the sorcerer was going to strike her. Instead, his hand went up to the hair above her eyes. Mystified, she stood silent as the elderly man searched for something.

"Aaaah! The growth is slower than I would've thought, but it seems to be different with each magic-user. Interesting. Ishmir was wrong."

"What—what are you talking about now?" She jerked her head away, as if suddenly feeling continued contact would affect her somehow. Simultaneously, Drayfitt released her hand.

"There is a lock of silver amongst your beautiful, golden tresses, Princess Erini. The silver will expand—*magically*, you might say—as your abilities grow. Soon—and sooner than you want, I know—it will be impossible to hide it. Before that point, you must decide what you will do."

This was the last thing she had expected to deal with this morning. Erini stepped back and smoothed her dress, more to try to calm herself than because it needed it. "You don't know what you're saying! If you will excuse me, Master Drayfitt, I believe I will retire to my chambers. I'm not feeling well."

She started to go around him, but the aged sorcerer took hold of her again. His strength was phenomenal, a complete contrast to his weakness a moment before. A fire burned in his eyes. "Don't make the mistake I did, milady. Even if you never need them, it is best to hone your skills. I can help you. I've lived through the pain and the fear—more than most, I regret to say. I can teach you. There is no choice; your abilities will grow with or without your permission."

"Let me go," Erini commanded icily.

Drayfitt obeyed, but he was not yet through speaking. "Think about it. I'll be honest. I may need your assistance later on." As her eyes widened, he immediately added, "What I ask of you will only benefit King Melicard, not hurt him. I want the best for him, as do you. I think that your marriage will may possibly save him from the fate of his father—or worse."

Erini could listen no more. There was too much in what Drayfitt had said that had the ring of truth or, at the very least, conviction. A part of her wanted to turn to him for whatever aid he could give her . . . but the fear of losing everything and the shame of what she was becoming held her back. Perhaps some time alone would let her clear the fog that had grown thick in her mind.

As she walked stiffly away, the sorcerer called after her, "I hope you feel better, your majesty. Let us talk again soon."

She did not respond.

THE THRONE FELT proper beneath him. Taloned hands stroked the cracked armrests. He smiled as he thought of the others making obeisance to him, awarding what was due to him after these frustrating past few years.

The hatchlings are tainted, the Silver Dragon decided. *They have lived with humans for too long.* That was the fault of the Green Dragon, master of the Dagora Forest and ally to the humans. When the Gold Dragon had been defeated, the royal hatchlings had been taken by traitorous Green and turned over to Cabe Bedlam, the foulest of the human race. Now, those hatchlings that would have become Dragon Kings were on their way to becoming human sheep instead.

It is the only thing to do. They must be eliminated eventually so that some other traitor does not try to use them as puppets. The line that rules all others will be mine. My claim is strongest. They will see that. I will make them see that.

"I didn't return to you so that you could sit dreaming in a broken-down chair."

The Dragon King jumped. "Curse you, warlock! Announce yourself from now on!"

Shade stepped out of the darkness of a nearby tunnel and looked around. "Where are your brave warriors? Out trying to scrounge up some more toys to replace your crystal bauble?"

"What of it?" The crystal had been a double blow to the drake's ambitions. Not only had it broken, but the chamber of the Vraad and several others nearby were now impassable. The smoky substance released by the artifact showed no sign of dissipating, either. Even Shade, who had come back to look for the Silver Dragon, would not enter.

The shadowy sorcerer had still not explained exactly why he had chosen to finally accept the drake's offer of an alliance. It was not for what the Dragon King had already discovered, though there was *one* item of interest that the warlock wanted—or at least *remembered*—nor was it because they shared common goals. Shade seemed to care little who was emperor, as it long as it did not interfere with his own goals, whatever those might be.

"Nothing," Shade finally replied in answer to the drake lord's question. "Let them search."

"What about you?" Silver's reptilian eyes narrowed sharply. "Did you find it?"

"You said it was in the palace."

"Correct."

The warlock shook his head. "I will try again later. Something went amiss." A slight hint of humor touched his normally indifferent voice. "I ended up in the personal chambers of the king's bride-to-be. She'll probably have nightmares for weeks and drive Melicard mad."

The Silver Dragon chuckled. "Such a tragedy is little in comparison to what I intend to do to that cowardly *scavenger* of a human! Talak will fall as Mito Pica fell—but, this time, there will not be enough left over to rise again. After Talak . . . Penacles, I think."

"Why not Gordag-Ai in the region of Esedi? Your 'brother' there is dead and few of his clan remain active; you've already taken claim to his kingdom. Teach your subjects that they must obey you. That is the point of having *true* power."

Shade watched the Dragon King visibly mull over the thought. Gordag-Ai would be easier pickings and boost the morale of the drake's clans. It would also guarantee that his erstwhile draconian ally would remain busy, thereby gaining Shade valuable time—time to remember what it was he had set out to do and whether he had any right to do it.

Staring at one of the majestic effigies lying broken on the cavern floor, the warlock tried to ignore the increased pressure building in his head. He knew his mind had changed again, simply by the added pain. Shade also knew that the fact that he could recall his personality changes meant that he was beginning to stabilize. What worried him was what he would be like at that point.

He felt some shame and remorse for his past actions, especially against Darkhorse, but yet, at the same time, it was his growing feeling that those who stood in his way, regardless of their reasons, were simply in the wrong. If they surrendered to the inevitable, the warlock would leave them be—maybe—but if they continued to oppose him, he felt he was justified in removing them in whatever way necessary.

Shade realized that the drake lord was speaking. "What was that you said?"

"I asked you what you think you are doing, human! Is this how you vent your frustrations?" The Dragon King pointed toward the spot Shade had been staring at moments before.

The warlock returned his gaze to the effigy—or to where it had once lain. Now, there was only a pile of fine dust. Very fine dust. Shade looked down at his hands. They literally glowed with the use of the powers.

"I am *Vraad*," he whispered to himself. "Vraad is power." The words had been spoken millennia before by many, all of whom, save Shade, were dead now. It had almost been a litany to the race, and his remembrance of it was yet another sign of what was happening to him. Still, it bothered the spellcaster that he had reduced the ancient statue to ash without realizing it. A warning beat briefly against the walls of his mind, but the pain drowned it out. He looked up at the impatient and somewhat nervous Dragon King. "Merely a little carelessness on my part."

The drake's burning red eyes narrowed. "Yesss. That is what got you into your predicament originally, is it not?"

"Watch your tongue, drake lord. It might dart too far out of your mouth once too often."

The Silver Dragon hissed anxiously. Because Shade had found a need for him, he had grown overly confident about his power. Only now did the drake realize that there were limits to which he could push the spellcaster. Both knew that the alliance was temporary at best. Quickly, the would-be emperor turned the conversation back to an earlier subject. "What do you sssseek in the book? Most of it makes little sense."

"A key, of sorts. I really don't know what. Not yet, but soon. Soon I'll be my old self again." A vague line that was what now passed for his smile surfaced briefly, faltered, and died. Shade wrapped his cloak about him and, as the Dragon King rose in the sudden realization that something was amiss, vanished.

Through his own words, the warlock had just rediscovered the purpose, the goal, of his search—and why he dared not let anyone, even Darkhorse, stand in his way.

VIII

THE PAIN INFLICTED upon him was like such he had not suffered in centuries. The human called Mal Quorin claimed it was on order of the king, but Darkhorse, in his more lucid moments, suspected that Melicard knew only vaguely what his underlings were doing. Something in the feline features of the counselor, as if he were toying with his prisoner the way the creature he so resembled toyed with its prey, told Darkhorse that.

It was obvious that the sorcerer was reluctant to question his rival and that alone spoke volumes as to their respective positions of influence with the king. Drayfitt's loss of face was the shadow steed's doing, made doubly worse by the successful destruction of the spellbook by the entranced mage. For that, even Drayfitt had exercised a bit of vengeance.

They had abandoned him for other matters some time back—how long, Darkhorse could not say. Now, the eternal recovered slowly in his accursed cage, his present form little more than a blot of shadow darker than the rest. Had he been human, he would have died several times over and that fact had not escaped him. With one part of his mind, he plotted the torture of his foes; with the other, he cursed himself for his stupidity and lack of foresight. Drayfitt had taken care with his original spell. Had the stallion delved deeply, he would have discovered the thin magical bond that still tied him to the sorcerer, a tie that the elderly human had used to recapture him. His escape, it seemed, had been no more than a farce.

So close! Shade was no doubt laughing at him even now. He had come so close, actually confronting the warlock. Darkhorse knew he should have come in striking, beating down Shade before the warlock had a chance to think. Hesitation had cost him the battle and his freedom.

Once more, he re-created the equine form he favored. A hollow victory, creating a form again, but a victory nonetheless. With nothing else to do, Darkhorse began a slow and thorough scan of his magical prison. Perhaps this time . . .

Nothing. If anything, Drayfitt had tightened the control of the pattern, used the power of the cell to cancel out the shadow steed's own abilities to the point where even eye contact would not help. The aged sorcerer was a survivor and learned readily from his mistakes.

Odd, he wondered, that Melicard's spellcaster would have access to a Vraad artifact at the same time that both Shade and the Silver Dragon were searching for such things. What was the connection? What did Shade *want* with a work from so ancient a time? Surely not to summon a true demon. Its power would be insignificant compared to his own. Was this latest madness just the product of his unstable mind? The warlock *had* undergone yet another personality change; in centuries past, he had done stranger things during various incarnations. These rapid and continuous changes, however, smelled of something different, something gone awry. When would they stop? Which "Shade" would be the final result?

Significant questions weaved in a hundred different directions like a swirling mass of tentacles, confusing and unanswerable for the most part. He soon realized there was little point in pursuing them for now, though he knew that forgetting them entirely would be impossible.

More time passed. All the while, Darkhorse stubbornly continued to raise, revise, and reject options as they occurred to him. There was no way that he could physically—so to speak—pass through the boundaries. His magical abilities all seemed useless while he languished in his prison. He did not even know what was going on; the Dragonrealm might be on the brink of destruction—

Darkhorse did not breathe, though he often pretended to for appearance. Nevertheless, he came close to holding that nonexistent breath when it occurred to him that, though his magical abilities were muted, there were natural ones—unnatural by human standards—that he might make use of. Regardless of his careful work, Drayfitt could not hope to completely understand the nature of the ebony stallion.

There were many over the centuries who had called the legendary Darkhorse the Child of the Void. They were closer and farther from the truth than they knew. Darkhorse was a creature of the border regions between reality and the Void who only *wandered* that empty realm, much akin to the mist dwellers who guarded the secret paths that crossed into and out of the world like portals. Through practice, Darkhorse had made himself stronger than most, though that had tied him to reality and lost him some mastery over the Void. He did not regret that; there was so much more to the multiverse. Had it not proved necessary in his prior struggle with the warlock, the shadow steed would have chosen never to return to the dismal domain he had dwelled in for so long.

Yet, it was the Void to which he now turned in hope.

While willing himself back into the form of a horse had proved difficult after his ordeal, the act of literally *separating* himself into two parts was sheer agony. The strain alone threatened to overcome him. Despite the horror, however, he was willing to suffer that pain and even the permanent loss of that smaller portion of self. What mattered most was learning what he could in the hope of using it to engineer his escape. There might even be a clue as to how he could stop Shade, though his hopes in that respect were less than nothing after what had happened.

He willed one of his hooves into a wide circular shape a little less than a foot in diameter. *That* was the easy part of his task. The second was far worse, a strain on his already worn consciousness. There was also the danger of losing too much of his essence. He planned to separate a tiny portion of himself from the main body. It was a dangerous thing, risking his very identity in the process, for a piece of his "self" would be lost along with his essence. Humans who had lost a limb might claim to have lost a part of who they were, but with Darkhorse it was literal. It would take him years to fully recover.

Straining his concentration to the limit, he forced the reshaped hoof to expand away from his leg. Slowly, as the two masses separated, the ankle grew thinner and thinner until it was little more than the thickness of a twig. Darkhorse felt his mind separate into two distinct "selves," one greater, one lesser. With one last effort, *they* broke the remaining physical link between the fragment and the main body.

What must be done . . . He wondered why such a thought would come to him unbidden—then paused in sudden guilt as he realized it was a fading thought from another, that piece of "self" he had sacrificed. Darkhorse stared at the black spot for several seconds before he could bring himself to work the rest of his plan. With great reluctance and a little revulsion, he extended his essence and created a new hoof to replace the old. The shadow steed could not help feeling as if he had abandoned himself.

"It is said," Darkhorse whispered to his other self pulsating on the floor, "that, from the Void, all places may be reached or viewed. The danger lies in forgetting yourself, losing the way home. I am my own home, yet I am also the path to the Void. I will consume you the same way that I have consumed so many of my adversaries, such as the drake in the cavern, over the endless years; but rather than be condemned to floating in the emptiness forever, you, who know the way as I do, will find the path and return through my body, the Void, and the border realms to this world, to the place called the Dragonrealm. Waste no energy in seeking the path closest to this palace, but enter at the first available. Entering reality will cost you your "self" and eventually your essence, but you will provide me with eyes and ears in the world out there—in the hope that there is still something that can be done."

He felt better saying it out loud, though communication between his two selves could have just as easily been accomplished by mere thought.

With a touch of the new hoof, he absorbed the lesser portion of his essence in the same way he had absorbed the drake who had tried to jump him in the cavern. It fell within him, growing smaller and smaller until it was beyond even his senses.

Darkhorse sighed—because it felt right to do so—and then stiffened as the world around him changed.

Mountains passed swiftly before his eyes, smaller than the Tybers, but still majestic in their own right. Green hills dotted the borders of that mountain chain and a few habitations could be seen in the distance.

Darkhorse jerked backwards, falling against the invisible barrier that held him. *By the twin moons! So quickly?*

It was impossible at first to separate the visions from his own sight, but gradually, they came under control. The journey his other self had taken went beyond things such as time, but even the eternal was surprised at the speed with which it had travelled. That surprise turned to worry, for the images he perceived were weak, as if the strain of the journey had been worse than he had hoped. Little of the fragment's essence survived. There was only one mind, too, for the other him no longer had the strength to preserve its own will. Darkhorse had gained his eyes and ears, but he had lost all else that mattered. Even though it had happened the way the stallion had thought it would, the pain was deep nonetheless.

The northwest. I have emerged into the northwest of the continent. It was now an easy matter to guide the fragment along the simpler paths he knew until it emerged again, this time in the outskirts of the city. Darkhorse could not recall the last time he had seen Talak. He wanted to know what sort of place was ruled by men like Melicard and the foulness calling itself Quorin.

Through the dim vision of the fragment, he observed the people. They seemed healthy, though he was no judge of human conditions, and relatively happy. Darkhorse moved on, intending to work his way to the palace. The more he saw, the more Talak resembled a prosperous and very normal city-state—not what he would have expected under a madman.

No sooner had Darkhorse thought that, when he caught sight of the first soldiers.

They were armored and very definitely hardened veterans. A full column rode through this section, evidently leaving on some military exercise. Dark-horse paused his tiny spy and observed the marching men closely. From the looks on their faces, they were almost fanatical in their devotion to the king. The shadow steed turned his gaze to the banners they carried. The stylized dragon made him chuckle in bitter humor. Melicard was preparing for all-out war and, judging by the size of this column, he was nearly ready.

He will have his glory . . . and the Lords of the Dead will have their bounty. Melicard had numbers, but the drakes had the ferocity. Either side had equal chances, which meant a long and bloody war that would strip the lands further of life.

Is that all there is to these mortal creatures? Are the humans, drakes, Seekers, and the rest all doomed to violent ends? Darkhorse tried not to think too hard about his own role; it was best to believe he had always worked for the quickest and most rational solution.

He wasted no further time. In seconds, his view had changed to that of the palace walls. The fragment, only a tiny part itself of what he had sacrificed, moved through those walls like a specter, entering the rear of the building. He ran it through corridor after corridor, room after room. Most of his observa-tions were of the ordinary type; servants going about their daily duties, guards standing at attention in various hallways, and officials running hither and yon-der with no evident purpose. Melicard was not in any of the rooms Darkhorse searched. There was also no trace of either the counselor or the sorcerer. So close, he was forced to slow his search. There were many risks, including exces-sive activity near Drayfitt, who might be sensitive enough to pick up the magical presence of Darkhorse's spy.

". . . and keep them prepared, Commander Fontaine! There's been report of activity in the Hell Plains. The remnants of the Red clans may be moving."

Counselor Quorin marched into sight, another man, a soldier, keeping pace. If Quorin had the face of a cat, his companion was just the opposite. Rough canine features and a bald head gave the human an ogreish cast. Like the ani-mals they resembled, the two men were bickering.

"I've not heard a thing about the Hell Plains! Damnation, man! It's east and north we have to watch! Drakes of the Silver clan have been spotted in the Ty-bers! *He's* the one we should be moving against!"

"You can always go *back* to the city guard, commander, if you can't obey a directive!"

The officer slammed his helm onto his head and marched stiffly away, mut-tering something about merchants and functionaries knowing less about wars than conscripted footsoldiers. Mal Quorin watched the fuming soldier vanish and smiled. It was the same sort of smile he had used on Darkhorse during the "punishment."

The smile quickly soured as some disturbing thought intruded. The counselor turned back the way he had come and moved on, his pace quick and determined. Darkhorse followed closely behind, curious. The path Quorin took led him toward an outdoor garden in the center of the palace. The human was halfway to an old door partially hidden in one of the vine-covered walls when another figure entered the garden from the opposite side. Both Quorin and Darkhorse stopped, the shadow steed quickly backing farther and farther away, hoping he had not reacted too slowly.

"Drayfitt!" The counselor spat out the spellcaster's name as he might have spat out a piece of rotten meat. The look on the sorcerer's face matched his own. There was no love lost between them.

"What do you want now, *Counselor* Quorin?"

As they neared one another, looking all the while like two fighting cocks, Darkhorse moved a bit closer again. Quorin was speaking quietly now, intending his words for his rival's ears alone. The eternal let his fragment drift close to the ground. If Drayfitt's mind remained occupied by the presence of his adversary, then it was not likely he would notice Darkhorse's spy. At least, that was the hope.

"Why aren't you attending to matters below?"

"There isn't much that creature can do at the moment—thanks to both of us! Melicard didn't even know I'd recaptured it, did he? In fact, he seemed quite surprised, *counselor!*"

"What of it?" Quorin bared his teeth in a parody of a smile. "I act in his name."

"Melicard would have never ordered such torture! I should have known better!"

"You seemed to be enjoying it somewhat."

The sorcerer's visage burned crimson. "I allowed my baser emotions to rule me that time, but not again! I care very little about what is ultimately done with that creature, but I will not see it abused!"

Mal Quorin leaned back and laughed loud. "Drayfitt—defender of the weak! That's not a pup down there, you old idiot! That's a demon older than time itself! Remember what it cost us—cost *you*—already! You're fortunate it didn't decide to take your head off while it was at it!"

Darkhorse heard the words faintly, his attention partially focused on the door Quorin had been heading for. The door, he realized, lead down to the chamber where he was being held—and both men had been heading toward it. For a brief moment, Darkhorse adjusted his senses, returning his full vision to the cramped room and his cage. If either man, especially Drayfitt, came while he was engaged with observing the palace, they would recognize that something was wrong. It was proving impossible to keep both positions in perspective and there was the danger that he might become so engrossed in spying on his adversaries that he might not even notice when one or the other visited his prison.

They were still arguing when the shadow steed reestablished contact with the fragment. The images were even more faded, a sign that the fragment was dissipating. Darkhorse knew he should have sacrificed more, but there was the danger of fragmenting himself into two greater yet weaker portions, neither of which could survive on its own. Only by utilizing a *small* piece of his "self" had he been able to do what he had.

"—before long! I expect it to be that way!" Quorin finished up. Darkhorse cursed himself for missing what might have been of great importance.

"We shall see. The book was fairly worthless in any case; most of it was notes, incomprehensible and, more often than not, complete foolishness. What little was useful was also insanely dangerous and destructive. I used what I could—and I still want to talk to the scoundrel you purchased it from. I want to find out *where* he stole or, more likely, scavenged it from."

"Why, if it was so useless to you?"

Drayfitt shook his head, now apparently a bit angry at himself for saying too much. "You wouldn't understand, Quorin. You could not *begin* to understand."

"Pfah! I've no more time for this!" Forgetting that it was he who had started the exchange, the counselor departed—in a direction that took him *away* from the door. Darkhorse hesitated, not knowing whether he should stay with the sorcerer or follow Quorin.

It was Drayfitt who decided for him. The elderly spellcaster started toward the door and then hesitated, as if he were noticing something for the first time. It was evidently not the stallion that had captured his attention, however, for Drayfitt also turned from the door and returned the way he had come.

Darkhorse watched him go, then drifted in the direction that the counselor had gone. *One wonders how anyone gets things done here, what with so many detours along their paths.* The tension in the palace was astounding. It was evident just from the two conversations he had followed that no one in charge trusted anyone else. This was a kingdom in danger of collapsing. Perhaps not now, but some time in the future.

They have no lives, just plots.

Quorin had disappeared somewhere in the cavernous corridors of the building, but Darkhorse did not have the power available to him to find out where. All the fragment could do was observe—and even that ability was faltering. So far, all that he had accomplished was to add to his list of questions. In his cage, the shadow steed laughed in self-mockery. He had outfoxed no one but himself with his trick. The sacrifice of this bit of his essence was proving to be worthless.

Despite the near hopelessness of his search, he endeavored to continue. So long as he could see and hear, there was a chance. Somewhere in this leviathan of a palace, he might still find something of value. Darkhorse regretted that he could not have severed a portion of himself strong enough to free him.

While he pondered his deficiencies, he guided what remained of the fragment, through the corridors leading to the main hall, or at least where he assumed it would be. Most palaces, while they reveled in their pomp and majesty, were very much the same inside. Unless the builder and the ruler he had designed it for were both insane, Darkhorse was fairly certain that things would be where he expected them.

He was not mistaken. Both the main hall and the throne room were where they were supposed to be. Regrettably, neither the king nor his underlings were present. The shadow steed cursed as the images grew dark. His lesser self was in the first stages of death—or nonexistence, at least. Something within the eternal twisted painfully at the thought.

"I must insist. He *will* see me."

The voice was female and off to the right. Darkhorse forced his pain down and drifted toward the voice. It had been raised to command, and a female authority in the palace of Melicard I was something worth investigating.

The owner of the voice was a small woman who seemed twice as tall as the sentries she was browbeating. All three stood before two massive, wooden doors. By human standards, she was beautiful, with a long, golden mane that would have put many a mare to shame. The female was not from Talak; her mannerisms and a slight accent spoke of the city-state of Gordag-Ai, which Darkhorse had visited once or twice in earlier centuries. Why she was here was a puzzle. There was only one reason that the stallion could think of, but—surely not with *Melicard!*

Unable to withstand his inbred training, one of the sentries finally stepped aside. The other followed suit immediately. The female, a princess if she had the authority to command the royal guard, waited until the chagrined soldiers opened the doors for her. Only then did she enter, and only after giving the two hapless men an imperial nod. It was almost enough to make Darkhorse laugh.

He followed her in, ignoring the doors as they passed through the misty form of the fragment.

The room was dark, making the dim images even harder to discern. Fortunately, the princess's first act was to walk determinedly over to a set of curtains rising from the floor to the ceiling and fling them aside. The room was bathed in a flood of sunlight. Darkhorse shifted to a corner less lit, knowing that the fragment, while insubstantial, would still make an odd shadow. A sudden movement from the other end of the room caught his attention. His spirits soared.

Melicard!

The split-faced monarch turned away from the female, but she would have none of his reluctance. Darkhorse admired her strength, though he could not say much for her taste. Evidently, here was a woman bent on saving a man from himself.

A waste of time, my lady, he chided, though he knew she did not hear him. *Why must mortal women always think they can bring out what no longer exists?*

"What's happened, Melicard? You act the way you did the first time we met. Have I given you some reason to think that I played you for a fool?"

The king did not respond at first, though he did look up at her from the chair he sat in. Darkhorse could not make out his face as well as he would have wished, but he thought that Melicard was nothing if not confused. Here was a man fighting himself. This was not the same man who had originally visited the imprisoned shadow steed. Darkhorse studied the female with new respect. She *had* accomplished something.

"I apologize—Erini. My work has become paramount. I cannot say how long it will demand precedence, but I suspect it will be some time. Rather than leave you alone for all that . . . time, perhaps it might . . . might be best if you returned to Gordag-Ai. When I can spare the time, I will summon you back."

The princess, "Erini," the king had called her, was not to be put off. With a bluntness that surprised both the eavesdropping specter and the disfigured monarch, she walked up to Melicard, put her hands on his face—on *both* sides of his face!—and replied, "Those are Counselor Quorin's words, are they not? I recognize the ruthlessness in them, a ruthlessness you could never match! Is he blaming me for some error of his? Am I accused of something? Do you remember the things we did and said the other day? Was that all amusement on your part?"

Melicard opened his mouth to respond, but the first try resulted in a silent swallow. After some effort, he said, "It would not be right to make you part of this. Not now. I don't dare allow anything to slow progress. I can't. Not after the setbacks."

Throughout all of this, Erini had refused to let go. Now, she pulled the king closer, so their faces were only inches apart. "Whatever you decide to do, I want to be at your side. Before I came here, it was infatuation with a memory and a dream. After seeing the real you, the one that men like that mouser you made counselor have tried to hide—with your help—it became *love.*"

Love? In his cage, Darkhorse snorted in disgust. *Love for this sorry creature?*

Melicard had as much trouble believing it. "After only a few days? Love . . . like that . . . happens only in the tales spun by the minstrels and storymen. How can . . . you be so certain?"

Erini smiled. "Because I know that you love me, as well."

She kissed him before he could even begin thinking of a response. Melicard, unprepared, pulled back. His eyes were wide in almost childlike disbelief at what had happened. He could not have had much experience with the complexities of women, not, at least, in the ten years since he had shut himself away.

This is a predatory woman, Darkhorse thought, amused by it all. *A capable woman.*

The king rose and stepped away from her, but each movement, each hesitation, was an indication that Princess Erini had dashed any argument Melicard might have brought up. He *did* love her; that was obvious even to Darkhorse, who had never quite understood the concept since it did not apply to him. The signs were all there, however.

He whirled on her. "How can you love *this*?" The elfwood arm came up so that the elfwood hand could touch the elfwood face. "This is no epic song. I am no hero. I cannot promise that we will live happily ever after, as they say. You will see this face and this arm every day of your life if you marry me! Do you really want that?"

"Yes."

Melicard, intending to say more, faltered at the quick, simple response. Erini pressed her advantage. "Even if you had neither the arm nor the reconstructed face, I would want that."

A knock interrupted them. The looks on both humans' faces said that an intrusion was the last thing either had wanted. A guard, visibly tense, announced that Drayfitt needed to speak to his majesty. Melicard looked at his betrothed and then at the sentry. "Have him wait just a moment."

"My liege." The sentry closed the door.

Turning, Melicard walked over to Erini and put his hands on her shoulders. She was forced to look up to see his face. "We *will* talk again before the day is over, I promise you that, Erini. I do."

She wanted to kiss him again and Darkhorse, though the images had become so black as to resemble night, could sense that Melicard wanted to kiss her back. Fear held him back, though. The princess smiled nonetheless. "I look forward to it, Melicard. Perhaps, dinner?"

"Dinner." He called out for the guard, who opened the door just in time to let the princess through. Darkhorse slowly followed her. Despite the gravity of his predicament and the definite possibility that the king and the sorcerer would be including him in their conversation, the eternal found himself with an overwhelming desire to know more about this woman who could turn Melicard around so. He wished he could contact her, speak to her, for he suspected she might be his key. Her sympathy might do what his powers could not: make the king forget his idiotic dream of harnessing a demon to his service and cause him to release the shadow steed. It was a futile wish, however, for Darkhorse could only see and hear, not speak, not with so weak a fragment, and what remained of this portion of his essence was no longer enough to even gain her attention.

The princess walked the corridors as one half-dreaming. Darkhorse, who recalled moments of similar reactions from past mortal acquaintances, knew she was picturing the days to come. The stallion wished her best, for here was a true queen who would rule wisely, but he suspected her path still had barriers, chief among them Mal Quorin. The counselor would never accept a role of lesser influence. Already, he had evidently tried to break up the two. Darkhorse wished again that he could speak to her.

She was barely visible now, a darkened figure wandering in the abyss. His sacrificed "self" was in the last stages of dying. With no other option remaining, he drifted as close as he could, hoping to pick up some last words, some last expression. It was foolish and highly useless, but, for reasons he could not understand, he felt drawn to her.

Erini stumbled as if pushed. She came to a sudden halt and looked around, her hands twitching nervously. The shadow steed, his perceptions less than perfect, tried to see what worried her so. He was not long in discovering what, for the princess finally turned in *his* direction.

"Who is that? Drayfitt? Is that you?" She reached up a hand toward the fading place. Darkhorse, stunned, could only watch as her hand went through.

"No, not Drayfitt, it can't be. Did—did I summon you?" She looked down at her hands in growing horror. "Rheena! Not now!"

Summon? In his prison, Darkhorse's ice-blue eyes glittered as the answer struck him. Small wonder he had been drawn to her! *A sorceress! A spellcaster untrained!*

She had the potential to release him! *She* had the power!

The last vestiges of strength burned away. The fragment slowly faded, the last of its essence sacrificed. Darkhorse wanted to *scream*. If she were truly a magic-user . . .

Listen to me! he called out. If she did have a natural ability, it might be enough to establish a link! *Listen to me!*

She looked up—and her image vanished even as the shadow steed sent one last message. *Below! Go below!*

The walls of the underground chamber greeted his eyes once more. The single torch flickered in seeming mockery at his attempt. Exhausted by more than his failed efforts, the shadow steed drew within himself. He had little hope that his final words had gotten through—and without that hope, there was nothing else he could do.

Darkhorse settled down, yearning for the dreamless unconsciousness that was the closest thing to true sleep he could ever know. He hoped his strength, sorely used by this poor attempt, would return long . . .

. . . before the *true* demon, Mal Quorin, paid him yet another *instructional* visit.

IX

IN ONE OF the many unused chambers of the vast palace, Shade returned to Talak.

This particular room had been closed down after the death of Rennek IV's young bride, Melicard's mother, though Shade neither knew that nor would have cared if he *had* known. It was a room where he would not be disturbed and that was all that mattered. Cloths, long buried under thick layers of dust, covered the furniture, blocked sunlight from entering through the windows, and hid the painful memories from the old king, who had come here once a year on the anniversary of his marriage. Melicard, while he did not follow his father's example and pay homage here, did leave a standing order that no one was allowed to enter this room unless on his command. As it was, more than four years had passed since a single soul had stepped in here for even a moment. Ironically, Melicard, wrapped up in his campaign, had forgotten about his mother's chamber completely.

"Light," the warlock whispered, as if reminding himself. A tiny pinprick of light, all that he needed for now, glimmered in the center of the room.

Shade studied his surroundings but briefly. In a time long removed from the present rulers of this city-state and during one of his more benevolent incarnations, he had stayed in one of these rooms, the guest of a thankful prince whose life he had saved. The warlock smiled thinly. *There* had been a man who knew how to treat his betters.

Lowering himself down on one knee, the cloaked figure stretched his arms forward, as if reaching for an invisible object. He whispered words of a language long forgotten, the language of Vraad sorcery. Like the spells of the present-day sorcerers, the words were more a memory trick, a way of reminding him how the powers had to be bent by his will so that he could achieve the results he desired. He knew he had succeeded when he felt something squirm within his sleeves.

They say the walls have eyes and ears in most palaces, he thought in growing amusement. *Now they will have noses as well.*

A tiny, wormlike thing poked out of his sleeve. Shade felt a number of miniature legs and hands on his wrist; on both wrists. The wormlike thing proved to be a long and narrow proboscis that twisted and turned as its owner cautiously made its way out from the safety of the warlock's sleeve. From the other sleeve, an identical trunk extended itself.

Shade said nothing, but he shook both arms lightly, stirring the creatures to renewed speed. Drones of his own making, they were prone to be lethargic at first. Given their own way, the simple creatures would remain on his arms for days, trying to draw strength from what they had once been part of. He had no inclination to let them do so. They were nothing to him, who had given them life of a sort. They were tools and nothing more.

A head popped out after the long trunk, a head that was little more than a single, wide orb that was nearly all pupil. Beneath the great eye, a pair each of pencil-thin legs and arms made up the rest of the tiny monstrosity that was the warlock's spy. It scuttled onto the dust-thick floor, crouching, where it was joined by the first from the other arm.

The eye-creatures began tumbling out in astonishing numbers, many, many more than could have been hidden by Shade's garments. As their numbers grew, the creatures began to wander about, inspecting their surroundings with great care, now eager to perform their function.

When he was at last satisfied with the quantity, Shade shook his arms once more, dislodging a final pair of the horrors. He rose and gazed down at his tiny servants.

"Find it," he whispered harshly. "Do not let yourself be seen. Sacrifice yourself, if necessary. When you have located it, I will know. Now *go!*"

Shade watched them scuttle away in every direction, each creature quickly disappearing into the first crack or hole it could find, whether that opening had been initially large enough or not. There were other ways he could have gone about this, but anonymity was his desire for now. Let the destruction of Talak fall to his erstwhile ally, the Silver Dragon. The ensuing chaos and bloodshed would decoy those few who might be able to delay the achieving of his goal and might even rid him of a few annoyances.

The warlock thought briefly about trying to explain to Darkhorse what it was he had to do, but he doubted his onetime companion would understand. There were lives that would be sacrificed in order to correct the error that had twisted him so, and Shade was now fully prepared to sacrifice those lives when necessary. What was the loss of a few transitory souls if it would gain him his proper immortality and the power that should have gone along with it? He was Vraad and the Vraad were absolute. All else was there to do his bidding—even if that meant forcing that obedience by punishing a few. Once he had reclaimed this land. . . .

Something glittered. Shade increased the intensity of the light a bit. The thing that had caught his attention increased by the same intensity. A reflection, which meant a mirrored surface. He walked over to the reflection and tore away the decrepit cloth, unveiling a full-length mirror embossed in silver. With the light floating behind and a little above him, the warlock stared intently at himself in the mirror.

A face stared back at him. The eyes and nostrils were dark spots and the mouth was a thin line, but it was still a face. A face that had been growing more distinct since his return to this world.

Shade put a hand to his reflection and drew a pattern across his face with his index finger.

The mirror cracked . . . and cracked . . . and *cracked*. Jagged lines crisscrossed the full length of the mirror. Pieces began to fall to the floor as the warlock stepped away, his face once again buried beneath his cowl.

Though the shattered mirror rained bits and pieces over the chamber floor, they made no sound as they hit. Odder still, the damage to the mirror did not stop there. Instead, those fragments that had fallen continued to crack, creating smaller and smaller parts which cracked further still. Shade watched silently, shaking, as a pile of dust formed beneath the rapidly disappearing mirror.

When nothing remained but a pile of fine ash, the warlock wrapped his cloak about him, twisted his body within himself, and vanished.

WHATEVER HAD STALKED her was no more. Erini felt its passing, felt that something had disappeared that would never return. Yet, she was also positive that the force behind the misty apparition was still very much alive.

Her first thought was that this was some spy of Drayfitt's, but the feel was not right. He was no more responsible for this than he had been responsible for the visitation in her chambers. Neither was this briefly lived specter the product of that other intruder. This was another presence, one that was somehow not quite *human*.

What sort of place have I come to? Magic flies left and right and, though there are high walls and armed guards, intruders go in and out with ease!

Erini had not spoken to anyone about the stranger in the mirror and she was not all that certain it would be wise to bring this encounter up, either. Again, she had no proof save her growing sensitivities—which would, of course, reveal her powers to Melicard.

Drayfitt? He knew already what she was. If his present conversation with her betrothed did not include exposing her secret, then she might be able to trust him. He *had* offered to help her learn to control herself . . . an idea with greater merit than she had originally supposed. Her initial reaction at discovering the sorcerous onlooker was to reach out with those powers and discover what it was. Only her own fear had held her back. Next time . . .

The princess stirred, abruptly realizing that she had been staring at the same area on the wall for several minutes. So far, no one had come by, but it would not be good to be found acting so strangely. Inhaling deeply, Erini turned and walked in the direction of her chambers. Until she came to a definite decision, it was the safest place for her to be.

As she walked, she could not help feeling that the tiny intruder had wanted something from her, something of importance. The apparition was a sacrifice on its part. Erini had felt the bond, though the fact of that was only just becoming apparent to her. Whatever its cause, the unknown presence was willing to give of itself, if necessary. That was more than most humans would have done.

So engrossed was the princess in her thoughts, she almost walked into two guards patrolling the halls. She succeeded in stepping out of the way at the last moment while they, being only soldiers, were the ones who immediately apologized. Embarrassed with herself, Erini hurried away without responding.

The chance encounter with the guards had steered her to the side of the corridor where windows overlooking the inner garden dotted the wall. Out of pure reflex, she glanced out at this one colorful place as she passed each window. At the fifth one, she froze and moved closer. The door in the far wall beckoned to her with a stronger pull than ever. In her mind, Erini felt the link between the door and the thing following her and found it amazing that she, who had wondered *what* might be down there, below the palace, had never stopped to think that the *what* might instead be a *who*.

Erini would have gone down into the garden then, using the very abilities she had always cursed if that was what it would take to open the door. It was a foolhardy notion, though, for the princess had no idea where the counselor was at this time and, even with sorcery at her command, she did not warm to the thought of confronting as dangerous a monster as Mal Quorin. Even Drayfitt, with much more skill, was cowed by the man.

Her fingers twitched of their own accord as she continued to stare intently at the door. Annoyed, Erini formed fists in an attempt to stifle this latest urge. This was twice now in the space of minutes. At this rate, she would soon be unable to suppress herself.

It's like breathing, Erini thought in defeat, *and I've been holding my breath all this time, building it up into something worse.*

The door still beckoned. Biting her lip, the princess took one last, lingering look—a grave mistake. Her curiosity overwhelmed her caution. She *had* to see what secret the palace held, regardless of the counselor or Melicard's desires.

This would be the true test to determine whether she was to be Talak's queen. If Melicard intended on keeping her in the dark as to his plans, then their marriage would be little more than a charade and something she would never be consonant to regardless of repercussions.

Having convinced herself of this, Erini sought out the nearest stairway leading down to the garden. All thoughts of sorcery were temporarily put aside as the anxiety of discovery replaced them. A tiny portion of her mind, buried deep within, warned her again and again about taking part in such foolishness, but Erini paid no attention to it.

The garden itself was beautiful, more so this close up. Any other time, she would have stopped to admire the lush, fragrant flowers and the thick, green bushes. Now, though, she had eyes only for the door. Erini took a quick glance around her, but there was no one else in sight. It disturbed her briefly that there were no guards in sight, but then she realized that the last thing anyone would want to do is draw more attention to the door by placing sentries near it. Unattended, it was just one more seldom-used passage not worth even a second look.

Erini felt a slight tingle pass through, but, unaware of the many abilities just developing within her, she thought it nothing more than nervousness. That delusion was quickly dispelled when a voice quietly but distinctly whispered in her ear.

"Enter there, your majesty, and I cannot promise to save you."

She whirled, saw no one, and whirled around again. Her hands came up in an instinctive offensive gesture.

"Peace, milady, peace! If you continue twirling like a child's top, someone is apt to wonder about your sanity—as I already do!"

The voice was Drayfitt's, but the elderly sorcerer was nowhere to be seen. In what was more a hiss than a whisper, the princess asked, "Where are you? Can you throw your voice a distance or is invisibility a trick you've learned?"

"Alas, invisibility has always been beyond me . . . but the secret of the chameleon is not. Turn slowly, as if admiring the flowers, and look at the wall behind you."

Following his odd instructions, Erini studied the vine-covered wall. At first, there was nothing new to see, but, as she studied it closely—a difficult task since she was also supposed to be admiring the garden flowers—Erini began to make out the shape of a cloaked figure standing at ease among the ivy and brick. His clothing and even his skin were colored and streaked in the same way as the wall, including the vines. The princess knew that if she ever hoped to see him clearly, she would have to walk straight up to him and touch his face.

"How do you do that?" Erini asked quietly. Unspoken was the second question: *Why did Drayfitt feel it necessary to disguise himself if only to reveal his presence to her? Because of Quorin?*

"Your majesty, if you would do an old man a great favor, I would ask of you that the two of us retire to a quieter place—such as my workroom."

"Why?" She was not entirely certain she was safe in trusting him after this peculiar display of his magical talents.

"Because I felt your struggle to control yourself even while I conversed with the king and I know you will not be able to hide your secret much longer. That was why I came, feigning weakness from some research."

Erini glanced wistfully at the door. "Very well."

"Excellent. We've been fortunate so far in that none of the guards have happened by here, but I assure you that our luck will not hold—and some of them are more loyal to Counselor Quorin than they are to King Melicard."

With that warning hanging over her head, Erini carefully made her way to the nearest exit. Her visible attitude was that of someone who has enjoyed the peace of a short walk but who now has become bored with matters. It was a look she had cultivated well over her short life.

Departing the garden, Erini continued to feign her disinterest in all things until she was well away. Certain that she was at last safe from prying eyes, she turned, expecting to see Drayfitt with her. The princess instead found herself to be utterly alone. Erini was about to call out his name when the sound of footfalls echoed from down the hall.

The ancient spellcaster stood before her, all smiles. "My dear princess, how nice to run into you!"

Confusion reigned supreme. "Why—?"

Her question went unasked as marching feet warned her that the two of them were no longer alone. Erini caught a glance from the sorcerer. *Play along!*

"I've just finished an interesting walk in the garden, Master Drayfitt. A pity you weren't able to join me; we could have walked while you told me more about Talak. There is so much I still have to learn and you must know more than anyone about the city."

Four well-armed guards turned the corner, marching with the same exacting precision that all Melicard's soldiers seemed to march with. The apparent squad leader, a stout man with a thin, graying beard, called his men to a halt. He stepped toward the anxious princess and bowed.

"Guard leader Sen Ostlich at your command, your majesty! May I say it's an honor then to meet with you! May we be of service to you?" He pointedly ignored Drayfitt.

This was something that Erini could handle with ease. Her face became a mask as she imperiously replied, "Nothing at this time, guard leader, but your attention is noted. Is there something you wanted of me? Has the king requested my presence?"

"Not to my knowledge, your majesty. We're merely making our rounds. It wouldn't have been proper to pass without acknowledging our queen-to-be. The captain would've had us all on double duty." Ostlich allowed himself a rueful smile.

Erini granted him a royal smile. "Then, I shall not keep you from your duties. Carry on."

"Your majesty."

Bowing, the guard leader returned to his squad and gave the order to resume the patrol. The princess and Drayfitt watched them go, a sardonic smile creeping across the lined visage of the elderly sorcerer.

"How *gracious* of them. How curious that they purposely changed their route to march by here while you were nearby."

"Isn't this their regular route?"

"By no means. Oh, they'll claim that it was changed only today—if you ask them, that is—but I've the distinct advantage of having seen them turn from their normal patrol because one of the other guards reported seeing you in the garden. The chameleon trick has its advantages. I saw the sentry just as you were leaving. He didn't see me." Drayfitt smiled, pleased with his own success.

"I wondered why you vanished."

"Enough of that. Now that we've *officially* met in this hall and you've expressed your interest in Talak—an *excellent* request and good, quick thinking on your part—I think no one will suspect, anymore than usual, that is, that we have anything else in mind. If you will accompany me to my workroom . . ."

"You are my guide," Erini answered gracefully. As Drayfitt led her down the hall, already into the beginnings of a lesson on the history of Talak, the princess looked back in the direction of the garden and the door. While she was grateful to Drayfitt for his concern for her well-being, the sorcerer's actions had not deterred Erini but rather fueled her determination. One way or another, she would return to the garden before long and discover the truth.

DRAYFITT'S WORKROOM WAS not what Erini had expected of a sorcerer. She had pictured a dark, moody place of vials and parchments, bones and the various parts of rare and magical creatures. There should have been ancient tomes on subjects such as necromancy and magical artifacts from civilizations long dead.

"Looks rather like the office of a minor bureaucrat, doesn't it?"

It was true. A high desk stood in the center of the tidy room, a set of candles and several sheets of parchment on top. There *were* books, countless books on shelves that ringed the room, but they were neatly stacked and fairly new. Some of them sounded fairly mysterious, but others were on classical plays or theories on government. Erini had not known that so many books on so many subjects even existed.

"Do you like them?" the sorcerer asked a bit wistfully. "I wrote most of them over the years. It's a shame that most city-states are not like Penacles, where writing and education are paramount. I understand that a few of the copies I made are now a part of the collection gathered first by the Lord Gryphon and now by Toos the Regent. I've made certain that at my death, accidental, natural, or otherwise, the Regent will get this collection."

Erini could not help smiling. "You do not remind me of what I was always told a spellcaster was like."

"Head bowed over a cauldron, arms waving in insane motions, and sinister, inhuman things waiting at my feet for some command? Some of those things are true, and, if you know the tales of foul Azran Bedlam, those images pale in comparison to what he was like. I was never happy with sorcery. I was quite happy to find myself a little niche in the controlling of Talak and stay there." The spellcaster's face darkened. "*Counselor* Quorin insured that I would never be able to return to that and so I've made a special point of making him regret that action ever since."

A twinge in Erini's right hand reminded her of why they were here. If Drayfitt could help her or, better yet, find her a way to rid herself of this curse, then she would take advantage of it. As if reading her thoughts, the sorcerer took her hands in his and looked them over.

"Tell me, when you observe the powers around us, do you see the lines and fields?"

She shook her head. "No, I see a rainbow, bright on one end and changing to black at the other."

"A spectrum. Pity. I see the former, myself. Well, at least you see the powers as something understandable. There are those who see them in radically different ways than we do, though such folk seem to be rare. The lines and the spectrum seem to dominate the minds of most—and before you ask, I have no idea why we see them at all. Some people discover them naturally; some, like myself, need training." Drayfitt released her hands. "You are a natural adept. With some assistance on my part, you could become very skilled."

Erini shook her head violently. "No! I want you to help me get *rid* of this curse, not *enhance* it!"

"Your majesty, the abilities you have are a part of you, a gift from—from whoever watches over us. It's the spellcaster who makes those abilities work for good or ill. How else could one family produce both a fiend like Azran Bedlam and good, strong men like his father, Nathan, or his son, Cabe. I understand your feelings. For years, I lived with the memory of my brother, Ishmir the Bird Master—Aaah! I see by your face that you know of him. Ishmir perished in the Turning War with most of the other Dragon Masters and it took me years to forgive him for that."

"Forgive him? For dying?"

The sorcerer looked chagrined. "He left me, a young man, then, half-trained, uncertain of what I was. I had your qualms, too, but Ishmir saw I had the potential, though it was buried deep. I forgave him eventually, but I kept my powers hidden, utilizing only those that would help me secure a place in Talak's government and keep me alive—I'm a coward when it comes to death. Since my forced re-education in the world of sorcery—only a short time ago—I've learned much about its benefits. If not for my efforts, Counselor Quorin's influence with the king would be much stronger. That alone I count as a reason to hone my skills."

Erini turned away, walking over to a shelf and running her fingers along the spines of some of Drayfitt's books. "It might be different if I were not a member of royalty, Master Drayfitt. Such things are not for us. In the eyes of my people, I would be considered tainted, a demon in human form."

"I think the only demon is in your own mind, if you'll pardon me for saying so, your majesty. There have been rulers aplenty who command in part through sorcery. The Lord Gryphon of Penacles is the best example. During his reign, it was his skill more than anything else that kept the Black Dragon at bay. He was even instrumental in the Turning War."

"The Gryphon was a magical creature, Master Drayfitt. The powers were a part of him."

The elderly spellcaster chuckled. "He may not like all this talk in past tense; he still lives, they say, but fights some war across the Eastern Seas—hence the title of Penacles's present ruler, Toos the Regent. That is neither here nor there, however; what I am trying to tell you is that the skill to manipulate the powers is as much a natural part of humanity as it is of the elves, the drakes, and the Seekers. We merely have a greater tendency to stifle those skills. *I* ought to know."

Erini slowly turned back to him, an idea forming. "Then, if you cannot help me rid myself of it, teach me how to control it so that I will never find myself 'accidentally' unleashing some spell at a courtier who has happened to annoy me. That is what I fear; the *powers* taking control instead of the other way."

A relieved sigh. "Thank you, your majesty, for making my task easier. Had you demanded I help you rid yourself of your growing abilities, I would have endeavored to do so, despite the impossibility. After all, you are to be my queen."

"That still remains questionable, Master Drayfitt."

"I doubt it. One reason it was so easy for me to leave the king abruptly was because he seemed distant himself, and the look on his face I have only seen when he thinks of you—favorably, that is."

The information earned the spellcaster one of Erini's few true smiles. "You have no idea how happy I am to hear that."

"I do and it makes me happy to say it. The two of you are well matched. Though it's only been a few days since you met as adults, I'm not above believing that a bond of love has already developed. There are those who are meant to be together. I—" Drayfitt suddenly paused, his eyes darting about the room.

"What is it?" Erini asked in hushed tones. To her horror, the sorcerer raised a hand toward her. She felt both the pull as he unleashed some powerful spell and her own instinctive response as she prepared to defend herself.

"Not *you!*" Drayfitt muttered at her. "Remain where you are!"

She froze in place. Behind her, the princess heard the thump of books falling from the shelves and—*the patter of tiny feet?* Something quick was running along the shelves, seeking a place it could hide from the spellcaster's attack. It might as well have been running from time itself.

Erini heard a tiny squeak, then Drayfitt's curse as something the old man had evidently not expected happened. A moment later, he lowered his arm, a look of disgust and worry on his face. He rose from the table toward the spot where the intruder had evidently met its fate.

Standing, the princess joined him. There was a strange odor emanating from the shelves and she sensed the remnants of some odd, disturbing sort of magic, something she had sensed briefly before. There was no sign of any creature.

"What was it? Did you destroy it?"

Abandoning his brief search, Drayfitt began picking up and reshelving his books. "As to what it was, I can only describe it as a little monstrosity obviously created to spy on others." He looked at Erini. "It's head and body were no more than an eye and a snout. A creature of magic. As to destroying it, that was not my intention. The creature destroyed itself. I wanted it alive—if it truly was— so that I could track it to its source, which is probably Quorin."

"He has no magic."

"Yes, you can tell that, can't you? Probably better than I. The only reason I noticed our spy was because this workroom is laced with spells sensitive to unwanted visitors. Here, of all places, I am most secure."

Erini hesitated before finally admitting, "I've felt something similar to that creature. The same sort of magic, different from you or me."

"What? When?"

"In my—my chambers. I was looking in the mirror when I saw him. When I turned around, there was nobody there. I thought I'd imagined him, but there was dirt on the floor where he had stood and—and when I touched it, the strangeness of it startled me so much I fell back."

Drayfitt's eyes narrowed and he scratched his head in thought. "Can you describe him, milady?"

"Not well. He wore a cloak and hood like you do, only they seemed older, out of style." The princess closed her eyes and tried to picture the dark figure. "All his clothing seemed a bit archaic."

"We are not always known for our sense of style. Forget his clothing, then. What did he look like? I may know his face if you describe it well."

She looked flustered. "I cannot help you there, Master Drayfitt. I was not able to get a good look at his face. My eyes must have been watery, because, no matter how I looked, it remained shadowy or blurry."

"His face was unclear but you could see that his clothing was old, archaic?"

"Yes, strange, isn't it? I remember them clearly enough, but not his visage. I think he had dark hair, perhaps brown, with a streak of silver."

"But his face you can't remember." The sorcerer pursed his lips in mounting frustration. "I wish—I truly wish, milady—that you could have given me a face to go by."

Erini could sense his worry. "Why? Who was it? Is it whoever you hide down below? Did he escape?"

Drayfitt gave her a dumbfounded look. "Soooo . . . you know about *that*, too. This gets worse and worse." He looked up at the ceiling, staring at something beyond it with eyes filled with dismay. "Aaaah, Ishmir! Would that you were here instead of me!"

"What is wrong, sorcerer?"

He went to the desk, opened a drawer, and pulled out a bottle caked in the dust of ages. Without asking whether the princess desired any, Drayfitt poured himself a goblet of what must have been wine and practically swallowed it in one gulp. Eyeing the shelves of books, he finally replied, "The one you described can only be the warlock Shade, who can only be here for two reasons; the first of which is caged deep below in a chamber forgotten until recently. Another creature of legend, a shadowy steed called Darkhorse."

"Darkhorse?" While everyone knew one tale or another concerning the tragic existence of Shade, forever cursed to live alternating incarnations of good or evil, it was the demon known as Darkhorse that had fascinated the princess more. Here was a magical creature from elsewhere, immortal, and the terror of drakes. Some stories made him as tragic as the warlock and there were many who feared him as much, but the image of a great stallion, blacker than a starless night, had captivated her. She had even dreamed, now and then, of riding through the darkness on his back.

A legend and a reality were two different things. The thought of riding whatever Drayfitt had imprisoned down below made her shiver—and not in anticipation.

"Darkhorse." The sorcerer nodded. "They have been friends and enemies for millennia. Yet, if he wanted the stallion, he could find him easily. There'd be no reason to materialize haphazardly in the palace unless he was searching for something better hidden, something like the book."

"What book?" Erini was becoming more and more confused.

Drayfitt sighed. "The book I used, half in ignorance, to summon a demon, or rather Darkhorse, to our world. A book he tricked me into destroying when he thought I wouldn't be able to recapture him again." The elderly spellcaster smiled a bit proudly at that; it had been a coup in ways, defeating the eternal twice. Then, he frowned. "I hope it's not the book he's after, though I can't think what else it might be."

All thought of her own problems had long ago vanished as Erini tried to make sense of everything. She had wanted answers for so long, but now that she had them, the princess was more at a loss than before. "Why do you say that? Is it something he should not have?"

"Probably not. That's academic, I'm afraid, your majesty. As I said, I destroyed it. He'll find nothing but ashes now."

IN A DARKENED corner of the ceiling, a small form scurried deep into a crack that should have been too tight for it. The sacrifice of its brother had proven worth the cost, for it had discovered what its master had wanted to know. Soon, it would be able to return to the warm nothingness he had summoned it from. Perhaps even as soon as it relayed the news to him.

Shade's eye-creature did not understand how its master would react to this particular bit of news. It would not be able to comprehend the fury nor would it comprehend that the warlock would destroy it, not because it had served him well, but because of a need to strike out at someone or something.

Least of all, it would not understand the danger the success of its mission had placed the sorcerer and the princess in. Nor would it have cared.

X

THE SILVER DRAGON watched from the throne he had usurped from his dead counterpart as his loyal subjects began the long process of clearing the central chamber of rubble. Under the light of many torches, warriors watched over the servitors, who seemed uneasy at invading the caverns of their cousins. The Dragon King shifted to a more imperious posture, the better to build the confidence of his people. It mattered not that the clans of Gold—those that still lived—were outraged at his actions. They had three choices: become part of the clans of Silver as the survivors of the clans of Bronze and Iron had, flee to their other cousins, or face execution. So far, none of the three choices had become a clear-cut victor, which was the best choice in the Silver Dragon's mind, for it meant that the remnants of Gold's people would never band together in sufficient strength to fight his rightful rule.

I should have taken this place after Gold's defeat. So many years wasted—but now the throne is mine. The days of the Thirteen Kingdoms are at an end. Eventually, the Dragonrealm will bow to one monarch alone with no council to voice their dissent. . . .

So far, none of his counterparts had raised more than an angry voice against him; proof, he believed, of their gradual willingness to accept him as emperor of all. Only Green openly denounced him, but that was to be expected from a traitor whose domain housed his race's greatest enemies, the Bedlams.

Ssssoon, he thought with a smile. *Soon we shall begin the cleansing process, sweeping down and bringing the upstart warm-bloods to their knees, where they will learn once again to give obeisance in the proper manner.*

One of his younger hatchlings, an unmarked male who served well in the hopes of securing a dukedom in the new regime of his sire, knelt before him. His false crest was less elaborate than some of his elders, a choice that the Dragon King approved of. He gestured for the warrior to speak.

"My sire, I give thanks to the Dragon of the Depths for your ascent to the throne of emperor."

Silver hissed as the flattery made him swell with pride. "What word of our chaotic ally?"

"None. Our spies search for him—cautiously, as you commanded. There *is* word on the book, however."

"And that is?"

"That the book is *ash*," a voice from behind the throne announced.

The Dragon King leaped from the throne and whirled around. The other drakes looked up from their tasks, but a chill glance from their monarch, who realized he had lost face by this cowardly action, sent them scurrying back to their duties with greater effort than before.

"How?"

"The sorcerer Drayfitt. Why would you give such an artifact to a human sorcerer?" Shade cocked his head, his voice soft and smooth, companionable even.

The Dragon King was not fooled for a moment. He knew that he was facing yet another variation of the warlock, one that he suspected was closer to the original than any of the rest. "He was to translate it. All others failed. It was said he had the skill and knowledge."

Shade walked slowly around the throne. The two drakes stepped back. "So the creature Mal Quorin is yours."

His draconian ally did not argue the point. "Only after the book wasss brought to him did we discover the truth. The human king was quickly made to believe that a ssspell had been found that would give him a demon servant and all he had to do was find a sorcerer—which proved *sssurprisingly* easssy. The one called Drayfitt would continue the translation—at the command of his king, of course—and also test the validity of his resultsss." Silver forced himself to stare into the two dark spots that passed for the warlock's eyes. "He would either fail and disssgrace himself or succeed, at which point, sssome accident would overtake him and the book would be returned to me. Any demon he had sssummoned would then be mine to control!"

"You are quite a gambler, evidently. I doubt if *I* would have done the same as you." With great deliberation, the warlock sat casually down on the throne. The drake who had reported to the would-be emperor hissed and bared his claws. Shade looked him over.

"One of *your* get?"

"What of it, *human?*" the defiant warrior hissed.

"He bears no markings," the hooded figure commented to his ally, ignoring the growing anger of the younger drake.

"What if I do not?"

The warlock finally seemed to notice him again. "Just so I know that I've eliminated nothing of importance."

The furious drake reached for him, then hissed in consternation as a great, black hole materialized in his stomach. While the rest of the drakes—unable to keep from looking despite their master's earlier glare—watched in horror, the hole expanded. The hapless victim, in a state of insane calm, put one hand into the gaping maw, unable to believe his eyes.

The hand and the arm were sucked in.

In less than a breath, the shoulders, head, and remaining arm followed after and, when they, too, were gone, the torso and legs vanished into the hole. A single black spot remained floating in the air for a second or two, then vanished, seeming to swallow itself.

Shade glanced in the direction of the Dragon King. "You've desired the power of the Vraad; that was a taste of what we could do."

"Am I next?"

"I was under the impression we had an alliance of sorts." The warlock leaned forward. "Don't we?"

"You recalled the book. That wasss why you returned to me. The book— *your book*—was destroyed. I assumed you had no further need to pursue our alliance and so I have moved on with my plansss."

"Subjugation and/or destruction of Talak. I remember. I would think it simple with the king's counselor at your beck and call."

"Nothing is simple except the belief in simplicity."

Rising, Shade straightened his cloak. "Continue with your plans. They coincide with my needs. There is only one thing you must remember."

"That is?"

"The sorcerer Drayfitt must not be harmed. I've need of him."

A wary look passed across the drake lord's half-hidden face. "Quorin's followers are to assassinate him—soon—while he travels with the army. What need do you have for a human spellcaster with little more than adequate ability?"

"It's not his abilities as a sorcerer that I want. It's his mind. You did say he set out to translate the entire book, didn't you?"

"So?"

Shade sighed, wondering how this creature could miss the obvious. "Never mind. Return to your plans."

"But *your* part of the bargain—"

"That?" The warlock smiled, a shadowy line slightly bent upward on each end. There was something dreadfully cold about his smiles, Silver thought.

"Neither Darkhorse nor the Bedlams will interfere. You may rest assured on that. They will be too busy with other, weightier matters." That said, the warlock curled within himself and vanished.

Almost the Dragon King felt sympathy for the warlock's adversaries—almost.

ANOTHER DAY HAD passed and Darkhorse once more studied the cracks of the chamber walls. Studied them while his mind sank deeper into a bottomless abyss.

Failure. Utter failure.

Darkhorse looked *again* at the chamber that was his world and would *be* his world for some time to come, apparently. His one hope had been crushed—and at the moment of greatest potential.

The human female called Erini, Melicard's betrothed—now *there* was irony—was a natural spellcaster of high potential, possibly as high as Cabe Bedlam or the Lady Gwen. She had noticed the fragment of self although even Drayfitt had not. In the last moment of vision, he had seen how her hands itched to reach out to the powers, manipulate them. The female was stifling those powers, though; that much he had seen as well. If that were the case, he would receive little aid from her. Likely, she had not even told Melicard her secret.

His thoughts were interrupted by the unlocking of the door. That made him chuckle in sour humor; who would want to come in and what would they do once they were here? If it was not to keep someone out, what other reason was there for locking the door? Darkhorse would have been as secure if the entire palace had been leveled. Even then, the barrier enclosing him would have stood.

The door swung open and Melicard himself, accompanied by his foul shadow, Quorin, and the pitiful mage, Drayfitt, entered. There was something different about the king, a humanity that had blossomed almost overnight. It was not complete humanity, not by far, but a great touch more than the split-faced monarch had had during his first visit.

Given time, this princess would make him a whole man again. The shadow steed studied Melicard's visage closer, especially the living eye and the set of his mouth.

Apparently, there will not be time after all.

The king was here with an ultimatum. Darkhorse could read that even before Melicard spoke.

"My army marches against the clans of Red in the Hell Plains at tomorrow's dawn. Men will die so that their children will live free. The Plains will drink their blood as it drinks the blood of drakes."

"A pretty speech . . . and very old."

"You have been told not to be disrespectful to his majesty, demon! Perhaps you need another lesson—"

Melicard curtly signalled for silence. "Quiet! I want this creature, this legendary Darkhorse who fought alongside the Dragon Masters, Cabe Bedlam, and other humans throughout the centuries, to tell me why he will not save the lives of men by ending those of drakes!"

The ebony stallion sighed. "You who would make history, have you not studied it? Are not the lessons of the Quel, the Seekers, and those who preceded even them evident? This land we now call the Dragonrealm is a harsh mother. It has watched the glory of many races and it has watched the downfall of each—all through bloodshed. Even the Quel, who succeeded where others failed and held onto a bit of their power when the Seekers took control, even they did not learn from their mistake and eventually lost what little they had in trying to destroy the new avian masters! As for the Seekers, in putting down the last gasp of the Quel, they planted the seeds of their own destruction!"

Melicard was silent, but Darkhorse could see his words had had no effect. *And I scoffed at his tired speech!*

The king's eventual response was what he had expected. "Though you are our prisoner, for some reason we cannot make you obey. Drayfitt has tried to explain, but that means nothing. Tomorrow, I will send the army out—without your magical aid. It will take them a week to ten days to reach the northern part of the Hell Plains, where the Red Dragon's revitalized clans prepare for their own assault. We shall catch them unprepared, however; and, where Azran Bedlam failed, we shall wipe them out to the last egg. One less clan. The others will follow."

"All hail the conquering heroes!" scoffed the shadow steed.

"Your *majesty*—" the counselor began to protest.

"You were overzealous before, Quorin. We will not punish this one, not this time. Perhaps he will reconsider before the deaths have grown too many."

Darkhorse refused to look at the king any longer, instead choosing to alternate his piercing gaze between Drayfitt, the weakest link, and Mal Quorin, the treacherous one. The elderly spellcaster looked pale, worn, as if he had just suffered a great disaster. If so, the malevolent cat who counseled the king had something to do with it because there was now a slight hint of satisfaction on Quorin's face that, under the circumstances, should not have been there. The counselor almost seemed pleased by events.

Something is not right where this tabby is concerned, Darkhorse decided. *What can I do about it now, though?*

"Come," Melicard commanded his two advisors. "There are more *fruitful* endeavors to pursue at the moment."

"The only fruitful endeavors will be those of the Lords of the Dead—after the battle."

The door shut behind them with a sinister note of finality. Darkhorse kicked at his invisible cage, frustrated more than before.

"Fools!" he cried, though he doubted they could hear him, sound-absorbing as this room was. "This will be far worse than the Turning War!"

He brooded after that, unheedful of the hours that soon passed by and wondering again and again if they now intended on abandoning him down here indefinitely. *Perhaps, as the years fall, some scavenger searching through the ruins of this once-proud city-state will find his way down here and pass on a word or two before leaving me alone again.*

The door jostled. Someone was trying to open it—but with little success.

Darkhorse gathered himself together, his interest in things revived by this sudden and possibly trivial incident. *It may only be a guard testing the lock . . .*

Nothing else happened for more than two minutes. The shadow steed's hopes sagged again.

A sudden groan of twisting metal informed him that the first time had not been an illusion. The area of the door where the handle and lock were situated had been torn asunder, rendering the whole thing useless. Someone standing on the other side of the door pushed it forward.

The eyes of the Princess Erini stared at him in awe and growing recognition.

"You. You were the shadow in the hall. The one that—that followed me and then vanished." While she talked, her hands continued to twitch, as if they were eager to perform yet more sorcery.

Darkhorse dipped his head in acknowledgment. "Princess Erini, I would assume." He indicated the door. "A trifle overdone, I'd think."

She looked embarrassed. "I was only trying to open it. Drayfitt said that if you concentrate, you can manipulate the spectrum and unlock it with little more than a look."

"Can you try that with my accursed cage here? Have you come to set me free?"

"Are you—are you Darkhorse?"

That made him laugh loudly. "Of course. Who else could I be? Who else would dare to be Darkhorse—or *want* to be, for that matter?"

"Not so loud, please!"

His manner became subdued. The shadow steed knew that this human held his freedom in her anxious hands. "Why did you come down here? Won't Melicard become wroth when he discovers his future bride has uncovered one of his secrets?"

"Melicard is busy. *Quorin*"—the look of disgust on her young face was evidence enough of her hatred for the man. The shadow steed's opinion of the princess rose further—"has convinced him that the time to move is now. Melicard is completing final preparations."

"He was here earlier. This is madness, you know." The ebony stallion shifted impatiently in the confined space of his prison. *Free me!* he wanted to shout at the human.

Erini looked up sharply. "I don't know if I should. I don't know if I can."

"Your powers are very formidable, gentle lady. I think you could undo the spell the elderly human wrought. The key is in the symbols on the floor. Look closely at them."

She started to, but then shook her head. "I can't! If I do, Melicard will never forgive me! If I betray him, he'll find out about these!"

"Your hands? They seem lovely, though I'm no judge of human standards. . . ."

"You know what I mean. These powers. I do not want them. They are a curse. If I thought that cutting off my hands would rid me of them, I'd be tempted to do it."

"It will not, so do not think about it again." *Madness! Am I to be tormented by the key to my freedom?*

If Erini caught that thought, she did not respond to it. Instead, the princess said, "Drayfitt told me the same thing. I know that."

"Is that why you came to me? To tell me you don't like your gifts and you won't use them to release me? Are you a greater sadist than the 'lovely' Counselor Quorin, then? He has only assaulted my physical form; you've torn at my hopes!"

"No! I—"

"Princess!" Drayfitt stood at the doorway. He had become even more worn and pale since the shadow steed had seen him hours before. Caught up in their own thoughts, neither Erini nor the eternal had noticed his nearby presence. He, on the other hand, had felt them all the way in the main hall, where he had just left the king after an unsuccessful attempt to, if not call off the march, postpone it until events became clearer. The intensity of the two had been enough to pierce the cloud of worry smothering his mind—and probably would have been enough had he been outside the walls of Talak itself.

The elderly mage inspected the damaged door and grew even more dismayed. "This will never do!" He touched the torn handle and lock. Before the eyes of Darkhorse and the princess, the metal reshaped itself, returned to what it had been like before Erini's impetuous entrance. Drayfitt glanced up again. "Your majesty! What do you hope to gain by coming here? I warned you to stay away!"

"I could not help it, Master Drayfitt!" She stepped back from both of them. "I saw the three of you come down here hours ago, then leave a few minutes later. When I saw the guards depart as well, I knew something had happened. I—I was not thinking properly. It took me this long to build up my determination, but eventually I had to come down here—I do not know why. Perhaps to see . . . to understand . . ." Erini trailed off, at a loss.

"She came to see a curiosity, sorcerer!" Darkhorse bellowed arrogantly. "She came to see the demon her love had chained to this world! Rest assured, she would not want to hurt his feelings by granting me my rightful freedom, oh no! I pleaded with her long enough to know that!"

Erini looked as if the shadow steed had kicked her violently—which was just what Darkhorse wanted. It was a terrible thing, he knew, that he was forced to resort to shaming her, but if the stallion had read her correctly, the princess would turn that shame around and come back to him—this time to free him.

I will make amends to her after Shade has been dealt with Darkhorse swore, shielding the thought from her already impressive abilities. He tried not think that by forcing her to look at her own conscience and free him, that she might lose the man she loved.

There were times when he did not envy humans the ability to love. It seemed to have more to do with pain than any other emotion.

Ignoring his outburst, Drayfitt confronted his queen-to-be. "Your majesty, tomorrow, thanks to the slippery words of the *loyal* Master Quorin, I will be enroute with the army. I must ask that you watch yourself while I'm gone, stay with the king at all times. The more Quorin has him alone, the more he can poison his mind—and diminish your hopes of a true relationship. I shall return when I can."

"*If* you can, spellcaster. Your kind has a limited lifespan in war. What happens to the city, then?"

"I will see to it that *nothing* happens. I've a stake in my life, Darkhorse." The elderly man took hold of one of Erini's arms in a gentle but determined manner. "Come, milady. Judging by your mishap with the door, there are things I need to show you before I leave come the morn."

"Wait, Drayfitt!" The shadow steed shifted as close to the door as the barrier would let him. "What about Shade? I've felt him here! You cannot deny his existence, I think."

The two humans looked at one another in a manner that answered one part of Darkhorse's question. The warlock had returned to Talak at least once and both of them knew about it. It was Erini who finally responded, much to the evident consternation of the sorcerer.

"He's been here at least *twice*, Lord Darkhorse. Once, for a brief moment, in my chambers; the second time, to release some foul creatures to spy on the palace."

"He wanted the book, apparently," her companion interrupted. "It was his, you know, but thanks to *you*, demon, *I* destroyed it."

"Then, you are in danger, human!"

"He's your foe. *You* were the one truly responsible. He has no further argument with me." The tone of Drayfitt's voice suggested he had worked hard to convince himself of that.

"Don't be a fool, mortal!"

Drayfitt turned from him. "Come, your majesty."

She accompanied him, but slowed long enough to study Darkhorse in detail.

Darkhorse returned her frank stare. This was a female who did not give in easily. There was hope after all.

As the door closed, the shadow steed laughed quietly. Now, if only it was not *too* late.

THE CLIMB UP was long and especially slow, despite Drayfitt's continual urging. Erini only partially heard him, her mind on the confrontation below.

Living darkness. An abyss that threatened to swallow all that stood too near it. More than a shadow, yet also less.

All these were apt descriptions of the astonishing being she had met. All were apt but greatly insufficient descriptions of the jet-black stallion calling itself Darkhorse. Majestic and terrible at the same time, he was far more than the legends had even hinted at. Small wonder he was held in both awe and fear by those who knew of him. There was a sense of time beyond eternity in his very presence. His chilling blue eyes, crystalline and lacking pupils, seemed capable of capturing her very soul.

His words came back to Erini and the shame burned brightly within her once more. For the sake of her relationship with Melicard, she had been willing to leave him a prisoner. It went against everything she believed in, and the fact that she had not done anything about it cut her deeply. She had once dreamed of a marriage based on love and trust; could she be satisfied with one that was also built on the sufferings of others?

Erini realized that Drayfitt had asked her something. "I'm sorry; what was it you asked, Master Drayfitt?"

The elderly man sighed. Somehow, he seemed even *more* drawn than when he had first discovered Erini. "I asked your majesty if she trusts her personal guard and her ladies-in-waiting."

"Completely. Why?"

Drayfitt's face revealed nothing. "No reason, milady. Only pleased to hear that there *are* those who can be trusted."

Neither spoke again, more to save breath than because of any other reason. The journey downward had seemed so much easier. At last, though, the door finally came into view.

I cannot leave him! the princess suddenly thought in a swelling panic, the sight of the door resurrecting her shame concerning her ill treatment of Darkhorse. *I have to do something for him even if—even if—*

"I've been wondering," Drayfitt began, "wondering why Quorin removed the guards from in here. They weren't necessary, but he seemed to think them so important before. If they'd been here, you wouldn't have gotten this far."

Erini neither knew nor cared what reason the counselor might have had to send the sentries away. Only one thing concerned her. The princess was not even certain it would work, but, based on what little she had learned from the sorcerer, it should at least be *possible*.

On the next step, she fell forward.

"Princess!" Drayfitt reached for her, almost losing his own balance in the process. He was unable to stop Erini, who turned so that her back was facing her would-be rescuer.

While her face and hands were not visible to Drayfitt and his mind was concerned solely with her safety, Erini unleashed a crude spell formulated only from half-formed thoughts and wishful thinking. The elderly spellcaster had explained that hand gestures were not necessary and mostly acted as a guide, but the princess did not trust her skills well enough to do without them. Her fingers wiggled in a maneuver that was pure instinct. Unfamiliar with the world of sorcery, she could not say whether she had accomplished her task or not. Whatever the case, Drayfitt was now standing over her and Erini knew that trying any longer would only give her away. As it was, she remained uncertain as to whether he knew or not. He had shown her how to shield her thoughts during their one session, but theory and practice were never the same, that held true in sorcery *and* governing.

"Are you all right, Princess Erini?"

She nodded slowly, trying to act dazed. "Yes—I missed my footing. Thank you."

The sorcerer helped her to her feet. "A fall here could prove fatal, milady. You would not stop for thirty or forty feet at least. Come, the sooner we leave here the better, as far as all is concerned."

Drayfitt opened the door, guiding Erini up to the surface with his other hand. The sun was going down and the garden was full of deep shadows, though none as deep as that which was Darkhorse, the princess thought.

Closing the door quietly, Drayfitt quietly said, "We will forget this happened, your majesty. Best for both of us, I'd say. Now go before someone asks why we were here."

"This is ridiculous! I am a princess! Am I not to be queen of Talak? Should I go skulking about? I won't be like you, Drayfitt! Not even for the love of Melicard!"

He frantically waved her quiet. In the distance, Erini heard the sounds of men in armor. "I only recommend it from past experience, your majesty. What you do is up to you, of course."

"Princess Erini."

Erini started and Drayfitt cursed under his breath. The princess calmed down, however, when she realized who it was. "Captain Iston!"

The Gordag-Ai officer bowed to her and, after a moment's hesitation, nodded briefly to the sorcerer. "Princess, you are making it extremely difficult for my men and I to perform our duties. So far, you've succeeded in evading every one of them."

"The princess is skilled at such things," Drayfitt interjected. To Erini, he said, "Think on what I said, milady, and, by all means, make use of such loyal men as your captain here."

"What's that supposed to mean, then?" Iston asked, his suspicion roused.

"Only that I hope her majesty will allow you to perform your function. It's sometimes hard to find a person you can trust so much. Good evening."

His eyes on the departing sorcerer, Iston frowned. "That sounds like a warning of sorts."

"It's nothing."

"As you command." Nevertheless, the captain continued to look thoughtful. "Might I be permitted to escort you back to your chambers, your majesty? I have a handful of anxious bodyguards waiting for the two of us."

"Why did you not bring them with you?"

Iston smiled enigmatically. "Some things are better handled by one man."

They walked quietly through the garden, the officer falling in place just behind his mistress. Erini allowed her thoughts to turn back to the events below and the question as to whether her spontaneous actions had freed Darkhorse or not. She also wondered what Melicard would say if it turned out the shadow steed *was* free. Drayfitt would be unable to say anything; come the morning, he would be gone with the army. Both the king and Quorin might assume that Darkhorse had either escaped on his own or that Shade had taken him away somewhere.

Her secret would remain safe . . . unless *she* chose to tell Melicard. He had to learn some time . . . but when?

As before, her questions went unanswered. She exited the garden, followed by Iston, of course, with the knowledge that sooner or later the truth would come out and that it might benefit her if it was *her* admission, not Quorin's, that Melicard heard first.

GUARD LEADER OSTLICH abandoned his hiding place overlooking the garden the moment the would-be queen and her lackey vanished back into the palace. His mind was aglow with the thought of the gold Counselor Quorin would pay him. What the princess from Gordag-Ai had been doing mattered as little to him as why Quorin had ordered the guards away from the area in the first place. He only knew that the counselor would pay for the knowledge that she had been down there and reward him further once the reins of rulership changed hands.

What happened to the princess was none of his concern.

XI

WITH THE GRAND crusade now ready to commence, no one had time to inspect the chamber where the King's reluctant demon had been locked away. Caught in the midst of final details that would keep them secluded all night, the king and his advisors saw no one except those who came to deliver information specifically on the march. Thus it was the Counselor Quorin remained ignorant of a fact that would have been of great import to both him and the king . . . for the barrier, the magical cage, and its sole occupant were no longer there. Had he received a message from one of the guard leaders to the Counselor Quorin, the advisor might have excused himself and investigated for himself, venturing down to the shadow steed's prison, and discovering something of such importance that even the king would have taken interest . . . because the barrier, the magical cage, and its sole occupant were no longer there.

THE BULK OF Talak's great army moved in swift and orderly fashion despite its impressive size. By dawn, more than half the column was outside the city gates. Around them, the citizens cheered their husbands, fathers, sons, and brothers. Cohorts four hundred strong marched by, most of them veterans eager to teach the monstrous drakes that humans of this particular city-state would never bow to the Dragon Kings again.

Lost in the cheers and commotion was one pessimistic sorcerer and several irritated commanders, all of whom felt they were moving in the wrong direction; but it was their duty to obey, and obey they would. The city was not undefended. There were garrisons posted all around the countryside, especially the northern and western borders. The city guard would keep order in Talak itself and the palace would be well-protected by the royal guard.

Unbeknownst to these forces, the northern garrisons, in response to orders received that very dawn, were preparing to move westward to meet with their counterparts there. For the next week, they were to face off in a series of war games designed to test their effectiveness in guerrilla fighting, much like the sort of war waged by Melicard in the early days of his crusade. While the commanders silently questioned the need for this, it was not the first time that some functionary in the government had decided to play up his own reputation by *cracking down* on the common soldier; and besides, the war was to be in the east for now, so no one would miss them for a few days, anyway.

No one argued the validity of the orders themselves; after all, they bore the king's seal, didn't they? Nobody but Melicard and his closest advisors used the seal.

The king saluted those riding out to do battle in his name, his visage somehow more regal than frightening this day. He had planned to lead them, as he had done in the past, but some of his advisors had recommended that he remain in the city. It would not do to have the crusade's driving force accidently struck down in the heat of combat. At the palace, Melicard could coordinate *all* of his activities. There was also continued talk of the eventual marriage of Melicard and the princess from neighboring Gordag-Ai, an event most everyone was looking forward to with eagerness. Those near enough to see the king were able to get a glimpse of the Princess Erini standing at his side. Counselor Mal Quorin, Melicard's chief advisor, stood on his other side.

In the shadow of a building near the city gate, a lone figure watched the ongoing procession with growing impatience. The shadows draped his visage, but even if they had not, it would have taken a long, close look to make out his patrician features and his arresting eyes—eyes with great, wide pupils not of any color, but instead glittering like fine crystal and seeming to see much more than the view before them. It was the face of one born to his place in the world, one who knew that all within his grasp was his. Azran Bedlam had worn such a look, but it paled in comparison with this one. This was the face of a Vraad sorcerer.

The true face of Shade.

FOOD. EAT. EAT. The others in the herd kept urging him. They had been doing so all day.

Provider. Walks-on-hind-hooves-and-smells-of-herd. Brings more food. Eat. The herd tried to watch out for one another, but the dark one kept refusing to be part of the herd, though he had said he was.

Not hungry. The dark one allowed the strange creature with the odd, loose skin to guide him. *Drink? Walks-on-hind-hooves-and-smells-of-herd leads to water. Smells puzzled. Not thirsty, provider. Provider smells of fear. Why fear of self? Self not harm provider.*

Self . . . not right.

Before him, the provider called to another of his own herd, a smaller walks-on-hind-hooves who often came to this herd and smoothed and washed their coats. The dark one could not recall ever having this done to him, but the others, who seemed very stupid to the dark one, had told him this. It was one of the happy times they had. The dark one did not care for their happy times. Their happy times were for stupid ones.

"Andru! When did they bring in this one?"

The boy—boy?—shook his head, his mane flying back and forth as he did. The dark one realized the boy could not speak.

The man—yes, *man!*—looked at the dark one. "He's magnificent, but he spooks me for sure! More like a demon than a horse!"

Horse? Demon? The dark one's mind stirred. He did not question for a moment that he understood the *man* so well, even though the rest of the herd seemed to only hear the tone of his voice. He was different. Far different. Memories began to stir, memories of confinement, of evil men and shadowed figures. Memories of a need to escape.

"Here! What's wrong with you?" The man—for the first time, the dark one saw that the man was tall, well-muscled, and graying—sought to bring his skittish charge under control. The dark one—there was *another* name!—easily fought him off.

"Andru! Boy! Get the others! We've gotta rogue on our hands!"

The young one ran off. The older man tried to get a grip on the bit that someone had dared put on the dark one, but failed.

Not dark one. Dark . . . horse. Darkhorse!

The shadow steed's memories returned in a torrent of mixed images and scraps of thought. Darkhorse froze as he tried to assimilate everything, and the handler chose that moment to grab the bit.

"I don't know which mule-headed lord or lady left you in the royal stables, but you're goin' to have to learn who's *master* 'round here!" He tugged hard on the bit, trying to force Darkhorse's head down. The horses around the ebony stallion shied away, already familiar with the strength and tactics of a man who had not yet met an animal he could not break.

Of course, the jet-black steed before him was far more than an animal.

Darkhorse, at last himself again, finally took notice of his would-be master. Soul-snaring blue orbs met the narrow eyes of the human—causing the latter to scream and release his hold. Stumbling backward, the man made a sign against evil.

Darkhorse laughed. Laughed, not only because of the futile gesture, but because he was *free!*

"Hela and Styx!" The horseman fell to his knees. "Spare me, demon! I couldn't have known!"

"Not known *me?* Not known Darkhorse? I am no demon, horseman, though neither am I one of your charges! Tell me quickly now and I will leave you be! What place is this and what day?"

The answers both amused and angered the phantom steed. This was *Gordag-Ai*, the Princess Erini's homeland! He could see what she had done. In haste, perhaps because she was still with the sorcerer, she had wanted him to be safe and secure. Her mind, however sharp, had thought of him in terms of a true animal—and why *not*? Very few people truly understood what he was. Therefore, when she had attempted to free him, her crude spell had sent him to a place her memories recalled as safe—the kingdom where she had been born and raised. Since he was a horse, her rescue attempt had sent him to the royal stables, surely the most secure place for one of his kind! Unfortunately, the side effect of so haphazard a spell had nearly made him just such a creature; and as much as he admired their forms and their loyalty, he had no desire to become one.

What frustrated him were the results of that side effect. Almost a full day had passed while he slowly reverted to himself. The massive army of Talak must already be far beyond the city, heading toward the Hell Plains; and though he had no proof to back up his fears, Darkhorse suspected that something terrible, something that Shade would have a hand in, was going to happen. Not just in Talak, either.

He realized that the human was still kneeling before him and that several others were standing at the entrance to the royal stables looking quite dumbfounded. Darkhorse laughed bitterly and said, "You have *nothing* to fear from *me*, little ones! Darkhorse has always been the friend of humanity, though there are those for whom my love has been tried! Fear not, for my time here with you is over!"

Rearing, the shadow steed summoned a portal. It flickered uncertainly for a moment, but the stallion, impatient to move against his adversaries after so long, paid it no mind. After his confinement and the stifling power of Drayfitt's magical cell, he expected his own abilities to be less than they should be. That was why it was time to include others in his battle with his friend/foe. It was time to seek the help of Cabe Bedlam.

The gate he opened flickered again—then *vanished*.

Cursing loudly—much to the panic of the few humans who had *not* run off already—Darkhorse tried to resummon the portal. It blinked into and out of existence almost too fast to be seen, enraging the frustrated eternal even more.

"I am Darkhorse!" he shouted at the disobedient hole. "A gate is less than nothing to me! Materialize!"

He was greeted by a complete lack of reaction. There was not even a flicker this time. His confinement had sapped his abilities far worse than he could have believed possible.

This was a spell with Vraad origins, the shadow steed finally concluded. *A treacherous, destructive thing like its creator!*

"Very well," he rumbled. "If, for the nonce, the paths beyond are forbidden to me, than I shall travel through the world of humanity!" Darkhorse looked down at the humans. "Be vigilant, mortals! The clans of Silver are awake and, though I suspect they look toward Talak, it would be safe in assuming that Gordag-Ai is also among their desires!"

When it appeared that his message had sunk in, the huge stallion reared and charged east. At first, the men in the stables grew panicked again, for there *was* no eastern entrance, only a solid wall. Then, before the unbelieving eyes of people who had thought they had already seen all there was to see, Darkhorse melted into the obstruction, like a ghost.

DARKHORSE HAD NO time for patience with the failings of humanity. If the fiery presence of a huge, jet-black stallion charging over their heads was enough to set them running in a hundred different directions, then that was their misfortune. What the shadow steed fought to stop was far worse than a little fear left in his wake. Shade, a Vraad sorcerer, would not settle for a little fear. As a Vraad, he would expect to control everything. It was not because he was necessarily evil; if anything, the Vraad had been, in Darkhorse's limited knowledge, amoral. They could not comprehend that something might be out of their reach unless another, stronger representative of their race had already claimed it. Even then, it was a matter of who had the upper hand.

The warlock would be working to divide and eliminate rivals, even potential rivals.

Darkhorse quickened his pace as Gordag-Ai fell behind him. Princess Erini's homeland had been given a warning about the drake menace near them. What concerned the phantom steed now was the very person he had looked to for aid. Cabe Bedlam and his family were in danger. A Vraad sorcerer would not let a spellcaster of young Bedlam's potential go unchecked; if he could not enlist their servitude, then he would destroy them the way one would destroy a pest.

Darkhorse pushed himself harder, only now realizing how accustomed he was to his magical abilities. Though he raced more swiftly than any common horse, the pace was infinitely slower than travelling the path beyond. Seconds, even minutes, had now become hours.

Hours he might not have.

What was occurring in Talak worried him also, but there was nothing he could do, and speaking to Cabe Bedlam and the Lady of the Amber was paramount. The city-state of mad Melicard would have to wait, despite the debt he owed its future queen—future queen *only* if Talak had a future. Darkhorse needed the mortal's aid.

Time continued to be his enemy, passing with a swiftness he could never match at his best. Night came, grew old, and began to dissolve. The lands of Esedi, where the Bronze Dragon had once ruled and where Gordag-Ai was situated, had given way to the southwest edge of cursed Silver's domain. As the sun began to climb, relief touched him. He was now in a region on fair terms with humanity and the Bedlams, the forest lands of the Green Dragon. Through the hateful words of Melicard and the confusing ones of Drayfitt, the stallion had learned how this one drake lord had done the unthinkable, worked it so that there might be a place for both races, so that his own would survive and not give way, which was inevitable to all save the other Dragon Kings.

His hooves grazed the tops of the tallest trees. Something large stirred and fluttered away into the depths of the woods below. Darkhorse thought it at first a small drake, but the glimpse he had of it showed it to be birdlike, yet with the shape and form of a man as well.

Seeker.

There were very few of them now. The brief, horrible winter that had taken place a year after the shadow steed's exile had apparently claimed many of these once-mighty rulers, predecessors to the Dragon Kings themselves. Confidentially, Drayfitt had indicated that the hordes of hungry, gigantic, digging creatures from the Northern Wastes, monstrosities who had followed the soul-numbing chill southward, had been responsible for the depletion of their numbers more than anything else.

Darkhorse, suddenly hesitated, almost landing on top of a tree. Of all creatures, the Seekers would surely know the Vraad. The avians had controlled this land before the coming of that race of men—and had fallen afterward to the might of the upstart drakes. Perhaps the Vraad had had something to do with that, though it was also possible they had no longer existed as a race by then. Something had changed their descendants into the humans of today. It was a time period that the eternal knew little about, having only known it through encounters with one Vraad, a good man. The shadow steed had not returned to this reality until long after the Dragon Kings had established their rule, long enough for all to have died who might have answered him.

Turning, Darkhorse dove into the forest. If he could only catch the Seeker . . .

The foliage whipped about the stallion as he entered the forest. The change in his form from phantasm to solid flesh startled him, as it had not been his desire. Darkhorse slowed and landed hooves-first on the ground, leaving deep imprints.

Thanks to the thick vegetation, it was impossible to locate the avian by normal sight. Those other senses that *should* have been able to aid him in his search failed just as miserably. The Seeker was nowhere to be found. Darkhorse trotted cautiously through the forest in the direction of his original goal, the Manor, while probing the visible world and those beyond for some sign of the Seeker or of any other creature out of the ordinary. It had occurred to him, belatedly, that the Green Dragon might not see him as the ally and friend of the warlock Bedlam. As peace-minded as this particular Dragon King had seemed, he might still consider Darkhorse as the enemy of *all* drakes.

He came upon a path that showed signs of regular use and chose to follow it, trying to indicate to any hidden sentinels of the Green Dragon that he was friendly. In times past he had travelled this region unharmed, but one could never completely trust what had once been. Perhaps the monarch of the Dagora Forest had not sought his death simply because of his strength. A struggle between titans would have destroyed this wooded land that the drake loved so much. Now, though, he was dealing with a much weakened stallion, a much more tempting target to those who believed they had a legitimate reason for vengeance.

Still the Seeker evaded his senses. It had either been able to shield itself or had fled long before. He knew the power of the avians could be formidable and that they might find him a useful tool in their efforts to regain the Dragonrealm, but if this was a trap, it was an odd one. Darkhorse cursed his present state; he was no longer certain if he could trust what his senses told him.

Darkhorse moved through the woods. The hours continued to become new memories, most of those concerning traipsing through endless forest and all thought of the Seeker was gradually abandoned as the shadow steed passed by tree after identical tree. As much as Darkhorse enjoyed nature, he soon lost all admiration for the color green. There was just too much of it. He was tempted to take to the sky again, but, with his abilities questionable, he preferred to be where he had the best chance of spotting hidden watchers, as futile as that seemed at the moment. The lush treetops made it virtually impossible to see anyone, either in the branches or on the ground. Here, at least, he could study both areas more thoroughly. His eyes and ears were now his foremost senses; they were far sharper than those of his animal counterparts' and thus afforded him a fairly accurate picture of what lurked nearby.

Though he appeared to be alone, he soon discovered that there *were* others. Those nearby, insofar as his limited skills could tell him, included small animals, a variety of birds and insects, and three creatures of vague shape and identity who could only be servants of the forest's master. It was possible, then, that there was presently a welcoming party of some sort on their way. Whether they would merely follow and shadow him was debatable. They *would* be there, however.

The land before him began to take on a familiar appearance. Darkhorse slowed to a more cautious pace, knowing that, like his cage, what he sought would be invisible to the eye. A decade was long enough in the mortal plane for an entire world to rearrange itself and, though he was not completely certain he had arrived at the outer grounds of young Bedlam's sanctum, it was best to approach things with the thought of traps in mind.

Darkhorse neared a copse of trees that had grown so close to one another as to be one. The shadow steed knew with little more than a glance that magic had been at work, for the trees wrapped around one another as loved ones might. The sight was a marker of sorts, for it told him that he was indeed close to his destination. The Manor grounds could be no more than—

He felt a great desire to go no farther. It was as if something pungent had been left under his nose. Darkhorse throttled back several steps, trying to recover. He snorted and glared at the location of the aromatic assault.

"Come now, Amber Lady," he jeered, certain that the horrid scent was a product of the Lady Gwen, Cabe's mate. "A little smell will not repel your enemies—nor those you insist of *thinking* as your enemies!"

The jet-black stallion reared and charged swiftly forward.

He found himself running the way he had come from.

"*What?!*" Darkhorse came to a dust-filled halt. He turned and stared at the direction he had originally charged. There was nothing to indicate when and how he had been turned. The spell was one of the smoothest he could recall seeing in centuries. Unlike many, there had been no sense of reversal, no noticeable tingling.

"Perhaps I've underestimated you, Lady Gwen!" He backed up and charged again, building his own defenses as he ran. No mere reversal spell would stop him *this* time.

It did not—but the sudden panic that he must have been *mad* to have even come this close to such a deadly, horrifying place sent him reeling back out of control.

Some distance from the stunning attack of nerves, he gathered himself. Darkhorse eyed his destination, then reared back his head and laughed. "My compliments, Lady of the Amber! This is far more an annoyance and far more creative than the original spell!"

She had placed at least three spells over the magical barrier that protected the Bedlams and their people from outsiders, and Darkhorse was not yet ready to see if there was a fourth. Each had been progressively better, and he suspected that any deeper level would stop being a deterrent and start becoming very, very painful. That left the eternal very few options. Once, when he had first met the confused young mortal name Cabe Bedlam, a Cabe who did not understand who he was and why the concerted efforts of more than one Dragon King had been focused on him, the shadow steed had called out in his mind to the un-trained warlock. Had not Cabe responded, the sorcerer would have fallen victim to the wiles of three temptresses, drakes in human disguise. Now, with his powers failing, Darkhorse would have to try again. Out of sheer pride, the shadow steed hesitated, but, in the end, there was not better way.

Slowly, his concentration on the mind of his human ally, Darkhorse made his way around the edges of the barrier. It was ironic, he realized, that he who had spent so much time fighting to free himself from one cage was now desperately seeking entry to another, possibly deadlier one.

Minutes passed. There was no response. He could not even feel the presence of another mind, though that did not necessarily mean anything. It was possible that this new series of spells, so intricate compared to the old one placed on it by one of the Manor's former tenants, also shielded those within from his silent plea. If so, he might find himself circling the grounds hour upon hour until either of the spellcasters or one of their servants happened to step without. Darkhorse's eyes narrowed to slits as he thought of the time wasted.

When he had circled the warlock's domain once, he paused, trying to assess the situation in the hopes that he had missed something earlier. The sun was almost gone and, standing in the midst of the deepest, darkest forest, Darkhorse was already in deep shadow. In a fit of unleashed fury, he gave up all thought of appearance and caution and, backing just a bit away from the edge of the barrier, called out in his loudest voice.

"Cabe Bedlam! Come! Give me entrance! I am Darkhorse, your friend and ally! Hurry, before the hand of Shade tears at the foundation of the Dragonrealm and lays waste to all!" *A bit flowery,* he decided once he had finished, *but it will bring him to me! It must!*

Several seconds later, something began to rustle through the brush. It kept itself well hidden behind the trees and bushes, but Darkhorse soon saw that it was too small to be a human of Cabe's size.

"Darkhorse." It was a statement, a child's statement, but with something odd about its tone.

"I will not harm you, youngling! I am indeed Darkhorse, friend and ally to the master of this place!" He tried to talk soothingly.

The boy moved closer, though he still kept himself fairly obscured. There was something a bit odd about his gait and his breathing was fast, as if he had been running. Perhaps he had. He might have been far from this place when he heard Darkhorse.

"Come closer to me, youngling! I mean no harm! If you will take a message to the warlock Cabe Bedlam, I'll be forever in your debt!"

"I don't like you. Go away."

Darkhorse kicked at the ground. He had little experience in dealing with young. Better a trial of combat with a Dragon King than to have to try to placate a child. It was a wonder humans survived to adulthood. "Your sire would do well to teach you manners, youngling!"

The boy straightened and hissed. Darkhorse, about to add further in the hopes that what humans termed a scolding would make the child obey him, hesitated. The boy's reaction was too violent, too—

"My sssire is dead."

The words were far too chilling for a human. The ebony stallion voiced his next words quietly and calmly. "You have my sorrow. Who was your sire, young one?"

He knew it would not be Cabe Bedlam, not after hearing the sibilant tones. It seemed impossible that the child before him could be what he believed it was.

As if emboldened by the question of his heritage, the boy stepped out of hiding. From his height, he was likely a decade old, maybe a year or two more. His height was the *least* of his characteristics. Darkhorse, who had once again come to believe that he had seen everything, found that the child left him speechless.

He had dark hair that flashed a hint of gold. His eyes were narrow, red ovals that burned bright in the darkness. His nose was tiny, almost imperceptible, and his mouth had a cruel yet majestic cut to it, thin-lipped and knowing. He was a child with a mind beyond his years.

The boy was handsome, but in an inhuman way.

The layer of scale that covered his face told the shadow steed what he was even before the boy opened his mouth and revealed sharp teeth and a tongue slightly forked. This close, Darkhorse could see the hatred in his eyes, an overwhelming hatred that no young one should have been allowed to grow up with. It had already twisted him.

"My sire'sss color wasss *gold*. My sire wasss an emperor." The drake child stared resolutely into the eyes of Darkhorse—and it was the eternal who looked away first.

The hatchling of the Dragon King Gold triumphantly added, "*I* will be emperor, too."

XII

KYL! WHERE ARE you?"

The unnerving drake child turned at the sound of a voice obviously familiar to him. Darkhorse looked up in the direction of the newcomer's voice as well.

He *knew* who it was who called out, though it was hard to believe that something had turned out right for once.

"There, guardian! He's there!"

"I see him, Grath. I see—*Darkhorse!*"

The shadow steed dipped his head in acknowledgment. "Greetings to you, good friend Cabe!"

Kyl, his visage now a mask hiding his earlier savagery, stepped aside as he watched the lean human clad in dark blue robes approach, accompanied by another child. Ten years had and had not changed Cabe Bedlam. With his masterful abilities, he could extend his lifespan and keep himself young for three hundred years or so, possibly longer if violent death, a common problem among spellcasters, did not claim him. He seemed taller, though that might be because of the confidence with which he walked. Cabe looked exactly as he had years before, like a youth in his twenties, but only until one studied his roughly handsome features. The basic face had not changed—attentive eyes that kept track of the disobedient hatchling while still maintaining a focus on Darkhorse, a nose slightly turned, and a strong chin reminiscent of his grandfather, Nathan. Yet, put together, they had an age and experience to them that had not been there before.

He will be greater than his father and his grandfather, the stallion decided. *May he live a more peaceful, fruitful life than they.*

"Darkhorse!" With a bit of wonder recalled from their time together, Cabe reached out to touch the shadow steed. However, just before he reached the limits of the protective barrier, he paused. His eyes narrowed and literally blazed with built-up power. The great silver streak in his otherwise dark hair seemed to glitter. "You *are* Darkhorse, aren't you? I'd hate to think what I might do if I found you were some drake from the Storm Lands or from Lochivar who thought he could sneak in here in the guise of an old and trusted friend. I might do something very, very damaging to you—say, turn you inside out."

Darkhorse laughed. "Friend Cabe, you have picked up a wicked streak in the years since we met! Of course, I am Darkhorse! Who would dare or *want* to be me, I ask you?"

To the side, Kyl, whose face had become animated at the talk of damage, lost interest again. The other boy—now the shadow steed saw that this, *too*, was a drake, but one more human, more *gentle*—looked relieved.

Cabe's grin returned. "Enter freely, then, old friend."

It was as if a portal had opened up in the protective barrier that had for so long frustrated him. Darkhorse stepped through as the others backed up to give him space. Grath, the other hatchling, wanted to touch him, but Kyl suddenly shook his head and hissed, "He'll suck you in and sssend you to the dark places!"

"That'll be enough of *that!*" Cabe reprimanded. He looked up at his former companion and apologized. "He hears the tales from other drakes—and humans, too. Stories, but what can I do? They've been around longer than me."

"Perhaps it might be best if I altered my appearance a little." Darkhorse became a true stallion, even altering the appearance of his eyes. "Is that better?"

"Much."

"I should speak to you as soon as we have some privacy, young Cabe! It concerns my—return—to your land."

As the four of them started out for the Manor, the warlock nodded. "I thought so. I didn't think you were ever coming back. The Gryphon said you'd sacrificed yourself to keep Sh—"

"Of *that* we shall talk—when we have more privacy, if you don't mind." He indicated the hatchlings, both of whom were openly curious about what the two were saying.

"Sorry."

Darkhorse shook his head. "There is no reason to be sorry! Come! While we have a few moments, tell me of yourself and what has become of the Gryphon. I only know tales that have been told to me by untrustworthy sources."

Cabe informed him first of the Gryphon's journey across the Eastern Seas to the land of his birth. The Gryphon had discovered his people, the denizens of some place called the Dream Lands, under siege by the black-armored wolf raiders, the Aramites. D'Shay, a particular wolf raider who had dealt with various Dragon Kings over a period of time, had evidently survived an encounter in Penacles that once supposedly had climaxed with his death. The missives, delivered to the Dragonrealm by drake ships of the neutral city of Irillian, did not go into detail on the subject of D'Shay. For the past few years, though, the lionbird had been aiding the revolt of many of the Aramites' conquered enemies. The wolf raiders' empire was crumbling, but it was a slow, bloody conflict. The ebony-armored soldiers had not conquered most of their continent by luck.

"Toos runs Penacles in his absence," Cabe concluded. "The general refuses to be named ruler, despite the pressure on him. He and I both wanted to go and aid the Gryphon, but that would have left no one to keep an eye on certain troublemakers."

"A wise decision, Cabe! Now, what of you? The Lady of the Amber is your mate, yes?"

It was informative to the shadow steed the way the mention of his wife made the otherwise confident warlock turn red. Darkhorse recognized the deep love the mortal had for his enchantress.

"She's my . . . mate. Yes. We have—we have two children."

"But this is *wonderful* news!" Darkhorse roared, unmindful at the moment of how his voice carried. After so many dismal events, the progression of life, something that both fascinated and puzzled him, cheered the stallion, especially as it dealt with one of the few mortals who fully trusted him. "You must introduce them to me—if that is acceptable to the Lady of the Amber!"

Cabe smiled in wry humor. "She doesn't like to be called that. It's either 'Lady Gwen' or 'the Lady Bedlam.' She's very much into the control of this place and our children . . . but then, so am I."

Darkhorse quieted as the four exited from the forest and entered the clearing where the unique structure called simply the "Manor" stood. Seeing the place reminded him again of that time when he had come to Cabe's rescue. The Manor was a perfect complement of nature and planned design. It was difficult to tell where the building ended and the natural contours of the great tree that made up at least half of the structure began. Some walls had been completely shaped by the tree; others had been built. It was at least three stories high, with windows everywhere. The grounds had been carefully shaped to match the land. There were other buildings as well; and, though they had not been designed with the efficiency and beauty of the ancient citadel, someone had taken great care to ensure that they did not detract from the splendor of the forest.

People looked up from their tasks—people and *drakes*, Darkhorse amended, trying to cope with the idea of such cooperation—and stared at the horse beside their lord. It was the stare of the mildly curious, not the panicked, which evidently meant that his disguise had succeeded. Both hatchlings suddenly ran off in the direction of the Manor itself, perhaps to give warning. The shadow steed wondered what sort of reception he could expect from the Manor's mistress. A cool one at best. Better that than open warfare.

There had to be several families of both races living here side-by-side, but everyone seemed to be taking it with stride. A man and a drake dealing with the horses broke off from their discussion to first acknowledge the warlock, then to admire the magnificent black animal trotting beside him. Darkhorse watched them in turn, amazed at such cooperation, such friendship. Even the humans of Irillian or Zuu, cities in which humans and drakes had lived together for centuries, were more polite and respectful to one another than they were friendly.

"She was in the garden when I went out to search for Kyl," Cabe whispered, nodding in turn to those who paid him homage as he passed. The embarrassed look on his face was a humorous sight to Darkhorse. "Hopefully, we should find her there."

With a brief nod of his head, Darkhorse signalled his understanding. Certain questions were beginning to eat at his patience, however, and he hoped that he and the two human spellcasters would be able to converse before long. As enjoyable as this reunion had been, Shade was a problem that could not be cut off.

They did find Gwen in the garden. Kyl and Grath stood patiently off to the side. With the witch were two strikingly beautiful women. Though no judge of human tastes, Darkhorse knew that they were capable of tempting many a man. He also knew that these women were not human. They were female drakes, far more adept at shapeshifting into such forms but less talented at sorcery.

Despite their beauty, however, the two drakes paled in comparison to the woman kneeling before them, who was bent on adjusting the clothing of a small human male perhaps two years younger than the hatchlings. Long, thick tresses crimson in color fell well below her shoulders and a silver streak, smaller and narrower than the one in Cabe's hair, added to the intensity of the fiery image. A form-fitting gown the color of emeralds revealed curves that were, by the standards of most human males Darkhorse had known through the ages, quite arresting. The Lady Bedlam rose and glanced their way, her perfect face with its glittering eyes—eyes that matched the gown absolutely—tiny nose, and full red lips marred only by the anxiety in her expression. Anxiety and distrust.

As they neared her, Darkhorse could not help feeling both relieved and disappointed that he was unique, that there was no female counterpart to him. Had there been, she surely would have resembled Cabe's mate in thought and action.

Even the multiverse is not ready for that! he thought with much humor and some passing regret.

"S'sseresa," Gwen called. The nearer of the two drake dams stepped closer. Her eyes still on the black steed, the witch said, "Take Aurim and the others to their rooms and please check on Valea. She should be waking from her nap soon."

"As you wish, Lady Bedlam." The two female drakes seemed to have no difficulty dealing with taking orders from a human, and Darkhorse slowly realized that they had probably had several years to get used to it. One dam took the two hatchlings; the other reached down and, whispering a few words to the golden-haired boy, took him by the hand. They followed after the others at a slower pace.

"Now, then." Gwen's expression was cold. "Kyl told me that *you* have somehow come back, but I was hoping he'd been imagining things. I see he wasn't."

"You were a bit warmer when last we parted company, Lady Bedlam—may I extend my congratulations?—and I see no reason for your continued distrust of me. I hardly came back by *choice*, much as I enjoy this world. I was *forced* back here by one of *your* kind."

The ice melted. Barely.

"Things have been fairly peaceful here the last few years. I have children now, Darkhorse. Children who should grow up in peace."

Darkhorse laughed, ignoring the fury on his hostess's visage. "I am so sorry that I have to awaken you from your dream, witch! If you have eyes at all, you should know that, despite their unwillingness to band together, the Dragon Kings are far from harmless! Even now, the clans of Silver prepare to strike— and with Shade loose—"

"Wait! What's that you said?" Cabe stepped between the two, his original intention being to keep one or both from striking out. Now, however, he was interested only in Darkhorse's words. "Is that what you came to tell us?"

Backing away for the sake of his friend, the shadow steed nodded. Even the Lady Gwen was now listening in rapt attention. The anger had vanished, re- placed by concern—concern for her husband and children.

"*Now* I have your attention! Good! It should have been obvious to you, Lady of the Amber, that if I've returned, then so has Shade! Our faceless comrade is worse than I can ever recall seeing him! Something in the spell that tore us from our exile has caused a reversion! Shade has been as a man gone truly mad, with personalities vying each time I've met him! I fear he is returning to his original mind-set—and I fear it may be the worst of all!"

Gwen sat down, her hands rubbing together tightly. "I owe you an apology, then. If what you say is true—"

"There is worse! I have sorely underestimated the age of my onetime com- rade! If I am correct, a Vraad sorcerer walks among us again!"

The name meant nothing to Cabe, though he carried within him some of the memories of his grandfather, who had studied the ancient races thoroughly. Gwen, on the other hand, turned pale and spat out an epithet concerning the shadowy warlock that made her husband look at her in mild shock.

"What's a Vraad sorcerer? Is he different from us?"

Lady Bedlam nodded slowly. Her jaw set tight as she looked at Darkhorse. "We've heard nothing out of the ordinary from the northern lands. The only reports that reach us concern the fact that Melicard is supposed to marry some princess from the west. I pity the woman."

"They are a fair match, witch. She may be his salvation. She is also a latent sorceress."

Cabe put a hand on his wife's shoulder. She reached up and placed her own on his. The warlock smiled sadly, as if acknowledging the end of a beautiful time. "You seem to know quite a bit, Darkhorse. Maybe you could tell us how you know so much."

He did. Drayfitt's abilities came as no surprise to Cabe, though the elder's actions in the name of his king did. Cabe had only met the man briefly, but he had come to respect him. Both spellcasters knew of Melicard's crusade and his overzealous advisor, Mal Quorin, but spies had reported nothing except the usual raids, though those had become fewer in the last couple years.

Of Shade and the plots of the Silver Dragon, they knew nothing, and what Darkhorse conveyed to them stunned both Bedlams. To Lady Gwen, it was the culmination of fears she had always harbored about the hooded warlock; to Cabe, it was a tragic conclusion to someone he had both befriended and pitied. That the true Shade might be a less than savory being saddened him further.

"I'd always assumed he was a basically decent man behind that curse."

"A fairy tale! This is true life! Shade is a Vraad and, with few exceptions, they were arrogant and amoral! The world did not weep at their passing, so I'm given to understand! It amazes me that you and yours could be descendents of their kind."

"Cabe." Gwen squeezed his hand tight. "If all he says is true—"

"I would not—"

She cut him off. "*As* all he says must be true, then we have been purposely led astray. Someone has been lulling us into a false sense of security."

The warlock nodded. "The Silver Dragon or Melicard; more likely it's his counselor, Quorin. I wonder if the lord of Dagora knows anything. He's been extremely quiet himself."

Growing unsettled, Darkhorse stamped the ground with his hoof. The words that fled his mouth had almost become an automatic ritual. "I was a fool! I should have come to you the moment freedom was mine! It may already be too late!"

Cabe grimaced. "It doesn't do any good to continually condemn yourself; I did that enough to know. What we have to do now is contact the Green Dragon and, with his aid, discover why there seems to be a curtain of silence between us and the north. You said that there may be a pact between the Dragon King Silver and Shade. Do you have any idea what that pact might entail?"

"I suspect part of it might have to do with a book—Shade's notes on his vile spells—but that book is dust, thanks to me. Without it, Shade will have to plan from scratch. At one point, he seemed to recall everything, but I think that must have proved a temporary state, else why his search?"

"Then you think he plans to recreate the original spell—but *why* if the curse is lifted?"

"It may not be lifted. Even if it has been, where would that *leave* him? Friend Bedlam, if Shade sought immortality long ago, why would he not seek it again?"

The warlock's mate, who had remained silent during this part of the exchange, turned to Darkhorse. "I worry about Talak. It sounds like a volatile situation. Do we dare let it continue that way?"

Darkhorse saw what she feared. Now would be a perfect time for the drakes to strike at Talak. "I would go back there now, since I owe the Princess Erini for my freedom, but I lack the strength and will to form a proper portal."

"Let me see." Gwen reached out with her hands, standing as if she were trying to ward off the stallion. Darkhorse could feel her probe as it danced over his essence, stopping here and there as she sought the cause of his weakness. When she was through with her examination, the Lady Bedlam lowered her arms and nodded to herself.

"There is a thin link between you and . . . someone else."

Incredulous, he searched for himself. His own probe was less efficient than hers, suffering as it did the way *all* of his abilities suffered, but he eventually found what she had located. Darkhorse laughed at the thin, magical strand, invisible and insubstantial, but virtually impossible to sever.

"Drayfitt's link! That's twice! Curse the mage! Am I never to be free of him?"

"Is it the same?" Lady Gwen asked. "Most links are forged in the same manner, but not this one."

Darkhorse inspected it again. "*No* . . . and it explains my weakness. I have become—a source—of strength for Drayfitt. The link is draining me slowly, but . . . this is too haphazard. I think the Princess Erini did this to me unintentionally."

"Sever it now," Cabe suggested.

"He cannot. If he does, he loses what Drayfitt has already." Gwen made a face. "You might say that the old sorcerer is stealing Darkhorse's essence, his being."

"I am being *devoured* alive, is what you're saying!"

"Essentially."

Cabe looked disgusted. "How can we stop it?"

"Killing Drayfitt is one way. With the link, all that he stole will return to its original place. Darkhorse might even gain something."

"I want nothing of Drayfitt's! I am not a ghoul—or a murderer!"

Lady Bedlam paced. "Nathan never taught me anything like this; I think he was as disgusted with the concept as you are, Cabe. Yet . . ."

"Yet what?" Darkhorse grew anxious. He enjoyed existence and planned to continue to enjoy it, despite the increasing odds against doing so.

"If you can persuade him to break the link from *his* end—"

"Why should *he* be able to do that when I cannot?"

"He forged the original." She looked at Darkhorse as he thought she must look at her children when they asked an obvious question.

"Forgive me, Lady of the Amber! I have not suffered so many calamities in centuries! I fear I am not taking them well! The frustration of being kept in check while Shade—"

Gwen cut him off. "Forget your apologies, eternal. Perhaps you're not quite the demon I cannot help thinking you are, but you always seem to be the harbinger of disaster. For the sake of my family and the peace of the lands, I want Shade stopped—even if that means dealing with you. I don't say that I'm right, but I'd feel the children especially safer with you far from here."

Darkhorse tilted his head to one side and looked at the two spellcasters, finishing up with Gwen. "Humans are a strange, convoluted people, and you, Lady Bedlam, are a prime example. There is a part of you that would accept friendship with me, but there is a part of you . . . I need not go on. When this is over—if it ever is—we must talk again."

More to turn the conversation to a safer course than because it was necessary to say, Cabe interjected, "If you need Drayfitt to break the link, then that means *you'll* have to go to him."

"I am aware of that. The thought does not stir joy within me. Drayfitt is not in Talak, I believe. That leaves the city virtually under Mal Quorin's control."

"We'll take care of that. It might be time for the master warlock Cabe Bedlam and his lovely bride, the powerful enchantress—enchantress of my *heart!*—Lady Gwen, to visit the city-state in typical sorcerous style."

His wife gave him a coy look. "Materialize on the steps of the palace?"

"Probably not a good idea. If it was that easy, the Dragon Kings would have done it long ago. I was thinking more at the city gates with a great fanfare and fireworks—all illusion, of course."

"What reason do we give, husband?"

"An offer of peace. Melicard was always good enough to hear such things out. There is still a good man beneath that horrible face."

"Princess Erini has brought much of that man out to the surface," Darkhorse added. "She would make a good ally, providing they *do* marry. Very well. I will leave now, then, since you seem to have things in hand! My relief is beyond measure—but what of the children while you two are gone?"

"Even Shade needed permission to enter this place. The children will be safe here."

Darkhorse did not ask the other question. *But can you trust the children?* he had wondered, thinking of the taller of the two hatchlings. What would this Kyl be like when he was mature? Already, he seemed too much a reflection of his sire.

There will be time to worry about that only if we succeed in solving the present crisis! Through habit, Darkhorse reared, intending to summon a portal for his journey to the north. Only when nothing materialized did he remember the extent of his plight.

Cabe was the first to understand what was wrong. "You don't have the strength or the will to summon a gate, do you?"

"I fear not."

The warlock thought about it, then, with some hesitation, said, "Neither of us have been in that region for years; most of our portals would depend upon blind luck, except . . ."

"Except?"

Cabe looked at Gwen. "I think there's one place I could never forget. Azran's citadel."

"There is little more than wreckage there. The spell protecting it from the violence of the Hell Plains and the ravages of time has long fled from it."

"You've been there?"

"Yes." Darkhorse decided it was better not to go into his encounter with the emissary from the Lords of the Dead.

"Still, I think I remember well enough to get you there safely. What do you say?"

"Since I have little to fear even if you should land me in molten earth or during some great tremor, I suppose so."

Cabe gave him a sour grin. "Thanks for your confidence."

The gate was there even as Cabe finished speaking, a sign of how accustomed he had become to his abilities since they had last met. Darkhorse inspected it briefly, more because of his own recent lack of success than because he did not trust the warlock's skill. When he was satisfied, he turned to bid the two farewell.

"Thank you for your aid, Cabe Bedlam—and yours, too, Lady of the Amber."

"Please don't call me that."

"My apologies! I was warned and I forgot."

She slowly shook her head. "*I* apologize. This is not the time for trivialities."

"Good luck, Darkhorse." Cabe waved a hand. "We'll leave on *our* journey as soon as possible."

"Do that. Things may be calm, but best not to take chances, eh?" The ebony stallion reared. "Beware, dear friends! Shade may strike at any time and in any way! Be vigilant!"

He heard Cabe call, "We will!" and then the world shifted as he crossed through the portal. Ahead of him, the fury of the Hell Plains exploded in a mocking salute to his return. The gate vanished as the shadow steed emerged. Darkhorse, wasting no time, immediately reached out through the link itself and noted that his quarry was somewhere south of him.

Darkhorse prayed that he would have some idea of how to convince the sorcerer to break the link before the two of them came face-to-face again. He was uncomfortably aware that he stood a good chance of becoming, for the *third* time, Drayfitt's prisoner.

The last thought might have been humorous . . . if not for the fact that he knew there would be no escape this time. Drayfitt would surely see to that.

IN THE GARDEN of the Manor, Cabe stood with one arm around his wife. The two of them stood staring at the spot where, moments before, the portal that Darkhorse had used had stood.

Cabe blinked and smiled. "We should do this more often."

"I keep telling you that. Why do you think that I bring the children out here? There's something about a walk around this place that puts one at ease."

The two walked slowly to one of the benches. The Lady Bedlam sat down, looking briefly confused.

"What's wrong?" Cabe asked, sitting down beside her.

"I keep thinking that Aurim was out here—but that's silly. He's not."

"You sent Aurim, Kyl, and Grath to their rooms, remember? We wanted privacy."

"Privacy." She kissed him. "We don't get enough of that, do we?"

"No. Still, we can't complain. Things have been pretty peaceful over the last few years. Even Talak's been quiet for months."

Gwen settled into his arms. "Let's hope it stays that way. I'd hate for something to ruin as lovely a day as this."

They kissed and then sat quietly on the bench, listening to the birds and enjoying the day. Neither of them spoke of the return of Darkhorse, Talak's army marching, or Shade's plot. What point *was* there in talking about such things?

None of them had *happened.*

XIII

A DAY HAD passed since the departure of the column, and it had been a day of change. It was not something that Erini found she could put her finger on at first. A glance from one of the palace guards, the curt words of one servant to another, and the politeness of Counselor Quorin. The last worried her most, for if the advisor had reason to be polite to her, it probably meant trouble.

Melicard's manner seemed to be the only positive result of yesterday's events. He was actually jubilant.

One final change confused more than worried her. After insisting that she allow him to protect her better, Iston had found reason after reason to summon his men away. From Galea, she had been told that the captain was out somewhere, honing his troops to battle-fitness as every good commander should; while from Magda, she received only an amused smile, a response to Galea's simplistic explanation. Erini suspected that neither of them really knew what Iston was actually doing.

Breakfast with Melicard went swimmingly, as her father would have put it. The princess was astounded at how pleasant he could be. More and more, his talk turned to peaceful times, times without the Dragon Kings and what he would then hope to accomplish. He even began talking about bridging the chasm that he had set up between himself and his neighbors, especially Penacles and Irillian. It would have been an idyllic world, the one he built up over the course of the meal, if it had not had one major flaw.

There was no mention of the drake race in his new world. From the way the king spoke, Erini knew that there would be no room for the drakes. It marred an otherwise wonderful morning. Finally, she put the thought aside, assuring herself that she would press him on it once they were married.

For the first time, Melicard broached the subject of marriage.

The two of them had walked outside onto one of the marble terraces that seemed to have been a preoccupation with one of the palace's designers. Two sentries stood stiffly at attention as the royal couple glided by. At home, Erini would have expected to see at least a dozen guards nearby—just for *her* protection. Melicard, however, seemed confident of his own safety. Erini was not so certain.

"You've made a change here, my princess. You know that, do you not?"

"What could I have done? I've only been here a short time."

The king closed his one eye (though the light made it seem as if *both* eyes closed) and appeared to make a rapid calculation. He opened his eye and smiled with the good half of his mouth.

"It *has* been only a short time, hasn't it? I've begun to feel as if you have been here always. Quorin says the same thing."

With a very different meaning behind it, the princess thought in grim satisfaction. "This is my home. I feel that way, too."

Melicard turned his gaze away from her, embarrassed. This was not the sort of thing he understood well. Battles and vengeance were his forte. "I told you something to the effect that love at first sight exists only in tales. I think I was wrong."

"You were. I know from personal experience."

Without thinking, he brought up the elfwood arm and took her hand. The arm was pleasantly cool to the touch, smooth without feeling lifeless. Erini noticed how its feel seemed to be dependent upon her betrothed's mood.

"I cannot say how long this crusade will last, or if it will even end during our lifetimes, for that matter. Regardless, if you are willing, I think it's time that we put an end to the 'royal courtship' and began planning for—the future."

She laughed lightly, positively delighted with the way he had put it. "Marriage? Is that the word you sought, your majesty?"

Melicard nodded with mock severity. "Yes, I think so."

Her kiss proved to be the proper response. As with the false arm, she hardly noticed that a part of the lips that touched her own was not real. The elfwood was wood only if the two of them saw it so. Now, their belief made it flesh.

"Your—*majesties*." Quorin's voice threw a deep chill on the day, dousing even the fires of happiness that had enveloped Erini during Melicard's proposal. Still, there was some pleasure in seeing the look on the counselor's face. He was confused and livid, and both those emotions were barely being kept in check. Erini gave him a polite but false smile.

"What *is* it, Quorin?" Melicard, unlike his future bride, bared his teeth in something that could never be termed a smile. Its ferocity surprised the advisor, who had probably never had it turned on *him* before. "I left orders that *no one* was to disturb us. That *included* you, I believe."

"Forgive me, my lord . . . I was under the impression . . ." He stared at the princess, who had the feeling that the man had not expected to find the two of them in so intimate a moment.

"Since you are here, Quorin, I have something for you to do."

"My lord?" Feral eyes drifted to Erini.

"Announce that, with the campaign underway and a new era beginning in which Talak will be at the forefront, the Princess Erini of Gordag-Ai has consented to be my queen. We will be married in a citywide ceremony in—how long would you say, my princess?"

She gave Melicard a smile. *At last!* "Since this marriage was arranged before I could walk, there is little preparation needed on my part. I would prefer it as soon as possible."

By now, the counselor had recovered somewhat. With a slight gleam in his eyes, he quickly said, "It would be remiss to have a less-than-regal wedding ceremony, your majesty. The princess's family will wish to attend and all of the nobles from both city-states will demand their rights, too. Such an event calls for extravagance."

Erini grew cold. "I've never been one for extravagance. If there is someone who can marry us now, so much the better."

Melicard patted her hand. "My sentiments exactly, but Quorin is, unfortunately, correct. We owe your family and the people a ceremony—a festival even."

"One month, your majesty! If I can help organize several thousand soldiers, a wedding will seem simple in comparison! One month!"

"That long?" The king seemed more reluctant now. "I was hoping two or three weeks at most. Make it a smaller ceremony. The nobles and the royal family of Gordag-Ai. Announce that a festival for the people will commence two weeks after that. They'll understand."

Quorin sighed in evident defeat. "Two weeks, then. May I be the first to extend my congratulations to both of you."

Melicard thanked him, but Erini could only nod her head. As the advisor turned to leave—supposedly to begin those preparations, especially the announcements that would have to be carried by courier to Gordag-Ai—the princess could not help thinking that he had given in too easily. In fact, it seemed that his main purpose had only been to assure that the wedding did not take place immediately. A month or two weeks; a delay was a delay.

"Is something wrong?"

"No. I just wish we could be married now."

"That would be pleasant, but we're already ignoring protocol. By rights, the courtship was to last a full month and the wedding date should have been set from four to six months later."

"Months in which anything could happen. Our fathers actually decided that?"

"It was how they were married to our mothers. Royalty sometimes requires setting odd examples. Enough of that. Now that Quorin has succeeded in interjecting his presence into my day, I am reminded of work that must be taken care of. The campaign has begun, but I have people to govern, too."

"If I am to be queen, should I not learn how you govern your people?"

Melicard smiled. "You have a point, though I fear that you will only distract me from my duties. Very well. Come with me and see how I protect my children. Perhaps you will even have a few suggestions on ways I can improve."

She refrained from commenting, wondering how he would react to her opinions.

As they left the terrace, Erini noted how the guards appeared to have been rotated. These were two new soldiers, men the princess vaguely recalled seeing in the patrol that had stopped her when she had been leaving the garden with Drayfitt. Ostlich's patrol.

"You're leaving me again," Melicard whispered from her side. "You have a mind that certainly loves to travel."

Erini suddenly tightened her grip on the king's arm. Had it not been the one made of elfwood, it was likely she would have cut off blood to the limb. Melicard's final words had struck her hard, for, as if having a premonition, she *had* seen herself leaving her betrothed—but only because both of them were dead.

SHADE WATCHED THE column come to a halt from what little remained of the tower he had usurped.

The tower had been built long ago as part of a sister city to Talak. However, at some point in recent times—recent time to the hooded spellcaster being anything in the past few centuries—the other city had been destroyed. The expedition steered clear of the crumbling tower, possibly because they felt that the ghosts of the dead would put a curse on their crusade.

It is not the ethereal phantoms of your minds that you must fear, the warlock thought with something almost approaching indifference. What became of Talak's great army did not interest him; what became of Drayfitt *did*. The elderly sorcerer was the only link he had to the spell. There were things he needed to know, things that had again escaped his mind after his brief fling with omniscience. He cursed the personality that had been dominant then. Instead of working with that knowledge, it had chosen to relax, to taunt, and to play the fool. There was little to redeem in any of his past incarnations. Madmen and fools all of them. To Shade, they were different people, not worthy of the Vraad race.

It had taken an accident to change things. To his regret, however, Drayfitt's misuse of the one spell offered Shade both immortality and final death. All that mattered was time.

I am Vraad. Tezerenee. The dragon banner rests in my *hands now.* Which tent would be the gaunt mortal's tent? Shade blinked and his view changed to a close-up of the massive camp, despite the fact that they were more than an hour to the south. He had no qualms about altering his body to suit his needs. Shapeshifting, however, was a costly and difficult spell for most sorcerers, and actual physical change was only a last resort because it required the most delicate of manipulations. They feared disrupting the natural forces of this world, something that had never stopped the Vraad. It was so very hard to believe that these people were descendents of his kind—except that there had been those, like the Bedlams, who had proved that magic was still the ultimate tool.

"Cabe," he muttered, recalling the first time they had met. The young boy had been frightened out of his senses, not understanding what he was.

A movement in the camp disturbed his reverie. Shade frowned, wondering why he should spend time reminiscing about something so inconsequential. This was not the first time, either. Everything he had done in the last few days had stirred some memory—and with the memories came emotions. The Vraad had never been immune to emotion; they had, in fact, been slaves to their passions at times. Yet, the memories he found he could not purge concerned these lesser creatures or those who could now only be called his enemies. It made no sense. They were transitory lives for the most part; thralls for his will as had been the way before the journey to this place.

He was saved further introspection by the appearance of his quarry.

Drayfitt looked worn out, unaccustomed, it seemed, to riding long distances. Shade clucked his disapproval; a competent spellcaster would have created his own, more comfortable transport and, since his companions were apparently mundane in nature, travelled at the head of the column as its supreme commander. Any idiotic officer who tried to argue otherwise would find himself without a mouth to curse with.

Shade watched as Drayfitt spoke briefly with two officers. Their words were of unimportant matters—the coming battle, what they possibly faced, and the continuing agreement that this was folly and the expedition should have actually been sent north or northwest to deal with the suddenly active clans of Silver. The warlock smiled; Talak would get to fight the Silver Dragon sooner than they expected.

The night would soon be upon them. Then he would go to the elderly sorcerer and relieve him of the burdensome knowledge locked in his subconscious. After that, the wrong that had been done to Shade could finally be corrected. He would be immortal, have control of the powers of this world, and have no rivals to argue his claim. There were good points to being the last of his kind. The Dragonrealm would be his to mold into a proper domain, and its inhabitants would adore him—because he would will it so.

A harsh voice, an old memory, thrust through his mind like a well-sharpened sword. *Do not dream! Act!*

The corners of his mouth curled downward as he observed Drayfitt departing for one of the larger tents.

"*Yes, father,*" he muttered coldly to the ghosts in his head.

AS THE LAST vestiges of an ignoble day departed beneath the horizon, Drayfitt discovered an odd thing about himself. The first few minutes on his feet— after a whole day's journey on the back of the monster some fool of a soldier had chosen for him—he had been totally exhausted and sore to the point of numbness. Now, only minutes after sitting down on the cot in his tent, he felt refreshed and actually stronger than ever. His abilities, too, seemed sharper. Drayfitt stared thoughtfully into space for several minutes, then looked up at a lantern someone had lit for his use. Pursing his lips, he whistled to the flame. To his delight, a tiny red figure immediately leaped out of the fire and down to the ground. Miniature plumes of smoke trailed after him. The figure was little more than a doll, lacking even a face. It walked up to the spellcaster and bowed gracefully.

Drayfitt whirled his finger once. The flame-creature did a flip, landing on its feet again. It repeated its bow.

Laughing quietly, the sorcerer whistled for another figure. The one that leaped out this time was female in shape. She joined her counterpart and executed a curtsy. At a silent command from their creator, the two fiery dolls stepped together and began to dance. Around and around they spun. Drayfitt watched them with a child's glee; Ishmir had performed a trick like this when Drayfitt had been little more than a baby. It was one of the reasons he had later tried to follow in his famous brother's footsteps. It was one of the first tricks he discovered he did not have the aptitude for. The potential was there, but the powers, for some reason, refused to respond properly. Ishmir had claimed on several occasions that the only difference between a Dragon Master and a simple street showman was strength of will.

Finally tiring of his little dancers, he dismissed them back to the flame. It was silly, he decided, to waste his newfound strength on so childish a spell. With his present level of competency, the aged spellcaster realized that an entire world had opened up to him. Up until now, his skills had served him adequately at best—lengthening his lifespan and blurring the memories of those around him when necessary. Now, he could take his place as a true sorcerer, one who did not have to worry about the Seeker talismans that Counselor Quorin wore upon his person to keep him safe from magical assault by *outside* foes. He, Drayfitt, would guide the king to a more reasonable course of action, make Talak truly a city guiding the Dragonrealm to peace.

"I hope you will excuse the intrusion," a mockingly polite voice asked quietly.

Drayfitt spun around, all his newfound strength at the forefront for this sudden attack. He knew whom he faced—even though he had not expected to actually *see* the other's visage.

"Yes, I am Shade." The hooded warlock bowed in what seemed a perfect imitation of the fire elemental's bow. He had something unidentifiable in each hand. For some reason, Drayfitt's stomach churned uneasily.

"I bring you—offerings." Shade threw the two objects to the ground. As they landed, legs and tails formed. Two very large and very nasty scorpions trundled toward one another, preparing to lock with one another in battle.

"They were partners in crime once. Sent by someone who would see you dead. Poison was to be their weapon, poison in your food this very night. Enough to kill a dragon."

Drayfitt turned pale. The scorpions sparred with their claws, their wicked tails waiting for some opening.

"I thought it only appropriate that they suffer justice akin to their crime. Don't you agree?" The expression on Shade's face—Drayfitt still marvelled over the fact that there *was* a face—was one of indifference. He might have been watching a leaf blown along by a gust of wind.

As if released from some spell, the two scorpions attacked in earnest now. Claws tore at legs. The tails darted forward and snapped back as if some mad puppeteer were controlling them. One creature succeeded in tearing a leg from his adversary. Overconfident, he was almost struck in the head by the wounded one's stinger. As it was, the near disaster put him off guard and his opponent, dripping ichor where the leg had been lost, forced him back.

Drayfitt looked from the scorpions to the warlock. Shade noted his emotions and snapped his fingers at the two duelists. Both backed away just far enough to separate themselves from one another, their stingers tensed.

Shade lowered his hand. The scorpions struck one another on the head again and again, piercing each other's brain. They continued to strike one another long after each should have been dead from the physical damage alone.

"Enough," the hooded figure commanded.

Two lifeless husks dropped to the ground. They decayed rapidly and within seconds there was no trace of either.

Summoning his courage, Drayfitt glared at the intruder. "Why have you come here? What was that damnable display supposed to prove?"

"Prove? They were going to kill you on Counselor Quorin's command."

"What?" Even having expected the answer to his second question, it was unsettling to actually hear it. "You could have left them alive rather than torture them so! This would've been what I needed to rid the king of that feline's poisonous words!"

"I wouldn't worry about your king. I think he's due to be toppled tomorrow." Shade scratched his chin. "Yes, tomorrow is correct."

"What sort of mad game are you playing?" Drayfitt readied himself. How his newfound strength would hold against the power of the eldest, most skilled spellcaster alive was difficult to say. *Not very well,* he supposed after a moment's consideration. "If you planned on killing me, why not simply have those two poor souls do the work for you?"

"*Kill* you?" The warlock looked openly startled. "I have no desire to kill you. Just give me what I want and I'll erase your memories of this night. Simple as that."

"Erase my memories? After you tell me my king is in danger?"

"He'll be toppled whether you know or not. Besides, I made a pact and I will abide by it. Be reasonable. I just want a piece of your mind." The ends of

Shade's mouth tilted upward and he stretched out a hand toward the elderly sorcerer. Drayfitt found that Shade's sense of humor escaped him.

Where are the sentries? he suddenly wondered. Shade was talking loud enough for anyone within the general area to hear him, yet no one had come to investigate. *And I didn't even notice the spell—whatever it was,* Drayfitt concluded. *What chance do I have? What* choice *do I have?*

"You will not take memories that are not yours!"

"Ohhh, but they *are!* My memories, I mean! You studied that book from end to end; I know. Even if you cannot recall its contents consciously, it remains trapped within you. I merely plan to sift through until I find them. You should be reasonable about this."

As Shade spoke, Drayfitt felt his arms and legs grow heavy. He took a step toward the warlock, thinking ruefully how much this resembled his failure during Darkhorse's temporary escape. That reminder seemed to give him the impetus he needed. Summoning his strength, he broke the spell the warlock had wound around him with such ease that it left him startled.

Shade did not look too pleased, either. "Do not resist me. You only play the role of mage; I *am* magic! Give me what is mine and I will leave you be."

Drayfitt made a circular motion with his left arm. "Anything of such value to you should be kept from you at all costs. I know what you are. I know the destructive effects of Vraad sorcery."

The sand began to creep up Shade's legs at a rate that caught the warlock unaware until it was up to his waist. He stopped it there with little more than a frown and sent the granules flying, creating a man-sized dust devil that swarmed over Drayfitt.

The elderly spellcaster dispersed it, but the motion cost him. Shade reached out with one hand and touched Drayfitt on the temple. Drayfitt let out a gurgle and fell to his knees. The warlock cradled his quarry's head in both hands.

Though physical resistance had failed the old man, Shade found his path no easier now. Drayfitt's will was stronger than Shade would have imagined it could be. It was almost as if the sorcerer were drawing from some secret reserve. He was actually succeeding in repelling the invasion of his mind.

Stepping up the intensity of his mental assault, the warlock began picking up random, insignificant memories. At first, he was pleased, thinking he had broken through. Then, he realized that Drayfitt had turned him toward a blind alley of sorts and that the other's resistance was still keeping him out.

Annoyed, Shade ceased holding back his full power.

Drayfitt's eyes widened and his mouth opened in silent agony. His hands clutched at his attacker's, but the will behind them was failing.

The memories began flowing like a river newly released from the winter ice. It did not take Shade long to find the ones he had wanted, for, being recent memories, they were clearer, more obvious. There were memories of Darkhorse mixed among them, but the warlock let them dwindle away, seeing no use in them. What could they tell him about the shadow steed that he did not know already?

When at last he had absorbed all he had desired, Shade released Drayfitt's head. The king's sorcerer crumpled to the ground, eyes staring sightlessly ahead. Drayfitt breathed, but that was nearly all he could do.

Shade knelt down beside him, putting one hand on the stricken figure's forehead. There was a mind there, but it was slowly ebbing away. He would be dead within the hour. The warlock generously closed Drayfitt's eyes. There was no remorse; had Drayfitt not resisted, Shade would not have been forced to take stricter measures. It was as simple as that.

Lying in the dirt, though, seemed an ignoble end for a mage who had, however briefly, had the strength to check him. Shade stared at the cot and slowly smiled.

It took him one breath to complete the scene . . . and then the warlock was gone.

JUST BEYOND SIGHT of the sprawling encampment, Darkhorse stumbled backward as what he had lost to the King's spellcaster returned to him in a heady rush. His initial thrill at becoming whole again was quickly smothered by the echoes of pain and suffering that accompanied the return. He knew instantly what had been wrought and by whom. Despite regaining everything, Darkhorse chose to continue on toward the camp and the tent of the sorcerer. There were things that Drayfitt might still be able to tell him—if the shadow steed could only reach him before the elderly mage expired.

He hoped desperately that one of those things might be *where* Shade would strike next.

XIV

FROM THE MIDST of the somber Tyber Mountains, another army set out on a crusade. A larger force coming from the west would join with them before dawn. Together, the combined legions of the new, self-proclaimed Emperor of Dragons would sweep down on the kingdom of the upstart human monarch and claim it for their lord. So as to seal his authority, the Dragon King Silver rode at the front of the horde, the huge riding drake beneath him the largest and deadliest of its kind, as befit an emperor.

The Silver Dragon's eyes burned hungrily as he stared south, where, if one used imagination, the gates of Talak already stood open to greet him.

SOMEONE ELSE SENSED the shock of Drayfitt's passing.

Erini had retired early and had just fallen asleep. The princess did not wake at that moment, but rather began to dream. She dreamed of the elderly sorcerer collapsing, his life ebbing away. She dreamed of a fearsome, hooded face made all the more terrible because the emotions that it displayed were not even evil; there was annoyance, irritation, and a cold indifference to the fate of the king's spellcaster. It was as if the life was next to nothing to this face.

The princess knew somehow that it was the face of the warlock Shade.

She dreamed of another, as well: the ebony stallion Darkhorse. He stood poised above a fairly stable hill, staring down at the camp. Though he had not yet entered, he *also* knew of the death and the bitter knowledge that he was too late.

Drayfitt had had his faults, but Erini mourned his passing. There had been a bond between them, the sharing of her secret, her *curse*. In a sense, she felt that Darkhorse had a similar bond with her, and her dream-self drew some relief from that. At that point, her subconscious turned to the one time she had truly met the shadow steed. The chamber beneath the palace. The meeting was fixed in her mind, as was the fact that she *had* succeeded in freeing him.

"Princess?" Darkhorse turned, as if realizing for the first time that she was there.

Erini woke—and found herself on a cold, stone floor in total darkness.

Fear struck, but it passed quickly. She seemed in no immediate danger, and hysteria might only lead her into something worse. Pulling her nightclothes tight, Erini wished for something warmer to wear, then almost panicked again when the fabric covering her form tingled and altered. For a moment, she thought something was trying to swallow her feet; only after touching them did she realize that she now wore boots.

With her growing skills, Erini had succeeded in reclothing herself. She so marvelled at the feat that it was some time before the princess returned to the problem of her present accommodations, and when she did, Erini decided that the first thing needed was light. Only then could she get an idea of where she was.

How? was something the novice sorceress already knew. Her abilities had brought her to this place, wherever it was, and those selfsame abilities would, the princess hoped, return her to her room. First, though, came the light.

Not knowing exactly how she was to do it, Erini tried picturing a candle-stick in a holder standing no more than three feet away from her. According to Drayfitt, a spell as simple as this would be almost automatic. She would not have to visibly reach out to the spectrum and touch the powers. Her natural skill would do that—hopefully.

When her first attempt yielded nothing but a slight throbbing in her temple, Erini shut her eyes tight and pictured the candle over and over, hoping that through constant repetition, she would achieve her goal.

The smell of melting wax informed her that she had succeeded. Then, the smell became a stench and brightness suddenly sought entrance through the lids of her eyes. Erini opened them wide and stared in disbelief as over a hundred candles, all burning like miniature suns, flickered and melted before her, an army come in response to her summons. The scene brought a brief smile to her lips—a smile that died when she recognized the room she had teleported herself to with her magic.

It was the chamber where Darkhorse had been held prisoner by Melicard.

There was no sign of the diagram that had made up the boundaries of the magical cage. Even the marks Drayfitt had etched into the stone floor were gone.

With the discovery that she was still within the palace and not that far from her chambers, Erini decided it might be best to *walk* back. Her success with sorcery had, thus far, been fair at best. Erini had altered her clothing—evidently to the type of brown leather and cloth riding suit, including pants, that was famous in Gordag-Ai—but the other spells had had wild results. Instead of one candle she had called up a hundred. In her sleep, she had teleported herself to another location. If she tried to send herself back to her bed, the princess knew that she *might* materialize there; however, it was just as likely she might appear back in her bedroom in her *father's* palace. Explaining *that* to the king and queen of Gordag-Ai, even despite the fact that Erini was their daughter, might prove scandalous. At the very least, her secret would be out before she had control of her abilities.

She picked up one of the candlesticks and, after a minor internal debate, snuffed out the rest as quickly as she could. Erini wondered what Quorin or Melicard would say when they came down here and found Darkhorse free and dozens of half-melted, unlit candles standing in the middle of the floor. While it had its amusing aspects, Erini knew that she wanted to be far away when it happened. If there was one thing that might still shatter her hopes with Melicard, it was her implication in the shadow steed's escape.

Erini stepped to the door, found it unlocked, and opened it.

Two bored guards turned in sudden shock and stared at her, openmouthed.

She tried to close the door, but one of the guards, quicker to react than his fellow, kept it open by thrusting one meaty arm against it. He was already pulling out his sword when the princess acted without thinking and thrust the candle toward his face, wishing desperately for something more effective to combat the two soldiers with than the tiny flame.

A ball of fire swelled *out* from the candlewick, engulfed the two hapless sentries, and dwindled back to a tiny, flickering flame . . . all before Erini had a chance to understand what she had wrought this time.

There was no trace of the two men. The flames had swallowed them completely, not even giving them time to recognize their fate—a minor blessing, the princess thought, her hand shaking. The candlestick and what remained of the candle itself, most of it having melted from the great burst of heat, fell from her untrustworthy grip and clattered to the floor. The stunning truth, that she had just *killed* two men with her unpredictable abilities, horrified her. Two men. Erini understood that they had been trying to kill or capture her, but that made it no better. She had not even been trying to hurt them; her desire for something deadlier had merely been in the hopes of stalling them long enough for her to think of something—anything.

Sleep! I could have put them to sleep! I know it! Instead, I murdered them! There's not even anything left for their families to mourn!

She knew then that she must not marry Melicard. She should not even be around people. Any passing thought might be the death of someone close to her—as if the death of some stranger was any better. Tears gave of themselves in great numbers as the princess stared at her hands. Even knowing that the magic was a part of her, hands or not, Erini could not help thinking of them as *the hands that have killed.*

Tonight, she decided abruptly. *I have to leave!* She refused to even consider utilizing her growing abilities to send herself far, far away by that method. There would be no sorcery. Everything would be done by physical means.

Torchlight illuminated the long, winding stairway. Erini, recalling the last trek up the maddening steps, took a deep breath and started up as fast as possible. She was able to keep her pace for the first fifty or so steps and then slowed continuously from there. Perhaps it was only because of her anxiety concerning her situation, but Erini felt as if the stairway had grown to twice its normal height, so long did it seem to take to reach the door to the garden. The princess was so happy to have finally arrived that she swung the door open carelessly. Only after it was out of her reach did she curse herself for forgetting that there might be sentries here, too.

There were none. The garden was dark and empty. Abandoning everyone was a bitter thought and, deep inside, she would have welcomed Melicard's sudden presence, even if his love turned to hate when he discovered what she was and how her lack of control had killed two men. The unfortunate guards had probably merely been performing their duties. They certainly could not have expected to see a royal princess step out of a chamber that supposedly housed only a magically ensnared creature from beyond. Their actions had made sense; an intruder had been emerging from a secured place. For their obedient performance, she had rewarded them with instant incineration.

Pushed forward by a new wave of guilt-ridden thoughts of the guards who had just been doing their duty, Erini started out in the direction of the royal stables. There, she would be able to find a proper steed, perhaps the bright devil Iston had ridden. She despised the thought of stealing another's horse, but her requirements included speed and stamina. Iston's horse more than measured up in both categories.

"A strange time of the night for walking the garden, don't you think, Princess Erini?"

Erini did not jump, though the voice floating from the darkness had actually shaken her already taut nerves badly. She stood her ground, putting on a frosty look and acting as if anything she did was not the business of a mere noble, even the king's special counselor.

"You weren't in your chambers, princess, and I became worried about you." Quorin stepped out from an entranceway to her right, looking unruffled. Behind him, Erini could barely make out the hulking shapes of at least two guards, one of whom was holding a torch.

"Of what concern is it to you whether I am in my chambers or out taking a walk in the garden? I find the night air and the life in the garden to be soothing."

"If you find walking so suits you, then I insist you join me. There's something fascinating you should see."

Mal Quorin took her arm. There was no pretense now, for his hand squeezed painfully tight. His men, four of them, formed an escort around the duo. Even though the counselor had not yet said what it was he wanted her to see, the princess knew already. She struggled briefly in what proved to be a futile attempt. Quorin was even stronger than his appearance indicated.

"*Counselor Quorin*," she grated angrily, trying a new tactic, "I have no desire to walk anymore, especially with you! If you do not cease this disrespectful manner, I shall be forced to mention it to my betrothed, *your king!*"

"Do so," the advisor responded indifferently. Without warning, he began walking, practically dragging Erini for the first few steps before she matched his pace. Two guards moved in front and the other two fell back to the rear, creating a square of sorts with the princess and her captor in the center. A glance from Quorin convinced Erini that it was not in her best interest to shout or make noise of any sort. She doubted he intended her any physical harm, but that might change at any moment, especially once they reached their destination.

There was only one way she could extricate herself, but it meant trusting in the very curse that had placed her in jeopardy initially. Erini could not bring herself to trust her abilities, not after the wasted death of two men. Even the slightest error in judgment might add five *more* lives to her burden of guilt, and as much as she despised and distrusted the counselor, Erini did not want his death on her conscience.

One of the men opened the door in the wall. Quorin pulled his reluctant guest bodily to the stairway and led her down. Whereas the journey upward had lasted an eternity, this one seemed to pass in little or even no time at all. Erini was down at the base of the steps, staring at the door through which she had released death, before her thoughts could even organize themselves.

"No," she gasped so quietly that her smiling escort did not hear her.

"These aren't your new quarters, your majesty," the advisor said wryly, mistaking the reason for her hesitation. "I thought you might like to see again what your *beloved* has wrought here. You do want to know what the true Melicard is like, don't you? I find it hard to believe that you could still stomach him after seeing his 'guest.'"

"Have you lost your mind, counselor? Do you think Melicard will let this pass? Even if I do not tell him, he will discover it for himself!"

"Undoubtedly. Given the opportunity, he might even be tempted to hand me my head—as he has done to so many!"

Erini had no time to ask for a clarification to the enigmatic statement, for Mal Quorin shoved her roughly against a wall and reached for the handle to the chamber door, evidently desiring to give the moment his personal touch.

In desperation, the princess gave in to temptation. Her muddled thoughts came up with a solution she believed would not result in death and, focusing her will, she struck out at her captors.

Nothing happened.

The princess tried again, gritting her teeth in frustrated concentration. Her original idea became murky; a solution of some sort was all she desired now.

Again nothing . . . nothing save that Mal Quorin, who had looked inside the chamber, was now stumbling back, his face red with rage and his anger focusing on the most likely target—her.

"What happened here? Where is he? Answer me!" Quorin slapped her hard, forgetting who it was he was assaulting and why he had dragged her down here in the first place. "This was Drayfitt's doing, wasn't it? He's the only one who could've done it!" Quorin the animal had resurfaced. His feral visage was filed with the need for blood.

It was that which strengthened Erini in the face of terrible danger. If she had so frustrated the counselor by freeing Darkhorse, then she had struck a heavy blow against his plans, whatever they were.

The soldiers had backed away from their master, obviously more familiar with his violent temper. He eyed them ferociously, knowing that someone had discovered the escape earlier but had been afraid to alert him, then sneered at his captive. One hand darted toward Erini's face, causing her to flinch. It stopped short of striking, instead seeming to caress her bruised chin. When his hand came away, there were drops of red on two of the fingers. For the first time, the princess tasted the blood on her lower lip.

Quorin took a deep breath. "You were an unexpected impediment! Melicard to have a queen? What sane creature would want that pathetic fool? You should've been well on your way back to Gordag-Ai within a day of meeting him, but *no*, you chose to play the heroine in one of your fainthearted ladies' tales, the woman who would rescue the enchanted king! This is what it gets you!" He held up the hand with the blood on it so that the stained fingers were directly before her eyes. "Even knowing that he would dare to summon up a demon, a fiend that might have killed hundreds of innocents if it got out of control, you convinced yourself that you loved him!"

Erini simply stared back. She knew Quorin's words for the twisted lies they were, however, and finally could no longer hold back. "And who was it who first suggested he seek out demons? Drayfitt would have never suggested such a dangerous, mad spell!"

"Drayfitt." Mal Quorin took hold of Erini's arm again and wiped the blood onto her sleeve. She did not give him the satisfaction of struggling, no matter how disgusted she had become with his true manner. Her abilities had failed her for reasons she could not fathom, but the princess had survived without them all of her life and would continue to do so, despite the odds. "What did he tell you? It doesn't matter now, princess, because that old charlatan is dead. Poisoned, I'd think."

Erini did not respond, and simply clamped her mouth shut, continuing to glare.

"Perhaps later," Quorin continued. He was slowly growing calm again, as if the discovery of Darkhorse's escape and Erini's questionable involvement did not really matter. "Perhaps later, when the last few items have been taken care of, we'll speak again. Your presence initially threw everything into chaos, but you may prove to be the key to adding Gordag-Ai to our winnings without so much as a struggle."

Responding to some silent signal, two of the guards took hold of Erini by her arms. She finally gave up all sense of caution. "You've overstepped yourself!

Melicard will not stand for this! Your influence over him is nothing now! He'll—"

He gave her a genuinely puzzled look. "Princess Erini! Do you mean to tell me that you, an intelligent if somewhat troublesome female, can't understand what's happening? Do I sound as if I care what your crippled lover does to me?" Quorin smiled as he watched Erini's belated reaction. "This is a *coup*, your majesty. Tonight, Talak will be without a *king* for the first time in centuries. Fortunately, the *rightful* one is on his way even now . . . and the gates will be open in greeting. Remove her from my sight but try not to damage her."

As she was dragged past him, Erini struck out at the counselor with the full force of her will, not caring what the results might do to her or even the palace, if it came down to it. The sole response to her efforts was a sudden movement of one of Quorin's hands to his chest, where he seemed to be reassuring himself that something still hung around his neck. He stared at the princess intently, his expression a mixed one of doubt and curiosity, until the twisting stairway took her out of sight. Erini wondered if he knew now what she was—and what that would mean to her eventual fate.

Melicard! Even though the evidence was all there, she could not bring herself to fully believe that the counselor's minions had taken over the palace so swiftly and silently. She had retired for the night only a few hours ago! Yet, Mal Quorin had had years to plan for this, slowly insinuating himself into the hierarchy of Talak, becoming the fellow crusader obsessed with the same goals as his master. The longer she dwelled upon it, the more the truth of those final words became evident. Probably more than three-quarters of the palace guard obeyed the advisor's commands. Melicard—Melicard had likely been cut down while he slept, a victim of the very men he had thought were protecting him.

Drained, Erini made no effort to free herself as she and her two companions reached the top of the stairway again and exited into the garden. The nearly starless night seemed a fitting symbol of the twilight of Melicard's rule. He had not needed her worthless curse to tear him down; his own obsession had done that.

Why her skills had suddenly abandoned her, she could not say, but, even if it had cost her his love, Erini would have utilized those abilities however possible to save his kingdom and his throne.

Her mind was numb and so she did not struggle as they passed through the garden and into one of the adjoining halls. Erini had never been through this area, but that made little difference to her now. All she wanted was to find some quiet place where she could bury herself in the darkness and not come out again.

Evidence of the coup mounted as they marched through the palace. Armed figures prodding men wearing the same uniforms, that of the palace guard, walked past them in the opposite direction. Erini rose from her stupor long enough to watch the unfortunates as they were herded away, wondering in the back of her mind where *she* was being taken, since it was safe to assume that the other prisoners were going to cells. Perhaps, Quorin had a separate area for prisoners of royal blood. Perhaps, Melicard's body would even be there.

They had gone through a number of unlit corridors, left darkened apparently because there were far more important things to attend to than lighting torches, and so neither Erini nor her captors paid any attention to the latest one. The two soldiers muttered to one another, but not loud enough for her to understand. By this time, they were leading her more or less as a puppet master might lead a marionette. Thus it was that she was totally caught unaware—as were her guides—when *hands* reached out from the walls and caught the soldiers by the necks.

Erini fell to the ground, bruising her shoulder but succeeding in preventing her head from striking the hard surface. She looked up and tried to make out more clearly what was happening. What little she *could* see left her completely baffled and even more frightened.

The hands had been joined by partial bodies. A darkly clad figure, consisting of the upper half of a man's form and one lone foot that seemed to hop by itself, had one victim down on his knees. The other attacker, no more than a head and two arms, was slowly dragging the other hapless soldier backwards. Both newcomers were using something akin to wire or string to choke their victims. With their windpipes expertly cut off, neither guard could even gasp loudly, much less summon help.

It was over in less than a minute. When both victims lay limply on the floor, one of the dark figures moved toward the princess. The other began removing evidence of the attack—that is, the bodies.

"Your majesty! I give thanks that we found you!" The man's voice was only a faint whisper, but Erini still recognized the tones of one of her own people. Were there *sorcerers* among her own subjects?

As if reading her thoughts, her rescuer pulled off the hood obscuring his features. In the darkness, she could only make out a soldier perhaps ten years older than she was with a face that only now, as her savior, could possibly have been termed handsome. "Don't be frightened, Princess Erini, of either what we did—or what I look like without a mask." The attempt at levity failed. "If you could please see to rising, my lady, we'd like very much to lead you to somewhere safer."

"Safer?"

He nodded. "Captain Iston holds a portion of the palace; he's been planning for this for days, ever since the rumors were first reported by our network here."

"Network? Days?" Reality was returning with less than savory surprises. "What do you m—?"

"Please!" he hissed. "When you're safe, your majesty, the captain will answer all your questions!"

The other man joined them. He was younger, almost as young as Erini and only a little taller. It amazed her to think that he had taken on a veteran more than a third again his size.

"We've gotta move! There's another batch comin' this way!"

"Please, your majesty?"

Too many men had died because of her already and the princess would not allow these men to become the next ones. Rising in one swift motion, she gave her hand to the first man, who immediately led them down the corridor in the same direction the guards had been taking her. At the first intersection between halls, however, they turned left. The sound of marching feet echoed for a time, then drifted away as the patrol the second man had noticed apparently turned in a different direction than the trio had gone.

As they moved, Erini caught a glimpse of the cloaks the two men were wearing. At first, they seemed incongruous, serving no apparent purpose, but then she noticed that, depending on how the cloaks twisted, her rescuers seemed to fade—no, not *fade*, but *blend* into their surroundings. The cloaks somehow cast some sort of illusion. Erini had heard tales of such things, though she had never seen anything like them before.

Twice, she tried to ask them something and twice they signalled for silence.

The second warning was punctuated by a short cry. The younger of her two companions suddenly clutched at his side where an arrow protruded. Stealth had required that neither of her rescuers wear much in the way of protection and that requirement was proving costly now.

Something thin and sharp appeared in the hand of her remaining guardian. He threw it at the archer who had seemed to materialize down the corridor. Though Erini could not see where it struck its target, the weapon did its work. The archer fell, his hands clutching at his chest.

More soldiers appeared, too many for any one of them to get off a safe shot at the escaping duo, but more than enough so that the odds against the two fugitives were overwhelming. Seeing that, Iston's man tore off the cloak of his dead companion and shoved it into his mistress's hands. Pushing her down the corridor, he whispered, "The stables! Head toward the stables! Down this corridor and then turn right at the third one you see! Keep running! It's the only way, my lady!"

"But *you*—"

"I do my duty! Run!"

Erini did, but there were more soldiers coming down the other way, cutting her off. As she slowed, trying to find another route, her lone defender went down. Another death on *her* hands.

Thinking of her hands, Erini suddenly noticed the subtle, familiar tingle in her fingers. How long since that feeling had returned, she could not say. Perhaps if she had kept her wits about her she would have noticed in time to save the others. Perhaps not. In a fatalistic move, Erini turned so that one outstretched hand pointed down each end of the corridor. If the results killed her as well, so be it. *These* men she felt no pity for. These men must *pay*.

She might have been influenced by the cloaks that had allowed her two rescuers to fade into their surroundings. The concept struck her as perversely appropriate for those who would play at loyalty and betray their good lords at first chance. They were not men; they were only the shadows of men, less than nothing—and Erini would make them so.

When the first screams rose, she tried to force her eyes shut and keep them shut, but failed, drawn somehow to the hideous tableau playing itself out on each side of her. From her fingers, glittering tendrils slithered forth, like serpents of the purest light, hungry avengers of her pain. As each broke free of her fingertips, they shot unerringly toward the nearest of her enemies. Nothing stopped them. One man put a shield up, but the tendril went through it like a ghost, continuing on unimpeded until it pierced the unfortunate in the chest and buried itself completely within his torso, leaving not the slightest trace of its passing.

As the man scratched desperately at his chest, a light seemed to come from within him, filling his eyes and his mouth with the same glittering illumination of Erini's creation. While Erini stared, unable to believe in what she herself had released, the light within intensified, becoming so brilliant that its glow shone *through* the soldier.

The man tried to take a step forward, but his body only rippled, as if lacking substance. For the space of a breath, a walking skeleton was outlined within the thinning frame of his body, then the struggling guard's legs collapsed underneath him, perhaps because those bones had finally melted away. He fell forward, arms outstretched in an instinctive effort to save himself, but, in a final sequence that would return in Erini's nightmares, first the hands and then the arms crumbled like ash against the hard surface and blew away. Unhindered, what remained of his torso struck the floor—and scattered into tiny particles that dwindled to nothing.

Not one man escaped that fate. The tendrils moved with the speed and tenacity of a plague, catching them even as they turned to run. By the time the first man had perished, the rest were infected. Even had she wanted to, Erini would not have been able to save them. The young princess, her face a sickly white by the glow of her instruments of vengeance, could only stand where she was, both fascinated and revolted by the results of her spell.

She had wanted something else, something *cleaner*. Only now did the princess know that there was nothing clean about death, especially death bought about by hatred and anger. They had killed two of her own and possibly the man she loved, but *this*—this was not what she had wanted. As the last man faded, still trying to remove his executioner from within his body, the last of her anger faded as well.

Erini slumped against the wall and slid down to a sitting position, her gaze focused on, but not seeing, the now-empty corridor where only a few loose weapons and an odd item or two were all that remained of probably a dozen men. Had anyone come now, she would not have fought them. It was as likely the princess would not even have noticed them. Now, she only saw darkness—a darkness she quickly welcomed as the one friend she could trust.

Her head tipped to one side as exhaustion and remorse finally carried her off to the only place she could now find peace.

XV

FULLY RESTORED, DARKHORSE nonetheless moved cautiously investigating the tent of the sorcerer Drayfitt. He could not feel the presence of Shade, but if there were anyone with the talent to muddle his senses to the point of uselessness, it was that one being who knew him best.

A careful probing of the areas surrounding the tent revealed nothing. There was a trace of strong, violent magic in the air, but such was to be expected when two spellcasters met. It said something for Shade's abilities that the two men had battled freely, yet no one knew even now that the king's sorcerer lay dead among them.

An interesting and devastating surprise awaits you all on the morrow, Darkhorse thought, wondering what the loss would mean to the crusade. If Shade was indeed working with the Silver Dragon, a killing as potentially demoralizing as this might send the entire military expedition back to Talak, the last place the drakes would want them, if the eternal had read the situation correctly.

Fairly certain he was not about to enter into a trap but unwilling to put his complete faith in such a belief, the shadow steed trotted quietly down toward the encampment. A portal would have been quicker and probably made discovery less likely, but materializing in an area that his adversary had just departed from was something he did not want to take a chance with this time. Besides, with Drayfitt dead, he faced only human soldiers, men whose weapons were nothing to him.

The tent was not quite on the edge of the camp and Darkhorse slowed as he entered the region. Whole at last, it proved little trouble for him to make a guard's eyes avert or cause a passing soldier to turn in another direction. A young recruit peeling an apple suddenly dropped his knife and, while he searched the dark ground for it, failed to notice the ebony form that flitted silently past. The shadow steed reminded himself what he had been through already so that the ease with which he now succeeded in his tasks did not create deadly overconfidence. It was at times like that when disaster struck—and Shade was a master of disaster.

Around the tent, the grounds were noticeably deserted. Though a sorcerer was generally invaluable in terms of combat, most of the soldiers, up to and including their officers, preferred, whenever possible, to keep a safe distance from those such as Drayfitt. One never knew what might crawl out of a spellcaster's confines.

Hmmph! Ice-blue eyes blinked as Darkhorse stared disbelievingly at the display only Shade could have wrought. The hypocrisy of his longtime friend/foe astounded him. *I grow less and less enchanted with the true you the more time that passes, dear Shade!*

There was no doubt that the warlock had honestly meant this as an honor of sorts, else he would not have taken the care with both the body and the bier that he had wrought. Darkhorse doubted that there had been much remorse; it hardly seemed the way of the new—that is, the *old and original*—Shade. Still, the stallion wondered how even his adversary could have not seen what he had created. Not a monument, but a mockery.

Drayfitt lay peacefully—the first time the shadow steed could recall seeing him so—with his arms crossed and his worn robes replaced by a fascinating, multicolored garment that the sorcerer would have never worn in life. A false smile graced his lips, obviously the warlock's doing, as Drayfitt had, in the shadow steed's limited experience, never been a man to smile freely. This was not the elderly sorcerer but some cruel parody.

The funeral bier was worse. As had been his people's way, Shade had created what might have been called a typical Vraad monument to opulence. Gilded and decorated freely with what were likely actual gemstones, it seemed more like an attraction in a city bazaar than the resting place of the unfortunate spellcaster. The base, in fact, was composed of four, intricately carved figurines designed to seem to be holding the bier level and representing the drake, human, Quel, and Seeker races. Darkhorse pondered briefly the potential significance of the four, but could think of nothing that related to his present situation. Desiring a closer look, he probed the immediate area again.

A thin tendril of life flickered *within* Drayfitt's body.

Untrusting, Darkhorse probed again. It *was* there! Only a trace and barely even that. He knew he could not save the aged mortal, but there was a chance, then, that Drayfitt might be able to tell him something about Shade's plans. Anything.

The essence of his probe altered. Where in the past few days he had twice been forced to part with a portion of his very being, Darkhorse now willingly gave of himself, a handful of water to a man dying of thirst. It was a slow, careful process. Too much and he might finish what Shade had started; too little, and he might not revive the sorcerer in time.

The cracked, gaunt face twisted suddenly as life fought back. Drayfitt coughed and choked, his fingers reaching out to claw at the air, perhaps in an unconscious attempt to further gather life to his thin shell.

Darkhorse silently cursed those who had given the original Shade his own life.

Eyelids fluttered open, but the eyes within did not see. The shadow steed moved closer, hoping that, even if the dying mortal could not see, then he could at least hear.

"Friend Drayfitt, it is I, Darkhorse," he whispered in one ear. "Do you hear me?"

Nothing.

"Drayfitt, I have done my best for you, but your time is short. Talak and your people still depend upon you, as they have for more than a century."

The sorcerer's mouth opened and closed. Darkhorse waited. The human's mouth opened again and a hiss escaped as Drayfitt sought to speak. Uncertain as to whether he might push too far, Darkhorse gave of himself again.

"*Draaa . . . aaa . . .* " the failing spellcaster managed to say.

"You are Drayfitt. That is true." Inwardly, the stallion wanted to roar. Would this be all his efforts came to? Was there nothing left of the human's mind?

"Draaag . . . King!"

Dragon King? Which one? The lord of clan Red?

"Tallll . . . aaak!" Drayfitt's left hand sought out his own chest. "Quorin!" It was the clearest, most precisely spoken word so far, an indication of the sorcerer's hatred for the counselor. Drayfitt clutched at his chest again, as if seeking something that had hung around his neck—or *Quorin's.*

While what he had heard had begun to form an ugly picture in Darkhorse's mind, none of it concerned the one the phantom steed was hunting. "What of Shade? Tell me of Shade!"

"Memmm . . . mrriess. Focus . . . child?" The eyes turned, seeing perhaps, at least shadows of what was around him. Drayfitt, with forethought that had kept him alive and secure for so long, was trying to economize his words to those that would mean the most. He knew that his life was ebbing away and that even Darkhorse's gift was failing him.

"Focus? Child?" *What did it mean?*

"Mistake again . . . again—"

"*Master Drayfitt!*" someone shouted from without. Darkhorse turned, then realized that the sorcerer was still saying something. By the time he turned again, Drayfitt had grown silent. His eyes were still open, but the only thing they might be seeing now was the final path that all mortals took at the end of life. His last words had been lost.

"Drayfitt!" An officer in his middle years barged through the tent flaps. Unlike most humans, who were properly in awe of the eternal, the newcomer took one stunned glance at the immense steed before him, drew a sword, and *charged*.

The image was so incredulous that Darkhorse laughed despite all that had happened. Ignoring the laughter, the soldier cut expertly at the stallion's legs. A true horse would have been too slow and would have fallen to its knees, its front legs useless. Darkhorse, though, nimbly stepped aside. Pulled off balance by the force of his own swing, the officer left his side open. Darkhorse seized the opportunity, sending the man flying with the gentlest of taps with his front hooves.

"*Now,*" he roared, ignoring the other humans who rushed through the entrance, "if you will be so kind as to *listen* instead of trying to kill everything in sight, I will—"

"You'll do nothing, *demon!*" A man clad in armor decorated intricately enough to designate him as the commander of the expedition pushed aside the rest and strode toward the shadow steed. He carried no sword, but something in his right hand emanated so much stored energy that Darkhorse grew uneasy. There had been, throughout the millennia, objects created by one race or another with more than enough killing power to destroy a hundred Darkhorses.

"Listen to me, you fools! Talak—"

"—will not suffer your masters' reign of tyranny ever again!" The commander held up a small black cube.

"My masters? I am no thrall of the Drag—"

Darkhorse got no further. The tent interior melted into a surreal, fog-shrouded picture. Darkhorse shook his head, trying to focus on reality. Through the haze, he could still hear the voice of the human.

"Think our king did not imagine your drake masters would try to summon such as you? This talisman is proof against *your* kind!"

The shadow steed tried to argue, but his words were muted by whatever trap he had been caught in.

"Would that I could command you to tear your masters apart, but such is not within the power of this object! I can only command *it* to perform its original function—and send you back to whatever hellhole spawned such as you! Begone now!"

"*Foooolssss!*" was all Darkhorse had time to cry.

"UTTER, ABYSMAL FOOLS!"

"Once there was a tiny dot," a voice floating in the nothingness commented blandly. "A tiny hole in reality, he was."

The shadow steed kicked uselessly at the empty space around him. He knew where he was—how could anyone fail to recognize a place as barren as the Void?

Whatever hellhole spawned me? This is not quite the hellhole that spawned me, but nearly enough, curse all meddling mortals! I should stay here and let them suffer their fates!

"The tiny dot grew over—*time* doesn't work, does it? I shall have to find something else later, when I have the"—the owner of the soft-spoken voice giggled insanely—"*time!*"

Darkhorse focused on the direction the voice seemed to be coming from. "Still composing your tales?"

"I compose *epics*; you *wear* tails." Another giggle.

"I've no time for your witticisms, gremlin."

"My name is *Yereel*, if you do not mind, and even if you do!" A tiny figure, like a child's doll, coalesced before him. It had no distinct features and was as black as Darkhorse. "And here, as you so well know, there *is* no time all the time! Have I said 'welcome home,' by the way?"

The shadow steed looked around him, noting, as he always did, the densely packed regions of empty space. Nothing crowded against nothing, which jostled even more nothing. Some of the nothing was forced to climb on top of the rest of the nothing just so there was room for all. It was astonishing that so much nothing could fit into so little space.

I begin to sound as bad as this one, Darkhorse thought wryly. To his puppetlike companion, he replied, "A welcome is hardly on my list of desires; I plan to leave here in a moment! You *know*, too, the mortal who saw you cried out 'You're real!' Hardly a masterful way of choosing a name!"

The puppet did a headstand in the emptiness. "And *you* chose *your* name so cleverly! You haven't commented on the start of my latest epic, dear one! I was thinking of calling it something nonsensical, like, *Darkhorse, the Hole That Would Be Whole!*" The tiny figure giggled again, then struck an upside-down orator's pose. "The hole, as it grew, matured into pretensions and delusions of grandeur. . . ."

Darkhorse had had enough. He physically turned himself from the other. "Goodbye, *Yereel.*"

"Let me *come!*" The black figure shifted form, becoming a miniature version of the shadow steed. It trotted through space to a point within eye-level. "Take me back! You know what it's like when we've touched the reality! I can't stand this emptiness!"

Darkhorse sighed. "I understand—more than you could ever imagine—but I cannot and *would* not even if I could! You were ousted and exiled here by those with greater power than me—and I cannot blame them!"

"It was all so glorious, I couldn't help myself!"

"Mortals *die*, Yereel," the stallion reminded his tiny twin. "*You* didn't care how many, either."

"I was *living!* I had *purpose!*"

Moving around his counterpart, Darkhorse began to drift away. He knew that Yereel could not follow him. Even the vast reaches of the Void were forbidden to him. The puppetlike creature could only travel in a small circle again and again. "*I* journeyed to reality. *I* learned about life and death. Your failure was your own, Yereel."

"I should *never* have *formed* you!" the other cried testily.

Darkhorse did not look back. "Perhaps, that would have been better."

As he moved faster and faster through the Void, the stallion heard the dwindling voice of Yereel.

"Then the hole, now a vast and mighty sea of false dreams and misconceptions. . . ."

In the Void, a trek could take no time or all time, including any interval in between. Had Darkhorse been the demon that others proclaimed him—or even one who had *played* at being a demon, like Yereel—it might have been different. He would have been condemned to stay here until some other spellcaster summoned him back. His self-exile had been such a one-way spell, though, in that instance, it was his cooperation that had given it the strength. Darkhorse, however, had a tie to the world of the Dragonrealm that was now at least as strong as his tie to the place that had spawned him. It should have been simple to pierce the barrier between here and there. Should have been, but was not.

He could sense the path, but it seemed endless. For a moment, he wondered if this were some trick of his counterpart, but Yereel's powers were limited to his tiny piece of emptiness. Nothing could change that. No, whatever interfered now, was the work of some *other* influence.

His intended destination had been the Manor, where the shadow steed had planned a quick discussion with Cabe and the Lady Gwen about all that had transpired in the short time since he had left them. Slowly, it occurred to him that the difficulty might not be with *him*. If there was a threat to Shade besides Darkhorse, then it was Cabe Bedlam. More and more, it seemed to make sense, although Darkhorse had little other than a feeling to go on.

"Well, if I cannot enter near the grounds of the Manor, then I shall open a path farther away!" He felt foolish that it had taken him that long to think of so simple an answer to his quandary. He recalled the area where he had entered the forest last time, the place where the Seeker had escaped him. This time, he felt the portal form. Pleased with his sudden change of luck, he laughed quietly and, when the shimmering gap fully materialized, he abandoned the Void without further delay. Had it been at all possible, Darkhorse would have wished that he would never have to return to this dismal, empty region again.

IT WAS STILL dark when he emerged into the Dagora Forest. Another stroke of luck. With time only an imaginary concept in the ageless Void, it sometimes happened that whole days, even weeks, could go by back in the worlds of reality. Darkhorse's journey had been, relatively speaking, a brief one and so he was fairly positive that this was still the same night that he had left only a short span earlier. Hopefully, he would not be proved incorrect.

Cautious of a trap, Darkhorse moved silently through the forest. Last time, his senses had been at their weakest. Now, though, they were at their peak, and he chose to make full use of them because of that. Whether those senses would prove equal to the task of locating and outwitting Shade was something that he would only discover at the worst possible moment.

The boundaries of the protective barrier were almost upon him before familiar landmarks informed him of where he was. The shadow steed backed away, not wanting to risk suffering through Lady Bedlam's attractive little curses again. He trotted back and forth for some time in an attempt to locate someone who could relay his messages. After a few minutes, however, he gave that idea up. Unlike Darkhorse, the humans—and even the drakes, for the most part— were creatures of the daylight only. With the spell protecting them, most, if not all, were asleep.

There was something amiss, but whatever it was, was not readily evident. He probed the area surrounding the grounds and found no trace of the presence he had felt earlier while still adrift in the Void. Something confusing attracted his attention and he extended his search. A low, disquieting laugh escaped him. He had found the paradox. A spell had been cast to prevent detection of another spell—but it had, at the same time, made magical detection of the Manor's protective measure impossible. Understanding that, Darkhorse adjusted his senses to a different level of comprehension, reaching into an area well beyond human limits, even Cabe's.

Well, well, my feathery little fiends!

The trees around him were aflutter with entranced Seekers. There were more than a score of the avian humanoids, all of whom seemed part of a pattern focused on the region of Cabe's home.

The threat was not Shade, then, but the former lords of this realm once again attempting to assert their power on a land that had passed them by so long ago. Darkhorse snorted in derision. He had no idea what the ultimate purpose of this pattern was, but, since it had been created by the Seekers, it could only be trouble.

Eyes glittering in anticipation, Darkhorse reared high and struck the nearest inhabited tree a harsh blow with his hooves.

Panic broke out above him as Seekers from the tree he had assaulted and many from those next to it took to the skies. He received confused images of indistinct attackers and realized he was picking up the avians' mental projections, the Seekers' method of communication. Some of them thought that the hordes of the Green Dragon had found them and were even now tearing down the trees. Others tried to calm their brethren while still maintaining the pattern. The latter, at least, proved an impossible task. With almost half their number fully awake, the avians lost control, breaking first the spell that had hidden them and, with much more of a struggle, the mysterious pattern that they had formed over the area.

Darkhorse laughed loudly, in part to keep his adversaries as confused as possible, but also to wake and alert those within the Manor confines.

"Come, oh lords of glories past! Darkhorse invites you to join him!" He kicked at another tree. The Seekers flew hither and yonder, trying to organize themselves. More images passed through the ebony stallion's mind, distorted views of himself as some horrendous creature from the netherworlds. There were few creatures that the avians feared; Darkhorse was among them.

"Come, come! I promise only to bite a few wings, pluck a few feathers, and stomp a few bony, beaked heads!"

One foolhardy male accepted the challenge, diving at Darkhorse with all four sets of claws ready. The shadow steed reared up and caught him in the chest with both hooves, smashing the creature's rib cage with that single blow. The Seeker squawked and collapsed to the ground. Darkhorse looked up at the others and laughed mockingly at them.

Slowly, the Seekers began to organize. Several older ones flew up above the rest and, as Darkhorse watched suspiciously, they formed a small circle. The shadow steed smiled grimly. *Think you that the air is safer?*

Other Seekers tried to form a protective wall in front of the circle. Darkhorse allowed them to organize no further, leaping into the air and soaring toward the avians at a velocity that sent the defenders scattering in sudden panic. One slashed wildly with its claws, sinking its hand into the eternal's body. Darkhorse absorbed him without noticing. Nothing would keep him from the circle.

He was halfway to them when, as one, they cocked their heads to one side and stared. Darkhorse knew then that he had *underestimated* the speed and ingenuity of the avians. That knowledge did him little good, however, as force buffetted him aside. He tried to counter it, but was then buffetted from another direction. One blow after another threw him back and forth across the sky. The constant battering made it impossible to think at all. Darkhorse cursed his own overconfidence and bravado. While he was struggling just to maintain some sort of defense, he knew that other Seekers would be preparing an attack of far more lethal measures than this.

A brilliant flash illuminated the heavens, sending *all* the Seekers into renewed confusion. Darkhorse heard shouts from below. Human and drake voices. The assault against him dropped abruptly as the members of the circle joined their retreating brethren. Darkhorse righted himself and gave chase, furious beyond the point of reason and more than ready to strike a few blows out of pure frustration.

He picked out one of the avians who had formed the circle and was probably one of the rookery elders. Even as he closed in on the creature, an image leaped to life in his head. Shade was in it, a tall and ominous monster whom the Seekers feared even more than they did the stallion. Darkhorse caught hints of a promise made and the results that failure would bring. There were random images of renewed glories and a land that the avians would have ruled again if they had succeeded.

I wonder what his draconian ally would say about such promises, Darkhorse thought as his prey continued its desperate, but seemingly hopeless escape.

The shadow steed slowed abruptly, soon letting the Seekers fly off into the night without further battle. For their failure to the rookery, many of them would pay dearly. For their failure to Shade, who *had* instigated this entire ploy, those who had *sent* this flock would also pay dearly—to the warlock himself. Darkhorse could think of no better justice than that. He turned, descending to the ground at the same time.

"Darkhorse!" a familiar and welcome figure cried out. Reforming himself into something more earthbound, the shadow steed touched earth just in front of the lord of the Manor.

"I'm glad you're safe!" Cabe wrapped his arms briefly around Darkhorse's neck, something that unnerved the eternal more than a hundred avenging Seekers would have. So open a display of affection for *him* was a rarity that he could count on one hoof. Several humans and drakes, who talked among one another like old friends, looked at their lord with renewed awe. After a decade they might be used to seeing many startling things, but how often did their great and powerful master greet a demonic horse with a simple hug?

Lady Gwen's greeting was cordial, but far less affectionate. "You have our gratitude, Darkhorse. When you broke their spell and woke us with your voice, we realized what had happened to us. My only regret is that we could not capture or kill a few more of those arrogant birds! They sometimes make the Dragon Kings seem *pleasant* in comparison!"

"And make *my* company acceptable, is that it, Lady Bedlam?"

She grimaced, then nodded her head slowly. "Sometimes, dark one. *Sometimes.*"

"What happened to you, Cabe Bedlam?"

The young warlock scratched his head. His open honesty was a great contrast to the secrecy and moodiness of Shade. After a moment's thought, Cabe smiled sourly and replied, "We've been living an idyllic life, thanks to the Seekers. They've had us taking walk after walk in the garden, playing with the children, relaxing, and," Cabe glanced at his bride and reddened, "doing whatever else gave us pleasure and took our minds off of the world."

Darkhorse laughed, but not at that. "What a fool I was! Never did it occur to me that the Seeker I pursued briefly might have some purpose for being so near! Now I see why I failed to find him, too! With my 'self' diminished and my impatience guiding me, I never noticed what they were about! They must have freed you briefly and in a subtle manner so that you would not be aware of what games they were playing! Tell me. Do you remember everything?"

Both humans nodded. Gwen added, "I can't help feeling that Shade had *something* to do with all of this."

"He did." Darkhorse explained what he had picked up from the Seeker's mind. There were benefits to the avians' method of communication, but there were disadvantages, too. Seekers, when in dire straits, often emitted their thoughts so powerfully that spellcasters of some ability could pick up the images in their own minds. For Darkhorse, it had been even easier.

"What now?" Cabe wanted to know. "Somehow, I don't think our original plan holds."

Darkhorse nodded. "I would say not. If only I knew where Shade was and what he now intends to do! Drayfitt is dead, Cabe, and his final words, if they were not another ploy engineered by the hooded warlock, are a mystery that I must solve before very long! Shade was never one to be inactive!"

"One thing," Lady Bedlam interrupted, "that we should still do is contact the Green Dragon. He may have some information for us or, at the very least, some suggestion."

"You do that, then," her husband suggested. "I want to check the area out. I want to make *certain* that there are no other surprises."

"That leaves only myself."

"What do you plan on doing?" Cabe asked the shadow steed.

"Return to Talak. If I am incorrect, things will be as they were when I—departed. If, however, things have gone the way I think they have," Darkhorse stared at them and his eyes glittered coldly, "it may already be too late to save the city."

XVI

SHADE STOOD STARING in open contempt at the putrefying column of mixed body parts and dripping ichor that was the guardian of this opening to the realms of the Lords of the Dead. He was not impressed. Not at all.

"Shoddy. I would've expected better of your masters. It appears that they, too, have fallen from the ranks of *pure* Vraad." He waved his hand and the guardian, with a wailing sound, crumbled into its component parts. "Is that the best you could do?" he called out to the mire-filled pit. The cavern around him echoed his growing annoyance.

Tendrils of thought reached out to him, some contemptuous, some defensive, all of them a bit fearful. What had *he* accomplished in all his existence? What had *he* accomplished other than creating an endless game between the opposing poles of his existence?

The warlock smiled coldly. "Too true. That changes now. *Your* existence changes now. You have a bauble of mine that I require." Protesting thoughts bombarded him, but he shook them off like droplets of water. "Don't bandy words with me! Return to me the *tripod*. Now."

Open fears now. Fears of control lost and rifts opened.

A sigh. "This world *has* changed you. Like all the rest. You are not worthy of the name Vraad. You are especially not, my cousins, worthy of the name Tezerenee."

A breath, perhaps two, passed before a dark and unprepossessing object formed at the warlock's feet. He picked it up and examined it thoroughly. It was, as he had termed it, a tripod perhaps a hand's length high. A black sphere, no bigger than one of his pupils, rested securely on the top. Finally satisfied, Shade thrust the artifact into the voluminous confines of his cloak.

"Thank you so *very* much," he acknowledged with a mocking bow. "Having taken such great care of it, I can almost forgive you for stealing it from my workshop after my—*death* just doesn't sound right, does it? My *temporary displacement*." He started to fold within himself, then changed his mind. "I did say 'almost forgive you,' didn't I?"

Panicked protests went unheeded as the warlock struck out.

When Shade at last left what remained of the cavern—and the now-ruined island that had once housed it—his thoughts turned immediately to the culmination of his millennia-long dream. Time was running out for him, he knew that. In two, maybe three centuries, his forcibly extended lifespan would reach its limit, but not with the normal aging results. The shadowy warlock knew what awaited him would be far worse, a last fifty or so years as a withered, decaying creature, a consciousness trapped alive in a dry husk. Only when the last vestiges of his earlier, more desperate spells dissipated would he be freed—freed to a death he had no desire to embrace. The others had given in to this world, let it *master* them, but not him.

He reentered the world in the emperor's cavern, only to find it abandoned. The Silver Dragon *had* moved on with his campaign, likely fearing that whatever Shade had in mind for Drayfitt would upset his carefully laid plan. He had taken everyone with him. The Dragon King's ideas had merit; planting a loyal human among his kind's worst enemies and then manipulating that man into a position of great authority had been a plan worthy of a Vraad—and why not?

He dropped that line of thinking, deciding it was hardly worth his time now that his dreams were nearing fruition. He had mapped things out carefully in his mind, seeing where he had made his mistakes, reassuring himself of those results with the memories taken from the sorcerer Drayfitt. It *had* to work this time!

With the tripod returned to him, there was only one other item he needed, but it was the most integral component of all, outweighing even the artifact that he had taken back from the Lords of the Dead. The tripod was the means of summoning, something Drayfitt could never have known since it had not been in the notes, but it could not function as the focus, the means by which the powers would be drawn together, bound, and turned to his will. His prior mistake had been making *himself* that focus. Forced to both contain and bind them simultaneously, even *he* had failed. No, the only way for the enchantment to succeed would be to find something else to serve as a focus.

Something? *Someone.* It had to be a living entity, one with the open gift that made one a spellcaster. As untrained as possible and young, for the spell would tear at the lifeforce, eating it away. Untrained and young also because those minds were more susceptible to the sort of commands he needed to ingrain upon them. A child would be perfect. A child was malleable.

A child with the potential he sought would also be nearly impossible to find. Since the days of the Turning War, when the human mages had almost defeated the Dragon Kings, the latter had tried very thoroughly to assure that there would never be a second such war. They had missed Cabe Bedlam because of his grandfather's interference. Likely they had missed others as well, since their control had slipped harshly after that near disaster. A long search might prove fruitful, but Shade knew that searching for an infant with latent abilities might very well consume more time than even he had.

There *was* one possibility, likely more, but he had found himself strangely reluctant to consider it. Memories of his addled past, the centuries of swinging back and forth between one mind or another, invaded again. A curse escaped his lips and a fissure suddenly burst into being in one of the cavern walls to his right. He paid it no mind. Breathing deeply, the warlock buried the alien thoughts and memories. It was not the first time he had done so, but he swore silently that it would be the last.

He had sworn so more than a dozen times this one day alone. Each time, they had returned stronger than before. Care. Guilt. *Friendship.* Unbecoming memories for one of his stature. Feelings for those who were not Vraad.

That settled it. He would hesitate no more. Not with so perfect a focus awaiting him. One whom the family would not even notice was missing, if he could help it. The last thought gave him a feeling of benevolence, like a master taking good care of his pets. For their sacrifice, they deserved that much. It would be as if the boy no longer existed.

Still, a tiny shadow of guilt lingered on.

MELICARD.

Erini stirred, her eyes slowly focusing on the darkened corridor. Her mind, a sluggish mire of self-disgust and defeat, refused to clear. She closed her eyes again. Melicard's visage was the only thing she could think about with any success. Her image of him had a strange quality to it, almost as if he were actually before her, propped up against the opposing wall. She saw him as unconscious. Dirt and blood streaked his face and—Erini choked—someone had torn the elfwood mask from his face, revealing the torn and burnt flesh that would never heal. She did not have to see his arm to know that the false one had been removed as well. It was a wonder he was still alive.

Still alive? The odd thought brought clarity to her clouded mind. Why would she think such a thing about her own imaginings? Why would she subscribe reality to delusion? Yet, there *was* something about the images, a continuity that seemed too real to be her own doing.

Could it be?

Erini tried to concentrate on his face, but that only made it less substantial, more that of a phantom than a living person. The princess thought quickly, recalling her state of mind. Leave her mind open? Let it happen naturally? Melicard's features were already almost invisible, little more than a true memory. Erini settled back and dreamed of Melicard the man. Where was he and what was he doing? She thought about him, but not at him. That, she hoped, was the key. If Drayfitt had only had the chance to teach her . . .

Melicard's face, which had been solidifying, dwindled away again. The princess quickly dropped all thought of the dead sorcerer. It was all to easy to let one's imagination turn to other things, even in times of a crisis.

Slowly, the picture of her betrothed returned to full clarity. It was almost as if, with her eyes closed, she could actually reach out and *touch* him. She saw the blood from his wounds, the bruises on his face and body. Mal Quorin's ogres had not been kind to him. Another thing the counselor would be called to account for—if Erini survived this terror.

She had, without thinking, reached out in an effort to ease his pain. The Melicard in her mind suddenly stirred, as if waking. The princess, startled, lost her concentration. Melicard's image faded away, this time permanently. Try as she might, Erini could not make it return.

He was *alive!* Battered and wounded, but Melicard was alive! New life surged through the princess despite all that had happened. As long as he was alive, there was reason to hope. Erini straightened into a standing position and gazed around her, finally realizing that more of Quorin's men might come pouring down one end of the hall or the other before very long. It was a wonder they had not already—unless there were other things on their minds. Like Captain Iston. Possibly loyal guard units, too. The suddenness of this coup could not have been completely planned. Despite the counselor's attitude earlier, there was too much evidence that all was not well in hand. Another sign of hope, as far as she was concerned.

What mattered now, Erini decided grimly, was to find Melicard. She could not draw Iston and his men into this. Two of them had already died on her behalf when she could have saved them. Her powers, the princess was slowly coming to realize, were as potentially beneficial as they were detrimental; it was her own attitude that determined which way she went. If she could turn her abilities to finding the king and overwhelming the rebels . . . The thought of a stunned and grovelling Quorin made her smile with dark pleasure.

How do I find him? came the unbidden thought. What little she recalled of the image had revealed a place far from the elegant rooms of a mighty king. More likely, he was in the lower depths of the palace, a dungeon or something. Unfortunately, Erini had a fair idea of how immense that network of underground passages and chambers was. She did not have the time to search *everywhere* and her attempts to recall Melicard's presence had, thus far, failed miserably.

There remained one option, then, that promised hope. It was the only possibility her mind could dream up. Given rest and some peace, the princess might have been able to devise something less daring, less risky. Time, however, was something she had already used up too much of. No, her only choice was to follow through with her decision.

She would simply *ask* someone where the king was held.

Drawing herself together, Erini stepped quietly down the corridor in the direction *opposite* that of where her loyal defenders had wanted her to run. Iston's stronghold—she wanted to know more about how *that* had come about—was probably watched by too many of Quorin's men. What she wanted was a lone sentry or two left to guard some secured hall. She would probably find such a place deeper in the sections of the palace that the treacherous advisor had under his control. Erini also suspected that, given Quorin's way of doing things, it was where she would be nearest to Melicard.

The nagging fear that her plots were all askew never left her during the entire nerve-wracking journey.

In the dark, Talak's royal palace proved to be quite a maze. Matters were not helped by her own lack of familiarity. Erini only hoped that by trying to keep a parallel course as much as possible, she would not lose herself in the vastness of the ancient structure. The palace of the king and queen of Gordag-Ai seemed almost like a cottage in comparison to the monstrous creation the princess was now forced to wander.

When she finally found what she sought, Erini hesitated. There were two of them, tall, ugly, and armed with blades longer than her legs, it seemed. The princess cursed herself for being so stupid as to not have taken one of the weapons scattered on the floor by her unfortunate attackers. Better still, a sharp, thin blade like the one the elder of her two defenders had utilized. *That* was a weapon she could use properly.

That would also not solve her present dilemma. Sorcery was her *only* chance of success. What sort of spell, though?

One of the men nodded off briefly and was knocked awake by his companion, who seemed none too lively himself. Their exhaustion reminded Erini of her own, but she dared not dwell on it too long for fear she would collapse. Still, the scene had given her the answer. It should not be too difficult to make men who were already tired slip far enough into slumber. From there, she could take one of them and try to coax the information from his unprotected mind.

Relaxing despite the natural tendency for just the opposite in such a situation, Erini found she knew which areas of the spectrum would aid her spell. In her mind, she saw the colors blend and shape themselves, forming a pattern. A part of her understood that what was happening was actually taking place in less than the time it takes a person to blink. This was what Drayfitt had been steering her toward. Soon, it might be so automatic to her that the actual process would seem instantaneous. Drayfitt had said that.

The results of her spell became noticeable instantly. The guard who had dozed off only moments before collapsed completely, falling back against the wall and sliding to the floor. His grip on his sword relaxed, but not until he was almost all the way down. The resulting clatter was hardly audible.

The second man's fall proved more nerve-wracking. He fought the spell, almost as if he had enough sense left to understand what was happening. He raised his sword arm up to his forehead, as if trying to support his sleep-laden mind, and *dropped* the blade. The weapon struck the hard floor with an echoing rattle that Erini was certain would bring new men rushing down the hall at any moment.

Unable to resist any longer, the second guard fell to his knees, then face-first onto the marble. His helmet added to the distant reverberations of the sword.

When neither man had moved after a minute and battle-ready newcomers had not charged madly into the hall from every direction, Erini stepped out from the corner she had been hiding behind and investigated the two men. The first guard was sleeping soundly; there was even a satisfied smile on his lips. The second man was not so well off. He slept, but his nose had been broken from the fall and blood spilled on the floor. Only the spell kept him sleeping. The pain was evident in his twitches. Erini wondered if the pain would eventually give him the strength to overcome her enchantment. If so, it meant that she had to work even faster than she had planned.

Turning back to the first man, she leaned near one of his ears and whispered commands . . .

The ensorcelled guard's arms hung limply by his sides. His eyes were closed. He looked as if someone had strung him up. That would never do. She gave him a few extra commands, hoping there was no immediate limit to such things. It would not do to have confusion stir him from the spell.

A minute later, he was ready. To all eyes, it now appeared as if *she* were *his* prisoner. The scowl on his face was very real. The gleam in his eyes made him a man carrying out orders from the *highest* authority: Quorin, of course. If anyone stopped him, he would say that the counselor had decided to give the two one last moment together so that the princess could see how handsome her betrothed was *without* his false face. Erini had trouble with the last, but it might prove necessary. Such comments would hopefully put the other men at ease.

While she stood there, assuring herself that all was in readiness, a sudden, horrible notion burst forth. She looked up at the mesmerized figure, who stared straight ahead, waiting to begin his new role. "Do you know where King Melicard is being held?"

"Eas'rn t'nnels. Rat land."

Rat land? She let that slide, happy that she had not gone to all this trouble for nothing. In her haste to test her abilities, Erini had totally forgotten to ask him the all-important question first.

From the other guard she took a small dagger. Not much of a threat, but one never knew. The princess secreted the blade in one boot, hoping she would not be forced to run very quickly while it was still hidden in there. Then, Erini turned to the guard and whispered, "Lead."

The next few minutes made the previous few seem almost heavenly. Erini's heart sounded like a stampede of heavily laden warhorses. It was astonishing that the sound did not echo through every corridor. She kept one hand close to the blade—on the off-chance that the soldier had completely fooled her and was even now bringing her to her own cell. The trek was taking her into regions of the palace that she had not known even existed. It amazed the princess to think that there was still so much she had not investigated. If she survived, Erini intended to survey every plan of this behemoth and then double-check every corridor and room personally.

Dreams of entering into such minor crusades kept her from going completely insane with anxiety. Too many things seemed to count on her. She had welcomed them in the past, but none had ever involved death—and so *much* of it—or the use of questionable abilities. Erini was no coward; that was not her fear. What ate at her was the fact that she might not be enough. Melicard, Iston, Galea, and Magda . . . they and so many others would likely die if she did not succeed.

A rough hand grabbed her arm. She almost lashed out with whatever her abilities would give her, then realized that she had fallen behind the ensorcelled sentry. He looked at her as if seeing someone else.

"Come on. This way." His voice was slurred, something that could be explained away as from exhaustion. She quickly reminded him of that fact. He coughed his acknowledgment of the command—a trick Erini had mixed in with the original commands—and resumed the journey. Erini kept pace with him this time, noting that they were heading toward a darkened stairway.

Down below the earth again. I should have known! It would make things that much *more* difficult—and that much *more* dependent on her abilities.

They descended together and, at the bottom of the stairway, her plan received its ultimate test. Four sentries stood guarding the underground passageway. Unlike the one beside her, these men did not look in the least bit tired. They studied the newcomers, first with veiled curiosity, then with eye-widening interest when they discovered who it was they were seeing.

One of them, possibly the leader, possibly not, pointed the tip of his mace at Erini's companion. The others were armed with blades of varying wear. All looked far more skilled at using the weapons than the mesmerized figure at her side. "The cripple's woman! You've caught her!"

"Yeah." The answer issued forth easy enough, but Erini's guard had been ordered not to continue unless pressed.

"Why bring her down here? The master said no one's to see the prisoner."

Erini forced herself not to look at her companion and try to guide his answer. It would have to be his response alone. "New orders. The counselor wants her to spend a last few minutes with him. See how pretty he is. See what she would've married."

There was a moment's hesitation, but then malicious grins began to appear. This was something they would have expected from a leader such as Mal Quorin. Destroy the last good memories of Melicard. Turn his betrothed's love to disgust. None of them could fathom a woman continuing to care for a "cripple," though Erini was of the silent opinion that, even without the elfwood to mask his face and replace his arm, Melicard was worth a thousand of these men.

"Go on," the leader signalled.

The princess's guard stumbled a little, nearly causing her heart to fail. Had they looked closely, they might have noticed the glazed look that was returning to his eyes. Fortunately, they assumed it was something else.

"You'd better report to Ostlich when you're through with her. He don't want anyone dropping on duty. Not tonight." The leader indicated a scar running across one of his men's face. "Edger here stays real alert now, don't you Edger? Sometimes up to *four* days!"

The one called Edger nodded, but said nothing. Erini's companion returned the nod automatically and added a slow "Yeah." His words were becoming more slurred. Fortunately, he was already leading her past them.

When they were out of sight, she started to breathe a sigh of relief—only to cut it short when two *more* guards came into view. They leaned against a wall in which several cell doors stood as grim reminders of some of Talak's less-than-pleasant history. One of them looked up.

"What's goin'? Why's *she* here?"

Her puppet did not respond. Erini pretended to stumble, prodding him into activity as she bumped into his side. He repeated his short explanation concerning Quorin's sadistic little game. His words were slow, but understandable.

The look that passed between the two sentries at the cell indicated that they thought something besides exhaustion had taken its toll on the newcomer, something with more than a little kick to it. One man licked his lips, evidently dreaming of what it would be like to have a drink after so long on duty.

Seemingly convinced, they unlocked the door. The princess wanted to rush in, take Melicard in her arms, but could not so long as she needed the charade to continue. That meant agonizing heartbeats as she forced herself to keep pace with the shuffling soul beside her.

A figure huddled against the far wall, chained by his hands and feet. There was no light in the cell; the prisoner's upper body was in complete darkness and the lower was only a vague shadow. Behind her, the cell door slammed shut. That was the ensorcelled soldier's cue. He released his hold on the princess and stared blankly in the direction of the prisoner. To outside eyes, he would be watching the two.

No longer able to contain herself, Erini rushed over to the worn figure. "Melicard?"

The head slowly turned toward her. It *was* Melicard! Until this moment, she had still feared that something was amiss.

His face, when she saw it, threatened to tear her heart asunder. They had *tortured* him! She forced herself to look closer and saw that she was not entirely correct. There were bruises and cuts, true. He *had* been beaten and badly. Quorin would pay dearly for that. What she thought were burns, however, were what had been hidden beneath the elfwood mask he had always worn. *This* was what was left of his true visage.

Deep pits of scorched and torn flesh streaked across the one side of his face. That was horrifying enough. The other side, the one that had received the brunt of the wild magic . . . Erini recalled only one thing in her life that had ever looked like this. A fire in the royal stables of Gordag-Ai. A fire that had burned to death four horses and injured one of the young boys that helped take care of the animals. One of those horses had broken free of the fire toward the end, a maddened, flame-drenched beast whose face, neck, and body had been burned to the bone at various points. It had run in confused circles for more than a minute, nearly spreading the fire further, before the life within that twisted shell had finally abandoned it. Like the horse, Melicard's face had been torn open to the very bone and, thanks to the power of the artifact that had caused it, those wounds would not heal. Even now, even in the dark, she could see them glisten moistly, as if inflicted only this day.

"The fruit . . . of . . . my labors." Melicard smiled grimly. The open side of his face looked like nothing less than a grinning corpse. Despite herself, Erini had to turn her eyes away for at least a moment.

He noted the reaction. "The storytellers never speak of this type . . . of scene. Either that . . . or they gloss . . . gloss over it."

"I'm sorry. It's not you—"

"It's never me." The sarcasm was biting.

Erini looked him squarely in the face. "It's *not* you. When I saw your face, I felt your pain, wondered how you could have gone on—I don't know if I could have—and cursed dear Counselor Quorin for every day of his existence!"

"Quorin." Melicard grew cold. "I was a fool of the highest rank, wasn't I? How many loyal humans and drakes did the Silver Dragon sacrifice to assure brave, clever Quorin's place at my side? How many? I never saw it once. I was so . . . so proud of myself and so ready to take them all on. Look what it has cost me. Part of my body. My kingdom. My life." He closed his good eye. "Worst of all, it's cost me you."

"No." She touched his hand. "It hasn't."

"I doubt if our future together is longer than another minute or two. Surely my esteemed advisor's man there has orders to drag you out of here. This is just a torturous game, letting us see one another and then separating us again."

It was time to explain. Erini leaned forward. "This is no game of that foul grimalkin! That is what the sentries outside are supposed to think. My guard is under my influence."

The king eyed her in open curiosity. "Influence?"

"Like—like mesmerism."

"Mesmerism." He did not seem completely convinced. Melicard indicated the chains that held him. "What about these? Mesmerism will not work on these, my princess."

"I—I can deal with them." She tried to reach for the cuff around his wrist, but he refused to let go of her hand for the moment. Trying to hide the worst of his face, he tilted his head to one side and gave her as honest a smile as he could manage.

"My princess . . . my queen."

When their hands finally separated, Erini took hold of the cuff and examined it. It had a simple lock on it—not that she knew anything about picking locks—and was worn with age. The rust interested her the most. She had succeeded in lulling to sleep two men who had already been tired. Could it be possible to use the same concept to encourage the spread of rust across the cuff? Make it so brittle that a simple tap or two would shatter it?

As she thought about it, her fingers unconsciously rubbed the cuff. Tiny streaks appeared. Erini gasped. Melicard, who could not see as well from his angle, grunted his curiosity. The princess did not respond, watching in fascination as the entire cuff and even part of the chain turned dark in the space of a few seconds.

She took his arm by the wrist and, sobbing like a grief-stricken, frail princess, muttered audibly, "Oh, Melicard! What will happen to us?"

The king offered no resistance, leaving things in her care. As Erini moved in what appeared to simply be a desperate hug of her beloved, she brought the cuff down against the wall. The sound was buried by her words and the rattle of the chains.

The cuff shattered.

"Impo—" was all that escaped from Melicard before he succeeded in smothering his surprise. Erini immediately went to work on the leg cuffs and found, to her joy, the spell working perfectly both times. She did not, however, try to share her joy with Melicard. Erini feared to even look at his face now. Not because of his appearance, but because of what he must by now have come to realize; his bride-to-be was a sorceress.

"Erini—" Melicard whispered.

"I think *that* verifies it, then," came the one voice she feared to hear.

Leaping to her feet, Erini shielded Melicard. Whatever aid her abilities would give her she would gladly accept. Anything, especially if it meant the end of Mal Quorin.

One of the guards unlocked the cell door and opened it. Quorin stepped through alone, confident in his power. Erini's mouth twitched upward. Not *this* time. She understood her abilities better. The traitor would soon find out what *power* actually was.

Behind her, Melicard had risen to his feet. He would not have someone like Quorin stand above him. Erini drew strength from his act.

The counselor still advanced, slowly and silently. He appeared very much the cat he resembled. His habit of always seeming to show up where and when others least expected him added to that effect. Even the smile.

Perhaps I will turn you into the mangy rat-eater you really are, Master Quorin! The thought appealed to the princess greatly. She would even let him stay and keep the stables free of other pests.

"Did you realize only now that your bride was a sorceress, your most royal majesty? I suspected as much, though I wasn't certain until she escaped from my men earlier." Quorin looked at Erini. "Of course, my lady, I knew where you would be rushing to and took a quicker, more direct route. Now I have you again. All that remains are your stubborn countrymen and a few random guards who escaped my net. Talak will not even know of its change of rulers until the northern gates open and my master comes riding triumphantly through."

"Bearing a silver banner?" Melicard asked grimly.

"Of course. This will be the true mark of his destiny, his right to be emperor of *all* races. The capture and destruction of the monster king. Your crusades will be at an end. A sign of strength will bring his brethren around—save the outcast lord of the Dagora Forest. With the united strength of the others, however, *no* opposition will stand in the Dragon Kings' way. They will bring this land back to the glory it had before the Turning War."

The king laughed, though it was evident that to do so hurt him further. "Did your master train you to say all of that? Look—look at him, Erini. Would you ever believe that he and these others were actually men and not drakes in disguise?"

The barb struck Quorin harder than he pretended it did. Erini, who had seen and felt his rage, watched him closely. She had just about formulated the sort of spell she felt appropriate for one such as him. Something *decorative*. A few seconds more and she would be ready.

Turning his attention to her, Mal Quorin said, "There was a chance you might have been useful in regard to Gordag-Ai—or even to my tastes in entertainment—but I don't care for the thought of a sorceress alive and neither does my lord. Your betrothed will get the opportunity to see you die more or less painlessly before we prepare him for the coming of Talak's new ruler."

Erini unleashed her spell at Quorin. If it worked, he would envy the men who had died trying to recapture the princess.

Nothing.

No! Erini stood drained, horrified. *Please! Not now!* Her abilities had abandoned her again!

"Have you never wondered why I feared no tricks by that doddering old fool, Drayfitt?"

To one side, the ensorcelled guard suddenly moaned and shook his head. Her other spell had failed now. Erini stared at Quorin, who was reaching into his uniform for something that hung around his neck. It proved to be a medallion the diameter of a walnut.

Melicard groaned, though whether from pain or what he saw was debatable. "A Seeker medallion, Erini. One he received from *me*. It mutes a spellcaster's abilities. Makes them . . . helpless."

"Helpless. Yes." The counselor snapped his fingers. Two of the sentries from the hallway joined him. One he ordered to assist the man who had just woken up. He looked at the second, then nodded toward Erini.

Beaten and worn, Melicard still tried to save Erini. He rushed past her and tried to tackle the oncoming soldier with his one good arm. Quorin's servant, however, was a massive ox and he threw the one-armed king against the far wall. Melicard slipped to the floor, still conscious but stunned.

As the man turned toward Erini, she saw Quorin watching her from behind him, his cat's smile wide across his face and a thin, jagged blade now waiting in one hand. Waiting for her.

XVII

WHILE THE NIGHT had brought chaos to Talak, it had brought something even more ominous to the Dagora Forest. Just beyond the protected grounds of the Bedlams' domain, a tree curled and twisted, becoming a gnarled thing that soon cracked and died. From its withering roots, a black blot seemed to spread to the plant life around it, creating a dead, barren patch of earth several yards wide.

Within the boundaries of the Manor, a separate but hauntingly similar incident passed. This one would have been less noticeable, save its victim was one of the birds that nested in the trees. The fate the lone tree had suffered had been kinder. What was left of the bird was barely recognizable.

In the darkened room of a young lad, a golden-haired boy who dreamt of amazing feats of magic he would some day perform, the night seemed to have eyes. Eyes and shape. A shape that slowly detached itself from the rest of the darkness and loomed over the sleeping child, noting even without light the tiny streak of silver in the youngster's hair.

Shade smiled almost fatherly. *Blood will tell, my young one! Great power courses through your parents' veins! Great power that has pooled together and formed you!*

There was a young girl, too, but she was too young, unpredictable. If this vessel proved insufficient, he would wait a few years and take the second. By then, she would be ready.

He touched the boy's forehead. A name came to his lips and he mouthed it in silence. *Aurim. The Golden Treasure.* The warlock frowned. He could feel the love the parents had for this child—both children—and it was beginning to disturb him in ways that were alien to him. He had taken subjects for his spells before. It was not as if they were Vraad. They were just . . . others.

His face resembles Cabe's, though his nose is his mother's. The uneasiness began spreading through him. Why was he not already gone? The task was a simple one! Take the child and depart. The defensive spells surrounding the Manor were laughingly simple to one with millennia and the powers of Vraad sorcery on his side.

Take the boy! he demanded of himself.

"Shade."

The hooded warlock looked up. Another figure stood on the other side of the bed, hands clenched and eyes narrowed. He wore a dark blue robe and much of his hair was silver.

"Cabe."

"My son, Shade. He's not for you to do with as you please. Get out of here now while I can still remain civil with you."

Moving almost like the shadow he resembled, Shade looked closely at the youngster. "He has striking golden hair . . . how is that possible?"

Cabe tried to contain himself. This *was* Shade. This man had been his friend. He had also tried to kill the younger warlock. Which stood before Cabe now? "We named him Aurim because, being our first, he seemed so precious. When he was old enough to understand what his name meant, he decided he should have golden hair. The next day . . . it simply was."

"A lad of great potential."

"If he lives to adulthood." The edge had returned to Cabe Bedlam's voice. "Which he won't if you take him."

"He might. He might not. I have need of him, though."

"You've no right to him." It was becoming harder for Cabe to maintain his composure. "You've no right to anything!"

The other warlock wrapped himself in his cloak. "I am Shade. I am Vraad. My existence is my right. My *continued* existence is my demand."

A hand rose. It blazed with green flames that danced about the fingertips. "You've lived long enough, Shade. He deserves his chance—and I won't let you take him."

Shade chuckled. "No longer the uncertain novice, are you? Is ten years enough? The skill is easy enough, but the reaction time is always the questionable part. Do you know your limits? I have *none*."

"You have more than you think. You still thought the Seekers controlled us until I materialized here. I made it seem so. I thought you might come back, Shade. I prayed you wouldn't, so that I wouldn't have to fight you. I'll see you dead a thousand times before I let you take my son."

"And I shall return a thousand and one times." The cowled visage lifted enough so that the glow from Cabe's hand allowed him to see Shade's true features for the first time. Cabe's mouth dropped open. "Or I will just take him *now*."

Tendrils burst from the cloaked figure of the one warlock and enshrouded sleeping Aurim. They started to withdraw into Shade's form until the hooded spellcaster checked himself.

"This is *not* your son."

"No, he and the other children are safely hidden—even from you. I've learned. I thought you might come back, so I laid a few snares. You chose the false Aurim, though I don't care to think why. It almost fooled you long enough. In fact, it *may* have."

A clear liquid showered down on Shade from nowhere. As it touched him, it solidified, becoming harder than marble. The torrent continued, forming a shell about its victim. Shade struggled, but seemed unable to move more than his fingers. Oddly, nothing but the warlock was covered by it.

"I never thought I would thank Azran Bedlam for an idea," Gwen said as she materialized out of the darkness behind Shade. "I never thought I would want to condemn anyone to this sort of hell—until *you* came back here for our child."

The shower ceased. As Gwen had once been imprisoned in a shell of amber by Cabe's mad father, so had she sought to snare Shade. Only Azran's fabled demon sword, the Nameless, had succeeded in breaking that prison, and only with an unconscious boost from Cabe.

"It's over," she continued, speaking to her husband. "It wor—"

The amber prison exploded, sending deadly fragments spilling across the room in every direction. A fair number flew with unerring accuracy toward the Bedlams. Only their automatic defensive spells saved them at all. Razor-sharp pieces tore into the walls, ceiling, and floor. Minor objects in the room were punctured or shattered. Cabe and his wife were battered into unconsciousness, though bruises were all they suffered. Not one jagged fragment had flown their directions.

When the last particles of the devastating assault had drifted floorward, Shade shook himself free of any remaining fragments and eyed the two spellcasters. Oddly, he was not angry, but rather, impressed.

"I am myself once again and there is *no* equal to me, Bedlams," he whispered. Shade turned to the false Aurim, undamaged by the assault. With a glance, he disposed of it in another realm where the surprise within would not threaten him. Two very deadly traps. Together, they might have succeeded.

"I am Vraad, Cabe. That was your undoing." He took a deep breath. "But you have earned the right to your children. I think there may be another who will serve instead—that is, if *his* memories serve me right."

He looked down at each of them and concentrated briefly. The walls groaned as if weakening, but he paid that only the least bit of attention, assuming the damage was due to his last assault. A new spell placed on each of them would assure that they would sleep a full day, maybe even two. More than enough time to deal with the other situations.

Taking one last—almost *fond*—glance at Cabe, Shade departed the Manor.

*   *   *

HOW COULD THERE be so many? Darkhorse wondered grimly. *How did so many still survive?*

The legions of the Silver Dragon were the stuff of epic. Not since the combined forces of Bronze and Iron had attempted to overthrow the emperor had there been a dragon host as great as this. Not all of them were of clan Silver, either. The two clans that had rebelled now had a new master. Remnants of both now rode, ran, or flew along with those of the Dragon King. There were even a few drakes of clan Gold, though they were the fewest of all. Darkhorse suspected that there *had* been other survivors, but not for very long. The would-be emperor had taken over their caverns, stolen their birthplace. Many drakes were too proud to stand for such things. Most of those that rode with him now were likely the dregs, perhaps even treacherous fools like Toma the renegade.

Though he could see them, Darkhorse knew that the night still gave him protection from the oncoming army. He had come here, rather than return immediately to Talak, because he had feared this very thing. His fears had proved far more than even he had supposed. The host here would have given a fully armed and ready Talak trouble—unless King Melicard had a trick or two up his sleeve. Perhaps that was one reason why he had agreed to summoning a demon; it was possible that he had suspected this invasion was coming.

Darkhorse laughed quietly. *Even a demon would think twice about taking on a legion of fiends such as this!*

A drake army was not an army in the traditional sense. The host included several castes and species from the lowest minor drake—huge reptiles almost as intelligent as horses and often used for the same purpose—to the elite of the ruling drake class, the humanoid warlords who drove their beastlike cousins and their lower-caste brethren before them. There were dragons in the air and on the ground. Some carried riders, others did not. Each one was as deadly as a score of more trained men; yet, they had been defeated in the past. There were weaknesses that men had learned to exploit, Talak most of all. That was why the Dragon King had worked to separate the forces of his human foe. He wanted an easy victory to prove his worth as emperor. Darkhorse knew he also wanted it because, of all his brethren, this drake lord was the most craven.

Yet, even this bully has the muscle to flex, the shadow steed thought with bitter humor. Alone, Darkhorse could harass the drakes and cause great damage, but he would eventually fall. Despite his cowardly ways, the Silver Dragon was quite possibly his equal or better in power; it was difficult to say. Surrounded by his own followers, each with their own measure of power, he would be nigh on invincible compared to Darkhorse.

Talak had to be alerted to the menace. If they had weapons to combat this host, so much the better. The Bedlams would lend their hand, also. This was not a battle to be won by a lone warrior, but only with the effort of many, himself included.

I shall see you before long, Dragon King. This I swear.

Summoning a portal, Darkhorse departed for Talak. He hoped and prayed that what he found there would be an improvement over this dismaying sight. He had his doubts, though.

MAY THE GODS who grant me my luck be cursed with the same ill sort!

As he stepped out into Talak, into the great hall near the front entrance of the royal palace, he sensed the wrongness of the place. *Blood had been spilled here! Much of it and only recently!*

Things were beginning to move too swiftly for him. A dragon host that would, by his estimate, be here just after dawn. A royal palace under attack— yet the city seemed its normal self! Was he mistaken about the bloodshed? Drayfitt could give him no answers, especially to the question that still plagued him from the back of his mind.

Where is Shade while the world turns mad? Is he orchestrating all of this?

He dared not linger on thoughts of Shade now. Like it or not, his first duty was to Talak and warning it of the threat moving toward its gate. Darkhorse concentrated his will on seeking the Princess Erini. As a sorceress—and an untrained one—she would unconsciously radiate a powerful presence. Training or pure luck would teach her to mask that presence. Death would completely eliminate the problem. For the moment, however, her ignorance was to Darkhorse's advantage.

Find her he did, in a place buried beneath the palace much the same way his prison had been, though not as deep. She was the only distinctive presence. There were others, perhaps as many as a dozen, but something interfered with his senses, making them appear as less than individuals. He did not have to think long to realize that she was probably a prisoner. There were fear and hatred; they were so strong they nearly radiated auras all their own.

If the Princess Erini was in danger, he could not hesitate. Summoning up a portal, Darkhorse reared and, laughing mockingly, leaped through it.

"Well! If there is to be a party, then surely Darkhorse is welcome, yes?"

His sudden, overwhelming appearance, coupled with his brash, confusing speech, stunned the humans in the chamber—a prison cell, he saw. There were several people in the room, as he had thought, and among them were two others he had wanted to find. The first was Melicard, mighty Melicard, looking more like something left behind by a playful and only slightly peckish dragon. He stood—with the aid of one captor—against the wall nearest the door.

The second and somewhat more irate of the two—and only *he* would be irate in the face of a creature as devastating as Darkhorse—was Counselor Mal Quorin. He had a long, ugly blade in his hand and had apparently been toying with the princess. There were no marks on her, but the look on her face indicated that, had she been able to, the advisor would have been dead a hundred times over. That verified what Darkhorse had already suspected. Quorin was the source of whatever was dampening his senses and the princess's abilities.

All this the ebony stallion took in during the first glance around him. He took a step forward now, his attention focused specifically on Quorin, who, with more courage than many, immediately moved closer to his prey. The knife touched the princess's throat.

"She dies if you even flinch, demon! She dies if you so much as blink my direction!"

Unimpressed by their master's defiant rhetoric, several of the guards deserted for safer climates. Only the ones in the cell, who probably knew they could not run away in time or were insane fanatics like the counselor, remained.

Darkhorse laughed in the face of Quorin's threat. "You are a true servant of your master! As much a fool as he!" An ice-blue eye narrowed at the traitor. "Think on what sort of mercy you will receive from me if you *do* kill her!"

"I can draw her agony out, demon! I will!" The counselor's eyes widened. Averting his gaze suddenly, he shouted to his men. "Don't stare into his eyes! He'll try to snare you like he did that bag-o'-bones charlatan!"

There was some nervous shifting. The man holding Melicard finally broke down and tore through the doorway, but not before shoving his charge to the floor. Melicard did not rise.

Cursing, Quorin stepped back a little, directing the others to do the same. Not once did his blade leave Erini's throat. She, in turn, continued to watch him with an obsessive loathing that disturbed even Darkhorse.

"Your men abandon you, Master Quorin! Their deep faith is *so* touching to observe!" The advisor was a very dangerous adversary. Even with his plots crumbling, he refused to give in to his fears. As long as he held the knife and prevented both himself and his men from falling to Darkhorse's gaze, there was little the eternal could do without causing harm to the princess. Anything he tried might still give Quorin enough time to cut her throat.

The key to this situation was whatever Quorin utilized to keep Erini's abilities in check and the shadow steed's senses a bit muted. It was likely a Seeker artifact—there were always too many of the blasted things around!—but Darkhorse knew of no way he could remove it from the chamber without Quorin reacting first.

It was Melicard who finally decided it. Melicard, ignored by all but Erini, considered helpless by even her. Beaten and minus one arm, he had lain as still as a corpse after being tossed to the floor. Quorin, of course, had had other, weightier matters on his mind. He did not, therefore, hear or see the king rise quietly from the floor, his one good eye fixed on the counselor's back. The advisor's remaining men, also more concerned about the foreboding steed pawing at the floor before them, paid him no mind, either. As for Erini, her view was obstructed by Quorin until the last moment. Even then, to her credit, she gave no sign, not even stiffening.

Darkhorse saw all and acted accordingly. Whether Melicard succeeded or failed, if there was an opening, the shadow steed would seize it.

The king stretched out his one good arm, tottered. Darkhorse quickly filled the silence that had been extending far too long already.

"What do you hope for now, human? To stand ready until the Dragon King himself stalks into this room?"

"If *need* be," Mal Quorin grated. "I doubt I'll have to wait that long. My only problem is to get rid of you somehow, and I think—"

Reaching forward, Melicard grabbed his treacherous aide by the collar and pulled him back. Quorin's hand went up, the blade briefly nicking Erini's chin, but no more. One of the remaining soldiers grabbed the two, who were falling down in one tangled pile of arms and legs.

Darkhorse struck. The man holding Erini, panicking, tried to shield himself with her. Against a physical attack, he would have succeeded. Darkhorse had other tools at his command, though. He hit the floor with his right front hoof, creating a wicked split in the stonework and the earth below. The crack that formed shot unerringly beneath the legs of both the princess and her captor. The soldier looked down in horror as an eye stared back at him from within the crevasse. In his shock, he loosened his grip on his prisoner. Erini suddenly went flying from his hands, pulled free by the power of Darkhorse. She landed softly by the eternal's side. As her feet touched the floor, the guard's left it, or rather, *it* left him. The floor where he stood collapsed into the crevasse, the guard with it. His screams had barely died before the floor had sealed itself back up, looking remarkably untouched.

"I was always a slave to the dramatic," Darkhorse rumbled to anyone who could hear him.

Erini was ignoring him, her only concern Melicard, whom she probably imagined dead by now. Her rescue had taken only a few seconds, though to her and her unfortunate captor, it must have seemed far longer. Darkhorse laughed. Concentrating now on Quorin, he used his powers to pull the hapless counselor into the air and, while the traitor struggled to regain control of his limbs, transported the medallion to a place that burned hot enough to melt even Seeker magic away. Darkhorse contemplated sending Mal Quorin there as well, but he knew that there might yet be need even for something as foul as this creature was.

The princess, however, was not so understanding. While her abilities had been hampered by the protective artifact the counselor had worn, her fury had grown unchecked. Now, feeling the release of those abilities, she struck without thinking. Mal Quorin screamed and tried to scratch off his own skin. The last of his men had run off the moment he had been thrust into the air. There was no one here left to save him. Erini planned to have her revenge now for everything he had done or planned to do.

"*Erini!*" Melicard's faint call went unheeded, so caught up was the princess in the full force of her own power.

"*PRINCESS!*" Darkhorse roared. His voice cut through where the king's had failed. "Princess Erini! Stop and think!"

Stop and think? The look on her bitter face indicated that she planned to do anything but that. The time for thinking was long past. Now, it was time for vengeance.

Darkhorse persisted. "Think what you do to *yourself*, princess, not this piece of rotting offal! You might become like Shade, so in love with your power that you lose your humanity."

She seemed to stir then, for her eyes travelled from her prey to the ebony stallion and finally to her betrothed. Melicard and Erini matched gazes briefly. Whatever the princess saw in the one eye of the king drained the need for vengeance from her heart. Darkhorse felt her withdraw her power back into herself. Above them, Mal Quorin, drenched in sweat and pale as bone, sighed and collapsed. The shadow steed brought him slowly back to the floor.

"Melicard." The princess looked ashamed, as if somehow her madness had made her less a creature than even Quorin was.

The king would have none of that. He had used the last of his strength in his battle and could only force himself up enough to lean on his elbow. He shook his head as his bride-to-be continued to berate herself and whispered something. Darkhorse, though he could have eavesdropped without either knowing, chose not to. There were some things that were meant to be private.

Whatever Melicard said soothed, if not completely convinced, Erini. She smiled and seemed to regain some of her confidence. Tenderly, the novice sorceress touched Melicard where he had been crippled by the one artifact so many years before.

His visage and arm became whole instantly. Darkhorse had to look closely before it became apparent that Erini had only given Melicard back his elfwood mask and limb and had not actually restored the missing pieces. Even for Darkhorse, that would have been an astounding achievement.

Aided by the princess, Melicard rose to his feet and walked up to the shadow steed. For a time, neither human said anything to the eternal. He waited patiently, knowing some of the limits of their kind. Both of them had suffered greatly at the hands of the crumpled heap on the floor.

"Thank you, dem—Darkhorse," Melicard finally began. He looked angry with himself. "And I dared to try and make you my slave. It's a wonder, great one, that you would even help one such as me."

"The past kindnesses of Counselor Quorin made it nearly impossible at first, I must admit," Darkhorse responded wryly. "I did it as much for my *own* benefactor here," he indicated the princess, "as anyone else, your majesty. I did it for your people as well. The Dragon King Silver is on his way even now with a host that may make all this subterfuge rather unnecessary."

"And Quorin's men still hold the palace and the northern gate."

"That is so, your majesty. Tell me, would your army turn back from its crusade into the Hell Plains if the sorcerer Drayfitt was found murdered?"

Melicard's mouth dropped open. "Drayfitt? Murdered?" He turned toward Quorin. "I should kill him now and forgo the niceties of a public trial and execution!"

Darkhorse shook his head. "While the effort was there, the true criminal is the warlock Shade—who has his own hand in this enterprise. He and the Dragon King have made a pact, though I would not trust either to adhere to it for very long. *Shade* is my true quest, but I will do what I have to in order to save your people from the more immediate threat."

"They will likely go on," Melicard said, responding to the stallion's original question. "We have many other tricks. Drayfitt is a great loss—both to my plans and personally—but his death does not mean that all is lost."

"Can you hold against the Silver Dragon's host?"

Melicard looked at Erini. "If my bride-to-be will add her strength, perhaps."

"My—what I am doesn't turn you?"

"No more than what I am turned you."

Perhaps it was a trick of the light, but Darkhorse swore that the elfwood mask moved exactly as the king's face would have. *There are all sorts of magic . . .*

Erini smiled gratefully. "I don't know what I can do, but I will help as I can."

Seeming to draw strength from that, Melicard looked up and said, "Then, the first thing we must do is take this palace back."

XVIII

THE WARLOCK SHADE haunted the halls and chambers of the vast imperial palace of Talak undetected amidst the chaos commencing around him. Sentries rushing to and fro—whether loyalists or traitors Shade could not say and did not care—did not so much as glance at the hooded figure they passed, even those within an arm's reach of him.

Unfolding himself at his destination, the warlock knelt down in the midst of the garden. Here, in such an excellent, centrally located area of the palace, he would release the last and largest clutch.

When emerged from his sleeves they were little more than amorphous shapes that flittered and darted about, as if in silent impatience. Unlike the bizarre searchers that he had summoned that other time, these were not living creatures in any sense of the word, merely bits of magical energy shaped to do a particular task. Shade counted out an even dozen before he broke off the spell. His head throbbed briefly, but he assured himself that it was only a headache this time. There had been no further losses of memory—as far as he knew—and his personality had been stable for days. He was himself at last and nothing would change that again.

Without a word, he sent the tiny shapes out and about. They would spread through the palace. No corner of the massive edifice would remain uninvaded.

He drew back into the shadows then, wondering how long it would take Darkhorse to detect him once the masking spell that had protected him thus far was removed. Not too long, he supposed, but long enough.

The warlock smiled to himself as pictured the scene to come.

RETAKING THE PALACE was child's play, as far as Darkhorse was concerned. Melicard found and freed a number of the prisoners the counselor's men had captured in the cells surrounding his own. Though still outnumbered and without weapons, they were a force to be reckoned with, even forgetting that the king also had a sorceress and a "demon" to aid him.

After a thorough search through more than half the building, it became apparent to all that the palace was, for the most part, deserted now. Only a few stragglers, looters generally, were uncovered. Melicard's men rearmed themselves quickly on weapons left abandoned in the corridors. The reason for the abandonment soon revealed itself to them, thanks to a looter caught trying to ransack the king's chambers. Staring up at Darkhorse all the while he spoke, the prisoner informed them of how Quorin's men knew now that Melicard had unleashed his personal horde of demons that he had saved just for this moment. Allowing the traitors to seize the palace had only been a ploy to discover who was guilty and who was not. Even now, men were fleeing for their lives from the monsters they knew were following them relentlessly.

Darkhorse understood. Seeing him and knowing that he had come for their master, Quorin's underlings had panicked. In their haste to get as far from the shadow steed as possible, they had likely rushed past their fellows without pausing, spouting out garbled warnings as they ran. As was always the case with fear, the stories had grown, each man shouting some tale of a demon come to get them. Panic escalated.

The eternal chuckled as he told Melicard, "Apparently, I *was* too pessimistic about your chances of quick success! You have my apologies, King Melicard!"

"We have you to thank for our easy victory. Let us hope that those at the gate surrender so easily."

"Shall I go there and see to it?"

The king shook his head. "I am grateful, but your appearance may panic people near the gate. I need as much order as possible."

Erini, who had vanished momentarily from the throne room, returned at that moment with another man, an officer in the dress of Gordag-Ai. Melicard knew him, but the princess introduced him to Darkhorse, who learned the man was a Captain Iston or something. Iston seemed in awe of the ebony stallion, but his military training succeeded in keeping him from making much of a spectacle of himself.

Captain Iston apologized profusely to the king for his failure to keep the princess safe. From the look on her face, Darkhorse hazarded a guess that Erini had heard the same thing only moments earlier.

"I've already explained to you," she said, interrupting his fourth apology, "I am a sorceress, captain. I transported myself out of the room by accident. There was no way for any of your men to keep watch over me." Beneath her calm tone, the eternal noted some bitterness. Erini had still not forgiven herself for the men who had died trying to rescue her.

While they talked, rather too idly in Darkhorse's opinion, something nagged at the corner of his mind. Something obvious that they had all been missing, something about the crooked counselor . . .

Of course! Darkhorse cursed himself for not thinking of it sooner. He turned immediately to King Melicard, who was engrossed in a discussion concerning the chameleon cloaks Iston's two men had worn. "*Your majesty!*"

When a tall, pitch-black stallion demands attention, he receives it instantly. Melicard fell back under the glittering gaze. "What is it? Is Shade within the palace walls?"

Darkhorse snorted. "I doubt I would be able to tell even if he was, but that is not what I wanted to say! I have a request of you!"

"Name it. I owe you too much to deny you anything."

"Mal Quorin's chambers. I want to see them."

Erini's face darkened. Melicard nodded grimly and looked rather irritated with himself. "I should've thought of that long before. He's the link, after all, to the Dragon King—and likely Shade, too."

"Yes! It was he who provided Drayfitt with the book that the drakes had uncovered! I wonder what else remains hidden in his rooms?"

"I'll have someone drag him back up here!" Melicard rubbed his chin. "He'll show you everything even if I have to remove a few fingers and toes to get him to do it."

The eternal disagreed. "Mal Quorin is the last creature I would want in that room. From the tricks he has already played, I would not put it past him to have a few more ready and waiting for him. No, I think I would prefer to probe his room on my own. Your good counselor is best left admiring the cobwebs of his new abode."

"There's much in what you say. Do you need someone to lead you to it?"

"It is not a place I think I would care to enter without some prior inspection. I am *not* impervious to everything."

Melicard smiled. "I was beginning to think you were unstoppable. However, if otherwise is the case, I can have one of my men show you the way."

Darkhorse dipped his head in the closest he could come to a bow. "That would be appreciated."

Little more than a few minutes passed before he was being led to the ex-advisor's personal sanctum by one nearly panic-stricken soldier. Even knowing that the great leviathan trotting next to him was an ally of the king did not stop the man from shaking and stuttering. It was an amusing sight, a soldier who was obviously a longtime veteran shaking in his boots, but Darkhorse forbore from saying or doing anything that would shame the human.

At last, they came to a set of doors that somehow arrogantly proclaimed power even though they were as plain as any Darkhorse had seen here. He was interested also to note how far they were from the king's chambers. Quorin had set up his own tiny little kingdom in the palace. It was a wonder that he had, according to Erini and Melicard, always seemed to be around when you expected him least.

Darkhorse dismissed his guide, who happily departed at the quickest walk he could manage while still seeming to keep his dignity. The ebony stallion waited until he was alone and then began to inspect the entrance for traps or tricks.

The first was simple yet devious. There was an intricate triple lock in the door. A normal key would merely cause one lock to be exchanged for another, all without the one turning the key realizing it. He would then find that the door was still locked. Trying again would set the third lock into play. It was an endless cycle. The secret, evidently, was a special key that Quorin had no doubt carried on his person, one that caught all three lock mechanisms simultaneously. A very impressive piece of work, the stallion decided, but not one that would give *him* any trouble. Darkhorse did not need a key and, in fact, could have ignored the lock altogether. The door was so reinforced that nothing short of a raging, full-grown bull would have been able to break it down, and that only after several painful attempts. That meant nothing to the creature who could create fissures in a mountain with the mere tap of his hooves. In respect to King Melicard and Princess Erini, however, Darkhorse decided to forgo splintering it into so much scrap. Instead, probing the locks again, he caused all three locks to open at the same time, as if the key were actually in there.

After that, it was an even simpler task to make the door open up by itself. Darkhorse laughed silently at the picture he knew he must have made. Not once, however, had he considered giving himself hands and arms, useful though they might have been. The form he wore was more his own than the shapeless mass he had originated with. With his abilities intact, it would serve him as well as any other.

The shadow steed peered inside.

"Curious," he finally muttered before stepping into the room.

Mal Quorin's personal chambers had an odd feel to them, as if the rooms, at least the front ones, were more for display than actual use. Things were just too perfect, too much what one would have expected, almost as if even the place-ment of the chair by the fireplace had been choreographed. This was *not* the sort of room a man like Quorin would have been happy with. This was a place where he spoke in private to the king or pretended to do work.

Moving swiftly to the next doorway, he noted that the bedroom was the same. Again, everything seemed appropriate for a man of Mal Quorin's rank and position. Too appropriate. The fixtures were just too gaudy to be believed. The bed was large, well-built and expensive, but hardly right. A row of well-preserved tomes on a shelf revealed the typical books concerning politics and history, including, ironically, several by the late Drayfitt.

Darkhorse laughed, his tone somewhat bitter, wondering if any of them had been read.

These were *not* Quorin's personal quarters, he concluded. These were the ones that the traitor had made up for the sake of appearances. Where then . . . ?

He backed out of the room and looked down both ends of the corridor. One would take him back toward the Princess Erini and the others. The opposite direction ended in a cul-de-sac and included two other doors on one wall. Darkhorse stared at the blank wall across from those two doors. Elegant paintings and intricate sculptures adorned it. Nothing seemed amiss . . . from the hallway.

Darkhorse reentered Quorin's chambers, heading straight into the bedroom. Probing with his mind, he soon discovered what he sought. There was a spell masking it, a strong one that even he had not noticed at first, caught up as he was by the general wrongness he had felt upon first arriving.

Not so clever, dear one! Someone, perhaps Mal Quorin, perhaps not, had sealed the other rooms on this side of the corridor, making it seem as if they had never existed. The only true way to enter them now was through the counselor's chambers. He found a switch of sorts hidden in the back wall of the bedroom. Darkhorse wasted no time, tripping the switch and immediately stepping back. After so many mishaps, the shadow steed was trying to be cautious. His senses had proven too little too often in the past few days.

The wall slid open without the slightest hint of any danger. Searching, Darkhorse detected nothing potentially threatening in the walls, ceiling, or floor. There was, though, a subtle spell emanating from the secret doorway that tried in vain to turn his thoughts to anything but the desire to enter. A human would have been affected and would have likely walked away, suddenly caught up in some other notion. Darkhorse overwhelmed the spell easily, eliminating it so that the king's men would have no difficulty entering at some later time. That done, the stallion nosed the secret door open further and slowly entered. Before he was even halfway in, he already sensed that here, indeed, was the true domicile of the traitorous advisor.

It was dark in here, as dark as the former inhabitant's life. Adjusting his physical senses, Darkhorse brought the world of Mal Quorin into focus. It was not a place he would have invited the Princess Erini.

"And they call *me* demon when abominations such as this roam freely, advising heads of state!"

The room he stood in was filled with grisly trophies. Skulls adorned one entire shelf, all of them polished smooth. Darkhorse wondered if each had died at the hands of the counselor himself. Possibly, they had all been rivals for power at one time or another. Hanging from the opposing wall, as if to allow the skulls something to gaze at, was an array of sinister and unusual weaponry. Most had not been designed to bring about a quick and painless death. Mal Quorin seemed to have a fondness for serrated edges.

Perhaps I should have let Princess Erini erase his existence from this world! Better yet, perhaps I should have done it myself instead of preserving his foul life!

Death had come freely to this room many times, he noted. The stench assaulted him on many planes. The room beyond emanated even worse. Dark-horse did not even bother stepping toward it. He knew what he would find. Quorin's *playroom*.

Does this truly fall under the definition of humanity? Darkhorse wondered. He knew there and then that he *should* have let the princess have her way with the fiend while they were in the cell. When this was over, Mal Quorin would pay . . . and pay . . . and pay. Darkhorse was not like humans; he had no qualms about the rights and wrongs of punishment. Mal Quorin had now forfeited any right he had to a continued existence. Whatever use he might have been, it was not worth it. Not now.

None of what he discovered so far, however, had any bearing on the reasons he had come here. Quorin's personal atrocities aside—though not *too* far aside—the man had left little other trace of his double side. Darkhorse had expected charts or something that would give an indication of what had been planned. There seemed to be nothing. His search would need to be more thorough. Frowning, the shadow steed concentrated.

Drawers slowly opened. Cabinets doors freely swung forward, revealing their contents. A panel hidden in the wall snapped into existence. Even the secret door through which he had entered opened wider.

"Show me what you have," he whispered to the room.

Parchments, maps, talismans . . . everything that had been stored over the years in one place or another came flying out into the air. One by one, they flew past the gaze of the eternal, who studied each with eyes that saw more than the physical. As each piece was dismissed, it would return to its point of origin, even placing itself in its original position. The last was not due to any courtesy toward the treacherous counselor, but rather because Melicard might find reason to inspect these belongings himself. What might have been of no significance to Darkhorse might prove vital to the king.

The speed with which he inspected each and every item would have horrified Erini or the others. Things flew by as little more than blurs, depending on what they were. Time was of the essence, true, but that in no way meant that Dark-horse was being careless. If there *was* something of importance to him among Quorin's effects, he would find it.

He *did*, though it took him more than half the search to find even that one item.

A tiny box, quite ordinary in appearance. To most, it would have seemed the sort of thing the man might have kept a keepsake or two in, save that the imprisoned counselor was hardly the sort of person to keep remembrances. Moreover, the box was not quite what it was supposed to be. Power had been infused into it; so much, in fact, that the lid refused his first attempts to open it, something that impressed upon him the abilities of the creator. There were few entities alive now with such power. A Dragon King would have the ability.

Darkhorse cursed and set the box aside. It would require his full concentration and that was not something he had command of, not, at least, until he was through with his search. Impatience was eating at his thoughts and Darkhorse knew he was going to grow more and more careless if he was not careful. So much to do and, despite what seemed an endless night, dawn was fast approaching. If the Silver Dragon and his host were not within sight of Talak already, they soon would be.

His search progressed with very little else to show for his efforts. Even the items of these rooms revealed little of Quorin's misdeeds or what the plots of his master still entailed. It was as if the man had only started his life a short time before joining the lower ranks of the city-state's government. Possibly it was so. Possibly it was also the case that Quorin kept most of what he needed to know in his head. Such agent would be useful to the Dragon King.

Just as the shadow steed was about to concede defeat, a yellowed parchment giving off a very distinctive aura caught his eye. Its age was uncalculable, save that he knew with only a glance that it was Vraad in origin. Darkhorse did not take time out to study it. Instead, he completed his search of the rest of the effects, moving more slowly and cautiously now.

Three other pieces caught his attention before he was finished. The first was a dagger with an inscription dating it to the time just prior to the Turning War. It had a taint to it that Darkhorse suspected belonged to Cabe's father, Azran. The second of the trio was another parchment, one of recent origin. While he could not sense anything overly malevolent about it, something disturbed him. The final addition was a talisman, obviously of Seeker origin, that he found in the same drawer as the box. Its purpose, too, escaped him for the moment, but any such item that Quorin would deem worthy of keeping interested him for that reason alone. The shadow steed's spirits both rose and fell as he surveyed his tiny collection. It was possible he had found what he had originally sought, but now came the difficulty of understanding just what it was he *had* found.

The box interested him most, but it would also probably be the most exasperating piece of the lot. He inspected the dagger first. It was, as he had suspected, a creation of Azran's and definitely one of his first attempts. The madman's mark was on it. The dagger would kill with only a touch. Even a nick was fatal. Close examination revealed the blade as nothing more than that. Unlike the other items he had looked over, Darkhorse did not replace the dagger in its original location. With some satisfaction, he raised it into the air before him and sent it on a journey that would only end when it reached the sun. Even a toy left behind by Azran had limits to its capacity to survive.

The Seeker talisman seemed to have little in the way of power and, though its use remained a mystery, Darkhorse doubted it could be of any importance. He returned it to where it had come from. That left the parchments and, of course, the box. After some deliberation, he had the Vraad parchment rise up before him. Defenses ready, the shadow steed slowly made the yellowed and crumbling sheet unfold. It had not survived the millennia as well as Shade's book apparently had, but that it still existed at all said something for the power invested in it. He only hoped that it was not protected by some secondary spell. His probing had revealed nothing of the sort, but one could never be too certain where the Vraad were concerned.

He recognized the mark, though he had seen it only once or twice, and that in the far, far distant past: the dragon banner. There was a Vraad clan name attached to that banner, but it escaped his memory at the moment. He could only recall that the warlock had been part of this selfsame clan.

It was a map. A map detailing the division of a land. There was a list of almost two dozen items, names perhaps, some of which had been crossed out and all of which were more or less illegible. Darkhorse discarded the parchment in disgust. Only the Vraad would think of preserving something so minor as a list of their division of spoils from some plot. The great conquerors. Despite himself, he laughed.

That left him only two items: the newer, or, at least more *recent* parchment and the box. Once more he tried to pry it open with his powers and once more he failed. Furious, he allowed it to drop heavily onto the floor. Darkhorse used his skills to snatch up the parchment in its place and, with thinning patience, unfurled the new item completely before common sense reminded him of the traps that might lurk within.

Something briefly struck at him. A human would have died from the blow, his heart literally bursting open. Darkhorse, on the other hand, suffered nothing more than annoyance at his own lack of thought. Had this been a stronger spell, he might have been injured—or worse.

The blow lessened until it was no longer noticeable. The ebony stallion inspected the parchment. It was blank. Its sole purpose had been to kill whoever had opened it. Darkhorse wondered if it had been meant as a last resort for Quorin should he have failed his master, or if the foul counselor had intended to give it to Erini or the king at some late point. Whatever the case, it was now no more than an unused sheet. He returned it to its original resting place and once again began inspecting the box.

"You, my friend," he muttered to the object, "have a story to tell! I wonder what lies within your maw—and what I must do to pry that maw open . . ."

The spell keeping it closed had an odd feel to it, almost as if it were incomplete and that, somehow, it was that incompleteness that gave it strength. The spell was a lock and completing it would be like using the key—but *what* key would fit?

I have no time for your little games! Darkhorse ranted silently at the box. The key would not be obvious to someone who had not searched the entire area already. If would have to be magical in some sense, but subtle as well. Only a tiny link was missing from the spell binding the box shut. What he needed was something almost insignificant in power but—

He recalled the Seeker talisman from where he had sent it. *Could it be?* It would explain why Quorin had kept such a weak artifact and why it seemed to have no detectable purpose. Add to that the fact that it had been located in the same drawer as the box. Why not put the key in the same place as the lock it was meant for, especially since most people would never connect the two. Like hiding something in plain sight. More and more, Darkhorse convinced himself that he had chosen correctly. In the end, however, there was only one way to find out, and that was to see if his "key" fit.

Recalling some of his past mistakes, he surrounded the container and the talisman before beginning. With so much effort put into keeping the box sealed, it was possible that what he unleashed might be devastating. Possible, but doubtful. Unlike the parchment, Darkhorse sensed that this item had a more useful purpose.

With his mind, he brought the talisman to the box and laid it on top. The pattern he sensed did not seem right. Darkhorse shifted the talisman to a standing position in front of the container. The binding field altered, but again it was not the complete pattern that he sought.

After a moment's thought, he caused the medallion to lay flat. This time, he brought the box to the talisman, carefully placing it directly on top of the Seeker device.

A perfectly formed pattern momentarily flickered into existence, then cancelled itself out completely. He had succeeded in unlocking the box.

That success did not ease his mind. Darkhorse still had to *open* the container.

Something nagged at the corner of his mind. He was beginning to dislike those feelings and, under present circumstances, chose to ignore it as simple growing paranoia. It might even be, the stallion decided, that the box itself was trying to turn him away before he opened it and discovered its secret.

Still, there was no sense in taking too many chances. . . .

He turned the container so that the lid would open toward *him*. In this way, the brunt of any blow would be away from where he stood. The precaution might be all for nought, but there was no harm in taking it.

With a careful touch of his will, Darkhorse raised the lid high.

Briefly, there was a flash of brilliant light, so brilliant that it illuminated the far half of the chamber as well as the sun might have, had it been brought inside. The flash lasted no longer than two, maybe three seconds and then died completely. Darkhorse's eyes, adjusted to the dark of the room, needed a moment to readjust. When they had, the shadow steed scanned his surroundings, searching for any minute difference. There was none. Despite the fact that he had shielded the box, he had expected some altering. Curious, he dissolved the shield.

The box looked and felt harmless. Darkhorse probed it closely. It was as if Quorin's toy had used up whatever power it had contained and now needed to be recharged. Where had the power gone, though? Darkhorse almost wondered what would have happened if he had taken the flash full on. It had been more than raw power, though time had not allowed him much of a chance to discover what *else* it had been. Some spell, but for what purpose?

In frustration, he dropped the box to the floor and crushed it beneath one of his hooves. "Curse your creator! If I should ever find that our paths have crossed . . ."

It was a foolish act and one he instantly regretted. Darkhorse kicked at the remnants of the container, knowing that it was likely he had destroyed his only clue.

Darkhorse was about to return to Melicard when he became aware of something—no! *Someone*—in the outer rooms. There was no mistaking *that* presence. Not so *close*.

"Your madness has finally led you to—" he burst into the room, defenses and offenses at the ready . . . only to find no sign of his adversary.

No sign of Shade.

Or was that the case? Darkhorse moved toward the wall to his left, sensing a slight trace emanating from that direction. Shade's magic. It was too distinctive, too *Vraad* to be any other's. There were cracks in the wall, too, as if the warlock had struck out against it before his abrupt departure.

Darkhorse laughed. Even now, he could sense the warlock's presence elsewhere in the palace. This time, there would be no escape. This time, Darkhorse *would* confront him.

And one of us will play the final hand . . . perhaps both of us, if need be!

The shadow steed laughed again, but it was a hollow laugh, devoid of even the least bit of humor.

IN THE PLACE where he had chosen to wait, Shade nodded to himself and whispered, "So. Now comes the time. At *last*."

XIX

Two MEN HAD been left to guard Mal Quorin's cell. Even though at the time the king had been shorthanded and no one had known that Quorin's men would rout, Melicard had decided that sparing two men was still worth the price. It said something about the importance of the prisoner—and how much King Melicard desperately wanted his former advisor to remain where he was until Talak could mete out proper justice to a man who had betrayed everyone.

For the last few hours, their prisoner had remained quiet. It had been a welcome change from the first hour, when Quorin had recovered somewhat from the princess's assault and started ranting how they would all pay when his lord and master crushed the city beneath his paw. The guards, still weak themselves from their own ordeal, had been taking turns napping, trying to build up their strength. Once in a while, the one awake would look through the barred window in the door of Quorin's cell and make certain that the prisoner had not slipped through the cracks in the cell walls or some such impossibility. Each time, Quorin had still been there. The ten-minute ritual quickly became something of a joke—until one of the sentries stood up, stretching his worn legs, and glanced inside.

The chains hung loosely. Of the traitor, there was not the slightest sign. The cell had no other openings . . . unless the prisoner *had* slithered through the cracks.

Though the panicked guard and his soon-to-be-panicked companion could not have known it, Mal Quorin had vanished from his place of confinement just about the time Darkhorse had opened the lid of the box. Even had they known and been able to make the connection, there still remained one more question, one that greatly outweighed the question of *how* he had escaped.

That question was, of course, *where was he?*

MELICARD PACED THE room, trying to explain again to his headstrong bride-to-be what he wanted of her and *why.*

"Erini, I want you to stay back here—"

"Where it's *safe?*" The princess shook her head vehemently. "This will one day be my kingdom, too—unless you've changed your mind about me—"

"Never!"

"Then let me defend it with you, Melicard." Erini took a deep breath and stepped away from the king. She was more nervous than she wanted to admit. *Does it ever become easier?* Darkhorse seemed to take the entire thing in stride, as if combatting immortal warlocks and sinister Dragon Kings was an everyday matter—and perhaps it was with *him*. The princess, on the other hand, while ready to give her life for the protection of her people, still contained within her a very human desire to be safe and secure from the troubles around her.

"Without Mal Quorin to lead them, the traitors have no one to turn to. It will be over in an hour, maybe less. We have a fair idea now who belonged to him, thanks to some of our prisoners. At worst, we shall round up everyone, replace the gate complement with men loyal to me, and sort out the innocent and guilty here in the palace. Crude but effective. Hardly something requiring your talents—which I *will* need when the drakes arrive."

"The drakes . . ." Erini shook her head, not because she disagreed with Melicard's summation but because the lack of sleep was finally taking its toll upon her. She stumbled momentarily.

Melicard succeeded in grabbing her arms, preventing her from causing herself any harm by slipping. "*This* is the reason I especially do not wish your aid in this matter. I *want* to protect you; I will not argue that point. I know, however, that your abilities make you invaluable to the safety of my—our—people. That is why I want you to take the time you have to *sleep*. Rest. You have not fought the battles I have. You have not had to go without sleep for days. What happens when the Dragon King arrives and you don't have the concentration to make use of your abilities? What happens then?"

What, indeed? Erini knew he was correct. Knew it, but did not like it. She wanted to be there at his side for every moment that became available to them, even in the middle of a battle if circumstances warranted it. Yet, if she truly wanted a future here, the princess knew that she would be best able to guarantee that by being fit and ready when the drake host arrived. Melicard admitted he had many tricks of his own, long-term preparations for just such a day, but the aid of a spellcaster of any sort would only strengthen their chances. They were hardly assured of victory. The Silver Dragon had been preparing for this day as well—with better success so far.

"You will face danger enough," her betrothed continued. His grip had changed from a spontaneous one designed to keep her from falling to one that threatened to never release her from his side. Erini would have been happy enough to suffer such a fate. "The Dragon King will note fairly quickly that there is a sorceress aiding in the defenses. You may be personally assaulted."

The princess shivered. She felt herself brave, but . . .

"I have something for you." One hand released its hold reluctantly, vanished, then returned, this time bearing a familiar-looking object.

"This is Quorin's talisman." Erini tried to push it away, wanting nothing to remind her of the insidious man.

"Not his, but one similar. Stronger. It was once mine. I've not worn it for some time, not since after the . . . you'll need it more."

She accepted it reluctantly, knowing this was one point it would be useless to argue over with him. As he placed it around her neck, a sudden, insane fear crept over her. "Melicard. Do you think we have any chance?"

"Talak has stood before. We also have Darkhorse. He's promised us the aid of the Bedlams, and I know from past experience that they are up to the task."

"Where are they? Why haven't they arrived yet?"

"Who can predict what these spellcasters will do?" He leaned closer and whispered, "I have enough trouble with just one. The one who so readily saved my soul after I twisted it into something of a mockery."

"It wasn't that difficult. You'd had nearly twenty years of free life. I only reminded you of what that life had offered once."

Melicard broke away from her. "Which reminds me also of the tasks at hand." He snapped his fingers, summoning four men he had borrowed from Iston's complement. "Escort her majesty to her quarters and remain there. See to it she gets some rest."

Both of them knew that the princess could easily bypass her watchers with the aid of her abilities, but Melicard also knew that Erini felt guilty about the trouble that her accidental departure had caused them during the coup. The princess knew he was counting on that.

Before allowing herself to be escorted away, Erini stepped over to Melicard for one final time, reached up, and kissed him in full view of the others. She was going to get a reputation for being brazen at this rate, she knew, but there was always the chance that something terrible might happen while they were separated. Reluctantly separating herself from the stunned king, Erini rejoined her escort and gave them permission to depart. For her own sake, she dared not look back until she knew for a fact that Melicard was no longer in sight.

In the halls, it seemed impossible that there was still a great threat to the safety of this city—*her* city. The palace was nearly silent. Only if she listened closely could she hear men running or marching in the distance. One last patrol was searching through this massive edifice in the remote possibility that some of Mal Quorin's men were still in hiding.

Captain Iston, on his way back to the king, stopped her in the hall. His face was worn, but he looked willing to take on the entire horde if that would keep his mistress safe. His mistress and one other, based on the first words that escaped his lips. "Galea! Your majesty! I—I beg your pardon! I wanted to ask—"

"—if I could see how Galea was doing?" Though they had failed to spirit her away, Iston and his men had succeeded in rescuing her two ladies. Unfortunately, Iston had never had any time to actually speak with Galea. Knowing how difficult it had been for her to leave Melicard, Erini smiled and added, "Of course, I will. You have my promise."

"My deepest gratitude, your majesty." The officer bowed and hurried on his way.

The walk to her personal chambers was uneventful, with the exception of the notion, which rose twice in her thoughts, that Shade was so very nearby. Once, she stared at one of the walls, thinking he was there. The second time, Erini had the oddest feeling that she had just walked *over* an area where the warlock should have been standing. It puzzled her once she realized that he was in neither of those two places. Why would she imagine such a thing? Had recent events finally taken its toll on her? Was Erini losing all sense of reality?

Sleep began to look very wonderful, very precious. Melicard was correct; if the princess did not sleep, she would be useless to him when the siege began.

Before dismissing her escort, she peeked into the rooms belonging to Magda and Galea. Magda, ever in control even after surviving a coup attempt, looked up from where she was sitting. Beside her and lying asleep in bed, was Galea. The tall woman rose and walked quietly over to her mistress.

"Yes, your majesty?"

"How is she? How are both of you?"

"She feared more for your life and that of her dashing captain that she did for her own. Galea is worn out, nothing more. I promised to sit with her for a while in order to calm her nerves. As for myself . . . I get along."

Erini could not help smiling slightly at Magda's attitude. "You are a rock that both of us sorely need."

"I live to serve my mistress."

"I'd be lost without you. When Galea awakes, tell her that her officer asked about her. He's fine. I also want you to get some rest, Magda. Even you have to sleep."

"The same could be said about you, your majesty. I'll tell her and do as you say. I must admit to some difficulty with keeping my eyes open."

"I know the feeling. Sleep well, Magda, for we may all need our wits about us come the morrow."

"The morrow is almost here already," the plain woman commented. "May you sleep well, also, my lady, and please summon me if you have need of my services."

"Thank you."

Her escort stayed with her to the very end, even insisting on following her into her chambers. Not until every corner and every closet had been inspected, evidently at Melicard's command, did they deign to depart. Even then, two of them went no farther than the corridor outside. Erini was tempted to tell them the futility of such an action, but knew it was likely her betrothed's way of eas-ing his own fears—though he knew as well as she that sorcery made it too easy for her to leave without anyone noticing.

Alone, the princess was tempted to fall face-down into her pillow and lay there until sleep overcame her, which would not have proven much of a strug-gle, judging by the way she felt merely *gazing* at the bed. She found her thoughts intruding again; this time concerning the terrible situation they would probably find themselves in come daylight. *If only Darkhorse had been able to warn them!* she thought wearily. *They would be here by now!*

He *had* tried. She knew that. Unfortunately, the commander had assumed it was the eternal who had killed Drayfitt and that he was a servant to one of the Dragon Kings. It was a wonder that all the stallion had suffered was a momentary exile to—to—whatever plane had apparently spawned him, if she understood correctly.

If only Melicard could have spoken with his men. He had mentioned once having methods for that, but, as with so many things, those methods had fallen under his "loyal" counselor's control. Now, they were no longer available. Quo-rin had been very thorough in his work.

Drayfitt, Erini thought sadly. *Drayfitt could have created something. He could have—*

It occurred to her at that point that she had the potential to do *anything* the elderly sorcerer had been capable of doing.

The notion excited her, brought new energy to her worn body and mind. If *she* could somehow contact Melicard's forces in the Hell Plains, she might be able to convince them to turn around. Then, it would be up to Talak to hold out until the army returned. Surely with foes coming at him from two sides, even the Dragon King would be forced to capitulate or flee. Melicard had also mentioned his smaller armies of the north and west. While the princess did not quite understand under what circumstances Quorin had tricked them, she could only assume that if she was successful with the first, then she stood a good chance of contacting them as well. From there, time would be what mattered. Erini hoped the Bedlams would arrive before it was too late.

How would she do it? Drayfitt had shown her little. Yet, the one thing he had always emphasized was, magic, in any form, worked more easily if one al-lowed it to come to oneself naturally. Allow her inner self to make each spell almost automatic. Few people had the ability or the patience to do that, which was why there had never been *that* many spellcasters of significant ability even prior to the Dragon Kings' secret purgings following the unsuccessful Turning War.

The first thing she needed, Erini decided, was a comfortable but firm place to sit. Had she been, say, the Lady Gwendolyn Bedlam, she knew that it would have taken perhaps just the blink of an eye or the wave of a hand to perform the deed. Not having experience or the feel of sorcery, the princess was forced to do everything step-by-step. Hopefully, there would be time later on for someone to assist her in her practice.

While the bed looked most comfortable, the floor seemed more practical. Erini did not want her spell ruined because the softness of her bed made her too sleepy. The floor was comfortable, but in no way conducive to rest—at least, not yet. Erini knew that, once her initial enthusiasm faded away, it would be near impossible for her to stay awake regardless of where she was or what she was doing.

Seating herself on one of the carpeted areas, she closed her eyes and tried to picture men encamped in a violent, smoke-filled land. They would be rising about now, Erini supposed. She pictured the tents, saw the sentries, and imagined the details of their armor, the last based on those she had seen the palace guards wearing. The images faded briefly as exhaustion tried to seize the moment while her eyes were closed tight. Blinking, the princess cursed under her breath and tried again.

The images grew sharper in her mind, but that was all they were—images. She could feel no connection between herself and anyone in the encampment. With growing disgust, Erini realized that she knew none of the officers by face, much less by name. How, then, could she hope to make contact with them? Was her only hope the possibility that she might be able to transport *herself* to the encampment? Would that even work? To date, her abilities had worked haphazardly at best, even taking into account Mal Quorin's damnable medallion.

Her concentration was interrupted for what she considered permanently by the return of the feeling that there was *another* in the room with her, another by the name of Shade. Erini leapt to her feet, teetering ever so slightly. Nothing. For the space of a breath, she had felt his presence so near that it would not have surprised her to find him staring over her shoulder. Her weary mind succeeded in coming up with an answer that satisfied her for the moment; her erratic senses had no doubt picked up on the traces left behind by his previous visitation. That she had not noted them in the days between now and the time of that incident did not occur to her.

Defeated, Erini slumped onto her bed. The appeal of falling asleep in her clothes renewed itself. Her arms were lead; the weight of the palace seemed to have been placed on her head. She wanted nothing but sleep now. Perhaps after some rest, the princess hoped, she would have some success.

A hesitant knock on her chamber doors stirred her. "You may enter."

It was Galea. There were rings under her eyes and it looked as if she had just woken up. She had dressed hastily, for her clothes were wrinkled and her hair was in complete disarray. "My lady?"

"What is it, Galea?"

The other woman looked perplexed. "You *summoned* me, your majesty."

Had she? Try as she might, Erini could not recall doing so. Perhaps Galea had only dreamt that she had. "I've no need of you now, but if you have a moment, I have a message for you from someone important to you."

From the way her companion's eyes lit up, the princess knew that Galea had already guessed who that certain someone was. Trying to smooth her hair into something more organized, the robust woman stepped respectfully inside, closing the door behind her. She hurried over to her mistress, unable to hide her anxiousness.

Erini started to speak, then clamped her mouth shut as the feeling of the two of them not being alone threatened to overwhelm her. She glanced quickly around the bedroom.

Galea looked at her in slight confusion. "Is something amiss, my lady?"

"I'm not—" the princess turned to her, intending to calm both Galea's worries and her own—and found herself staring into eyes that no longer saw, but gazed blindly into the emptiness next to her. "Galea?"

The gentle woman did not move. Erini could not even tell if she was breathing.

It had *not* been her imagination and in her weariness she had failed to understand that.

"Greetings to your majesty," a voice uttered indifferently.

Even before her gaze turned on him, she knew it was Shade. He stood near the mirrors, which had turned black and opaque in his presence. Erini idly wondered whether there was something the warlock did not want to see.

Shade slowly strode toward her. His face, though shadowed by the immense hood, was quite distinct this time, a complete change from their accidental meeting. A lock of silver hair hung down across his forehead. Erini shook her head, not believing any of this. *Not now! Not after everything else!*

"I find I have need of you, Princess Erini. Other matters . . . well, you wouldn't understand, I imagine."

She tried to open her mouth to scream for help, not knowing who or what could save her from this, but her lips seemed sewn shut.

"My apologies, but I have more to say and much to do." He reached forward, not for her, Erini noticed, but for Galea. The princess reached out to block him, but her movements were uncoordinated for some reason and she only succeeded in falling over herself. As she tried to rise, Erini caught a glimpse of Shade whispering to the other woman. Galea nodded, still deep in the trance.

Darkhorse! Where was Darkhorse? Managing to come to a kneeling position, the novice sorceress tried a spell, any spell, that would alert someone, preferably the ebony stallion, to her predicament.

"Mustn't do that," Shade's hand was suddenly on her shoulder, though the warlock had been elsewhere a moment before. Galea was nowhere to be seen. Tears of frustration tumbled down her cheeks. She looked up into the cursed warlock's visage and tried to convey her anger with her eyes.

He almost looked sympathetic. His next words even carried a tone of slight remorse with them. "I do not know why I am explaining myself to you. You are my only choice. I have to act now—who can say how long a better choice than you might take to come along? My time is limited and I find I grow more impatient."

Her eyes narrowed as she pictured Darkhorse confronting and defeating him. Shade smiled knowingly, almost as if he could read those harsh thoughts. "Your savior will not notice your absence for some time to come. At present, he is chasing . . . me, you might say. Something to keep him busy." Shade held up the fingers of both hands and counted names off. "The Bedlams sleep. I owe them that much for now. They will sleep for quite some time. Your Melicard has a mighty horde approaching his very doorstep and, counterwise, the Dragon King Silver has an entire city prepared to face him. Poor Drayfitt, my sad benefactor, is dead—an unfortunate accident of his own doing."

There were still several fingers up as the warlock completed his insane recital. Erini studied them closely, still keeping a faint hope alive. Shade looked from her to the raised fingers and then slowly lowered them. "The rest were merely spares, I'm afraid. There's no one else."

He pointed a single finger in her direction and indicated that she should rise. There was no choice in the matter; Erini's body responded without her cooperation. The hooded warlock nodded in satisfaction.

"I could have taken you in a much more violent manner, princess, but I'm trying to be reasonable. You have no idea how calm I've been. I could have leveled this city with your precious Melicard in it. The Dragon King would've been annoyed; he so wants to take Talak in one piece. There's so much I could have done, but things turned out for the best after all, so I suppose there's no use pursuing the subject."

Erini could say nothing, do nothing. Only her eyes allowed her any opinion at all. They spoke volumes, mostly concerning the madness of the creature before her.

Shade frowned and purposely looked away, only to find the blackened mirrors confronting his gaze. Turning back to his captive, he smiled again. It was a different sort of smile, though, one tinged with guilt; an emotion Erini

found it hard to accept that the warlock would feel under the present circumstances.

"You may survive," he added, almost hopefully. "If you do, I'll return you
safe and sound to here—or Gordag-Ai if the drakes succeed here. You have my
oath on that."

She gave him one last glare, telling him what she thought of his promises.

The warlock grew oddly unsettled. "We have to go now."

As Erini struggled futilely to make her body respond, Shade wrapped his
seemingly endless cloak about both of them and pulled her toward him. The
world seemed to warp around them—and then they were elsewhere.

XX

Shade!"

Darkhorse struck the wall of the cellar he had materialized in only a few
seconds before. As with his previous stops, the only trace of his adversary was a
minute trail left behind by the warlock's method of travel. The previous thread
had led him *here*—but then, the last trail before that and the ones before that
had *all* led him along.

That was the truth of the matter, Darkhorse finally admitted to himself. He
had been *led along*. He had fallen for yet another ploy by the warlock, who had
spent each and every lifetime during his curse plotting and planning tricks for
the incarnation yet to come, not to mention the hundreds of enemies he had
gathered over the centuries.

"Damn you!" The shadow steed kicked through the wall. He stepped back,
annoyed and embarrassed. If he was not more careful, he would do the Dragon
King's work for him. How ironic it would be for the inhabitants to discover
that the palace had collapsed due to the efforts of one of its defenders.

After his fourth miss, Darkhorse suspected he was being led astray; suspected it, but could not be certain. There was always the chance that Shade
wanted him to believe he was on a false trail. As he had thought so often in the
past, the only thing predictable about the warlock was his unpredictability. That
convoluted sort of reasoning had forced him to pursue the trail again and again.
This visitation, however, had finally settled it for him. Shade had made a fool
out of the eternal once more.

What is your purpose for all of this, Shade? What plot have you unleashed now?

Was there danger to Melicard or the Princess Erini? The possibility was
too great to ignore. Darkhorse departed the damaged cellar posthaste. In his
imagination, he saw the king and all his soldiers scattered about like so many

toys. Worse yet, he pictured the novice spellcaster, Erini, desperately battling for herself and her betrothed against a foe she could not hope to withstand. It was not that she was weak or that she was a female; it was because the warlock had the experience of the ages to draw upon, whereas she had only a handful of suggestions given to her by Drayfitt and him.

He burst through the portal's other end, landing amidst a conference between Melicard and several officers. A few could not help gasping at the imposing sight. Melicard flinched, but otherwise held his shock back respectably.

"Darkhorse! Where have you been? Dawn is almost upon us! The first rays are already doing battle with the weakening night!"

"Already?" The eternal sought out a window facing the proper direction. Sure enough, there was an aura of light growing steadily upward from the horizon. Had he been occupied *that* long? Either his obsession had finally grown completely out of control, or Shade had added a slight twist to the trail, secretly slowing Darkhorse's time perspective. True, he had also taken quite some time with his search of Quorin's belongings, but that still was not sufficient. It would have been an astounding feat, slowing time, that is, but hardly something beyond the abilities of a Vraad. Darkhorse prayed he was incorrect; if Shade was playing with time, then the entire world was threatened. The Vraad had a tendency to eventually destroy everything they utilized.

Melicard sensed Darkhorse's sinking mood. "What is it? What did you find in Quorin's chambers? Something of great importance?"

Shaking dark thoughts from his mind, the shadow steed finally replied. "There is nothing of value to us that I could discover. Perhaps you will find it different. My sincere recommendation, however, is to either seal or strip those chambers as soon as you can. I, myself, would prefer everything burned—with the fiend bound, gagged, and laid out on top of the pyre!"

"Gods! What *did* you find?"

"That is unimportant to us at the moment! The Princess Erini! Where is she?"

"I sent her to get some rest some time ago. We'll need her if we're to stand off the Dragon King's oncoming host. By the way," Melicard gave him a triumphant smile that somehow stretched across the mask, too, "the gate is ours. It was almost too simple—even more so than retaking the palace. They virtually threw themselves at us and begged for imprisonment rather than face the demons! You have quite a reputation now, Darkhorse."

"One that I would gladly trade for another, I think. Is the princess guarded?"

"I believe so. She will be safe."

Darkhorse shook his head. "I think I would prefer to look in—"

"Your majesty!" An officer clad in the same sort of uniform as Erini's

Captain Iston barged through the heavy doors. He had apparently been running all the way from wherever he had come. "I brought the news myself, in case you had questions!"

"Questions about what, man?" Melicard demanded.

Between gulps of air, the soldier replied, "The lookouts have identified the first signs of the drakes' approach!"

"Already!" Melicard took a deep breath and looked at everyone, even Darkhorse. "Come. I want to see it for myself and I want each and every one of you to give me *any* observations about them as they draw nearer."

Darkhorse hesitated, caught between his fear for his benefactress, the princess, and his concern for Talak. Talak won out, though the steed swore to himself that he would look in on Erini once he had seen whatever there was to see of Silver's horrible army.

Out on one of the highest balconies of the palace, they gathered to watch. One of his aides handed the king a long tube, which Melicard put to his eye. Darkhorse did not have to ask the purpose of the device, which obviously gave the king a better view of the distant reaches. Sorcerers had created similar tools before, though this one had evidently been crafted by hand.

"I see them," Melicard commented at last. "By my father, it looks to be a vast legion! I don't think there's been a drake host this great since perhaps the siege of Penacles!"

While others gazed on or waited for the opportunity, Darkhorse adjusted his own senses, allowing him a view that even the mechanical toys of the king could not match. Melicard was correct; this was a vast host—and at its head rode the Dragon King himself. Oddly, Silver seemed almost apprehensive. Bully and coward though the drake lord was, Darkhorse would have expected him to be in a far more triumphant mood. With such an army behind him and the city gate supposedly ready to welcome him in without a struggle, he should have been confident. Was it just the drake's way, or did he know something?

Surveying the drake warriors who rode beside their master, Darkhorse finally discovered the horrible truth. Seated behind one warrior and looking distinctly distressed was none other than *Mal Quorin*.

"King Melicard!" The eternal returned his senses to normal.

"What now, friend Darkhorse? Do you see something?"

The shadow steed laughed. "Do I *see* something? Your majesty, was it your intention to perhaps draw the drakes unsuspectingly to your gates? Did you hope to fool them into thinking that the traitors still controlled the city?"

From the flushed look on Melicard's face, he had intended something very close to that. Darkhorse was not surprised; it would have been a fairly logical maneuver.

The stallion dipped his head so that he was almost on a level with the mortal. "Your majesty, the plan will fail now! Mal Quorin *rides* with the drakes!"

"Impossible!" Melicard raised the tube to his eye again and tried to see what his ally had. Unfortunately, the device was not up to the task. He threw it to the floor in disgust, where the glass lens on one end cracked from the force. The king did not even notice. "I believe you, Darkhorse, even if I can't see it for myself! How, though? What sort of trick?" He turned to one of his aides. "Alert the gate! Tell them that our plan is known!" To another, he added, "Go to our treacherous counselor's cell! Find out from the guards posted there what happened and why I was not informed!"

"Go easy on the sentries, your highness," Darkhorse commented, somewhat subdued. His mind had been racing and he suspected he knew the secret of Quorin's escape. "They are probably confused and fearful. I think that I may have accidently been the catalyst for the devil's escape." He did not elaborate, intending that for a time when things were more peaceful—if such a rarity were ever to occur.

Melicard nodded, reading the eternal's attitude and knowing Darkhorse was angry toward himself. Fear suddenly raged across the monarch's odd features. Not fear for himself, but for his bride-to-be. "Erini! He might have done some something to her!"

That was doubtful, in Darkhorse's opinion. He suspected now that the box was a last resort saved by Mal Quorin on the off-chance that he had to flee to his master. In opening up the container, the shadow steed had unwittingly unleashed the spell, which apparently had been specifically tied to the imprisoned advisor.

The king would not listen to those around him. If he had not been informed of Quorin's escape, then it followed that he might also have not been informed of any new attempt to kill or kidnap Princess Erini. Darkhorse was on the verge of stating that *he* would investigate, having already desired to do so since first arriving, when a new voice broke through the chaos.

"What's wrong? Darkhorse! Melicard! Are the drakes already at the gate?"

"Erini!" At the sight of his beloved, the king rushed to her and took her in his arms, ignoring the embarrassed looks on the face of his subordinates. The princess held him briefly, but seemed more interested in what was going on that would require everyone's presence here. "I couldn't sleep any more," she commented as she broke away and walked toward the rail of the balcony. "I was worried that something might happen while I was resting."

Melicard, a little at a loss due to the chaos his mind had been struggling with, joined her. "The drakes are out on the horizon. There. Darkhorse says that Quorin is with them."

"Quorin? That's terrible." Erini stared northward, as if trying to see the drake army without the aid of any device or her own sorcery.

Darkhorse snorted. *Terrible?* He would have expected a far more virulent response from the princess, who probably hated Quorin more than anyone else here. Studying her closely, he noted her pale, almost unresponsive features. It was likely that her lackluster response was due in great part to a surge of fatalism concerning the coming day or even simply because she had only slept a short while. Unlike Melicard and his men, who were long used to staying awake for a day or more, she had never had the need to do so. *Would that I could sleep! I would sleep for a year if such was possible!*

But not until Shade has been dealt with, he reminded himself.

Shade. Darkhorse still wondered what purpose the warlock had had in setting him off on the endless and pointless chase. Shade had wanted him occupied. Why?

He realized belatedly that Melicard was speaking to him. "What was that, your majesty?"

"I asked what might be taking your friends so long? We have need of the Bedlams, Darkhorse. I would like to discuss our options with them beforehand—unless they feel they can arrive at the last moment and remove the threat with a wave of their hands." The king's voice was tinged with aggravation. His kingdom's existence was hanging in the balance and two of his greatest allies were among the missing.

Darkhorse, too, began to wonder. Cabe had fallen prey to Shade's machinations earlier. Had the warlock struck twice? "I will go seek them now! There is still time before the Silver Dragon can strike! Will you be safe?"

"I would never leave my kingdom defenseless against a threat like the drakes. I swore that Duke Toma would be the last of his kind to ever enter Talak with his head still attached to his body."

The shadow steed chuckled. "Indeed. You also have your personal sorceress, too." He indicated a somber Erini with a nod of his head. She looked at Darkhorse, smiled briefly, then returned to her dreamlike gazing. "Yes. I will return before long, King Melicard! You have my oath on that!"

"I would prefer your presence instead. We will await your return."

Summoning a portal, Darkhorse leapt from the balcony and vanished into it. The transition was swift this time and he barely noticed his brief passage through the emptiness. In mere breaths, he was exiting the other side, his destination as near to the protective barrier as he could get. This time, he hoped for a simpler visit.

He sent a probe first, hoping that it would engage the attention of one of those he sought. With the Bedlams sorely needed elsewhere, Darkhorse wanted to keep his return as quiet as possible so as to not panic the others who lived here. Unfortunately, he received no response, which, when he thought about it, left him few other choices than to call out.

Trotting closer to where the Manor itself stood, Darkhorse shouted, "Bedlams! Cabe! It is I, Darkhorse! I have need of you!"

He heard confused shouts and the mutters of angry folk. Several anxious minutes went by before someone responded to his summons. It was *not* Cabe. It was an uncrested drake, one of the servitor caste, who finally dared to challenge him.

"What isss it? What do you ssseek?"

"What do I *seek*? Your master and mistress, drake! The warlock Cabe Bedlam and his mate, the Lady of the Amber!"

The drake seemed more interested in the ebony stallion than locating those he served. "I have never ssseen a beassst such as you!"

"I was here earlier! I am Darkhorse!"

"*Darkhorssse!*" The drake hissed in pleasure. "The massster has ssspoken of you! I wasss sorry that I misssed you! I am Ssarekai, one who trains and cares for riding drakes and sssteeds such as your magnificent ssself!"

As much as Darkhorse normally delighted in being appreciated, he had no time for such flattery now. "Your *master*, scaly one! I have need to speak with *him*!"

"Yesss, forgive me! Your appearance here has excited me! Others have been searching for them!"

"Searching? No one knows where they are?"

"They were not in their room."

Ssarekai would have said more, but a human female materialized through the trees and rushed to his side. Glancing at Darkhorse with more than a little fear, she whispered to the drake. It was an odd sight. Though humans and drakes intermingled in some places, such as Irillian, there was generally a sense of separation even when they spoke to one another. Here, on the other hand, the woman stood somewhat behind Ssarekai, as if she depended on him for protection from *Darkhorse*.

Curious things are being done here, the shadow steed thought wryly.

The drake looked upset. His hissing became more evident and his blunted, nearly human tongue darted in and out every now and then as he spoke. "Great Darkhorse, sssomething is amisssss! No one can find the massster and mistress! Someone sssays—"

He did not hear what the drake had to say next, for another voice intruded, this one threatening to tear his mind apart, so intensely did it strike him. Ssarekai stepped back, his next words forgotten. Behind him, the female human tried to make herself as small as possible.

Darkhorse!

That was all. His name. His name echoing again and again. Shaking his head, he succeeded in clearing the echoes from his mind, but not from his thoughts.

"Great Darkhorse?" Ssarekai tentatively called.

The eternal paid him no mind. *Erini!* She was calling for his help! The Dragon King must have struck somehow!

His task here forgotten, the eternal summoned forth a new portal. Had the drakes waited until *he* was gone before beginning some insidious assault? What?

"Great One?" the drake Ssarekai called again, this time more urgently. His voice went unheeded.

"STAND FAST! THOSE who would touch the friends of Darkhorse must be willing to pay in full for their misdeeds!"

The fearsome statements were out of his mouth before his eyes acknowledged the obvious fact that *no one* standing within sight appeared to be under attack by so much as a flea. Nothing seemed to be happening at all, save that Darkhorse once again found himself facing a sea of startled looks from every pair of eyes in the room. It was something he was becoming very annoyed about. The stallion was beginning to feel as if *he* were the intruder, not Shade or the Silver Dragon.

Scanning those around him, Darkhorse spotted Erini. She was staring at him in mild surprise. Confused, the shadow steed turned away from her gaze and focused on Melicard. The king flashed an uncertain smile in his direction.

"While we—appreciate—the sentiment, Darkhorse, I think the time for theatrics is long past."

Something is dreadfully wrong here! Had it been possible, his face would have turned crimson. "I received a desperate summons for help—from the Princess Erini!"

Melicard looked at his future queen. "Erini?"

The princess shook her head silently. She seemed almost disinterested.

The king turned back to the imposing figure before him and said, "Nothing has happened since you departed a moment ago save that the drakes have moved a little closer and we still await your friends, the Lord and Lady Bedlam. When do they arrive? I would rather not put my faith entirely in my own tricks, not if there are two master spellcasters available."

"I—I cannot say when they will arrive or if they even *ever* will. There was no sign of them. Their own people cannot find them!"

"Cannot find them?"

"I fear Shade has struck again!" Darkhorse could not help looking skyward. "I rue that this time should have ever come! He was my friend during many an adventure, but he has also been my sworn foe in times past! This day, however, washes away all the good that he has ever performed! If Cabe and his mate have suffered because of the warlock . . ." Darkhorse could not finish, unable to find a punishment strong enough to mete out.

The cry had seemed so *real*. He studied the princess, who idly stood by, waiting for something to happen. Why was she so indifferent now? Even with the lack of true sleep, she was not acting as he would have imagined her to act. The Erini he had met would have continued pushing until unconsciousness took her. This one seemed to hardly care.

There was one other thing that disturbed him—or perhaps it was the *absence* of something.

Several men came marching into the chamber, Captain Iston in their lead. A gasp escaped Erini and she took a tentative step forward before catching herself and settling back into her look of indifference. Darkhorse's ice-blue eyes narrowed.

Iston saluted. "My men are ready when you give the signal, your majesty."

Darkhorse listened to the officer's words, but his eyes remained fixed on the princess. There was a look of longing growing in her eyes that had nothing to do with Melicard. Her attention appeared to be focused on the captain.

He knew that the princess was a woman of passions, but the shadow steed knew that her love could have never turned so easily. Erini had been prepared to give her life several times over for the sake of her betrothed. This Erini acted as if she had never cared at all.

This Erini?

Forgetting Melicard and the others, he trotted toward the princess. She could not help turning to him, so impressive a sight he was, especially moving toward her with such evident purpose. Strangely, there was a level of fear noticeable in her eyes that also did not match the Erini he had come to know well, even despite what little time they had spent together.

"Your majesty is not looking well," he rumbled.

"A lack of sleep," she murmured. It was evident that the woman before him did not want him so near.

"How is your concentration? Will you be able to aid in the cause?"

"I hope so." Her tone suggested otherwise.

Darkhorse fixed his glittering eyes on hers. Erini tried to struggle, but her will was surprisingly weak and she quickly succumbed.

"I know *now* what so disturbed me about you! I know now that you could not have summoned my aid!"

Behind him, Melicard moved quickly to stand beside his bride-to-be. He faced Darkhorse with blood in his good eye.

"What *are* you doing to her? What in the name of the Tybers are you doing?"

"Resolving my own uncertainties about a few things—and cursing myself anew for missing the obvious!" Darkhorse drew Erini toward him, repelling Melicard at the same time. While the king struggled in vain and his men watched in stunned confusion, the shadow steed probed the human before him. He was not surprised at the results.

"This is *not* your future bride, King Melicard! This woman has no sorcerous ability whatsoever! She who stands before you, though she looks like the Princess Erini, is but a poor creature caught in a spell whose origins can only derive from that master of mayhem, Shade!"

Melicard's jaw dropped. "Not Erini?"

"No, *not* the princess! I should have noticed instantly that she projected no sorcerous presence! Princess Erini did not have the skill yet to mask that presence, at least not so completely!"

The false Erini was struggling with the spell that held her. A spellcaster she might not have been, but whoever—and that was likely to be Shade—had ensorcelled her had shrouded her in a few defensive spells. Darkhorse, though, strengthened by his own fury, tore away each of them, until only the illusion remained. While everyone waited—Melicard shaking—the shadow steed removed that last spell, revealing a shorter, slightly stout woman.

"Galea!" Captain Iston surged forth, trying to reach the woman. Darkhorse nodded imperceptibly. The female's deepest emotions had forced themselves to the surface the moment the officer had entered the room. Only strong love or hate was capable of that and Darkhorse knew enough to tell which was which. He released the confused Galea, who turned to her soldier and buried herself in his arms. A quick glance into her thoughts had already revealed that she knew nothing.

"Erini! Where's Erini?" Melicard demanded of him.

"I do not know, your majesty! When the summons reached me, I paid its point of origin no attention, assuming that since little time had passed, she must be in the palace with you!" The ebony stallion laughed madly, mocking his own stupidity and carelessness. "Every turn! Every direction! He trips me each time and I continue to take the falls!"

The king's split visage became a grim mask. Staring at some point in space, he calmly and quietly commanded, "Find her, Child of the Void. Find my queen and save her. I don't care what the cost might be. Start now."

"Now?" Darkhorse studied the human incredulously. "I cannot search for her now, though a part of me screams to do just that! Talak is endangered and the life of one being cannot outweigh the fate of an entire kingdom!"

"I have no need of you. We *will* hold. We will hold until the end of everything, if necessary. Go! I refuse your help! Will *that* free you of your obligation?"

The shadow steed stamped a hoof against the marble floor. He knew what the king was doing and liked it not at all. All of Talak! "King Melicard . . . I cannot do this—"

"Get out of my sight, then, *demon!* I want nothing of you if you will not do this for me!"

Melicard's subordinates were finding everything else to do other than stare at their ranting monarch. Darkhorse knew that the king's ravings were only an act. An act of love.

Sighing, Melicard visibly pulled himself together. "We will still be here when you return. As I have said, Talak has long been prepared for such an invasion—even if most of my forces are scattered elsewhere."

They would be arguing until the Silver Dragon himself burst through the chamber doors, Darkhorse finally realized. There was no changing the king's mind. The eternal knew that accepting the human's decision was not the correct thing to do, but it was too close to his own desires for him to fight it. He felt he owed much to Erini for releasing him—and much more because there was a quality about her that he had found in so few others, making it all the more admirable. There was no one name for it and he did not care to think of one. What mattered was the princess.

"Very well," he finally replied, his words as close to a whisper as he could manage.

The look he received from Melicard was a mixture of gratitude and relief.

"I do not even know where to look." That was somewhat of a lie. Darkhorse did know where to look; the only trouble was that there were *too* many places and certainly not enough time.

"You do what you can." With that final statement, the king turned away, momentarily unable to continue.

Deciding silence was more appropriate than any response he could give, the shadow steed departed immediately—for where, he could not say.

WITH THE IMPOSING presence of Darkhorse gone, Melicard was slowly able to get his thoughts under control. He had sworn that he would make Talak hold, and hold it would. The defenses had never been tested in actual combat, but he tried not to think about that. Ironically, Melicard no longer thought about the potential for destruction. That hundreds of the cursed drakes would die meant little to him. His own people would die as well and the kingdom might fall.

"Captain Iston!" He had come to rely heavily on the foreigner, impressed as he was with the man's loyalty and experience. If they somehow survived, he would offer the soldier a permanent position on his staff—if Iston still wanted to remain in Talak. Should Darkhorse *fail*—and the horrid thought refused to die—the complement from Gordag-Ai would likely return to their homeland, having no further ties with his own kingdom.

"Your majesty?" The officer reluctantly abandoned his woman's side. Melicard felt a twinge within.

"You have your orders. I must ask that you now follow them."

"Yes, your majesty."

As an afterthought, the king added, "You may say your farewells before you depart."

"Thank you." Iston saluted, took Galea's hand, and led her away.

Melicard turned to the others. Several already had their orders and these he dismissed immediately. The rest waited, somewhat reassured now that their liege had taken control again.

The king surveyed the horizon. Was it his imagination or was the Dragon King's host moving more slowly? He grimaced. Wishful thinking, no doubt.

"We have," he finally began, "only a few hours before havoc reigns. The others know their duties. What I want from each of you are suggestions—or comments on anything I've forgotten about. I want anything that will buy us time." He also wished he had at least one spellcaster. Thanks to the talismans he had kept, despite his own dislike for them since his disfigurement and what little Drayfitt—poor *Drayfitt*—had succeeded in accomplishing, the king had assumed his palace was fairly safe from the invasions of spell-throwing drakes and such. Now, however, he was not so certain. Darkhorse's ability to come and go as he pleased did not bother him. Shade's did, but here was a warlock with the knowledge of millennia. What bothered him was that an agent of the Silver Dragon had worked actively underneath his very nose and there was no doubt that Quorin had been in contact with his true master several times. It would take only one breach in those sorcerous defenses . . .

"My lord!" A guard stood by the doorway, awaiting permission to enter.

"Yes, what is it?" Were there not enough troubles?

"There is a drake demanding entrance to the city!"

"A drake?" How had they missed that? No doubt an emissary from the Silver Dragon, here to issue the demands of his lord. Best to kill him . . . no. Best to send him back with a message! "Tell the reptile that his master will never have this city and that I have said his head will hang alongside the banners when we have crushed gaggle of monstrosities!"

"My lord—"

The king knew it was emotion speaking, not thought, but he hardly cared.

The *audacity* of his foe angered him. "You heard me! Go!"

The sentry bowed low, but did not move. He had something he felt *had* to be said, regardless of the king's anger. Melicard nodded permission.

"The drake is not at the northern gate, my lord, and he does not appear to be of the clan Silver."

"No?"

"He claims to have ridden from south."

South? "The Dagora Forest?"

"That was what he said."

Melicard did not know whether to laugh or curse. The Green Dragon had sent an emissary, but, considering that Talak and the monarch of the Dagora Forest had clashed in the past, the question was—was he here as an *ally* or a new *foe?*

There was only one way to find out.

XXI

ERINI WAS FRIGHTENED, though she tried as best she could not to show it. She was frightened of many things, but what frightened the princess most was the curious behavior of her captor.

Despite his claims to the contrary, she doubted that Shade's mind was as complete as he thought it to be. His personality seemed fluid to her, changing from one extreme to another. So close to what he believed would be his triumph, Shade was beginning to recall more and more about his tragic failure—and he insisted on sharing each detail with her, as if trying to purge himself of the memories.

"When men came back to this land," he was telling her companionably, "and settled, bowing for a time to the will of the first Dragon Kings, I moved back among them. Weaklings! Their ancestors had given in to this world, taking up its magic instead of strengthening their own! There were a few who could do outstanding things with that magic, though, and from them I learned much of what I had dared not attempt for fear of losing myself as my counterparts had."

Erini, held by his spells in a standing position with her arms outstretched—as if challenging the world, she thought bitterly—did not understand half of what he said. He was talking for himself. As long as it kept her from the fate he had planned, Erini did not object.

"I took many names and many guises in those days, learning what I could. Several times, I renewed my lifespan. Someday, though, I knew that *those* spells would fail me. I would die and the Vraad would pass from this world forever, a world ours by *right*." He smiled coldly. "There were a few others who survived, in a sense, but they had also given themselves over to this world's nature, becoming less Vraad and more—more—"

Shade rose, seeming to forget his tale completely. It was not the first time he had changed so abruptly. Shade stretched out one arm and caused the blue ball of light floating high above them to increase in intensity. The warlock's stronghold, little more than shadow prior to this, was revealed to his captive for the first time. Erini was properly awed.

Erini had never seen the throne room of the drake emperor, so it was understandable that she would miss the incredible similarity between that place and this. Grand effigies of people and creatures long dead or vanished lined the walls on each side. Some were so real as to force the princess to look elsewhere, for fear one of them would start staring back at her. Erini was brave, but, even with her limited experience in magic, she could sense the cold presence within each one. These things *were* alive, although hardly in the sense that most people thought of as living. In some ways, they almost reminded her of Darkhorse, though she hated even considering such a thought.

"My cache. Plundered by those scaly wretches above. This was where I formulated my spell and stored all my notes and special—toys. A Vraad habit. Though I performed my spells among humans and lived in human communities, it was here, in this place, that I first conceived of my notion. It was here that I found and began to travel the path of immortality and *true* power such as even the Vraad had never dreamed."

As he spoke, Shade reached into his cloak and removed a rather ordinary-looking tripod. The care with which he handled it told Erini it was anything but ordinary. She watched in helpless frustration as the warlock placed it at her feet.

"The concept came to me early on, but the doing of it escaped me for centuries. I feared I was lost. To understand what I needed, I would have to give myself. Become changed by this world—have I said that already?" Shade looked up from what he was doing, uncertain. There was a slight trace of fear in his tone, as if he were finally realizing that his mind was not as it should be.

While he puzzled over his own question, Erini continued her own struggle. Though she could not move, her mind was still free. Shade needed her mind free yet malleable. The princess desperately tried to capitalize on that, continually summoning up whatever strength she could find within herself and sending out a sorcerous cry for aid that she hoped Darkhorse would detect. It was a slim, almost mad hope, but it was all she had. She lacked the skill and experience she needed to break free of her physical predicament. The warlock knew too many tricks.

"It won't even hurt—not much, that is," Shade suddenly told her, coming within a hand's width of her face. She tried to close her eyes, but his spell prevented that. Instead, she was forced to stare into his glimmering, seemingly multifaceted orbs. There were those who said that the eyes were the mirror of the soul, and what there was of Shade was more reflection than substance. More than life, but also less.

He was no longer human and likely had not been since the very day that he had fallen victim to his own obsessive desires.

His hand came up before her eyes, his voice was soothing, yet with that undercurrent of anxiety and fear. "Listen to me now. I'm going to begin. I don't need your cooperation, but I ask it. Give me what I want and I'll see what I can do for you afterward. You will give it to me regardless of your desires, but the transition will be easier on both of us if you do your part willingly."

Frozen as she was, Erini could only respond with her eyes, which she did promptly. Shade backed away, his face initially the picture of remorse, then, in an abrupt change, arrogant and lordly. "Very well, then. I offered for your sake, really. Suffer if you like. Here is what you will do for me."

The warlock reached up and touched her forehead. Erini's mind was suddenly filled with images and instructions. She found herself unable to continue her desperate summons under such circumstances and finally gave in. Her only consolation was the thin hope that something in the shadowy warlock's instructions might give her an idea.

Erini's task, as he had defined it, was to be the vessel in which two radically different forms of sorcery would be meshed together. Unlike the tales the princess had heard as a child, it was not the powers of darkness and light that Shade had sought to master. It was the vestiges of a power that lingered from whatever world the Vraad had originated from and this world's own strength. The images both horrified and fascinated her.

"We will begin *now*." Wrapping himself deep within his cloak, Shade leaned forward and focused his gaze on the tripod.

Though she could see little, Erini felt everything. She felt the power that she summoned forth fill the chamber—*she* summoned forth? No, it only appeared that way. From the instructions that the warlock had implanted in her mind, she understood that he was utilizing the tripod in order to draw energy through *her*. To draw upon so much power himself would be to risk the success of his plan. He had to be free to control the situation, and without her that would have been impossible.

Erini knew that there must be defenses she could summon, things that would disrupt his spell permanently, but her mind was not skilled enough to cope with the influx of power and still concentrate on shielding herself. The princess now saw why Shade desired an untrained and inexperienced spellcaster with high potential. Even Drayfitt's mind would have been too closed for Shade to have trusted the outcome of his experiment. Erini was like a child, uncertain of what her limitations were; an open book on which Shade could write what he pleased.

"You feel the power flowing into your soul." A statement, not a question. "Hold it there. Let it gather."

She did as he bid her, unable to do anything else. It was frustrating to feel so strong and yet be so helpless. The strength of the world seemed to flow into her. For the first time, Erini saw the world in terms of the lines and fields of energy that many spellcasters did. Yet, the spectrum remained there as well. The two were one. It was impossible to tell if one had resulted because of the other or if they had both sprung into existence simultaneously. There was so much potential here that even the greatest sorcerers of legend had probably never known the like. There was power enough here to make one almost a god—

—and this was only a *part* of what Shade desired. Shade, not her. She was a vessel, the princess reminded herself, for all the power that she contained was for her captor, not herself.

"The flow will continue slowly. You must guide its intensity, make certain it does not overwhelm you—and be prepared to accept the next offering."

It was too much! Erini panicked. How could she hope to contain so much energy, so much pure power? Erini struggled to assert her mind. *Darkhorse! If only I could summon him!*

Erini?

It was brief and lost to her completely after that single word, after the calling of her name, but she knew that she *had* touched the eternal's thoughts. Her mind filled with hope.

A cold, loathsome essence entered Erini just as she sought Darkhorse again, caressing her soul as if tasting a treat. Caught unaware, the princess wanted to scream and scream and *scream*, but Shade's earlier spell prevented such a release of her horror at the unthinkable invasion. The world around her shrank away, as if she were looking at it from above. The warlock looked into her eyes, curiosity and anticipation at the forefront. She wanted to ram him through the earth, peel away every layer of skin while he writhed in agony—*anything*—as long as it would free her mind from the unspeakable presence seeking to become a part of her.

"Accept it, princess. You have no choice."

She didn't. Erini wanted to destroy, to tear her *own* body apart and remove the cancerous thing from her soul. Shade's commands prevented all but the weakest resistance. This was the essence of the power that the warlock's kind had utilized in that nameless hell they had been—forced?—to leave. It was alien to the Dragonrealm, following different, twisted laws of nature that should not—could not—exist here.

There is a way around that.

The thought was not her own, but rather one of Shade's imprinted instructions, rising forth, now that its task was at hand. It felt like something almost alive, as if it had been imbued with a tiny piece of the Vraad's being.

There are points of binding, places where the two realities may be joined. You have only to look.

Joined. They had to be joined. Erini saw that now. It was the only possible way to keep herself from suffering a similar fate to that which Shade had suffered, if not something worse. Either force within her was capable of scattering her body and mind beyond the reaches of forever. If she was to have any chance to survive, she would have to do as her captor's instructions indicated.

Of course you do, the piece of Shade reminded her. Erini wondered if it was her own mind that made it seem so *much* alive and, if so, was she going mad?

You have a task. Do it.

That was the only truth she did have at the moment. With growing disgust, she accepted the foreign sorcery completely into her being. In her imagination, it seemed to squirm like a worm trying to burrow deeper. Erini almost rejected it then, but knew that, by doing so, she would condemn herself. What sort of world had the Vraad come from, and how could they possibly be the ancestors of the humans alive today? There were hints of those answers now and then, vague, ghostlike images that danced around her, almost distracting her from the horrid task. None of them were distinct and Erini felt some relief at that. Despite her wonder, these were things she actually had little desire to learn about. They all bore the same stench as the sorcery.

See the points. Take them and marry them to their counterparts. Here. Here. Here.

This part of her task seemed almost laughingly simple now, though she knew that here was where Shade had originally begun his downward spiral to damnation. Erini could not see why. The points her mind saw met willingly with one another. Perhaps it was, as the warlock had indicated, only because she was the vessel—or rather the catalyst—and not the final recipient of the spell's outcome. She had only one purpose, not several as he had had.

While a portion of her consciousness worked automatically, having no choice to do otherwise, Erini found a change occurring throughout her mind, throughout her very *soul.* The princess could no more deny the transformation than she could her earlier acceptance of the alien sorcery. After a few seconds—perhaps minutes or even *hours,* she could not say—Erini even began to *welcome* the change. Her perspective grew and grew and her comprehension of what her world was truly like expanded until Erini felt she *was* the Dragonrealm, the vast eastern continent, the smaller southern continents, the islands, the seas . . . everything.

Shade's spell became a secondary thing to her, something that had to be done but that did not require more than a trace of her concentration. All events, all people, became known to her. Unconsciously, Erini focused on Talak and her betrothed.

It was there before her gaze, a thought came to life. The drakes were within striking range of the city. The princess gained some perspective on how much time had passed, for the sun was already high and it appeared as if the first blows had already fallen. There were dead, drakes on the landscape between the Dragon King's host and the city walls, and settlements unfortunate enough to have sprung up near the northern wall were little more than splintered wood and scattered articles. The inhabitants, she remembered, had been ordered in at some point before her kidnapping. There was also damage to the city itself. *An aerial assault,* some corner of her mind told her. It sounded astonishingly like her grandfather, general-consort to her grandmother, the queen at that time. He had been dead for almost seven years. She studied the dragons. Something pierced their hearts. *Something magic.*

Melicard. Her view did not alter, for she saw all things at once, but the image of the king somehow was foremost among them. He was in the throne room, giving orders, caught up in the battle. A few of his men were injured and there was a sticky, dark fluid covering one of the walls. Erini belatedly noticed the sky where the ceiling had once been. A drake had nearly broken through *all* of their defenses. Somehow, though, the magical defenses of Talak—she could not recall if she had ever known about them prior to this—had been restored and, in fact, improved. The Dragon King would find Talak a costly victory.

Victory. It was still within the drake lord's grasp. At the very least, Talak would be in shambles and most of its population would be dead. Another Mito Pica.

The two magics were nearly one now. Erini's perspective altered again, this time in a puzzling manner. A bit worrisome, too, though that emotion was becoming less and less a part of her. The princess, despite the understanding of her world that she had gained earlier, could not fathom what was happening now. In some ways, it reminded her of how the world looked when the spectrum was visible to her. Like one image superimposed upon another. It was an apt comparison, she decided, but hardly one that explained *what* was overlaying the Dragonrealm and the rest like a shroud.

There were mountains where mountains should not have been. There were seas and rivers where only dry sand or lush forests existed now. Where Talak stood, another city, smaller in width yet stretching far higher into the heavens, also rose, ziggurats of Melicard's kingdom fighting for supremacy with odd, twisted towers that ended in spearlike points. It was and was not the same world.

Though she felt life on this world, something warned her not to seek it out. Instead, she turned her inner gaze to the most fascinating and most chilling sight visible. The heavens themselves. The beautiful blue of her world had been replaced by a green of dark intensity. Not a green such as a leaf might be colored, however, but a green that reminded Erini of nothing more than rot. Decay. A world that was festering and had *been* festering for over thousands and thousands of years.

The world which Shade and the Vraad had abandoned for this one. A world they had *made* into this putrefying abomination.

This was the potential that Shade represented.

Without willing it, her view turned to the warlock himself. He knelt before her, enraptured by the progress of his spell, almost ready to accept the fruits of her forced labor. To her shock, she saw things about him she doubted even *he* had ever known. Not just his myriad incarnations, but what the distorted spell had done to his essence over the millennia. Shade was far from whole, far from untouched by the world to which his people had fled. He was possibly in a worse condition than he had been during the time of his previous incarnations—and he refused to see that.

She was astounded at his latent abilities. He had held back throughout all of this, the princess realized. In the hooded warlock was the potential to devastate a region larger than the Tyber Mountains themselves. Shade had hinted at the godlike powers of his kind, but the truth was far more overwhelming. It had only been his desire to complete his lifelong goal that had checked a madness that might have seen the Dragonrealm in complete ruins in less than a week. That and a tiny, nagging doubt—*guilt*, she correct herself—about what he was doing. There was more good in Shade than he realized. There had been more in the original, too. His own memories were playing him false.

This is a new form of incarnation, Erini concluded. *Shade has not escaped his previous failure; he has become even more mired in it than before.*

What would happen when his power increased a hundredfold?

Erini found she was growing beyond the point of caring. Her perceptions continued to expand. Soon, she would no longer be a part of her world, not in the true sense. This was the fate that Shade had suffered, but Erini would not be returning in any form. Shade's variation on his original work would guarantee that. He would gain command of the powers he sought, but lose his vessel in the prospect.

What remained of Erini sought to fight that fate, but she lacked any weapon with which to do it. She did not have the concentration to strike back with her own insignificant talent—and what good would it have done, anyway? Shade would have dismissed any assault on a magical level with as much effort as what he needed to breathe.

Erini felt herself beginning to fragment. Her task was almost complete, but she would never see the outcome. The strain was too much.

She thought of Melicard, who would have no one to keep him from falling into the same darkness that he had lived within before her coming. His image, commanding his aides in the defense of Talak, flickered before Erini. She thought of her parents, who would never know what fate had befallen their daughter. Melicard seemed to fade as the king and queen of Gordag-Ai took precedence. Lastly, Erini thought of Darkhorse, a being she had known only for a short time, but with whom she felt a rapport, a bond.

Erini?

The image of Darkhorse strengthened. He stood, confused, in an area she recognized from its ungodly bleakness as the Northern Wastes. The cold and snow did not bother him in the least. Darkhorse remained where he was, his head cocked to one side, almost as if he were listening to-something.

Erini!

Had he sensed her? The novice sorceress was no longer certain she cared. Still, because of their bond, she acknowledged her presence to him.

Now he stood ready, seeking a direction in which to run. *Erini! Where are you?*

Where was she? "Everywhere" seemed the most appropriate response, but she knew that was not what the shadow steed meant. He was searching for her physical form.

A wave of urgency washed across her consciousness. Erini could not be certain whether it was a stray emotion of her own or one of Darkhorse's, relayed somehow by their contact. Whichever was the case, she acted upon that urgency and allowed him to see, to experience, where she was.

The eternal grew very grim and shot back, *I know where your are! Do not lose yourself! Keep a hold on your existence, Erini!*

She lost track of him, then, for, to obey his instructions, on top of all else, the princess was forced to concentrate her remaining will on maintaining her essence. She was uncertain as to how long she could do this, for the intensity of the warlock's spell was becoming more and more difficult to withstand. It would not be long, regardless of her efforts.

Erini wondered whether Darkhorse would find her in time—and whether even *he* now stood a chance against the powers of Shade.

In that part of her that was puppet to the warlock, the final binding was at last completed.

* * *

IN THE CHAMBER, below the watchful eyes of the effigies, a triumphant Shade, hood pulled low over his face, reached forth with those abilities at his command and prepared to at last accept what he felt was his due. The faces of Vraad he had known, most of them clan, others friends or, more often, foes, drifted in and out of his memories. He would have life eternal now, and power to make even those who watched over the Dragonrealm and the other lands, those would-be gods, acknowledge his mastery.

He would have a world to play with. No Vraad had ever had an *entire* world to play with.

Most of all, he would not *die*. The Vraad would not become a shadow of the past.

A presence oh so familiar to him forced the sorcerer from his dreams. He felt a barrier form about the princess.

"The last false trail has been removed, Shade! Come! Turn around and greet your old friend! Have you no words for Darkhorse—words that I may have them etch upon your crypt?"

The hooded warlock turned slowly toward his ancient adversary, his friend of old. "You took long enough getting here."

Darkhorse stepped back anxiously, but not because he was frightened by the Vraad's confident words. Of course, Shade had known the shadow steed would be coming. He would have expected nothing else. No, what disturbed Darkhorse was something that Shade from his angle, could not see—and, as a matter of fact, neither could the stallion.

Nothing met his gaze from beneath the deep hood save a blur that *might* have been a face.

XXII

THE DRAGON KING Silver hissed bitterly as he watched Talak fend off another assault. Somehow, the crippled vermin that fancied himself a ruler had overcome all obstacles placed before him, save the loss of much of his army. The drake lord glanced briefly to his right, where his human agent stood surveying the same scene with emotions that mirrored the Dragon King's own. He had no idea why he was letting the creature Quorin live, save that he had a desire to prove to him, to prove to *all* of them, that he would take Talak if it cost every possible weapon and life at his command.

Shade was next. The alliance had been a fallacy, one the drake lord had thought he needed during a desperate moment and one that neither had followed from the first. The Silver Dragon wondered if the warlock knew yet that his curse had not been lifted. That had been obvious to him, but the arrogant warm-blood had been certain he was whole once more. The drake laughed, making those around him eye him discreetly while they tried to discern what it was their master found amusing at a time such as this.

Shade had taken his information from the mind of the sorcerer Drayfitt, knowing that the elderly spellcaster had studied the warlock's book thoroughly. Unfortunately for Shade, Drayfitt had never seen some of the final notes. Though the drake lord had had to wait until the sorcerer's translations of the other pages were passed on to him, that wait had been worthwhile. They had provided the dragon king with the basis of translating the remaining sheets, which were where he had successfully guessed the most valuable information had been written down. The pages contained clues to the foundation of Vraad sorcery and, by sheer coincidence, integral comments that the warlock had written about his original theories. Somewhere along the way, those notes had been forgotten by Shade. The Dragon King had ensured that they would remain forgotten until *he* could find some use for them.

Yes, Shade would be next . . . if there was anything left of him for the drakes to kill.

The Dragon King straightened and gave a signal to one of his dukes, a warrior whose clutch he himself had fathered. Most of those around him were his offspring, though none bore the markings of succession. They could never be heirs: All they could be were warriors who gave their lives for him—as they might do now.

The signal was what the main host had waited for. The Silver Dragon King knew what defenses were weakest now. He would throw everything he had at them. He had wanted Talak in one piece. A prize. Now, the drake lord did not care if one stone remained standing, even if it took the last of his force.

One of his offspring had argued that such an assault was madness, that it would only cost lives. His carcass was even now being digested by the Dragon King's riding beast. No one else had dared speak out and no one else would ever dare hint that he was an incompetent ruler, that he had only thrived in the shadow of his more powerful brother, the Dragon Gold.

No one else would dare call him a coward.

There was no reasoning behind the last, but none was needed. A Dragon King was answerable to no one save himself.

They moved on Talak.

A BLUR.

The passage through the barriers between the Void and reality of the

Dragonrealm had *not* reversed the spell Shade had unleashed. It had, evidently, altered it in such a way that there was no telling what would happen next. The period of sanity had been little more than a time of dormancy while the next phase of the warlock's "disease" built up. From his manner, Darkhorse knew that his companion of old did not even realize what had happened. Shade still believed he was back to where he had started, that he was mortal, but whole.

What would this new spell do to him, then?

Erini, locked frozen in the final stage of Shade's gambit, seemed to fade just a bit. Darkhorse turned his gaze back and forth, his fear for Erini, but his fury for the warlock. The female had little time remaining to her. Darkhorse's quick action had bought her a delay, but how long that delay would be was questionable. He was forced to expend energy at a growing rate merely to keep the forces gathered within her in check. The ghostly steed had great doubts as to his ability to face Shade and still maintain that balance. He knew that, by rights, his first and foremost duty was to stop Shade at all costs . . . but that cost would include his benefactress.

Barely more than two or three breaths had passed since his arrival. Seeking to borrow time, he slowly replied to the warlock's initial statement, "You expected me."

"There was nothing planned that did not foresee your eventual success at tracking me down," the faceless figure returned. Shade seemed entirely too much at ease. "Almost everything I have done was merely to maintain your curiosity and stubbornness until our final meeting."

That caused Darkhorse to laugh. "There are few with the audacity to seek an audience with me—and you are foremost among them, my former friend and current nemesis!"

"That's because I have nothing more to fear from you, eternal—*Eternal!*" Shade might have smiled; it was truly impossible to say. Watching him, Darkhorse actually pitied the warlock. To have come so close to escaping his endless curse . . . "I am one with you now, Child of the Void! I am *immortal.* I have succeeded *at last.*"

"Not yet, Vraad. The key is in the lock, but it has not yet turned."

Shade said nothing, but Darkhorse suddenly became certain that the warlock *did* wear a smile.

A bitter-tasting wind swept through the chamber, so swiftly birthed that it was near tornado proportions before Darkhorse could even acknowledge its existence. If Shade had created it to destroy him, it was a feeble attempt. Formed in a place between chaos and order, such a wind was little more than a breeze to him and, protected by the shadow steed's power, it did not even touch the helpless Erini.

What it *was* doing, however, was tearing the chamber—even the *mountain* under which the cavern lay—to fragments that flew madly into the air, colliding with one another and flying off into a darkness that was not night. Darkhorse found his footing growing unstable and his bond with Erini being stretched to its utmost. It was too late to stop whatever spell Shade—and it could only be the warlock's doing—had cast. The eternal could only shield himself and the princess and wait for the storm to pass. If it would.

As the last of the cavern walls tore free from the earth and vanished, a new land formed around the three. A land that seemed out of sync with reality. Its colors were haphazard, clashing, and the landscape was twisted and dying. The sky was an odd shade of green, much like mold or something dead left too long to decay on its own.

Throughout all of this, Shade stood where he was, seemingly passive. As the wind died down, to be replaced by a stale, sulfurous stench, the warlock spoke one word ever so softly. In the still of this ugly, decrepit land, he might have been shouting, for Darkhorse heard that word all too clearly.

"Nimth."

A single word that spoke volumes. It told Darkhorse where he was. It told him what sort of power Shade must have had to break a barrier that had remained unbroken since the Vraads' escape from their tortured world, Nimth. It told him something of Shade that he had failed to see upon his arrival.

The warlock had moved more quickly than the eternal had guessed. He had *already* claimed his due from the princess by the time Darkhorse had thrown up the protective shield around her.

Darkhorse had *failed*.

"I restore the balance," Shade abruptly whispered. Again, his voice carried as if he had shouted with all his might.

They were once more in the cavernous chamber in which the warlock had performed his experiment. This time, the transfer was immediate. Shade evidently assumed that there was no reason for further theatrics.

The message behind the sudden return to the Dragonrealm was not lost upon the shadow steed. Shade was telling him through actions that there were deeds within his power that stretched even beyond the laws of nature, beyond the rule of reality.

In the midst of mulling over those thoughts—a period which the warlock was apparently magnanimously willing to grant to his ancient comrade—one realization raised itself above all else and made the huge stallion laugh mockingly.

Shade, who would not have been able to appreciate the humor had he understood what it was that Darkhorse laughed at, lost his calm demeanor. Though his expression was lost to all but himself, his change in stance was message enough. Darkhorse quieted, knowing he had touched the greatest weakness of his adversary and knowing that his chances of capitalizing on that weakness were minimal at best. Better to try and create a friendly peace between the Silver Dragon and King Melicard.

Tiny whips of controlled energy darted from the spellcaster's arms and struck the stallion like a thousand accurate shafts released by master archers. With each blow, Darkhorse felt a little of his essence fade. He repelled what he could, sending a few back at their creator, but there were too many and they continued to come. There was one certain way he knew that would rid him of the deadly rain, but it would require releasing Erini to her fate and Darkhorse refused to do that. It did not escape him that his death would be followed almost immediately by her own, regardless. Only an ever-increasing output of his own power kept her from being scattered throughout all. Soon, he would have none left to defend and heal himself.

The last of the wriggling missiles faded before they touched the shadow steed. Shade seemed to regain control of himself. His tone was near apologetic. "I was trying to show you what I am capable of, Darkhorse. I am beyond even you now. It would be pointless to pursue your death—and it would be *your* death, not mine."

"You have only succeeded in revealing to me how much I dare not allow you to escape me."

"Your efforts go beyond the point of futility now. I could exile you to a place that would make the Void seem a paradise. I could compact you into a tiny sphere and drop you into the deepest sea." Shade's voice was almost pleading, as if he truly did not want to continue this confrontation. "I could do so much more, but there is no point to it, anymore. I'm willing to forget our past differences."

Darkhorse met his threats and condescending words with disdain. "I think it might be a bit difficult to forget our past *differences*, considering how they have affected so many. Exile me and I will find my way back. Seal me up and I will outlive my prison. *Destroy* me . . . and you will defeat yourself." The stallion kicked at the floor. "Destroy me and condemn yourself to your fate, to your selfmade curse."

The warlock straightened, the tension within him visibly mounting. After so many failures, there still remained anxieties. Had he seen his visage or lack of it . . . "I am free of my past errors. I am whole."

One of the statues, the one nearest to the faceless spellcaster, collapsed. Darkhorse felt a shrill cry that coursed through his mind as that which had lived within perished. The others quivered in sudden anxiety. The floor of the chamber slowly developed cracks.

Darkhorse knew what was happening, though he doubted the other did. "Listen to me—"

Too late. His adversary was beyond listening. Any hope of a peaceful accord between them had been shattered and Darkhorse knew that it was his own fault as well as Shade's.

His mind already a sea of confusion and turmoil, Shade saw the destruction around him as an attack and the shadow steed's words as a ploy to gain time. A hint of sadness touched him. *That Darkhorse would act so!* That there might be another cause did not occur to him. He, after all, was himself again—and the warlock was not about to give up so quickly what he had sought for so long. Even if it meant killing the one closest to him.

The air around Darkhorse grew oppressively thick. So thick, in fact, that it began to squeeze him. Had he been an actual horse, he would have been crushed in the first seconds. Instead, the eternal found himself being compressed smaller and smaller. The warlock was making good his threat. If Darkhorse failed to resist, Shade would reduce him to the size of a pebble and throw him somewhere where no one would be likely to find him. The hooded spellcaster might even choose to keep him as a memento.

He resisted instantly, of course, but with only a portion of the strength normally available to him. Erini's life was demanding almost as much of his energy as his own rescue. It took him far too much time to finally free himself. The next assault took him even before the last vestiges of the first had faded away. A tear in reality sought to draw him inside, pulling at his form with such persistence that he almost succumbed before he was able to fashion a defense. Darkhorse sealed the rip and let it vanish. It lasted long enough, however, to give him a glimpse of where Shade had intended on sending him.

The festering sore that the Vraads had once called home. Nimth.

He had not wanted to do it this way, but Shade was leaving him no options. Unless Darkhorse struck back with the one weapon he knew would be effective, the warlock would take him with his next attack—and success or not, this ploy would likely drive the final wedge between them.

The unsavory deed was done even as Darkhorse pictured it. Shade, sensing something materializing before him, struck at its heart. His target shattered into dozens of glittering fragments, which immediately expanded into exact copies of the original. As one, they focused on their attacker, who could not help but look up at them. Darkhorse, watching, could not help but flinch.

Shade stared, possibly openmouthed, at repetition after repetition of his own blurred, featureless visage. They were everywhere and each told him the one thing he could not face. The truth of his condition.

He screamed denial even as his pent-up power caused each mirror to melt like a single snowflake on a raging campfire. Darkhorse himself was buffeted to the ground by the wild forces unleashed. He barely maintained his bond with Erini. Other than the energy utilized to keep her from dissipating like a wisp of smoke, the shadow steed had little more to call upon. What remained he needed just to survive this latest and most horrid onslaught. It was all he could do just to keep his mind coherent.

"Nonononononononononooooo!" Shade was screaming. Rocking back and forth, he *clawed* at his own face, trying to remove what could not be removed. Portions of the chamber ceiling collapsed, but none so much as struck within two yards of the warlock. Somehow, his own defenses were still intact.

He cannot contain the power and the more he releases, the more destruction! It was worse than Darkhorse had feared. Vraad sorcery had destroyed one world already. It tore at the laws of nature rather than worked with them. As with the sorcery of the Dragonrealm, it was oft times an almost unconscious, automatic thing and the more it was used, the more chaos it caused. Shade, trapped in his own horror, was allowing it to run rampant. Darkhorse wondered if there might have been *some* other way.

The warlock was on his knees and facing the ground, unmindful of what havoc he was unleashing. Darkhorse had wondered what this new spell would do; the answer seemed to be *create more destruction*. It was as if the intensity of the original curse had been doubled in scope.

"Shade!" he called out, his voice booming above all else. "You must listen to me! A part of you must know the chaos you have invited into this world! I know from the past few days that there is, within you, a desire to end this madness peacefully! If you would hear me—"

Surprisingly, the warlock *did* look up. There was a tenseness in his movements. He had heard Darkhorse's voice, but not the shadow steed's warning. A fierce presence rose about the warlock as his tortured mind mixed facts and suppositions until they no longer had any true meaning. From that came one final, insane conclusion.

"*You!*" Shade rose, all fury. His mind, the stallion noted, was shifting from one extreme emotion to another—and with this particular emotion, he needed a focal point. "You *did* this to me!"

It would have been one of the most absurd things that Darkhorse had ever heard, save that he could have predicted it would be so. Shade could not accept that the grand spell had failed again or that he had not even recovered from the first attempt. He needed a scapegoat in order to preserve what little remained of his sanity—if there *was* anything left. The warlock needed something to lash out at.

What he does next could level settled areas, the eternal realized. *And being in the Tybers,*

one of those places might be Talak! How ironic it would be if the Dragon King captured Melicard's kingdom, only to have it sink beneath the earth or simply cease
to be.

That image in mind, Darkhorse vanished—

—and reentered the world in the desolate, blistering cold of the Northern
Wastes.

Before him, almost as if he had known where the shadow steed had intended
fleeing, was Shade. Despite the wind, his cloak remained still, covering him like
a shroud. Darkhorse had wondered what death would look like when it finally
claimed him. He now knew. There would be no escaping Shade, then. Whatever
it took, the warlock would track him down, laying waste to whatever happened
to cross his path in the meantime. Perhaps, letting the axe fall here would at
least save the Dragonrealm, thought Darkhorse somewhat fatalistically, though
he suspected that the tortured figure before him would not completely spend
his madness here.

"For our friendship," the spectral figure said, his calm words more chilling
than his angered ones, "I would have left you in peace. I would have. Then, you
did *this* to me! Now, I have only—"

"Shade, if you would just listen to me!"

"—one question to ask of you before I treat you as you've chosen to treat
me. Why do it? Tell me that."

There was no correct response and Darkhorse knew that. The best he could
do was give no answer at all. Shade's twisted thought had condemned him already.

"Goodbye, then, my comrade of old."

Despite the distance now separating them, Darkhorse still maintained the
shell protecting the helpless Erini, although it sapped almost all of what remained of his strength. He prepared himself now for the worst. Death or, at the
very least, the absence of life. Having never died, he could not say what awaited
him, if anything. Certainly, he did not fall within the realms of human afterlife.

Scattered thoughts touched him. Curiosity concerning the eventual fate of
Talak. Questions as to where the Bedlams had gone. He wondered what their
children would grow up to be like. Most of all, Darkhorse wondered what fate
awaited the world of the Dragonrealm, with or without the interference and
chaos created by its new, blur-visaged demigod.

He would protect Erini with the last vestiges of his power. When Shade
finally took him, the shadow steed would give his essence to her. Perhaps it
would buy her time enough for Cabe to find her. Likely not.

I have erred every step of the way, Darkhorse decided. *Most of all, I erred in thinking of
this one as still human—when all he truly was, was a Vraad!*

Shade moved, but slowly, as if unwell. Darkhorse saw little of consequence in that at the moment, instead concerned with bracing himself against what would surely be the warlock's final blow. His own nature would protect him briefly, but hardly long enough to matter. He only hoped, a foolish hope, that the warlock would feel regret afterward. It might stave off some of the coming devastation.

If only there was some way to take from the warlock the powers he had usurped . . .

There *was*. There *WAS*.

The answer came to him too late. Something darted around Darkhorse like a mad horsefly, something that grew as it circled him. He tried fending it off, but his power was too weak. It expanded as it moved, rapidly wrapping him within a shell whose very presence chilled his form, froze lifelessly his very essence. Given time, it would make of him a monument to his own futility. Given time, there would be nothing more than a shell shaped like a huge, writhing steed.

Given a little more time, there would not even be that.

Darkhorse struggled to maintain his senses. The key was his. He had controlled it all this time, but his own foolish sense of "noble sacrifice" had left him blind to the potential before him. Now, it might be too late.

Entangled in the warlock's death trap, Darkhorse tumbled into the snow and ice. The link with Erini, the one that still kept her alive, was his only chance. Summoning up his will and foregoing his own defense, he called out to her in his mind. *Erini!*

If he was wrong, it hardly mattered. Neither he nor she had more than a few minutes left either way.

A dim shadow fell over him. Through partially obscured vision, he saw a spectral Shade loom over him, likely come to gloat over his throes. To the eternal's confusion, the hooded figure sighed and reached out to touch his foe on the head. Briefly, Darkhorse entertained the thought of absorbing his adversary and trapping him within the emptiness that was his inner self, but he knew that the power of Shade was more than capable of withstanding even that. True enough, the Vraad's hand pulsated with energy.

The fiendish thing—did it live?—had sealed his mouth and Darkhorse found himself unable to form another. He lay there, silent and nearly mummified, as the warlock continued to move his hand along the shadow steed's neck and to his head.

For the first time, he felt the probe of Shade's mind. It was the final defeat. Darkhorse no longer even had the will with which to combat his longtime nemesis and companion.

"Soooo, that's why you fell so easily," the shadow lurking above him whispered. He had discovered the stallion's refusal to abandon Erini. Darkhorse shook, but was no longer able to do anything else . . . unless . . .

The shadow steed opened his mind completely and let his captor see *everything*, but, most especially, what he knew about Shade's *condition*.

The warlock shook and pulled his hand away as if touching something unclean. He remained stooped over his defeated adversary for some time, muttering things that Darkhorse could not make out save that Shade seemed to be arguing with *himself* adamantly. Finally, however, he came to some fateful decision and wrapped himself in his cloak, staring at the point somewhere beyond Darkhorse's limited range of vision.

"I'll need the girl again," he whispered to himself as he rose to a standing position. With an almost careless dismissal of the muffled figure at his feet, Shade stepped over Darkhorse and vanished into the tundra.

The eternal cursed himself. Of course Shade's first thought would be to recapture Erini! Darkhorse had let him see what was happening: instead of becoming a near-perfect demigod, the warlock was threatened with an existence even less real than in his prior incarnations. As powerful as he had become, Shade was still at the mercy of his self-made curse. The shadow steed had hoped that, knowing this, Shade might come to his senses.

Forgive me, Erini! Oddly, Darkhorse's error gave him the glimmer of hope. He had been abandoned and the deadly spell that had almost ended his existence had stopped, apparently dormant without its master's guidance. Given time, he would be able to free himself.

At that moment, he felt the link between himself and the princess break. Shade had reclaimed her for his dire purposes.

A dangerous error on your part, my dear, deadly friend!

No longer forced to divide his strength between his own defense and the protection of the fading Erini, the eternal's might returned much more rapidly. He had still nearly burned himself out, but now he had at least the ghost of an opportunity. Shade would be vulnerable now, mentally if not magically, and Darkhorse was already devising a way to increase that vulnerability. He no longer felt much remorse about what he plotted to do; Shade's apparent denial of his own condition had made it clear that the spellcaster was beyond aid. It was either defeat Shade or watch as the Dragonrealm and the rest of this world suffered the same fate as long-forgotten Nimth.

A storm was brewing, one that threatened to become a fullscale blizzard. There was a touch of sorcery about it and Darkhorse knew then that there was no time to waste. Shade had already begun whatever new experiment he planned. If there was a time to catch him with his guard down, it was before the plan reached fruition. The shadow steed had failed at that once. This time, though, the tale would end differently.

Darkhorse rose quickly, tearing and snapping the bonds that had ensnared him. Where they had sought to leech from him, he now returned the favor, causing them to dissipate in mere seconds. Things of sorcery, they left no remains. The only regrets Darkhorse had was the vile taste of them; they were filled with the taint of Vraad sorcery.

In the distance, he witnessed a vast aurora and knew immediately that there was where he needed to go. There, he would finally have Shade where he wanted him.

A portal offered too much risk. Darkhorse raced across the empty land, feeling somewhat at sympathy with it for all it had been through. Once, there had been trees here, life. Now, nothing but emptiness. The land looked much the way the eternal felt.

It was, he thought, a fitting place for what would be coming next.

Erini was the first to come within sight. She stood much the way she had in the chamber, save that her eyes were open and she seemed to be saying something. Darkhorse slowed. Something seemed wrong. When a rise brought Shade into view, the shadow steed *knew* that the scene before him was not as it should have been, that something was amiss.

The warlock was seated before his captive, his head low and his arms outstretched as if *he* were the one giving of himself.

Darkhorse sped across the remaining tundra and began casting his first—and likely last—spell. Entranced as he seemed to be, Shade would not notice until it struck. From the corner of his eyes, Darkhorse noted Erini's gaze turning toward him. Her mouth opened as if she intended to say something, but the ebony stallion ignored her. For the moment, it was only Shade that mattered.

When the attack caught him unaware, the shadow steed's first angry thought was how the warlock had tricked him again, laying some trap that he *knew* Darkhorse would be unable to resist. Then, as the world turned upside-down, he realized that it was not his ancient adversary who had caught him by surprise, but *Erini*. Erini had attacked *him*, as if she actually wanted her captor's spell completed.

Before he could rise and demand explanations, Shade's voice suddenly rose above the howling wind. "No, princess. It's all right. He doesn't understand—and, besides, it's taking its own course now. He won't be able to touch me; no one will."

"I can only try!" Darkhorse roared, standing. The snow fell from his huge form as if glad to abandon his fearsome presence. "Stand away, Erini! You shall be compelled no further!"

"Darkhorse!"

He ignored her shout, supposing her to be under the warlock's influence. "The female is under my protection, Shade! You will release her will and face me!"

Shade lifted his head toward Darkhorse. It was pale and drawn, but *distinct*. The stallion's first thought was that he had failed *again*. Cursing, he kicked at the snow and readied himself to perish fighting. The warlock, however, rose on surprisingly unsteady feet and shook his head at the leviathan ready to charge him.

"I'll face you, Darkhorse, but only to say goodbye."

"You will not leave me behind again!"

Shade smiled without malice. His face was as pale as the snow—or *was* that the snow Darkhorse saw? The warlock stepped toward him, leaving no trail. His movements were slow and he seemed to *ripple* with the wind. The warlock paused just out of arm's length from his adversary.

"You can't follow me where I'm going."

Darkhorse lashed out with his hooves, hoping to take Shade by surprise with a physical attack. To his dismay, he struck only air. Behind him, the massive stallion heard Erini gasp.

Wrapped in his cloak, the warlock stepped back so that he now faced both Darkhorse and Erini. Turning to the latter, he said politely, "You have what you wanted in return, sorceress. May it please you."

Erini would not respond, but her face grew almost as deathlike as the warlock's. She suddenly shook her head and sat in the snow, shivering from something other than the cold. The princess buried her face in her hands.

"What we gain is never quite what we originally wanted, is it, Darkhorse?" It was impossible to deny anymore; Shade *was* little more than a ghost in form, a memory more than a man.

"What have you done now, warlock? What have you demanded of Erini that leaves her in such pain?"

"She cries at the vast extent of her reward, Darkhorse. I leave that for her to explain. As for me, I have taken the only path left to me. A *final* path, you might say."

"Final—!" Darkhorse probed the figure before him—and found nothing but a dying emanation of power. Nothing physical stood there; what remained was of magic. Magic that was fleeing even now to where it belonged. The farthest stretches of the Dragonrealm and a crippled, tortured place called Nimth.

Shade had made Erini *reverse* his earlier spell, drawing forth not only his newly accumulated powers, but those forces within him that had originally cursed him to what had once seemed an endless chain of phantom incarnations, personalities that existed, but did not truly *live*.

Sorcery was all that truly remained of the original spellcaster and, when the last of it had dissipated, there would be nothing. No Shade. Not even the ever-present cloak. *All* of him was magic, nothing more.

"All that power, all that glory, was not worth facing—facing?—a continuation of that damned, horrible mockery of immortality, of life." There was little left of the warlock now. He looked like a reflection in a piece of glass, wavering in the wind. The storm that had threatened seemed to be dying with the man who had likely been its cause, but the wind, oddly, was picking up in intensity.

Or *was* that so odd? Darkhorse gaze locked with Shade's. The warlock smiled again and nodded ever so slightly.

"I had another name, once," he started, as if seeking to take both of their minds off of the truth. "It was . . ."

Words and warlock drifted away with the wind.

His name. He wanted to say his name to me. The black steed stared at the place where his adversary, his other half, had last stood. There were no tracks, of course. The last tracks were those where Shade had stood and given himself to Erini. Where he had finally, absolutely, ended his curse in the only way left to him.

"Darkhorse?"

Erini. He had forgotten her presence.

"I will never know love as you do, princess," he rumbled without removing his gaze from Shade's last stand. "But I know that I have lost one who could be considered a brother to me despite the evils he caused."

The sorceress was silent. Darkhorse, urged by a feeling he barely understood, trotted forward and kicked snow across the warlock's remaining tracks, not pausing until they were buried. Gruffly, he turned to his companion. For the first time, the stallion seemed to see her. Though her abilities protected her from the elements, she had suffered as few others had. Twice Shade had used her, forced her to touch something of a world that was little more than a sick parody of this one. He hoped she would recover once they returned to—

His ice-blue eyes widened as he recalled what was occurring in their absence. "Talak! Lords of the Dead, Erini! You should have said something!"

The human was drawn and weaker than he would have suspected, considering the power she had absorbed. Darkhorse sensed also a loss to the aura, the presence, about her. She was worn to the bone, too, but none of that was why she now sat in the snow, gazing at the emptiness without truly seeing it.

"There's no need to hurry," she stated quietly, finally responding to his words.

"No need to hurry? With Talak under siege by the drakes?" Had her ordeal at last overtaken her mind, too?

"Shade said that I had been rewarded." Erini laughed bitterly. "It seemed so perfect. They didn't deserve to survive. I keep telling myself that they would have killed Melicard and all the rest if I hadn't agreed." Her voice caught. "Yet, for some unfathomable reason, I can't help crying at the suffering they must have gone through, the shock when they realized what was happening."

"You make no sense, mortal!" She did, but Darkhorse had trouble believing what he was imagining.

She looked up, so pale he almost expected her to dissipate in the wind as Shade had done. "I want nothing to do with sorcery, Darkhorse. It seemed the best way to rid us of them, but . . . so many lives!"

"The drake host?" he finally asked with some misgivings.

She nodded, putting her head in her hands again. "All of them. Swallowed up without damage to anything or anyone else—save Mal Quorin, I suppose. I even pity him, if you can believe it. Shade killed them all with my permission.

Now it was Darkhorse who could say nothing. He wondered at the carnage they would see when they returned. In some ways, it had been necessary, but *the scope of what the warlock had been capable of* . . .

Erini looked up again, tears for her enemies in her eyes. "Take me back to Talak, Darkhorse. I—I can't do it myself. I might—might appear in the middle of—I want Melicard!"

The eternal let her cry some of the pain away as he slowly formed a sphere around them. A variation on the portal, it would allow them to travel without forcing the princess to act herself. When they arrived in Talak, he would see to speaking to Melicard privately about her immediate needs.

He welcomed her sorrow and her need for his aid. Her trials would give him purpose and allow him another chance to learn. Some day, he might yet understand the mortal creatures he had chosen to make his own. Some day, he might understand their path through life and, because of that, the definition of life itself. Perhaps then, the shadow steed might one day come to understand what could have created the man who had become known in legend and face as simply Shade.

Perhaps then, he might also make sense of the continuous, wrenching feeling that had begun within him when he realized that the warlock had surrendered his life.

XXIII

CABE BEDLAM FOUND the eternal overlooking the northern lands from one of the palace balconies. A vast, well-cultivated field, half wheat and half oat, covered nearly every inch of the level plain before them. Upon first glance, there seemed nothing out of the ordinary, aside from the fact that this was hardly the time of year for such a mature crop. What made the sight stunning, however, was the fact that it was out there where the army of the Dragon King had once stood. It was out there that settlements, wooded areas, and roads had existed prior to this day.

It was there that the drake host had perished down to the least of the minor drakes.

"I'll never forget the sight," Cabe said quietly, eyes fixed on the innocent-looking field. "We had barely arrived here ourselves, and then only thanks to the Dragon King Green, who arrived at the Manor and broke the spell Shade had cast over us." He had already relayed that story earlier, telling how, in response to word from the Lady Bedlam, the master of Dagora Forest had gained entrance and found the two, victims of Shade's attempt to kidnap their son Aurim. Neither the Bedlams nor their Dragon King ally, Green, could explain why the warlock had abandoned his plan after successfully dealing with the only two standing in his way.

Darkhorse thought he knew, but did not say so to Cabe. It would only make what had happened to the ancient warlock more difficult to accept.

Cabe moved on to the shocking fate that had befallen the charging drakes. "Even with our sorcery, we were only keeping them in check. Some of their number got through from time to time and wreaked havoc until each was killed or driven off. Some of their spells succeeded as well." The sorcerer shivered, remembering some of the more dire ones. "Word reached us at one point that the expedition to the Hell Plains *had* turned around, apparently because of some message etched into the ground by a spell of Drayfitt's just before his death—" Cabe did not notice Darkhorse flinch. *That* explained the final words he had not heard, the ones the elderly sorcerer had spoken before expiring! To the end, Drayfitt had served Talak with the utmost efficiency. "Though the reinforcements were on their way, the fighting was becoming so fierce that we suspected the drakes would be through Talak's defenses before they arrived. It was just after that when the ground to the north began to split *open*."

What had happened next had driven even stone-hearted Melicard to pity the deaths of his enemies. Great gaps and ravines opened in the earth, but only in and around the moving host. Some estimated that nearly half of the drakes perished in the first minute, as the warriors tried frantically and uselessly to control the sudden panic of their lesser cousins. Warriors and mounts fell screaming into the gaps, which closed up instantly, only to be replaced by others. Many of those who managed to find stable footing during the first onslaught fell easy prey when that ground beneath *them* suddenly yawned wide.

"Did none of them fly away?"

"Seems logical, doesn't it?" Cabe wore a grim smile. "They tried it. The sky over the area was literally filled with them—until the winds began to buffet them *back* to the earth!"

"Winds?"

"Winds followed by lightning followed by a downpour that would have crushed in the roof of the palace had the storms touched the city—which they did not with amazing accuracy! Everything was confined to the area where Silver's horde was trapped."

Quakes, wind, lightning, and rain. Earth, air, fire, and water. Darkhorse had to admire Shade's work. *How extravagantly traditional.*

No one had seen the Dragon King himself perish nor, for that matter, Mal Quorin's fate, either. It was safe to assume, however, that they had fallen with the rest. The entire horrible sight had lasted perhaps five minutes. When the last drake had perished, the wounds in the earth healed themselves and the storms dwindled to nothing. No one could really say when exactly the field had risen up, though everyone swore it was there only moments later.

Voices within informed him that the one he had been waiting for had finally recovered enough to join the rest. Darkhorse excused himself from Cabe.

"I'll not forget the good he did, Darkhorse," Cabe called after him.

"Do not forget the evil, either." He trotted into the vast room.

Her face lit up as she noticed him.

"Princess Erini!" He dipped his head in her honor. "Glad I am to see you better! Cherish this woman, King Melicard, for there are few as worthy as she!"

The king had one arm securely wrapped around his betrothed. The love he bore for her was spread equally across *both* sides of his face. The elfwood arm, the one that held Erini, looked as supple and lifelike as the real thing.

It is the spirit of the wearer that makes of the elfwood what it will be. With love comes life, it seems!

"Darkhorse." Erini separated herself from Melicard, walked up to the shadow steed, and hugged him by the neck. Off to the side, the Lady Bedlam smiled sourly. "Thank you for giving me my life again!" the princess added.

"It is I who should thank you! Are you truly better?"

"It will take me some time to learn not to shiver each time my eyes turn north and see the field."

Darkhorse laughed. "Think of the field as the first heralds of peace! What Shade did was horrendous, but did not cowardly Silver bring it upon himself?"

"I suppose." The princess looked down, as if remembering. Then, she looked back up, staring into his glittering eyes. "What happens to you now?"

The shadow steed felt as if all eyes in the room were now on him. "I shall roam the Dragonrealm as I always have! For Darkhorse, there is no grand scheme, no destiny! I shall roam and see what there is to see! I—"

It was the Lady Bedlam who spoke the words that he would not. "You shall search the lands to see if, somehow, *he* survived, won't you?"

The room grew silent as he stared first at her and then at Erini. She looked puzzled, having seen Shade freely end his tortured existence. Slowly, he nodded. "Yes, I will search the Dragonrealm for him. There must be *no* doubt. If he *has* survived, he may need help." Darkhorse absently pawed at the floor, leaving scars. "He may also need *destroying* again."

The ebony stallion stepped back from the mortal creatures around him. "It is past the time for me to leave! I am glad you are all well and that most of us have lived to see this peace." He looked specifically at Melicard and the Dragon King Green. There was hope there for some sort of compromise, a lessening of Talak's zeal toward those drakes who sought peace between the races. Erini caught his stare and looked at her betrothed, who nodded noncommittedly. "I now bid you farewell!"

"Come back to Talak when you wish," the princess called.

Darkhorse nodded to her and also to Cabe, who had rejoined his mate. He reared, summoning a portal.

"Come to the Manor sometime," Gwen said, startling both Cabe and the eternal. "You must meet the children. They would love you."

The shadow steed laughed cheerfully, the echoes resounding through the palace. "This, then, is truly a day of miracles! I shall take you up on that offer soon, Lady Bedlam. Ha!"

He entered the portal still laughing, his destination—and his destiny—unknown even to him.

THE
SHROUDED REALM

PROLOGUE

Toos the Regent, ruler of Penacles, stared down at the rolled missive the courier had just left in his hands. Undistinguished as it looked, the crimson-tressed ruler knew it for a thing of potentially great importance. It was the latest in a series of communications he had had with Cabe Bedlam, the warlock of the Dagora Forest. They were comrades of some fifteen years, and spellcasters both.

As he carefully broke the seals, both seen and unseen, he pictured in his mind the youthful visage of the warlock. Cabe's more regular features contrasted sharply to his own older, foxlike image, and it was hard to believe that so much knowledge and power rested within a man who was less than a third of the regent's own hundred-plus years. Of course, Cabe would probably look the same even when he was two hundred. There were benefits to having a talent for spells.

Alone in his study, Toos unfurled the parchment and started to read.

My greetings as ever to the regent, it began.

Toos chuckled. Cabe insisted on using the self-chosen title as much as possible. Each year, the people of Talak had presented the former mercenary with the crown and each year Toos had declined it. Someday, his lord and master, the Gryphon, would return and on that joyous occasion, he would return control of the city-state to him and quickly and quietly resume his position at the legendary monarch's side. No one had, so far, succeeded in eroding his determination, for the regent was the most stubborn of men.

Dismissing his thoughts, Toos continued reading, suspecting he already knew much of what the warlock's communication was going to reveal.

The death of Drayfitt of Talak still leaves a dark blot in what has been, for the past two years, a relatively peaceful time. His papers, of which there seem an endless tide, fill all corners of the room at the time of this writing. My wife and children claim I neglect them and I am apt to agree. Still, it was not my choice to begin this project, since the Gryphon, a scholar at heart, would have eagerly plunged into this mire, which I, instead, must battle through. Unfortunately for both of us, he is across the sea and there is no news as to when he and his brood may return. That leaves it to me, though I've not yet been able to figure out why. Since I am the chosen one, however, and it's you who read the fruits of my research, I will once more make no apologies for my rambling style and merely continue on.

My admiration goes out to Drayfitt. I find it difficult to understand a fraction of what he'd gathered even with so much knowledge passed down directly to me from my grandfather, Nathan. One thing I have discovered is that my own pet project will go for naught. The information concerning the mysterious Vraad is, at best, a thin veneer of half-hinted legends and exaggerated rumors masking a gulf of ignorance as vast as the Void itself. The bulk of his work perished at the hands of Mal Quorin, advisor to King Melicard I of Talak and agent of evil for the late and truly unlamented Dragon King, Silver. King Melicard, whose capable queen, Erini, I trust to keep him honest, assured me that what I received was all that remained. Those writings by Drayfitt that I have succeeded in organizing will be sent to you by separate couriers, likely a drake-human pair, as I would prefer to keep the two races working together as much as possible.

These, then, are my conclusions concerning the Vraad, of whom poor mad Shade was the last—I hesitate to use the word "living"—representative.

Toos found suddenly that he was sweating despite the coolness of the evening.

Drayfitt used many words to describe them, but arrogant and frightening seem to sum them up best. If I read his notes correctly, at their peak they were able to tear the heavens and earth asunder . . . you recall what Shade, in his final moments, did to the army of the Silver Dragon. Not a trace left. That was nothing. I think when you read some of what I am sending you, you will see as I did how fortunate we were that it was only Shade who defeated death for so long. The greatest irony in all this is that they were also our ancestors. We have the Vraad to thank for being here instead of that place I mentioned in several of the earlier missives, that twisted world they called Nimth.

I've found even less on that dark, fearsome domain than I have on those who once dwelled there. The Vraad left it a ruined place, abandoning it like the gnawed core of a srevo. The succulent flesh of the fruit had been eaten; they had no use for what was left.

Something must have gone awry, for they came here and vanished as a distinct race almost overnight . . . leaving us lesser spellcasters as their only legacy.

I'm sorry that there isn't more. A pity the libraries beneath your kingdom have chosen to be especially vague concerning the Vraad, though somehow that doesn't surprise me as much as it should. Darkhorse, our great, eternal friend, refuses my inquiries when he makes one of his rare visits—he still cannot accept that Shade is truly dead—and says only that the Vraad are better left a fading memory. Once, though, when he said that, I caught a wistful tone in his stentorian voice. It makes me wonder.

Gwen gives her love, you old fox. The children are fine . . . both human and drake.

Yours,

Cabe Bedlam

The regent allowed the parchment to roll closed, his mind sifting through what the warlock had and had not said. A world of *Shades!* A chilling thought. Standing up and walking over to the fire that kept his study warm, he threw the parchment into the greedy flames. It was difficult to say why he thought that necessary. There was nothing in the missive that was earth-shattering to him, not after the past notes. It was only that he found within himself, as Cabe had confessed he *also* had, a desire to forget anything concerning the arrogant, destructive Vraad . . . and a crippled, murdered place once called Nimth.

I

IN ALL OF Nimth, there stood only one true city. It was a tall, jagged thing so diverse in design that the best way to describe it was that it was a reflection of its creators. There were spires, ziggurats, towers that leaned at horrific angles . . . no one style dominated, unless *madness* could be called a style. Those selfsame beings who had built it with their sorcerous abilities even now gathered, as they did every few years, within its walls. It was the time of coming for the Vraad . . . perhaps the last to ever be held here in Nimth.

In deference to its neutral nature, the city had no name. It was simply *the city* to one and all. The Tezerenee had taken to utilizing it for their own needs, and who was about to make feud with a clan as huge and deadly as theirs? The rest of the Vraad patently ignored the slap in their faces, pretending it was beneath spellcasters as mighty as themselves.

Despite the supposed neutrality of the city, sorcery was very much in evidence. Brilliant auras clashed with one another, and new and old arrivals paraded about with entourages consisting chiefly of their own creations . . . beasts that moved as men, living stick figures, myriad sentient lights.

The Vraad themselves were no exceptions. Most of them were tall and beautiful, gods and goddesses come to life. Few of them wore the faces and bodies they had been given at birth. Long, flowing hair was popular now, as were bright chameleon tunics, flowing from one shape and design to another depending on the tastes of those who wore them. Not to be outdone, other Vraad wore suits of mist and light, seeking to both tantalize and distract.

The air crackled with so much pent-up magic. The sky, ever warring of late between shades of bloody crimson and a dark green touching on decay, stirred itself to greater fury this day because of all that power. Outside, the rumbling of yet another tremor to the west gave voice to the earth's protest at this latest coming of Nimth's masters. Once, the land had been a rolling field of green grass and the heavens a blue so brilliant even the otherwise indifferent race of sorcerers had often paused to admire it. No more.

"We have finally created a world *suitable* to our personalities."

So Dru Zeree felt as he looked from the assembled throng well below his perch to the bitter sky above.

"You think *that* spectacular, Sil?" someone in the crowd taunted, intensifying the loudness of his voice so that the one the words were intended for could not escape hearing them. "Your skills as well as your tastes have reached new lows!"

The second half of the exchange was lost in a thunderous explosion that was part of no natural phenomenon. Dru waited, but the aftermath he had expected did not occur.

"Not *yet*," he whispered to himself.

Nearly seven feet in height and somewhat narrower than his counterparts, Dru was markedly unique among the many spellcasters who strove for that very effect. His narrow face was handsome, true, but not in the beautiful way that most had chosen to sculpt their features. The somber mage had a hawk-like appearance that was complemented by a thin, well-trimmed beard the same dark brown as the rest of his hair. It was, in contrast to the blues, greens, and multihued tresses of the others, his original hair color. A *real* novelty among the Vraad, save for the Tezerenee, who prided themselves on maintaining their original outward appearances as much as possible.

Dru was a Vraad in the end, however. For this coming, he had added to his hair a streak of silver directly down the center. Simple as it was, it had earned him his share of stares, as had the plain, unmarked gray robe he generally wore. Perhaps, he thought wryly, he would be responsible for starting a trend toward basics . . . a trend very *un*-Vraad-like, considering their tendency for excesses.

A black and gold beast fluttered onto his broad shoulder and hissed, "Dekkarrrr. Silestiii. Seeee."

The Vraad scratched his familiar on the fur beneath its predatory beak. The familiar opened its maw wide in pleasure, revealing an incongruous set of sharp teeth within that beak. Had someone taken a sleek wolf and combined its parts with that of a swift, huge eagle, they would have found themselves confronting something resembling Dru's familiar. The torso, tail, and upper legs were lupine. The head, though furred, was more avian, and the lower extremities ended in claws capable of tearing apart creatures far bigger and stronger-looking than their owner. The round, amethyst eyes that gazed into his had no pupils. Dru was, in Vraadish fashion, quite proud of his handiwork.

"Where are they exactly, Sirvak?"

"There. There." The beast pointed its head toward the eastern side of the great courtyard, where most of the newcomers entered.

He saw Dekkar first. Tall but exceedingly wide, a living wall of strength, both sorcerous and physical. Dekkar had a striking visage, though it was made less so by the fact that it was, in many ways, much too much like the faces of those around him. He was clean-shaven and his long, orange/blue hair fell back behind his head like vast tentacles. The expression on the other Vraad's face was typically arrogant. The sorcerer wore a tunic of rainbows that literally shifted with each breath . . . a masterful piece of work, it had to be admitted. Dekkar had put a vast amount of detail into the subtleties of its design.

It was a pity he could not put in as much effort in aiding the coming exodus of the Vraad.

"The epitome of predictability." Dru followed his counterpart's gaze, knowing he would find Silesti at the other end. "And there is his brother, *foolishness incarnate.*" The other Vraad had evidently noticed his rival, for he stared back at Dekkar with a look that so matched the broader sorcerer that it was no wonder some took them to be kin. In point of fact, Silesti had always chosen to look very much like Dekkar, and Dru found himself wondering if there might have been a reason for that. No one could recall what had started their thousand-year feud, likely not even the combatants themselves. A thousand years was a long time, even for a race that was nigh immortal. Dru suspected that the two Vraad had continued on with their battle long after the original reason was lost strictly because it kept them from falling to the deep ennui that so many Vraad suffered.

That made them no less mad than the rest, Dru himself included.

"Seeee, masterrr! Seee!"

"I see, Sirvak. Hush now."

Silesti was wearing a brilliant black suit that clung to his form and covered all but his head. As his eyes narrowed on Dekkar, one gloved hand went to a pouch hanging from a belt around his waist. Many of the assembled Vraad watched the two with mild interest, though a good number ignored them completely. Feuds were just one more thing in the life of the sorcerous race. The only interest was in what sort of action the combatants might take.

Dekkar struck first, creating a miniature rainstorm above Silesti's head. Without pausing from his own task, the latter sorcerer created a shield that made the rain bounce off and slide down to the earth around him, leaving Silesti high and dry. Dekkar, however, seemed none too upset over that abrupt change. He stood quietly, openly challenging his adversary to do his worst.

The other Vraad was only too happy to do so. From his pouch, Silesti took out a tiny, wiggling form that Dru could not make out even when he amplified his vision. With careful precision, Silesti tossed it toward the expectant Dekkar.

True to form, Dekkar did not wait for the creature to reach him. With a wave of his hand, he stole from his own raging storm a single bolt of lightning. It struck the hapless servant of Silesti and sent the bits scattering. A wind rose up, blowing them toward their original target, but Dekkar was hardly in danger from ash.

On Dru's shoulder, the familiar shifted, raising one claw and then another as it tried to comprehend the apparently useless assaults by the two spellcasters . . . men capable of raising mountains, if need be.

"Masterrrr . . ."

Dru smiled grimly and shushed the beast. He understood what Sirvak could not. After so long a struggle, the feud had become ceremonial. What seemed like minor touches of Vraad power would soon lead to far more.

As if in response to his thoughts, the true assaults took place.

From around Silesti's feet, the torrent of rain rose upward *around* his shield, creating a cocoon of some silky substance whose binding force was the counterspell the ebony-clad sorcerer himself had cast. Dru knew, as Silesti now knew, that the trap also grew beneath the latter's feet, essentially sealing him in.

While Dekkar laughed and some of the spectating Vraad clapped their approval, Silesti's spell came to full fruition. The ash had settled on the broad Vraad's person, including his face and arms. Dekkar had, of course, ignored it, and it came as quite a surprise, then, when he found himself suddenly sprouting tiny, toothsome heads that rose on serpentine bodies and proceeded to viciously bite their host. More and more vermin sprouted from his clothing and his flesh, taking root wherever possible. There were even a few on the ground near his feet, but Dekkar stomped them to death.

Many of the Vraad thought that they were finally seeing the culmination of the millennium-old struggle. Dru doubted that it was so. Both adversaries had faced a vast array of traps in that time. It would take more than these to kill the two.

True enough, both assaults began to falter. From within the cocoon there rose a tremendous heat, one that even touched Dru despite the height and distance separating the balcony he stood on from the site of the duel. A simple spell of his own cooled the area around Dru, but Silesti's prison lacked any such protection. It sizzled and melted, evaporating to nothing by the time the residue reached the ground again. Even the cloud had dissipated.

Dekkar, meanwhile, did little but stand and wait. Once his initial surprise had passed, he stood smiling despite the bites he had suffered. It was soon easy to see why. The vermin began falling off, first a few, then in great numbers. Each one was dead, that is, each one that had *bitten* the sorcerer. Dru caught sight of one of the last, true to its mission, snapping at Dekkar's unprotected hand. Once the creature drew blood, it instantly recoiled, as if ready to strike again. Instead, the monstrosity shook, spat the blood of its victim from its mouth . . . and fell to the earth, its grip and its life both things of the past.

"Masterrrr?"

"Poisoned, Sirvak. Dekkar's blood is poisoned. I wonder how he survives it? It would have to be a strong poison to kill one of those creatures, I suspect."

Like two bedraggled but triumphant bookends, Dekkar and Silesti faced one another, each ready for the second round.

"Masterrr!" Sirvak's talons bit deep into Dru Zeree's shoulder, a signal that the familiar was more than just apprehensive. A dark shadow blotted out all but the artificial illumination the Vraad themselves had created for the coming.

The sky was filled with dragons. Huge monsters, larger than the tallest horses and quite able to fell said animals with one blow of their massive forepaws. There was a rider on the back of each emerald horror, a sure enough sign, not that one had been needed, of who the newcomers were.

"Tezerenee . . ." Dru muttered to himself.

Below him, the crowd, whose interest in the duel had grown with each passing second, suddenly became silent save for a few hardy souls who dared to whisper what Zeree himself had just said.

Tezerenee.

There were more than forty and Dru knew that these were only a token representation of the clan. Vraad, by nature of their egos, were not a familial race. Dru and his daughter, Sharissa, were a rarity. Under the draconian rule of their patriarch, the Lord Barakas, the Tezerenee were a cohesive and masterful family of sorcerers. They were also skilled fighters, another aberration in a race that relied so heavily on their magical prowess.

Dragons began to land on the roofs and walls of the city.

From a distance, each rider seemed identical. Dark green armor covered them from head to toe, forged from the scales of the very beasts the Tezerenee rode. Ferocious dragon-crested helms all but obscured the savage faces of the Tezerenee. Two of them wore crimson capes, Lord Barakas and his eldest son, Reegan. Nearly a third of the riders were sons of the patriarch, spread across the five thousand years of his life. (How many more there were and how many had died one way or another during those millennia was something no one spoke about within earshot of the Lord Tezerenee.)

Barakas Tezerenee had landed on the roof of a building that had flattened itself out at the moment of arrival. From his vantage point, the overwhelming figure overlooked all but Dru. Barakas stroked his heavy beard and stared long and hard at the two duelists.

"This is the final coming." His voice, augmented by his power, sent a tremor literally through the city. Oddly, despite his bearlike appearance, the Lord Tezerenee's voice was smooth and calculated. It was also the voice of one so used to commanding that even a simple "good day" would have seemed an order to be obeyed.

"This is the *final* coming, Masters Dekkar and Silesti. From here, the Vraad will be moving on to a better, less disreputable home." The warring sky rumbled, as if punctuating his statements.

The two feuding sorcerers glanced at each other with disquieting looks.

"See that these two finish their absurd duel once and for all." It was not evident at first to whom the patriarch was speaking, for he still studied Dekkar and Silesti. Then, two riders remounted their reptilian steeds and rose into the sky. The two rivals began to protest, but a sharp glance from Barakas froze them where they stood.

Dru blinked, leaned over the rail of the balcony, and studied Dekkar and Silesti closer. *Frozen, indeed.* Neither sorcerer was moving, save to look around futilely for someone who would free them from the Lord Tezerenee's spell. The dragons descended to points just above the heads of each hapless Vraad, raising dust storms that sent the throngs backing away, and, at a command from their riders, grasped Dekkar and Silesti in their forepaws.

The riders looked to their clan master for further orders. Barakas Tezerenee considered, then said, "Take them west. Do not come back until there is a victor . . . or until both of them are *dead.*"

With a renewed flapping of their huge wings, the dragons rose swiftly into the air. In seconds, they were mere dots in the sky to even the most skilled of observers. In less than a minute, they were out of sight.

Barakas scanned the remaining Vraad—who were still uncharacteristically silent—and finally said in the same tone of voice he had used to dispose of Silesti and Dekkar, "May the spirit of the coming be with you."

Without another word, he turned, visibly dismissing the throng from his interest, and eyed the waiting Dru.

Dru inclined his head briefly toward the patriarch. "I came as you directed."

In the next instant, the Lord Tezerenee was standing beside him. Sirvak, who had a distinct dislike for anything of draconian nature, let out a low hiss. Dru quieted him while Barakas looked on, a cold smile playing across his lips.

"It is only fitting that you should be here, Zeree. This is your doing as well as mine."

The intended compliment did nothing for Dru, though he pretended to be honored. "The credit goes to you, Barakas. To you and your sons, Rendel and Gerrod."

For the first time since he had arrived, the patriarch looked uncomfortable. Dru noted with particular interest his discomfort at the mention of those two sons. "Yes. Yes, they've done their parts. You laid the groundwork, though."

Below, the other Vraad had returned to their other interests, Dekkar, Silesti, and even the watchful Tezerenee forgotten for the most part. Barakas laughed harshly.

"Weak fools! Children! If not for us they'd still be bemoaning their fate!" He took Dru by the arm. "Come! The tests draw near, Zeree. I want *you* to be there when the time comes."

The world around them seemed to curl within itself.

When it had unfurled again, their surroundings had changed. They were now in a vast chamber in which nearly a dozen Tezerenee sat on the outline of a pentagram, one at each point and corner of the design. A single hooded figure sat quietly in the center, different from the rest by nature of the long cloak, scaled tunic, and high boots he wore. Wisps of ice-white hair dangled free of the encompassing hood, identifying him readily enough for Dru.

"Father." Another Tezerenee, clad identically to the one in the center, knelt before the clan patriarch. Barakas deigned to put a hand on his son's hooded head.

"Gerrod. Explain what occurs here." Beneath the calm tones, there was an undercurrent of suspicion and the first traces of righteous fury.

Gerrod looked up. In contrast to most of the male members of the Tezerenee, he was handsome. Dark hair hung down slightly on an aristocratic visage that took greatly from his mother's side. He was slim compared to such as Barakas or Reegan and hardly the warrior type. He and the still figure at the heart of the pentagram might have been twins, so much did they resemble each other. Yet, there were more than a thousand years separating their births. Twins they were, but in the soul, not the body.

"Rendel couldn't wait, Father," Gerrod informed Barakas, speaking with much more calmness than Dru thought he himself would have been able to muster.

"Couldn't *wait?*" Suddenly it struck Dru what Gerrod was implying.

The younger Tezerenee inclined his head toward his father, shivering slightly as the patriarch's grip on his head tightened. Barakas could crush his son's skull like a piece of soft fruit if he so desired.

The Lord Tezerenee glanced imperiously at his companion. "Rendel, it seems, Zeree, has jumped the chasm. His ka is now over *there*—in the *Dragonrealm.*"

II

"THE *WHAT?*"

Stirred by the tensing of its master's body, Sirvak opened its eyes and hissed. A small wyvern perched on a ledge returned the familiar's angry sibilation and stretched its wings in challenge. Dru silenced Sirvak with a few whispered words while a single glare from the Lord Tezerenee quieted the wyvern.

Lord Barakas smiled, a feeble attempt, if it *was* one, to reassure Dru. "Forgive me, Zeree. We have come to call the realm beyond the veil the Dragonrealm.

Since no one else has put forward a name for it, we thought this one would do just as well."

We meaning *you*, Dru thought sourly. The patriarch of the Tezerenee, who had personally raised the dragon up as the symbol of his clan, knew he had the rest of the Vraad at a distinct and unique disadvantage. Each day, since the first discovery that another domain, unblighted, lay just beyond their own, Barakas Tezerenee had worked to ensure that it was he who commanded the situation. When the first mad attempts at crossing over physically had failed shamefully, Barakas had turned his talents to studying the works of his rivals. It was only because of Dru's own experiments that he now shared in the successes of the clan. He had devised what had become the Vraad's hope, the Vraad's *triumph*.

It galled the rest of the race and made Dru careful as to whom he spoke with. Vraad were nothing if not vindictive.

A disturbed Dru, in an attempt to keep from commenting on the Tezerenee's presumptions, studied the prone form of Rendel. The patriarch's son might have been dead, so limp was his body. It was quite possible, in fact, that Rendel *was* dead, his ka trapped in some endless limbo. What the Tezerenee proposed to do was lofty, even by Vraad standards.

Which left another question, one that Barakas had, as yet, left even his "partner" in the dark concerning.

Of what use was transferring the ka of oneself if there was no suitable vessel awaiting it at the other end of the journey?

The Lord Tezerenee had promised success to his rivals and counterparts. Even he knew better than to fail in those promises. Failure would erode not only his standing with those outside of the clan, but with the rest of the Tezerenee themselves. He had trained them to be too much like himself and that, Dru Zeree had always thought, was the most dangerous mistake that Barakas had ever made.

As fearful as they were of their lord, enough Tezerenee banding against him would send even the overwhelming Barakas to the dragon spirit he so revered.

"Rendel's . . . enthusiasm . . . is commendable." With great effort, Barakas removed his hand from Gerrod's head. Dru was certain he heard the younger Tezerenee exhale in relief, though that would have been considered a sign of weakness by Gerrod's parent. The patriarch's son rose and stepped quickly aside.

Walking at a measured pace, Barakas led Dru forward. The method of ka travel was his own idea, but one, in his mind, that he had always restricted to Nimth. After all, where else *had* there been to go besides the Vraad's own world?

The realm behind the veil—the *shrouded* realm, as Dru had first called it— had altered the lives of the near ageless Vraad as nothing else had. The ghostly domain had flaunted its rolling hills and lushly forested lands in their faces as far as they were concerned because, quite simply, it could not be *touched*.

Some had immediately scoffed, claiming the trees and mountains that superimposed themselves on Nimth's own battered and unstable landscape had been nothing more than a prankster's illusion. No one laid claim to the supposed trick, however, and it soon became obvious that this was no mirage after all. With that, the Vraad began to study the place in earnest . . . as a second home.

When was the last time the sky was blue? Sharissa had asked her father once. Dru could not recall then as he could not recall now. Not in her lifetime, short as that had been so far. Of that he was certain. Nimth had started dying long ago. Its death was a slow, lingering one that might go on for millennia . . . save that long before then it would be unsuitable even for the Vraad.

Gerrod shadowed them every step of the way. There was more beneath that hood than either Barakas or even Rendel knew, Dru suspected. Gerrod observed everything with a cunning eye. He was keenly interested in what the outsider his father had brought with him had to say about the spells cast here, of that much Zeree was certain. Interested in a way that puzzled Dru, for it was almost as if the younger Tezerenee hoped to find fault with what he himself had helped create under the very nose of his lord and progenitor.

"Here it is, Dru Zeree. The missing link in your work and our salvation."

Following the grand wave of the Lord Tezerenee's arm, Dru gazed upon a body. He knew what it was, having created such beings before, but the size and scope of it made any initial comment superfluous. Under the waiting gazes of his two companions, he dared to reach out and touch the nearer arm. It was warm and very much living to the touch. Dru wanted to shrink back from it, but knew that only he would suffer from such a cowardly act. The Tezerenee neither respected nor worked with those they considered lacking in nerve. At this point in the alliance, such an action might have been tantamount to suicide on his part.

"A golem made of flesh," Gerrod informed him needlessly.

Had it been standing rather than lying flat on a marble platform, it would have come to Dru's chest. *The same height as Sharissa.* Zeree had no idea why that should come to mind now, save that he had already been away from her longer than he had planned. It was also for her sake that he had accepted the patriarch's original offer. A solution, however insane, that saved her life was worth entering the domain of a horde of ravaging dragons like the Tezerenee. It was not a Vraadish notion, to be sure. Most elder Vraad would have gladly given up their offsprings' lives to save their *own* hides.

"You may be wondering about its . . . incomplete construction," Gerrod prodded in a more daring manner.

Dru grunted. *Incomplete, indeed!* A poor excuse of a golem, taken on face value . . . or rather on *faceless* value, seeing as how it lacked a visage of any sort. In fact, it was lacking in much more than merely features. There was no hair, no mark upon its person. Its hands and feet, he saw, were little more than stubs at the end of each appendage. The golem was neither male nor female, an asexual, living puppet.

As a Vraad over three thousand years old, Dru had seen far worse than this . . . yet the golem had some quality about it that made him want to shiver. Some difference beyond its visual deficiencies.

Then it struck him as to what it was he sensed.

"This was *grown*, not fashioned from bits and pieces."

Gerrod's eyes brightened. For the first time, Dru noted how crystalline they were. Barakas, meanwhile, smiled approvingly at the befuddled spellcaster. He indicated to Dru that he should continue with his guesswork.

The narrow Vraad did, forcing himself to touch the golem's bare torso again. The skin had a peculiar leathery feel to it, almost like . . .

"Not Vraad after all." He ran his finger along the arm, forgetting, in his dreaming, the dread he had been experiencing previously. What did he know that felt like this?

It came to him and the realization rekindled his dread of the gloom. "This has been spawned from a *dragon!*"

"You see, Gerrod, Master Zeree has a nimble mind. A mind worthy of a Tezerenee."

The hooded figure bowed, his reaction, if any, totally shrouded by the cloak. Dru wondered if Barakas simply pretended not to notice or was so caught up in his belief in his control of the Tezerenee that Gerrod's actions escaped him.

That was a question for another time. "This is to be the vessel for the ka."

"Yes." Barakas reached out and caressed the golem's shoulder as one might a lover. "The golem has no ka, being neither dragon nor Vraad. It is a shell, open to possession, that has no true essence, no life of its own. The only thing it carries is the inherent magic of the dragon. Only a carefully structured spell gives it the appearance of life. A Vraad ka, entering, will find no resistance to its presence and take it over completely. The golem is malleable; it will become what the Vraad wants it to become."

"A superior body for a new world," Gerrod added, speaking as if by rote. He had evidently heard his progenitor preach this often.

The Lord Tezerenee nodded approval to his son. "So it will be." His attention returned to his guest. "It will be a true combining of our soul with the magic of the dragon. Through that, the Vraad will be more than they could have ever *hoped.*"

Dru kept his expression indifferent, but, inside, the disturbing feeling was growing. It was more than just the golem now. The Vraad had a new world awaiting them, but it was one that Barakas Tezerenee was mapping out to his own desires. The anxious sorcerer looked down at the still form lying next to them and could no longer repress the shudder.

"Is something wrong, Zeree?"

Before he could respond, Gerrod spoke. "Father, Rendel will need some watching for the next hour. Despite earlier expectations, he is not yet in the Dragonrealm. We have judged the cross-over to be a slower and more tedious process than originally calculated and his body must be kept well during that extra time. If I have your permission, I would like to discuss with Master Zeree what opinions he has concerning our progress here and the possible difficulties we may not have foreseen . . . unless, of course, you have need of him still. . . ."

The Lord Tezerenee's gaze measured Dru. "I have no need of him now. What say you, Zeree?"

"I would be only too happy to add whatever I could to ensure the success of your spell."

"Very good." The patriarch reached up and took Sirvak's beaked countenance in his hand. Dru could feel the familiar's nervous breathing against his neck, but Sirvak, to its credit, did nothing otherwise during the span in which the large Vraad studied it. When Barakas finally released it, the creature carefully lowered its head and pretended to resume its napping.

"A splendid piece of workmanship. How would it fare, do you think, against a wyvern?"

"Sirvak has a certain skill in combat." Dru purposely smiled as he looked at the beast and scratched its throat. "As for wyverns . . . he killed both of them in under a minute."

The patriarch's face darkened, but he kept his voice composed. "A splendid piece of work, as I said." To his son, he commanded, "I am to be notified the moment something occurs. The *exact* moment."

"Father." Gerrod bowed, staying in the subservient position even after the Lord Tezerenee had vanished in a verdant cloud that threatened to spread throughout the chamber. Finally standing, the younger Tezerenee dispersed the greenish mist through an open window with a violent twist of his hand. He glanced at Dru. "He's quite mad, Master Zeree, even more than the rest of us." When there was no response, he added, "And we would have to be mad indeed to think of toppling him. Come take a look at this."

With that last peculiar twist, Gerrod had turned toward the pentagram and those who maintained the spell. Dru followed silently, thinking about how much truth there was in his guide's words.

"You have, of course, thought of the one difficulty with my father's plan, haven't you?" With his back turned to Dru, Gerrod looked like nothing more than a vast piece of cloth hung up to air out. His steps were surprisingly inaudible, a contrast to the heavy thuds that generally accompanied his armored relations.

Dru knew what the hooded figure was talking about. "Your golem is here; how will he get it to the Drag— How will he get it to the other side?"

"It was *my* idea . . . mine and Rendel's, that is. A matter of power, as Father would say. Power will always prevail if you have it in sufficient quantities." A low laugh escaped the all-encompassing hood. "Father is such a philosopher."

"And what *was* that idea?"

Gerrod turned and indicated the pentagram. At that moment, the smile on his face was all too much a copy of his father's. "What one Vraad cannot do, perhaps more, acting in concert, *can*. A group like this is out in the middle of the phantom forest, sitting among trees that are not quite there, stretching forth with the might of the Tezerenee, and creating for Rendel—and those who follow—vessels drawn from sources of the shrouded realm itself."

It made sense of a sort and would only work with such as the Tezerenee. Only they could gather enough Vraad willing to work together to have a chance at success, even if that success was no more than a ghostly hand invading a ghostly world. The Vraad could not travel physically to their new home, but their power would build them another path.

Dru blinked. "Are there *dragons* over there?"

"Of course. It was—let me see—a cousin or brother or maybe even a sister, I forget which, who saw it. You can imagine how *thrilled* Father was. Our destiny was clear then. Until we found the beast, Father had intended on using some of those damn elves."

Whispers of creatures inhabiting the shadow lands had slowly circulated through the network of spies and allies among the various Vraad. The elves were the most interesting, being a race long extinct on Nimth. They had been the first to suffer at the hands of the early Vraad. As Serkadion Manee, a singular sorcerer who had decided to chronicle the rise of his kind, had written, the elves had been too peaceful and giving to coexist with the new race. They had vanished virtually overnight. Nimth had seemed to die a little then, if Manee's words were to be believed.

Living elves meant only one thing to the Vraad. Slaves and toys. It burned deep within Dru that his initial reaction had almost been as terrible as that of the rest; he had thought of what it would be like to study one, to take it apart and see how it differed from his own kind.

Sharissa would have abandoned him there and then had she only known.

He realized that Gerrod was staring at him, the younger Vraad's eyes glistening.

"I want it to *fail.*"

At first, Dru was uncertain that he had heard the other correctly. When Gerrod's expression did not change, however, he knew that the sons of the dragon were indeed all insane. In the end, Dru could only ask a simple "Why?"

The hooded Vraad looked at him helplessly. He seemed unconcerned that anyone might hear his traitorous words—traitorous to both his clan and the Vraad race as a whole.

"I don't *know!* I feel it sometimes, as if my head were about to split in two! That something very wrong awaits us, something that means death . . . and more . . . to the Vraad, *all* Vraad!"

Suddenly Gerrod stared up at the ceiling. His mouth drew shut, a tight, thin line across his countenance. His head snapped down a second later. The eyes that met Dru's were full of both relief and despair.

"Rendel's made it. I can feel him. His ka now definitely inhabits the realm beyond. Our success"—Gerrod hesitated, visibly tasting the words and disliking their content—"is a *certainty* now!"

For the second time in only a matter of minutes, Dru could not hold back the shiver that coursed through him.

THOUGH IT HAD no mouth, it screamed.

Though it had no eyes, it turned its head toward the dark, raging heavens, as if seeking some power to end its agony.

Its visage was blank. No mark, no hair, graced its head. There were no ears, though it seemed to listen. Naked, it stumbled to its feet, which had no toes, and grasped the tree it had fallen against with hands that were little more than stubs. It was a sexless being, devoid of any distinguishing feature over the expanse of its entire body. It could feel the elements warring around it, but could do little else.

It was a golem, the first to be grown and the first to be claimed by the Vraad.

A flock of wyverns, half as tall as the helpless creature staggering below but capable of tearing asunder predators thrice their size, huddled fearfully in the few trees dotting this area of the storm-drenched field. It was not the wind and the lightning that sent shivers through their reptilian forms. What they feared was the being feeling its way around the trunk of the tree on which many of them perched. It was not exactly the scent that stirred their anxiety, but a presence of power so foreign to their limited existences that it frightened them into immobility.

The faceless monstrosity guided a foot over the upturned root it had previously tripped over. As it did, bulbous growths sprouted from the end, twisting and shaping themselves into individual toes. The other foot was also whole now, though the change went unnoticed by the creature itself. It could only feel its pain.

The storm had swept across a clear evening sky mere moments before, but it was already at its height. As it vented itself, the thing paused, seeming to consider something.

It suddenly pulled back its fist and, for no apparent reason, harshly struck the trunk of the tree. The wyverns squawked in panic; the blow nearly cracked the trunk in half. Sorcery crackled in the air around the blind wanderer. As it pulled the hand back for a second try, blood dripping to the already-soaked earth, stubs emerged from the front, mad little points that stretched and wriggled, creating fingers and forming a true hand in the space of a single breath. The blow stopped in midflight, the hand's owner only now becoming aware of what was happening. If its empty visage could have indicated anything now, it would have been pleasure—the pleasure of a dead man who had been given a reprieve.

It wiggled the fingers on both hands, seeming to admire the movement that it could not see. The storm was a thing forgotten. The creature put a hand to each side of its head, feeling for and finally locating the budding ears. Like a child, it became aware of yet other alterations in its form. Pale white hair sprouted with astonishing alacrity, lightly covering the body and richly overwhelming the top, back, and sides of the head. He was male, too, a fact that he had known always but could not have proven before this instant. The body itself grew until it was well over six feet in height and swelled as the rib cage expanded and muscles stretched into being.

As the torso transformed, so, too, did the blank countenance. A tiny protuberance rose near the center. Below it, a slit formed, first little more than a tear in the skin, but soon a gap that spread across the emerging visage. Above, two tiny folds twitched, the beginnings of eyes.

Through the thin-lipped mouth and the arrogantly curved nose, he breathed deeply, for the first time, the air of this land. A smile, with just a touch of self-congratulation imbued in it, curled into life. Teeth gleamed white.

The eyes opened, glittery, multihued orbs that saw everything and forgot nothing. For a time, they studied the eye of the storm, a black abyss that was no cloud but the remaining effect of his passage to this new world. Even as he watched, it began to recede, giving way to the heavens once more. He sighed in relief, pleased now where he had been in agony moments before.

Fully whole, Rendel gazed down at himself, assuring that all was in order. The smile broadened.

The chill wind, a last remnant of the storm he had helped cause, reminded him of his lack of protection. The smile died, replaced by a look of petulance with just a hint of confusion added. He gestured angrily at his form.

A dark suit of the finest scale, scale from the greater cousin to the hapless beasts above, wrapped him from neck to toe. A green cloak and hip-high boots completed the image of some majestic but frightful forest king. Rendel left the hood of the cloak back, enjoying the feel of the wind on his face. He laughed, his triumph, which he had begun to doubt more than once since his arrival, completely erasing the earlier pain and fear. That, of all things, pleased him most. To one who had suffered little in the areas of pain and fear before this day, such emotions were doubly strong.

The wind was dying down now. Rendel turned his gaze toward a distant chain of mountains. Among them, he spied a giant among giants, a peak that seemed to summon him.

Turning briefly to the field and the spot on which the golem had lain, the mage executed a low and somewhat sardonic bow. That done, he straightened and, without hesitation, walked off in the direction of the mountains. An arrogant smile dominated his features.

The wyverns watched him depart, now bunched together so tightly that they threatened the stability of their perches. Beyond them and hidden by the tall grass, something else watched the receding figure of the Vraad with deadly interest.

III

With Rendel's apparent success, Gerrod chose to speak no more concerning his conflicting desires. Dru knew better than to press him. There was enough to ponder and enough to worry about, and joining the other Vraad in the coming was proving a two-pronged decision. What Dru had learned so far only emphasized the need to continue his secret work, which even the Lord Tezerenee, with his multitude of prying eyes, had no knowledge of—he hoped. On the other hand, what Dru had learned also made that work seem superfluous, for what support would he get once Barakas announced to the others that *he* held the solution to their growing predicament?

Dru left the chamber by himself, Gerrod preferring to monitor the health of his brother's body rather than join in their father's encroaching triumph. The news would reach Barakas nonetheless; Gerrod evidently did not want to have to be the bearer, not after what he had confided earlier.

Walking was not a necessity in a city designed to supply its users with all comforts. Dru could have commanded the citadel to carry him along until he arrived at his destination or he could have teleported, but the tall Vraad cared for neither choice. A long, mind-calming trek through the myriad corridors and staircases of the structure was what he needed . . . that and his daughter.

He had wandered in a gradual upward direction, slowly making his way to where Barakas and the others were gathering, when a slim figure materialized around the corner of the stairway. There was no going around her and it was too late to turn back.

"Dru, sweet thing, I was wondering where you were!"

She had her arms around him and kissed him soundly before he could peel her clinging claws away. The struggle was made all the more difficult by the fact that part of him did not *want* to break away.

"Melenea . . . I didn't see you earlier."

"Didn't see or don't want to, sweet thing? Am I so bland and undesirable?"

In a world where beauty was commonplace, there was nothing common about the scarlet- and ebony-tressed sorceress. *Enchantress* was a word whose definition included Melenea. Her oval face was the color of pearl. Her lips, round and sensual—and *soft*, Dru recalled almost with shame—complemented her partly upturned nose and the narrow, tear-shaped eyes. Her brows were arched high, which tended to give her a calculating and commanding look. She had chosen to emphasize her cheekbones further than in the past and the effect was such that the memories it brought to life made Dru regret his not having departed instantly upon first sighting her. Her hair was short and tightly wrapped about her head, almost like a helm. Wisps of hair darted across her cheeks from each side, complementing her bone structure.

Where many of the female Vraad openly displayed their continually changing attributes, Melenea had, in contrast to the last time they had met, worn a form-fitting, glittering dress of deep green. The dress, by virtue of its clinging, displayed her full shape to far greater success than her counterparts. One reason Dru suspected he had not seen her earlier—and he had been watching just so he could have avoided this moment—was that she had likely been surrounded by admirers of both sexes vying for her favors.

Once, Dru had been one of the more ardent.

Melenea laughed lightly, pure music, and Dru's pulse quickened. He realized he had been staring.

"Sweet thing." She put a hand on his cheek and caressed it. Dru wanted to but did not move. "You're so much more fun than the rest." Her eyes twinkled, a trick she had mastered as no other had. The smile grew knowing. "You play the games with more feeling, more defiance."

That snapped the spell. He reached up and grabbed her tiny, firm hand, but not before she left bloody memories of her long, sharp nails in his cheek. With a careless twitch, he healed the wounds.

"I don't play your games. Not anymore."

The laugh, the *smile*, they both taunted and tempted him. He knew his face had grown crimson long ago, but that was one thing beyond his abilities to prevent.

"You will, dear sweet Dru. You'll come to me because I am the only way you can pass the centuries without thinking *too* deeply." She artfully turned his grip on her hand into an opportunity to let her lips brush against his knuckles. Dru released her hand instantly, pulling his own to his side.

She took a step toward him and watched with visible amusement as he forced himself to stand his ground. "How is darling Sharissa? It's been *so* long since I saw her. She must be a beautiful and desirable woman by now . . . and so *new*."

"Sharissa is well . . . and no longer any concern of yours." He would *not* give her this victory! He would not flee from her!

"She will always be my concern, if only because she's your concern." Melenea waved off the subject as if it no longer entertained her. "Barakas is making his silly speech and simply destroying the mood of the coming. A shame what he did to Dekkar and Silesti, isn't it? I understand neither of them will be coming back."

Dru gritted his teeth. There was no way to avoid some loss of face; he *had* to get away from her now!

"If Barakas is speaking, I should be up there. I trust you will be able to do without my company, Melenea"—he executed a mock bow—"as I have been more than able to do without yours."

Now it was her visage that shone scarlet, the smile faltering just a little and the eyes narrowing. Some of Dru's confidence returned. He started to walk past her, indicating to Melenea, he hoped, that her presence bothered him so little that he felt no need to instantly teleport far away.

Her voice snared him as he continued up the steps. "Lady Tezerenee is here, Dru sweet. I think she, too, would like to give her love to Sharissa. She seems to have been looking for both of you, in fact."

He stood on the steps, his face carefully kept from her sight . . . a futile gesture since his sudden immobility spoke volumes concerning the success of her barb. It was the one thing Dru had not expected because it was the one thing he thought Melenea could not understand.

With her low, knowing laughter cutting through his heart, Dru curled within himself and vanished from the stairway.

His new destination was far from the balcony on which Barakas Tezerenee, his eldest son Reegan, and a host of other Tezerenee stood, overlooking the expectant throngs. The patriarch was already into the thrust of his speech and his presence could be felt even from where Dru stood. Yet another shiver coursed through the tall sorcerer, but this time he could not say as to which reason was the cause.

"Masterrrr?"

Sirvak! In all that had happened, Dru had completely forgotten the familiar, despite it being perched on his shoulder and wrapped around the back of his neck. Despite its seemingly awkward size, the familiar could make itself virtually unnoticeable, an ability that Dru himself had personally added during Sirvak's creation.

"What is it, friend?"

The familiar gently licked its master's cheek with its long, narrow tongue. Being a part of Dru, it sometimes understood him better than he himself did. "Meleneaaaa."

"She caught me unawares, nothing more."

"Frightens, masterrrrr. Lady frightensss."

"She's disturbing, Sirvak, but hardly frightening." The creature's fears, however, transmitted themselves to him. He knew Melenea's tastes—all *too* well—and knew her propensity for games that tended to leave others damaged or, at the very least, in disarray.

Dru shook his head. She had just been *toying* with him, nothing more. Petty cruelty was a streak common in the Vraad race and more so in the temptress. That was all it was.

And you make yourself such an open target, he scolded himself.

The sky flashed, the green and crimson clouds swirling violently as if in response to the explosion. Dru turned at the sound of thunder, wondering it if was going to rain for once. There had not been any rain for over three years now. If not for the powers of the Vraad, Nimth would have perished from thirst.

A second flash lit the heavens in the direction of his own domain.

A massive peak, clearly seen and as solid as any, stood in the distance, its white tip and vegetation-enshrouded base taunting him. Dru gaped.

It was—it *had* to be—a piece of the shrouded realm thrusting through the veil *into* his own world!

"There you are!"

Dru whirled around, but saw nothing. He glanced up and discovered the source of the voice directly above him. A Tezerenee riding a dragon. From where he stood, Dru could not make out the features of the rider. It could have been one of the patriarch's sons or a cousin. In fact, if he had not heard the voice, Dru would have been hard-pressed to identify the newcomer as male or female without augmenting his vision again.

The rider urged his mount lower. "The Lord Barakas Tezerenee has dispatched myself and several others to search for you! You were to be at his side by the time he began to speak before the crowds!"

"I found it necessary to be away. It seems my absence had little effect on his speech, anyway." Dru desperately wanted to leave the city, to explore the rift. If there was truly a physical way through . . .

The Tezerenee seemed horribly ignorant of the vast sight in the distance. He only had eyes for the object of his mission, a protesting outsider. "The clan master still desires your presence! You will return with me!"

Dru felt all the anger and frustration of the past hour battle against his slipping self-control. He eyed the rider and the beast. "I am not one of your toy-soldier brethren, Tezerenee! I come when I wish to! Matters have come up that demand my return to my own domain! You can convey my *regrets* to Lord Barakas, but not me!"

"You—"

"That is all I have to say to you, Tezerenee!" Raw power crackled like an aura around the narrow spellcaster, a sign of the fury within him straining to be released.

The dragon protested the difficulty of continuing to hover, but the rider ignored him. Dru matched stares with the airborne Vraad. At last, the Tezerenee signaled for the dragon to rise again.

"The clan master will be furious!"

"You may relay to him my apologies and my wishes for the best in the hours to come! I will contact him when it proves possible!"

In the end, it was likely the authoritative tone that backed the dragon rider away. From his time in the company of the patriarch, Dru had picked up on the voice that Barakas utilized to exercise his control. Trained from birth to obey that voice, the rider could not, in the end, match wills with Zeree. With a final muttered response that the wind, which had picked up despite protective spells surrounding the city, carried away, the Tezerenee rode off.

Dru sighed and smiled. Sirvak hissed in satisfaction. It was always nice to gain a victory, however small. The rider would probably wait until his master was finished speaking, rather than disrupt the patriarch's great moment. That gave Dru a little more time before Barakas began trying to contact him. Time enough, if he hurried, to see his daughter.

The claws of his familiar tightened on his shoulder. The creature had gone from pleased to dismayed in only seconds. Even before he turned, Dru suspected what he would see.

The peak was fading. Slowly, to be sure, but far too quickly for Dru's needs.

It was with a mixture of relief and anxiety that he vanished from the city only a breath later.

"*SHARISSA!*"

A soft mist settled around Dru as he appeared in the central chamber of his gleaming citadel. The pearl luster of his home generally filled him with a feeling of peace, of sanctuary. Not so, now.

"Sharissa!"

His call echoed through the corridors. When he had created this castle centuries before, he had added a spell that would relay sounds from one room to the next. For the most part, it had protected him from several angry rivals over the years and kept his most important work secret from even the best of his counterparts. In the twenty years since his daughter's birth, Dru had essentially used it to locate her. Two people did little in the way of filling a void so large as this structure.

"Father?"

"Where are you?"

"In the theater."

"Stay there." Dru curled within himself and vanished again, almost losing Sirvak, who had carelessly assumed it was safe to climb off. The familiar let out an annoyed cry and dug its talons in deeper. This time, Dru winced.

The scene that he found himself in the midst of threw the sorcerer completely off balance. He was in a chamber filled with dancing couples. They twirled and twirled, completely ignorant of the towering figure caught in the center of the ball. To the side, a nonsensical group of animals that were also instruments played the music. A huge, furred thing, loosely related to Sirvak's lupine half, beat on a drum in its middle while a four-legged monstrosity with a pipe-stem mouth played a merry tune.

One of the male dancers came within arm's reach of Dru. The spellcaster's eyes narrowed; it was his own face, but as it might look if he had allowed it to age more. Lines crisscrossed his features and the visage as a whole had filled out. Dru quickly turned and studied another dancer. Again, it was his face, but clean-shaven and with a somewhat bulbous nose. This one was also shorter by half a foot.

A quick scan revealed that *all* of the male dancers were variations on his appearance. Tall, short, fat, thin, old, and young . . . he was astonished at how numerous the combinations were.

Then his attention fell on the women.

They were *Sharissa.*

It did not surprise him, not really, since she had no one but the two of them to really go by. Nonetheless, as he watched the couples sweep across the floor, Dru was struck by a feeling of dread. Looking at them, he could see her as other Vraad would see her . . . fully adult and ready, physically, at least, to make her mark among them.

To use and *be* used, as was the Vraad way.

With a furious gesture, he dismissed the dancers. They dwindled instantly into tiny whirlwinds of dust, puppet images drawn from the life of the world itself. Unlike golems, who had some solidity and could comprehend orders, the dancers were no more than intricate toys, an art form that occasionally amused Vraad. He had taught it to his daughter when she was only a few years old and had been pleased with her immediate skill with the not-so-simple spell.

Dru was not so pleased now. There were too many things to worry about to keep adding to the list, though this was really part of his first and foremost fear, he supposed.

"Sharissa!"

"Here, Father."

She came to him as more of a mist than the child that he had expected. The billowing silver dress that clung to her proportions reminded him of what he had just tried to force from his mind, that, though only two decades old, his daughter was a woman. For someone three millennia old, two decades seemed hardly enough time to learn to walk.

Tall, though she only came to his chin, Sharissa was not willowy. She had grown to fit her frame, looking exactly as she should have looked if she were a foot shorter. Her hair was silver-blue—natural, as far as Dru knew—and flowed down her backside to a point just below her waist. Like many Vraad, she had crystalline eyes, aquamarine gemstones that shone brightly when she was pleased with something. Her lips were thin, but perpetually curled upward at the ends. Even when Sharissa was angry, it was all she could do to force those lips into a straight line much less a frown.

"What is it, Father? Did something happen at the coming? Was there a duel?"

He stirred. Caught up in *dreaming*, again! "No, no duel. One, actually, but the Lord Tezerenee put an end to it."

"That's no good! A duel should reach a dramatic conclusion on its own!"

Among Dru's earliest attempts to entertain his daughter had been tales of some of the more interesting duels he had witnessed . . . and occasionally been part of. Much to his regret, Sharissa had proven to have a Vraadish taste for such things. It was one of the chief reasons she had begged to go to the coming and one of the chief reasons Dru had not taken her. He was thankful that she had listened. By this stage of her powers, she could have easily ignored him and gone on her own.

"Never mind that now! I gave you some duties to perform while I was away." Those duties had been partly to keep her busy for a time, but *some* of them had had true purposes. "Did you take care of them?"

Sharissa looked down. "Some of them . . . I . . . I was bored with them. I thought I'd finish in a few minutes." Her eyes were wide with worry. "I only had the ball running for two or three minutes; that's all!"

Dru forced himself to breathe calmly. "The crystals. That's what I want to know about. Did you adjust their settings? Did you refocus the spell as I asked?"

"Oh, *yes!* I did that first because you made it sound the most important!"

"Serkadion Manee be praised!"

Hugging his daughter, Dru felt the first relief he had experienced since before his departure for the coming. If things were as they should be . . .

"What happened? What about the Lord Tezerenee's plan? Did something go wrong?"

"I'll tell you later. For the time being, we have work to do, you and I." Releasing his daughter, Dru twisted his head around so that he could look Sirvak more or less in the eye. "To your sentinel duties, my friend. Some young drake of the patriarch's might come looking for me. I want to know before he or they get here. I also want no one else prying into this!"

"Masterrrr." The familiar stretched, spread its magnificent wings, and flew off. Dru had complete faith in the creature's abilities; Sirvak was single-minded when it came to its duties. It would monitor and protect the castle better than either the sorcerer or his daughter.

"Come." He took Sharissa's hand. "This may literally prove to be a key to our predicament!"

As one, they folded inward and vanished from the theater—only to *reappear* at their exact starting point a second later.

Sharissa moaned, holding her head as if struck by some unseen assailant. Dru felt little better, finding even his legs unsteady.

"Father . . . the spell . . . like yesterday . . ."

"I know." Yesterday, Dru had found it necessary to adjust the design of the eastern tower so as to allow for the softening of the soil beneath. From a base of rock, the earth had turned to so much mud. Despite his best efforts, however, the Vraad could not alter the composition of the ground. Mud it had become and mud it was determined to stay. In the end, Dru had been forced to create a bridge and pylon system . . . and *that* had taken two attempts. For a time, his spells had either gone awry or failed completely.

"Why not just let the castle take us there?"

Dru considered the plan and dismissed it. "I would rather not be caught between floors if the castle magic began to fail."

"We walk, then."

"That we do."

Fortunately, their trek was a brief one. Had he chosen to visit his sanctum for any other reason, it was probable that he would have walked in the first place. His excitement was leading to carelessness, something the spellcaster knew was far too dangerous at this juncture. The two of them had been fortunate that they had only returned to their starting point. Another time and they might have materialized in the midst of a wall or floor.

A gigantic, metallic figure blocked the doorway through which Dru and Sharissa wished to pass. Its features were roughly hewed and vaguely reminiscent of a hound. The leviathan stood on a pair of blocky legs and held in its two enormous hands a shield taller than its master. A stylized gryphon decorated the shield.

Sharissa mouthed a single world. Though her voice was nearly inaudible, the golem understood. It stepped aside and went down on one knee, a supplicant before its lord and lady.

"Did you teach it to do that?" Dru asked, eyeing the unliving servant with distaste.

A momentary look of guilt passed across his daughter's otherwise perfect visage. "Only this morning! I just thought it would be amusing to see such a horrible-looking creature act so civilly."

"It will do this no more." The other Vraad would have laughed at him. Kneeling was one of the least commands they would have given their own golems. Dru, though, had found it too ridiculous. There was nothing magnificent about commanding a chunk of metal that could walk and kill. The golem was still no more than a toy.

Another sign of how he had changed. Once, he too, would have laughed.

The golem rose silently, Dru's words now law. The two Vraad continued on, the massive doors swinging open for them as they neared.

The sanctum of a Vraad was a far more individualistic thing than his or her outer appearance. Here, the subconscious played an active role in the design and maintenance. Here, a sorcerer's mind was free to act and create, with varying results. In the chambers of his counterparts, Dru knew, one could expect to find anything within the realms of the imagination . . . and often beyond.

Dru's own chambers, on the other hand, were bare—bare, that is, with the exception of countless crystals of all shapes and sizes orbiting or floating all about the room.

The spell, of which the gems were only the physical aspect, was the culmination of his work so far. Since the discovery of the realm beyond the veil, Dru had cleared out the paraphernalia from all past experiments—some of those items raising protest—and set aside everything for research into the nature of the wraith world. While others were pounding their magical might futilely against its phantom boundaries, he and a few of the more patient had sought out answers through careful study. That study had brought about, as a side result, the rediscovery—not *discovery*, as Barakas had put it—of the method of ka travel. The early Vraad had known of it, but for vague reasons no one could explain, they had forgotten soon after the founding generation of the Vraad race had passed on. He had discovered many other secrets as well, but all of them paled in the face of the greatest challenge. Somehow, the stubborn spellcaster still tried to believe, there was a way to travel physically to this other place.

Perhaps now . . .

Dru and his daughter stared curiously at the patterns formed by the floating crystals. The primary crystals, larger and generally fixed in one place, were, as he had hoped, arranged in the pattern he had asked Sharissa to set them in. It was something that had to be done by hand and his requested appearance at the coming had made that impossible. Sharissa, while occasionally prone to dreaming, was as excellent a helper as he could have dared hope. Soon, she would be able to conduct her own series of experiments and—

And that would only happen if they found a solution before Nimth began to pull the Vraad down with it in its death struggles.

The secondary crystals, which had been organized to catch the natural emanations of any sighting and record them for his later need, floated in a complex spiral cluster near the focus, a foot-wide black sphere that kept surveillance on the nearby regions surrounding his own domain. Principal study of late had been on the very area where Dru had seen the rift.

Sightings, the sorcerer had noted early on, always occurred near unstable regions. Whether one resulted from the other—it was debatable which way *that* worked, too—he could not say. They just seemed to be related, like opposite ends of a magical beast.

His eyes took in the myriad pattern of colors and shapes in the spiral, noting what changes had resulted from this latest opportunity and wondering what they would reveal. The crystals were still absorbing information, so all he could do for the moment was wait.

An irregularity caught his eye.

There were three crystals, two golden and one turquoise, that should *not* have been part of the spiral.

"Sharissa," he started quietly as he studied the possible ramifications of the error. "Did something happen to the spiral? Did the spell fail? Did you try re-creating it without my guidance?"

Knowing her father as she did, his daughter waited until he had exhausted all questions. When Dru grew silent, attention still focused on the crystals swirling about, she replied, "Nothing happened to the spiral, Father. I added those three on my own."

He turned, unable to believe his ears. "You did that of your own volition?"

"It makes sense, Father. See how they play off the amethyst and emerald ones below them."

"They cannot! To do that would mean—" Mouth still open, the gray-robed figure could only blink. The new additions were indeed playing off of the crystals Sharissa had mentioned and to far greater effect than he could have believed. But . . . "Impossible!"

"It works!"

"They should make the spiral unstable, cause it to explode!" Dru walked toward the spiral and dared to touch one of the golden gems. It pulsated in perfect harmony with the rest. "The combination has never held before!"

Sharissa held her ground. "I saw that it would work the moment I started adjusting the primaries. You've always taught me to use my initiative."

"Not like this." Still awed, Dru stepped back. They *were* functioning. Crystal work was very delicate, even for beings as powerful as the Vraad. Many of the sorcerous race could not even work that particular magic successfully. The ability to move mountains, while it tore asunder the natural laws of Nimth—what remained of them—was far and away more simple. That required only will and power. Crystal work required patience and finesse. Sharissa, to have seen what was needed, had developed a skill that would soon surpass her parent.

There was more to this, however, than met the physical eye. Dru turned his gaze to another plane of sight.

The world remained the same, but now he could see the jagged patterns that bound Nimth. Spirals, once neatly formed and organized, had reconnected in haphazard fashion, the world's own natural attempt to make up for the damage the careless Vraad had done to it. Things were far beyond repair, however.

All seemed as it had been until Dru looked closer. Then he began to notice the intruding lines, forces that came from nowhere, but bound themselves to the fabric of Nimth.

But from where?

Where else? Dru followed the invaders as far back as he could and found that all of them dwindled at the same point. The region where he had noted the rift.

The Vraad had been trying with little success to break into the shrouded realm . . . and here it was, *encroaching* now upon their own!

IV

GERROD STOOD ON the plain where a group of Tezerenee, led by his cousin Ephraim, worked to provide the clan and those allied with it the bodies they would need in the days to come. The other Vraad as yet did not know that proving one's loyalty to the sons of the dragon would be a prerequisite for their survival.

He had come here to escape the wrath of his father, if only for a time, who had been livid from the moment it was discovered the outsider Zeree had left the city. Gerrod both admired and scorned the outsider. Admired him for both defying Barakas and providing the research that had been of such immeasurable value. Scorned him as an outsider and weak man when it came to certain necessities. Still, Dru Zeree had been the only man Gerrod felt safe admitting at least some of his feelings to for now. He had not told him everything, but it was safe to assume that a quick mind like Zeree's was capable of reading much from the tone of his voice.

The deeper truth was that unlike his multitude of obedient relations, the young Tezerenee had no desire to live in a world formed by his progenitor's continually growing religious fervor. As a matter of fact, he had no desire to live anywhere his father lived, dragon spirit or not.

Ephraim, his armor hanging oddly loose on his body, finally rose from the center of the pentagram etched in the earth. Gerrod frowned impatiently. He had stood here for nearly twenty minutes, far too long for a respectful wait. That was one of the problems. Among his own clan, he felt out of place, unnecessary except as an assistant to Rendel. This despite all the work that *he* had done.

"What is it you want?"

The voice was horribly dead of any emotion, something terribly alien in the violent Tezerenee. Gerrod studied his cousin before answering. Ephraim's face was pale and gaunt, hardly the heavy, weather-beaten figure who had come here only three days ago. There was also a faraway look in his eyes that chilled Gerrod.

"Did you feel it when Rendel took over the first golem?"

"Yes. It was painful for him." Ephraim's eyes would not meet his but insisted on staring beyond the hooded Tezerenee's shoulder.

"You've made changes, then?"

"We have."

"How soon can you begin on the others?"

"We have nearly a dozen completed." The pale face broke into a thin, satisfied smile.

"Already?" Gerrod was taken aback. Small wonder that his cousin was so pale, if they were already hard at work on the hosts for the Vraad ka.

"There seemed no reason to wait. It's quite . . . entertaining." The ghostly smile remained fixed, as if forgotten by its bearer.

This was news Gerrod knew he would have to take to his father personally. He could ill afford to hesitate with this, despite his lack of desire for the crossover's success. Not just the jump on creation of the golems, but the effort being put in by the group. If Ephraim was any indication, the strain must be terrible. Barakas would have him punished if something went wrong and it could be proved that Gerrod had been at fault.

"You'll need help. Father will send others to replace those who cannot go on."

"*No!*" A white, cold hand reached out and snared one of Gerrod's wrists. "*We* will not falter! This is our calling!"

The eyes of his cousin blazed bright. Gerrod peeled his hand free. Ephraim's gaze finally met his own. It was not one the hooded Vraad cared to stare into for very long.

"As you wish, Ephraim. If you need anything, though, you must—"

The other interrupted in the same monotone voice he had utilized earlier. "Do you know that it should be possible to take a portion of a ka and keep it after the one to whom it belongs has died? We've discussed it, the others and I. No one would truly ever be dead, then. They could be called up, using golems for temporary form, and made to—"

"What are you talking about?"

Ephraim quieted. "Nothing. We have found that we only need a part of our selves now and so we talk. The strain lessens with each one. Perhaps we are adapting to the Dragonrealm."

Gerrod had heard more than enough. The strain might be lessening, but it had evidently already driven the group mad if its leader was any example. He doubted that his sire would send anyone to spell the group until they began dying. Why waste any more? If Ephraim and the others lived long enough to complete their task, that was all that his father would want.

He wrapped the shroudlike cloak about himself, once more becoming more of a shadow than a man. Ephraim took a step away. Gerrod hesitated, then said, "I will inform Father of your success and your confidence concerning your ability to continue."

"That would be good."

Perhaps they will die when no one is around to see, Gerrod thought. *If only there was another way than Father's, I would* . . . He curled within himself, feeling, as he had the last couple of times, a curious hesitation, as if the teleportation spell did not wish to work. It did, however, and he gratefully left his cousin and the others.

Ephraim, for his part, waited until Gerrod had left. Then, he silently returned to the center of the pentagram. The others looked up in unison, and had anybody watched them then, it would have seemed that they were one mind with eleven bodies . . . a mind that was no longer Tezerenee.

Dru LOOKED OVER the information his crystals had gathered for him and compared them to those he had utilized in the past. There were definite signs of a potential breakthrough, yet there were aberrations that still made no sense.

Made no sense unless . . .

He recalled the change in the pattern that Sharissa had wrought. A pattern that should not have been stable. The intruding forces from the other realm were affecting the natural laws of his own world in much the same way as Vraad sorcery did, only without the damage. Could it be that what Dru thought made no sense merely did not because his mind refused to accept that the binding forces of Nimth had been altered by the intruding power?

"A change in the laws of power like none before," he muttered.

"What will you do now?"

"What will *we* do? Don't look at me like that. I'm beginning to think that you know more than I do . . . or *will*, before long. Besides, what I hope to do will take two people and I think I prefer to trust *you*."

Her eyes were wide with realization. "You think you can *cross!*"

Again, she had anticipated his next moves. Dru's smile masked mixed emotions. "It may be possible. What we have to do is go to the point where the forces from the other realm merge and fade away. *That* is the point of weakness, I hope." It was also quite possible that due to the combination of Nimth's power and that of the other, the location would actually be the point of greatest strength. If such were the case, Dru might find himself beating against a wall so incredibly hard that not all the Vraad in the world, even had they been able to cooperate, would have been able to bring it down.

"Will we have to walk there?"

He considered their options. "I do not care to try to teleport, especially not after what I've seen and what the crystals have verified." His eyebrow arched. "We can *ride* there."

Sharissa caught his meaning. "I'll saddle them up!"

Dru watched her hurry off, her childlike glee a direct contrast to her elegant face and form. If there was one thing that she had never outgrown, it was her fondness for the creatures of the stable, specifically the horses. They were rare and wonderful beasts taller than Dru, and fearsome to all save his daughter. She rode them expertly and without the aid of sorcery. They might not be as powerful or majestic as the gryphons, which she also enjoyed, but they were swifter and more companionable.

While Sharissa went about her task, Dru reached out with his mind and strengthened the link between himself and Sirvak. The familiar's mind opened, knowing that orders were about to be given. Dru informed it of his intentions to investigate and how long he thought they would be. To his surprise, instead of acknowledging all and returning to its duties, the beast protested.

Masterrr! Take Sirvak with! Will need!

Not for this, friend. I only go to research, as I have done in the past.

Do not leave Sirvakkkk! Sirvak will guard!

Your duties are here! Enough of this! What's gotten into you?

The creature sulked and would say no more. Still perturbed, Dru broke contact. As if he did not have enough difficulties! Now, even Sirvak was causing him worry!

"Father, the horses are ready." Along with Sharissa's words came the echoes of animal sounds, hooves clattering on hard earth and the snorts of the two mighty steeds.

"I'm on my way."

The walk to the stables was not as long as it sometimes was, especially when one was propelled, as the sorcerer was now, by a desire to be done with things. Sharissa waited at the mouth of the central stable, a horse on each side of her, their reins in her hands. Again, she had used no magic save her own charm and skill. It was not due in any part to the gentle nature of the horses, either. As one Vraad—sardonic Krystos, wasn't it? Dru remembered vaguely—had once discovered, these animals were particular as to whom they allowed close. Krystos had escaped with his fingers intact, at least. A few more arrogant visitors, invited and not, had discovered that the stables of Dru Zeree were no place to vent their arrogance. Like their master, the animals were willing to strike back . . . and were doubly protected by the spells that he had layered over their forms.

"Was Sirvak upset?"

"Yes, how did you know?"

"It just seemed that way. I could feel the poor thing all the way here. Why not take Sirvak with, Father? The castle will defend itself adequately."

Dru shrugged off her suggestion. "And Sirvak will defend it superbly. Never underestimate others, Sharissa. A Vraad always has rivals and those rivals always look for weaknesses in your defense. With Sirvak there, it will be as if they are fighting me . . . and you know what success they've had so far."

Sharissa's perpetual smile broadened. Despite his more peaceful way of life since her birth, her father was not one to be underestimated. After the Lord Tezerenee, Dru was one of the most respected of the Vraad. Even his most bitter rivals occasionally came to him for assistance and advice.

Taking the reins of the larger of the two animals, Dru mounted. In general shape and color, the two steeds were identical—proud, auburn-furred animals built for both speed and battle. Dru had chosen to forgo the use of sorcery when breeding them and had found, to his pleasure, that the results exceeded what he had originally wanted. As with many things over the past few years, he had discovered a diverse pleasure in not performing spells to accomplish his needs.

When both of them were ready, Dru urged his horse forward. Sharissa's steed followed close behind. With the cool wind in his face, the sorcerer slowly calmed. Things were moving in the proper direction for once, and if his theories held out, the Vraad would not have to bow to the will of the Lord Tezerenee. Barakas would be upset about that, to be sure, but Dru had no qualms about destroying his "partner's" dream. It was only because there had seemed no other way at the time that he had let the situation go on for as long as it had. Now, the cross-over would no longer be necessary.

The sky rumbled again, tearing him from his musings and making him look up. The dark, foreboding green was dominant for the first time in months. Dru frowned, recalling the violent changes in the land when that had last happened. The dominance of either color in the sky spoke ill for Nimth. Things were always best when the two were more or less even.

Change could have only come about from some extensive use of Vraad sorcery. Dru knew of only one cause . . . the spells of the Tezerenee tearing at the boundaries and beyond. The great cross-over was *hastening* the death of the world, if Dru read the signs right. Now, more than ever, the importance of his *own* plan became unmistakable. Unconsciously, he urged the horse to greater speed.

"Father!" Sharissa suddenly called out, her voice partly obscured by the continued rumbling.

He turned toward her, careful to make certain that the steed was following a safe path, and saw what had caught her attention.

A crack had opened in the earth far to the north of their present location. It was small now, little more than a scar, but it was widening with each passing moment. The walls of each side of the growing ravine crumbled, causing a rain of rock and dirt. The sight would not have disturbed Dru save for the fact that the path of the tear would cut through his own domain closer than any such vast instability had prior to this. In fact, the horses might not be able to clear it on the way back. He would be *forced* to use his sorcery . . . and so near to an untrustworthy region.

Complications and disaster; it seemed he was never to be free of them. Dru hoped that the point of intersection would at least prove peaceful, like the eye of a storm.

The horse stumbled, nearly causing him to lose the reins. The path was rocky and rose higher than he recalled. When he pulled on the reins in order to slow the animal, it gave him no argument. Sharissa's mount caught up to them, then slowed to a similar pace as the young woman copied her father's action.

The wind was picking up, much the way it had at the city. There seemed, however, no one direction to its movement, for it struck the tiny party from all sides, changing with each passing breath. Dru cursed his own impatience, for they had left their cloaks behind. With some trepidation, he stretched out his left arm and summoned one for each of them.

On his outstretched arm appeared two brown cloaks with hoods. Sharissa took hers and gratefully put it on, drawing the hood partly over her massive waves of hair. Dru donned his own, but left the hood down for the time being. He had simply wanted the garment as a precaution.

"How much farther?"

Dru pointed at a ridge. Though both of them could follow the lines of binding, the odd strings of power cut through the ridge and came out somewhere on the other side, completely hidden. "Over that ridge! This must be where the rift was birthed!"

"But that was elsewhere!"

"The power . . . the flow from the other realm . . . spreads as it enters Nimth! The rift was the weakest of spots, perhaps created by some surge! I don't know yet!"

Their conversation continued as they encouraged their mounts around the ridge. As they drew closer to their destination, the wind abruptly changed again, this time dying to next to nothing. It was so calm, in fact, that Dru felt as if he had ridden into a tomb. The only sounds were the clatter of hooves against loose rock and the breathing of the riders and steeds.

"Serkadion Manee!" Dru tugged tight on the reins as he spoke, for the horse had begun to shy at the disquieting sight before them.

"It's—" Sharissa struggled futilely for words and finally just let her silence speak for her.

Dru had seen the phantom lands three times before, but they never ceased to stun him. A part of his mind that still functioned understood what Sharissa, who had *never* seen such a sight, must be feeling.

The ridge that was truly a part of the Vraad's world was a sharp, twisted thing that rose high in the air and went on for some distance. A few scraggly trees stood here and there, along with some equally misshapen bushes. Of animal life, there was no trace. The ridge was more or less a great gray-brown mass of dirt and rock, hardly worth looking at by itself.

Not so, the *other* realm.

A forest of spectral trees, high and strong, seemed to stand guard at the base of the ridge. When Dru looked closer, he saw that the forest went *into* the ridge itself, much the same way the lines of force had on the other side. Transparent waves of grass, knee-high to the spellcaster, dipped back and forth, brushed gently by some breeze that existed *there*, but *not* in Nimth. A tiny form flitted beyond, an avian of some sort, though it looked like no more than a shadow. The curious mist hung over all, making both regions appear blurred.

"It's frightening . . . and *beautiful*," Sharissa finally managed to say.

"Yes." Dru stirred, knowing he was wasting valuable time. "Stay where you are. I want to go farther."

"Father! You can't do that! This isn't like the others, the intruding power—"

He was already dismounting. "I won't be able to find out what I want unless I walk through it." That was not quite true, but he could not resist. This was not the solid, absolutely real mountain peak he had spotted earlier, but it was the most complete image yet. More important still, the point of intersection was almost in sight. There, he would learn the most.

Dru started to hand the reins of his mount over to Sharissa, then decided it might be better to have the horse handy. He whispered a short spell to the animal, calming it in case the unnatural landscape made it too distraught.

"Be careful."

"I will. You watch. Let me know if you see anything out of the ordinary."

"Everything *here* is out of the ordinary."

He chuckled. "True."

Leading the horse he slowly walked into the chaotic region. Even the ground, the watchful spellcaster noted, had its wraithlike counterpart. Twice, he stepped into depressions that he had assumed were not part of his reality and once he nearly tripped when what he thought was better footing proved to be a slightly more solid-looking bit of the other realm.

The translucent field of grass invited him to enter. After a moment of hesitation, he put a foot forward. Finding nothing but the hard soil of his own world, he grew more confident.

All around him, Dru began to feel a tingling. He was close to the invading lines of force. For reasons the sorcerer could not fathom, a great revulsion at the thought of using Vraad magic overwhelmed him. He had not had any desire to cast a spell, but the feeling was with him, regardless. Dru steadied himself and pushed the emotion to the back of his mind. It continued to nag him, but no more than if he had been experiencing a mild headache.

Halfway through the field, Dru paused. The forest was far more solid now and tinges of color pervaded it. The lines converged within the forest after all, but he could still not make out where.

"Father!"

Dru whirled back, but all he saw were Sharissa and the other horse. She did not appear fearful, only worried. He waited for her to say or do something.

Sharissa pointed at the treetops, which Dru had more or less ignored. It was hard to hear her; the shrouded realm seemed to deaden sound. All that he could make out from her shouts and gesturing was that she had seen some fairly large shape in the trees. The master mage turned and studied them for more than a minute, waiting for some sign of whatever it was his daughter had noticed. His own impatience, however, got hold of him and he finally turned back to her and shrugged. She still looked disturbed, but indicated her willingness for him to continue if he wished.

His steed was beginning to act up now, despite the spell. Dru held tight to the reins and talked to it. Slowly, he got the animal under control. When he was at last able to gaze upon the forest again, it had grown even more real. Now, he could almost imagine the sounds of wildlife.

Within a few yards of the first trees, Dru paused again. The true landscape of Nimth was no longer visible through the trunks; he might have very well been standing at the edge of an actual forest, though none such remained in his world. Leading the reluctant horse on, Dru moved to within arm's length of the nearest tree. Slowly, cautiously, he reached out.

His hand waded through something that had the consistency of mud. It was as if the tree was there, but not quite.

The horse reared, screaming as it did.

A man-sized shape with a wingspan greater than the length of the maddened steed fell upon the startled Vraad. Dru saw taloned hands and feet and a beak designed for tearing flesh come racing at him. So sudden was the attack that it was all he could do to raise his arms in a feeble effort to block the airborne monstrosity. There were spells that he wore upon his person that *should* protect him, but *should* and *would* were two different things. Whatever assaulted him was a creature of the other realm and there was no way of telling what powers it might have.

An odd twinge coursed through Dru's body. He stared in amazement as his adversary fell *through* him. In his surprise, the sorcerer had forgotten that any creature of the land beyond the veil would have the same consistency as its habitation.

It seemed that the winged horror would continue down, battering itself against the earth of its phantom plain. Then the creature somehow managed to flap hard enough to keep it above ground level. With great strain, it rose swiftly into the air and back toward the forest. Throughout most of the moment, Dru saw little more than wings, feathers, and limbs all tangled together. Not until the attacker was disappearing into the treetops did the spellcaster get a good look at it.

Avian it was, but also manlike. It could walk on its hind legs and grasp things in its hands, of that he was certain. Standing, it was probably nearly as tall as he was. From its ability to compensate for its mistakes and the nearly human form it wore, Dru knew that it was likely that it was intelligent as well. If such was the case, then the Lord Tezerenee's precious Dragonrealm might not prove so idyllic a place . . . although the sons of the dragon *might* actually look forward to fighting an actual foe for a change. Perhaps Barakas already *knew* what awaited the Vraad.

Barely audible, the worried voice of Sharissa finally broke into his reveries. "Father! Are you all right? Father?"

The disheveled spellcaster scanned the region for the horse. There was no sign. For some reason, that did not sit right with the Vraad. His horse *had* to be somewhere nearby. At the very least, Dru should have been able to sense the equine. As hard as he tried, however, there was no trace. It was as if the horse had vanished. . . .

"Father! Did it hurt you? I think that was what I saw!" Sharissa reined her mount to a stop and leaped off. She rushed over to Dru and wrapped her arms tightly around his torso. She buried her tear-tracked features in his chest. "I was certain you were dead! It was all over you and then I suddenly remembered that it had to be a wraith just like where it came from and—"

"Hush, daughter. Take a deep breath and calm yourself. I'm fine. Like you said, it was only a wraith. Perfectly harmless." Though his words were for his daughter, Dru's attention was still focused on the missing horse. Was it possible, he wondered, that the animal was no longer in Nimth? Could it be . . .

"Sharissa." He stroked her silver-blue hair. "Can you tell me what happened to my horse? Did you see where it ran off to?"

Her emotions slowly coming under control again, the young Vraad looked up at her father. "Your horse? Can't *you* find it?"

"I find no trace."

"That cannot be so!" With the determination of youth, she utilized her own powers to seek out the errant steed. After a few moments, she frowned and said, "You are right! I cannot feel its presence anywhere! I think I do recall seeing it . . ." Sharissa hesitated, replaying the chaotic scene. "I think it . . . oh, Father!" Her eyes grew round. "It ran *into* the forest!"

"As I thought." Dru separated the two of them and turned to study the forest. A thin mist still permeated it, but, for the moment, it looked more real than the landscape it had replaced.

"Is it one of those rifts you mentioned?"

"Possibly. I have to go see."

Sharissa nodded. "I guess you'll be safe if those things can't touch you, but be careful!"

"I will, even if it means using sorcery. I want you, though, to ride back to where I left you and stay there this time. Keep an eye on the lines . . . if they change, I want to know when I get back."

"All right." With some reluctance, Sharissa obeyed his orders. Dru forced himself to wait until she was beyond the edge of the translucent field and then turned to face the dark woods.

As a Vraad, he should have had no fear, yet Dru felt his heart pound wildly and could hear his own rapid breathing as if someone had magnified the sound a thousandfold. Those two sensations were beginning to become normal with him it seemed, the spellcaster thought sourly. Nevertheless, curiosity held the edge. A cautious curiosity, to be sure, but one that would not, in the end, be denied.

Dru entered the forest.

Just past the first trees, he paused. Becoming lost would have been the culmination of all his troubles. Reaching into a pocket of his robe, the sorcerer pulled out a small, glittering cube. It was a beacon of sorts, one that he had shaped gradually over the past few years so as to give it great strength. He had meant to give it to his daughter, but had forgotten because of his excitement. Still, knowing where the edge of the forest was would do just as well. The horse might be beyond his other sight, but not so this device. It would allow him to backtrack to this spot without error. He placed it on the ground where he had previously walked and made certain that it was secure. Feeling a bit more confident now, Dru moved on, picking up his pace and anxiously waiting for the first sign that he had *finally* reached the point of intersection.

He was careful to note his path as he wandered among the tall trees. Though the cube would lead him back, it could not warn him of the obstacles that he might have to deal with, or of those things that might lurk in the forest itself. He had not mentioned it to Sharissa, but if the forest continued to grow more solid, it was more than likely that the denizens, including the avian monster that had attacked him, would follow suit. Dru had a spell handy, just to be on the safe side, but hoped he would not need it. In this place, it was possible that his spell might not even go off properly.

Now several yards into the woods, Dru could still feel no trace of the animal. More annoying, however, was a new obstacle to his success. Here in the forest, it seemed, the lines *curved*, moving off to the right and bisecting trees here and there. For some reason, he could still not see the intersection. A Vraadish temper Dru had once thought he had tamed completely rose for the second time this day, bathing him in a golden aura of his own sorcerous might. That action, however, caused disruptions in his sight, distorting his view of the lines he had been following. Breathing deeply, the Vraad fought back his anger. Not now. Not so close to his goal.

He had to be close, even with this latest twist. A few more steps and he would be there. Dru kept telling himself that, unconsciously turning it into a litany.

It was tempting to try to walk *through* the trees in order to take a more direct route, but Dru decided it would be safe not to aggravate things. The gray trunks were more solid than not and he might find himself trapped within one. Not a pretty way to die and certainly not a dignified one.

A horse neighed somewhere ahead of him. Oddly, he could still not feel its mind.

How far had he walked now, the sorcerer wondered suddenly. The second ridge, the one in which the forest actually continued on as if the massive formation were so much air and not stubborn rock, had to be nearby, yet Dru could not find it. The canopy formed by the treetops made seeing the heavens nearly impossible. The lack of illumination made it troublesome enough to see his path . . . though he was not tempted in the least to alter his vision to compensate for the darkness. He might turn himself blind instead.

One thought that he instantly dismissed was the possibility that he might have walked *into* the ridge. Dru was of Nimth, as was the ridge. If he needed proof of which reality he belonged to, he only had to look at the wavering, dull gray trees around him.

Wavering? Dull gray?

The forest was fading. Slowly, yes, but definitely fading. The Vraad cursed. He had wasted too much time with his thoughts!

Throwing caution to the wind, Dru ran on, following the lines of power as best he could. Trees constantly blocked his way, almost as if intentional, but

Dru, even knowing that they were growing more and more insubstantial by the minute, insisted on going around them rather than through. Even still, the spellcaster could see that he was drawing closer. A few of the lines had already begun to merge. Why he could still not make out his goal nagged him. Only a step or two more. That was all. Only a step or two more.

In this one instance, his thoughts proved all too correct. Dru *did* find the point of intersection . . . or perhaps it could have been said just as easily that the point had found *him*.

It sprang to life before his very eyes, a huge, pulsating thing of light and darkness. As it swelled, it burned as bright as any sun. As it contracted, it turned as black as the deepest cavern. Dru, his foot raised for his next step, was caught unawares. He twisted in surprise and lost his footing. The ground—both of them—rose to meet his face as he tumbled forward.

Dru felt the padding of wild grass attempt to soften his fall, grass that had not existed in the landscape surrounding the Nimthian ridge.

"Serkadion Man—" The oath died as he looked up and caught sight of the vast mass of energy before him.

The darkness, a black far deeper than that of the forest, was growing faster than its opposite . . . and with each increase in size, the forest faded more.

He had no intention of finding out what would happen to him if he stayed so close. Curiosity was one thing, but in the end survival won out. As he rose, Dru cursed his Vraadish arrogance for leading him to this predicament. There were other ways he could have dealt with this situation, only he had refused to see them, preferring to face the mystery personally. Now, it was possible he would pay for that mistake.

His dignity a moot point, the sorcerer fled the way he had come. This time, he ignored the unsettling presence of the trees and charged through them, hoping deep inside that he would not find one that had, for his benefit, chosen to remain solid. That would end his flight very quickly and very painfully.

The mist was thickening even as the phantom landscape was fading. The trees were no more than shadows now, but the uninviting terrain of Nimth was just as murky. It was as if he were caught in between both of them, yet existed in *neither*. Full panic attempted a coup and was only barely beaten back. Dru stumbled to a halt. So far, he had not been thinking very much and that could prove more treacherous than the mists. Somewhere out there was the cube, his beacon back to reality. All he had to do was feel its presence.

That was *all* he had to do, yet he could not. Seeking out the cube proved no more simple than seeking out his steed. Nothing met his heightened senses no matter which direction he turned. The sorcerer might as well have been buried deep within the earth, so thoroughly was he cut off from everything. Dru could not even sense the lines of force. It was as if he were trapped in some sort of limbo.

He had only one choice. Though something within him warned that Vraad sorcery stood an equal chance of being either his salvation or his *death*, Dru had to make use of the one tool still remaining to him . . . *if* it still remained.

Curling within himself, Dru forced the teleportation spell through. Where once he could have performed it without conscious thought, now he had to complete the spell a bit at a time, urging each successive step on.

Slowly, the last bits of landscape—both Nimth and its wraithlike brother—dwindled to nothing, and only the mist and a peculiar whiteness that seemed like pure *nothing* remained. Dru, his body wracked with pain, did not relax, knowing that he was not safe until he stood on solid earth once more.

"Father . . ."

Sharissa's voice! Encouraged, the spellcaster pressed harder. In all his existence, he had never struggled so with a spell. The sweat covered his body and every muscle was taut with pain. Only a little more now. . . .

Where had he heard *that* before?

No! he screamed within his own mind. *I will succeed! I will!*

A rocky, wind-torn land abruptly greeted his eyes, almost jarring his senses with its sudden appearance. Never before had Dru thought he would be so happy to see the unfriendly domain of Nimth.

"Father! I'm coming! Hold on!"

Straightening, though every muscle shrieked during the process, Dru saw the tiny figure of his daughter running toward him. He stood, it appeared, in the center of where the field had been. Not his destination, not exactly, but close enough. Just so long as he was free of that other place.

With great relief, Dru put his hands to his face and wiped the sweat away. Blinking the moisture from his eyes, he happened to stare at his palms.

They were fading, already translucent enough that he could see Sharissa through them.

"No!" Something that would not be denied began pulling at him. He felt as if his body were being torn asunder. Nimth . . . and Sharissa . . . began to fade away once more.

"Father! Run to me! You're still too cl—"

Her words faded away along with the rest of the world. Dru's eyes flashed this way and that, seeking some object, however tiny, that he could fix on. There was nothing. Even the mist was gone. The only thing remaining was the white emptiness that he had noted briefly during his attempt at teleportation.

Dru now floated alone in that emptiness . . . with *no* idea as to where he was or *how* he could escape.

V

Gerrod kept his head down as he stood by his father, thankful that the bulky cloak he wore covered so much of his body. Barakas could not see—at least Gerrod thought—that his son was trembling.

Rendel would not have been treated with such scorn. That was true as far as it went. Rendel *would*, however, face much worse if he did not contact the clan before long. It was not due to any problem with the spell; Rendel had either left the region where he had crossed over or simply refused to respond.

That had only been the latest thrust. The outsider Zeree's departure—and his refusal to return—were eating at the patriarch as nothing else had. For the first few minutes Lord Barakas had ranted and raved. Then he had fallen into one of his deathly silent moods. Gerrod, who had been the object of his parent's anger more than once, would have preferred the ranting.

"I wonder what he plots?"

The question, the patriarch's first spoken words in over two hours, caught Gerrod and the others assembled by surprise simply because they had all been resigned to waiting in silence for the rest of the evening. That was how things normally went. A change in tradition now meant disaster for someone.

"The outsider?" Gerrod ventured.

"Zeree, yes, who *else*?"

Rendel. Perhaps Ephraim. Are you so blind, Father? The young Tezerenee wanted to shout at the clan master, but knew what results that would bring.

"You said nothing more to him than what you told me?"

"Nothing of importance, Father." Nothing save his desperate words toward the end.

"Leave it alone, Barakas dear."

The throaty voice belonged to perhaps the only member of the Tezerenee who could dare to speak back to the patriarch. She strode elegantly into the chamber that the clan had usurped from the city as sort of a second throne room. Clad in green scale, a living warrior queen, she stood nearly as tall as Lord Barakas himself. Her face was more striking than actually beautiful, but the grace with which she moved—or even breathed—was such that it added an entire dimension to her that most female Vraad lacked. The newcomer was desirable, but where Melenea had been a temptress, this woman was a queen.

The patriarch moved to take her hand. "Alcia."

Around them, the rest of the Tezerenee, Gerrod foremost, knelt before her in obeisance. Most of the clan whispered, "Lady Alcia."

Gerrod and a few select others simply said, "Mother."

"The others are getting restless out there, Barakas. You might have another duel or dozen if you don't let them enjoy themselves."

"I gave them permission."

"You have dragon riders perched on every roof nearby. *They* don't draw the comfort from them that you do." She smiled through perfect lips, assuring him that she, unlike the Vraad outside, *did* share his appreciation.

"It will be done." Barakas pointed indifferently toward the nearest of his people and snapped his fingers. The appointed messenger rose, bowed to his lord and lady, and vanished. "Where have you been, Alcia? Were you looking for someone?"

"Hardly. I was accosted by that she-devil earlier, though, the one Reegan seems so *fond* of." She stared pointedly at their eldest. Not all of the patriarch's sons were hers, indiscretion a fact of life for beings with countless millennia on their hands, but the heir and Gerrod were. Rendel was also. It sometimes amazed Gerrod that he and Rendel were related to a creature like the burly Reegan.

The heir, titled so only because Barakas felt it necessary to appoint his eldest to such a role, looked sheepish. His lust for Melenea was an open secret with the Tezerenee, made more comical in some eyes by the fact that the temptress could, when she so desired, make him look like nothing more than a great pup. Alcia did not care for her people, especially her offspring, to be made fools of even if they themselves had had a part in the process.

"Have you been outside in the last hour?" Alcia asked her husband.

"No. There have been complications—minor ones—with the various aspects of the cross-over. I've been busy sorting them out."

The Lady Tezerenee tensed. "Rendel! Is something wrong? Has he—?"

"Rendel is fine," the patriarch lied. No one dared to contradict him, although Gerrod was sorely tempted. "He proceeds with his tasks. There's nothing to worry about. You had something you wished to convey to me, however."

"Yes. The city is being buffeted by powerful winds. The protective spells seem to be weakening."

"It's to be expected. *Nimth* is weakening. That's why smooth progression of our work is so important. Gerrod!"

The hooded Tezerenee leaped to his feet and straightened as his father whirled on him. "I await your command."

Barakas looked him over, as if seeking fault. Alcia, on the other hand, beamed proudly. Reegan and the rest might be her husband's, but Rendel and Gerrod were *her* favorites. Unlike most of the clan, she had been born an outsider, and in those two sons, the matriarch saw her identity passed on.

"You seem to get along with Master Zeree fairly well," the Lord Tezerenee commented. "I give you the task of visiting his domain and bringing him back here. It looks bad when one's partner seems . . . reluctant to be present at the culmination of his work."

"We don't need him, Father!" growled Reegan.

Gerrod smiled from within the shadowy confines of his hood. When Reegan spoke, it was generally to put his foot in his mouth.

"We don't need him!" the heir continued. "The outsider gave us everything of use! Let him take his place in the courtyard with the rest! Better yet, see that he gets left behind!"

Barakas stood silent for several moments. Then he walked over to his eldest and slapped him across his furred visage. It was not a gentle slap, Gerrod noted with some satisfaction. The heir struck the stone floor end first, causing a yard-long crack along the surface. Lady Alcia remained stone-faced throughout the incident.

"He was given the bond of the dragon—*my* bond of honor! Never speak that way again unless I permit you!" Barakas focused on his younger son. "Go, Gerrod! Leave now!" The patriarch's voice was more of a dragon's roar. The young Tezerenee hastened to obey, folding within himself and vanishing from the room instantly, secretly gleeful to have any excuse to be far away from the mad rabble he was forced to call his family.

EMPTINESS.

What could one do with so much emptiness?

That was the question that pervaded Dru's thoughts as he continued to float helplessly in . . . in . . . this *void*, he finally decided. It was a shorter, more succinct name and, more importantly, had pushed back his boredom for at least a hundred or so breaths.

Breaths. There was no way of telling time here, if time was even a familiar concept in this nondimension. The number of breaths he took was the only way he could make any estimate. Even then, it was tricky, for Dru had discovered earlier that it was not *necessary* to breathe in the *Void*.

He was at a loss as to what to do. Several failed attempts had proven to him the uselessness of Vraad sorcery here. That had come as a shock. Even with all the chaos on Nimth, Dru had never conceived that there might be a time when he had *no* sorcery at his command. There had been times when he had abstained from the use of it, but he had always known the magic was ready should he need it.

In growing desperation, he had tried pushing himself along with his arms and legs, an awkward parody of swimming. There were problems with that, however, chief among them being that it was impossible to tell if he was making any progress. Everything looked the same and he could feel nothing on his face. He soon gave the attempt up. Where was there to go, even if he was moving? There was nothing to see from his position save for *more* nothing.

A part of him did marvel at this place, however. The realm beyond the veil had been amazing enough, but this was truly something the Vraad had never conceived of in all their years. What was the Void? he wondered. Just emptiness? If he had accidentally fallen into it, had others? If so, what had happened to *them?*

With nothing else to do, Dru chose to rest. He was only now feeling the exhaustion caused by his transition from Nimth to this place. Perhaps, the sorcerer hoped, when he was rested he would be able to conceive a feasible plan. Perhaps something in his surroundings would change by the time he woke.

No sooner had he closed his eyes than he opened them again with a start. Suddenly Dru felt refreshed, as if he had slept for hours. The Vraad frowned, puzzled at the change. What could have given him so much energy?

Then a tiny orb floated into his range of vision. It shocked him at first, being the one object other than himself that he had seen, but then he recognized it as one of his own possessions. As he retrieved it, he noted other objects from his pockets. They all floated in lazy fashion about his person. Two questions were answered then. He *was* moving, albeit at an incredibly slow rate, else his belongings would have been scattered farther apart. He had also *slept,* yet there had been no feeling of time passage. It dawned on Dru then that he might float here for the rest of . . . of *whatever* . . . with only sleep to entertain him.

It was a Vraadish version of hell.

One by one the sorcerer retrieved his errant possessions, studying each in turn in the hopes of finding something that would aid him in his escape from this horrible place. They were all useless trinkets now, even the ones that had once been his most powerful tools. Everything he had derived from Vraad sorcery . . . and he could not touch upon that here, it seemed.

In a fit of anger, he took a hand mirror, once used for scrying but now only sufficient for staring at his frustrated features, and threw it from him. To his horror, while the mirror went one way, *he* went the opposite. Not far at first, but far enough so that the remainder of his escaped items were now out of reach.

The horror was quickly exchanged with an almost childlike glee. He *could* travel. There might not be anything to find, but at least Dru now knew that he could explore. His exploring was limited, however. Waving his arms did little to keep him moving; throwing an object in the opposite direction—a *nebulous* term at best—was the only way to assure himself of momentum.

Reaching into one of his voluminous pockets, he pulled out the orb that had originally begun the present chain of events. It was no more than a piece of metal now, but one that should start him on his way. Using the other floating trinkets as his means of perspective, the sorcerer threw the orb. His momentum was not great, but he slowly returned to somewhere very near his earlier position. Utilizing the cloak he wore, Dru scooped up as many of the other pieces as he could. He might need them later.

The drifting spellcaster's present course took him nowhere in particular, which was the only place to go in the Void. Nonetheless, he now had purpose. As he floated, an act he more or less had to assume, he kept watch for something, anything, that might also exist here.

His euphoria passed into boredom again without one change in his surroundings. Dru could not say whether he had been floating for a very long time, but he knew that more than a thousand breaths had passed before he lost count. Still his eyes were greeted with nothing, great and endless quantities of nothing. There was nothing as far as the eye could see. Dru wondered if he would know when he finally turned completely mad at the sight . . . if one could call emptiness a sight.

Then, an object in the distance caught his eyes. It was only a speck, but, in so much emptiness, it stood out like a glittering crystal beacon. Dru discarded another of his items and altered his direction. Perspective was a problem, he realized. The object might be very close and very small or it might be far, far away and larger than his castle of pearl.

More than two hundred breaths passed before he was close enough to make out what it was. Deep disappointment vied with the simple pleasure of actually touching something else.

It was a rock. A jagged, brown rock that looked as if it had been torn from some hillside.

Through sheer luck, he had aimed himself near enough so that the rock would pass within arm's reach of him. As the two of them closed the gap, Dru stretched his left arm out, intending on taking hold of the object and using it to send him in another direction.

He caught the rock . . . and was sent *spinning* away madly, his arm *twisted* back and wracked with mind-piercing pain. The rock continued on its oblivious way.

Despite the agony, the calculating portion of Dru's mind knew what had happened. He had assumed, because it seemed to float so serenely, that the massive stone had been moving slowly. Not so. The Void had played him for a fool. Perhaps the rock had been falling when it entered this place; he could not be certain. Dru only knew that what he had tried to catch had been moving faster than the swiftest steed, so fast, in fact, that it had *broken* his arm.

It was an arm that would remain broken, too, for he had no sorcery with which to repair it.

With deliberate effort, he forced himself to put the broken limb back in place. It was a difficult enough task, what with the unceasing spin. Dru screamed readily, unashamed to do so since no one would hear him. Pain gripped him without pause. Once he had the arm back the way it should have been, he pulled off his cloak and turned it into a sling of sorts.

The pain still rocked him, but Dru knew he would have to live with that. His next quest was to cease his twirling before he grew too dizzy. The arm was draining his strength too much already.

How could he stop himself? Dru reached into his pocket, but the angle at which he was spinning made it an awkward movement that in turn put pressure on his broken limb. The Vraad screamed again and nearly passed out.

"It does! It makes sounds! Loud ones!"

The voice seemed to boom within his head. Through tear-drenched eyes, Dru hurriedly scanned his vicinity. More nothing, yet . . . he had heard a voice. *Felt* was perhaps just as good a description, but the point was that he was not alone.

So where was the other?

"Hello, little one! Do you talk? I am coming to you!"

"Where?" the sorcerer managed to choke out. His arm was on fire now; at least, that was how it felt.

"You *do* talk! Patience, patience! This is one is not far!"

Dru screamed once more, but not because of pain. He screamed now because the emptiness to his right had suddenly burst into a huge, ever-shifting field of darkness. His first thought was that it was the point of intersection and he had somehow been drawn back to it. Then it shifted form, as if an inky liquid. It was no liquid, however; Dru, staring at it, felt himself seem to fall toward the thing, as if it were a bottomless pit and he had been thrown into it. Fear battled with pain.

The massive blot changed form again, solidifying a bit. The falling sensation passed.

"There! That is better!"

"What—what's better?" He could still see no sign of the newcomer. Was the blot his method of travel? Is that why Dru had felt he could fall into it? Hope for an escape from the Void stimulated him. "Where are you?"

"Here! Where else is there, little voice?"

"But . . ." The sorcerer's gaze narrowed on the inky darkness through which he had expected the other to enter. "Are you . . . is that . . ."

This time, he saw the darkness quiver. "You are a funny thing! I will not have you join with me yet!"

The blot was no path, save perhaps to *death*. It was, despite Dru's inner protest, a living *thing*. *It* was the voice he had heard in his head.

"What do you mean about 'joining with you'?"

The sensation of falling into the darkness overwhelmed him once more. It lasted only a moment, however. That was far and away more than enough for Dru. It was all he could do to keep from passing out.

"I have not taken from you, have I? You seem to be less than whole." The thing sounded annoyed, as if it had underestimated itself.

"My arm . . . this"—he indicated the broken appendage—"I injured it badly."

"Injured?"

Did this monstrosity not comprehend pain? the sorcerer wondered. Perhaps not. How could one harm a blot?

"It does not work properly."

"Silly little voice! Take it in and make another!"

Now it was Dru who did not comprehend again. "Take it in?"

"As I." A crude limb formed, little more than a narrow bit of darkness. It stretched forth for nearly a yard, then slowly sank back into the primary mass of the blot. "How else?"

Dru shook his head, partly in response and partly because it kept him conscious. "I cannot do what you do and the way I heal does not work here."

"Too bad! Would you prefer I take you now? You will no longer know pain."

"*No!*"

"Your voice grows! I must *try* that!" The blot commenced with a variety of sounds, some higher and some lower than what so far had passed for its voice. Dru did not interrupt; if such entertainment took the creature's mind from the prospect of devouring him, then so much the better. As it was, the agony continually raking through his system was making it impossible to think of any other way to save himself.

The ever-shifting creature's interest in the noises it was making soon waned. "Not so much fun after all! Tell me, one of many voices, why you cannot do like I do?"

It took Dru a moment to realize his unnerving companion was speaking of the broken arm again. "I am a man. A Vraad. We can shift our forms, but not like you and not without sorcery."

"What is sorcery?"

This creature did not know what sorcery was? The Vraad was astonished. Based on what little he had already seen, Dru was certain that the entity was part inherent magic itself. How else to explain its existence and its method of travel?

If he could somehow get it to take him back to Nimth . . .

"It's . . ." Pain made him grimace. "It's an ability that allows one to change things about them."

"What is there to change? With the exception of curious little entertainments—like you—all is as it always is."

Dru shook his head. "Not where I come from. If I was there, for instance, I could make this arm work properly again. I could make the hair on my head"—he indicated each part of his body that he spoke of in case the creature did not understand—"so long that it would go down to my knees."

"Is *that* all? I know this 'sorcery'!"

"So I thought. Tell me—do you have a name?"

"Name?"

"I am Dru. Dru is my name. If we had a third voice with us and he wanted to speak to me but not you, he would say something like 'I will speak with Dru.'" The explanation sounded weak to the sorcerer, but it was the best he could do. Unconsciousness was becoming more and more inviting and he did not dare let that happen until he was certain he would wake up again.

The mass of darkness grew and shrunk, twisted and reshaped itself. Several breaths passed before it finally replied. "I am 'I' or 'Other.'"

"No . . ." Dru held his forehead as he tried to think. "That's not what . . . not what . . ."

"Come! This is too interesting! Do not fade away!"

The Vraad shrieked as raw power filled his being. He felt both omnipotent and helpless. The world was at his beck and call, yet he was the lowest form of existence. Pain and rapture tossed him from one to another like a rag doll.

He was suddenly himself again and the initial sensation was like striking the earth after falling from the highest peak. When that had passed, Dru found himself feeling stronger and more alive than he had ever felt before. The amazed spellcaster undid the makeshift sling; his arm was whole again!

"You were saying I could not be called 'I'! Why is that?"

Dru flexed the arm. It was perfect. "You did this?"

"You did not finish explaining this thing about names and I thought I would help if I gave to you a little of I!"

"Thank you." His mind as clear of fog as the Void was of everything but itself, Dru asked a question that had just occurred to him. "How is it we can speak? Are you—?"

"We speak because I *wished* to speak! That is nothing! I want to know about names!" The darkness shifted menacingly.

The entity had somehow picked at his surface thoughts, the sorcerer suspected, and learned the language of the Vraad instantly in that way. Yet, it did not understand many concepts, which either meant that it lacked the power to delve deeper or it had not wanted to damage him. Dru was willing to bet on the latter.

"Perhaps I shall take you now."

"Names!" Dru shouted with such vehemence that the living hole shifted away despite its obvious superiority. "What do you want to know?"

"Know? I *want* a name! Can I be *Dru* also?"

"That wouldn't do for you." A huge, living pit of darkness bearing *his* name! It might have been humorous if his predicament had not been so tense.

"What, then?"

What, indeed? If he could give the creature some name it found entertaining enough, it might reward him by helping to find a way out of here . . . providing there *was* one.

Descriptions! Descriptions were always a good starting point! "Let's draw a name from the way you look and act."

"I act like me!"

"But what are you? Powerful, ever-changing, dark, compassionate . . ." Dru trailed off, hoping his strange companion would pick up on the flattery while it pondered what it wished to be called. At this point, ingratiating himself in any way to the shifting horror seemed his only hope.

"I am all that and more, but 'Powerfuleverchangingdark' is too long a name for my tastes! I want something short, like you have!"

The sorcerer was willing to just fling names at the monster and let it pick one, but he suspected that such an act might just bore the entity into forgetting the entire thing. If that happened, the blot might decide it was time to absorb him.

The mass of darkness pulsated, evidently pondering its choices so far. Apparently unable to come to any decision, it flowed nearer to the hapless mage and said, "I see only me! I cannot describe me! Give me more to choose from!"

Dru took a deep breath. Much of what he would have liked to have said would probably stir the dark creature to anger. Still, it might pick up on *something*. . . . "I was not whole when you first came to me, so my thoughts were muddled . . . there was a burst . . . the darkness was suddenly there before me . . . where there had only been emptiness before." The nebulous form was still. "I thought you were a hole yourself, an emptiness that led to . . . to a place far from where I float now. I—"

"I *like* that! That will be my name!"

"Your name?" Already? What had he said?

"Not so short as yours, but I am more than you! It has good, strong sounds!"

After a brief moment of soul-searching, the Vraad dared ask, "What *is* your name now?"

"I am the *Darkness!* Does it not ring with me?"

"Ring with . . ." Dru could not help smiling. "Darkness is truly a good name for you!"

Darkness shifted form again and again, openly gleeful about its new possession. "A name! I have a name! It is a good thing!"

"No one can take it from you, either. No matter what they do it will always be yours." The sorcerer was reminded of Sharissa as a tiny child. The blot—*Darkness*, Dru corrected himself—was as much an infant as a godlike entity.

Sharissa. Thinking of her made Dru double his efforts now to gain his odd companion's aid.

"I've helped to give you that name, Darkness," he pointedly reminded the other. "Will you give *me* something now?"

"You wish to be taken? Very well—"

"I do *not* wish to be taken! No, I want you to help me find my way home. You have the power, don't you?"

Swelling, Darkness responded, "I can do anything . . . and if *I* cannot, then Other I can!"

Dru puzzled over the being's words. " 'Other I'?"

"The one from which Darkness was formed, of course!"

"Of course." The sorcerer decided not to press, suspecting he would not care for the answer.

"So tell me. . . . Dru . . . what 'home' is."

Another concept his companion did not understand. "Home is where I came from, where I stay when I am not doing anything—hmmm—where I was *made.*" He spread his arms wide. "The Void is your home, though you were only made in one particular portion of it."

An appendage rose from the creature's disturbing form. It came toward Dru, pausing only a foot or two from him. To his surprise, part of it folded away, revealing . . . an *eye.* It was an ice-blue eye with no pupil and a stare that made the Vraad turn away before he became lost in it. Darkness pulled the ghastly eye away, using it to scan their very meager surroundings.

"This is called the Void? I did not know that!"

Dru was beginning to have visions of floating for the rest of his existence, trying to fight his way through a convoluted conversation with something that half of the time viewed him as a meal. "Do you understand what I mean?"

Stentorian laughter nearly deafened the mage. He put his hands to his ears, but the effect that had was less than negligible. The laughter went on and on until Dru thought his ears would burst. Then, as quickly as it had begun, the raucous sounds died.

"That was entertaining!"

"What . . . was?"

"I got bored listening to this voice so I thought I would listen to your other one as well! It says such humorous things! Fright is a fun thing! Do I frighten you much?"

Piecing together the full situation from the mad comments of Darkness, Dru realized that the unnerving creature had chosen to spy upon his thoughts. It now knew of the sorcerer's fear and desperation. There was no saying how deep the probe had been, but it had been deep enough.

There was no sense lying . . . for now. As he worked to shield future thoughts, Dru answered, "Yes, you frighten me very much, Darkness! You remind me too much of what my kind are like, what I was once like! You could swallow me up with hardly a care! You've invaded my mind! Shouldn't I be frightened?"

To his surprise, the entity contracted until it was only half its original size. The eye stalk sank back into the depths from which it had come. "I did wrong, it seems. I understand that now. I understand more, having listened to your inner voice." Darkness *sighed,* a sound so human that Dru could only stare in astonishment. "I will help you however I can to take you home."

"Thank you."

Darkness grew jubilant again. "So, my little friend! Where is it?"

Dru had been so desperate to get this far that he had not even thought about what to do when the moment came. "It's . . ." He paused. How could he explain to Darkness what he himself did not understand. "I . . . wasn't prepared when I was thrown here."

The inky blot laughed again, albeit much quieter this time. The sorcerer silently thanked him for the sake of his ears. "You are such an entertaining little Dru! Are all Drus like you?" Before the Vraad could explain how names worked, Darkness continued, "Give me access to your inner voice again! Let me experience your arrival again!"

It made sense to let Darkness survey his memories of the incident, but Dru could not help feeling as if the creature might tear his mind apart seeking those particular memories. They were not surface thoughts; they were conscious and subconscious impressions that even under the best of circumstances the Vraad would have been hard-pressed to recall.

"Come, come! Are you afraid of *me?* I am *gentle!*"

Shuddering, Dru finally nodded. When there was no reaction from his amorphous companion, he realized that Darkness did not know what the nod meant and quickly added, "Go ahead. Do it."

He expected the worst. He waited for the blot's probing to wrack his mind. Dru waited for something, *anything*, but felt only his own heart as it beat anxiously.

"But this is *fascinating!* Unbelievable! I must see these things! So much . . . so much *filled* Void! How do you stand being so *cluttered?* How can you not feel squeezed together?" As Darkness spoke, his shape contracted farther until he was only a little larger than the floating spellcaster. There was awe in his thunderous tones, awe at the existence of so many things, so many *solid* things.

Dru feared that the blot had experienced too much, was no longer able to cope with the situation, but that was dispelled when Darkness suddenly expanded again, growing and growing and *growing* . . . until it seemed he—*he?*—would fill the entire Void with his ebony self.

"I *must* go there! I must go with you! The *forms!* The . . . the . . ." Darkness apparently had no words for many of the things he had experienced in Dru's head. The Vraad made a note of that; his nebulous friend was not perfect.

"Can you find a path out of here?"

"To be sure! Can you not feel the many ways? Can you not feel the paths that cross through here? There are endless choices, though some I will avoid since you are so fragile! I think I know the best way!"

Hope sprang to full life within the breast of the sorcerer. Freedom would soon be his! At the moment, it mattered not to him that his freedom would also mean letting the creature sorcerer loose upon Nimth. Darkness was no worse a threat to the world than the Vraad race had ever been, and with power once more his to command, he believed that he could hold his own against the black entity.

His thoughts were interrupted by yet another change in his unnerving companion. Darkness was contracting again, but now his form was also shifting. More and more, he resembled a crude black mouth, like the maw of some huge beast. The maw was disturbingly close to Dru and was getting closer with each passing breath.

"Darkness! Wait! What are you *doing?*"

Did the mouth actually smile? "Have no fear, little Dru! I am only making myself into a form that will be able to carry you! I will not, as you constantly fear, take from you! You have given me too much entertainment and I owe you! In fact, I owe you for an entire existence! To think of all that solidity together!"

Closing his eyes and gritting his teeth, Dru waited for the creature to envelop him. When he felt nothing, the sorcerer dared look.

"Serkadion Manee!" He floated in the center of a huge bubble in which there was no light save two pinpricks of an ice-blue color. There had been no feeling of transition, no sense of being swallowed whole. He breathed a sigh of relief, then nearly choked when the two blue dots swelled and became a very real pair of glittering eyes that lacked pupils.

"You are whole?"

"Yes . . . yes. Thank you."

"You will be cushioned in here. I will let you see how we travel. Perhaps you will be able to do it yourself . . . should you need to, that is." Darkness's understanding of the Vraad language was becoming stronger and stronger. Except for an excess of formality, he spoke as well as any Vraad.

The bubble began moving; Dru knew this only because Darkness *informed* him of the fact. The sorcerer tried to brace himself for anything, then realized the futility of the attempt. What could he do, lacking power as he did?

For a long time—several hundred breaths, by Dru's count—nothing happened. The Vraad watched as emptiness was replaced by more emptiness. His companion spoke little during that period, a sign that this was a tense situation even for the nearly omnipotent creature. Safe and secure within, Dru began to wonder more about the thing now calling itself by so apt a title as Darkness. Was it a demon of legend? Serkadion Manee's books had mentioned the summoning of such spirits, but no Vraad living now had ever succeeded in summoning them. It had long ago been assumed that demons were either the products of great imagination or golems of fanciful design. Yet, his companion certainly fit the descriptions of a demon.

Could it be, Dru pondered, that some being much like Darkness had been the truth behind the legends?

He was never able to answer his question, for in the next breath, Dru collapsed, his mind suddenly a chaotic cornucopia of intense sensations. Pain, happiness, fear, sadness, indifference, anger . . . he went through each emotion in the blink of an eye. Other feelings that he could not exactly identify intermingled with the rest. The Vraad crawled to his knees and put a hand to his head. Darkness said nothing, but the bubble that was his form trembled constantly. The sorcerer fell again, but struggled forward even still. His eyesight was blurred, giving him liquidy images of the same emptiness that he had become so sick of and—

And was there something out there now?

Still Darkness did not speak, but Dru knew that the "demon" did not have the effort to spare for such a minuscule thing as conversation. His unearthly companion had located what appeared to be the way out of the Void and the two of them were even now breaking through. The emptiness had finally been replaced, but by *what* was hard to say for certain.

It looked very much like a pale path of light . . . a path that, when Dru looked behind them, seemed to run on into infinity. Ahead of them was a different tale. The path continued on for some distance—as well as the Vraad could judge—but then faded away slowly until it became—Dru forced his eyes to focus—until it became a mist *very* much akin to that which had blanketed the wraithlike forest.

"Free!" the sorcerer hissed without realizing it.

His joy turned to panic as the path before them suddenly split into one and then countless identical paths that turned in all directions and faded away in the same manner as the first. Which one led to *his* world, the Vraad fretted silently, and *where* did the others go?

One path that Dru did not want Darkness taking was a single path that appeared to curl within itself like some perpetual double loop. It was exceedingly inviting, for reasons that Dru could not define, yet it also filled him with a sense of mortality, of the death that had nearly claimed him. He breathed a sigh of relief when his companion ignored it.

At some point, the overwhelming assault on his brain had ended. Dru hardly felt comforted by that fact, faced with what seemed the impossible task of choosing a path.

"So many . . ." he whispered. To Darkness, the hapless sorcerer quickly asked, "Do you know which one?"

The icy orbs stared at him in resolute silence. Whatever decision Darkness had come to, the Void dweller had chosen not to include the tiny, insignificant human in it. Perhaps that was for the best, but Dru could not help feeling a bit of Vraadish indignation at the exclusion.

They alighted onto one of the paths.

Around them, the others faded completely away.

Darkness had made his decision and there was no time to turn back. Already, the incredible creature was nearing the mist. Dru closed his eyes, hoping that a repeat of the onrush of sensations was not in the offing. Hoping, too, that they would not be destroyed or, worse yet, left again marooned in the midst of the hellish Void, this time with the knowledge that there *was* no escape.

Absorption by Darkness would be preferable to an eternity here.

They plunged into the mist . . . and a tear—a literal *rip* in the emptiness— opened wide before them. Dru waited for some horrific assault on his mind and body. It never came. A brilliant glow temporarily blinded him.

"Through!" Darkness laughed gleefully, a child who had succeeded in some great task his parent had set for him. "I am Darkness! I am truly amazing!"

Dru made no attempt to argue with him. He only wanted to step onto the scarred surface of Nimth and take his daughter into his arms. At this point, he was even willing to take Barakas in his arms. Anything, so long as he was free again . . . and once more a mighty Vraad.

"Such a wonderful place! Are all these green things the trees that I learned of from your inner voice?"

Green things? Trees?

Dru frantically pressed himself against the clear body of his "demonic" savior and peered at the world to which he had been brought.

Trees, hundreds of trees, a vast forest, greeted his eyes. A mountain range stood proud in the background.

A resplendent blue sky completed an image of beauty and tranquility.

"So overwhelming! Nimth is truly a wonderful place!"

The Vraad could not respond. In his desperation to be free of the Void, he had forgotten of the two lands, the two worlds, buried in his memories. Darkness, as was his way, had dug only so far into those memories . . . and had pulled up the most recent, the most vivid.

The *wrong* ones.

Darkness had brought him to the other side of the veil . . . and to the shrouded realm.

VI

IT HAD TAKEN Rendel far longer than he had supposed it would to reach the outskirts of the immense mountain chain. His barely constrained impatience, however, had gradually been supplanted by an even more virulent emotion—anger.

None of his spells worked as they should. Oh, they did what he wanted them to do, but generally to a lesser degree. They also had a tendency to fail the first time, as if the something did not *want* the spells completed. His growing distrust had forced him to walk the entire trip and suffer the effects of an unbroken world. Rendel stared with arrogant distaste at the scenery around him. It was pretty, yes, but hardly interesting, especially after having seen so much of it. Someday soon, though, he and the others would subdue the Dragonrealm and make it as it *should* be.

By now, Rendel thought, choosing a rock upon which to sit for a moment, his father and the others knew he had abandoned the plan. Barakas had probably taken much of his anger out on Gerrod, but the pale-haired Vraad could do nothing about that. That was what his younger brother was for, taking the brunt of things. Rendel liked Gerrod as much as he liked *any* of his brothers, sisters, and cousins—which was not *that* much at all—but, in the end, it was his own concerns that mattered. And was that not what his father had always taught them?

Rendel had his own agenda, one only he was privy to. The Lord Tezerenee had always been bringing up the outsider, the fool Zeree, as the one most knowledgeable about the ka and the nature of the realm beyond the veil. Never had the patriarch really asked his son if he knew more than he said. Rendel knew *far* more, having studied greatly in secret. Each sighting had been personally visited, albeit surreptitiously. Each phantom land had been carefully mapped. Each had been scanned for anything out of the ordinary . . . or perhaps it was best to say anything out of the extraordinary, for even Rendel had to admit that as a whole the Dragonrealm was truly different from his Nimth. Trouble was, most of it had no place in his grand designs.

Eyeing the first intrusion of night in the early evening sky, the Vraad cursed the time differences between Nimth and the Dragonrealm. Three days of walking and now the setting sun reminded him again that he had to push on before the trek became too treacherous. Until he had a better grasp of the intricacies involved in utilizing his powers, he would keep their use to a minimum. That meant facing an even harder walk than the one he had just completed. Yet, if he persevered—and Rendel had confidence in his ability to eventually turn every situation to his own advantage—then all his plotting would have been worth it.

In the mountains, he knew, there was a place he could rest, a place where he could attend to his needs, and begin to carve out a domain of his own, one that would equal, nay, *surpass* his father's and all the rest. One where Rendel could at last be *alone*.

Inspired, the Vraad rose from his resting place, ready to continue even if it meant wandering through the dark of night. Only a little farther and the cavern he had discovered, along with all its treasures, would be his.

His higher senses chose that moment to warn him of the closing presence of one or more creatures. Rendel whirled and studied the trees he was leaving behind. The damnable forest. All throughout his journey, he had felt the eyes upon him. Not merely the eyes of beasts, but ones belonging to other observers, observers who succeeded in staying beyond his reach. They had let him be so far, but he knew that was about to end. Rendel did not fear them. Even with his abilities hampered as they were, he was still a Tezerenee . . . and a Vraad, of course. There was nothing more potent than that combination. His kind had conquered and broken one world; the Dragonrealm would be no different.

The grandiose visions forming in his mind were shattered by the fluttering of massive wings all about him. Rendel summoned a fiery staff, then summoned it *again* when the first attempt gained him nothing but smoke. Simultaneous with his spell, the rock he had been sitting on *melted*. Rendel grinned at the feeble attempt on his life and took a step toward the trees. Large things flittered about the treetops, but always just out of sight. His watchers had finally chosen to come for him. He would make them regret that decision.

Raising the flaming staff high, the Vraad put both hands at the center and twirled his weapon around and around, building speed as he did. When the staff was little more than a blur, tiny balls of fire shot forth in every direction. Treetops became orange infernos in a matter of seconds. If his adversaries would hide from him, then he would just remove their cover.

As the seconds passed, he heard no shrieks and saw no winged figures fleeing from the damage he had caused. The fire continued to spread, reaching other trees through intermingling branches. If left unchecked, it would likely spread throughout the entire forest. Rendel was unconcerned about that; all that mattered was mastering his unseen companions.

Then, as swiftly as the fire had grown, it began to die. The sorcerer glared at the treetops as, one by one, the flames were snuffed out by magical forces. Rendel swore. This was not how it should have gone. The staff had always been one of his favorite and most potent devices. The magical flames were stronger, more resistant to counterspells or even natural attacks, like wind and water. They should not have died out so easily. Rendel had underestimated his foes.

Dismissing his staff—which, as it happened, coincided with the withering of a pair of trees to his left—the Tezerenee folded his arms and gazed intently at the area where he had heard the rustling of wings. He stood motionless, forcing his will upon the world, taking from it what he needed for *this* assault.

A wind rose. It was a light breeze in its infancy, but Rendel pushed it beyond that. From breeze it became a prestorm wind, full of vibrant life and shaking even the stoutest of limbs as it coursed through the nearby forest. Still not satisfied, Rendel pushed harder, turning the wind upon itself, making it follow its own tail around and around. Leaves, dirt—anything loose and tiny enough— were swept into the funnel. It continued to grow, a tornado twice as tall as any of the brown and green leviathans it stood among.

Rendel was still not satisfied; he wanted a rampaging maelstrom that would tear the forest out by its roots . . . and with it his shadows.

The unseen watchers had not counterattacked, which to Rendel meant that they had used what they had and were even now cowering in the trees, holding on for dear life. He was slightly curious as to what they looked like, if only because they might prove useful slaves, but it would be just as satisfying if the elemental force he had unleashed tore their limbs from them and battered their bodies into pulp. Rendel had never fought a foe who was not one of his kin or at least one of the other Vraad. The golems and other constructs his clan used in mock combat did not count. His would-be attackers here had been a real, albeit minuscule, threat. The Tezerenee allowed the satisfied smile to spread farther across his face. He felt a growing pleasure at his handling of the brief affair. His had been the *first* conquering blow. His enemies had fallen before him like . . . like leaves in the wind, he decided, laughing.

The maelstrom he had created chose that moment to completely *dissipate*. A brief shower of refuse buffeted the treetops and then nothing was moving. No wind. No birds. No animals. Rendel stood frozen, suddenly uncertain as to *who* commanded the situation now.

The silence was broken at last by a sound already familiar to the stunned Vraad.

A great rustling of wings, as if a score of massive birds were taking to the sky, filled his ears, echoed in his head.

Shadows dotted the clearing around him. Rendel looked up.

Their wingspans were at least the length of his frame. They were vaguely Vraad-shaped, having arms and legs and a narrow torso. How the wings, as long as they were, succeeded in lifting all that perplexed the studious side of Rendel. Sorcery, perhaps. The creatures glided effortlessly to the ground, more than a dozen of them surrounding him. A part of Rendel demanded to know why he was standing here like a fool and not striking. Yet, the Vraad could not push himself to even the slightest of efforts. His only inclination was to gaze upon those who, in his misplaced arrogance, he had thought he could so easily better.

One of the avian beings walked up to him, contempt for Rendel in every movement, every breath. It came within reach and simply matched his gaze. The Tezerenee found he could not turn away from the visage before him. His counterpart opened its sharp, savage beak and squawked something at him. Rendel wanted to shake his head, tell the creature that he could not understand it, but even that seemed hardly worth the trouble. In the back of his head, the same part that had fruitlessly demanded action now informed him bitterly that he was under a spell. He, who had been so confident of his power, had been captured effortlessly by his shadows. Rendel had not even felt the spell.

The avian leader, for that was who he assumed the creature was, leaned closer, cocking its head to one side so as to better observe him. That one eye, inhuman as it was, reminded Rendel all too much of another eye. His father's. In his captors, the Vraad had found a race whose arrogance appeared to match that of his own kind.

Seeming to find nothing of worth in what stood before it, the leader started to turn away. It paused midway, however, and slowly turned back, visibly contemplating something.

A taloned hand shot out toward the startled and helpless Rendel's face. He would have screamed, picturing in his mind what those long, needle-sharp claws would do, but the world—the world he had thought *he* would conquer—suddenly turned into a welcome darkness that enveloped Rendel and took him away to a place where he could hide.

"EAT THIS, GIRL."

Sharissa shook her head, not wanting anything from the Tezerenee woman who stood above her. For three days, since the dark one called Gerrod had found her lying near where the rift had last been, she had been a "guest" of the clan of the dragon. For three days, she had been questioned, in order that they might *help* her, yet she had not spoken a word to them. The first two days, the patriarch, a man who made Sharissa shiver when he stared at her, had chalked it down to panic. Why not? Something had happened to her father, something unexpected. What they wanted to know—what the Lord Tezerenee in particular wanted to know—was exactly *what* had happened to him?

Gerrod, who unnerved her with his ghostly appearance, had explained how he had found her there, still sobbing and unable to say anything coherent. It seemed to her that the patriarch frightened his own son as much as he frightened her, for the half-seen Tezerenee continually shrank deeper into the protective folds of his cloak, becoming, by tale's end, little more than a walking piece of cloth.

Lord Barakas had been gruff and his lady had been sweet, caring almost, but Sharissa had said nothing. They did not push her after a certain point, likely because they still wanted, at the very least, the semblance of cooperation between the elder Zeree and the clan. A sudden break between the partners would raise the already strained suspicions of the rest of the Vraad. It pained her to remain silent, since if anyone was capable of aiding her in rescuing her father, it was the clan master. He had the most knowledge of the phantom realm.

The strain of three days of fighting her own fears had taken their toll. She was worn, thin, and unable to think. What was worse was that they would not let her alone, not allow her the needed privacy to work things out. Their "concern," as Lady Alcia had put it, forced them to watch her day and night.

An impatient sigh from her latest guardian stirred her. "Weakling! I'll leave it here. Maybe when you stop blubbering, you'll be able to swallow it . . . though anyone who can't conjure themselves up a meal on their own . . ."

Even as the voice faded off, Sharissa knew she was now alone. Like most Vraad, the Tezerenee had little patience for those unable to fend for themselves. Another one would be replacing the snide woman shortly, though, so Sharissa's privacy was temporary, at best.

They are right! Nothing but a weakling! Sharissa scolded herself bitterly. She raised herself to a sitting position and slowly dragged the food over to her. A delicious odor drifted past her nose. There was no denying that the patriarch *was* treating her well—on the surface. What could she do now, however? There was no possibility of leaving the city without a score or more of the Tezerenee, not to mention any exceptionally paranoid Vraad celebrating the coming down below, from noting her departure. Sharissa was uncertain of her father's true present status with the patriarch. Would he send dragon riders after her? Would he actually lay siege to the castle? Even Sirvak, skilled as the familiar was with its master's defenses, would be hard-pressed to keep them out.

"Sharissa Zeree."

A deathly cold wrapped itself about her spine and spread quickly throughout her person.

Gerrod's shrouded figure stood at the doorway. "Are you better?"

He had treated her with nothing but respect and could have been considered harmless in comparison to those others she had met, but Sharissa could not warm to him. Gerrod lived in two worlds, and had hid too many things from even his lord and progenitor. He was, Dru would have said, an outstanding example of Vraad duplicity. Sharissa could feel that even though they had actually spoken very little.

"What do you want?"

Gerrod folded his legs and sat down on empty air. He floated nearer to her, *much* too near for Sharissa's tastes. "This is foolish. Each moment that passes lessens the chances of Master Zeree's survival. *I* know where he must be; I've searched everywhere *else* for him." From the bitterness in his tones, Sharissa guessed that the bulk of the task had, indeed, been foisted upon her visitor. For the first time, she was able to sympathize with Gerrod. "I know he must be across the veil." The half-seen face moved closer. "How did he do it? Tell me."

"It doesn't matter," she finally replied, deciding that a partial truth might aid her. "The way through is no more. He can't come back and no one can go after him."

"Oh?" Gerrod straightened. His glittering eyes, temporarily visible, widened. "Then there *is* a way in which to—?"

Whatever his next words were to have been was something Sharissa would never discover, for one of the countless multitude of armored Tezerenee cousins or brothers materialized between them, anxiety evident in his agitated manner.

"Gerrod. Father wants you! Something—" The newcomer glanced at Sharissa, but appeared to find her of little importance. "Something is amiss! Go to him now!"

The hooded figure shifted, as if about to protest, then gradually sunk deeper within the protective layers of his cloak. "Where is he, Lochivan?"

"Ephraim." It was all the other brother had to say. One moment, both

Tezerenee faced each other in uneasy silence, then Sharissa was alone again. The clan of the dragon were not known for their long farewells, she decided.

The patriarch's grand design was in jeopardy. That much was evident from Lochivan's distress and Gerrod's instant compliance at the mere mention of that other name. Sharissa had no proof that there was any connection between whatever the Tezerenee struggled with and the disappearance of her father save that both were tied to the land beyond the veil. Nonetheless, the feeling swept over her that the Vraad were facing something beyond their arrogant plans, beyond, perhaps, their varied and supposedly limitless abilities.

And here she sat, doing *nothing*.

Sharissa had spent most of her brief life secluded from the rest of her race. Dru Zeree, knowing the Vraad as he did—and remembering his own excesses—had wanted his sole child to have nothing to do with the others until he felt she was ready. The only question was, when was that to have been? As skilled as she had become with the use of sorcery, Sharissa was still an infant when it came to dealing with her kind. There had been a few scattered individuals throughout her life, but none who her father had wanted her to know intimately. Only a handful of names came to her from those passersby. One she remembered better than others, so alive had that particular Vraad been.

Perhaps . . .

Mistressss?

Sirvak? It was only the second time the familiar had contacted her since the horrifying events at the ridge. The first time, Sirvak had witnessed with her the fading of the forest and her father's last desperate attempt to escape his fate. The familiar had broken contact with her moments after Gerrod had reached her, emphasizing that *it* would reestablish the link. Sirvak distrusted the Tezerenee—all Vraad, in fact—more than even Dru had.

Alone, mistressss?

Yes. Is Father—

The creature silenced her with a mental hiss. *No, mistressss. Masterrrr issss still away.* Sirvak apparently refused to accept the possibility that its master was dead. Sharissa wondered if there was an even stronger link between the magical beast and her father than the one of blood between Dru and herself. *Come home, mistressss.*

What is it?

Hesitation formed a silence that stretched Sharissa's nerves taut. When she could wait no longer, the young Vraad asked again, this time with more emphasis in case the familiar was forgetting *who* she was.

May be a way to find masterrr, mistressss.

She almost shouted out loud, so overjoyed did the startling announcement

make her. Sirvak, however, was quick to dampen her spirits before she grew too
happy.

May, mistresss! Not certain! Need your guidance!

I'll come instantly! There's no need to wait!

Must not! It was as if her father himself had scolded her. *Must take care. Never
trust a Vraad, master always said.*

They're busy with their own problems, she retorted.

The familiar let loose with a mental sigh. *Do as you must then, mistress. Take care,
though.*

Sirvak broke the link.

Rising, Sharissa stepped over to the doorway and leaned outside. The hall
was empty. The young Vraad stepped back inside and moved to the sole window of her chambers. Her view overlooked the courtyards where the Vraad
still gathered, talking and attempting to outshine one another. The coming had
spread to the surrounding lands—as her father had said it usually did, and she
could see some of her more flamboyant counterparts showing off. There was
now a mountain of glittering diamond beyond the northern walls and a vast
lake of *water*—truly a difficult spell, she acknowledged silently—on the eastern
edge of the mountain. Beyond, there were flashes and sounds, none of which
Sharissa could identify with anything that she had learned.

Dru had spoken of the subdued manner of this, the last coming. Only
those with long-standing grudges, like Silesti and Dekkar, were likely to stir
things up. Such massive displays of sorcery, however, spoke for the confidence
of the Vraad race in the Lord Tezerenee's plans. Everyone understood, at least
somewhat, that the more sorcery unleashed, the worse Nimth grew. Already, the
sickening green covered the murky sky. It saddened Sharissa to think of what
her kind would be leaving behind and she hoped that the new land would not
suffer the same.

That was if they ever succeeded in migrating over there.

No one would miss her for some time; Sharissa was certain of that now.
Lord Barakas would have his entire clan working to solve whatever disaster had
befallen his dreams. He would have no time for her or her father's disappearance. Other than Gerrod, they probably thought he was dead by now, not that
she had not thought of that herself constantly. With great effort, Sharissa once
again pushed the ugly vision from her mind. Sirvak's confidence bolstered her.
It had to; it was the only thing she had to lean on.

Sharissa gazed down at the throngs one last time and her eyes caught on a
lone figure seeming to watch the rest with barely constrained amusement. She
leaned forward, not thinking to adjust her sight accordingly.

As if feeling the eyes upon her, the single Vraad looked up. Sharissa was greeted by a vibrant smile that washed away the terror and distress of the last few days. It was such a wonderful feeling that she could not help being caught up in it. She smiled in return.

In the next breath, Sharissa was no longer alone in the chamber. The other female was with her, reaching out to take her in her arms, ready to comfort the younger woman. Sharissa went to her gladly, knowing that she had found someone with whom she could share her problem.

"You look both distraught and beautiful, dear sweet Shari! What has that beast Barakas been doing to you? Why are you here instead of with your father?"

"Father's in terrible trouble!" Sharissa burst out. It had been so long since the two of them had seen each other, but the feeling of safety and assurance she felt now washed away the years of absence.

"Why don't you tell me all about it," her companion said, smoothing Sharissa's wild, tangled hair. "Then we can see about doing something." Sharissa started to speak, but was cut off. "No, on second thought, let us go elsewhere; too many Tezerenee here for my tastes."

"I was going to go home. Sirvak said I should. He said—"

"Hush! Let us depart for your father's wondrous castle of pearl, then, sweet Shari." The smile broadened, smothering any doubts Sharissa still had. "You'll have to do it, however. Your father lets no one in and I think Sirvak must be the same. So very distrustful."

"Sirvak has no say in what I do," the young Zeree commented defiantly. "If I want you with me, he'll obey."

Melenea stroked Sharissa's hair again. "That's exactly what I *thought*."

VII

"COME, COME! I grow bored at this! How long will you dawdle there, little Dru?"

Dru did not answer him at first, still caught up in his thoughts. Day had given way to night—a night *filled* with stars and *two* moons!—and yet the sorcerer was only beginning to comprehend the patterns of the world around him. Unlike Barakas, he had never intended on charging into the phantom domain, uncaring of what obstacles might lay in the immigrants' path. Dru knew that even with the tremendous abilities of the creature who floated beside him, there might be dangers too great to combat. His own powers, while they *had* returned, were unpredictable, even more so than they had of late been back in Nimth.

Shifting form again, Darkness once more tried to berate his companion into movement. Behind the blustery tones were undercurrents of fear and excitement. "You can protest all you want, little Dru, but I *have* brought you home! Even if you cannot remember it, *I* can!"

That was the other thing that kept Dru from moving on, the shadowy blot's insistence that this *was* Nimth. Even after the sorcerer had given Darkness permission to search his memories again, the entity had argued that he had not made an error. Dru had decided not to push too hard; Darkness had an ego as great as his interior, the latter of which seemed to go on into infinity when the spellcaster stared long enough.

Somewhere along the way, Dru had chosen to think of the creature as male. Perhaps it was the deepness of the blot's voice or perhaps it was the overbearing arrogance. In some ways, his companion reminded him of Barakas. Knowing that Darkness could pick up the thought, Dru had buried it deep. He suspected Darkness already knew how he felt about the patriarch of the dragon clan.

"I want to try something," Dru finally said. "When I'm through, then we can move on for a short while."

"What is a 'while'?" Darkness pulsated. Despite the light of the two moons and the stars, the lands around them were barely visible. Darkness, however, was blacker than the night, so much so that he almost stood out as a beacon.

Dru knew better than to try to explain time to a creature who dwelled in a place that itself did not comprehend the concept. Instead, he concentrated on a tree before him and muttered a memory-jogging phrase.

The tree should have withered, should have dwindled to a dry husk and crumbled before his eyes. It did nothing, but a black death spread across the grass beneath the sorcerer's feet. He leaped away, forgoing pride for safety.

"Good! Now we can depart!" Darkness rumbled, ignorant of the failure of the Vraad's spell.

"Wait!"

"What is it *now*?"

Kneeling by the blackened, dead blades, Dru tried to inspect the damage in the dim illumination. As he had spoken the fanciful phrase, he had felt the familiar twinge as the essence of Nimth bowed to his overpowering will, but it had been checked by a fierce protesting force from the shrouded realm itself. The sorcerer touched the grass, only to have it disintegrate into a fine powder. Dru cleared his throat at the thought of what might have happened if he had remained standing on the spot.

This world will not bend to us so easily as the last, he concluded nervously. This was not just spell failure; this was a battle of wills, so to speak. He already knew that a second or even a third attempt would gain him the results he had intended, but that was only a pitifully tiny victory. Like Nimth, which had turned mad from the massive abuses of Vraad sorcery, the stronger the spell the more this domain would battle back.

Suddenly, a world-heavy weariness swept over the frustrated Dru. He slumped back, visions of a land swallowing up each and every Vraad dancing about his tired mind.

The entity Darkness shifted closer to him, the two icy orbs staring down at him in what the Vraad vaguely recognized as anxiety for the sorcerer's well-being.

"You are fading? You lack essence?"

"I'm tired."

"What *is* that?"

"It means that I must lay for a time in quiet. Probably until after the sun has returned." When that was, Dru had no idea. Time felt different somehow, almost as if the shrouded realm moved more swiftly.

The creature seemed annoyed that nothing else would be accomplished for now, but evidently understood that his tiny associate was lacking in many ways. "What shall I do while you lay down?"

"Remain nearby. I cannot protect myself as I thought I would be able to. I'll have to ask for your aid in case something tries to attack me."

"They would not *dare*! Not while *I* am here!"

Dru winced. "One more thing. *Please* make as little sound as possible while I sleep . . . lay down, that is. It will help me to recover my strength sooner."

"As you wish," Darkness replied in a rumble only slightly less deafening.

The sorcerer grimaced, but consoled himself in the fact that anything nearby would get as little sleep as he did. Still kneeling, he looked around for a more comfortable place to rest. At the moment, he was too tired to trust another spell, yet there was no area around him that looked inviting. Dru sighed and, pulling his cloak tight around him, simply lay down where he was. He wondered briefly at the sudden intensity of his exhaustion, then drifted off.

"ARE YOU RESTED yet?"

Dru straightened with a start, turning his head this way and that. The sun was just over the horizon and the sounds of the day were already well into their second movement. Gradually, his eyes focused on the huge, ungodly thing next to him.

Darkness was a contrast to all around him, *unlife* surrounded by life. Even the period in the Void, where the gigantic horror had been the only thing visible other than the helpless Vraad himself, could not compare to the scene now unfolding before Dru. Yesterday, he had been so turned around that he had failed to notice it. Now, though, Darkness's disturbing form fairly shouted at him. This was the creature who had befriended him.

"Are we to do *nothing* again? You promised that once you were whole we could move on! I want to see all there is to see! All this solidity!"

The rest had aided in rebuilding Dru's reserves, but not completely. Nonetheless, the sorcerer himself was now eager to move on, if only to get a better idea of what he might have to face. He also wanted to find the way back, something he now knew still existed. At a vague point in his slumber, it had occurred to his unconscious mind that the fact that he could still draw upon his power in Nimth meant that there *was* a gap between the two realms. One of them had to be like the tear that he had fallen prey to. This time, though, he would not run. This time, Dru would make use of the rip in reality.

He stood up and looked the Void dweller straight in the two pupilless eyes. "Let us go."

"At last!" Like a child unleashed from his studies, Darkness bounded forward, a hole of black space frolicking among the trees. Dru heard the frightened cries of birds and watched as many flew into the sky at insane speeds. In the woods themselves, small animals departed with equal haste.

Both amused and dismayed by the entity's antics, the spellcaster followed close behind.

Dru had tried to map as carefully as he could the translucent sightings, but none that he had studied resembled this one; though, being in a forest, it was possible that he just did not recognize where he was yet. He supposed it did not really matter save that he was interested in locating Rendel and the Tezerenees' point of arrival. Dru imagined the countless dragon-borne golems, a sea of still, blank-visaged beings who contained no true life of their own, who were merely vessels for the migrating Vraad. The sorcerer shuddered. If—*no*—*when* he found the way back, the Tezerenee plan would be abandoned. Barakas might still desire to cross and seize control of a body, if only because of their draconian origins, but none of the others would.

"Something watches us."

"Where?" Dru could sense nothing, but he knew how faulty his senses might be.

"It is gone now." Had he shoulders, Darkness would have shrugged off the incident.

Dru would not allow that. "What was it? Where did it go?"

His nebulous companion seemed more interested in a stream that was just coming into sight ahead of them. Darkness had never seen water and was visibly attracted to its fluid nature. Dru was forced to repeat himself, this time in much more demanding tones.

"It was Dru-sized! How does this solid move as it does? It seems almost like me! Look how it races and shapes itself! It went away. It was there and then it was not there."

It took the Vraad a moment or two to understand that the latter portions of the creature's comments were in response to his question. "The watcher simply vanished?"

"Yes, yes!" Darkness moved closer to the water. A rough limb extended from its central mass. The limb dipped into the water. "What a truly fascinating sensation! This is the most fun yet! Come feel it, little Dru!"

Dru glanced around, wondering where the unknown watcher had vanished to after its discovery by Darkness. He wished he had asked the entity to alert him more cautiously about intruders. He wished he could trust his own senses better.

Water splashed all over the sorcerer. Darkness was tossing the clear liquid about, awed at how it allowed itself to be scattered all over the area and yet seeming to re-form in the steam. Dru was reminded once more of how child-like the astonishing creature actually was. No, he thought, it would never do to thrust Darkness among the other Vraad. His innocence would be his downfall.

Shaking his head and momentarily putting his present worries aside, Dru wandered over to the stream and kneeled down to drink. He cupped his hands and swallowed mouthful after sweet, cool mouthful, allowing it to dribble down his chin and onto his gray clothing. To his left, Darkness stopped playing, now interested in the novel entertainment his tiny companion was performing for him.

"You are *taking* it within you! I did not know you could do that! We are much alike!"

Dru paid him no mind. With the acknowledgment of his thirst, he was forced to acknowledge his great hunger as well. It stunned him to think that he had not thought of either since arriving here, almost as if he had not, until his first drink, actually been a part of this realm. The spellcaster stood, eyeing the forest around him. It appeared much more real now; his higher senses now functioned more as they should have. He could even sense the passage that the unseen watcher had taken when it had departed. Darkness had been correct; it *had* vanished. What it was, however, remained a mystery.

Aside from hunger, other functions were now demanding their due. Dru spent more than an hour near the stream, the bulk of time involving the picking of berries from a lengthy expanse of bushes and fruit from a tree overshadowing the stream just south of his original location. Darkness took everything as part of his continual game of discovery, much to the Vraad's annoyance.

When he was at last ready to depart, Dru had a destination in mind. The intruder had been in the woods to the north and the stream originated from somewhere in the same direction. That meant that there might be civilization there. There was also a distant chain of mountains that Dru hoped *might* be the ones Barakas had mentioned once or twice. Rendel would be there, directing efforts on this side of the veil, so the tall Vraad assumed.

Their journey that day was uneventful, something Dru felt very grateful about. While he walked, the sorcerer continually investigated the binding structure of this world. With his higher senses, he surveyed the lines of force running gridlike throughout everything. It was a much more basic, more stable pattern than Nimth's spirals, stronger, too. This was indeed a world that would resist the coming of the Vraad.

A chill wind came up at that point, a wind in Dru's mind. The uncomfortable idea of a land consciously resisting outside invaders stirred. He shook his head, trying to rid himself of such a mad concept. The idea retreated, but did not leave. Dru threw himself back into the trek and his studies and was able to at least temporarily bury the unnerving theory.

Surprisingly, it was Darkness who called for a halt as the sun neared the evening horizon. The entity was unusually subdued. "I would have us stop here, Dru."

The sorcerer was all for stopping himself—the berries and fruit from the stream insufficient for an entire day's activity—but he wondered at his huge companion's change of attitude. "Is there something wrong, Darkness?"

"I must . . ." The creature was at a loss for the proper words. "This form is not right for this world. I do not fit in. I am not part of the world."

It was the same feeling Dru had had earlier, but he had not thought Darkness would suffer from anything similar. "What do you plan to do?"

"I think . . . I think it will be as close to your sleep as I can come. I wish to make myself over into something acceptable."

"How long will it take?"

The blot pulsated. "I cannot say. I have never done anything like this . . . ah, how your land affects me! I never want to return to the foul emptiness again!"

That was the last Darkness spoke. As the Vraad watched, the huge, pulsating hole drew within itself, becoming more compact. The sorcerer had had enough trouble dealing with a hole that also had mass; he wondered what new miracle Darkness would present to him . . . and how long it would take. With the creature's notions of time, or lack thereof, it might be years before the transformation completed itself. Dru could hardly wait years, but his companion had not given him an opportunity to say so.

He had no choice, anyway, not now. Whatever Darkness had decided to do, he was doing it. Dru was left to fend for himself and hope that the wait would not be for the rest of his life.

It occurred to him then how much he had come to depend on his unusual ally, both for protection and *friendship*.

Food became his own priority. He wanted something solid, something that would give him the energy he needed. Throughout the day's travels, he had picked at berries that seemed safe enough. There was no denying the bounty of this land. It was merely a matter of the Vraad taking what he wanted, and that was surely an easy enough thought for one who had grown up on that very principle. It had only been his uncertainty that had prevented him from attempting sorcery. Now, however, Dru was willing to take risks, if only because his stomach now controlled his reactions.

His first thought was to merely conjure up a sumptuous feast, table and wine included, but a part of his mind fairly shrieked at such a wasteful display of power. It was a sensation that Dru had felt ever since his arrival here, but not to such a degree. He dropped the notion instantly, suspecting that it would not have worked out the way he wanted it to, regardless.

"Am I to starve, then?" he muttered. His mind turned to other methods. Perhaps it was the intensity of his sorcery that created the problem. If so, the safest use of his power might be a mere summoning spell, something that would allow him to bring a bird or small animal near enough so that he could capture and kill it. Dru could not cook, but he hoped that a second minor spell would prepare his feast for him. He grimaced at the image of himself physically preparing a bird for eating. No Vraad dirtied themselves with such menial tasks, but then, no Vraad had ever been in his position before. If it came down to it, he would do what he had to do; that was one Vraadish conceit Dru adhered to.

The first elements of the spell went smoothly. Dru worked slowly, hoping that by doing so he would ease his spell into completion. Then, the resistance began, first softly, then harder as the Vraad lost his patience and began to batter it. A wind rose, but Dru scarcely noticed it.

The summoning went out. The sorcerer felt as if he had been struck by a bolt of lightning, but at least the spell had held. There had to be another way, however. Continually fighting against the land each time he attempted to use his powers would drain him. He could not rely on Darkness for everything, especially now.

He heard the animal well before it came into sight. A large creature, far larger than he had wanted to call. If it was a predator, Dru had doubts about his survival. The renewed fear over his own mortality froze the Vraad for a moment, allowing the oncoming beast to step close enough to see.

It was a *horse. Dru's* horse, in fact.

The steed snorted and trotted closer, visibly pleased to have found its master. The sorcerer was at least as pleased and hugged the animal tight. It was a childish notion, but here was the only other creature from his home, the only link he really had to his citadel, Sharissa, and even Sirvak. More importantly, it was proof positive that had he remained where he was, he could have easily passed through to the shrouded realm. Surely, Dru pondered as he calmed the excited horse, the path worked both ways. He just had to keep going until he found one . . . that is, if Rendel and the Tezerenee monstrosities were not to be found.

"Good boy," the Vraad whispered. He stroked the steed's backside, smoothing out its coat. As his hand went across again, it froze midway back.

Where were the saddle and bridle?

Dru carefully inspected the horse's mouth. There were no bloody marks that indicated the animal had pulled itself loose. Nor were there signs that the saddle had been dragged off as the steed had moved through the woods. There was only one explanation that fit what the spellcaster saw before him; someone had removed the saddle.

A quick scan of the darkening landscape brought no answers. He could not see a stranger simply removing the saddle and letting a horse as fine as this one run free. It now seemed too coincidental, too, that Dru's spell had summoned his very own animal.

His senses touched nothing out of the ordinary in the trees and bushes, yet Dru was almost certain that he was under the scrutiny of others.

The horse chose at that moment to pull away and trot back toward the direction it had originally come. Physically, the Vraad was no match for him. Used to controlling the steed by power alone, he fought fruitlessly to keep it from going any farther.

"Come back here, you misbegotten—" Sharissa had always had the way with animals. They tolerated, even liked Dru, but obeyed more because they had never had much choice.

He turned briefly to see if there was any change in Darkness, but the entity was still rolled up into some sort of obscene ball, pulsating all the while. Unwilling to lose the massive horse a second time, Dru reluctantly followed after it. He was not certain as to what he would do, but he had to do something.

It had never left his mind that this might be part of some trap. Yet, the value of the steed, for travel alone, pushed him on. If worse came to worst, he would unleash his sorcery and damn the agony it caused him afterward. A strong enough will would put down the protests of the land. He was, after all, a Vraad.

The horse continued to evade him, turning to the northeast as it somehow trotted through the wooded area without so much as a pause. Dru stumbled after it, hampered by both the clutching branches and the continual rise of the earth. He was near a hill or a ridge. The trees had obscured this fact. It could not be a high one since he had always had a fair view of the regions in the distant north, but it was high enough to tire him further than the day's trek already had. His determination did not waver; in fact, Dru actually began to look forward to any challenge before him. His growing anger would fuel his will. Anyone seeking to cross his path would be in for a terrible awakening.

At last, he came near the top of the formation. The horse vanished over the other side, which told Dru that it was a hill, for he could hear the steed's steps as it continued on its way. The Vraad reached the uppermost edge and took his first look at what lay on the other side.

What had been a fairly low hill on his side was a *vast* ridge on the other. Dru gazed down at a valley that had once likely been fertile, but had given way to dust over the centuries. That, however, was not nearly so interesting as what stood within perhaps half a mile from his present location.

A city! Not a leviathan stretching out to the horizon, but a large city nonetheless.

Dru squinted, correcting his first observation. The *ruins* of a city. Even from where he stood it was evident that the place was in disarray. Several towers had crumbled and the walls were little more than a jumbled mass of rock. Once, it had been a sprawling place covering a hill at least as great as the one he stood on. It was perhaps more of a vast citadel, for Dru could see that each and every building within was connected. Most were round, like spheres buried partly in the sand, but there were rectangular structures as well and even a courtyard barely visible.

Despite its ragged appearance, he knew it to have once been a place of power. The builders had been on a level equal to that of Vraad, which stirred up the question of what had happened to them. Why was this place now abandoned?

The horse had paused at the bottom of the incline, gazing up at its master with an almost impatient look. Despite the height, there was a path that allowed one fairly easy access to the valley. Dru knew he was supposed to follow the animal and knew also that whoever had sent it *wanted* him to know that the sorcerer was being purposely guided. That spoke of someone who wished to converse, not to kill.

"And shall we enter the dragon's maw?" Dru whispered nonsensically to himself.

He thought of Darkness, who might revive and find him missing. Separating was perhaps not the most prudent of choices in this land, but Dru's inquisitive, arrogant nature would not let him miss this opportunity. Even with his skills hampered, he felt more assured. Someone obviously wished to speak to him and his mind interpreted that as a need for his aid. Being Vraad, it appealed to him, eradicating all other possibilities, including a few which likely would have been seen to bear more merit, had Dru thought them through.

He started down the hill, his eyes focused more often on the decaying citadel than the path he took. Twice he almost tripped, which would have ended with him rolling the rest of the way, but luck was always with him.

At the bottom, he almost tripped again, but this time because the body in his path was so much the color of the earth it lay half-buried in, that he almost did not see it in time.

Dru's entire situation altered in the single breath it took the sorcerer to recognize the form for what it was. Near him, the horse waited silently. It no longer seemed impatient, but rather expectant.

The Vraad reached down and touched the corpse. It lay on its stomach, but he could tell it was manlike at least. Nearly as tall as the spellcaster, it had worn finely crafted cloth garments that crumbled when his fingers ran across them. To Dru's shock and wonder, the body, too, crumbled, collapsing within itself and blowing away with the breeze. Nothing remained after the first few seconds save a collection of fragments, mostly decor from the clothing.

How old? Dru wondered. *How old and in what way would one have to die to be preserved like this?*

The ravaged city no longer seemed such a wondrous place to visit. The sorcerer wiped dust from his eyes and glanced back up the way he had come. It would not be *too* terrible a climb. . . .

The sun was little more than a tired remnant of its once-glorious self. Climbing the hill might not be so terrible, but could he find his way back to his companion? Even granting that Darkness stood out even in the . . . the *true* darkness . . . he was still too far away for Dru to locate immediately. In the dark, the spellcaster might wander off in the wrong direction.

"Serkadion Manee!" Dru cursed his own stupidity. His powers and senses now functioned, at least somewhat. It would be a simple matter of focusing on—

Something snagged his left foot and threatened to topple him to the ground. Dru looked down to see the foot, up to and including the ankle, sink beneath the rocky surface. The grip that held him was tight enough to cut off circulation. His first attempt to free himself was to kick at the slowly encroaching ground. When his mind registered the idiocy of that act, the Vraad threw caution to the wind and summoned forth his powers as best he could. Whether they worked sufficiently or not, he would strike at the underground nemesis with everything within him.

The earth shook violently and the hillside threatened to collapse on the sorcerer. It was *not* the result Dru had intended and he wondered whether he had hastened his own death. Then whatever had hold of him lost its grip and the startled spellcaster fell back, arms akimbo as he sought uselessly to halt his descent. Dru stuck the ground hard.

A huge, monstrous shape rose out of the earth, filling Dru's vision. The Vraad looked into a visage of savagery, a long-snouted, red-orbed beast that seemed to glitter. The creature was covered with a natural body armor and stood on two bulky legs. It had clawed appendages large enough to grasp him by the neck and rip his head off, if it so decided.

The terror let loose with a maddened hooting noise that threatened to pierce Dru's eardrums. It raised a claw, obviously intending to rend the sprawled Vraad's midsection. The harried sorcerer desperately sought for control, hoping to make one last strike with his haphazard skills. The claws came down.

A black aura surrounded the attacking beast. It let out one frightened hoot, and toppled toward its intended victim.

Dru had, at the very least, enough sense to roll away from the collapsing figure. He had no idea what had happened, save that he had escaped death again—with help from someone or something. The sorcerer ended his rolling by returning to his feet, crouched low in case of a second assault. There was none.

Cautiously approaching his would-be killer, Dru frowned. The creature blended into the region around him with the exception of little spots of glitter buried in the folds of its armor. Suspicions already forming, Dru carefully prodded the huge corpse.

It collapsed the way the first had.

At the same time, the Vraad heard the flutter of wings. He looked up.

More than a dozen copies of the avian horror that had tried to kill him back in Nimth hovered overhead. The largest of them wore a medallion about its neck and cradled the artifact with one of its hands. Dru had no doubt that this was what had killed the armored creature.

It was now focused on *him*.

VIII

AMONG THE CELEBRATING Vraad, enmities began to spill over the mental dams in what could best be described as the first forerunners of one massive flood of hatred.

Gerrod noted it first in a Vraad called Lord Highcort, a pretty man bedecked in huge, glistening baubles. Highcort wore rings on each finger and was clad in a robe of majestic purple, giving him the appearance of some jaded monarch. The object of his wrath was a female who had once been his mate, or was it twice? She wore nothing but a multicolored streamer of light that occasionally revealed her charms for the briefest of times. Her hair hung low over her face, almost obscuring her eyes. She was presently taller than Highcort, though that could change depending on their moods. What her name was, Gerrod could not recall.

Highcort had evidently had no such trouble finding names for her. The last was the least in a long line that had initially alerted Gerrod to the argument down in the courtyard. "Minx! I grow annoyed at your toying! If you will not cease your diatribes, then I will have to remove the troublesome tongue that makes them!"

"You've been trying to remove that tongue for years, Highcort! What's the matter? Have I struck so close with the truth that you cannot take it anymore?"

The male gritted his teeth. A haze started to form around him, first simply a cloud, then a whirlwind that began circling around.

What the woman was doing, Gerrod had no idea, but he could sense her own powers at work.

Just as the two were about to strike, a pair of dragon riders materialized above them. Both Vraad turned their attention skyward, knowing where the more dangerous threat lay.

"What is it? What goes on?" His father's booming voice pulled the hooded Tezerenee from the window. Gerrod found he was disappointed that the combatants had not been allowed to continue. At least the others would have been thoroughly entertained and the mutterings would have ceased for a while.

"We can't mislead them for much longer, Father. The feuds are starting to brew anew."

The Lord Tezerenee was presently hunched over charts and notations that Gerrod and Rendel had made concerning the passage over to the Dragonrealm. Barakas absently stroked the head of the small wyvern perched on his armored shoulder as he digested both what lay revealed before him and his son's warning.

Reegan, ever a champion of the head-on charge, slammed a mailed fist onto the table and, ignoring the splintered remnants where his hand had gone through, said, "They should be brought under control, informed of who is in command here! If they knew their true standing, they would abase themselves before us and beg for a place in the new kingdom!"

Gerrod had had enough foolishness. The words escaped his mouth before he considered that he was turning attention away from his brother and back onto himself. "A kingdom we can no longer promise to deliver to them!"

His father jerked straight, causing the wyvern to flutter off in shrieking panic, but the Lady Tezerenee, standing to his left and just behind him, put a steady hand on his shoulder.

"Hush, darling. Gerrod is correct. The thing to do now is recoup our losses and see if we can salvage some sort of victory."

"I would rather recoup the *heads* of Ephraim and his band." Barakas took a deep breath, which threatened to exhaust the air supply in the room, and calmed himself. He turned away from Gerrod, who let out a silent sigh, and focused on one of the coven assigned to monitor Rendel's passage. They had given up trying to keep the body alive; it had passed away shortly after the initial news that the cross-over itself was in danger. "Esad! How many golems remain?"

The newcomer knelt instantly. "Father, there are some two hundred plus golems ready. That is the best we can say at this point."

"Acceptable." Barakas scratched his chin. "More than enough for us to cross over and still have some left for those we deem our allies. As for the rest"—he shrugged uncaringly—"they, being mighty Vraad, should be able to fend for themselves."

Which still did not answer the initial questions raised earlier, Gerrod thought bitterly. What had actually happened to Ephraim and those of the clan whose task it had been to create and shape the golems? Those shells were to act as the Vraads' receptacles when their kas passed across to their new domain. When it was reported that they had not responded to a summons, the Lord Tezerenee himself had gone out to find the reason why. All they had found were the pentagram etched in the dead soil and a few minor items that individuals in the band had carried with them. There had been no sign of a struggle and no misty apparition marking an intrusion by the other domain.

The patriarch was of the opinion that the band had somehow crossed, abandoning their bodies in some well-hidden cave so as to delay discovery of their deed. It was possible to create a lifeline of sorts that would enable the kas of each of them to cross, down to and including the last man. Such a task would require the first arrivals to remain linked mentally with those to follow. It was that part of the plan that Rendel had abandoned earlier.

"It is settled, then."

The gathered Tezerenee, mostly the combined sons and daughters of the lord and lady, grew silent, whispered conversations dying in midsentence. When no one else dared to ask, Gerrod took the burden onto his shoulders, as it always seemed he did, despite a continuing lack of gratitude on the parts of his siblings. "*What* is settled, Father?"

Lord Barakas glared at his son as if Gerrod had turned into an imbecile. "Pay attention! Our course is settled! We begin transferring over to the

Dragonrealm before this day is over. I will summon those who will join our ranks. The announcement will go out that they will be but the first, overall order being done by lottery."

"They will never believe that."

The patriarch gave his son an imperious glare. "They *will* believe that because I will stake the bond of the dragon on it."

So it had come to that, the younger Tezerenee marveled with distaste. *The fine line of honor!*

In truth, his father could not be said to be lying, for lottery was to have been the original system, albeit with a few strings. The supposedly random pattern of who would depart first had been first suggested by Rendel. Gerrod's elder brother had reminded them that no Vraad felt they should come second to another. The lottery, with a promise that no influence would be made when the names were chosen, had subdued many arguments. What the other Vraad did *not* know, however, was that only certain names went into the first batch. Those were the ones Barakas knew could either be turned or bullied into submission. The rest would have eventually found themselves offering up their own wills in return for survival.

With the rampant displays of Vraad sorcery going on even now, Nimth would not last half as long as had once been supposed. The Vraad, certain of their continued existence, assumed that there was no reason to hold back and were celebrating accordingly.

Gerrod, his mind on such thoughts, abruptly found his air cut off and his body being dragged by some invisible force around his neck toward his father. The Lady Tezerenee gasped, but that was the only sound other than Gerrod's futile attempts for breath.

"You are proving yourself to be quite *inadequate,* my son," the patriarch said in the smooth voice that unnerved all, especially those for whom his words were intended. "I left you to organize the transfer. Its control escaped you. I left you to organize the creation of the golems, our hope for the future. Control of *that* escaped you as well. I placed the young Zeree female in your hands . . . and now she has run off to her father's citadel, no doubt." The spell holding Gerrod ceased, leaving the younger Tezerenee to gasp in precious air. "You constantly question my wisdom when you cannot trust your own." Barakas turned from him to his bride. "I have done all I can with our son. If he cannot redeem himself, there are others willing to take his place once the cross-over commences."

Lady Alcia started to protest, but noticed something in her husband's eye that warned her to remain quiet.

Barakas took her arm and started to lead her out. As the two departed, the patriarch calmly commanded to those behind him, "Begin the transfer. Reegan, you control it." The Lord Tezerenee gave Gerrod one last withering glance. "As for you . . . find out what the Zeree hatchling has in mind that she first holds back information and then sneaks off to the protection of her father's domain. If you manage to succeed, there will still be a place for you."

Gerrod nodded, keeping his visage composed since his father's sorcerous reprimand had knocked the hood back. Deep inside, however, he seethed. His progenitor was insane, highly so, though there were none here who would back up such a notion. Each of the "failures" mentioned had hardly been the fault of Gerrod, yet it was on him whom the iron hand of Barakas had fallen. Simply because he would not be one of the clan. How Rendel managed all this time, the young Tezerenee could not say, but he now understood that there might have been *many* reasons Rendel had chosen to abandon them.

When the lord and lady of the clan had departed, Reegan regained his nerve and began giving orders. Most of them were more apt for going into battle than organizing the cross-over, but he had been given control of the plan and there was nothing Gerrod could do about it. With his eldest brother in charge, though, he wondered whether *any* of them would make it across.

He began to wonder again if he really wanted to cross at all.

It was a ridiculous thought. Here, he only faced death. In the realm beyond the veil, there was a chance for survival. Even despite his feeling that colonizing the so-called Dragonrealm would not prove so simple as his father had thought, it was better than remaining here and watching Nimth simply rot away over the centuries. He would not even survive long enough to see its end.

That in mind, Gerrod drew his cloak about him and departed from the domain of Dru Zeree.

IN THE SELFSAME castle that Gerrod sought to reach, Sharissa berated Sirvak. The familiar crouched before her, pitiful but still unremorseful about its actions.

"You disobeyed me, Sirvak! How many times do I have to tell you before you understand that?"

"Understand, mistressss! Only obeying master'sss ordersss! No one but you to enter here!"

"Father isn't here! I'm trying to save him and she can help!" Sharissa waved a hand in the direction of a bemused Melenea.

"Calm yourself, sweet thing," Melenea said soothingly. "I'm certain Sirvak meant well. You cannot expect it to so easily disobey an order given to it by Dru. After all," she added, smiling at the nervous familiar, "it has a limited imagination, a limited mind."

Sirvak dared a hiss at the intruder. Sharissa would have been dumbstruck if she knew all that the beast struggled with in that "limited mind." Powerful as it was, the familiar was next to nothing to Melenea now that she was inside. With the defenses of the citadel behind it, Sirvak could have matched her and more. Inside, however, the familiar faced her with only its own abilities. Sirvak feared for Sharissa's life if it dared reveal what it knew of the enchantress. From experience, the winged beast knew that Melenea would not hesitate to kill both of them. Sirvak could only wait and hope.

Dru was greatly to blame and even the familiar would have acknowledged that. Unwilling to reveal to his daughter any more than he had to about his past indiscretions, he had forbidden the familiar from speaking of those like the beautiful but dark sorceress. That command had now come back to haunt them. Sirvak hissed again, not so much at the enemy before it but at the unfortunate beast's own inability to protect its charge.

Sharissa, unmindful of the mass confusion in the beast's mind, stared it back into silence. "No more! You said you had something for me, something that might help us find Father! What is it?"

The creature looked from its mistress to the hated one and back again, frustration written across its odd visage.

"Sirvak, this is Father's *life* we're talking about!"

Reluctantly, the familiar told her. "The crystalsss. All information liesss in the crystalsss. Can predict when rip will open again, perhapsss."

It was obvious that the creature was uncertain and the idea did not sit well with Sharissa, either. Melenea watched them both, waiting, it seemed, for some explanation. Sharissa realized that her friend did not know about the spell her father had cast and explained it, going into careful detail as to how the crystals recorded images and sorcerous energy so that Dru could later study those memories at his leisure.

Melenea was fascinated. "Dear wonderful Dru! I always knew he was a brilliant thinker! So much potential in this! Do you realize the advantages this could give one over rivals?"

Sharissa had never considered that point but could understand how gaining knowledge of the magical patterns of both Nimth and what the Tezerenee called the Dragonrealm could teach a sorcerer ways of better utilizing the natural power. That was hardly a consideration now, however.

"What Sirvak says is true," Sharissa replied, forgetting Melenea's comment. "The crystals might lead us to another tear, another intense appearance by the shrouded realm. It might even show us a way to travel there with little danger."

The other Vraad's eyes glowed, a sight that Sharissa found both fascinating and disturbing. She had never seen such a sight before. There was so much that Melenea could teach her. . . .

"Shari darling, you may be correct! Wouldn't *that* turn Barakas's beard around? He'd be livid if he found out, you know."

It was a confirmation of everything the younger female had thought of already. She knew she could not allow the Tezerenee to know the truth, no matter how much aid they were capable of giving her. With Melenea to help guide her, Sharissa was certain they could do it on their own.

"Why don't you show me the crystals, sweet thing?" Melenea put a comforting arm around her shoulders. Sharissa took heart from the moral support.

Sirvak chose the moment to raise its head and cry out at something unseen. "Warning, mistresss! Someone stands without the bordersss of the master'sss domain!"

"Let me see." Melenea withdrew from Sharissa and, as the young woman watched, stared blankly into space for a short time. When the eyes focused again, Melenea smiled wryly. "It's your cloth-covered shadow. He's trying to find a way around Dru's defenses."

"Gerrod?" *They suspect*, Sharissa thought in panic. Then she realized that they could not. No, Gerrod was here for the simple reason that his father had likely thrown it upon him to drag her back. Again, she felt sympathy for his plight, but not enough to give herself up. "He can't get in. Father planned the defenses too carefully."

Melenea was thoughtful. "If this were that mountain Reegan, I might be inclined to believe you, but this Gerrod has a sharp mind . . . a treacherous one. He might be able to outthink a series of spells."

"Not if Sirvak is also monitoring things." Sharissa turned back to the familiar. "See to it that he does not gain entrance."

The magical creature looked upset, looked as if it wanted to say something else, but it finally bowed its head in obedience and simply replied, "As you say, mistresss."

"Go now! What are you waiting for?"

With much hesitation, the familiar rose slowly into the air and, looking briefly at Melenea with an unreadable expression, flew off.

"Where is it going?"

"There's a tower it uses for a roost. Sirvak prefers to observe from there."

"It has *preferences*? How odd to find so much personality in a familiar! I'd forgotten! Still, Dru did create it, so it shouldn't surprise me so much!"

Sharissa smiled at the compliment, then pointed at a hallway to her left. "This way. We bypass Father's iron golem."

"Then let us go. Let Gerrod hammer away until he exhausts himself." The other Vraad made as if to teleport. When nothing happened, she tried again. It was only then that the young Zeree recalled the earlier troubles she and her father had suffered.

"The rift was near here. It makes some spells more difficult. We finally found it easier to just walk. I think Father actually grew to like the physical activity."

"Did he?" Melenea sounded quite the contrary, but she finally shrugged. "I suppose it could be novel for a time. Very well, then. Lead on, Shari sweet."

Sharissa found herself talking incessantly. There was something about having another woman to talk to that allowed her to say things she would not have spoken of even with her father. Melenea seemed so interested, too. Adding a point here or there and listening very attentively when the younger Vraad spoke of her mother.

"Father says I look like she did when they first met. I don't know if that means anything; everyone keeps changing their appearances so. I don't remember her. She died in some duel. It seems like such a useless way to die." Sharissa looked at her companion. "I know I sound uncaring, but I'm not. It's just that it was so long ago and I hardly knew her in the first place."

An arm pulled her near the other woman. "I understand. The thing to do is harden yourself to the trials of life. To make everything, no matter how sad, into some sort of game. It is the only way to keep going after the initial four or five centuries. I have found life so much more fulfilling since I began looking at it that way."

"A game?" Sharissa had difficulty with imagining all that had happened in the past few days as part of a game, but Melenea had the centuries of experience backing up her claim. Perhaps when this was over—*if* it was ever over— Sharissa would try to take her advice.

They came upon Dru's inner sanctum. The two attempted to enter, but something refused to give them leave.

"I don't understand this!" The young Zeree stepped forward and put a hand out. She met with no resistance and kept walking until she was completely inside. Melenea also put a hand out, but hers was repelled. Annoyed, she put the hand to her hair and tugged on one of the locks tracing her cheekbones.

"One of Dru's safety precautions, lovely Shari," the enchantress commented. Her smile was a bit forced.

"I'm so sorry!" Reaching out with her mind, Dru's daughter disrupted the spell long enough for Melenea to walk through. "I grow so used to them that I sometimes forget, though I think this must have been a new one. It's keyed only to Father and me and follows the changes in Nimth that I discovered before . . . before Father went out and . . ."

Again, Melenea was there beside her, giving comfort when it was needed. Sharissa wondered why she had stopped coming years ago, but did not dare ask. It was almost like having a sister—or even a *mother*—and she did not want to break the bond they had been forming.

"Oh, darling Dru! This is fabulous!" The comforting arms pulled away without ceremony as Melenea moved quickly toward the far side of the chamber and the glorious spectacle of the magical crystals. She eyed each and every one separately, it seemed to Sharissa, mouthing silent comments about the patterns and colors. The elder woman knew much about the use of crystals, that was evident. Sharissa's hopes flamed higher; while she understood much of what her father had taught her, there were many things she suspected he had not thought she was ready for. Perhaps Melenea knew what to do.

After several long, agonizing minutes, the enchantress said, "The phantom lands . . . the shrouded realm as Dru called it; it affects the nature of Nimth, does it not? More so, I mean, than was assumed earlier."

She *did* understand! Sharissa nodded rapidly, adding, "It has intruded in some places so much that like the ridge, no one can predict how sorcery will work. That was why Father waited so long before he tried to teleport away."

Melenea nodded in turn. Sharissa had explained this to her earlier; had gone through each agonizing moment again and again. It had hurt her deeply to relive that time, but the other woman had insisted that she needed to know exactly what had happened.

"I wonder . . ."

"What?"

The enchantress shook her head. "Nothing. Idle thoughts, sweet one."

Sharissa came over and pointed at the additions she had made. "There's where I had to alter what Father had created."

"That pattern should not be *possible*," Melenea breathed in astonishment.

"Father said the same thing, but when he looked close, he saw that the other realm was intruding into our own. That was what sent us out to the ridge and . . ." She trailed off.

"Don't trouble yourself with that anymore." Circling the astonishing panorama once more, Melenea smiled. It was a smile unlike the others Sharissa had seen. This smile denoted satisfaction, great satisfaction. She wondered whether the enchantress had indeed discovered a way to recover her father.

"I think, pretty Shari, that you should add something here." A thin, elegant finger pointed toward the very center of the spiral. "And here." The finger now pointed toward a spot near the ceiling.

"Are you certain?" The locations that Melenea pointed to were certainly open to stable additions, but their purposes escaped the younger Vraad.

The brilliant smile banished her fears. "Oh, *yes*, Shari! We don't dare go on until you add crystals to those two points."

"All right." Sharissa walked over to a case on a worktable. The lock spell protecting it was one she knew, having opened it often in the past. The case itself was wooden, with intricate scrollwork. Dru Zeree's mark was upon it, emblazoned in the center. This was where he kept the crystals he used in his work.

"I—" She was about to tell Melenea that she knew neither the size nor the color of the proper crystals, but then another mind entered hers, interrupting her chain of thought.

It was Sirvak. *Mistressss, Tezerenee Gerrod departss.*

So soon? That did not sound like Gerrod. *Are you certain?*

There was a moment of hesitation, which Sharissa took as the familiar's attempt to confirm its own statement. *The Tezerenee is nowhere outside, mistressss. I have protected home asss best asss I deemed posssible.*

It was a peculiar way to put it, but she understood. *Keep vigilant, though, Sirvak. He may try to gain entry again. Do what you have to in order to protect the castle. Father's safety relies on you.*

I do what I mussst, mistress. Mistress, I cannot enter the master'ss sanctum.

If I need you, I'll let you in. It would be too time-consuming for now, Sirvak, and there's no need. Father's darkdwellers will assist with the work, if necessary. The darkdwellers were creatures of shadow that lived in the rafters above. They acted as extra hands for Dru when he experimented.

They are weak, mistress, I—

That will be all, Sirvak!

I do what I must for the master and you, mistressss, Sirvak repeated again before breaking contact.

Sharissa briefly wondered at the last statement, not so much because of the words but the tone that Sirvak had used. The gold and black beast had sounded almost fatalistic.

"Shari, sweet thing?"

The crystals! "Sirvak linked with me, Melenea! Gerrod has departed, likely back to the Lord and Lady Tezerenee."

"Has he now?" Melenea smiled thinly. "Watch him, Shari. He is likely the most devious of them. You cannot trust his words or his actions at any time."

It fit with the way Sharissa had pictured the hooded Vraad. Gerrod was both a Vraad and a Tezerenee. What could be a *worse* combination?

"The *crystals*, Sharissa dear." The enchantress tugged at one of the locks of hair following the line of her cheekbones. She seemed to be holding back a building excitement within her. Sharissa took that as indication of their eventual success. It made the need for proper crystals even more urgent.

"Which ones do you need?"

"Any will do."

Sharissa's head jerked upward and she stared at the other Vraad. "But the size and color! You can't just put *anything* in there! You might destroy Father's work and then we'd never be able to find him!"

With swift strides, the magnificent sorceress devoured the distance between them and took hold of her younger counterpart by the shoulders. The grip was perhaps a bit stronger than Sharissa would have liked. "Shari, dear little one, I know the workings of the crystals. Don't you worry. Here." Melenea took out two of the larger ones, a blue and a clear. "You need not worry. These two will do *just* fine."

While Sharissa watched, still uneasy about the carefree choices, the enchantress returned to the brilliantly illuminated artifact and quite casually tossed the two new crystals into the center. Propelled by her power, the blue one immediately shot ceilingward. The clear crystal, meanwhile, struggled against the spiral pattern, which seemed to resist its addition with an almost living determination. Supported by Melenea's will, however, the clear gem soon overcame opposition and took its place within the structure of the one spiral.

Her own additions had made perfect sense to her father once he had inspected the final results, but the younger Zeree, even after several seconds of careful study, could not comprehend what purpose these new pieces served. She said as much to Melenea, who gave her a smile that warmed Sharissa so because of the care that she read in it.

"It will become obvious over time. I promise you that. Now, there's just one more thing. I'd like you to remove the crystals that would contain knowledge of the sighting where poor Dru vanished."

That was easy enough. Happy to be once more an active part in her father's rescue—and happy to understand what she was doing this time—Sharissa joined Melenea by the artifact. With deft skill, she summoned forth the magical gems in question, smiling as they broke away from their positions and fluttered to her waiting hand. While that went on, she brought forth replacements from the protective case. The newcomers fit into the places vacated by their predecessors with perfect ease.

Her skill earned her the praise of her friend. "How wonderfully deft you are, Shari sweet! Had I a daughter of my own, I could not be so proud as I am of you! Dru has raised you so well!"

Sharissa blushed deeply under the barrage of compliments from someone who was *not* her father.

"Now," Melenea added, holding out one smooth, pale hand. "Give me the crystals and we can be on our way."

"'On our way'?" Sharissa almost dropped the gems. "Where are we going?"

Taking the younger woman's hand in her own, the enchantress replied, "This is best done back in my own sanctum, dear love. I have methods I doubt Dru even knows . . . and I think you would be quite a bit safer there if blustery Barakas sends Gerrod back with a few more of his endless supply of relations. You see what I'm talking about?"

Sharissa did. No one really knew that Melenea was aiding her. The Tezerenee would hound her father's castle, wasting time in which the two women could study the crystals' findings. It made perfect sense to her and once more Sharissa was grateful for having the help of so good a friend as the caring enchantress.

"There are notes Father compiled that we'll need. He has them in his private chambers, but I'll be able to get them easily enough."

"That's fine. While you do that, I'd like the opportunity to inspect this chamber for anything else of importance to our goal." Melenea squeezed Sharissa tight for a brief time. "Soon, you'll see Dru again!"

Separating, Sharissa rushed from the room, the quicker to retrieve her father's work and return. Her mind had slipped from the present moment to her eventual reunion with her father. It was because of those dreams that she passed the shadow without noting how it differed from the rest.

"Sharissa."

She stumbled and fell back against one of the walls, disbelieving what she had heard. Her eyes scanned the corridor behind her, at last sighting the shadow that was no shadow.

It unfolded before her, revealing what she had known but had hoped was only her panicked imagination.

"Gerrod!"

"Zeree, listen to me! Sirvak tells me that—"

Sirvak! The familiar had betrayed her? How was that possible . . . unless Gerrod, cunning as Melenea had said, had somehow overwhelmed the beast's mind, making it a creature of his. "Stay away from me, Tezerenee!"

"Little fool! Your father protected you too well! You have no concept of what Vraad mentalities are like! If you only—"

Sharissa, taking advantage of his pontificating, rushed past him back in the direction of the chamber where she had left Melenea and safety. Not expecting such bold, nonmagical action from her, likely because he assumed her a weak, sobbing child, Gerrod was caught by surprise. His reflexes, a product of his upbringing, were exceptional, however, and he barely missed grabbing hold of her arm.

"Sharissa! No! Come back! Talk to Sirvak!"

She paid him no mind, knowing that the familiar would puppet the hooded

Vraad's words. Her only hope, she decided, lay in Melenea and escape from the castle.

As she reached the doorway, through which Gerrod would *not* be able to touch her, she felt a tingling in the air around her. The Tezerenee was casting a spell. Without caring where she landed, Sharissa leaped into the room.

"Melenea, I—"

"Shari! Call these vermin *off* of me!"

The darkdwellers, little more than rags of darkness, flittered about the enchantress, moving in on one side to strike at her as she attempted to defend the other. A few marks on the floor spoke of those who had met their fate at Melenea's hands.

It made too much sense to Sharissa's distraught imagination. Through Sirvak, Gerrod must now control the darkdwellers, too. The citadel was no longer secure; even this room, where she thought to have a chance to think, was threatened by the Tezerenee.

"Sharissa!" Gerrod stood at the entranceway, pushing futilely at the barrier. How long that would last, she had no idea. Trying to ignore the threat behind her, she turned her attention to her friend. At her presence, the ebony creatures flew away, reluctant but obedient to her will. The younger sorceress did not question her luck, wishing only to see if her companion was injured or not.

Several scratches marred the ivory skin of Melenea, but the enchantress ignored them, choosing instead to grasp Sharissa's wrist painfully and pull her closer.

"We leave now! Hold on to me!"

"Zeree! You can't trust—"

The remainder of Gerrod's words were lost as the castle ceased to exist around them and Sharissa suddenly found herself in what could only be the domain of Melenea.

FAILUREFAILUREFAILUREFAILURE . . .

Gerrod struggled against the mad panic of Sirvak's mind. The beast had lost control the second its mistress had departed with Melenea. Even as he forced the familiar back to a state of sanity, he himself could not help fearing for the young Zeree. Gerrod was not fond of her, but no one deserved the ministrations of the enchantress . . . save perhaps Reegan, who would have likely reveled in them.

Sirvak! Listen to me!

He had succeeded in convincing the familiar that an alliance with him was the best hope. The familiar's fairly quick agreement had stemmed mostly from its knowledge of the Lady Melenea. It was a case of *the enemy of my enemy*. . . .

Whatever the reason, they had hoped to catch Sharissa at a time when she would be willing to listen. Gerrod himself felt bitter about the failure, for that had been strictly his own fault. It called to mind what his father had said earlier and he now began to question the truth of that reprimand.

In the end, it likely did not matter. Gerrod had failed at his task and he could not go back empty-handed. Now, Dru Zeree's theoretical pathway to the shrouded realm was looking to be *his* only chance for survival. When the Lord Tezerenee hinted that he would leave a body behind, it was not a jest.

Failure. . . . The familiar was much more calm now, but it still was in no condition to aid in planning. That would fall to Gerrod again.

Though he could not enter the chamber, he *had* spied upon its occupants for a short time. Sharissa had mentioned Dru's earlier work involving the sightings and the binding forces of the two worlds. Perhaps there lay the key.

Sirvak! He treated the familiar as he would have treated one of the wyverns back in the clan's domain. The winged creation responded as if its own master had summoned it.

Listen to me closely, he began, *and we may yet save your master and mistress . . . not to mention myself.* He added the last slowly, knowing it was all too true. *This is what I think we must do. . . .*

IX

DRU WOKE TO a new dawn not even knowing when he had blacked out. The last thing he recalled was the sudden descent of a number of the bird people, creating, in the process, a circle around him. He had tried to act, his mind screeching that he moved in slow motion, but was too late. The blackout occurred then.

His bonds held when he tested them. Attempts at spells left his head pounding at first and then filled with a buzzing that would not depart for several minutes. He gave up after two attempts, knowing that he was very much a helpless prisoner. With escape impossible for now, the sorcerer began to work on satisfying his ever-hungry curiosity. Studying his dusky brown captors in the early morning light, Dru supposed that they were nearly all male. None of them had any special characteristics that were visible, but four of the avians appeared adult even though they were shorter and slighter than their companions. Not knowing any better, he assumed these were the females. If so, the birdlike creatures were great believers in equality, for the four smaller ones worked as hard as the rest and were treated with equal respect.

The avians were little more familiar with this territory than Dru was; it was evident from their jerking movements, their constant vigilance. Territory had been secured, but they were surrounded by unknown lands. Likely, they were also more at home in trees, mountainsides, and, of course, the sky. His captors were in awe of the abandoned city and more than a little afraid of it as well, though they tried to hide both emotions under a mask of arrogance worthy of Barakas. Dru tried to speak to them, but all he received for his attempts were slaps across the face and unintelligible squawks. From their gestures during one of those sessions, he suspected that they had a way of communicating with him, but had debated whether it was necessary to do so. In the end, his captors chose to merely drag him along.

Dru wondered about the beast they had saved him from. Judging by the reaction of the bird creatures, its death was a cause for celebration. *Like the killing of a blood enemy,* he noted. It would not have surprised him if a war was going on between these two horrific races. From what little experience he had enjoyed so far, neither seemed any better than his own race and bloodshed was quite a favorite pastime of the Vraad.

That they had killed the other figure, the one that the sorcerer assumed must have been one of Barakas's elves, went without saying. What interested Dru most, despite the danger he was in, was why his captor and members of two other races would come to this place. What did it have that they all wanted so badly? Granted, most of his ideas were pure conjecture, but Dru was fairly certain he was on the right path.

As they grew nearer and nearer to the avians'—and his own, admittedly—goal, Dru wondered what had become of Darkness. A wild notion that his captors had instigated the entity's odd withdrawal passed quickly from his mind; certainly they would not have left such a threat at their backside. Neither had they been the ones responsible for his horse's odd actions. The avians had totally ignored the steed other than to initially note its presence. Horses were apparently common here and one wandering loose in the vicinity of the ancient city was beneath their concern. It had, in fact, wandered off at some point after his blackout. The trail it left steered to the north, but that was all Dru knew, unable to track it farther.

Up close, the ruins were even vaster. The outer walls had been more than five times the sorcerer's height; massive fragments of some still remained standing. The towers, those that had not collapsed, were much taller and easily comparable to anything the Vraad had created. Little remained of any writing or decoration; they had been worn away by the weather of millennia. The city was incredibly old. It had probably already been in ruins when the first of the Vraad race proclaimed themselves.

The party stood near what had been the city gates, the avians evidently preparing themselves mentally for entering the ruins. Only Dru noticed the tremors when they first began and, being so used to such in Nimth, he hardly paid attention.

The ground suddenly ripped open as huge, clawed hands tore at those above.

Dru, stumbling madly away from one claw, instantly recognized the creatures attacking them. The thing that had tried to kill him had not been alone, though the truth of that was only just sinking into the minds of the party. Dru swore at his captors while he tried to evade another grasping hand sprouting from the earth by his right foot. His captors *should* have searched more carefully; he had assumed they knew to do that much. Like some of his former rivals, however, the birds suffered from too much pride in themselves. They had been certain that they had contained the problem. Now, the problem threatened to contain them.

With a pain-filled shriek, one of the taller creatures was pulled swiftly into the earth regardless of the fact that the jagged crevice was too small for his winged form. Before Dru's disgusted and horrified gaze, the avian was reduced to a mass of mangled limbs and blood that, after all too long a time, completely sank into the soil. The Vraad renewed his efforts to evade the hands groping for him, wishing that, as his captors were belatedly doing, he could take to the sky.

Of the fourteen avians, all but the unfortunate who had just died made it into the air. Several reached for their medallions.

The air proved no more of a haven than the ground had been. From the earth rose one of the snouted monstrosities, a deep, challenging sound accompanying its appearance. It carried with it a needlelike spear as long as its body. The spear was hurtling toward the avians before the attacker was even completely free of the soil. Its accuracy was perfection itself; another of the bird people died, plummeting to the ground no farther than a yard from the hapless Vraad. The spear stood like a banner, one that had been planted so firmly into the victim's chest that it even came out the other side.

The avians finally struck back. Dru steadied himself, expecting the foul mummification spell he had witnessed earlier. Instead, a mist formed swiftly around the monster that had come to the surface. The sorcerer frowned. The intended victim hooted its contempt, waving one arm to dispel the light fog. It did not clear, despite the beast's attempts, but rather continued to thicken, so quickly, in fact, that the blinded earth-dweller was, after only a breath or two, no longer visible. A breath, perhaps two, passed, and then the wind, which itself had pounded fruitlessly at the fog, finally began to have an effect, slowly banishing the magical mist.

When it had at last cleared, there was no sign of the hulking creature it had enveloped. He might have never been, save that the earth was still marred by his initial eruption to the surface.

Another of the winged beings fell prey to a perfect strike, but that was where the newcomers' luck ended. Two more that rose to the surface suffered the same fate as the first; a fourth shriveled to a stomach-wrenching mass directly in front of Dru. After that, the assault ceased. Either the avians had killed all of their adversaries or the underground dwellers had retreated.

In pairs, the surviving creatures descended to deal with their dead. Two separated from the rest and took hold of the sorcerer, lifting him high into the air before he even had the breath to protest. Accompanied by a third, they made for the city, passing over the ruins of the gateway instead of trying to walk through.

Dru was brought unceremoniously to the ground in what had been a well-crafted street but was now a jumbled pile of smooth, broken stepping stones.

The Vraad had finally had enough. Bound and with death likely facing him, he turned on his captors, almost daring them to strike him down, and shouted, "Listen to me! I don't know what you search for, but tell me and I can help! At least have the courtesy to talk to me! I may know something you don't! I demand that you listen to me!"

He doubted that he knew much of value to his captors, but was not about to reveal that to the avians. The trio stared at him with identical one-eyed looks. Under the unblinking gazes, Dru shifted impatiently.

Without warning and with a speed that left Dru breathless, the two avians who had carried him suddenly stepped forward and took him by the arms. Uncertain as to what they planned, the Vraad could not help struggling, though he might as well have been a tiny child fighting a raging wolf, so powerful a grip the creatures had. The third one, once he saw that the sorcerer was held tight, slowly stepped up to his prisoner, halting within arm's reach and glaring haughtily at the human.

A clawed hand thrust out so swiftly that the spellcaster did not even have time to fear for his life. The leader's long hand covered the upper half of Dru's visage. The palm flattened against his forehead.

The world about him *altered*, shifting from a scene of long-lost glory to a dark and unsettling place. Somehow, his mind knew this to be a cavern in one of the mountains of a chain—*across a vast sea?* Yes, it was true. Darkness had brought his tiny companion to the realm beyond the veil, but apparently there was more than just one continent. He had been right in assuming that the bird people were unfamiliar with this land. They had traveled here after an arduous journey that had cut their numbers by a third before they even reached the shore of this place. All this Dru knew through feelings and images filling every niche of his mind.

Dru's view of the cavern widened until he realized that the central cavern housed a vast chamber that had, in the far past, been used as a throne room or a temple. A dim light illuminated the cavern, but its source was not readily noticeable. There were bizarre stone effigies, things that seemed alive in their own way. Some were human, some were not, but the amazing detail of each remained as testimony to the skill of some ancient master. The Vraad recognized something inherent in the tall statues, in the ancient chamber itself, that reminded him of the ruined city, as if both had been built by the same race despite the gulf of water separating them.

"That's it, isn't it?" he asked the avian leader, even though the latter was not visible to him for the moment. "You found the cavern and traced its origin to here."

A sensation that somehow indicated acknowledgment coursed through him. He did not try to comprehend how the sensations could possibly be translated into replies; that demanded much too much time of its own. Dru knew only that he had guessed correctly about the ruins and the winged creature had informed him so in its own way.

Dru watched as a figure he recognized as himself searched the city alongside the—Sheeka?—seeking something. The . . . there was the name again, the Sheeka, but somehow it did not work with him. The seekers . . . yes, the observing sorcerer decided, they were the *Seekers*. It was as apt a name as the one Darkness had chosen for himself and much more tolerable to the Vraad's ears and mouth.

The Seekers had found something—what it had been was carefully kept hidden from the sorcerer's mind—in the cavern, and that had led them to their journey to this other continent. Unfortunately, it had also led their bitter rivals, the ground diggers, to the same place. Dru tried to catch the term for the enemy, but the avian used only the most derogatory symbols for the huge monstrosities, none of which were at all suitable to the mage. He did gather, however, that the other race was more ancient than his captors' was and its power was waning . . . but not fast enough, as far as the avians were concerned. That might have merely been the arrogant opinion of the party's leader, but Dru took it at face value for the time being.

As abruptly as he had been thrust into the cavern, the Vraad was shifted to another scene, this time of vast rookeries, some natural, some created, and the glory that was the Seeker people. Their world, a combination of nature and design, began to fascinate Dru more than the reason for their being on this side of the world. The avians melded the forms of trees and hills with elaborate living quarters that might easily have been constructed by the mage's own race. It was evident that much of their society demanded that the Seekers be groundlocked at times and so it was no surprise that their buildings resembled those of the Vraad. Cities like these dotted most of the other continent, allowing the race to breed yet not destroying the nature.

Recalling his own world, Dru envied the skill of his captors.

The leader chose that moment to remove his hand from his prisoner's forehead. Dru had been correct in his assumption; the taller ones *were* the males.

Although it was guesswork at best in trying to read the more subtle expressions of the birdlike beings, the sorcerer caught what appeared to be a look of disgust and amazement on the leader's visage. It then occurred to him for the first time that the unique method of communication that the Seekers utilized worked *both* ways. Dru had unwittingly revealed to them his own origins, including the all-important fact that he was *not* of this world!

The Seekers evidently needed no physical contact to communicate with one another, for the look of revulsion spread to the two holding him still. He knew they were considering Nimth and its decaying state. He knew also what they must think of him, one of those responsible for spoiling a once-wondrous world.

He was not questioned further, which surprised him. Whatever the avians sought here, they considered it of far more importance than a lone representative of a decadent race from beyond. When the rest of what remained of the party materialized over the walls and landed around them, careful this time to observe the ground beneath their feet, the leader did not even take time to allow the others to digest what he had torn from Dru. Nonetheless, the Vraad was fairly certain that all of them knew what he had let slip, if only because of the difference in the disdainful glances they gave him at various times. Before, it had simply been arrogance at one who was not a member of their "superior" race. Now, it was that arrogance, but peppered with the look Dru's own race reserved for those Vraad with tastes even too perverse for their brethren to accept.

With Dru in their center, the two guards still holding him by the arms, the party journeyed deeper into the remnants of the city. Now and then, members would flutter off for several minutes, inspecting nearby structures and getting a cloud's view of the ruins themselves. Gradually, they began to steer toward the east. It was not the center of the city, but it was where the greatest of the rounded buildings lay. So great a building, in fact, that it could have easily housed the several thousand individuals who made up the Vraad race.

The sun was already nearing its zenith when they came upon the cracked and rubble-strewn clearing between themselves and the huge structure that his captors had chosen as their ultimate destination. Dru wondered briefly what, if anything, was happening to Darkness. He had hoped that the entity would revive before the Seekers located their prize and decided they needed their "guest" no longer.

One of the avians squawked and reached down to pluck something from the fragments covering most of the area before them. This had likely been a square, complete with statuary, but one of the towers nearby had completely collapsed and the remains were scattered all over, making even travel awkward. Several treacherous crevices crisscrossing the square bespoke of just a few of the possible dangers awaiting them.

It was not some shard from a crushed statue that the Seekers had noted. Things could not have been *that* simple. Rather, the object turned out to be a small pouch made of leather and decorated with symbols. Dru's own view was cursory at best, but he thought it looked akin to the style of the clothing the dead elf—if it *had* been an elf, that was still not clear—had worn. That was probably the case; the Seekers were certainly upset about it. Dru was caught between renewed hope and increased fear. This third party might be his salvation, providing he survived any pitched battle between his captors and them, but they also might prove no more hospitable than the avians had been. At this point, however, Dru was willing to take the chance.

The discovery of the pouch changed the attitude of the party. Already having lost three of their number—after having lost so many during the crossing of the seas—the Seekers evidently felt they could not spare any more of their kind. It was thus that Dru found himself walking before them, within easy enough range to be struck down if he attempted to escape, acting as unwilling first scout. Each Seekers had a hand on the medallion that they wore on their chests. Their vision identical to that of true birds, they kept one eye on their destination and the other on the ruins around them, waiting for any potential ambush.

Nothing happened. Dru reached the steps of the building and turned, uncertain as to whether the leader wanted him to continue on or not. The response he received indicated the latter, at least for the time being. The Seekers gathered at the steps, the sorcerer once more under the watchful gaze of two he suspected were the same ones who had acted as his jailers before. He still had trouble telling them apart, save for the leader, who somehow Dru could readily identify, now that they had linked minds.

After some silent discussion that the Vraad could only guess at, he was prodded up the steps. Though they had survived relatively intact, there were places that needed only slight encouragement to collapse, which they did several times for the bound spellcaster. It took more than twice as long to climb than it should have and Dru was out of breath by the time they reached the top.

Dru was tugged back from the doorway he had been about to walk through.

He cursed the avian who had pulled him and who had nearly succeeded in sending him falling backward down the way he had come.

"What now?" he grumbled, more to himself than the avian who had manhandled him.

A Seeker, one of the females, moved in front of Dru and kicked at the rusted relics that had once been doors. They fell with a clatter that not only vibrated through Dru, but echoed again and again all through the building. A layer of dust rose up, creating a miniature storm. After allowing the dirt to settle again, the Seekers prodded their captive on. The female stood aside as he walked through the doorway, wondering what fate awaited him. A Vraad would have had a thousand lethal snares awaiting intruders, even if that Vraad had died a thousand years before. As old as the ruins seemed, they were in fairly remarkable condition. His fear of some lurking danger was soothed in no way by the actions of the avians, who obviously wanted him to act as a sacrificial lamb.

The builders of this edifice had not been raised on Vraadish ways, though, for nothing struck him down, no ancient spell tore the flesh from his skin, and no metal bolt pierced his chest. The structure, at least the front hall, was safe. Dru would have sighed in relief, but his companions shoved him forward again, eager to explore this place.

Reptilian eyes met his own as he moved into the first chamber, a black place without windows. A maw, opened wide enough to swallow the entire party, beckoned. In the darkness of the windowless room, Dru believed he had finally come face-to-face with one of the Lord Tezerenee's dragons. Only when one of the Seekers summoned forth light did he realize that what he had seen was actually a huge stone representation. Dru froze where he was, but no one disciplined him for his actions; the avians were as overwhelmed as he was.

Unlike the dragons of his own world, big, lumbering beasts that acted as little more than pets and steeds for those like Barakas, this dragon was a monarch. The unknown artist had chosen to keep its vast wings folded—likely because of the difficulty it would have caused with the statue's balance—but it was still the largest, most majestic of its kind that the Vraad had ever seen. Here was a leviathan who ruled through both power and intelligence. There was no denying what the sculptor had intended; this was a master of all it surveyed, one who could outwit all but the craftiest of adversaries.

Unbidden returned the question of what had happened to the race that had ruled from here.

Excitement rose among the Seekers; they had recognized a row of items lying on a dais before the overwhelming statue. Dru only now noticed them, the eyes of the giant continually drawing his own despite his efforts.

The dais was more of a display, a platform on which tiny figurines that

looked distinctly familiar to Dru stood even after all so much time. In this
place, he did not question that. The city, for all its decaying state, was remarkably preserved for having been abandoned so long. The platform and its contents were the only items in the room, which was *not* to say it was bare. The
walls, the floor, even the curved *ceiling*, were covered with somewhat surreal rep-
resentations of worlds and races, most of whom the Vraad could not identify.
He saw a tiny sphere that contained a Seeker and another that contained one of
the avians' enemies. There was also what Dru assumed was an elf and another
that reminded him too much of his own kind.

What is *this place?*

So many races were represented, but only he had eyes for them. The Seekers
were far too interested in the figurines, squawking like excited children . . . like
Sharissa.

Dru wondered if she was safe. In the citadel, she would have Sirvak to watch
over her, but he knew that being his daughter, she would be seeking some clue
as to his fate. That worried him, for it would be easy for her to gain the notice
of one or more of his rivals and, especially, the Tezerenee. They *might* see Dru's
accident as a new means of escape from Nimth, but it was not past the patriarch's madness to assume that Barakas *might* choose to destroy Dru's work. It
would, after all, weaken the Lord Tezerenee's tightening grip on his fellow Vraad.

A crash made Dru turn back to see what was happening with his captors.
Four, including the leader, had been inspecting the artifacts. The care with
which they had studied each minute curve of each figurine spoke volumes of
their interest. Now, however, something had occurred that infuriated them. The
leader had taken one small statuette and flung it at the towering figure of the
dragon lord, as Dru was coming to think of it. The relic had shattered, spreading fragments about the room, but the statue had been unmarred.

The sorcerer watched silently. Bitter avians abandoned the figurines, returning to the rest of the party. The leader, frustration and anger at the forefront,
pointed at the entranceway, indicating that Dru was to lead them back out. He
dared one last glance at the majestic dragon and again felt it return his gaze.
The Seeker leader, however, had no patience left and swung a taloned hand at
him. Dru fell back, the taste of blood on his tongue, and would have collapsed
to the floor if not for his two bodyguards. They kept him on his feet until he
had recovered his wits, then pushed him forward, always staying close behind.

In the same manner as they had inspected the first room, the party went
through the next dozen. If anything, they were more disappointing than the
first. More than one turned out to be nothing but a pile of mortar and rock,
the ceilings having collapsed long ago. A few of those chambers that were still
whole held nothing but generation upon generation of dust. If the occupants

had died here, it had been so long ago that their corpses, even their skeletons, had faded away with time.

They found no trace of the other intruders, although, with the jagged and rocky surfaces they clambered over, it would have been near impossible to find any sort of tracks. Dru suffered over the worst of the treks, his bound arms making it impossible for him to protect his face when he slipped forward. Concerned with their own footing, his two guards often could do nothing for him. By the time they had explored the first floor, the Vraad's face and body were one mass of bruises and cuts. Given the opportunity, he could have easily repaired the damage, but his health was low on his captors' priorities. Dru wondered why they had bothered to even keep him alive, so unconcerned did they seem.

The sun moved ever closer to its daily death. The Seekers' leader grew more and more frustrated and his emotions were echoed by the others. Dru was beyond caring; the sorcerer only wanted to lie down, go to sleep, and wake up in his castle of pearl. He wanted to never have found the tear, the hole between this place and Nimth, even though that meant bowing to Barakas and his clan.

At what had once been the stairway leading to the upper floors but was now a jumble of rock, the Seekers finally lost their last reserves of patience. A look from the leader sent four of them leaping into the air. Dru stirred briefly from his worn musings to watch them fly through the hole where the upper portion of the steps had once led. Although it was a dangerous move, considering there still might be foes lurking somewhere nearby, the avians had chosen to split their numbers in order to facilitate their mad search.

Dragging the harried sorcerer with them, the seven remaining creatures continued their scouring of the main floor. They had come to such a point of desperation that they began to sift through the wreckage of each chamber the instant they entered. Under the watchful, one-eyed gaze of the leader, who held Dru while the search progressed, the avians picked at whatever seemed out of the ordinary among the chunks of ceiling and wall. A few items that they unearthed encouraged them and stirred Dru's curiosity. One or two artifacts that the birds seemed to puzzle over, he recognized but was careful to pretend otherwise. Slowly, some of the ancient race's prowess was revealed to the sorcerer. They knew much about crystal magic, that he could tell from the glittering fragments that the avians shoved rudely aside in their quest. What the Seekers sought, however, evidently had nothing to do with that; they seemed far more interested in objects that represented forms, such as dragons, animals, and things that might have been, in a vague way, referred to as human.

The leader, who still held him by the arm, suddenly cocked his head to one side, as if listening to something outside. Dru strained, but heard nothing but the clatter of rubble as the avians tossed bits of ceiling away in order to burrow deeper into the wreckage. A breath later, the rest had paused in their work, also listening.

Dru heard nothing save the beat of his own heart . . . until he realized that the clap-clap pattern could hardly be coming from him if the others heard it. No, the sounds issued from an unknown location near the main hall, and were getting closer by the second.

Rising, the Seekers looked to their leader. He eyed Dru, then tugged the spellcaster around him and tossed him toward the doorway. Stumbling, Dru stepped out into the corridor. The unsettling clap-clap sounds continued to rise in volume, in some way as familiar to the sorcerer as the icons had been earlier. He tried to recall what made that sort of sound, but his attempt to harness his scattered thoughts into something functional was cut off by a harsh shove from the Seekers' leader. Lacking any choice in the matter—and that was becoming too common a way for one who had grown knowing there was little he could *not* have—Dru walked slowly down the corridor in the direction of the noise's source. The avians followed, spreading out as they moved. Two took to the air, hovering near the ceiling.

The sounds echoed continuously throughout the vast structure, almost to the point where it grew difficult for the hapless sorcerer to estimate where he had to turn. He turned back, and as if knowing his confusion, the leader pointed ahead.

"*Thank you*," Dru whispered in bitter tones. There was no hope of avoiding a confrontation with whatever sought out the party. It did not sound like the massive creatures who burrowed beneath the earth—the Vraad would have expected their footfalls to be near silent, considering that blood enemies lurked somewhere within the edifice—and neither did he think it was the elves, whom he had still not seen. They, too, would have taken more caution.

What then lurked in the main hall and had the effrontery to move without care of detection into a place of possible danger?

He was so near now that the clap-clap sounds made it impossible to wonder further. The avian leader put a taloned hand around his neck, essentially turning the Vraad into a living shield. The two of them, with the others following as if all were puppets commanded by the same strings, stepped into the main hall and, all too soon, the confrontation.

Behind him, the avian started, almost losing his grip on the human. Dru could in no way blame him.

It was a *stallion* of the deepest ebony, an impossible and grand creature more massive than any the sorcerer had ever seen. As it slowed to a halt, the clap-clap noise, the sound of its hooves striking the hard surface of the floor, died. The steed stood taller than either the human or the avian. The animal shook its head, sending the wild mane fluttering. It looked at the two tiny figures before it as if they were specks of dust needing to be swept away and began pawing at the rock-hard floor.

Dru tried to step back, but the leader's stiff form prevented him from doing so. Before the eyes of the party, the stallion continued to paw at the floor with its hoof . . . and was quickly succeeding in gouging a *crevice* in it!

The steed lifted its head high and, instead of a loud neigh, *laughed* at their dismay.

X

LOCHIVAN CEASED SCREAMING the moment he felt the hands upon him, knowing that he had already shamed himself before his clan. The raging wind and the stormy heavens could not take his mind from that fact.

"Have no fear concerning your reaction to the cross-over," he heard Esad, his brother, whisper. "Most of us screamed and the rest have all felt the pain. *No one* will speak of it when Father arrives."

The newly arrived Vraad gazed down at his naked form, at last feeling the effects of the storm. "My clothing—" He looked up at Esad, who was clad in armor identical to that which they had been forced to abandon back in Nimth . . . along with their *old* bodies. The armor and the rest had been conjured, no doubt, but then why could Lochivan not emulate his brother's work? Why did the magic resist him?

"The first arrivals clothed me," the other Tezerenee said, reading Lochivan's mind. "It takes great effort and often more than one person to push the spell to completion." Even with the helm covering much of his features, it was obvious that Esad was under tremendous strain.

As Lochivan stood and shook his head, causing several locks of brown and gray hair to obscure his vision, he found himself clad once more in the comfortable feel of cloth and dragon scale. The Tezerenee nodded his gratitude to those of his kin who had aided him. "Have we all made it across so far?"

"Yes."

Something in Esad's tone encouraged his brother to survey the others assembled. There were ten, so far, including himself, and he could see that each and every one was there. Still, something was amiss. There was no mistaking the worry in Esad's voice, and Lochivan knew it was not for him. "Tell me what is wrong, brother?"

"A number of the golems are missing."

"Missing?" The Vraad whirled about until he caught sight of the still forms.

Seeing them even now made his stomach turn, though he would not admit that to the others. That the body he wore had once been as these. . . .

It took him a moment to estimate their numbers and then he saw that what Esad said was true; there were perhaps a hundred of the flesh-and-blood golems remaining where Esad had reported two hundred or more. "The dragons!" Lochivan snarled, recalling the beasts that the golems had been formed from. "Ephraim will pay dearly for his betrayal! With he and his band of traitors gone, the dragons returned and devoured the—"

"No." It was not Esad who spoke, but one of their sisters, a tall, slender woman who favored their mother in form. *Tamara* was her name, if Lochivan recalled correctly. She had been born some eight or nine centuries prior to both of them. It was sometimes so difficult to keep track of those within the clan, much less the outsiders as well. "No," she repeated. "It was not dragons. There are no traces, no blood. The bodies vanished in too orderly a manner, as if those who had taken them had stood in line, one following after another."

"Logan will be crossing in one quarter hour," Esad reminded the two of them. "We should be preparing to guide him on this side of the veil. If we don't, there is always the chance his ka may become lost." The chances of such were slim as long as those back in Nimth still controlled matters; both Lochivan and Tamara knew that Esad was trying to steer them both away from a subject he found unnerving. Father would not be pleased and he would want someone physical to blame. For the moment, Ephraim was beyond his capacity to punish, but they were not.

Lochivan shook his head again. "Father must know before long. The greater our delay in informing him of this latest debacle, the worse it will be."

"We will still have to wait for Logan," Tamara reminded them. "We need at least eleven to reach through the veil and establish a *true* link of communications with the others. Any word we send now would likely be garbled, and I, for one, want everything perfectly clear when we report this to Father."

The storm, a side effect of the transfer, was rapidly dwindling to nil. Gazing up at the wondrous blue color replacing the dark gray clouds, the latest immigrant quietly cursed the misleading innocence that lay all about him. At any other time, the clear sky would have entranced Lochivan, who had never seen such a thing. Now, though, he thought of the problems the plan had suffered of late and how the Dragonrealm was not going to fall to Barakas's might so easily.

"Very well." Unconsciously, he stood in a pose that mimicked the patriarch almost exactly. If his relations paid no notice to it, it was only because they themselves were often guilty of the same mannerisms.

"We have a little over a quarter hour to decide *exactly* how we'll tell Father . . . and *how* we'll avoid his anger!"

DRU STARTED TO speak, but his mouth refused to answer his desperate summons. The laughter died away, though its echo would continue on for several seconds. Trotting closer, the huge ebony steed eyed the avian party with blue orbs that chilled any who stared in them. It chuckled, a low, spine-scraping sound that mocked those who would stand against it.

One of the Seekers held up a medallion and focused on the demon horse. Dru recognized the terrible mist. It started to form around its intended victim in the exact manner it had around the hapless earth dweller earlier. In the space of a breath, it was nearly impossible to see the stallion. The Vraad could feel the sense of triumph that flashed between his captors.

The ebony steed trotted forward, ignoring the mist as the sorcerer might ignore the very air he breathed.

"If that is the best you can do," the animal boomed, and its voice stunned Dru, for he recognized it instantly, "you should not have struck at all!"

Laughing, the entity calling itself Darkness winked at the captive spellcaster. "You should not run off, little Dru! I was most distressed when I found you missing! At least *I* waited while *you* slept!"

Two brown shapes dove down from behind the Void dweller, talons poised, while his attention was focused on the human.

"Look—" A backhand slap from the Seekers' leader silenced him before he could warn Darkness of the danger to him. Nonetheless, the massive stallion understood enough to twist his head around, though it was too late to avoid the attack.

The first avian struck, his clawed feet ready to rend the back of the impudent creature below. To his horror and that of the rest of the party, the diving attacker found *no* solid flesh beneath his talons. Instead, he kept diving, sinking into the darker than dark mass that was the phantom steed. The Seeker screeched once, then seemed to dwindle as he sank completely into Darkness. It was as if he had fallen into a bottomless crevice that sucked him ever deeper despite his efforts to the contrary. In mere moments, the would-be killer had vanished, taken completely in by Darkness.

A raucous noise rose among the Seekers as they voiced their dismay.

That was what he meant by taking me, Dru realized when thought was finally possible again. He swallowed hard, thankful for his escape from such a fate.

Unable to combat his own momentum, the second winged fury joined his brother, dwindling and vanishing even faster than the first had. It was almost anticlimactic after the first, though no less horrible, and in less than a minute, Darkness had destroyed—*devoured?*—two opponents without even striking.

"And *who* will be next? All you really need do is release my friend to me! What say you?" The shadowy steed indicated Dru with a nod of his head. Once, the thought of a talking horse would have been simply a matter of amusement to the Vraad; not so now. There was nothing humorous about the astonishing stallion that the Seekers faced.

The leader glanced at Dru, at his remaining fellows, and then back at Darkness. He released his grip on the spellcaster's neck, for which the Vraad was extremely grateful. The bonds vanished as quickly.

As one, the avians spread their wings and took to the air. With equally swift speed, they abandoned the hall—and, apparently, their goal—and flew out the same tall doorway through which the party had initially entered. All the while, Darkness kept a cold blue eye on them, openly daring them to face him down. As the last departed, he let loose with another earsplitting laugh, his final cut at the fleeing foe.

"This is too amusing! One adventure after another! I shall ever be in your debt, little Dru!"

The sorcerer did not answer, choosing to collapse to the floor, the first time he had been able to rest without the painful interference from his captors. Darkness trotted toward him, still chuckling. Dru shook his head at the incongruous sight, as yet unable to believe either the entity's new appearance or his own luck.

"It's fortunate that you left a trail for me to follow, friend Dru. Those *things* did not seem friendly sorts; I suspect they would have harmed you."

"They certainly seemed to not be." The weary sorcerer knew that he should move on, but the opportunity to rest unhindered for once was too sweet to pass on.

"You have not commented on my form! Is it not exceptional? Truly, the sensations and movements are nearly overwhelming! I felt the urge to push to greater and greater speeds and never slow down again . . . it took some doing to not keep going once I did reach this place." The shadow steed peered around at the ruins, his attention wandering as he finally got a good look at the ancient wonders around him.

"How did you . . . how did you come to take that form?"

Darkness snorted, recalling what he had been speaking of. "This *magnificent* creature strode up to me as I unfolded, altered but still at a loss as to a final form. I thought of shaping myself into something akin to you, but the creature was so fascinating that I could not help but wonder what it would be like to move as it did, to live as it did." The ebony stallion laughed low. "It was a most prepossessing being! Once it saw what I wanted, it allowed me to examine it.

Then, when I was at last complete, it showed me the path you had taken. What do you call such a remarkable creature?"

The Vraad had grown colder with each passing word. "A horse. My kind calls such a creature a horse." No horse was so knowing, however, at least none that Dru had ever raised. He was certain that the animal Darkness had met was the very same horse that he had once ridden. Yet, its actions had not been that of the true beast, but that of an intelligent mind. "Where is it now?"

"Hmm?" Darkness seemed distracted in his thoughts. He shook his head, sending his mane whipping back and forth. It took him another moment to answer. "It departed! I do not know where. 'Horse'! I like it, but it lacks something!"

Dru puzzled over the last. "What about it?"

The ghostly stallion gazed at his tiny companion as if he could not comprehend the latter's confusion. "I have a brand-new *form*! I need a *new* name!"

This was hardly the time for such things and Dru tried to tell the entity so, but the shadow steed was already tossing words about, seeking a combination that would please himself. "Mighty . . . black . . . amazing . . . majestic . . ."

"Dark—" The tired spellcaster rose, trying again to cut into the creature's musings, but luck was not with him.

"Dark? Hmmm. Frightening . . . shadow . . . wondrous . . ." The ice-blue eyes focused on the human. "What say you to *Darkhorse*? I like the old name, but Darknesshorse runs too long."

"It's . . . descriptive of your nature." Dru refused to even mention some of the meanings the name brought to mind. No one would jest about the appropriateness, not to such a being as this.

"Darkhorse it is, then!" The huge stallion shouted his name so that it echoed and echoed through the ruins. "Darkhorse! Darkhorse!"

Cursing, the sorcerer tried desperately to get his companion to quiet down but it was already too late. If there was anyone else in the city—and he knew that the Seekers, at least, would still be lurking about, waiting their chance— then they knew exactly where the twosome were.

Darkness—*Darkhorse*, the Vraad thought, correcting himself—seemed willing to listen now that he had found himself a new name. Hopefully, it would be more permanent than the last.

With the magic of the Seekers no longer dampening his own abilities and senses, Dru was becoming more and more aware of the aura surrounding— *overwhelming*—the ancient citadel. The building he stood in was especially awash in the sorceries of the long-dead race. It had the same feel as the natural forces of the shrouded realm itself, save that it was far more concentrated, as if the inhabitants of this place had filled their home with raw power drawn from the world. It would not have surprised him; the Vraad were capable of such, but not on the grand scale he suspected these ancients had.

"Those things that captured me—the Seekers—were looking for something in these ruins. Do you feel anything at all?"

Darkhorse sniffed the air, an act which put Dru off for a moment. Then the stallion replied, "There is a great concentration of power nearby, several such, actually. They tend to be moving, however."

"The power moves of its own accord?" Dru had never come across anything like that on Nimth. Wandering concentrations of sorcerous energy?

"That is how it appears. What is this place, little Dru? This is the most magnificent sight you have shown me so far! So much solidity, in some ways so random and some ways so orderly!" Coming from a place where matter was nearly as rare as a clear sky was in Nimth, Darkhorse did not know what ruins were.

The Vraad did his best to explain to him his theory about the ruins. Darkhorse became so interested that he interrupted only twice, curious both instances about the passage of time, a concept he was still having trouble comprehending. After the second interruption, he angrily dropped his queries and went back to the enjoyment of what, to him, was an exciting story.

When the tale was finished, Dru sighed. Even if Darkhorse only saw the theory as a great story, at least he understood most of what had been said.

"I have told you again and again, friend Dru, that this *is* your world! It may not be the location you desired, but this *is* where you asked to be taken!"

Dru gave in, knowing the futility of arguing. Perhaps later he would broach the subject again.

"And now," Darkhorse was continuing, "where do we find this 'goal' of theirs?"

"Find it?" The sorcerer had not had time to consider that. His mind was only now becoming organized enough to plan the future . . . and an important aspect of that future was finding a way back to Nimth, Darkhorse or no Darkhorse. Still, if the avians believed that what they sought was so important, then it might hold some key, for certainly, if anyone had ever known about the veil and Nimth, it would have been the builders of this edifice. Straightening, Dru smiled grimly. "Yes, let's find it. They thought it was in here, but I don't think that's the way to go about it."

The shadow steed had an eager gleam in his unsettling eyes. He was all ready for another game of discovery. "And how shall we go about it?"

"I can't sense the distinctive areas of power that you can and I doubt if the Seekers can, either. Tell me, are they in a pattern—a circle or something?"

Darkhorse shook his head after a moment. "They have no pattern. Their movements show judgment, but not a regular path."

The Vraad did not like the way his companion spoke of the power as something with intelligence. Darkhorse himself was difficult enough to accept. Dru was still getting used to the entity.

He considered further. "Is there any one area they tend to avoid or congregate near?"

When the wraithlike stallion answered, Dru's hopes rose dramatically. "There is a place they move near and then away from. There is no place they seem to avoid completely. They . . ." The blue orbs dulled a touch.

"They *what*?"

"I do not know. It escapes me for now."

Curious but also cautious, Dru asked, "Have any of those . . . concentrations . . . shifted near us?"

"They have all crossed this place since I arrived. Some have even passed through this very chamber while we spoke."

"*What?*" The sorcerer's mouth fell open and remained that way until he was able to force his next question to the surface. "Why didn't you—?" Dru clamped his mouth shut and berated himself. Darkhorse was an innocent in many ways; the manner with which he had dispatched the two avians had made the human forget that. "Forget it. You didn't tell me because I didn't ask and you felt it was nothing dangerous, correct?"

"On the contrary! I only recalled when you asked me. For reasons I cannot fathom, my recollection of many things has become faulty. Is this what you termed 'exhaustion'?"

"Possibly." The worried spellcaster doubted such was actually the reason. From what he had seen, his companion from beyond did not suffer exhaustion as others did. Once again, the shrouded realm itself was acting against the outsiders.

"Shall we go to this place, then?"

"This—" Dru had forgotten about the location the black horse had mentioned, the one that the sorcerer suspected might house whatever it was the Seekers had wanted so desperately. "You know where it is?"

"Little Dru! I can find it easily! It has an aura of its own, one far different from that which surrounds this place."

"Does it?" That interested Dru. He started to move again, eager suddenly to be on the trail, but his body protested. "I need to rest a little. I don't think that I have the strength to go climbing over more wreckage just yet."

"There is no need for you to do so if it wearies you! Simply climb atop my back and I will carry you to our destination."

"Your *back*?" Memories of the two Seekers swallowed whole were enough to make Dru reject such a mad plan without further thought. "That would—"

Darkhorse laughed. "Poor, simple Dru! Of course my backside will be solid! You are too good of an entertainment for me to take you as I did those others! You are my *friend!*"

Mounting the shadow steed proved a bit difficult for the tired sorcerer, partly because Darkhorse had no bridle or saddle. There were those, like Sharissa, who could ride a horse bareback if the whim was upon them. Dru preferred his comforts. Once he was aboard, however, things changed. Darkhorse was not built exactly like the animal he had so boldly copied. Despite his muscular appearance, the ebony stallion's back was soft, almost padded. It was, in fact, better than a saddle. Dru wished all horses had been designed like his companion and decided that any he raised from now on would have a few minor magical alterations made.

He found it easy to accept Darkhorse as some fantastic steed. Thinking of him as such was easier than trying to cope with the concept of an intelligent black hole . . . not that Dru was going to truly forget what the entity was. It was just more comfortable thinking of Darkhorse as a physical being, especially now that he was riding the creature.

The fearsome stallion picked his way through the rubble to the doorway leading out of the ancient structure. Dru worried about some trap laid by the Seekers, but Darkhorse sensed nothing. The spellcaster wished his own senses were so infallible. He was lucky to even sense the aura of raw power that covered most of the city. Dru wondered if at one time a shield of such power had enveloped the entire citadel. The sorcerer who cast it could have literally made for himself a world of his own, for no one would be able to enter—or *exit*, if that was his desire—without his permission.

Useless conjecture, he reprimanded himself. Best to keep his eyes upon the ruins around him, just in case there was some threat that Darkhorse did *not* notice in time. What he would do if such happened was beyond him; Dru trusted his own abilities as much as he trusted the Seekers not to attempt one last ploy.

"How odd!" The shadow steed's booming words bounced again and again throughout the devastated city.

"What is it?" Dru peered around, looking for Seekers or elves or *anything* to justify his companion's cry.

"I saw a figure, but only as a vague form! It was built akin to you, but that was all I could tell."

An elf, perhaps. Yet, what was there about an elf that Darkhorse found so disquieting? "Why do you find that odd?"

"Because I could sense nothing from him. No presence. No . . . *existence.*"

"An illusion?"

Darkhorse evidently knew the term now, for he shook his head with great vehemence. "Not an illusion. I think I would sense the . . . the sorcery . . . at least."

"Where was it?" The Vraad cursed whatever fickle trait made him miss everything that happened until it came crashing down on him.

"Directly ahead. It stood on our very path."

The sorcerer reached down to his belt, wishing he had a sword. While spells had always been a way of life, he, like many Vraad, dabbled in the physical, especially when it involved violence toward another. Dru was adept with many blades and had even killed one rival in a duel using nothing but a sword. "I was looking ahead. *I* didn't see anything up there."

"Beyond the tall structure leaning to one side."

The "tall structure" was a tower, far in the distance, that had partially fallen onto a smaller building on the other side of the street they were following. The only thing that it now revealed to the sorcerer was that they might have trouble getting around it unless they took a different path. Darkhorse's vision was evidently much more efficient than his own. The Vraad was not quite desperate enough to start experimenting with his eyes.

A low grumble from his stomach informed him of other matters he would also soon have to deal with if he hoped to continue on. The Seekers had fed him, but only small portions of some vile meat that tasted as if it had been stored in salt and left to age for a few years. All that could be said for it was that it had assuaged his hunger for a time.

Darkhorse continued on the route he had chosen, despite the mysterious appearance. The demon steed was confident in his ability to handle whatever threats confronted them and so was becoming more and more lost in his ongoing game of discovery. A statue that had somehow stood the test of time made him pause for a moment. It was unremarkable save that it was whole. Like the stone behemoth that the sorcerer had come across while a prisoner of the avians, this, too, was a dragon. In fact, it was identical to the other save in size. There were a few other statues and some had recognizable attributes, though they were, for the most part, cluttered together and broken. One was a wolf and another a human garbed in a robe. The rest were too broken up to identify readily, though Dru imagined he saw the gryphon and a cat in the pile.

They eventually reached a point where the Vraad saw that his fears about the fallen tower were true; the opening it left was too small for the sorcerer, much less the huge stallion.

Darkhorse was in the process of locating a new path free of blockage when they came across the elf.

She was young in appearance—though with elves that meant as much as it did with the Vraad—athletic in build, and had straight silver hair that would have reached her waist had she been standing. This elf would stand no more, however, for she was dead, a needle spear that had pierced her chest a certain sign as to who her murderers had been. Dru wondered how long ago she had died; the blood had congealed, but she still appeared too close to life to have perished very long ago.

"What is that?" Darkhorse asked innocently, curious as to this new form.

"An elf." The sorcerer recalled his one-time desire to capture an elf so that he could dissect it. That desire, that *Dru*, turned his stomach now. "There have been none in Nimth for thousands and thousands of years."

"Obviously there are. *She* is here."

Dru held back from commenting, having no desire at present to argue about whether this was Nimth or not. He dismounted and looked over the corpse for any clues, any bits of information that would better help him understand his situation. Unfortunately, the elf had nothing with her save her clothing and a tiny knife. The Vraad took the knife gratefully. As tiny as it was, it was still a physical weapon.

At last satisfied that he would find nothing more, Dru mounted up again, saying to Darkhorse, "The things that killed her have a habit of rising from the earth. It would be an excellent idea to keep an eye out . . . just in case."

"As you say, little Dru."

The sorcerer, about to suggest that they move on, shivered as something cold seemed to brush by him. He twisted back, scanning the area around him, but saw nothing. Dru was too experienced to think that he had imagined the sensation. "Darkhorse, was there something near us?"

"One of the concentrations of power passed *through* us. I think it wanted to know more."

"It wanted to *know*?"

"It exists, after a fashion. Much the way you think of me."

Dru gripped his companion's mane tight. "It thinks? Why didn't you say something *before*? I—"

"I did not know until it actually crossed me. Then I felt its thirst for knowledge—fascinating! Your world never ceases to amaze me! Shall we go forward again?"

"I don't—" Dru was unable to finish his sentence, for Darkhorse pushed ahead immediately after asking the question, despite whatever opinion his friend might have had. The sorcerer clamped his mouth shut and opened his senses as much as they allowed. Oddly, there was no resistance this time, possibly because he was now attempting to work *with* the land. In a vague way, the Vraad felt the massive concentrations of power around him and how they moved with purpose, though their patterns might have once appeared random. Dru knew he could not be far from the place that Darkhorse had spoken of. Whether he found anything there . . .

"You are so very quiet, friend Dru! Are you whole!"

A feeling of unease was gradually creeping over the weary spellcaster. It was as if every bit of rubble had eyes and ears and was following each move the duo made.

"I feel like a blind lamb about to enter the den of a pack of silent, starving wolves."

Wolves.

Dru gave a start. Darkhorse also tensed. "They are concentrating more and more in one location!"

The Vraad nodded, sensing an overwhelming level of raw power ahead of them. Though other structures still blocked their view, he knew that what he and the ebony stallion sought was very, very near . . . and it was there that the power concentrated.

Wolves.

There it was again! As if the wind itself had spoken!

"Something happens, friend Dru! Prepare yourself!"

Prepare himself? The sorcerer wanted to know *how*. His senses warned him that the danger lay everywhere, including above and below him. With his present distrust of his skills, how could he even consider fighting back against . . .

Against the ruins of the city.

It began with a tremor far worse in intensity than that which had signaled the rise of the underdwellers, the armored monstrosities from below. No, whatever caused the ground to quiver so, if it was not an actual earthquake, was far greater than them.

A building before them *exploded*, but the fragments, instead of raining down upon the two, flew high into the air above where the edifice had stood. Rubble from the streets flew up after them, joining together and forming great clusters. Nothing was spared; mortar, bits of marble from shattered statues, even vast pieces of the tower they had bypassed . . . all gathered together.

Beneath the Vraad, Darkhorse shied. There was a limit, evidently, to even his bravery. Had he turned and charged off madly, Dru would have urged him on. As it was, neither of them took up the option of flight. The form slowly taking on vague shape had them almost entranced. It stood taller than the great domed building where the demon steed had rescued his companion. There were four limbs, a tail, which was made at least partially from a column, and, if one stretched the imagination to the limit, a head.

Only when it opened its mockery of a mouth, revealing teeth formed from jagged, broken pieces of stone, did Dru identify it as any particular beast.

It was, as the wind had whispered to him, a wolf . . . more than forty feet *tall*.

XI

"Do you like my home, Shari darling?"

"It's so . . . *alive!*" the younger woman breathed. Melenea's citadel, what Sharissa could see of it, was awash with gay colors and glittering crystals. Silk was everywhere. Figurines of fantastical design capered and celebrated. A furry carpet that Dru's daughter was tempted to lose herself in covered the entire floor. Bright candles lit up the vast room they had materialized in, candles whose flames were of all sizes and more than a dozen different flickering colors. Panoramas of women and men competing in game after game covered one wall. The Vraadish symbol of gaming, used most often when announcing a form-ing duel, was the centerpiece of the wall across from the entranceway of the chamber. It would be the first thing someone saw when they entered here. The symbol consisted of two masks, one crying and one laughing, with the former partly obscuring the latter. Sharissa knew that the masks represented the basic aspects of the Vraad mentality.

Her father had summed it up in his own special way. "When your enemy flaunts his weakness, look to your back. When your allies grow too friendly, trust in your enemies."

Sharissa was not certain she liked what she read into her father's definition, but she allowed that there was probably some truth to it.

"Have a seat, sweet thing! Rest yourself. I know how terrible things have been for you of late. There's so much I have to prepare, anyway."

"I really couldn't . . ." Despite her words, Sharissa wanted all too much to relax, to sleep. Her constant fears, the race against time, and the very dominant worry that it might all be for nothing, that her father might be dead, were tak-ing their toll on her again.

"I insist." Melenea shoved her backward. As Sharissa fell, the thick, shaggy carpet swelled upward, catching her softly in what was, a second later, a com-fortable couch. The soothing fur encouraged the young Zeree to rest. "I prom-ise that I will not forget you, Shari. You may count on that."

It was too overpowering. Sharissa settled in and nodded, already half asleep.

"That's fine," the enchantress said, smiling at her guest. She raised a hand, palm upward, and formed a fist. When she opened it again, a small pouch lay within. Melenea took hold of the pouch and opened it. She reached in and pulled out a tiny, squirming figure.

Sharissa, though a part of her wondered what her companion attempted, could not rouse herself to do more than watch through half-closed eyes. Even when the tiny creature, now set loose on the floor, began to grow and grow, the novice sorceress simply stared. It was as if everything around her had taken on a dreamlike quality.

"Come, Cabal," she heard Melenea say to the creature, a blue-green wolf already as tall as its mistress. It had fangs that seemed as long as Sharissa's forearm, and though she was in no state to truly count them, she was certain that its teeth numbered more than a thousand.

When it was almost a foot taller than Melenea, the wolf ceased growing. Sharissa focused long enough to know that she was staring at the enchantress's familiar.

"I live to serve you, lady." The wolf's voice was little more than a deep growl.

"We have a guest with us, Cabal. Her name is Sharissa Zeree." Melenea turned and smiled at the younger Vraad. "This is Cabal, Shari sweet. It'll watch over you so that you can rest easy. Cabal will let nothing happen to you."

"Will I get to play with her, lady?" Cabal asked, eyeing Sharissa in a manner that seemed more suited for sizing up a snack as opposed to studying a potential playmate.

"Perhaps later. I have given you a duty to perform. You will watch Shari at all times, make certain she is secure."

"I obey knowing my life is yours."

"That's as it should be." Melenea stroked the head of the massive wolf, then stepped closer to Sharissa, who tried in vain to concentrate enough to rise. The beautiful enchantress sat down beside her and stroked her hair. "No need to rise," she heard Melenea say, though the voice sounded as if it had passed through a long tunnel. "You sleep. Later, you'll have my undivided attention."

The kiss on her forehead tickled Sharissa, making her giggle rather giddily. Her last view of Melenea was of the sorceress rising and smiling to herself. The crystals she had gotten from Sharissa were in her hand. There was something not quite right about the image, for the smile had no warmth in it. Dru's daughter shifted uneasily, rest momentarily put off.

Melenea had vanished by the time she forced herself to look again, but the familiar, Cabal, lay watching her from no more than ten feet away. It had an eager expression on its lupine visage, as if looking forward to something. Its size further unsettled Sharissa. She rolled over so that if she opened her eyes again, they would not settle immediately on the massive wolf.

The masks stared back at her.

Frustrated, more awake than asleep now, the young Zeree squeezed her eyes closed. Of all places, this was the one in which she should have felt most at ease. Here, Sharissa should be able to get the rest that she *knew* she needed. It was only a matter of letting her exhaustion take over again. That was all.

Lying on the floor, with its gaze ever on its charge, the huge Cabal opened its mouth wide and yawned its boredom. Its eyes glittered in the candlelight, black, pupilless things that never blinked.

Outside, a storm was brewing. Such was not uncommon on magic-torn Nimth and, especially, near the domain of one such as Melenea, who cast spells almost wantonly. There would be no rain . . . there was never any rain. Sharissa enjoyed the sounds of a storm even though she knew that the storm itself was a product of Nimth's twisted nature. The thunder eased her troubled mind . . . and at last allowed her to sleep.

THE STONEWORK MONSTER snapped its peculiar jaws closed, sending bits of mortar and marble flying. It was constantly losing pieces of itself, but new fragments continually replenished its form.

Go! Flee! The words sprang to life within Dru's head unbidden. He was sorely tempted to follow them, but some deep, arrogant pride kept him from doing so.

Below him, Darkhorse shook his head, as if trying to clear it of noise. The sorcerer suspected that his companion was hearing the same words, that those words had been planted by the chaotic creature before them.

Fear! Death!

On cue, the leviathan stretched forward, snapping its make-shift jaws at them. A shower of dust and fragments threatened to smother Dru. Fortunately, none of the fragments was large enough to injure him.

"They are all around us, friend Dru! One of them has taken on this form! I find it interesting, but also highly annoying! Must it shout within our minds so? Does it need us to fear it so much?"

That was the question that the sorcerer had been asking himself. For all its size and apparent strength, the behemoth was holding back. Why? If it meant to destroy them, it certainly had the opportunity.

Darkhorse had said that one of the unseen beings—they could no longer be simply thought of as concentrations of sorcerous power—had clothed itself in this form. The beings had known about them since at least the huge, circular edifice, yet had not confronted them sooner. That meant that they were guardians, yet as guardians, would they not be able to strike back?

Somehow, Dru suspected that they could or would not. The only question remained—if it was a case of the latter, was there a point that he might cross that would unleash their strength?

"Ride forward, Darkhorse."

"At our peculiar friend? Little Dru, you never cease to entertain me!" Laughing, the ebony steed pushed forward.

Wolves! Teeth that tear! Mangled bodies! Blood!

The words by themselves would not have bothered Dru, but each was accompanied by images of his corpse—what was left of it—scattered about on the rocky surface of the city. He saw the wolf grinding up his bones in its stony teeth. Despite his attempts, he could not help feeling more than a little uneasy as they drew nearer and nearer to the odd horror.

When they were within what the Vraad estimated was no more than twenty feet of the monster, it *collapsed*.

The ensuing storm of dust and rock caught Dru by surprise. He coughed for several seconds, trying to breathe in a cloud of dirt. Darkhorse froze where he was, evidently knowing that the sorcerer's grip was nonexistent and a wrong step would send him falling. The ebony stallion's grasp of human frailties was growing.

It took some time for the dust to settle, but when it had, Dru's view left him puzzled. There was nothing before him that seemed to warrant such protection. Yet, this close he could feel the consternation of the unseen beings, the questioning sensation, as if they did not know what to do about the twosome. In Darkhorse they must have sensed incredible ability. Dru pictured servants, much like his darkdwellers, whose ultimate purpose was something other than fighting. The darkdwellers would attack his enemies if there was no one else to protect his sanctum, but they would do so haphazardly, lacking as they did any real knowledge of combat. The guardians of this place, he decided, were much the same.

Wisdom, a voice, different from the first, whispered in his mind. *Understanding.*

Aberration, came another. *Not to be here.*

Darkhorse roared at the unseen speakers, shouting sentiments that matched Dru's quite closely. "Enough voices in my mind! Speak to us or be gone! Come! Are you so afraid of us?"

That was the truth of it, the sorcerer knew. The guardians *did* fear them. Not just because the two of them had come this far, either. It was because they knew the two to be different, to be outsiders.

Remove them! That was the first voice, the one that had taken the thought of wolves from the Vraad's mind and attempted to use it as a means of scaring them off. *Remove them!*

No, the one who had commented on wisdom said calmly. Each of the guardians seemed to have a separate personality or perhaps a separate characteristic.

There were more than the three who had spoken, but Dru took these as the more dominant of the guardians.

No interference, the one who had called them aberrations said, almost as if reminding the others of something. *All must proceed.*

Darkhorse kicked at the rubble, frustrated that the beings would not speak directly to them. The sorcerer put a warning hand against the shadow steed's side. In his ear, Dru whispered, "Calm yourself. I think they may leave."

"Why should they leave?" Darkhorse asked much too loudly. The tired Vraad winced, knowing that the guardians must have heard his companion. For that matter, they probably knew what the sorcerer himself had said, so easily did they touch the mind.

No interference, a multitude of ghostly voices echoed suddenly in Dru's head. With that, the entities withdrew from both his mind and the vicinity. One breath they were there, the next they were gone. Dru could sense no trace of them.

"They have departed," Darkhorse announced needlessly. "Good! They were hardly entertaining company after the one dropped the fascinating form!"

Somehow, the ebony stallion's almost humorous attitude eased the tension that Dru was suffering. He leaned forward and stared at the visibly unprepossessing area they had been protecting. He could still see nothing of value and there seemed only the slightest touch of power.

"Do you know where they went?" he finally asked Darkhorse.

"I cannot feel them," the steed replied.

"What about the region before us? Do you sense anything there?"

"Only what I felt before."

The tall sorcerer straightened and rubbed his chin, which had developed stubble, he noted belatedly. "We may as well go and see what they thought was so worth protecting."

"Of course! Did you actually consider otherwise?" Still sounding amazed that his companion had even thought of turning away, Darkhorse worked his way across the rubble.

Dru turned his head this way and that as the phantom steed moved. He fully expected the guardians to return, this time with more than just bluffs as weapons. What sort of beings were they? Certainly not the builders of this city. If they were akin to familiars, as Dru thought they were, why did they remain so long after their masters had turned to memories?

The air shimmered before them, slowly peeling away. It took the sorcerer time to recognize what lay before them and Darkhorse, ever curious, had picked up his pace at first sign of this latest phenomenon.

"Darkhorse! No! Stop!"

The demon horse backstepped quickly, coming to a stop only a few feet from the shimmering gap, a tear in reality.

"What is the matter? I find nothing dangerous about this! Do you fear it?"

"It . . . it's like the thing I investigated just before I was cast adrift in the Void."

"Ah! Then perhaps this will get you to the home you keep complaining I have not brought you to! Shall we enter, then?"

Dru had not considered the idea that this might be exactly what he had been looking for. Whatever lay within the tear was not yet visible. Likely, they would have to literally be standing in it to see their destination. It was still a hope, however, and one that Dru was willing to cling to if it meant reuniting himself with Sharissa.

"Go in." He tightened his grip and prayed to some of his less repugnant ancestors that he was not making the final mistake of his existence.

Darkhorse stepped into the tear, which seemed to widen so as to admit him more easily.

At first, Dru was aware of nothing but bright illumination, as if he were staring into the sun of the shroud realm. Then, while his eyes were still recuperating, sound returned. The sorcerer had not even been aware of the fact that there had been no sounds until they had returned. With them also came touch and smell. Dru felt the cool breeze and smelled the flowers. He heard the small birds singing where there had been none in the abandoned city.

His eyes finally focused. Before Dru could speak, a voice from below him boomed, "Worlds within worlds! I shall never tire of your fantastic home, little Dru!"

The Vraad, on the other hand, was growing tired of being shocked all the time, though he was no less astonished this time than he had been when he had met his companion, been delivered to the shrouded realm, and discovered the city—was there nothing simple and straightforward in this domain? It was as if someone had designed everything as in a game or a vast experiment.

Where the two of them had once stood in the midst of an ancient, ruined citadel, they now stood at the bottom of a grassy hill on which was perched a beautiful and not at all ruined castle. Banners still fluttered in the wind, crisp and new, not tattered and torn. The castle consisted of spiral towers and a great wall, at least as far as Dru could see, with more buildings likely hidden. The grassy field that covered the rest of the hill was neat and orderly. Someone might have trimmed it only yesterday, so immaculate it was.

Dru did not even hesitate. Things had gone on too long for his strained nerves. He wanted answers, not to mention food, drink, and rest. "We go inside. Now."

The ebony stallion said nothing, but his laughter cut across the hillside as he reared and charged up toward the castle. They were at the gates before Dru even blinked. Regaining his breath, the startled mage wondered exactly how swift his companion was. If the time came, he would question Darkhorse thoroughly. Now, however, this *new* castle was priority.

The gate was open. Dru could sense nothing, but as usual did not trust himself. Darkhorse seemed disinclined to hold back. They were through the gate and into the courtyard in the next breath. As with the outside, the courtyard was in perfect condition. The inhabitants might have stepped out only this very morning. For all the sorcerer knew, they *had*.

Sculpted bushes and vast, colorful flower beds added to the feeling of walking into someone's home while they were away for a moment. Dru admired the marble benches and a tiny bit of his mind noted the style for later use when the Vraad settled in their new world . . . *if* they did.

"Hold up," he whispered to Darkhorse. The phantom steed came to a halt and Dru dismounted. For their purposes, he preferred to continue on foot.

"Worlds within worlds within worlds . . ." Darkhorse was saying. "What fun it would be if we entered and found a way to yet another! Just imagine if they went on forever!"

"I'd rather not! Nimth is the only world I want . . . *my* Nimth," he added quickly, noting his companion ready to argue the point *again*. Studying the buildings, Dru settled on the largest, the one whose towers they had seen from beyond the walls. "That's where I want to go."

Not waiting for Darkhorse, the sorcerer crossed the courtyard. He heard a chuckle from behind him. "And has impatience now become a *virtue*?"

Dru ignored him, fairly rushing through the open doorway. The main hall sparkled; he had not doubted it would by this point. From the doorway the sorcerer had just entered, Darkhorse stepped within, his hooves making the same clap-clap sound they had when he had followed Dru and the avians into the one rounded edifice. The sounds echoed throughout the building.

For reasons he could not explain, the Vraad felt ashamed of the harsh noise Darkhorse was making. The castle touched him in an unusual way; Dru felt as though the sounds violated a peace that had reigned here for thousands upon thousands of years. It was a different sensation than what he had felt in the ruined city. There, he had felt the ghosts of memory and the remnants of power. Here was tranquility, a rare thing to a Vraad. If he died, this was where Dru wanted to be laid to rest. Here, he could—

The sorcerer shivered. Beside him now, Darkhorse asked, "Is there something amiss with you?"

"No. Nothing." Merely, Dru thought, that he had been almost willing to lie down right here and now and wait for death to claim him.

More cautious now, he strode ahead. There were two massive iron doors at the end of the hall, each more than twice as tall as the Vraad. Somehow, he could feel their importance. Behind them were the answers to the endless questions filling his mind. Whether he understood those answers was yet another question, but one Dru was willing to live with for the time being.

Putting a hand out to where the doors came together, the sorcerer pushed gently. The hinges groaned, but access was still denied him. He pushed harder, leaning into the two doors, but was granted no greater success than in the initial attempt.

Putting his shoulder to the crack, Dru angrily threw his weight against the obstructions. For his trouble he received a sore shoulder. Even though there was nothing to indicate that the way was locked, the Vraad could not get the doors to swing back.

"Perhaps if I—" Darkhorse began.

"No!" This was one that the angered spellcaster wanted for himself. Worn beyond his limits, Dru could no longer check his Vraadish temper. It swept over him, a crimson curse that seized control of his body. Shouting words he would not recall later, Dru raised his left hand and brought it down on the massive metal doors.

With a spark that seemed to course from his fist to the entire doorway, the Vraad opened the way. "Opened" was perhaps misleading. What actually happened, if Dru could still believe his eyes, was that the two doors flung back, going the full turn of their hinges and then tearing free of the walls themselves. While the two watched, Dru in dismay and the shadow steed in growing amusement, the doors, now free of all restriction, teetered for a breath . . . and then fell with a resounding clatter that shattered forever any remaining feeling of tranquility that the spellcaster might have retained.

"Nicely done," Darkhorse commented wryly. He had quickly developed a knack of sarcasm equal to any Vraad.

"It wasn't . . . I didn't . . ." Dru gazed at his fist, then at the battered doors.

"Would it be of interest to mention that the boundaries of this place seem to have suffered from your calm, collected solution?"

Dru turned and eyed the walls of the hallway. An intricate system of fine cracks ran along each wall. The ceiling and floor had suffered from a similar network of these skeletal branches, and Dru could see where bits of ceiling had fallen. "I did this?"

"It seemed a reaction to your power. I noted resistance, but you overwhelmed it."

His madness had defeated the shrouded realm's resistance . . . that is, if this was still the shrouded realm. He wondered how well it would work back in the ruined city. There was also the question of what these side effects had to do with it. They were too akin to what Nimth suffered each time the Vraad utilized their abilities. Was this how his world's death had begun? *Were* the Vraad going to destroy their new home as well?

Too many questions. Dru snarled and turned back to the chamber that his fury had finally allowed him entry to.

His eyes widened to saucers and his mouth grew dry. It seemed the realm beyond the veil was not yet depleted of surprises.

Before him, obscured by robes that made them resemble lumpy sacks; knelt more than a hundred figures. They had their backs to the newcomers and all faced a clear crystal in the center of a pentagram that covered the entire floor. The crystal stood on a bronze, pyramid-shaped platform. As with all else, the ages had been unable to touch either the focus, for that was what the sorcerer knew the crystal to be, or the base upon which it stood.

Dru backed up a step. The figures remained motionless despite the noise and damage he had caused. They were, he noted quickly, lined along the points, corners, and sides of the pattern, creating, by themselves, a second pentagram atop the one etched in stone.

"Where did they come from?" he whispered to Darkhorse. The tall Vraad knew that they had *not* been there when the doors had fallen.

His companion did not reply and a glance at the creature's equine visage helped little. Darkhorse's eyes stared vaguely at the chamber, as if he had trouble seeing anything in there at all. A repeat of his question gave Dru an equally silent response.

Admittedly more secure now that he knew he could summon up tremendous power—despite the effect Dru knew it likely had on the land—the sorcerer stepped forward again. He made no attempt to walk silently, knowing that any folk who could ignore the earsplitting sound of two gigantic metal doors collapsing would hardly notice his footfalls.

Dru studied the area with his higher senses, noting how the lines crisscrossed exactly at the point where the focus stood. There were secondary lines as well, weaker links that followed the pattern of the pentagram . . . and piercing each cowled figure from back to chest.

He blinked, then squinted, returning his vision to the normal plane. There was something *wrong* with the meditators. Too much of what he saw already reminded him of something else, something back in Nimth.

"What do you do?" Darkhorse asked from behind him. A few hesitant steps informed him that his companion was following the sorcerer inside.

"I don't know," he muttered, running one hand through his hair as he pushed himself toward the nearest of the baggy forms. Was he mad to risk himself?

Stretching his left hand forward, calmly this time, Dru touched the figure.

Tried to touch it. His hand went through in much the same manner as it had in the wraithlike forest. Both emboldened and frustrated, he waved the hand back and forth, trying to draw *some* response.

"They don't exist," Dru finally told the shadow steed. "They're ghosts . . . no . . . they're *memories*."

"Memories?"

Nodding, the fascinated mage walked around the one he had tried to touch. Its visage was fairly covered by the hood, but he saw that the being before him had been human and male. The visage was disquieting in some ways, though. It was and it was not the features of a Vraad. Not quite elfin, either. The man's eyes were open and in them Dru noted an age far greater than the figure's appearance would appear. So great, in fact, that any Vraad would have been but a toddler in comparison. "You can still feel the vestiges of their power if you stand among them. It was so intense that even after all this time, the shadows of their faces and forms have been imposed upon reality . . . *burned* into it, you might say. I think my use of sorcery, even Vraad sorcery, was all they needed to grow substantial enough to see."

"All I know," the majestic stallion snorted, "was that they unnerved me. I could make no sense of their existence whatsoever." It was a deep admission, coming as it did from the amazing creature.

Dru continued to study the wraiths. There were men and women, all handsome in the same disturbing way, as if they were part of one tremendous clan, even more so than the Tezerenee. All stared at the focus and the image of so many sightless gazes chilled even the centuries-old spellcaster.

"These fantastical images that you call pictures . . . were they not also in the ruined city?"

Darkhorse's words broke the spell that had tied Dru to the lifelike images. He looked up, annoyed that he had been so engrossed in phantoms of the far past that he had not seen what might prove far more important to his immediate needs.

The ceiling was rounded, which gave it and the walls the appearance of being one. That in itself was nothing, but the pictures that covered the entire chamber stirred the sorcerer's memories of another place, a place where a dragon lord had gazed with stone eyes down at the avians and their mystified prisoner.

Again, Dru looked over countless little worlds, each with their own representative. The Seeker was there, as was the enemy. The elf, the Vraad-like human, a figure that looked like a walking salamander . . . there seemed to be more here than in the first building.

Directly above the focus was the only illustration lacking a living figure. It was also the largest, and in the place of a representative race, it had a city . . . one very familiar, despite the differences time had wrought on the actual one.

The Vraad's mind worked quickly. With growing suspicions, he looked down at the focus . . . or rather, the floor beneath it.

Another world was illustrated there, this one greater than the one above. In its center was the very castle they stood in.

"Let us go view something else! I grow bored in here!"

"Not yet." Dru studied the phantoms—who seemed just a bit translucent now—and then gazed at the worlds above and below him. There was no denying the similarity between what he saw here and what he had devised when researching ka travel. Yet, if the images around him—the races and the worlds they stood within—meant what he had concluded, then the ghostly inhabitants of this place had been to the Vraad as the Vraad were to a lowly insect or, worse yet, a simple grain of sand.

Dru had a great urge to be elsewhere—*anywhere*—as long as it was far away from these ancient masters of power.

"We're leaving. Now."

"As you like it." The shaken sorcerer quickly mounted and the black steed turned and trotted swiftly through the doorway. In less than a breath, they were already back in the courtyard. Another and they were out the citadel gates and heading back to where the tear had been.

There had probably been so much more that Dru knew he should have investigated, but what little he had seen with what little he had theorized was enough. There had to be another solution that would gain him Nimth. He wanted nothing to do with the memories within that place. Even the ruined city—*their* ruined city—was better than this.

A horrible notion crossed him mind. "Darkhorse! Can you see the way in which we entered here?"

"I cannot!" Despite the incredible speed at which the dweller from the Void raced, he sounded perfectly normal. Sometimes, it was difficult for Dru to recall that his companion did not have to breathe as he did. "But we are nearly at the spot, I think!"

"Then what will we do if it isn't—"

A gaping hole opened before them and, at the heartrending speed they were moving, swallowed them before the Vraad could finish.

"—there?" Dru stuttered.

They were back among the ruins, but, this time, they were not alone.

The Seekers had returned, apparently having followed the duo's trail, and among them, they now had a captive, who struggled vainly against their might.

An elf.

XII

NIGHT, SUCH AS it was, had come to Nimth. With it came the beginning of the end, as far as Gerrod was concerned. He had returned briefly to the Tezer-enee stronghold, a vicious-looking iron building that, if Gerrod had been asked his opinion, reflected his clan's personality perfectly. It was a toothy structure and cold to both the body and the soul. Wyverns and young dragons constantly flew among its dragon-head banners, while the elder beasts slept in their pens. Besides a nasty array of sorcerous defenses, more than a dozen riders generally patrolled the perimeter of the domain.

Not so now. The stronghold was abandoned forever, though it seemed at first glance that the inhabitants had every intention of coming back. Personal effects lay where their owners had last left them. Charts and books gathered dust. Some of the wyverns flew loose through parts of the edifice they would normally have shied away from. Food was left rotting. Even projects, such as those he and Rendel had been working on, were forever abandoned. The Tezer-enee could take nothing with them.

It was Rendel's notes Gerrod wanted. Rendel knew more than he did about the shrouded realm. Not all of it had been shared with his closest brother, though Gerrod doubted they had been as close as *he* had once supposed. *You left me behind with the rest, brother dear.* He only hoped that Rendel had also left behind his work. It was quite possible that his elder sibling had destroyed everything so as to keep that much longer whatever advantages he had uncovered in his research.

Fortune was with him. Not only were the notes he sought easy to locate, but they had been so meticulously organized that Gerrod found the proper sections within seconds. Evidently, Rendel was unconcerned about what these notes contained. They verified what he had read in Dru Zeree's notes and added new information that the outsider had not known . . . or perhaps purposely ignored, dealing as they did with the region in which Melenea made her home. Gerrod allowed himself a quick, triumphant smile and closed the book. He knew that there were other notes, much more well hidden, but there was no time to search for those. What he had would suffice, anyway.

"So it *is* you."

"Mother!" Gerrod turned on her, wondering desperately how she had been able to sneak up on him and also wondering if there were others behind her whom he also could not sense.

"I came back to see our home once more. Silly sentimentalism, isn't it, my son?" The look on her face was unreadable, suggesting both mockery and truth.

"Some would not see it so," he responded in neutral tones, hoping she would draw her own conclusions.

"The plan falls apart, Gerrod."

He had suspected as much, but hearing it from the mouth of one of the few he trusted, the hooded Vraad shivered. "What happens *now?*"

Her smile held no humor in it, only bitter irony. "It would seem that the golems, not all of them but a great many, have vanished."

"How *many* are left, Mother?" The noose he had felt tightening around his neck since his last confrontation with his father began to choke him.

"Barely enough for the clan. To assuage suspicions, Barakas has selected a few outsiders already."

"And *me?*"

"For the moment, there is still a place for you. You know that much of the anger your father throws at you should rightfully be directed at Rendel?"

"I know." Gerrod smiled darkly. Rendel was his mother's favorite, but he saw no reason to hide his feelings of betrayal.

"You are your father's sons in the end, Gerrod."

"Speaking of dear Father—much as I'd like to avoid doing so—you may tell him that Melenea has the Zeree brat. It was not my fault; she must have been the one who instigated the girl's departure in the first place." Whether that was true or false, he could not say. What it *would* do, however, was steer some of the trouble from his shoulders to those of the enchantress. Perhaps even Reegan, Melenea's toy, would feel some sort of backlash.

"Leave her, Gerrod. There's no time to get her out. As it is, she probably would have been left behind, regardless." There was a trace of regret in his mother's face, but she was hardly willing to risk one of her offspring being left behind. Alcia despised Melenea as much as any being did, but there were higher priorities than the daughter of Dru. "I do not think Barakas will wait too much longer before he decides to finish the cross-over. Some of the outsiders have been raising a fuss. The coming has broken up."

Gerrod rubbed his chin. "How long left?"

"By dawn, your father wants everyone over. He will be the last to go."

"How brave."

She gave him a silent reprimand. "I cannot promise he will hold a place for you even that long."

"Then *damn* him, Mother!" He would have thrown the notebook, but recalled in time what vital information it held. "Perhaps I'm better off here!"

Lady Alcia wrapped her cloak about herself. In the flickering light, she looked as if she wore a shroud. "It may be so, my son."

Gerrod found himself alone. Snarling, he buried the notebook in the deep confines of his own cloak and also departed, leaving the keep of the Tezerenee and possibly his own future to the whims of crippled Nimth.

WHERE IT HAD still been day in the tiny, hidden world Dru and his companion had discovered, it was now night. With the return to the ruined city, the sorcerer's weariness and hunger had increased a hundredfold, as if being in that other place had held back time for a space. Dru found concentration impossible, despite the threat before him. This time, the spellcaster knew that there would be no second or even third wind; his body had reached its limitations. He prayed that Darkhorse was still fit, else the two were lost.

The Seekers were late in noticing the newcomers, concentrating as they had on their captive. The elf was the first to become aware of the tall figure astride the demonic steed and it was her inability to hide her shock that alerted the avians to their danger. In the pale light of the one full moon, Dru knew that he and his companion must appear fearsome, but appearances and reality often had little in common. He clutched Darkhorse's mane tightly to keep from falling and whispered, "You have to deal with them! I . . . won't be much use!"

The shadow steed's laughter rang through the night, bouncing eerily throughout the skeleton of the once-mighty place. "They are hardly a matter of concern! Hold tight!"

"Don't hurt the elf!" Dru added, suddenly fearful that the Seekers' captive, possibly someone who *might* verify what the Vraad had guessed about the worlds within worlds, would perish in the course of the ebony stallion's rampage.

"Is *that* what you called an elf? Have no fear! It has not made itself worthy of my caring attention yet!"

Dru shivered. His companion, growing more and more comfortable in his form and role, was also growing more frightening.

The avians scattered, two carrying the prisoner into the sky while she fought them tooth and nail, crying out words that Dru, holding on for dear life, could not understand. One Seeker foolishly held her ground, locating but fumbling with her medallion. Darkhorse ran *through* her. The sorcerer, pressed against the entity's backside, caught a brief flash of a horrified visage . . . and then the female was no more.

"Ha! Let that—" The words never came. Dru heard a *swish!* and then he was being thrown into the air, his grip broken as easily as the sorcerer might have snapped a twig beneath his boots. He lacked the air to scream and so could only wait in silence for the ground to come up and shatter his body. His thoughts refused to go beyond his imminent destruction. The moons flashed by twice, a glimmering circle and a dim slash, one crimson and the other the pale of death, and their appearances remained fixed in his mind even as he noted that his descent was about to come to a very final finish.

No, said a voice within his head.

The earth was cheated of its prey. Dru felt everything freeze. Though his eyes were open, he could see nothing save the memories of the moons. It occurred to him that no sounds could be heard and he wondered what had become of the Seekers and Darkhorse.

No interference, came another familiar voice.

We are beyond that, added the third, almost eagerly.

We are, agreed the first. *They have all come to this place. To not interfere is to allow all else to fail.*

Dru could feel endless voices arguing for and against what the first being had said. Though the argument seemed to go on forever, the confused sorcerer knew that only seconds had likely passed when it drew to a conclusion. In the end, the first being's opinion was upheld, but only barely.

That was the last he knew. The world, *all worlds,* ceased to be of any import to him.

YOU ARE VRAAD.

The defiant sorcerer nodded, not knowing where he was or how he had come to this place from the chaos of the ancient city. Dru looked around, but could make out nothing save the chair he sat on and his own body. He felt refreshed, capable of doing combat with the strongest of adversaries, but knew better than to attempt any assault now.

He cannot be Vraad! They are rejected!

It was the second voice again. The tall sorcerer stared defiantly into the darkness and said, "I *am* Vraad! I am Dru Zeree!"

He has life! the third being mocked. Of the three who acted as speakers, this was the one who repelled Dru the most. It reminded him far too much of Melenea and her games, of how she looked at *everything* in life as some wicked game.

Games . . . I like that! We have played such a long, boring game . . . until now! the third commented playfully.

A cold sweat formed on Dru's brow. He shielded his thoughts better, though he supposed the effort was little more than futile. In these creatures Dru had found power that dwarfed even that of his companion.

What is the thing? asked the first.

When the sorcerer finally understood the question, he shook his head. Answering the question could do him no more harm than he was already due. "I don't know for certain. I met Darkhorse in an empty place I call the Void. He seems to come from there."

There was silence as he felt the beings mull over his words and his thoughts. They did not reprimand him when he spoke out loud and he wondered if they had their limitations as Darkhorse did or whether they merely knew he felt more comfortable hearing his own voice in this place where other noises did not exist.

How did he come to be here? the second voice asked. Of the three, it seemed the most indecisive.

You have seen it, the first reminded. They seemed indifferent to the fact that Dru listened into their conversation.

It was not made to be that way.

It was too long ago. You know that time drains, time turns all away from the purpose.

And we do nothing! *Always nothing!* the third interjected with disgust. *We who have the power to do anything!*

Such is not our purpose. The response came from several minds and reminded Dru of nothing so much as a litany repeated from generation to generation.

Our purpose is dead!

Perhaps, shot back the first. *Perhaps not. It may be these Vraad who provide what the masters sought.*

"What?" Dru blurted out. He cursed himself even as he spoke. The debate had already given him an insight far greater than he could have hoped and now he had brought himself back to their attention.

All of them must be returned to their places with their minds cleansed. This was a new voice.

The first voice, the one who seemed most commanding of the unseen beings, replied, *The Sheeka and the Quel cannot be cleansed of their knowledge so easily. Neither can we touch the elves here, who serve as we do, though they do not know why. Would you have us interfere more than we have already?*

There is no real choice! the sinister third voice said, cutting off any other response. *It is time we took control!*

No!

Dru screamed and clutched the sides of his head in vain as he sought release from the multitude of shouting voices vibrating through his mind. He collapsed against the chair he had been seated in.

Are you ill? Have we damaged you? It was the first voice again, concern weighing heavy in its tone.

The concern so startled Dru that he almost forgot his pain. "I'm . . . well . . . as well as can be expected."

We did not wish to cause pain. Despite the being's words, the Vraad thought he felt one bit of dissension among the ranks at this statement. He did not have to hazard a guess as to which one of his odd captors it was.

"Where am I?" Dru asked, deciding it was time to take control of the situation, if possible.

In one of the many pieces of the world that the masters cut free. It was never used so we thought it best to bring you here.

"And the—I find it hard to talk to nothing! Can you show yourself to me?" He pictured in his mind something akin to the rubble-grown wolf. "Not quite like that, please."

There was hesitation . . . underlined by worry, the anxious spellcaster noted. *Very well.*

Something glittered before him. Slowly, Dru made out two golden orbs and the faint outline of some great beast. The shape looked vaguely familiar, but he could not place where he had seen it.

It is the dragon lord you came across in the old ones' first city, where they lived when there were many. I took the form because you admired it. I will add scent if you like.

Dru recalled the smell of the Tezerenees' many wyverns and drakes. "The form will suffice."

The mock dragon dipped its half-seen head. *You wished to know of the others. They sleep.*

"Even . . ."

Even the enigma you call Darkhorse. He is not a creation of the old ones. He is from the rim areas between the Void, as you call it, and the true world. We did not recognize this until now.

"Why have you chosen me?"

The shadowy form moved, spreading wings that were and were not there. *You are closest to the masters. The Sheeka—you call them "Seekers"—have not become what they should have. Soon, they will join the Quel in the list of failures. Then there will be nothing left.*

Dru wanted to stand, but he was not certain there was actually a floor on which to do so. He squirmed uneasily on the chair. "The Seekers control this world?"

The greatest of the continents.

"You make it sound as if you put them there."

He could almost see the being shake its head. *The masters set such in operation. They made the tiny worlds so that when the turn came, each would open again unto this, the true world. They hoped that one would prove a successor to their own kind.*

The creature had informed him of everything in a simple, unattached manner, which was why its words did not penetrate immediately. Dru sat still as the impact of what his captor had said burrowed its way into his mind.

You understand correctly. The places from which the Sheeka, the Quel, and even you originated are slices of this world.

"Nimth . . . Nimth isn't . . . isn't real?" *Not possible!* the sorcerer wanted to shout. The birthplace of the Vraad a falsehood? A . . . *zoo?*

He could sense the sadness around him, a sadness that deepened his own horror at what he had come to realize. The mighty Vraad race had risen to supremacy of a cage, another race's toy!

Not so, the ghostly dragon emphasized. *Not a cage. More of a birthing place for the masters' successors. They were old; their race was tired. The masters wanted to leave behind a legacy, so they took from their own and worked to make them better. Then they set them in worlds of their own and let each grow. See it as it was.*

The dragon sank completely into the darkness and was replaced by a tiny image that expanded gradually, filling more and more of Dru's vision until he actually felt he was standing in another place, in another time. In some ways, it was like communicating with the Seekers, save that what Dru saw was not forced upon him. He could accept it or not.

He had no intention of refusing such an opportunity.

There were beings he could call human and many he would not have guessed could ever have been. The ancient race had chosen every conceivable variation they could think of, some of which even Dru, who had witnessed much over his gray life, found so revolting he was astonished that they even lived.

Many attempts did not. There were scores of empty little worlds, worlds created by slicing reality itself. Each had once housed a hope, but those hopes had died for one reason or another, sometimes in great wars that destroyed everything. More than a few were judged failures even if the race within survived; the elders had searched for certain traits among their children. Eventually, most of those failures destroyed themselves, only one had not . . . so far.

Dru knew without asking that Nimth was the one failure that had, up until now, not succeeded in destroying itself completely. The time was nearing, however.

"What about those that succeeded?"

There were those that matured to the second stage, the mock dragon responded. Images of various civilizations passed before Dru. He recognized only two. The Seekers and their enemy, the armadillolike beings called the Quel.

"But you said . . ."

They have failed. The Quel hang on, but nothing more. They will never rise to greatness again. The Seekers have begun their own descent. Their arrogance and communal thinking make them unwilling to face ultimate change. As for the elves . . . they will survive and aid us, but they lack the drive to become what they are capable of becoming. Because of that, they are lost to the plan as well.

"And we have also failed you."

Perhaps. Perhaps not. With time . . .

With time, they, too, will fade, the one who chilled Dru's spirit whispered.

Their death knell has begun already, added the fourth voice.

Dru shook his head, trying to clear away the confusing echoes within.

Not so! the mock dragon overwhelmed his counterparts. *There is still time.*

We have interfered enough, the fourth countered, but uncertainly now.

Give me leave to do what must be done. . . .

The sorcerer found himself in the midst of darkness again as the entities evidently discussed something *not* for his ears.

So many questions continued to clamor for answers, but Dru doubted he would ever learn everything. Still . . .

His musings were forgotten as the world returned.

The sun was in the sky, a brilliant, burning orb that the mage had never thought to see again.

The Seekers who came here have been taken care of. You will think of them no longer. It was the first voice, but there was no sign of the dragon form.

It will not be needed for this short time. You will listen, Dru Zeree of the Vraad. A wind picked up as the being spoke. *I have removed the one called Darkhorse from this place and returned it to its own domain. It should have never come here. It does not belong.*

"He did nothing to harm you!"

A strong gust blew a cloud of dirt into Dru's face, blinding him and causing him to choke for a few seconds.

It . . . he . . . has not been harmed. We have merely placed him where he should be. His presence was only one more catalyst for chaos in something we have been commanded to preserve.

"You interfere quite easily for something that isn't supposed to interfere!" the Vraad snapped. Darkhorse had aided him, had saved him several times. To be so carelessly removed was unfair to the ebony creature.

I leave you the elf, Vraad. That is all I can do for you. That your kind have breached their boundaries is a matter of importance. I must study what can be done to return things to what they were. If the Vraad are to succeed, they must follow the path set by the old ones.

Dru could not resist one more barb before his *benefactor* departed. "*Things as they were?* Complete collapse of your masters' hopes is all that remains if you steer things back that way. We're entering this world at this very moment. It's too late to turn things back!"

A mocking laugh made the embittered sorcerer start. He knew it was not the laugh of the servant he had been speaking to. He knew which of the entities now enjoyed his discomfort.

It will be easier than you think!

He was alone in his mind again. Around him, the wind died abruptly, a sign that the guardians had abandoned him.

A moan behind him reminded Dru that he had been promised someone who could guide him.

"You . . . you are not an elf or one of those monsters, are you?"

The Vraad turned to his new companion. "Obviously not, as you can see."

She was slighter than the dead female he had seen earlier, but identical in appearance otherwise. Her hair was bound back. Her eyes scoured his form, at last resting on his visage. Dru doubted that it was because she found him attractive.

"You are Vraad."

He looked at her with renewed interest. "How did you know that?"

The elf rose, doubling the distance between them as she did. Loathing coated her words. "We thought we had left you behind forever! Now all of our work is for nothing! There's nowhere left to hide! No hope of turning this insane sorcerer's experiment in our favor!"

A knife materialized from her left hand. She had moved so quickly, Dru would have almost sworn it was magic.

"I will still get the satisfaction of killing you, though!"

XIII

I'VE GIVEN UP my future . . . and for what? The imbecilic child of an outsider!

Gerrod knelt behind a ridge on the outskirts of Melenea's domain. She could not possibly know he was so near, not if his calculations based on his brother's work were correct. This region would be in the midst of one of the greatest instabilities existing, nearly as great as the area where the fool Dru Zeree had vanished. Already, the hooded Tezerenee had caught glimpses of a ghostly elsewhere that he knew had to be the shrouded realm intruding into Nimth. Would that his father's so-called Dragonrealm would fully overwhelm the decaying world. Then, at least that problem would be solved.

It would still not solve the Vraad problem concerning colonizing a land that Gerrod felt wanted nothing to do with his kind . . . and *that* was likely why he had finally, in the hours since his last words with his mother, chosen to stay clear of the city. Missing the cross-over had likely cost him his life, yet he had not cared enough to abandon his plan to rescue Zeree's daughter.

There were more reasons than that. A matter of honor probably held as much sway as his insane fear of the land beyond the veil. His progenitor had questioned his abilities, and like any good Tezerenee, he had fallen into the trap of honor. He had gone out to redeem himself even if it meant his end.

Gerrod swore under his breath. He could go around and around with his reasons, some of which even *he* would have admitted were complete mysteries, but that would not remove Sharissa Zeree from the ministrations of the viperous Lady Melenea.

"Masterrr Gerrod!" Beside him, crouched low, was Sirvak. The familiar was in what seemed to the warlock a constant state of frenzied anxiousness. "She could be dead! She could be dead!"

"She's not, Sirvak. Now be quiet." He was, admittedly, a bit uncertain himself. Things had taken much longer than he would have liked. Day, such as it was, had returned to Nimth before he was confident enough of his own plan. All of it had depended on just how well the temptress's home was being affected by the instabilities.

"It must be as physical as possible," he reminded Sirvak. "Trust sorcery only when needed." Sirvak, out of necessity, had drawn first strike. It could fly. Gerrod would have to trust to small teleports and simple running.

"Understand, Masterrr Gerrod." Eagerness suddenly flooded the familiar's unsettling eyes. Its mistress was within the citadel. It had the help of a powerful ally, one it could trust as much as Vraad could be trusted. Gerrod could see that it would perform its task to perfection or die valiantly in the attempt.

Under former circumstances, the Tezerenee would not have feared for himself. Even Melenea had respected the clan of the dragon. With anarchy soon to erupt (if it had not *already*), she would have no qualms about killing both Gerrod and Sharissa. Worse yet, death might prove slow in coming. Gerrod respected Melenea's deceit. Her citadel might be one massive trap waiting to be sprung . . . if his theory proved inadequate.

The shrouded images of the other realm grew more distinct. "Go now!"

Sirvak leaped into the air and was gone from sight a moment later.

The wait tore at Gerrod's patience. His active imagination conceived of every flaw, every overlooked threat. His memories reminded him of Melenea's past *games.* He shivered.

When the time finally arrived for his part, he was thankful. His mind turned to the patriarch as he rose.

"Charging headlong into the enemy. I *am* your son in the end, just as Mother said."

He dared to teleport.

SHARISSA WOKE, KNOWING she had slept for quite some time, but barely able to keep from falling once more into a deep slumber. She struggled against the urge, forcing herself to a sitting position.

A form shuffled near her. Through sleep-filled eyes, the young sorceress caught sight of the overwhelming form of Cabal, Melenea's familiar. The massive blue-green wolf yawned in her direction, once more revealing to her a multitude of savage teeth.

"Mistress says for you to lie down. To rest." Its rough voice assaulted her ears and made her head pound.

"I've rested long enough. It's day outside, isn't it?" She shifted closer to the edge of the furry bed. Doing so seemed to clear her mind more.

Cabal did not answer her. Unlike Sirvak, the wolf seemed more an extension of its mistress. What was it the creature had said to Melenea? The words were slow in coming, but Sharissa finally recalled them.

I obey knowing my life is yours or something to that effect. She frowned. Not at all a pleasant phrase. It almost indicated that Cabal expected death if it failed in its duty. Not like the Melenea that Sharissa knew.

With the wolf following every movement, she dared to stand. There was a brief instant when the sorceress thought the familiar was about to pounce on her, but it turned out Cabal was only resettling itself so that it could watch her better. Though it seemed foolish to believe anything would happen to her here, Sharissa could not help being cautious.

"Cabal? Where's Melenea?"

"The mistress rests also. She has worked hard. You should rest, too. Sleep until the mistress comes again."

"I'm not tired." It was true. Now that she was away from the soothing confines of the bed, Sharissa was wide awake. It was almost as if the bed encouraged slumber.

Cabal said nothing more, but it continued to play the role of sentinel.

Sharissa wandered about the room, admiring the statuary and other items that decorated it. During her arrival, she had only given the chamber a cursory scan. Now, however, the young Zeree was able to study detail. The capering figurines at first seemed comical until she leaned forward and looked again. Up close, the expressions on the tiny faces gained a cruel twist, as if the statuettes had no desire to play whatever game it was they played. She also read new actions in their movements. Instead of dancing, it seemed more likely that they were fleeing or, at least, trying to flee. Unsuccessfully, too.

Disturbed, Sharissa turned from her inspection of the figurines and walked toward one of the windows. This one faced the direction of her own home, and though she knew seeing the Zeree dominion from Melenea's citadel was impossible, Sharissa felt an undeniable urge to seek it nonetheless.

The heavens were one massive cloud of putrefying green that rolled and twisted within itself, seeming to gather strength in the process. A storm of gargantuan proportions was preparing to rage. The novice sorceress temporarily abandoned her initial desires and turned to better view the growing storm. Its center, she suspected, hung over the Vraad communal city. She wondered what could draw together such a force. Only an epic unleashing of sorcery could create such a magic storm. Her father's research had taught her enough to realize that. The cross-over might be enough, but she doubted that. No, something else was happening in the city.

A tiny figure cutting valiantly through the rising winds caught her attention briefly before vanishing into the clouds. Sharissa blinked and looked again. Nimth still had wildlife, as twisted as much as the world itself, but this figure had looked familiar. Likely, she assumed after a minute or two of useless searching, it had been her own desires that had made her believe she had seen Sirvak. The familiar was lost to her. Sirvak was now a puppet of the unsettling Gerrod. The hooded Tezerenee had no doubt taken the small beast and every bit of lore her father had collected and brought them back to the patriarch as an offering. At this late stage, there was no reason for him to come searching for her; the Tezerenee hardly needed her for their cross-over.

Behind her, Cabal began to growl.

"What is it?" she asked, turning at the same time.

The familiar stood, its imposing form nearly making the sorceress gasp. Like all else she had seen after her arrival here, she had forgotten exactly how huge the beast was. It towered over her. One paw the size of her head scratched at the floor. Cabal sniffed the air and continued to growl, curling its lip back as it did. Though the familiar looked at its charge as it snarled, Sharissa knew it was not her the beast challenged.

A swift black and gold figure burst through the window, shrieking a challenge as it soared toward the sinister lupine familiar.

"Sirvak!"

A gloved hand covered her mouth. "We are here to *save* you from yourself, Zeree! Don't let your pet die for the sake of your innocence and ignorance!"

Gerrod! Sharissa fought wildly, locating and kicking the Tezerenee's shin. Startled by her viciousness, Gerrod almost released her. He cursed loudly and said something else she could not catch.

Savage cries alerted her to the battle taking place. Sharissa stared in horror as Sirvak took on Cabal. The tinier familiar looked pathetic in comparison to Melenea's behemoth and she was filled with fear that Sirvak would be torn apart as easily as Cabal might have torn apart one of the drapes. Somehow, though, the winged creature easily dodged the wolf's initial attack and, in fact, struck the huge beast a powerful blow to the head. Jagged scars now decorated Cabal's left side. It roared at the insignificant little annoyance buzzing about its head.

"Don't fight me, Zeree!" Gerrod hissed. "Think for a change!"

Sharissa ignored him and continued to struggle. With great effort, she twisted her right hand free and unleashed the quickest, simplest spell that might serve her against her would-be attacker.

The Tezerenee lost control as a brilliant flash blinded him. Sharissa pulled away immediately. She had to find Melenea. The enchantress would be more of a match for the hooded kidnapper. Sharissa knew that her odds against Gerrod could only worsen if she continued to battle him alone.

Leaving, however, proved far more difficult than she had hoped. Cabal's huge frame blocked the doorway, and in its combat with Sirvak, it was not unlikely that the beast would accidentally crush her.

"The dragon take you, you stupid—" Gerrod's hood had fallen back and the anger Sharissa read on his patrician visage urged her to take her chances with the doorway.

"Mistress! No! Listen to Sirvak!"

The imploring tone made her pause and she looked up at her father's familiar . . . only to watch in horror as the winged creature, evidently caught up in its concern for her, forgot its own safety.

Cabal's mighty jaws caught the smaller familiar's right foreleg. The blue-green wolf bit hard. Sirvak shrieked in agony and quickly pulled away.

The tattered remnants of Sirvak's leg hung uselessly. Cabal laughed and swallowed the limb.

"Good meat," it rumbled. "Come and let me taste more."

"You will taste your own blood!" Sirvak howled back. The wounded animal started to shimmer, a sign that it was about to make use of its own sorcery.

"Sirvak! No!" Gerrod ceased his assault on Sharissa, though she made no use of the advantage, also caught up in the struggle of the two familiars.

Cabal, meanwhile, was preparing its own magical attack. The lupine form wavered, as if not quite real. Two forces stretched out and met between the beasts. Being constructs, the familiars used the most basic sorceries in attack. Basic, but very, very dangerous. Sharissa knew that Sirvak was capable of destroying a good portion of Melenea's home and assumed that Cabal was of at least equal ability. Despite her belief that her father's creation now obeyed a new master, she could not help fearing for it. Wounded, Sirvak might not be a match for Melenea's creature.

Her hesitation cost Sharissa her freedom. Gerrod caught her again, this time in a grip she knew would be unbreakable. He pulled her head back so that she was forced to look him in the eye. "Despite yourself, Zeree, we are going to save you from that witch you think is your friend! Did your father never tell you about why he demanded she never see either of you again?"

"I neither know nor care what you're talking about!" Sharissa tried to spit in the Tezerenee's face, but he turned her head away in time.

"You *will* . . . someday!"

"What have we here? Cabal! How did they get inside so easily?"

"Melenea!" Gerrod snarled under his breath, disgust emphasized in each syllable of the beautiful enchantress's name.

At its mistress's appearance, the huge familiar backed away. Its breath came in harsh gasps, as if its sorcerous battle had taken a toll not noticeable until now. Sirvak, too, looked fatigued, Sharissa noted, but that might have been from the wound that, while sealed by the winged familiar's own powers, still must have pained it dearly.

"I'll thank you to release my guest, Tezerenee."

"And leave her to *you*? I think not. Even a naive fool like this deserves better than *your* tender care!"

The stunning sorceress laughed, a melodious sound that, had he not known her reputation so well, might have lessened Gerrod's guard. "And she should trust *your* care? I think Sharissa knows who her friends are." Clad in a glistening silk robe that did nothing to hide her body, Melenea strode toward Cabal, placing an arm around the blue-green wolf's neck. "I've only done my best for her. I'm probably the only one who can save her father."

"Did you find something?" Even with Gerrod's arm around her, Sharissa forgot her predicament as visions of her father's rescue blossomed in her mind.

"I most certainly did, Shari sweet."

"Don't listen to her!" the hooded figure whispered in frantic tones. "The only thing she has waiting for you is a slow and painful death after she's done toying with you! Ask Sirvak what she's like!"

"Ask away! Shari knows that you control the poor beast." Melenea's visage expressed her deep pity for Sirvak's fate. "I'm afraid you can probably never trust the familiar again. It will have to be destroyed, I imagine."

Sirvak squawked. "No, mistress! Sirvak is good! Sirvak wants only to protect you!"

With a speed worthy of Sharissa's swiftest steed, Melenea reached out and pointed at the flying familiar. Sirvak shrieked in agony and started to glow blue. Sharissa gasped and struggled with renewed urgency.

"I'll regret this; I know I will!" she heard Gerrod mutter. Suddenly she was being pushed aside by the warlock, who pointed at the writhing black and gold familiar and mouthed something. Sharissa fell against the couch she had been sleeping on and stared in amazement as Gerrod actually worked to save Sirvak's existence. There was no reason why he should do so. Whatever knowledge her father's creation carried could have easily been supplied by his notes, which the Tezerenee surely had access to.

"Cabal!"

At the mention of its name by its mistress, the hulking figure charged directly toward the shrouded Vraad. Caught off guard, Gerrod tried to shield himself. Sharissa, for reasons not entirely clear to her, struck even as the monstrous familiar leaped into the air, jaws wide open.

As if caught by a net that was not there, Cabal stopped in midair, struggled futilely with the nothingness surrounding it, and finally fell to the floor with a howl of frustration and pain.

The citadel shook.

"I *knew* it!" Gerrod stumbled toward her, trying to reach out. Sharissa remained where she was, her thoughts in turmoil. She still trusted Melenea, but the young Tezerenee's nearly suicidal rescue of Sirvak, who could serve him no useful purpose, touched her. If there was a grain of truth in anything he had told her . . .

"What have you done, Tezerenee?" demanded Melenea. She fell against Cabal. The familiar somehow succeeded in regaining and then maintaining its balance, unlike Sharissa, who rolled helplessly on the carpet as the building trembled again and again.

"I only added to an overfilled pot, witch!" He groped for Sharissa, but she succeeded in steering herself away.

Though Melenea failed to understand, Sharissa did. She realized that this stronghold sat near an area that had grown unstable. Her companion had continually utilized her sorcery as if nothing had changed, as if the Vraad were still in full command of Nimth. Gerrod must have known what an effect such a concentration of power would have and how this battle would only serve to aggravate things. It was unlikely that he could have predicted the tremors so precisely, but the clever Tezerenee had probably researched her father's work enough to know that the potential for *some* disaster was high.

Above her, Sirvak hovered. The beaked familiar's wings beat slowly, barely enough to keep the creature aloft. Sirvak appeared not to notice, evidently still more concerned with its mistress and her safety than its own magical existence. "Mistressss! Are you injured?"

"No, Sirvak, I'm not!" Its concern was so genuine she could no longer believe the familiar was a puppet of Gerrod. Either Sirvak had broken free of whatever spell the shadowy Vraad had cast upon it, or it had never been under a spell at all. If the latter was the case, then much of what Melenea had said became questionable.

"Sirvak! Does Gerrod speak the truth?"

"Shari darling, you cannot—"

"He speaks *truth!*" the flying beast shrieked, purposely drowning out the enchantress. "She is evil! She only loves pain, mistresss! *Others'* pain! That is the nature of her gamesss!"

A portion of the ceiling gave way, crashing down very near Sharissa. Reacting instinctively, she rolled away. Her maneuver brought her nearer Melenea.

"Cabal!" the enchantress shouted.

The deadly familiar suddenly stood over Sharissa, its hot, stinking breath bathing her face. She grimaced and tried to drag herself away from the stench.

The wolf laughed. "Play with Cabal!"

"No, Cabal!" Melenea commanded. "Gently!"

Twisting its visage into an expression of annoyance, the massive beast bent its head low and caught Sharissa by the arm. The jaws clamped tight, not enough to cause great pain, but enough to keep the young Zeree from daring to pull free.

"Mistresss!" Sirvak came down low, but the winged familiar dared not attack. Cabal had bitten off its foreleg with the least of efforts; it would not take much more for the huge wolf to snap Sharissa's arm apart. Any assault by Sirvak would endanger her further.

A burst of thunder deafened the novice sorceress. As she pulled without success, she saw some of the statuettes leap off their pedestals and run off, scampering through doorways and windows before the startled Vraad. The pedestals themselves were melting.

"Bring her, Cabal!"

The familiar tried, but the floor beneath its feet had begun to grow soft, and though it did not yet impair Sharissa's own progress, the tremendous mass of the monster was enough to make its paws sink. It growled, all the while maintaining its hold on its unwilling companion, and tried to lift one of the paws out. Sharissa ran her free hand across the floor; it felt more like soft butter than marble. Her father had warned her that this sort of thing would happen. Random waves of wild magic, the culmination of centuries of misuse. It would pass eventually, but other waves would come as the days progressed, until there came a time when the area would be forever beyond the control of anyone and nothing would be safe from change.

"Nimth's blood!" Melenea was wiping at her arm, where the sleeve of her gown now moved of its own volition. It appeared to be attempting to envelop her hand, almost like a mouth. As Sharissa watched, the enchantress, modesty the least of her interests at this point, tore off the crawling garment and threw it to the floor, where it attempted to return to her. Melenea pointed at the gown, fury marring her perfect features. The gown froze, but the new spell only increased the general havoc being caused. The chamber began to tilt to the side.

Sharissa heard a painful *crunch!* and found herself falling to the floor, her arm freed from Cabal's toothy grip. Her elbow sank into the floor, but she pulled it free, not suffering from the problems of mass that the familiar did.

Cabal was whining and growling, too maddened to see that its anger and pain were making it sink deeper. Gerrod stood just out of range of its claws and teeth, the shattered pieces of a stool in his hands and a satisfied smile on his half-seen face. While Cabal had been occupied with the task of releasing its limbs, the hooded Vraad had evidently come around the monster's blind side and, timing his attack perfectly, smashed the wolf's nose with the stool. It was probably the only attack that would have succeeded in releasing Sharissa without the loss of her arm.

"Mistresss!" Sirvak alighted on the edge of the couch, or what was left of it. The magically formed piece of furniture had sunk halfway into the carpet again, making it more of a lump. Sirvak carefully balanced itself on what remained, the lack of the one forelimb making it more difficult than normal. "Come, mistressss! Trussst Sirvak!"

Sharissa did . . . now. The beautiful gold and black beast was probably the only one she trusted. Gerrod had succeeded in raising doubts as to Melenea's interests, but his own were just as debatable. One thing she felt certain of, however, was that Sirvak, even if the familiar *had* worked with the Tezerenee, was still loyal to her and her father.

"Plaything! You are being naughty!" Cabal had managed to lift one paw out of the soupy floor and was trying to reach her. Of Gerrod there was no trace, and for the first time, she feared for him. He *had* freed her from the horrible creature before her.

As the massive paw neared her, Sirvak flew from the couch and, paying no heed to its own safety again, attacked the limb with great relish. Cabal took an unsteady swing at the winged attacker, but the horror's lack of full movement made it impossible for the creature to twist far enough to make contact. Sirvak backed away from the paw until it was obvious that the blue-green wolf had overextended its reach, then moved in close enough to snap at the struggling adversary.

Cabal roared in pain. The toothsome beak of Dru's creation tore into the limb just above the paw. Sirvak ripped a chunk of flesh from its counterpart and quickly abandoned the attack before the huge monstrosity recovered. It had not been a total payback for the smaller familiar's loss, but Sirvak's triumphant cry spoke nearly as much about the extent of the damage inflicted as Cabal's howl did.

Sharissa felt the floor stiffening. Things were returning to normal, such as that was. She would have to make a decision now. Either she stayed and trusted

Melenea or she left and trusted Gerrod the way Sirvak seemed to. It was not a choice that filled her with anticipation. She wished her father was here to make the decision for her.

He may be dead! she berated herself. It was up to her to decide her own fate. When her father had vanished, she had let Gerrod lead her to the Tezerenee. Her first attempts at independence had consisted of refusing to share what she knew with the overbearing patriarch, Barakas. Unfortunately, just as she had been deciding to lead her own life, the young Zeree had found Melenea, someone from her childhood. She had allowed the enchantress to lead her as if Sharissa were still a small child. No more.

The crystals. I have to find the crystals! I can't leave without them! Only Melenea knew where they were, however. Only Melenea could give her access to the crystals that might lead her to her father. They somehow held the key to passing from Nimth to the realm beyond the veil. Sharissa knew she could not leave this place without them, regardless of the danger that the enchantress possibly represented to her if Gerrod had been telling the truth.

"Damn you! Not again!"

She only barely recognized the Tezerenee's furious voice before something struck her from behind and sent her facedown into the carpet. Sirvak called out her name.

Someone bundled her up. "We're leaving! Now!"

Before she could protest, Gerrod brought his cloak around the two of them and started a teleportation spell. Sharissa knew she should warn him about something, but the pain at the back of her head made it impossible to recall exactly what it was that the hooded figure had to beware of. By then, it was already too late. She felt the chamber shift around them, melt away, and become another place.

"Dragon's blood! This isn't where I wanted to go!"

"You're . . . you're lucky to have made it at all," she managed to gasp out. "We might have ended up in the shrouded realm . . . or some place even farther away!"

Gerrod's laugh was bitter. "That might have been better for both of us! Look about you!"

"I can't . . . wait . . . my eyes are clearing." The blow, obviously her unwanted companion's doing, had blurred her vision. The teleport spell had not helped matters. Fortunately, as the pain eased, her eyesight returned to normal. "Where have we . . . Serkadion Manee!"

"I think Father's betrayal has angered the rest of the Vraad." The sardonic tone in Gerrod's voice was unmistakable.

They stood in what had once been the courtyard of the Vraad communal city, a place where only days before the race had first started to gather for the coming. It was a city now ravaged by those who had created it and who, Sharissa suspected, would likely greet a Tezerenee and the daughter of the patriarch's supposed ally with even *deadlier* fury.

XIV

BARAKAS, LORD AND patriarch of the Tezerenee, the clan of the dragon, gazed at what would be the beginning of his new empire. Gone were the ways of old Nimth, when he had been forced to share the world with so many arrogant and maddening outsiders. Now, only a handful of outsiders remained, all manageable. Most of those were female, too, for the patriarch knew that to start any new civilization required new blood. He had kept his clan to certain numbers because of the restrictions of space in Nimth. That was no longer necessary.

"Those mountains over there." He gestured at the same peaks Rendel, days ago, had set out for. "I want them explored."

Reegan looked abashed. "We have no flying drakes and our powers work haphazardly, sire."

"Do not state the obvious with me, Reegan. I have trained you to do what you must to obey my commands. See to it that what I say is done." Though Barakas almost looked peaceful, his eldest son, reading into the patriarch's eyes, bowed quickly and rushed off to see what suggestions some of his brethren might have.

Lady Alcia, stepping away from a conversation with someone who was either a daughter or a niece—Barakas felt it unnecessary to try to keep track of *all* of his people as long as they did what they were told—joined her husband as he surveyed the fields and forest around them.

"You seem flushed with excitement," she murmured.

"I have a world to conquer. I have my people to obey me. What more could one ask for?"

"Your son?"

Barakas looked at her in distaste. "Which one, my bride? Rendel, who betrayed us once he was on this side of the veil, or Gerrod, who failed to do anything I asked of him?"

"I can't say anything concerning Rendel, but Gerrod did as he was commanded. You never paid attention to that fact, however. It may interest you to know that I ran across Gerrod before I returned from our old keep. Even though time was running out, he was determined to find Dru Zeree's daughter, as you commanded, despite the fact that he believed she was a 'guest' of Melenea."

"I waited as long as possible, Alcia. You saw how they were acting. Any longer and *we* might not have crossed in time." The patriarch's attention wandered to where Lochivan was trying to look busy. He still feared his father's wrath, though there was nothing he or the others could have done to prevent the disappearance of the golems. That had been Rendel's province. "Lochivan!"

"Father!" Despite the fear, the Lord Tezerenee's son rushed to his side and knelt. "You have a task for me?"

"This will be our initial camp. Begin expanding our perimeter. We need drakes, too. If you—"

Both Lochivan and the Lady Alcia looked at the patriarch, curious as to why he had stopped speaking.

"There!" Barakas pointed a finger at one of the nearby treetops. A horrible, agonized shriek filled the ears and souls of the assembled Tezerenee, all of whom turned to stare in the direction of the cry as if mesmerized by the strident sound.

A winged figure, now only a corpse, plummeted to the earth. It landed with a dull thud, a crumpled and twisted rag doll. Even from where he stood, the Lord Tezerenee could see that while it was avian, it was also humanoid. It had most certainly been spying on them, so he knew it was also intelligent. He wondered how long it—and likely others—had watched his people, all the while undetected. Though Barakas had appeared to know where the spy was, it had actually been a fluke; he had spotted a movement as he had surveyed that part of his new kingdom. No one would need to know that, however.

Pain abruptly wracked the hand from which he had directed his deadly spell. Barakas swore and rubbed at the sore spot. He felt as if part of his assault had backfired, though there was no method by which that could have happened so far as he knew.

"Lochivan!" His pain was assuaged a bit by the speed with which his son came once more to attention. "This is a hostile region! We have an enemy to confront! I want the immediate area cleared of any other spying eyes."

"We dare not trust our power, Father. Already, three who attempted spells have been injured. There is something amiss with the magic of this world."

Barakas released his injured hand as if nothing had happened to it. "I felt nothing. The spell worked as it should have." That was not true; it had been his intention to *capture* whatever had lurked in the tree for interrogation or, if it had proven to be merely an animal, examination as a potential food or sport source. For some unfathomable reason, he had unleashed a spell more powerful by at least a hundredfold. "I have commanded; your duty is to *obey*."

"Father." Lochivan bowed and backed away. It was evident in his movements that he would have preferred the patriarch's reprimand to such an impossible task. Yet, being Tezerenee, he would work to fulfill Barakas's command, no matter what the cost.

The Lord Tezerenee gestured to two clan members who stood nearby, still stunned by what their master had done. With their helms on, he could not judge whether they were his children or merely relations. It did not matter as long as they performed their duties. "Bring that carcass to me. I want to know what our enemy is capable of."

The Lady Alcia tried to bring the conversation back to Gerrod. "If you could only—"

She was cut off with an imperialistic wave of one gauntleted hand. "Gerrod is dead. Everyone back in Nimth is dead . . . or as *good* as dead. I will hear no more about them." Anticipation tinged his next words. "We must prepare for our first battle. It will be *glorious!*"

As she watched her husband stalk off to oversee the disposal of the monstrous corpse, the matriarch frowned. Barakas had found new playmates, actual adversaries. There would be no turning him from the task he had set for himself now. The role of conqueror was at last his to claim. Gerrod was no more than a soon-to-be-forgotten memory, as far as the lord of the dragon clan was concerned.

Glancing at the limp bundle of flesh being dragged to the waiting patriarch and thinking of what other potential dangers the new world might yet offer, the Lady Tezerenee wondered if the clan itself would be such a memory before long.

"Perhaps it would be for the best," she murmured, then strode off herself to help organize her people for the coming threat.

VRAAD AND ELF faced each other, eyes locked. Considering the speed with which she moved, Dru questioned his chances of unleashing a spell before the knife struck home. He also wondered what sort of sorcery she might have to back up her assault, for the stories had always hinted that to some extent the elfin race had had its share of potent spellcasters. Somehow, he could not see the knife as her only weapon; his Vraadish mind-set could not comprehend a foe who would take on a mage with only a small hand weapon. No one was that insane.

Another thing occurred to him as he readied himself for the worst. He knew time had passed, for the sun was bright in the sky. Yet Dru could not recall either sleeping or eating. He was, however, fully rested and not the least bit hungry. The sorcerer thanked the guardians for small favors; maybe they had wanted him to be at his best when he died.

"What did they tell you in there?" she suddenly asked, the blade still poised for immediate use.

He almost laughed. Questions at a time like this? He would have expected such from himself had his mind not still been at least partly back with the very creatures she asked about. "They told me about this place . . . and about Nimth."

"It is all falling apart, is it not? Nimth, that is."

His gaze shifted briefly from her green, almond-shaped eyes to the knife and then back again. "Yes, it is."

"You destroyed Nimth. You destroyed it the way you destroyed everything else on it other than yourselves."

"Yes."

Confusion spread onto her face, lessening the anger a bit. "You admit it? You are very cooperative. Why is that? What are you planning?"

"I have no quarrel with you, elf. If I have a quarrel with anyone, it is our former hosts."

"Do you think I am a fool because I use a knife against a Vraad? I know how chancy your spells are, but I also know how devious you are said to be. We went through the same difficulty with our own magic, for a short time, when we first came here. I can easily kill you before you take another breath."

Dru believed her. The grace with which she moved, even seemed to breathe, spoke of skill surpassing his. Still, if it came to a battle, he had a few tricks she could not know about. "The guardians put us together to survive."

"Or *kill* one another and save them the problem of dealing with two more who know about this place."

The sorcerer had considered that but had chosen not to mention it. He had not even dared to ask what had actually been done with the Seekers. The elf was no one's fool. "Do we do it, then? Would you like to kill me?"

She hesitated. "A trick?"

"Hardly. I would rather form an alliance than fight." A gust of wind blew his hair in his eyes. He pushed it aside, wondering if this breeze meant that some of the guardians remained, shielded from his senses. That might have been the true reason they had ejected Darkhorse from their world; he represented a potential threat to their security—to their *legacy*.

"You are Vraad." Was there just a hint of uncertainty in her tone? Dru wondered.

"A chance of birth," he replied.

She smiled at his poor attempt at humor, an effect that nearly dazzled him. So used to the unreal and exceedingly arrogant beauty of his kind, he was unprepared for the beauty that nature itself could offer. Dru forgot himself and simply stared. Only Sharissa could claim similar beauty.

Sharissa and her mother . . .

The knife was suddenly at his *throat.* "I could have killed you now. You didn't even bother to move."

He had been too engrossed in admiring her . . . something that *had* to be the work of this land and not his own doing. Dru had not survived all these centuries by letting his mind wander to pleasant things in times of crisis. No, it *had* to be the land playing with his thoughts. Yet, Dru realized that his adversary *did* remind him of his wife and daughter, too, so perhaps . . .

When her enemy continued to pay no heed to the death tickling his neck, the elf withdrew her blade and, after what must have been a tremendous debate with herself, sheathed it. "If you would desire an alliance, I can see no reason to turn you down. Not for the time being. You can call me Xiri. Not my birth name."

"Xiri." The Vraad did not ask what she meant by it not being her birth name. Elfin ways were mystery to his kind, who could only go by what little had been passed down over the millennia. Even Serkadion Manee, who seemed to want to chronicle everything, had been sparse in his details of the one other significant race in Nimth history. "Call me Dru, Xiri. My *birth* name, if you are interested. How did you know I was a Vraad?"

"It is *not* because I am *so* old that I remember your arrogant race," she bit back, though again with a touch of humor. "Those who passed to this place made certain we would remember the forms of our foes." She sized him up. "You do not seem exceptionally sinister. Merely tall and a touch too confident in yourself."

"You'll find enough of my kind that fit your darkest fears. Overall, we are probably everything your ancestors claimed we were, which is why we ourselves have been trying to escape Nimth." It was peculiar, he thought, how easy it was to talk to her even though she had come close to slitting his throat only a breath or two earlier.

"How terrible is it?"

Gazing around at the remnants of a civilization far older than his own, Dru pictured Nimth in a few thousand years. "These ruins will look picturesque in comparison to what we have left as a legacy."

"And now you've come here to spread your poison." The hostility had returned to Xiri's voice, but it was not meant for Dru personally. "The land will not permit it."

The sorcerer shivered as she said the last. "Why do you say that?"

Xiri began walking, if only, it seemed, to burn off nervous energy. Without thinking, Dru moved beside her, keeping pace. He was taller than she by nearly two feet and his stride was nearly double her own, but the Vraad was still forced to walk faster to keep up with his new companion.

"You mean you cannot feel it? You cannot feel the presence that is the land itself?"

He had. More than once. He also believed it was the same force that had guided him into this world and then used his horse to lead him here. If what he supposed had truth in it, then there was a purpose for his being in the shrouded realm. Dru was not certain whether he should be pleased or worried.

"I see you have." Xiri had used Dru's musings as an opportunity to study his face, reading there the answer he had not given to her in words.

"Do the . . . the guardians know of it?"

She shrugged. "I am as much of a newcomer to this continent as you. Maybe. It could be that what we feel is like them, though you would know that better than I. Another 'guardian,' as you called them." Xiri mulled over his term. "Guardians. I suppose that describes them better than anything else."

They were taking a path that would more or less lead them back to where Dru, as a prisoner of the avians, had entered the city. The sorcerer did not ask if there was a reason for this particular direction; he was learning too much to be concerned with anything else. He found he also enjoyed Xiri's company, she being a more pleasant, straightforward companion than most Vraad . . . when she was not trying to kill him, that is.

"How long have the elves been here?"

"Thousands of years. We really do not keep track of time as precisely as you do."

He took a breath before asking his next question. They were on fair terms at the moment, but he knew that there were areas that she might not wish to talk about. Her skill with the blade had been impressed upon him quite sufficiently. Still, he had a question that had to be asked. *"How did you escape Nimth?"*

To his amazement and relief, she appeared undisturbed by what he had asked. "There is debate as to that. Some claim we found a hole in the fabric of Nimth that led us to here. Some claim the hole was opened *for* us.

"I think they made a mistake, whoever created all this. I think we were not supposed to be in the same place as your kind, but it took them time to correct that mistake."

That was likely close to the truth, the overwhelmed spellcaster thought. "How much did the guardians tell *you*? They'd indicated that they chose to speak to me because I resembled their ancient masters. I thought that I was the only one they spoke with because of that."

"Enough." Xiri, her eyes closing to little more than slits, related a tale much like that which Dru had suffered through, but less informative. She knew about the old race and how, for reasons she found insulting, her kind had been judged lacking and left to live out their existence in a place where others were to rule, such as the Seekers and, before them, the Quel. The guardians had said no more, not even telling her that they were leaving her with a Vraad. That the Vraad had been left to face eventual destruction at their own hands had long satisfied the elves. To find herself with Dru had come as a great shock to her. His presence meant that the elves had not left the evil behind them as they had hoped.

When she was finished, Dru told her his own story, including events leading up to the city itself. For reasons he felt were justified, the mage made no mention of the final world, the one in which he had found all that remained of the elder race. He wanted to forget that place. Where the citadel with the ghostly memories had once soothed him, it now filled the Vraad with dread. There were too many parallels to the cross-over and its potential results.

"I am alone, Dru," Xiri commented without warning.

"The others . . ."

"Dead. Some during the crossing—the seas between this continent and ours are extremely violent—the rest at the claws of either the birds or the shell-backs."

"How do you intend to return?"

She turned and faced him. In the midst of so much devastation, the two of them seemed so tiny to the sorcerer. He wanted to go somewhere and hide, a very un-Vraad-like reaction. Of course, Dru had not felt like a Vraad for the past twenty years, especially the last few days.

"I really do not know."

He laughed despite his efforts not to and when she asked what he found so humorous, her hand straying to the blade at her side, Dru pointed out his own predicament. They were two strangers in a land that did not want them with no idea how to get back to where they had come from. A teleport across a distance as vast as the seas that Xiri described would have been nearly impossible even at his peak of power. He did not know the other continent well enough, having seen it only as a ghostly image, and blind teleports, especially so lengthy, generally proved treacherous. It was easy to end up in the wrong place, such as the bottom of the sea.

Xiri sat down. She did not care that the ground was covered with broken marble. The elf sat as if it were the most important thing she could do. One hand toyed with a pouch akin to the one the Seekers had found. On it was a symbol that resembled the sun. Dru was uncertain as to whether it was decorative or representative of some belief and decided not to ask.

"What do we do, then?" she asked in a monotone voice.

If she was an example of the elfin race, Dru could understand how they might be found lacking by the guardians. Xiri was mercurial in nature, ready to

kill him one moment and walking along with him the next. Her abrupt pause
now was a surprise, but not great when Dru contemplated it in comparison to
how she had acted in the few minutes he had known her. She was a confusing
woman . . . more so than any whose path he had crossed in his long life.

"Where were we walking to?" he finally asked. Dru assumed the elf had a
destination in mind.

"I do not know. I merely walked to put distance between myself and the
guardians." A touch of bitterness underscored her next words. "I did not want
to *offend* them any longer with my less-than-perfect presence, I suppose." Xiri
clutched the pouch tighter. "All our work for naught."

"The Seekers and the . . . the Quel . . . didn't find whatever it was they
sought. That should be something." The sorcerer knew it gave *him* some satisfaction.

Xiri looked up at the spellcaster, who felt uncomfortable at what he read in
her expression. "They wanted to seize control of the power that made all of
this. They found caverns left behind by the builders of this city, caverns that
whispered some of the truth about this world and promised many things for
those willing to look for the source."

That was what the figurines in the chamber of the dragon lord had reminded
him of. They were akin to some of the talismans the Seeker leader had revealed
to him through the avians' peculiar method of communication. "So they found
a chamber carved out by the former lords of . . . is there no name for this
world?"

"None that I know of. We did not feel it was our right to give it another."

It may yet be called the Dragonrealm, then, for lack of a better title, Dru thought sourly.
He refrained from telling Xiri, not wanting to arouse her anger. "What purpose
did the chamber serve?"

"I do not know. The Seekers control that region. The Quel . . . no one knows
how the Quel learn what they learn. They just seem to know." The elf rose,
stretching her slender legs, much to Dru's discomfort. He had stayed clear of
the female of the species since the idiotic duel that his wife had died fighting.
Again, he noted how Xiri reminded him of . . . of . . .

He had tried so hard to forget her death, to forget the pain *he* had suffered . . . that Dru had forgotten her *name.*

"Is something amiss?"

"Nothing," he snapped back. The shamed sorcerer knew his face was crimson. "My memory has failed me. That's all it was."

"I see." She did, in a sense. He could see that. Xiri knew that whatever had
disturbed the Vraad had been very personal. It was a comfort that, unlike Melenea, the elf did not probe the open wound merely for her own amusement.

Instead, Xiri glanced up at the blue sky and said, "The day will be gone and we will still be here wondering what to do."

Dru hesitated. Their key to escape might lie within the empty square where the rift was. Despite his desire to never return there—and the possible threat of the guardians, who might decide that eliminating an elf and a Vraad was worth breaking their own rules—the rift was probably the only hope they had. Even if Sharissa crossed over with the rest, there was no way she would be able to locate him. Not here.

They had to go back.

"I know a way." When she waited, a slight, patient smile enhancing her smooth, pale features, he forced himself to go on. "Do you remember when I rode into sight?"

"I remember. Your steed frightened me. I had never seen such an animal. Are all your horses like that?"

The thought of a stable filled with Darkhorses eased the tension in his mind and almost made him smile. "Hardly. What I ask is if you remember *how* I appeared?"

"I did not see that. I assumed you came from behind some building."

He had forgotten that no one had noticed the two of them until he and Darkhorse were already riding toward them. Dru shook his head. "No, we didn't. What you and the avians missed was the rift in reality through which we emerged. *A hole,* if that brings to mind what I'm trying to explain."

"A hole?" She rose, ever lithe in her movements. "You found a hole such as the one my people are supposed to have used?"

"Not just any. It leads to where the originators of this . . . experiment . . . last lived. It may hold the key to controlling everything."

Xiri gazed back in the direction of the clearing where she had first seen Dru. "The Sheeka never knew how close they were." Turning to the tall Vraad, she asked suspiciously, "Why did you 'forget' to tell me this before?"

There had been a time when nothing would have shamed the master sorcerer. Now, it felt as if his face burned all the time. "I was frightened. I . . . didn't want to . . . return to the central chamber."

"What was in there?" Her suspicion had turned to sympathy. From all she had likely been told about his kind, shame was not something Xiri would have expected from him.

Now it was his turn to gaze back in the direction of that terrible place. "The memories of the last of that race. The truth about Nimth. A feeling that the Vraad are too much like them and will fade away even as they have."

"All races fade with time. The Quel, the Sheeka, and their predecessors are all examples of that. Even the elves will pass on." Xiri gave the ruined city a

look of contempt as she added, "For all our 'failure' to live up to their expectations, we elves have lasted longer than most."

"I don't believe we have to fall. Not until all reality itself fades away." Dru
clenched his fists. "I can find it fairly easy. I could never forget now."

"What about the guardians?"

He met her eyes, found no fear in them, only honest worry. "You're the one
who reminded me we have no choice. I'd hoped you had a way out of here, a
way to travel to where my . . . to where your people are."

Xiri put a hand on his arm. "I know the Vraad have come. You could not
exactly hide it, Dru. We will deal with them when we return home."

She had not said "if," which strengthened the sorcerer's resolve a bit, though
he was certain Xiri had used the word for her own sake. Neither of them
wanted to think what would happen if the guardians, especially one of them,
did, indeed, decide the Vraad and the elf *could* be removed despite the rules laid
down by the long-gone lords.

"You are not so bad, for an ancient and terrible enemy," she commented without warning. "You might be elfin if not for your height and your odd visage."

"And you," he replied, starting back to the inner city as he spoke, "are not so
mystically withdrawn as I thought elves were supposed to be."

"There are always those caught up in the wonder of themselves. Most of us
have learned to relax. We find we get along much better now. There was a point
where we were nearly at war with ourselves, because of our strict, pompous ways."

"What happened?"

She had moved ahead of him, again building a pace he had to work hard
to match. "Our elders reminded us of the Vraad and how we were acting too
much like them."

Dru could only see the back of her head, but he was of the suspicion that
his companion was smiling.

Throughout the return, they sensed no presence other than their own. Xiri
pointed out that it was hardly proof that the two of them were alone and Dru
readily agreed. He kept waiting for the end to come, for the magical beings to
take them up like rag dolls and drop them wherever they had disposed of the
avians.

What *had* they done to the Seekers?

Xiri froze. "Wait."

"What is it?" He peered ahead, but saw nothing.

"I thought I saw a shape, elf or Vraad, but when I blinked, it was not there
anymore."

Darkhorse had said something similar . . . in the same region, Dru noticed.
Who else was here? "Not a Seeker or a Quel?"

"Neither. I would recognize a Shee—Seeker, if you prefer, quite easily. No, it looked manlike, but *incomplete*." She shrugged. "I cannot explain the last."

Dru moved with more caution, expecting trouble at any moment. As for Xiri, the Vraad was unsettled by her almost casual manner. It was clear that she felt that at this point they had nothing to gain by stealth. A quick, direct march to their destination was what she obviously had in mind and Dru, understanding her more and more, knew the senselessness of trying to stop the elf now that she had decided on her course of action.

Before he was ready to be there, they had arrived at the square where the rift waited.

"I do not see anything."

"Did you see anything before I burst into sight?"

"No," she admitted. "It just seems wrong to not see something."

"If it had been so visible, the Seekers would have found it before either of us."

"But would the guardians have let them?" she countered.

It was one of many questions he could not answer. The sorcerous creatures had likely interfered because of the number of intruders, not the mere fact that there *had* been intruders in the first place. They had not disturbed Dru and Darkhorse after their initial attempt to frighten the duo away. In what was a somewhat naive manner of thought, they had probably hoped the two would leave without disturbing too much. The mage was astonished at how rule-bound such godlike beings were, even considering the fact that they had been as familiars to their ancient masters. To remain at their tasks this long, with the cracks in their ranks only beginning to form, was astounding. Yet, if the one sinister guardian was a sign of what was to come, Dru worried that the future held even greater danger than the refugees from Nimth had ever imagined could confront them.

"No one has stopped us so far. We might as well go on." Though Xiri made it sound like a suggestion, Dru understood that it was more of a gentle nudge. Without realizing it, he had already stepped back a foot or so, as if his deep fear were stealing control of his body.

"It was this way." The reluctant sorcerer urged his legs into motion, leading his elfin companion to where he estimated the rift would be.

They saw nothing save more ruins. Dru began to worry that he had lost the gap, that they would wander this area for hours and find nothing but more rubble. Xiri would think him a fool. . . .

"There!" the elf shouted, her voice almost gleeful.

He saw it now, a tiny tear just below eye level. In that tear was a glimpse of another place, a wondrous place.

I said so! I said they would return! They must be removed! The savage voice in their minds made both explorers fall to their knees. Dru needed no help in identify-ing the creature that ravaged his brain merely by speaking.

Should not! came the voice that the Vraad had deemed the fourth. It sounded reluctant, as if it, too, no longer believed that noninterference was possible.

They had their chance! They betrayed our good faith! roared the attacker. Dru held his head, trying to keep it from bursting. *They—*

Dru's mind cleared.

Beside him, Xiri rose, her body trembling. "What happened? Where did they go?"

The sorcerer shook his head, then regretted the action as the world swam. Of the mental intrusion by the guardians, there was no trace. It was as if they had been cut off . . . or *fled.*

"Something frightened them." His head cleared.

Dru and his companion heard the scuffling sound at the same time. Xiri was the swifter of the two, so she was first to turn and see what stumbled toward them. It did her little good; the sorcerer could read the confusion on her vis-age even as he himself was turning to see what new twist the once-supposedly peaceful world had for him.

The newcomer shambled toward them, clad in a simple robe and cowl that covered its body all the way to the earth. It stumbled again, walking as if it did not really know where it was going. Not surprising, as far as Dru was con-cerned, considering it had no eyes. It also had no ears, nose, mouth, or hair . . . in fact, no markings whatsoever.

One of Barakas's golems, larger than before, but instantly recognizable as such.

How had it gotten here, when the cross-over had been set to occur on the other continent?

Dru forgot that question, forgot *all* thoughts, as the faceless golem was joined by a second and then a third.

Then they began swarming out of the ruins from all sides, the Vraad, the elf, and the rift their obvious destination.

XV

A TALONED HAND thrust itself into his scarred face, making new trails of blood.

Rendel did not scream. He had stopped screaming after the first day. That did not mean that the pain was any less, however.

Images swarmed into his tortured mind. Humans in dark dragon-scale armor, at least a hundred. The death of a flock member, who had watched and relayed the information. The realization that these were as Rendel was.

"So . . . what do . . . you need me for?" They obviously knew everything. Why then would his captors turn to him? Did they not know, too, that he had betrayed his kind, seeking, in typical Vraadish fashion, to rise above the rest by deceit? He shivered slightly, both from his anticipation of the torture he was certain was coming and the simple fact that they had stripped him of his clothing, allowing the damp, cool air to play havoc with his unprotected body.

The aerie overlord pulled away his hand and stepped back while two females brought water and some sort of meat to the prisoner. Rendel had a blurry view of his surroundings, not that he needed it. The Tezerenee already knew what the aerie looked like, a natural set of caverns within and beneath the mountain he had dubbed Kivan Grath. It was the chief aerie of the bird people since their setbacks in a war with what looked like two-legged armadillos, if the images Rendel had been shown were correct. The avians still controlled most of the continent, but their adversaries had a nasty habit of springing suicide raids from underneath the earth that had caused the collapse of more than one of the lesser dwellings of the race. The purpose had not been the death of the warriors; it was the next generation of avians that had suffered. The young, not yet able to fly, had suffered heavy casualties. Aeries could be rebuilt; the future was much more difficult to replace.

Rendel could care less for his captors' war. All he wanted was what the leader had taunted him with since his arrival. Just beyond the circle of bird people watching over his questioning were the towering and seductive effigies he had discovered in his research. How ironic that they should stand as silent monitors of the Vraad's torture. There was power in this cavern, power more ancient than that of the birds. They understood that, somewhat, and he knew that they had been attempting to both utilize what they had found and also locate the original home of those who had created this edifice within the mountain. It lay across a vast expanse of water, however, and so they had no way of knowing how their explorers were doing. He already knew that the overlord was growing impatient. The avian leader had already taken out his frustration on the prisoner twice.

When they were finished with feeding and watering him, he repeated his question. "What do you need *me* for?"

One of the other avians, an elder by the looks of his balding form, cocked his head so that one eye was focused on the leader and squawked at him for several seconds. The overlord's reply was short and succinct. It was also unnerving. The others instantly knelt, spreading their wings, smoothing their feathers, and cocking one eye earthward, essentially showing their trust in the leader by making themselves blind to his presence. He could have struck any of them down.

It was a sign of submission, of course. Submission to whatever plan he had . . . *hatched*, Rendel though wryly. A plan that the sorcerer was evidently an integral part of.

He had an inkling of what it was even before the overlord reestablished contact. Unlike most times, Rendel now welcomed communication. It might be his only path to freedom.

Images of his clan, especially a bird's view of the most dangerous, a huge monster that Rendel knew could only be his father. The imprisoned spellcaster relayed an image of his own. His father as a leader. His father as a sorcerer of great strength. His father as an adversary who would crush the avians' bodies beneath his boots and plant the dragon banner in their blood-smeared chests.

From the earsplitting shrieks that filled the cavern and echoed until Rendel thought he would go deaf, he gathered that the entire aerie knew what he had told the leader.

A new image was directed back at him with such force that Rendel nearly passed out. It showed the Tezerenee scattered about the landscape, their bloody corpses all that remained of the once-proud clan. The dragon banner still stood, but this time it protruded from a gaping hole in the throat of the patriarch himself.

"A pretty picture," Rendel choked, "but not so easily accomplished."

Now it was his own image that appeared in his thoughts. He stood a free man, one working beside those of the aerie, unlocking the mysteries of the ancient lords. The avians' discoveries were his to share. He saw himself seated in a vast citadel of his own, a massive manor partly built, partly grown from the soil. It already existed, a ruined artifact from an even older race than theirs that the bird people had rebuilt to greater glory. It only lacked a master.

They wanted him to betray his clan again, to lead the Tezerenee into a trap in which they would perish to the man. In return, Rendel would receive his heart's desire . . . his own domain and the secrets he had sought for upon crossing to this world.

Not for one moment did the captive sorcerer believe he would ever live to see the day of reward. They *might* let him live long enough to aid them in their attempts to understand the talismans of the long-dead race, but Rendel would never see the domain they had promised him.

Nonetheless, he nodded his head in agreement, hoping they understood the movement. Apparently they did, for there was a sense of approval from the leader, who removed his hand from the Vraad's face and signaled once more to the two females who had fed the prisoner. Another avian, a tall male, undid the bonds that held him to the wall and caught him as he collapsed. The females took him by the arms, surprisingly strong for being so much smaller, and carried him from the council. He assumed that was what he had faced.

They brought him to a mat and assisted him as he slowly lay down on it. It was soft, so very soft. Every bone in the Vraad's body screamed as he moved. He would, he thought, be very stiff when he awoke . . . if he ever did.

When he had settled, the two females left. They were replaced immediately by four others, one carrying a bowl. Despite his sparse meal, Rendel was not hungry; he wanted only to sleep for the rest of eternity.

Two avians stood on each side of him now. The one with the bowl held it out to the others, who reached in and scooped out a thick soup substance that dripped all over his prone figure.

"Dragon's blood! Watch where you're dripping that muck!" What were they going to do?

When all four had a handful of the substance, they poured it on his naked form and began rubbing. Weakened as he was, the sorcerer struggled in vain against their combined might. The avians were quite capable of going about their task with one hand while holding him down with the other. With this method, they massaged his body from top to bottom.

There was no feeling of arousal, not when a talon reminded him now and then what his half-closed eyes could only vaguely still make out . . . that his companions were not human, but a vicious race of bird people. What they did, he realized as consciousness began to slip away, was necessary if the spellcaster wanted to be able to move when he woke. The massage and the substance, combined together, had already eased some of the pain. It made sense; his captors hardly had the time to wait for his recovery, not if he knew his father. The patriarch, once alerted to the presence of enemies, would not rest until they were beaten. The birds, meanwhile, hoped for a quick and treacherous victory, with their willing prisoner as the key.

Rendel's last conscious thoughts, concerning what *he* would do when the time came, left a smile on his face long after he fell asleep.

THE GOLEMS CONTINUED to stagger toward them, like unliving horrors from a nightmare. Xiri had her knife out and was muttering something under her breath.

What were the golems doing here? How had they crossed the violent seas?

"These . . ." the elf finally managed. "These are what I saw! What are they?"

"Golems." He watched one fall, then right itself. After a moment, Dru realized that they did not walk as the blind in an unfamiliar place, but rather as children did who were not quite used to walking. The Vraad recalled his own daughter's first steps and how similar these were. The uneven ground certainly did not help.

There was something else, though. No matter what direction that golems came from, they all stared toward the same location, as if drawn by a great treasure.

"Xiri! Take my hand!"

He was pleased when she did not question his action. Cautiously, the sorcerer walked toward an area where there was somewhat of a gap between the faceless horde. "Be ready for anything!"

Dru allowed the golems to continue on unhindered, only making certain that he and the elf were not directly in the path of any of them. As he had surmised, they steered, not toward the two intruders but rather in the direction of the rift.

Xiri choked back a gasp as one of the robed creatures brushed her backside on its trek toward the tear. "They do not want us at all!"

"No. They want what lies beyond the tear."

"You called them golems. You recognized them."

The last of the unnerving figures had stumbled past them. The first were nearly at the rift. The fascinated sorcerer released the elf's hand and took a step toward the line of steadily moving figures. "We made them. The Tezerenee, that is. I worked with them, though. These were supposed to be our new bodies when our ka shifted to this world. We could touch the land here—the shrouded realm, as I called it—but not physically cross."

"Then, these are your people." She shifted the blade, debating whether to throw it or not. Her skin was even paler than before.

Dru shook his head and started back toward the tear. Now that he knew the golems did not want him, he was curious as to what they sought. "No, those aren't Vraad. They would look like me, if they were."

"Then what *are* they?"

"I think we should follow and see." Whatever his feelings toward the citadel on the hill, they were secondary now.

"You know," she said, lowering but not sheathing the knife, "that they must be what the guardians feared."

"I know." Dru had a theory, but was afraid to tell it to the elf. He could scarcely believe it himself.

The first of the golems, walking a little more confidently now, stepped through the rift and vanished. The others began lining up and marching through two at a time. The sorcerer likened the image before him to a parade of macabre marionettes. In swift fashion, the golems entered the tear, never hesitating. The last crossed into the ancient realm of the creators, leaving only the elf and the Vraad in the ruined square.

"Do we wait?" Xiri asked.

Dru realized he had been hesitating again. This time it was more from awe than fear. Nevertheless, he knew that the longer they waited, the more chance that something might pass that they would miss.

"Follow me."

She took his hand in her free one. When he looked at her, Xiri smiled uncertainly and said, "I would rather not end up alone in a place I have never been to before."

He could have assured her that such would not be the place, that they would find themselves near each other in the gardenlike field at the bottom of the hill. He could have told her, but he did not. "Time to cross, then."

The sensation was akin to what he had felt earlier, a blinding brilliance and the late realization that all sound had ceased during the transfer.

"Rheena!" Xiri froze the moment they entered the world of the citadel. She looked at the birds flying merrily above and the trimmed, grassy field in which they were now standing. "It is so beautiful! As if someone had sculpted it!"

Not far from the truth, as far as Dru was concerned. Seeing it again, with Xiri, made him appreciate it that much more. Had it not been for the presence of the determined golems, he might have lost his fear of this place. They served, however, to remind him of what he might expect.

Unmindful of the beauty around them, the faceless figures strode upward, no longer awkward in their movements despite the climb. The closer they got to the castle, the more confident the creatures moved. It was clear they had some true purpose in mind.

"They know this place." Xiri was the first to utter what they both had known for some time. "They move as if they are returning home."

"I think they are." He recalled the ghostly watchers hunched about the crystal and the pentagram. How many had there been? How many more had existed besides these? He had hardly taken the time to inspect the rest of the massive structure.

"Guardians?" From the tone of her voice, it seemed that the elf wanted him to agree, even though neither of them believed that.

Dru shrugged, trying hard to keep the golems from getting too far ahead. Xiri was now leading *him*. "I doubt it, though I won't rule it out. I think the guardians in the ruined city gave evidence to what those things truly are. The exodus to this place only confirms it, as far as I see."

They were nearly at the top of the hill. The cowled figures were already vanishing through the open gate. Both the Vraad and the elf could see that the golems were spreading out as they entered the edifice. The newcomers appeared quite at home.

"I think that says it all," Dru whispered. He took a breath before finishing. "I think the masters of the house have finally *returned*."

Indeed, there seemed no arguing with the statement. Following the last of the figures into the courtyard, the sorcerer and his companion watched in silent regard as Barakas's usurped creations entered buildings, climbed stairways, or simply studied their surroundings with eyes that were not there. None of them appeared to care about the two intruders.

Finally regaining control of himself, Dru leaned over and whispered, "The chamber we want is through there." He pointed in the direction of the building he and Darkhorse had entered on his previous visitation. A number of the featureless beings had already entered.

"There?" Xiri did not sound so certain, still overwhelmed and understandably anxious around the strange figures wandering about. Dru, knowing the forms from his time with the Tezerenee, was, if not comfortable with the golems, at least used to their appearances . . . or lack thereof.

"It's where I saw the crystal. In the room of worlds."

"All right." She had the knife in her free hand. Dru had thought she had sheathed it at some point, but could no longer recall. He pushed the hand down by the wrist.

"I doubt that will do you much good. It might even be detrimental for *us*." He gave her a smile that likely did not reassure her any more than it did him. "I thought *I* came from the bloodthirsty race, not you."

"As I said, we have changed since escaping Nimth." Xiri nonetheless did sheathe the blade. "You have a point about the knife, though, Vraad."

They moved slowly across the courtyard, partly due to caution and partly due to Xiri's fascination with the lifelike images sculpted from the shrubbery. "This reminds me of something back in my village," she whispered, smiling all the while. "There are those among us who can persuade the trees and bushes to take on new and fantastic forms."

"Is that what the Seekers do?" He recalled the unique aeries of the race, places both constructed and grown. The ones his captor had revealed to him had been stupendous works of art.

"In a sense. Like the Vraad, however, they *demand* more than request cooperation." The flat line formed by her mouth was sign enough that she would speak no more on that particular subject.

No one barred their way when they reached the open entrance and so the two entered the long hall. The female elf was awed by the grandness of the inner hallway. She glanced around as if expecting it all to vanish. It was not that the corridor was so richly decorated, but rather that it carried about it a feeling of majesty, a reflection, perhaps, of the builder's skill.

Dru, only slightly less awed even though he had seen the corridor before, led her farther inside. It was then that the sorcerer noticed a smaller room to the left that he would have been willing to swear had not existed the first time he had entered the castle.

A slave to his curiosity, he stepped closer to the entranceway of the new chamber . . . and nearly bumped into one of the silent figures as it departed that very room. Dru and Xiri kept a careful eye on the faceless wanderer until it departed through the front doorway. Dru cautiously peered into the chamber . . . and gasped.

"What is it?" Xiri circled around him so that she could see.

The room was immaculate and glowed with a brilliant illumination. Down to and including the overwhelming figure poised before them, it was identical to the chamber of the dragon lord that he had been nearly tossed into by the Seekers back in the devastated city. Yet, that first chamber was a pale memory in comparison to this one. Here was the dragon lord in all his glory, looking ready to leap into the air. If the other had seemed almost living, Dru was nearly certain this one was. Despite its wary eyes, he could have believed it was merely pausing to consider its next action. Even its muscles, carved taut by that long-dead master sculptor, emphasized the readiness with which the dragon lord waited.

The same statuettes were also there, and better able to view them this time, he realized that they also resembled the figures from the mind message relayed to him by the Seeker leader. One of the tiny artifacts reminded the sorcerer of the figurine that the avian had thrown and broken in anger. Emboldened by their luck so far, Dru stepped inside in order to learn more. Xiri, also very curious as to the purpose of this place, not only followed the Vraad in, but twisted around her companion and walked swiftly to the tiny effigies, her hands out before her as if she intended to pick one up.

"Wait!" He rushed toward her, fully expecting every golem in the citadel to come storming into the chamber, ready to strike the impudent twosome down for their transgressions. If, as he believed, they *were* the ancient race that had built all of this, they might take *special* measures for the disturbance of their most precious artifacts. The figurines themselves might be protected by a hundred different spells, all deadly, though it hardly seemed there had been enough time for the faceless ones to have affixed so many magical traps. Dru knew that he might be placing Vraadish paranoia before common sense, but the sorcerer also understood that he and Xiri knew next to nothing about the originators and their power, save that it made the Vraad race look childlike in comparison.

Xiri had stopped at his shout. She realized instantly what he feared and frowned in annoyance. "I know better than to touch something that I have not observed closely first."

Embarrassed by his own fears, a reddened Dru joined her. He pointed out the similarity of the carvings to both what his captors had discovered and what they themselves had revealed to him. The sorcerer also mentioned the shattered statuette and pointed to one that vaguely resembled the one he believed had been destroyed. Xiri was upset about the latter; anything created by the founding race should have been treated with the utmost respect as far as she was concerned.

"They feel almost alive when you stand this close to them." She had put her hands near the artifacts, but was careful to leave enough empty space in case of an accident. Neither of them cared for the thought of stumbling into the figurines.

"I don't recall the others feeling so." Though he had not been allowed to study them, Dru was certain he would have felt the aura surrounding the objects from where the avians had deposited him. "I wonder . . ." He took a closer look. The detail was so precise that he almost believed the gryphon he stared at would snap at him if his fingers came too near. "I wonder what they *do*?"

A scuffling sound alerted them to the entrance of three figures. The featureless golems might have been copied from one original, so identical were they down to their very movements. Somehow, they communicated, that much was evident. Dru supposed that they communicated in a fashion akin to the method utilized by the Seekers. That still did not make it any less unnerving. It was the silence that unsettled the sorcerer the most.

The three figures walked purposely toward the area where Xiri and the Vraad stood.

"I think they want to do something with the figurines," Dru suggested, whispering despite himself. "Now, maybe we'll find out what the purpose of this chamber is."

Since the two explorers stood in the way, they separated, each moving to one side of the platform where the figurines stood. As long as the duo did not interfere, Dru felt confident that the newcomers would ignore them as they had before.

Two of the oncoming creatures turned toward the tall mage. The other shifted to intercept Xiri.

Though initially stunned, the elf recovered instantly and reached for her blade. To her horror, the golem moved even *more* swiftly, trapping her wrist even before she could begin to unsheathe the weapon. Xiri struck her attacker with her free hand, but the blow, which would have stunned most adversaries, did not even slow the faceless construct.

The spellcaster had troubles of his own. His mind was a maelstrom of resurging doubts. He was caught between defending himself against a power incredibly old and the possible repercussions of unleashing his own strength in a place where it might do him more harm than help.

His hesitation cost him. The golems secured his arms and one of them put a hand to his temple. Dru felt as if his head swelled to twice its normal size. He tried to concentrate on a spell, but his mind wandered during the attempt. A second and third try yielded the same results. They had effectively blocked his abilities. Each time he tried to defend himself, his attention would turn to some triviality. He was barely able to concentrate on the mere fact that he was a prisoner, let alone how the two of them could escape.

Xiri was brought to his side and they were led from the dragon lord's chamber. The faceless beings were not harsh; they used only what force they needed to control their prisoners. Dru noted the direction they were going and smiled grimly. "They're taking us to the very place we wanted to go. The room of worlds."

"What do you think they will do?" The elf shut her eyes and the irritated expression on her otherwise perfect face told the sorcerer that she, too, had been prevented from using any magical abilities. "Why did they suddenly notice us? We touched nothing. We *did* nothing."

Dru had no answer this time. The faceless ones were complete enigmas to him. Everything about them had a question mark attached to it. Why return after all this time and why in such a manner? More to the point, what frightened the guardians so much? If these were their masters come home, should not the servants have been delighted? Their loyalty, with one or two exceptions, had seemed quite firm even after millennia of abandonment by those very same lords.

As they were marched toward the massive doors of the room of worlds—doors that the Vraad remembered demolishing during the peak of his earlier anger, but which now stood new and shining and *very* open—Dru noticed alterations in the corridor itself. It seemed higher and there were doors that like the first he could not recall seeing his first time through. *Redecorating?* he wondered in momentary amusement. Why not? It *had* been a few years.

His amusement was not long in lasting. At the doorway, two more of the faceless creatures met them. The ones that held Dru and Xiri released their grips, but did not move away. Not for a moment did either the Vraad or the elf think to fight or run. Both knew how little a chance they stood.

One of the newcomers pointed at the sorcerer and gestured that he should follow. The other turned to Xiri and mimicked its counterpart's actions.

Dru glanced at his companion, who met his gaze with a look of uncertainty that mirrored his own expression. Before either could speak, the two who had met the party at the doorway turned and walked into the chamber, moving in opposite directions once inside. No one pushed them forward, but their former guards pointed at the receding figures. The two prisoners hurried to catch up to their respective guides.

"Rheena!"

Xiri's words, the only sound other than the heavy falls of Dru's boots, reverberated throughout the room. She stumbled into the one leading her, her attention focused on the walls and the ceiling, and instantly sprang back, fearing a reprisal. The golem did not even appear to notice once it had rebalanced itself. It continued to walk to the opposite side of the room, always succeeding in matching the pace and movements of Dru's own guide.

When they stood across from one another, bisecting the chamber, the cowled figures halted. The sorcerer and the elf stared at one another from beside each. Dru managed a shrug in response to Xiri's anxious visage.

Other than the two who had led them inside and the three who still stood by the doorway, there were only four other golems in the room. Even the spectral impressions of the ancients were no longer visible. It was as if they were no longer needed now that the originals, albeit changed, had returned to claim their castle.

The four in the center of the room knelt before the crystal, as if inspecting it. One touched the top, which caused the focus to glow like a dim fire. It seemed to satisfy the creatures, for they rose and took a step back from the crystal as if expecting something.

Neither they nor the two prisoners were disappointed.

Dru leaned forward, careful to avoid the attention of his guide. The entire focus wavered as if it were composed of smoke rather than crystal and metal. The four near the center stepped back again, but it was due more to some ritual, the sorcerer believed, than any fear on their part.

The focus was no longer visible as such; it now swirled, a tiny, gray whirlwind. No, not a whirlwind, for it had shape of some sort, almost a crude rectangle. What had caused him to see it as a whirlwind were tiny shapes that ran madly across its surface in an eternal chase. It was going through a metamorphosis, becoming some other artifact. Dru wondered if it would have done the same for him or whether he would have ended up killing himself.

Xiri caught his eye. She frowned and indicated the odd form growing in the center of the room. It was hardly what she had expected. The Vraad was equally confused.

Again the four who had been the catalyst for the change stepped away, this time giving the object—or perhaps it *was* a familiar or demon of some sort—a far greater space into which to spread. That proved a wise move, for in seconds the rectangular shape had risen to a height nearly half again as tall as those who had summoned it. As it had grown, so too had the shapes scurrying about its frame. They were black and might have been reptilian in nature, though they moved with such speed that they were generally little more than blurs. Staring at them for more than the blink of an eye stirred an uneasy feeling in the disconcerted spellcaster's stomach. He had no desire to study them closely.

Returning his attention to the structure as a whole, he finally recognized what stood before them. Xiri had mentioned that her ancestors had discovered a hole . . . or a hole had *discovered* them, for as with so much that this ancient race had created, it had a life of sorts. A life in a similar sense to the way Darkhorse had a life. Certainly, it did not live as she or Dru did.

It was a *gate*. No, not merely a gate. That was hardly suitable for the pulsating, magical doorway standing before them. Rather, it was the *Gate*. A name more than a description since it lived. Dru dared to take a few steps to one side. No matter what direction he looked at it, it always seemed to face him. He knew that Xiri would see it the same way.

Glancing at the worlds painted on the walls and ceiling, he understood now how the founders might have crossed from here to any of their creations.

Nimth.

He caught sight of the image, stared at the figure of a Vraad, then felt an uncontrollable urge to face the Gate once more.

"Serkadion Manee!"

Within the frame of the Gate, there now stood the entrance to another world. Dru did not have to ask to know it was his own.

His guide left his side and stepped toward the waiting artifact. The shapes on its frame seemed to slow, though they were still not quite in focus.

Less than an arm's length from the passageway to Dru's world, the golem halted. It raised one hand, then lowered it in one harsh swing.

Nimth vanished, to be replaced by . . . nothing. More than nothing. The sorcerer knew what doorway had now been opened. His recognition of the Void was accompanied by a sense of growing dread.

The faceless being who had stood beside him turned then and, indicating the vast emptiness within the Gate, gestured for Dru to step forward.

XVI

THERE WERE STILL angry Vraad moving about what remained of the communal city, but most had departed. Ever distrusting of their brethren, the majority had returned to the safety of their private domains, there to brood and pout at the trick that had been played on them. They would be so engrossed in their self-pity and their eternal plots for vengeance that they would probably never get around to devising their own ways of escaping . . . something the Tezerenee had proved quite able to do.

It was those few who still remained, still seeking to find some stray ally of the dragon clan or merely desiring to unleash their frustration, who worried Gerrod. Having had one attempt at teleportation misdirected, he was not looking forward to a second try at any point in the near future. Sharissa shared his fear in that respect, which was why the two of them still remained in hiding, despite the occasional passing of a blood-thirsty sorcerer. The room they presently called safety was a tiny storage chamber in a flat, black building on the opposite side of the city from the building where the Lord Barakas had made many of his fine speeches of cooperation, including the one in which he had seemed to promise that *all* Vraad would indeed be crossing into the new world.

Oddly, it was Dru's daughter who had finally had enough. She stalked over to her hooded companion and leaned over him, arms crossed. "The great and powerful Tezerenee! To think that I was afraid of you! What have you brought us to? How could you abandon Sirvak?"

Gerrod had no answer for the first question and he had already answered the second one more than a dozen times in the past few minutes alone. That, by no means, prevented Sharissa from asking it again. With her father gone, Sirvak was all she had. She no longer trusted Melenea, which, as far as the young Tezerenee was concerned, was the only good that had come of the whole incident.

"I told you, child! Sirvak flew out one of the windows the moment I snared you! It is likely back in your domain, awaiting us!" He looked up at her, more than matching her glare. "Try and remember that for at least a second or two, will you? I need to think!"

"Maybe one of those grateful folk outside would be willing to help you think! You've done nothing but brood since we found this place!"

He started to snap back at her, then saw that she spoke the truth. He was acting much like those he had always despised. The Zeree whelp had not helped his situation, however. He spread his hands wide and replied, "I would welcome whatever masterful plan you have conceived during all the time you've been berating me."

Sharissa clamped her mouth shut and gave him a stare that should have, by rights, burned a hole through his head.

"I thought as much." Stimulated by both her words and his growing shame, Gerrod pushed himself harder.

"Have you noticed something?" she asked, disturbing the peace he had *finally* gained.

"Besides the inability on your part to remain silent for more than a breath?"

She ignored his remark. "For all the damage they did to the city, it should have been far worse."

"I think they're doing an admirable job."

"I mean that they're in the same predicament as we are! They can't trust their spells!"

Gerrod straightened, feeling very stupid. He had understood that when dealing with Melenea, understood it because he knew she lived near an unstable region. The warlock had not considered it in respect to Nimth as a whole. *Sleep. I need sleep!* That was why he could not think straight. When was the last time he had slept? "And so? What else does that suggest to you?"

"I don't know." Sharissa looked crestfallen.

The Tezerenee slumped again. "Waste of *time!*"

"At least we could accomplish something if we were back home! I haven't given up on Father! I know he's alive somewhere!"

The eternal optimism of the child, Gerrod thought bitterly. It *did* gall him, however, to sit here, virtually helpless. He was used to acting—not without thought, of course—but what could he do? The business with Melenea was not finished; he knew her too well to think she would simply lie down and wait for the end of Nimth. No, to her thinking, he had made a master move. Now, it was her turn . . . and, perhaps, that was the fear that kept him sitting in this hole rather than doing his best to find a way to cross. As much as he despised the company of his clan, the shrouded realm did represent continued life and that was the hooded Vraad's primary goal now that he had the Zeree child.

He had hoped she knew more than she had let on, but such was not the case. The information was there, but . . .

Fool! His laughter, full and vibrant, brought a panicked look from Sharissa, who could not understand what he found so amusing. She would not have understood how the laughter was both a sign of his relief and his way of mocking himself for being so blind. He stood up and, in his merriment, took Sharissa and hugged her tight. Even after he finally released her, she stood there, stunned into immobility.

It was not his fault entirely. Tunnel vision was a trait that his race could claim as one of their most dominant features. A Vraad who deeply believed in or desperately wanted something would concentrate on that one thing with an obsession that would make them ignore a hundred more reasonable solutions or beliefs. It was what had kept many a feud going for centuries. It was why few Vraad mixed with one another for more than a few years, if that long. It was a stubbornness of sorts, one that made a solution to the eventual death of Nimth and its inhabitants impossible, for that meant putting aside their arrogant belief in themselves and working in cooperation with one another.

"We're leaving! Somehow, we're leaving! Even if we have to walk back to your domain!"

"Why? What do you have in mind?" Sharissa was smiling, caught up in his enthusiasm and the dream of returning to the citadel of pearl.

"We've both been wrong. You wanted to find a way to bring your father back here. So did I. Why?"

"I . . . he's my father!"

Gerrod sighed. "And you worry about him. Fine. Let me rephrase it, then! What was *he* hoping to accomplish?"

"He hoped to find a different way to cross over to the realm beyond the—oh!"

"He *found* one! He has to be over there! Why bring him here, something we don't know how to do, when we can follow him there! If it worked for Master Zeree, then it should work just as easily for us!"

The fear had returned to mar her delicate features. She was not unattractive, he knew, but she had a way of grating on him that the young Tezerenee could not explain even to himself. "What is it now?"

Sharissa described her father's departure, including his struggle to escape.

Gerrod saw the problem instantly. "Then we shall be careful not to teleport during the change. That leaves us with only two more problems."

Emboldened once more—and evidently more willing to trust him now that he had made concrete suggestions in regard to her father—Sharissa responded, "One is the timing. It fluctuates. We don't know how long we might have to wait . . . if it will happen at all."

"Oh, it *will*." Having had both Dru Zeree's notes and those of his brother's to add to his own knowledge, he probably now knew more about the unstable regions of Nimth than anyone did, especially concerning the rapid rate of growth they had achieved. Nimth did not have half as long as his father had once believed. Of course, the Vraad would still all be dead before then, the wild magic of the world and their own stupidity a combination they could not possibly survive. "I doubt we'll have to wait for very long."

He started walking to the door, deciding that things were not yet desperate enough for sorcery, but she stopped him with a question. "What was the other problem?"

Gerrod looked at her in surprise. "Surviving long enough to get there."

DRU SHOOK HIS head at the creature who stood near the Gate. If it came down to it, he would fight them with his fists and his teeth. A spell might be beyond him, but he would not go passively back into the Void.

The golem gestured again . . . and the Vraad's *body* obeyed even while the mind began to struggle against it.

Something flashed in the light of the chamber, a metallic missile that flew toward the pointing golem with remarkable accuracy. It would have struck the being squarely in the side of the throat . . . had it reached its target.

Less than a foot from the open flesh, the blade Xiri had thrown in a futile attempt to save him ceased moving and fell straight down. It did not even make a clatter when it struck the floor. The assembled golems, even the one who had stood beside her, failed to even look her way. They remained intent on the portal and the Vraad, who was nearly at the base of the huge artifact.

Only two or three steps from an eternity of endless nothing, Dru's body stopped. In the short walk, he had sweated profusely. Somewhere out in the Void, Darkhorse wandered, possibly looking for a way back, unless the guardians had broken yet another of their rules and removed that knowledge from his mind. It was a slim hope, but if they did send him through, the shadowy steed might find him again.

If not, Dru would float forever.

He readied himself, waiting the final push that would send him falling into the Void. When it did not come, he tried to observe the one who had forced him to this point. It was impossible; though the Vraad's eyes could move, his head would not. He was transfixed before the Gate.

When his body became his once more, the sorcerer was so startled he nearly condemned himself to the very fate he had thought the faceless ones had planned for him. A hand caught the back of his robe and pulled him to a position farther from the menacing portal. The Gate closed off the pathway to the Void. Its sleek companions increased their pace once again, ever chasing one another over and over the artifact's surface.

"Dru!" Xiri had her arms around him in a grip worthy of a Seeker. None of their "hosts" moved to separate the two and so they held one another tight in relief. Finally, the elf whispered, "I thought they would walk you straight into that . . . that . . ."

"It's the Void."

Her eyes widened. "Why do you suppose they put you through that torture?"

He shrugged. He had no intention of second-guessing the masters of this place if he could avoid it. Their ways were as different as those of the Seekers, perhaps even more so.

Hands reached out and finally pulled the two free of one another. A pair of the golems, possibly the same two who had led them into the chamber, took the intruders by the arm and indicated the doorway. Puzzled but relieved to be away from the Gate and its deadly potential, the Vraad and the elf accompanied them without protest.

Their guides walked them swiftly out of the room of worlds and back down the magnificent hallway. It was evident within seconds that they intended to deliver their charges back to the chamber of the dragon lord. Dru and his companion exchanged bewildered expressions even as they were ushered inside.

Nothing had changed within, which was almost a disappointment to the sorcerer. He had nearly expected the huge figure of the dragon lord to suddenly squat down, stare them in the eye, and speak. It *did* stare at him, but only as its counterpart in the ruined city had. Any life the statue contained was strictly a figment of Dru's nerve-wracked imagination.

A second pair of the faceless beings entered the chamber and moved past the foursome. It began to irk the Vraad that he could not tell any of them apart. Had he not followed them through the rift and into the castle, ever mindful of the numbers, Dru might have wondered if there were only a handful who ran back and forth merely to fool their two prisoners into believing they were many. The sorcerer knew it was a foolish thought, but his predicament was tearing at his sanity. There might actually come a point, he feared, when he might prefer the Void to remaining among the faceless ones any longer.

The newcomers stepped up to the figurines and passed their hands over each. A few of the statuettes were removed and hidden from sight, somehow, in the robes of the two. With what was evident satisfaction, they backed away and indicated the remaining artifacts. Dru and Xiri were led forward.

"They want us to choose," the elf whispered.

She was correct. One of their unsettling companions indicated each of the fantastic figurines, then pointed at the two reluctant outsiders.

Dru studied the carvings. Choose a figurine, but for what reason and what result? Would the wrong choices kill them?

Most of the figures were of creatures magical in nature. There was the gryphon, the dragon, a unicorn, a dwarf, an elf—he glanced sideways at Xiri at that point—and others whose names escaped him. Included also were beasts and a few human figures.

"Let me choose first." Xiri did not wait for his answer. She reached out and took hold of the elf. A reasonable, safe choice. Both waited for some grand reaction, but still nothing happened. One of the golems eventually took the figurine from her hands and replaced it among the others.

The sorcerer held his breath as he tried to choose. There seemed no particular purpose to what he was being asked to do. It was tempting to reach out and seize the statuette that most resembled a Vraad, but for various reasons he chose not to. He glanced at the gryphon again, thinking of how much it resembled Sirvak, and nearly picked it up. Then his eyes focused on the dragon, almost a miniature version of the overshadowing form before him, and he almost chose that one instead.

While he debated his choices, the faceless ones waited patiently. Dru knew, however, that he would have to make a decision soon. His hand wavered by the dragon, then by the gryphon.

Abruptly, the Vraad withdrew from the artifacts. He met the eyeless gaze of one of their disturbing hosts and said, "I make no choice at all. I want nothing from here."

An interesting choice.

The chamber had vanished. Dru, Xiri, and their silent companions stood within a place of darkness. The sorcerer did not have to ask to know where he was, especially when two gleaming eyes formed and the vague outline of a huge dragon emerged partway from the black depths.

The voice that had filled his head was the only one that would have given him hope at this late point. "You've returned."

From the glance Xiri gave him, it was evident that she, too, was included in the conversation.

Yes, both choices affect the outcome, the guardian whom Dru had labeled first among the commanding voices added with mild satisfaction. *They are pleased with your choice, though it also confuses them.*

As if in response to the mock dragon's words, the blank-visaged figures withdrew to arm's length of the Vraad and the elf.

"Are they your masters? Was I correct in my assumptions?"

The hesitation that followed chipped away at the confidence that had only just been returning to the spellcaster. After a time, however, the half-seen entity replied, *Yes and no.*

"Yes and no?" This from Xiri. "How can they be your masters and yet not be your masters?"

To explain that, I would need to explain their final leaving . . . a cross-over of a different yet similar sort than what the Vraad have undertaken.

The guardian's words were both confusing and enlightening. "If they will permit you, please do."

I am not exactly certain if they permit me or do not care. What inhabits your golems are a shadow of our lords. We communicate with them almost as little as you do. The others struggle to understand, to know their places. Some have even argued that this is proof we are now our own masters.

Dru grimaced. As before, he knew which one of his fellows the dragon spoke of.

I digress. Was there an undercurrent of annoyance with itself? Anxiety? Dru could not be certain, but there *was* something. However confident the guardian acted, the truth was otherwise.

They were few when it finally became obvious that they would not live to see the culmination—or failure—of their dream. They had us to do their work, but we were limited in what we could do.

The sorcerer found it hard to believe that such as this could be wanting in power. The guardian *was* power, even more so than Darkhorse.

We are . . . aspects . . . of their minds. Bits of personality traits. Your choice of the term "familiar" is as close as we can come. They formed us as such so that, together, we would preserve all that they were, should the worst befall them.

What part did the rebellious guardian represent, the Vraad wondered, and *how* dominant a trait was it?

There came a point, the ghostly figure went on, when the race had two options. They could use the Gate and seek out something, anything, that would revitalize their life force, give them the strength to continue on. It was an option steered toward failure and possibly even a quicker end to their kind. The second choice was the one that promised the most hope for their legacy, but like the first would mean a finish to all they had raised up over the millennia.

They chose the second. With it, though they would no longer exist as they were, they might still direct the course and final outcome of their grand plan. The true world might still one day greet the successors to the elder race.

Dru interrupted at that point, despite the uncomfortable feeling that the faceless ones were eyeing him with particular interest now. "Did they have no name? You say 'they' and 'them' but you give no name."

He could almost feel the other's embarrassment. *It has been so long, manling, that we have forgotten it. Even we are not immortal, though it might seem that way. With the passage of century after century, we have become a little less than we once were. There will come a time when we will fade as a dying wind.*

"Don't *they* know their name?" Xiri asked, her eyes ever keeping track of the movements of the blank-visaged beings.

In what they allow me to still tell you lies the answer to that . . . and perhaps other things. You, Vraad, have talked of the ka and how one can travel with it to places the body cannot reach. So it was with the elders. You saw the pentagram in the place you call the room of worlds. An apt name that, for with the Gate they could observe or travel to any of their creations. This last time, however, they chose to do something different.

The dying race numbered no more than a thousand or so by the time they came to their final decision, a thousand where there had once been millions. The guardian's tone was wistful, recalling the glory of those earlier days. In groups numbering close to one hundred apiece, they stepped into the room of worlds and never came out. Not until the last group was ready to enter did the founders deign to reveal what they were doing to their servants, their familiars.

We feared for them, but we were only the servants and so we obeyed when they commanded us to return to our duties and not interfere. We have never been allowed to interfere, save when they gave such orders. Still, their plan gave us fright, for it would place them beyond our limits, leave us with no one to guide us. You see, as with your kind, Vraad, their kas, their spirits, were liberated from their physical forms. The image of a hundred departing specters made both Dru and the elf uneasy, but they remained silent. *Your people created for themselves new bodies so that they could continue as they had always been. The founders did not. They had chosen instead a receptacle that would contain their collective consciousness, but it was more than a body, much, much more. It was intended that in some way, they would always watch over the world that had spawned them. They would be their world as much as the trees, the fields, and the animal life were.*

Dru blurted it out before the tale could go any further. "The *land!* The land itself! When I felt as if this realm would protect itself, it was more than my imagination, then."

The land. You, elf. When you spoke of the land being alive, you spoke truer than you thought. It is. It has a mind, albeit different from what you might consider one. It knows what those who live upon it do and moves to affect things in its favor. Yet I think that such a change affected those who created us, for the land is different. It is and is not our masters. Until your interference, we had thought the land dead once more, the founders having passed on despite their determination. Fools we were to be so presumptuous. Subtlety is not our forte. We could not see what the land was doing . . . even when it sought to bring you here, Vraad.

"Me?"

The dragon shape moved, as if uncertain itself about what it said next. *You or your kind. They have chosen to give the Vraad race a second chance.*

"It wasn't our own doing that weakened the barriers between Nimth and here?"

Hardly. The guardian paused again. When it spoke, it was already fading away. *I have said as much as they desire me to say for now.*

"What about our choices? What did they represent?"

A laugh, self-mocking, echoed through Dru's head. *I do not know. If you find out, I would be interested.*

The chamber of the dragon lord rematerialized around them.

A golem put its hand on the dumbfounded spellcaster's shoulder. Dru turned and fairly snarled at the creature before him. "*What?* What else do you want to amaze and confuse us with? Do you even understand what you're doing? Are you so little a shadow of what you once were that you perform movements without truly thinking? Why did you even return?"

He knew the answer to the last question, at least, or hoped he did. The guardian had said that the Vraad had been given an opportunity to redeem themselves. If they failed, the experiment failed and the ancients' dreams would die. The stolen golems gave the land hands to work with if it came down to the physical. Perhaps some elements of the presence had also simply yearned once more for solid flesh.

Dru got no further in his thoughts, for the faceless ones, for lack of a better name, indicated they wanted the twosome to follow them yet again. With little true choice in the matter, the sorcerer and the elf followed wordlessly. Xiri did shift over so that the two of them touched, but they did not so much as glance at one another during the duration of the walk.

Once more, they were returning to the room of worlds.

At the doorway, Dru and his companion finally exchanged looks of frustration. Were they to be shuttled back and forth from the two chambers until they collapsed?

The answer stood before them, its glimmering interior more reminiscent of a predator's maw than a portal to other worlds.

This time, Dru could sense that there would be no last-minute reprieve. Whatever world the cowled figures had chosen was to be their new home.

Xiri had apparently realized this at the same time, for she tried to push her guide away and break a path to freedom for Dru and herself. As with her earlier attempt, when she had thrown the knife at one of their captors, the golem was barely affected. The elf, despite her speed and obvious battle skill, bounced off the side of the robed creature and into the unprepared sorcerer. It was all Dru could do to keep both of them from falling to the floor. As they regained their footing, their guides reached out and took each by one arm. Both prisoners discovered that struggling from that point on was impossible. Having attempted violence, they had been stripped of control over their very bodies. Helplessly moving in time to their guides' steps, they walked to the center of the chamber and the patiently waiting Gate.

The spellcaster wished the guardian had not abandoned them back in the other chamber, but he knew that the mock dragon had really had little say. The guardians were used to obeying their masters blindly, and even though they *had* come to the point of questioning that blind obedience, it was not yet enough to save the two outsiders.

Vraad! the voice of the dragon guardian hurriedly called. *They have faith in you.*

That was all. One of the blank visages looked to the side, as if seeing to something. Dru felt the guardian retreat in something akin to fright.

They have faith in me? What did that mean?

The Gate shimmered again, causing renewed agitation among its dark denizens. They scurried, if it was possible, even more frantically than earlier.

Nimth greeted the sorcerer's eyes. He took a deep breath, waiting for it to change to the Void or some other place, but Nimth still beckoned after nearly a minute had passed.

He was to go to Nimth . . . and they had *faith* in him. Faith to do what?

"Is that . . . is that Nimth?"

"Yes." Dru looked at Xiri. "They want me to go there. I think they want me to bring the Vraad to this world."

The concept still did not sit well with the elf, though both knew she no longer hated Dru. He, however, was only one Vraad. Dru himself had told her how terrible his kind could be.

"They'll change when they've been here for a time. They have to. The land won't accept them any other way."

"What about me?"

He had not thought of that. "They can probably send you to your own people. You can prepare them for our coming." The Vraad smiled in a cynical way. "Providing they aren't as bloodthirsty as you, we should be able to live together."

"I am not going back to my people, not yet." Xiri looked up into his eyes with a determination worthy of any of his own race. "I think it would be better if I came with you back to Nimth."

"You don't want to do that. Not when there must be so many bitter Vraad. Not now."

"Yes." She took hold of his hand. He could not have peeled her hand from his even if he had wanted to do so. "Now. With you. I want to see this through to the end."

Dru looked up and met the sightless gaze of one of the ancients. Even without eyes of any sort, he could feel the creature absorbing every movement, every facial expression. The golems saw more than many who had perfect vision.

"We're stepping through now," he told it.

To his surprise, the blank visage dipped in what might have been a nod. The way before them cleared. The Gate waited expectantly, pulsating, it seemed, to the sorcerer's rapid heartbeat.

Tightening his own grip on Xiri's hand, he led her into the portal and onto the soil of treacherous Nimth.

XVII

THE TEZERENEE HAD planned to strike first, attacking their foes while they slept. Those sent by Barakas to explore the mountains had returned prematurely, bearing a tale of discovery. An aerie existed, a vast cavern from which they had seen the bird people enter and depart.

Lord Barakas had slowly formed a fist when all was said and done, saying, "We will crush them while they still prepare! I want the drakes ready for flight!"

The clan of the dragon had only six representatives of their totem, not counting the eight small wyverns they had come across by sheer accident. The wyverns made good hunting creatures and pets—the first one mindbroken by the trainers had been given to the patriarch as a symbol of luck—but they were ineffective fighters for a foe such as this. Of the six drakes, only four were mindbroken and one of those had struggled too much during the spell, addling its brain. Mindbreaking, the method by which the Tezerenee could quickly and efficiently control and train their beasts, was more of an all or nothing method here in the Dragonrealm. Precision was impossible, and after the damage caused on the one dragon, the trainers had ceased their work, hoping to find a better way.

It was not a well-armed armada that would have flown off to do battle, but they were Tezerenee and that was all that had mattered.

Barakas knew, from examination of the corpse, that the avians were diurnal like his own people. Most would be caught napping. Time after time, the Tezerenee had played their games of war, preparing, through mock combat, for daring strikes such as this. Even though there were probably at least twice as many of the birds as there were the drangonhelmed warriors, the advantage would be on the side of the clan.

"We are might. We are power. The name Tezerenee *is* power!" Barakas had said. It was a ritual saying, one the clan had heard often in the past, but spoken with the fervor that only the patriarch could summon, it was *truth.*

It was unfortunate, then, after all that had been planned, that the avians attacked while the Tezerenee were still organizing themselves.

The new keep was little more than a dark, morbid box around which a pathetic, half-grown wall stood. As with the drakes, it was all the clan sorcery could provide under present circumstances. There was only one room, a communal hall. Most of the Tezerenee were presently occupied with matters outside. Esad, chosen for the dubious honor of being one of the three dragon riders, was working with his mount, letting the large green beast familiarize itself with his scent. He and the other riders had the task of taking out whatever sentries the avians had posted. They were also supposed to prevent too many of the birds from gaining a flying advantage. Esad had his doubts about his ability to perform his task, but his fear of his father prevented him from doing anything about it.

He looked up and barely saw the winged silhouette in the thin sliver of the pale moon.

"Dragon's blood!" The Tezerenee abandoned his mount and went rushing to the keep. He kept silent, hoping that he could spread the word through contact and give the clan some slight advantage of surprise yet. Esad knew that if he died *before* he was able to alert someone, the blame for the deaths that followed would fall to him.

An armored figure, female, nearly collided with him. He grabbed her by the shoulders and whispered, "The birds attack any moment! Spread the word, but do it quietly!"

She nodded her understanding and started to move away.

A bolt of blue lightning caught her in midstep . . . and left only a thin trail of smoke to mark her passing.

The time for silence, Esad realized in horror, was over.

"Defend yourselves! We are attacked from above!"

The air was swarming with black shapes that fluttered into and out of the dim light of the two moons.

THEY HAD LET him watch. Watch as they began what would, it seemed, be the end of the Vraad race. He was treated well, since it was his knowledge of the tactics of the Tezerenee that the avians had used and might still need, yet he was still a prisoner, not the ally they pretended he was. Bereft of his powers and watched over by fierce companions, it was a wonder the avians even made the pretense of *calling* him an ally.

Despite all that, Rendel was quite satisfied, though he knew better than to show it. It was not the destruction of his kind that pleased the sorcerer, but rather that his *own* plans still moved on unimpeded. The cavern was virtually empty of its inhabitants, Rendel's practiced words—*images?*—impressing upon the aerie's overlord that nearly every able fighter was needed. It was a lie not *that* far from truth. Even with the advantages of first strike and dominance in the night sky, the birds would take hard losses. The Tezerenee would not die without a fight . . . and would not even die, if things went as planned.

After all, he preferred human subjects to feathered monsters like his captors.

The young who had been deemed too untrained to fight and those responsible for their care had retreated to lower caverns on the off chance that some danger might threaten the aerie. That fear had been planted, albeit surreptitiously, by the Vraad during his communications with what he still liked to term the council of elders for lack of a more defined description. To the avians, it seemed a reasonable precaution. As with now, he had barely been unable to suppress his pleasure. Rendel had succeeded in assuring that he would be left with only a few guards to watch over him.

In fact, there were three. A few others were scattered about the mountain and the mouth of the cavern, but the arrogant creatures actually believed that *they* had tricked their captive. Glancing at those standing around him, Rendel marveled that this race had become the dominant one in the Dragonrealm. Two were tall, muscular warriors, one of whom the Tezerenee believed was the leader of the patrol that had taken him prisoner. His remaining watchdog was the balding elder who had spoken out during the offer of alliance. The overlord was not here, having chosen to lead the attack, something that would have earned Barakas's respect, but received only silent amusement from Rendel. It had never made sense to him to dangle such a prize as a leader before an enemy. Let the lessers take the damage. There were always more of them.

The male he believed was his original captor squawked something. Rendel turned completely from the glittering crystal that acted as his eyes in the attack and allowed the avian to touch him, establishing the link between the two of them.

The vision of two birds falling prey to a dragon rider's mount was followed by a wave of anger. Rendel surmised that the image he had been shown was only one example of how the clan was fighting back. His erstwhile allies could evidently see in the dark better than he could, either that or the mind link was even stronger than he supposed, for the Vraad could not recall any such image in the viewing crystal. That did not matter; he believed the avian when it spoke of the dragons and their deadly strength. Much larger than either a Vraad or bird man, the three flying drakes were wreaking havoc. The invaders, Rendel was informed, were refraining from using their medallions for fear of striking down their own. Drakes were swift and agile despite their girth. It would require a practiced aim and great daring to bring down the beasts without adding a few feathered misfits, too.

Rendel shot back the image of his people as warriors, leaving an unformed question concerning the avians' abilities in the same role. As he had expected, it made the huge figure furious. He removed his hand from Rendel's forehead and pulled the hapless sorcerer forward so that the razorlike beak was within snapping range of the spellcaster's pale visage. The Tezerenee stumbled at the last moment, falling against his irate captor. The creature pushed the cloaked figure back. With its great strength, Rendel fairly flew, landing several paces from where he had stood. To his surprise, the two warriors dismissed him from their attention, refocusing on the scene in the crystal. They apparently felt they had no more use for his knowledge, something he was not ready to dissuade them concerning. Only the elder still eyed him.

Rising to his feet, the sorcerer pretended to brush himself off. The damnable, half-plucked bird was still staring at him when he finally gave up the effort. Rendel put one hand to his mouth and coughed, starting back to the trio at the same time.

The elder's attention strayed back to the images of the battle before it evidently occurred to him that their prisoner was a thing not to be trusted despite the dampening of his sorcery. A watery but wary eye looked Rendel's way.

It was a decision made a breath too late. The unsupervised moment was all the Tezerenee needed. The one thing Barakas had taught him that Rendel had come to appreciate was to use anything possible as a means to an end. He had planned something similar to the provoked attack by his one guard, but a bit later. Circumstances had, however, worked to his benefit.

He had the medallion focused on the trio even as the ancient one became aware of the threat the Vraad intended.

Rendel had palmed the medallion knowing only that it had been designed to kill. He neither knew nor cared what sort of deadly force had been trapped inside by its maker, only that it would suffice as a means of removing the three tensed figures before him. The avians had assumed he did not know how to utilize it, but the spellcaster had used every glance to study the artifacts, noting how the markings were fingered and how it had to be focused. Now, his studies had rewarded him. He concentrated, willing the spell of the medallion to come forth and looking forward to the pathetic cries of those who had dared to make him their slave.

Nothing happened.

The amusement in the eyes of the one he had stolen the magical item from told the story. Rendel's prize was an empty vessel, a useless ornament. They had allowed him to betray himself, to pick the time of his own demise. As his face reddened in anger—anger at himself for being so easy a pawn—Rendel thought how like the clan of the dragon these creatures were. How often had Barakas employed similar methods?

The patrol leader strode toward him, needle-sharp claws waiting to rend, beak open in the closest the avian could come to a cold smile. A low, reverberating sound issued forth, laughter of a sort.

Rendel did the only thing left to him—he ran. The entrance to the caverns themselves was blocked by his executioner. That left only one path. He would have to hope he could escape to the lower tunnels and lose himself.

A malevolent form swooped down before him. The avian had flown over his head and blocked his way. Rendel swore and ducked among the stone leviathans, wishing he knew how to tap into the power he felt within them. Yet the birds had tried countless times and they had not succeeded. It was why they had sent explorers overseas. There likely lay the key to understanding and utilizing the elemental forces sleeping deep inside each figure.

Claws struck stone just inches from his throat. Rendel let out a yelp and scurried to a different effigy, this one a muscular, horned beast that looked as if the artist had caught it in the midst of contemplating its own mortality. The figure wobbled when the Tezerenee fell against it, the ground beneath broken from some past tremor.

It was not fair, he thought in bitter fear. At his best, the Vraad would have taken his attacker apart with the simplest of spells. The avians had refused to release him from the enchantment that dulled his abilities, their reason being that he had to prove himself first. Rendel had thought he had planned for even that hurdle, but once more he had overplayed a bad hand. Now, it would be he who was torn asunder, ripped to bloody gobbets by a freak of the heavens.

He screamed as a pair of taloned feet scored his backside, tearing apart the cloak and shirt in the process. They had disposed of his dragon-scale clothing and given him simple cloth ones for the time being. He now knew why. Talons alone would have been inefficient weapons against the likes of dragon scale and a long, torturous death was evidently what they had chosen for him.

As the avian rose for what was certainly the final assault, Rendel threw himself once more against the stone figure, trying in desperation to push through or climb over it . . . he could not say *what* it was he wanted to do, not now.

The ancient carving teetered, then started to collapse on its side.

It was debatable as to who was more horrified, Rendel or his captors. Impending death could not take from the frantic sorcerer's mind the fact that he was destroying the very things he had risked himself for. Rendel grasped the nearest edges of the statue in a foolish attempt to right a massive stone artifact with only his own physical strength.

"No!" The Tezerenee was thrown forward as the effigy came crashing down on its neighbor, shattering *that* figure as well. A horrible sensation of pain and loss flowed like a wave over the central chamber. The avians fluttered back, acting as if they had been physically buffeted by the death throes of the dwellers within. Rendel pictured a terrible domino effect in which more than half of the artifacts were reduced to rubble and his mind was ravaged by an undeniable flood of agony that he would be forced to share as one after another of the elemental spirits, if that was truly what they were, died.

He was fortunate. The second statue collapsed in a dust-enshrouded pile without so much as nicking the one next to it. The Vraad fought for breath and heard harsh, choking sounds from somewhere above him. He peered through the cloud that had risen and saw the other two birds rushing his direction in rather unsteady movements. The time for games was over. Despite the loss he had brought about, Rendel knew he could at least die with the satisfaction that these three would be made to pay for the damage he had caused in his desperate attempt to escape. The laws by which the avians lived were simple and harsh.

Dust continued to fill his lungs. Why was the cloud not settling? Rendel stood, hoping to evade his executioners for at least a little longer, when the rubble began to *move*. It was not merely a tremor, though. The broken statues were moving of their *own* accord, not merely being jostled by the quaking earth . . . and what tremor localized itself so precisely?

Hope and fear vied for Rendel, neither emotion able to gain the upper hand. His first thought was that the things within had survived and were coming to the aid of the one who had released them. That was impossible. Rendel had felt the deaths and knew that what now stirred was not the same. The battered Tezerenee stumbled back as the mound began to rise higher and higher.

An elemental force permeated the huge chamber, living and not living. It was and was not dissimilar to those he had accidentally destroyed, but it was certainly far more, too. Rendel found he did not really care what it was; he only knew that here surely must be what he had sought.

"Mine! You're mine!" the weary yet triumphant spellcaster shouted. The pain that coursed through his system was forgotten. "Come to me! Fill me with the power that is mine!" He had summoned it, accidentally the sorcerer supposed, but that *must* make it *his* to control. . . .

Despite his demands, the force appeared disinclined to obey. Earth and fragments of the statues flew upward, nearly striking the top of the cavern and bringing light that frightened off numerous tiny forms. The avians, who had frozen at the sight of it, began to stir. Rendel was ignored. They, too, had sought whatever treasure the ancients had left here. Whichever one of them mastered it would become the new overlord, not merely of this region but of the entire land.

Is there no end to the chaos your kinds bring? A vague, animallike shape formed. Molten earth burbled from the inner depths of the world, joining the dirt and stone in creating the image of life. Despite so much flying about, not one particle of dust or one drop of melted earth so much as touched the Tezerenee. Even the statues, so close to the center, remained unaffected.

Is there truly hope for such as you?

Though no one looked in his direction, unless those *were* eyes in the midst of the jumbled pile, Rendel knew it was he who had been asked the question.

"Cease your prattle! I am the one who commands! I am the one who judges!" Rendel's doubt added a quiver to his voice.

Fiery wings spread, composed almost entirely of burning earth. What had once been the mouth of the horned beast was now the mouth of an entirely different monster, but one growing all too familiar in shape with each passing breath.

You have daring . . . and nothing more. My obedience is not yours to demand. Nor theirs, either.

It spoke of the avians. Rendel started, wondering how he could have forgotten the onrushing creatures. He looked around, but the three had vanished.

They have been redirected elsewhere until something can be done with them. It is you who I have come for, Vraad, at the command of those who rule here.

"You can't take me from this! Not now! It's why I worked so hard to make the cross-over work! It's why I risked all, coming here alone though I knew there was the threat of danger!" Rendel knew he was babbling, but it was buying him time. His mind raced, seeking some solution to his predicament. He had been rescued from death for . . . for *what* he did not know, save that it would separate him from what was his by right.

Manling, I found much to admire in one of your kind, but I see little of those traits within you. Do not stir me to measures that I will be forced to regret . . . later. I have already interfered more than I am supposed to. Your destruction of this place, of those who preceded my kind in the aid of our masters—elementals, you might call them—was accidental, but your desire to abuse their purpose was not.

Rendel no longer had any thoughts concerning the glory that was to have been his. Instead, he wondered whether he was going to leave this place alive.

The mock dragon dipped its macabre head, the burning earth giving it the appearance of a fire-breathing beast. It filled the Tezerenee's entire field of vision.

You have no more need to wonder, manling.

The false jaws opened.

Rendel shut his eyes and screamed.

XVIII

"Is this what it all comes to? Does nothing but ruin follow the Vraad?"

Dru could not respond to Xiri's question, not at first. The portal, through either the whims of its creators or, as he personally believed, *its* own, had returned them to Nimth near the Vraad communal city. Though it was night, a dim glow from above left the land in the equivalent of sunset, enabling them to see. Even from the slope on which they had materialized, it was evident that some catastrophe had struck. From what he could see, Dru knew already that the catastrophe had not been natural. The destruction was too well organized. Someone had *wanted* to destroy the only thing that had ever linked the individuals of his race together. The Vraad swore quietly, both saddened and ashamed.

"I've never seen such a *green* before," the elf whispered. "I feel as if it eats the soul of Nimth." She was gazing skyward, watching the maelstrom above. A massive storm was forming, one that looked to cover *everything*, for it stretched as far as the sky itself. Dru did not want to be caught outside when it broke; what rained down upon Nimth would not be so simple and harmless as water.

"Take my hand again."

She did, squeezing it tight. The sorcerer drew some comfort from having another person to touch during this period of chaos.

"Do you plan to teleport?"

He nodded. "At least try, anyway. I have to chance it. Time is short. Nimth won't die today, but *we* might."

Xiri looked up again. "The sky?"

"This glow from the clouds is a new phenomenon . . . very new, I think. There is also a storm brewing. It won't be a normal rain like you might expect. We've not had a rainstorm for years. If it strikes, it will be magical."

"Which means it could produce *anything*. Will it necessarily be bad?"

He swept his arm across what lay before them. "Look around you. Do you see anything good coming from what the Vraad have done so far?"

His point was obvious, but something seemed to disturb her. "Will not your spell aggravate conditions? Is there not a chance it will act as a catalyst?"

"It might, but our choices are few. I either use my sorcery or we walk."

Her hand slipped from his as she visibly struggled with herself. "There is one other way."

"What might that be?"

Elfin eyes lowered. "I could try my own powers. Like you, mine have been returned to me."

In the suddenness of their release by the founders, Dru had forgotten that his companion also worked magic of some kind. "Do you need anything?"

Xiri smiled. "Luck?"

He stepped back as she concentrated. The natural, if they could still be called such, forces of Nimth stirred as they were summoned. Her way felt different from that of his kind, however. It was more gentle, asking instead of taking. A glimmer of light materialized before the elf. Dru rubbed his chin, trying to understand the nuances of her spell. Was this the course in which Vraad sorcery *should* have developed?

He heard a gasp then, and saw Xiri starting to crumple. Instead of following her desires, it almost appeared as if Nimth sought to use *her*. Not only had power answered her summons, but it was trying to pervert her spell, almost as if it consciously desired to do so. With the swiftness born of centuries of careful practice, Dru seized control of her spell. The power fought back, not as a living thing but in the way that a raging river might fight against a dam that had broken partly away. Yet he did not turn the spell to the way it would have been had he been the originator. Instead, the spellcaster strained to make a hybrid of the two sorceries, at least long enough to perform the spell. Dru doubted the two could really be joined without a cataclysm resulting.

The strain was horrible, but in the end a shining, circular portal stood open before them. His concentration still monitoring the strength of the spell, Dru reached down and helped Xiri to regain her footing.

"That should never have happened!"

Dru knew better. "You tried to use the binding forces of Nimth as you would those of your own world. Nimth no longer follows the same laws of nature, if it ever actually did. We Vraad have made it too much like ourselves. Vicious and hungry. Still," he added as encouragement, "I think what you accomplished was likely more effective than the results I would have obtained."

"We have not crossed through yet. Save your congratulations for then."

Stepping through the portal was only slightly less unnerving than entering the founders' living gateway. Dru had a brief vision of a path, one that reminded him greatly of those Darkhorse had utilized to escape the Void, before he and his companion stood once more on the surface of his home world.

They stood in the courtyard that Dru had stared down at only . . . only . . . the Vraad gave up trying to count the days since his unexpected departure. After all, those who had ripped the massive structure apart had probably only needed hours, not days. He could not help glancing away from his companion, however. Seen up close, the devastation that had overcome the city was even worse than he had imagined.

"The city of the elders fell to time," Dru whispered, again shamed of his kind. "Before a fraction of the same time has passed, this place will be a foul blot in comparison."

"A ruin is a ruin," Xiri said, more to mollify him than because she believed in the simple statement. "What do you hope to find here?"

"Nothing. I hoped that there might be someone. They can't have all crossed over. Not so many and not so quickly. This was done by those left behind . . . the ones I'm supposed to help."

"What do we do now?" Xiri clearly did not want one of their choices to be to remain in this dark and ugly place. Dru was not so fond of the idea himself. He had hoped part of the city still lived, that some of the magic that enabled it to serve the Vraad still functioned. From what his higher senses told him, nothing had been left undamaged. There would be no food, no water.

It seems I am destined to never eat a normal meal again! The guardians and their masters had removed his hunger and thirst more than once, but they were not available. Dru glanced at his companion. Could Xiri's sorcery provide them with the sustenance they would be needing before long? "Can you conjure food and drink?"

She mulled it over. "After what happened, I think I might be able to, but there could be a better way."

"Such as?"

"If we work the spell together, as we did more or less before, then it should be possible."

It made as much sense to Dru as anything else had in a long time. "Let's try it, then. We shouldn't go on without dealing with the problem. I'd hate to think what would happen if we needed food or water in some desperate moment and found we couldn't do a thing about it."

He began first this time, determined to keep the forces of Nimth under control from the start. The slow work annoyed him; it was like learning the use of his sorcery all over again. After a moment's consideration, the spellcaster decided that this was what he *was* doing.

"I have it," he told her.

Nodding, Xiri reached out and coaxed the power to work with her. The firm hold that Dru's consciousness had on it prevented a magical assault akin to that taking place during the teleportation attempt. He felt the elf turn the land's binding force to the task she had wished completed.

The sorcerer blinked. The abrupt completion of the spell left him dizzy. Xiri, too, was trying to reorient herself. Dru looked down at the broken courtyard floor.

A loaf of bread, some fruit, a bit of meat, and a jug of some liquid made an incongruous image when surrounded by so much destruction.

"Better than I could have hoped," he said, smiling.

They split every item into equal portions, save the contents of the jug since neither of them had thought to conjure cups. Dru was surprised when Xiri sank her teeth into the meat. He had supposed that being an elf she would abhor the thought of eating the flesh of some wild creature, even if what they ate now was actually magical in origin.

"Eating meat does not decrease my spiritual nature," she said, swallowing a piece. "*Wasting* meat would. A diet of plants is lacking in a few necessities. There are a few I know who believe it is the only way we can become more than we are now, but I notice they are usually the ones lacking in strength and mind as time progresses." With her fingers, Xiri tore off another piece. "I *do* give thanks to the creature that provided me with sustenance, though it might be impossible in this case since the beast never existed."

The jug proved to contain wine that tasted vaguely familiar to Dru. It took him several swallows to recall that it was one of his own creations. He wondered if the spell had somehow tapped into his own mind, then decided that it was a matter for a more peaceful time.

It took only minutes to satisfy themselves. Dru noticed that the food and drink had materialized in quantities exactly matching their present needs. Again, it was a thought for another day, but he did want to ask Xiri if she had planned it so or somehow the spell itself had known. He rose and stared in the direction of his own domain. A part of him wanted to fly directly there to see if Sharissa was there. She *should* have crossed over, but the signs and what the one guardian had said hinted that more than a few Vraad had been abandoned by Barakas. Unless they had dragged her to the pentagram themselves, the Tezerenee had likely just forgotten her. Dru could not say why, but he felt that left to her own devices, his daughter would still be here.

"Dru! There is another nearby!"

The sorcerer sensed it, too. It was almost as if the newcomer had literally *popped* into the city . . . and why not if he or she were a Vraad?

Someone laughed. It was loud and lacking somewhat in sanity. Male, that was all the duo could tell other than the fact that they were mere seconds away. It was as if he had been searching for them.

"What should we do?" Xiri asked, deferring to Dru since this was his world, *his* madness. She knew little about the Vraad and looked as if she would have liked to keep it so.

"We find out who it is." A dangerous decision, the sorcerer knew, but it might also be their best way to find out the state of things. Between the two of them, he felt they had a definite edge over the newcomer. It was even possible that they would find the intruder friendly. Not likely, of course, but still a possibility to consider.

The real reason, though Dru would have denied it after all he had been through, was that he was simply curious. His unexpected exodus had only temporarily cooled his inquisitiveness.

With the care only experience can bring, Dru and the elf made their way through the rubble of the courtyard and toward the sound of laughter. Neither was too concerned with silence. The newcomer's laugh continually rose so high in volume that they doubted he could have heard them even if they had stood behind him and shouted.

Xiri was the first to see him as she peeked around the corner of a roofless building that had been, as far as Dru's memory served, the place where he had first discussed his theories of ka travel with the patriarch. "He just sits there and *laughs!*"

Dru, looking over her, held his breath. "Rendel?"

It was indeed Rendel. The Tezerenee, clad in torn garments and looking as if he had risen from a harsh burial, sat on a battered bench. He was silent for the moment save for the gasping sounds he made as he gulped in air. *Readying himself for another round of madness,* Dru decided. What was Rendel doing here and where had he been?

"You know him?"

The tall Vraad nodded, unmindful of the fact that the elf had her back to him. "I'm going out there."

"You should not!"

Her words went unheeded. Dru stepped out and walked toward Rendel, trying, all the while, to maintain an image of confidence he knew to be false. When he saw that the Tezerenee intended to laugh once more, Dru called out.

"Rendel! It's me! Dru Zeree!"

The other Vraad leaped to his feet and shook his head. He was silent, though his mouth kept forming words.

"Rendel. I'm real. Where have you been? What happened to you?"

"What happened to me?" Rendel almost began laughing, but found the strength to resist. "What has not happened to me? You should ask *that!*"

Dru forced his own voice steady. "All right, Rendel. What happeened? Tell me."

"It took everything away from me." The tattered Tezerenee's eyes revealed his close battle between sanity and madness. "Took it all away! I had worked so hard, given so much up!"

"Who did? Who took it from you?" Rendel's lost prize did not concern Dru so much as what power had returned him from the realm beyond the veil to dark Nimth.

"A dragon. It rose from the depths of the earth . . . only it was *not* a dragon! It was the *earth!*"

A dragon formed from the earth itself? One of the guardians. One with a fondness, it seemed, for the form of that particular leviathan. "The guardian brought you here?"

If Rendel noted the familiarity with which Dru spoke of the ancient familiar the latter had befriended, then he made no sign. "Sent me here. Said it had already interfered more than it had been allowed. Assumed that if I made it back to . . . to where I was . . . from Nimth, then I was meant to be there." His eyes snared Dru's. "But there is *no* way to cross! We are trapped here, Master Dru!"

The brown- and silver-tressed spellcaster hesitated, wondering whether his response would weaken or strengthen Rendel's sanity. He also wondered if he really *wanted* to tell the Tezerenee his belief.

Rendel, the remnants of his cloak wrapped around him, started to sit again.

It was not clear whether he desired to continue with his pointless laughter, but Dru knew that listening to *that* much longer would drive *him* insane.

"There may be a way back . . . if you'll listen to me."

"There *is* no way back!"

Dru stepped closer. "I crossed to the shrouded realm and back again. It's possible."

For the first time, hope crossed the Tezerenee's scarred visage. Dru wondered what he had gone through over in the other domain.

"Possible?"

"It is."

Drawing himself straight, Rendel managed a shadow of his old, arrogant self. "Then we can still win."

Rendel's widening eyes told Dru that the Tezerenee had finally noticed Xiri, who had joined them. A strange look crossed the battered figure's face for the merest of moments. "Who is that?"

"Xiri. My friend and companion." The description sounded inane and inefficient to Dru, but he was not about to attempt to define his growing relationship with Xiri at this time, not when he himself was not certain in what manner it had grown. "She's an elf. We met on the other side, when both our lives were in danger."

"An *elf*." Rendel looked her over as one might look over a prize pet. "I had forgotten there were elves."

"We have not forgotten the Vraad," she returned, her voice chilling.

"So I see." With each passing second, Rendel was becoming more and more his old self. Dru wondered if he *had* made a mistake.

His worries lessened a bit when the pale-haired Vraad turned back to him and asked, "What about this way across? How did you find it? Can we get there easily?"

"It found me." Dru described his involuntary crossing and went into vagaries about how he had returned. Rendel's eyes lit up at talk of the founders and the news that the golems' purpose had been usurped made him smile.

"Father must have been furious."

"I suppose." Dru tried to remain unsuspicious. "I would have thought you'd have come across Barakas and the rest."

"Circumstances separated me from where they were to arrive." Rendel would say nothing more about the subject. Taken with what the Tezerenee had said during his less lucid moments, however, a specter of the truth began to form. It was not a truth Dru appreciated.

"Well." The other Vraad crossed his arms. He still wore his tattered outfit, but no longer looked like one of the walking dead. His bearing was that of a man fully in control of his life. "What now?"

"We have to find whoever is left here. We all have to cross. I have this feeling that Nimth will be cut off at some point soon and left to rot. I don't want to be left here to rot with it."

"No, neither do I." Rendel growled. His anger, it seemed, was for someone else, likely the guardian who had delivered him back to the dying world. "I have a suggestion, however."

"What might *that* be?" Xiri asked, moving close to Dru, as if to show Rendel that the two of them were a united force. Neither Dru nor his companion wanted the Tezerenee to become the dominant partner. Their trust hardly ran that deep.

"Instead of seeking them out, let *them* come to us."

"Why should they come to us?" Dru rubbed his chin. "They came here once, expecting to begin a new life, and were betrayed. Why should they come here again?"

Rendel uncrossed his arms and indicated himself. A wry smile spread across his face. "Tell them that you have a Tezerenee, myself in particular, and they will come with the speed that only the hunger for revenge can give them."

He was offering himself as bait, in a ploy that could end in his slow, nighmarish death. Dru had to admire his daring, if nothing else.

"They will blame everything on you," the elf remarked needlessly.

"Concerned, little one? Let them, if it pleases them. They will forget when we show them there is a true path, one which would ensure they were never in debt to my father."

"Only to us. Only to you," Dru added.

"They *might* feel some debt to you, outsider, but not to an elf—whom you had better protect—or from me. From me it will only be a balancing of scales."

"He is correct, Dru."

"I know." He did not trust Rendel, knowing there was too much that the Tezerenee had not told them. Yet, the plan had merit. Further argument would only waste time they might not have.

"The only question remains," the other Vraad interjected, "is how to contact the rest. It will be a long task, I think. My own power works haphazardly, as yours likely does."

Dru looked down at Xiri, who returned his gaze with a smile, too. "We have a way around that."

Rendel glanced from one to the other, openly puzzled. "Do you really?"

It would have been impossible to perform the spell and keep their new companion from discovering the truth. Any attempt to hide their secret from Rendel would have only further weakened the bond they had forged. Dru wanted no trouble from the Tezerenee and admitted to himself that, of all other Vraad, it was Rendel who had the most knowledge concerning the shrouded realm, knowledge they might still need before all this was over.

"Step back." The curious Tezerenee obeyed without question. Dru and Xiri sat, the better to concentrate fully on their new task. Alone or with another Vraad, Dru doubted the summoning could have been performed with so much chance for success. Even Rendel's clan would have found themselves hard-pressed at this point. Oh, their summoning might have gone out, but not so clearly or so far. Besides, would anyone believe Dru if they knew that his sup-posed prisoner was *aiding* him in the spell?

Though much more complex due to the area that they were forced to cover, the spell proved far more willing than the last. What was sent out was not so much actual words, but images and sensations that repeated and repeated. Dru had intended on sending out an actual message, but it was Xiri who had per-formed that part of the spell and she had followed elfin ways. It really mattered little so long as what they desired was clear, but the end results reminded the sorcerer too much of the method by which the Seekers had communicated with him.

A glance at Rendel's suddenly chalky features made him wonder how well the Tezerenee knew the avians.

Dru had hoped that Sharissa would be the first to respond, but as the min-utes passed, his daughter made no attempt to contact him, though she had to have noted the message. Instead, when the first response *did* come, it was as if the maelstrom that he had been eyeing anxiously had finally let loose with a rage intended to tear Nimth apart.

What was left of the tallest tower shook as if coming to life. Several frag-ments broke loose and struck the battered courtyard. A blue fire spread across the northwest edge of the city, burning solid rock as if it were dry kindling. A ferocious wind threatened to topple one of the smaller, outer towers. Cracks formed in the earth. Rendel had a grim smile on his face, well aware that who-ever was coming wanted his head. Dru kept his eyes focused in the direction of the source of the attack, waiting for the Vraad to reveal his or her identity.

It was not *one* Vraad who finally materialized before them nor was it two. Dru almost wanted to laugh. If there was one other motive than survival that could band life enemies together, it was vengeance.

A full score and more faced them down. Dru was certain he counted at least three dozen, most of them the strongest among the Vraad, and leading them was one with a special hatred for the Tezerenee, a Vraad who should have been *dead*.

"Silesti," Rendel hissed. "Where is Dekkar, do you suppose?"

Dru stirred, realizing that the Tezerenee did not know about the patriarch's command that both Dekkar and Silesti finish their feud. He was certain that both of them had died, but if the black-garbed figure was truly who he appeared to be, then Rendel faced an added danger. Silesti was one of the deadliest sorcerers, his millennium-old feud having honed his skills. Nimth's situation had apparently not caused him much difficulty, if his entrance was anything to go by. It was evident that *he* had brought the others with him.

"Dru Zeree." Silesti dipped his head in formal greeting. "I had thought the reptiles had done away with you." His eyes were wide and bright. He wore the same darkly elegant bodysuit that he had been clad in the moment when Barakas had condemned the two rivals. There had been only one change, a small rainbow crest on the shoulder that Dru recollected had once been the symbol of his eternal adversary, Dekkar. It was a homage to a worthy foe.

"It was by my own doing that I was lost."

The leader of the unlikely band shrugged. "We have until Nimth takes us to talk of that. What concerns me, concerns *all* of us, is *that* one."

It was to Rendel's credit that he merely acknowledged the remark and made no sudden attempt to flee. Dru knew that in the Tezerenee's place he would have been considering any option that would have gained him freedom.

"Before you attempt anything, Silesti, I have a proposition."

"You want him first? By all means! You deserve it, only see that you keep him living!" He indicated those with him, a sea of nearly identical images with the *exact* same expression. Had looks actually been able to kill someone, there would have remained only a scorched mark where Rendel now stood.

"That's not what I meant." This would be delicate. If what Dru said failed to placate the bitter spellcasters, then he and Xiri would probably share Rendel's fate. He took a long breath and then, before the restless muttering grew any louder, presented them with the carrot on the stick. "I have a path of escape for us . . . all of us."

Several faces grew hopeful, but more than a few darkened. They had been betrayed once, and because they were Vraad, it was easy for them to imagine someone pulling the same ploy. Silesti's expression was unreadable, but his skin had turned a deep crimson.

"You . . . intrigue us. Tell us more."

There was a protest from within the group, but it quickly subsided after a single glance from their chosen spokesman.

Wishing he had the oratory skills of the patriarch, Dru detailed his mishap and what had become of him. The faces before him kept changing as emotions rose and fell. He said as little as possible about the guardians and their masters, deciding it was not yet time to tell as arrogant a people as his that they had been a failed experiment, but emphasized how there were those who shared their desire to survive. When he had finished, Silesti and the others conferred with one another.

Dru squeezed Xiri's hand and met Rendel's wary gaze. Neither could guess whether the vengeful band believed them. Dru was ready to defend both himself and Xiri with whatever it cost and Rendel would do no less for himself.

It was Silesti, as was expected, who announced the decision. His eyes kept switching from Dru to Rendel as he spoke. "If you were *this* one"—he indicated the Tezerenee with a savage jerk of his head—"we would already be taking our pleasure with your agonized screams. Because it is you, however, I, at least, am inclined to risk trusting you. That reptile . . . is there reason to spare him?"

"If you want my aid. Rendel is as trapped as we are. He knows more about the realm beyond than even I do." That was a matter of debate, but he was not going to tell them so. "We'll also need him when we confront Barakas . . . or would you care to begin your first moments after the cross-over fighting the Tezerenee?"

As angered as they were, Silesti's people were no fools. "Others might not agree with what you say."

"Between us, I think they'll force themselves to listen. Isn't life more important at this point? Do any of *you* want to remain in this hellhole *we* created?"

That was the point that none of them could deny. Even Silesti looked weary, now that the desire for vengeance was forced to subside. It was raw emotion that had kept these Vraad going. How were those with less strength surviving?

They were all looking at him in expectation, waiting to be told what to do. Why was *he* forced to lead them? All he wanted was to find his daughter and leave this place. When had he developed such a care for the survival of his undeserving race?

"I need help. From you, if possible. Many of the others will probably make their way here as the hours pass, and I don't think I can control them all. We might even have to fetch some of those still drowning in self-pity and convince them that I speak the truth. That's assuming *you* believe me. This is a sick jest. If I lie, you know I have nowhere to run from you. I swear I speak the truth. My life is my—" He stopped. His pledge would have sounded much too like the ones given by Barakas. Dru did not want to remind his counterparts of what had happened last time they had believed a pledge of honor. "I won't fail you," he finished up, wishing that he could have thought of something better to say.

"We've already given our assent, Zeree," Silesti commented. "You should have guessed that by the fact that the Tezerenee had not been flayed already."

Dru nodded in relieved gratitude. He knew what he had to say next. "I ask you to help coordinate steps, Silesti."

The mob leader's chest swelled. He acquiesced with a slight tip of his head. His eyes were gleaming.

The choice was the best one. Silesti's control of the band proved he had the presence and might necessary. It also gave the plan a look of cooperation. Making others an integral part of the plan would build up their faith in Dru. Unobserved for once, Dru tried to relax. It was a fruitless attempt. There was too much to do and he still worried over the fact that Sharissa had not shown up yet. Dru had expected her to be one of the first. More worries. *Would* it ever end?

"My father could not have handled it better." Rendel had come up behind him, but Dru had been too overwrought to notice. Xiri made it a point of switching sides so that she would be farther away from the Tezerenee. "You left out quite a bit, didn't you?"

"What if I did? Some of it probably would have resulted in your demise . . . and perhaps ours, too."

Rendel shrugged. "I meant nothing by it." He smiled in gracious fashion. "You have only my admiration."

There was a way that the Tezerenee had about him that demanded questioning by Dru. "You seem very pleased, more so than I would have thought."

"Why not?" With visible effort, Rendel created an emerald dragon-scale suit with a glittering cloak that moved even when there was no wind. He was greatly satisfied with his results and smiled again. "Despite that thing you call a guardian, I *will* cross again. I *will* have what is rightfully mine."

Dru wished he shared the pale-haired spellcaster's confidence. Rendel's words had stirred a nameless fear within him, a fear that the journey to the shrouded realm would be far from simple.

A fear that Nimth itself would not let them leave.

XIX

The night passed, though it was nearly impossible to believe that since the sky remained unchanged. The storm still grew, yet did not unleash its fury. Illumination from the green mass above still kept Nimth bathed in a parody of sunset. Xiri forced Dru to rest and he perhaps succeeded in sleeping an hour, but overall it was no use. Too much preyed on his torn mind. Vraad gathered in greater and greater numbers and still there was no Sharissa. Unable to rest any longer, Dru wandered among his people and asked several of those he knew if they had seen her. Several could not be bothered to remember. In some ways he could not blame them. They wanted to leave Nimth and be done with it. To most Vraad, the only reason to ask the whereabouts of a child of theirs was so that said off-spring would not be able to mount a surprise assault on their domain.

Only when he realized that Melenea was also among those still missing did the tall sorcerer have an inkling of why his daughter might not have been able to reach him.

"I have to leave," he whispered to Xiri. "We have to leave. There is an en-chantress called Melenea." Dru could not recall at the moment whether he had told the elf of his former lover, but that did not matter. Even if he had said something, he needed to say it *now*. "She's a Vraad of the worst extremes. Her entire life is built around what she likes to call games, but which others have often called insanity."

The Tezerenee returned. His eyes burned with anger and not a little fear. The more Vraad who arrived, the less comfortable he felt. Only Dru's presence and word of honor kept the growing mass from trying to take him.

"Going somewhere? I think not," Rendel warned, keeping his voice low so that the rest of the Vraad could not hear him. He had remained close by, drawing protection from Dru's mere presence. An unwelcome, eavesdropping shadow that Dru was regretting. "Not, at least, until I'm across!"

The two faced off. "It's a fallacy that the Tezerenee understand what caring for a son or daughter means, but that doesn't give you the right to command me, Rendel!"

"Would you like me to tell *them* that you plan to abandon them? I doubt whether I'd have to worry much about my hide if I did! It would be you they were after, outsider! You and your sweet pet here!"

Xiri had already proven her bravery time and again, but the covetous look Rendel gave her turned her face pale. Her eyes were daggers as she tried to pre-tend his implications meant nothing to her.

"They'd still take you, don't think otherwise! I won't be bullied, dragon! You don't want me as your enemy!"

Rendel tried a new tactic. "You were given a purpose when the guardians sent you back here."

It could not be denied. Dru took a deep breath. "Rendel, I don't even know what I'm supposed to do except probably bring you all to the one rift that I know of, the one in the far reaches of *my* lands."

"Is *that* it?" The Tezerenee laughed out loud, causing more than one head to turn. "I'll take them there! Go on and find your get! I'll make certain they cross safely."

Dru could read some of what Rendel planned by the minute but visible changes in his expression. Somehow, Rendel would try to make certain it was he to whom the other Vraad owed a debt. He wondered just how much of a fool Rendel was. Most of the Vraad would still want his hide even after the crossing, preferably in many screaming pieces. He was a part of something they hated and this was their opportunity to strike back.

"If anyone leads them, it should be the one called Silesti," Xiri suggested. Her dislike for the Vraad race was still strong, but if there were any who could be trusted other than Dru, it was the somber Silesti. Dru agreed. Silesti's contribution to the new plan was growing with each addition to the ranks. He appeared to have been born for this moment. Everyone looked to him as the symbol of defiance, defiance against the draconian Tezerenee clan. Barakas had tried to kill him, so the rumors now went, and had failed.

Silesti had already proved his ability as a leader, something that came as a bit of a shock to Dru and possibly the somber warlock himself. Dru wondered if it was his way of filling the void left by the abrupt end of his lifelong duel with Dekkar. Thinking of the duel, he wondered again how Silesti had survived. The other Vraad had not offered a reason and no one had the audacity to ask. For now, it did not really matter. What mattered to him was that he and Silesti both trusted and *respected* each other now. Had he dared to consider the black-suited Vraad's last conversation with him, a simple talk over questions raised by some of the newcomers, Dru might have even gone so far as to say the two of them *liked* one another . . . at least a tiny bit.

"It will be Silesti."

Rendel's mask of calm nearly slipped away. Rage spread like wildfire and it was all he could do to keep from screaming. "As you like it! We will speak again in the Dragonrealm."

He turned and caught sight of Silesti and several others, all of whom had an avid interest in the conversation between Dru and the Tezerenee. It was clear that they were hoping for some kind of break between the two so that Rendel would no longer be protected from their wrath.

The Tezerenee paused, measuring their emotions, and stepped back until he was next to Dru. Without meeting Dru's eyes, he whispered in a cold tone, "I will be waiting for you, Zeree. Waiting for all of you to bow to me, not my father."

The pale-haired warlock pushed past Dru and strode off into the deserted sectors of the city.

"Perhaps someone will find him alone and unprotected among the ruins," Xiri suggested, watching the receding figure with disgust. "What did he mean by that last?"

Several Vraad had stirred the moment Rendel had walked away. Silesti rushed over to Dru and Xiri.

"What happened? Where did that reptile go? Is he coming back?"

It had only become clear to Dru now what the Tezerenee had meant. A search of the city would reveal nothing of him. "He's gone. He won't be with us."

"Will he escape to the Dragonrealm?" The ebony-garbed figure spouted. Not having another name for it, the Vraad as a whole had unconsciously adopted the one coined by Barakas.

First victory to you, patriarch! Dru thought in sour humor. "He may. Rendel knows where I planned to go and he knows much concerning the shrouded realm and its intrusions here. Still . . ." An idea dawned, one that he did not care for. "I could be wrong about the location. The place I fell through might not be our way out. Rendel might be following a dead trail!"

"If he gets left behind . . ." Silesti smiled at the image. "What a perfect fate! Better than any torture! Nimth will kill him far more slowly than we would!"

"Yet he may escape to the other side if the rift *does* prove open," Xiri pointed out.

Silesti still had a bit of trouble dealing with an elf. Because she was Dru's close companion, he had succeeded so far in treating her with at least some respect. "Then we will track him down at our leisure once *we* have finally reached our new home!"

That was Dru's opening. What Rendel did could be dealt with once they were all safe and secure, but Sharissa was a subject that could wait no longer. "I think it might be best to see if there is another path through. I know what to look for now. If the way I know of is closed or if it only opens periodically, then I should find that out before we dare lead the others there. Are there those you can trust to act in concert with you? Those who can keep our people trusting for a time longer? It might take into the morning to do what I must."

The other Vraad frowned. "That sounds as if you will be leaving us."

"I won't be here for a time, that's all. There's still more I have to do. I want the cross-over to work."

"You underestimate me." Silesti's visage grew troubled. "Or perhaps you do not trust me. That you care for your daughter is a mystery to many of us. Now she is missing and you want to find her; that is what you are really thinking about. You asked where Melenea was and I know that she's also among the missing. I, for one, would draw the same conclusion as you have, that Melenea has your Sharissa. She has always been a vindictive and deadly bitch and this smells like one of her mad games! Only she would play when the world is crumbling about her!"

As opposed to the rest of the Vraad, Dru thought with what he considered justified criticism. Left abandoned by Lord Barakas, had they attempted their *own* plan of escape? Hardly. He did not, of course, reveal any of this to Silesti. It would have been unfair, anyway. Dru was just as guilty as the rest. Only the past two decades had he attempted to redeem himself. "I meant what I said about the cross-over, Silesti. I *do* want to check my work before we try. We know what will happen if the others feel they've been betrayed again."

"And I would join you as one of those facing their combined wrath." Silesti gave him a brief smile that would have looked more appropriate on an animal being led to slaughter. "I really have no choice, do I? Get your little hellion and make certain that you have a destination for us, that's all I care." The other sorcerer's voice grew fatalistic. "If you don't return by a reasonable time, I'll do my best to see that *I* lead the mob that comes for you."

Though Xiri was taken aback by the threat, Dru accepted it as normal. With time ever passing too quickly, he outlined the basics of what he had in mind concerning the second cross-over, only vaguely making references to the guardian who had aided him. Dru hoped he himself understood what he was doing. The guardian had said that he was to lead them to the shrouded realm, but had never actually said that the rift the sorcerer had fallen through was the correct path or that there might be some other way altogether. The magical creature had inferred a few things, but . . .

With an effort born of anger, Dru ousted the worries and the second thoughts from his mind. He would defeat himself without aid from either Melenea or Rendel if he fell prey to his own fears.

Silesti nodded his understanding when Dru concluded. "I have it. Remarkable!" he added, his dark mood fading as he once more fell victim to the wonder of it all. "To think escape stood there waiting for us and we thought it was merely an aberration, a part of Nimth's long dying! Why is it these others sought us out in the first place?"

"That's something that must wait until we've crossed."

"Not going to tell me. As you wish. You can count on me, Zeree, if only so that I can be around to see the dragon lord's sickened face."

Dru's jaw nearly dropped until it occurred to him that Silesti was speaking of Barakas, not the statue whose likeness the guardian had taken on.

"What are you waiting for?" Silesti asked. "You of all people should know how quickly time is running out."

Dru's growing guilt made him offer the other Vraad one last chance to back down, though he prayed Silesti would not take it. "There will be several thousand, Silesti. We're talking about *all* of our people, you know. We can't leave anyone behind."

"I have some concept of the numbers. They will be here. Anyone foolish enough to want to remain behind deserves their fate, but we will try to convince them otherwise." A pause. "In fact, it will keep them busy and give them a reason why we have to delay! Perfect!" More confident now, he waved Dru and the elf away. "That settles everything. Now go! I want you here when the time comes . . . or I cannot promise what will happen afterward!"

Both men locked gazes for a time, the truth of Silesti's words a grim reminder of the fickleness and pettiness of their kind. Neither could claim to be above such things, either.

It was the other mage who broke contact first, physically turning away from the two. "Find the bitch and get your daughter back! I just hope your youngster doesn't pay you back with typical kindness when she finally *does* leave you!"

Dru watched him walk back toward the expanding crowd, then led Xiri away from the sight of the milling Vraad. When they were alone, she turned to him with a questioning expression. The elf wanted an explanation for the other sorcerer's last statement.

"It's good that Vraad live so long," he said in a hushed voice. "Most offspring die trying to murder at least one of their parents."

The horrified look he received made him burn with bitterness. "Yes, the founders and the guardians are very desperate if they think we are their last chance for a future! I thought you knew that already."

"You are not like that! You could not have . . ." Though it was a denial, there was a hint of question in it.

His lack of reply was response enough.

They found a building that still retained enough roof to give them shelter for the brief time while they worked the spell that would send them to Melenea's realm. Facing Xiri but avoiding her, Dru took her hands. He was becoming tired, so very tired, but it was not yet the time to sleep. Xiri squeezed tightly, not from disgust but rather from understanding. Dru felt like a corpse given a second life. He dared to kiss the top of her head just before they teleported.

To ENTER THE heart of a raging storm would have seemed a pleasant task in comparison to what Dru and Xiri found themselves in the midst of when they appeared. The duo was thrown to the ground as a quake rocked everything. Dru was certain he felt the earth *ripple* like a wave. A frog with tiny human legs rushed past his dust-covered face. Something he was thankful he could not see slithered over his backside. Beside him, Xiri coughed hard in an attempt to empty her lungs of dirt that she had swallowed.

"What in the name of Rheena?" she finally managed.

Turning over, Dru found that his vision had gone mad. That was the first and most sensible explanation for what he saw. The spellcaster almost wished the dim glow in the sky would fade, if only so that he would not have to see what was happening around him.

They were only a short distance from their intended destination, but that minute gap had probably saved them from disaster. Melenea's stronghold was only a chaotic memory of what he recalled. Its walls and cloud-capped towers twisted and swayed, snakes of marble and ivory. The entire edifice wriggled, a thing pretending at life. Things crawled all around it, nonsense creatures that existed only in the Vraad subconscious . . . until now. It was magic gone wild, a region madly unstable. He should have known that her domain would be one of the first to be lost. Melenea had always been free with her spells, more so than even the Tezerenee. Worse yet, what they had seen so far was only the first stage. Anything would eventually be possible in an area like this and there was no way to turn it back once the instability had established itself so. Even as Dru stared, dumbfounded, one of the walls grew a score of mouths, each of which began babbling words of no meaning. The land itself turned and shaped itself like soft clay, hills rising and sinking at random moments. Now and then, some new aberration would go running by them. Plants, as twisted as any Nimth now produced, sprouted, grew, tried to reach them, then withered and died . . . all in the time it took to blink.

There could be no one in the citadel itself. Melenea would have no desire for a place that was no longer hers to mold as she willed. Thankfully, it also meant that Sharissa could not be there. If she *was* a captive of the deadly enchantress, Melenea would hardly waste her. This was one of her games and Sharissa was her prize piece. Her bait. The game he had unwittingly joined when he had taken her as a lover had never truly ended, not for Melenea. Dru had defied her in ways that none of the others had. It would not be over until he succumbed to her will.

Or when I kill you. That would end her games once and for all. The grim choice made, Dru rose and helped Xiri to her feet. "They have to be back in my lands. Melenea will be waiting for us there, ready to play a final hand."

"She must be mad!"

"No more than any other Vraad! Longevity has its price. Perhaps that's why the young try to kill their progenitors . . . to either unconsciously save their elders from further madness or prevent themselves from ever having to suffer it. Reaching adulthood is insanity enough!"

One of the sky-scraping towers twisted toward the duo, sighting upon them like a great serpent. Melenea had always been proud of her achievement. There were none stretched so high, not even in the communal city. Seen acting as some living creature, they were even more astounding.

"Time to leave," Dru whispered. "Serkadion Manee! I pray I'm right!"

"What if Sharissa is not there?"

His skin was white and he knew his present appearance chilled the elf. At the moment, Dru did not care.

"Then Melenea will learn—"

Blue-green fur swarmed over them.

Xiri was tossed aside, only to land like a wet cloth on the ever-shifting earth. The monstrous form ignored her. Dru stared into a maw filled with teeth.

"Lady said that someone would come, sorcerer! Said that I could play with you if you came!" The massive wolf loomed over the battered spellcaster. "You are Dru Zeree. Delicious! She would never let me play with you before, but she is gone now! Lady said I could have *anyone* who came, anyone at all!"

Dru had forgotten Cabal, though he found it amazing that he could have ever erased the memory of this monstrosity. Cabal was Melenea as she should have been. Her alter ego. Yet . . . yet now painfully reminded of its existence, he also recalled something else about the wolf. Melenea had destroyed the familiar in a fit of anger when it had tried to take Dru while he slept. Destroyed it with hardly a care for the loyalty it had always given her. That was why he had forgotten Cabal; it had not existed anymore.

This was hardly an illusion that stood over him. Dru could feel and smell its hot, nauseating breath.

Seeming to understand the changing emotion in its victim's expression, Cabal laughed again. "A long time, yes. You remember. A good trick she played, not telling you about me. Lady has punished me often, but there are always *other* Cabals!"

"I am legion!" laughed an identical voice.

A *second* Cabal emerged from hiding and joined the first, eyeing the limp elf with interest before turning a hungry gaze at the Vraad.

It should not have surprised Dru that there were more than one; it was typical Melenea. How many *did* she have? Dru envisioned an endless array of huge, blue-green wolves, all of them extensions of her twisted personality.

For all their strength, however, the familiars also suffered from her weaknesses. It was his only hope. With Xiri unconscious, Dru could not leave . . . even supposing his spell did work the first time.

Behind them, several of the towers had twisted their way, rippling pseudo-snakes drawn by the movements. Dru developed a wild, desperate plan.

"Who plays with me first, then?" he asked, trying to seem interested rather than anxious. Their response would indicate just how much like their mistress they were.

"I caught you! I am first!" growled the one who had knocked the Vraad and the elf over.

The other snarled. "I saw them! I let you have first strike, but I play first with him!"

"Play with the elf!"

"No!" The second Cabal narrowed its eyes, studying the hapless spellcaster as it might a favorite treat. "I want *him!* He is mine!"

"After I am done!"

"I don't think I'll be much fun to play with after the first of you," Dru interjected when he saw the second reconsidering its position.

"I want him first!" it finally responded.

The twin behemoths turned and bared their multitude of sharp teeth at one another. As he had suspected, they were as possessive as Melenea. It was a common failing with familiars. Other than a few exceptions such as Sirvak, whom Dru had worked to make as separate an individual mind as possible, most were nearly perfect reflections of their masters and mistresses. Cabal was even more extreme than most.

"I will have him!"

"*I* will have him!"

The first one snapped at its doppelganger. That led to a snap from the second. Both were working to make the other back down, a futile ploy considering they were equally stubborn. Melenea would have never backed down and Dru hoped her pets would follow suit.

"Mine!" The two beasts shouted in simultaneous fashion. They leaped as one, coming together in the air, jaws biting and claws tearing. Dru crawled backward as fast as he could to avoid being crushed by their falling bodies.

Both Cabals landed on their feet, still locked together in combat. Identical scars decorated their shoulders and blood dripped from their jaws as each tried to tear out the other's throat. *There is no worse enemy than one's self,* Dru thought as he watched in horrified fascination. He still dared not take Xiri and attempt to flee. The moment the Vraad moved to escape, the twin familiars would forget their feud and turn on him. Of that he was certain.

The battling beasts stepped back from each other, blood spattering their faces. Magical though they were, in order to be useful to a Vraad, a familiar had to be flesh and bone. The wary combatants circled one another, baring their fangs and again seeking to frighten off one another.

Xiri stirred at that point, both cheering Dru with the fact that she was still alive and adding to the sorcerer's fear by moving so near the creatures. If she caught their attention, they might break off the battle long enough to make certain she did not try to escape.

Once again, the Cabals joined. So evenly matched, they might fight for days without pause, neither ever gaining an upper hand. Dru could hardly wait out all that time. Had this been the Nimth of long ago or even a few months past,

Cabal would have been nothing to him. Yet, in a place where his sorcery was suspect, Melenea's familiar, doubly strong now, could easily be his equal or even his superior.

He glanced briefly at the wriggling towers, his thin hope there fading away. The citadel still acted like a living creature. Two smaller towers even sparred with one another, a reflection of the battle between the familiars. A portion of the edifice now seemed to be flowing down and away, not molten, for the walls and buildings still held some semblance of their function. As with so many things of late, it was a phenomenon that he would have dearly loved to study, but not during his present predicament.

It was now impossible to tell which of the wolves was which, not that it really mattered. They rolled in a jumble of fur, blood, and dust, their snarls loud enough to hurt Dru's ears. The two leviathans crashed into a low overhang and the rubble that fell to the ground sprouted arms and legs. A hundred or more magic-spawned gargoyles scattered to escape further fragmentation.

Even if the familiars never ceased their fight, how long would it be before the wild power affected Dru and his companion? He had no idea how much resistance elves had to such chaos.

Some of the living towers had returned their attention to the movements of the familiars. Dru studied the back and forth swaying of the snakelike bodies and tried to make himself as still as possible. The two Cabals had broken from one another again. Both turned one wary eye toward the Vraad, as if to warn that he had better not try to escape. Dru tried to look panic-stricken, which proved to be easy since he was not, in truth, far from that point already.

Satisfied, the twin wolves backed away. They had not abandoned their fight. Instead, each sought to find better ground from which to attack. It was their only venue left. An advantage of position would break the deadlock created by their identical abilities.

"*Dru.*" It was a whisper, one barely heard among so much noise.

He blinked, trying not to show his shock. "Xiri?"

"What do we do? They won't fight forever."

That was debatable, based on what he knew of Melenea's nature, but it was still important that they escape before too long. Not merely for their sakes, but for Sharissa's.

"Can we outrun them?"

Dru shook his head, and whispered back, "They could catch us even if each of them had two broken legs and half their bodies ripped apart. Melenea knows her sorcery well. What they lack in personality and intelligence, they make up for in ability. They have reflexes a thousand times greater than the animal they resemble."

"What do we do?" Xiri's voice cracked for the first time that he could recall. He wanted to go to her and hold her, for *both* of their well-beings.

Dru looked up once more at the nearly hypnotic swaying of the towers. "We hope that it won't take much more."

Before she could question his statement, the familiars charged at one another. One Cabal had taken to a hill that kept crumbling. The second had opted for lower but more stable ground for its starting point. Each evidently hoped the earth itself would prove the deciding point. If the one above stumbled, it might lose its footing and fall, leaving it open to its counterpart's attack. If it maintained its balance, it would have the opportunity to leap onto its twin, crushing the other beneath it and enabling it to reach the neck.

As the two monsters closed, Dru caught a twitch of movement from the living citadel.

With a swiftness even the wolves would have had trouble matching, the largest of the towers, so very much serpentine in movement, *struck* at the charging combatants. It had no mouth, though it might have thought it did, but its girth and the pointed tip were sufficient. The living tower caught both wolves, coming down upon them with a mass so great that it continued on even after meeting the ground. It withdrew almost instantly, leaving behind a deep crater.

The wolves had never even noted its coming.

Dru was already moving, hoping that the actions of the one spire would hold the others back for a moment. Xiri was on her feet even as he reached her and the two ran with all the speed they could muster. Neither dared to look back, even when they heard movement.

A powerful shock wave sent them flying forward. As Dru tumbled, he saw another of the towers retreat, its strike having fallen short by only a few yards.

There was one benefit of the second assault. Dru and Xiri had been tossed out of reach of the murderous spires. The two of them lay where they had fallen until their hearts had slowed to something approaching normal. Beyond them, the towers of the citadel started to collapse like wax candles tossed into a fire. Even still, the tallest made one token attempt to reach them. It fell far short. A moment later, the entire tower fell for a final time, its base no longer solid enough to support it. It continued to flop around for a few seconds more, a horror suffering its death throes.

"That . . . was . . ." Xiri took another breath and tried again. "That was . . . I cannot find a word that satisfies me!"

"Astonishing, amazing, horrible, terrible, insane, unbelievable, impossible . . ." Dru's smile was wan. "Use all of them and more. It's the only way you might ever describe it in sufficient fashion."

She squinted, trying to locate something. "Do you think that those creatures are dead?"

"Cabal? I doubt there's much left that could do anything to us. For a time, I was afraid it wouldn't happen."

Her eyes became dishes. "You *knew* the citadel would attack them?"

"It was watching like a snake, striking at movement. I hoped that it would attack them before they decided to make peace."

"What if they had?"

He stood up and stared grimly back at the gaping crater that was all that remained of the wolves. "I'd rather not think about it. Let's hope there are no more of them."

"We should leave here," the elf said. She did not want to have to face more of those obscene creatures if they could avoid it. "But where should we go?"

Dru was still pondering the familiars and whether Melenea had truly wanted them to kill him. He would have thought her too possessive to let others, even bits of her own personality, do it for her. That was verification enough that she was not here.

"She could only be in my lands . . . as I said earlier. Where best to humiliate me and take from me everything I care for than my own home?"

"She must have loved you deeply at one time," Xiri whispered in a hesitant manner.

He was stunned. How could she think that? "Melenea loves no one. I thought that was obvious."

"Then why has she such a marked interest in you? I gather many have known her over the centuries."

"We're wasting time!" Dru barked, taking Xiri's hands a little more tightly than he had planned. She remained passive, knowing his anger would fade . . . and knowing it was aimed at himself, not her.

Behind them, Melenea's stronghold started its final collapse within itself. Melting yet not melting, it looked like a water-soaked drawing rather than an actual castle. That such power was now unchecked . . .

If it was a sign, neither of them wanted to know. They closed their eyes and were, a heartbeat later, at their destination.

XX

THE DISCONCERTING IMAGE of one land imposed upon another was possibly the most refreshing vision that Dru had experienced in some time. The shrouded realm was a victim of paradox; its presence was one of the few *stable* things that the sorcerer could still recall. Where everything else was suffering chaotic change in one manner or another, the region where he had made his accidental pilgrimage to the Void and beyond was nearly the same as it had been at that time.

"This is . . . beautiful." Xiri brushed a hand through several blades of ghostly grass. "Like seeing the spirit of the forest and the field."

"But not enough." The realm beyond the veil was too vague an image, too much like so many others he had investigated early on. Even from where he stood, he could see that the rift area was only a vague shadow of its once-mighty self. He could not say whether the spectral land would fade to nothing or strengthen until it was more real than the piece of Nimth it was displacing. Whichever, it was evident that for at least the time being, they would find no accessible path to the founders' world. Perhaps later, but not now.

Dru imagined several thousand vengeful faces and shuddered at what sort of reward Vraad imagination would create for him if his promises proved as transparent as the woods in the distance.

"I do not see him."

He did not have to ask who it was she meant. Rendel would have known after a few moments that there was no escape using this place. Dru had not expected to find him here, though he had scanned the region with care, just in case. The Tezerenee was none of his concern, however. Rendel had chosen to go his own way.

The sorcerer shifted, anxious to be gone from here. He had fulfilled his duties to the other Vraad; it now was necessary, not just for his own sake but theirs as well, that he return to his domicile. That his concern presently centered more on Sharissa than the fate of his race did not disturb him.

He sent his mind out, seeking the link.

Sirvak?

Xiri watched, both interested and anxious. He had explained earlier about Sirvak and how the familiar, like Cabal, protected the pearl edifice from outsiders.

Dru frowned. Sirvak rarely took so long to respond. The link between them was strong . . . or had been until now. Concentrating harder, he discovered only the barest thread keeping his mind in tune with the creature. Sirvak's end was a complete mystery. There was a fuzziness, as if the familiar was not quite there. Dru grew more uneasy. He called to the familiar again, this time pressing to the limits of his will.

After another long, nerve-twisting silence, a distant, tentative voice filled his head. *Masterrr?*

He knew that Xiri was aware of his success by the look of relief she flashed at him. Likely the same expression was plastered over his own. *Sirvak! What happened to you? Why didn't you respond? Is Sharissa all right?*

Masterrr. There are troublesss! You must come here!

"What about Sharissa?" Dru realized he had shouted, so frustrated had he become in the few seconds since contacting his creation. Why was Sirvak acting so upset? Why would the familiar not answer a question concerning Sharissa? *I'm coming! You will wait for me by the entrance to my work chamber!*

Masterrr, no! Danger! Let Sirvak guide you in! Will explain when you are safe!

Very well! Just do it! Dru broke the link, confused and very angry. He reached out to his right and took Xiri's hand. "My familiar will teleport us into my home. It seems quite agitated."

"Something to do with your daughter?"

"It must be. Sirvak wouldn't say a thing concerning her, but kept speaking of trouble. I—"

Nimth was no more. Dru suffered a brief period of total chaos where he floated in a dark limbo. He had lost his grip on Xiri, somehow and realized that he had never brought her up to Sirvak. Had the familiar left her outside?

His feet touched the cold, hard surface of one of the castle's floors.

"Sirvak? Xiri?" His eyes refused to focus. "Sirvak? What kind of spell *was* that? What happened? Xiri?"

After a moment, a delicate hand touched his. "Hush, Dru. I'm right here."

He blinked, slowly making out vague shapes. The shapes tightened until they were actual forms . . . walls, doorways, torches, and, to his left, his elfin companion.

"How are you feeling?" she asked in concern. Her eyes were bright, as if she had actually enjoyed the transfer.

"Better than I did when I first arrived. Didn't you feel the disorientation? A sensation of being held in place for a moment or two?"

"A little. Perhaps it didn't affect me as much since I'm an elf." Xiri said the last with a touch of amusement in her voice.

Dru was unable to see the humor. He turned around and looked for the gold and black form of his winged familiar. Sirvak was nowhere in sight.

Sirvak?

Masterrr?

Where are you? Dru let his rising anger wash over the disobedient creature.

I come. The great reluctance with which the familiar responded caught the spellcaster by surprise. He would have questioned Sirvak then, but Xiri chose that moment to desire his attention.

"What is that in there, Dru?" She had drawn closer to him, nearly clinging to his arm. To his surprise, he felt uneasy rather than pleased with her nearness.

Stirring himself, he followed her finger, which pointed at the doorway to his work chamber.

"That's our destination. That's where the key to crossing the ghost lands into the realm beyond waits. It should—" He broke off and stretched a hand out toward the unimpressive-looking doorway. "It's *open!*"

"Of course it is."

"That's not what I mean! Sirvak!"

There was no response from the familiar. With a new fear stirring in the pit of his stomach, Dru raced through the unprotected entrance. He had improved on the magical barricade surrounding this, one of the most important of his chambers, and left it active prior to his last departure from the castle. By rights, only he and Sharissa could have entered and neither of them would have removed the spell, even with all the other defenses implanted throughout Dru's domicile. Did this have anything to do with the dangers that Sirvak had mentioned in his ravings? Where *was* the familiar? Where was *Sharissa*, the only other person who had access?

When Dru saw the crumpled figure buried beneath the long cloak, he thought his worst fears had finally caught up to him. Then the sorcerer stared more closely and saw that it was a male body sprawled before them.

Rendel.

From the awkward angle that his body lay in, it was quite impossible that the Tezerenee had survived. Dru stepped closer, cautious because he still did not know what had killed the other Vraad. He also wanted to know how Rendel had gained entrance in the first place.

He touched the body. It was still warm, which was not too surprising since Rendel had only departed the communal city a short time before Dru and Xiri had. The dead Vraad's expression was that of puzzlement, as if even then he could not believe that something had, in absolute fashion, ensured that he would *not* return to the shrouded realm. He felt no remorse for the arrogant Tezerenee. As intelligent as Rendel had been, his ego had made him blind to common sense. He could not see the abrupt end his ways would bring him. Nothing had been beyond him, as far as Rendel was concerned.

Dru wondered what it was that the Tezerenee had desired so much that he would grow so careless. If it did lie in the realm beyond the veil, then someone else would someday claim it. Dru hoped he would not be around when that happened. Anything that so obsessed a Tezerenee could only be a danger to all others.

Stepping back from the corpse, he saw the cracked blue crystal, no more than the size of a nut, that lay nestled in the crook of Rendel's arm. Dru forgot about the body at his feet.

"Serkadion Manee!" He had slim hope that he was wrong, but a simple turn of the head was enough to show him the worst.

His experiment, the spiral patterns and the orbiting crystals, the work that was to have given him the answers he needed, was in disarray. A few stones still circled, but in mad curves that no longer had meaning. Several had fallen to the floor. The spiral patterns still existed, but they had deteriorated beyond repair. Rendel had destroyed not only the culmination of his research but the patterns that had been needed to find the nearest opening.

The master mage frowned. Viewing things, he saw it was not so much Rendel who had destroyed the artifact but rather the artifact that had killed the Tezerenee. But how? As he had created it, the experiment should have been harmless. This one had unleashed enough magic to make an end of the intruder.

"Sirvak!" Dru shouted, more out of anger than because he thought that it would have any more success in summoning the familiar than the mind link had.

"Masterrr."

The gold and black beast was a pitiful sight as it fluttered into the room. It gave Xiri a wide berth, glancing at her with pain-wracked eyes as it passed, and settled down on a table nearby. Dru studied the animal, taken aback by its disheveled appearance. Its fur and feathers were matted heavily with dirt and blood and it was even missing most of one of its forelegs. The spellcaster's anger deflated as he imagined the cause of the beast's injuries.

Sirvak stretched its ravaged wings, the effort visibly painful. "Masterrr."

Xiri moved to join Dru, taking his arm and watching the familiar from his side. Sirvak hissed in her direction, but shrank into itself when the sorcerer gave it a withering look. A slight smile spread across the elf's face.

"What happened here, Sirvak?" he finally asked. "Where is Sharissa? How did Rendel get in here and what killed him? Tell me."

The familiar opened its toothy beak and squawked in frustration. It could not take its eyes from Xiri, though it was evident that Sirvak could not abide her being here. Dru knew that not trusting outsiders was part of the creature's training, but it should have been able to make the distinction between those like Melenea and one who was so obviously the master's companion.

"I'm still waiting."

"Answer your master, familiar," the elf urged, still wearing the smile.

"The Mistressss Sharissa, masterrr. It was by her doing that this one"—it indicated Rendel—"gained entrance here."

"What killed him? Was it my experiment?"

Sirvak's eyes were narrow slits that followed each movement Xiri made. "Yessss. It was the experiment."

Dru had been afraid of that. He had no doubt that the trap had been set for him, which meant that Melenea had been here at least once before. Had Sharissa let her inside? He recalled his own commands to the familiar, the ones that had made it virtually impossible for the winged creature to tell his daughter anything about Dru's time with the enchantress. Once again, the fault was his. Sirvak had only done the best it could under the circumstances.

"Where is Sharissa?"

"Sirvak does not know."

"Not know?" He quieted as the injured creature shut its eyes in shame. "I'm sorry, Sirvak. When was the last time you saw her?"

The familiar opened its brilliant eyes wide. "Mistress was with Tezerenee! Hood-faced one. Like this one."

Dru gave Rendel's body a glimpse and asked, "Gerrod? Do you mean she's with Gerrod?"

"Gerrod, yesss."

"This Gerrod is like his brother?" Xiri asked.

"Like Rendel, yes, but I didn't think he was quite so bad." He studied Sirvak's wounds. The familiar had fought wyverns before, but none had caused such damage. A larger beast, like Cabal, would have been more of a threat. Something did not sit right. "You've no idea what happened to them."

"No, masterrr." Sirvak was upset with itself. It kept staring at its lord's companion with loathing. Dru stroked the creature's head, trying to soothe it.

"It's been terribly damaged," the elf said, looking over the ruined limb and the scars. "Perhaps it might be better if you destroyed it and made a new one."

Dru said nothing, but rather stared into Sirvak's eyes. When the gold and black animal closed its eyes again, its body shivering, he leaned close to it and, in a quiet, companionable tone, asked, "Sirvak, will you do something for me?"

"Master?" It looked at him, weariness and pain giving its voice an unsteady pitch.

"I want you to go outside and search. Find Sharissa."

"Masterrr—"

"Do as I say."

Sirvak hesitated. It eyed the elf, then Dru again. Something changed in its manner. It spread its wings and shifted. "I will obey."

"You always know what I want, Sirvak. I trust you do now."

The familiar dipped its head. "Sirvak will not fail you."

Both Dru and Xiri stepped back as the once-magnificent creature flapped its wings and rose with awkward movements into the air.

"Are you certain it can handle this task? It looks nearly dead."

"Things are not always what they appear," was his reply. "Sirvak will do what it must, regardless of the handicaps it now suffers."

"And what do we do in the meantime?" Again, her arm was around his. "What do we do with him?"

She spoke of Rendel. Dru did not bother with the still shape. "The castle will take care of his remains. It, like Sirvak, owes its ultimate loyalty to me."

The downward corners of her mouth revealed her uncertainty concerning the phrasing of his response, but the elf did not say anything more, allowing Dru to bring her along as he suddenly started for the doorway.

"Have I raised any doubts in your mind?" he asked when they were out in the hallway.

"What?" She stumbled as she blurted out the question.

"Have I raised any doubts? Do you still want to remain with a Vraad? One of the unholy race?"

"You're not so evil." Xiri caressed his cheek.

Dru watched the hall ahead of them. "No, there are far worse."

"Melenea."

"And Barakas, for one, though he's been rather tame. I wonder if he has his empire yet or if the Seekers have left his bones to the scavengers. Have you ever seen one of their cities? What is it like?"

They moved through one hallway to another. Ahead of them, Dru knew, lay the theater where Sharissa had created and manipulated her fanciful dancers.

The woman at his side shrugged. "I'd rather not say too much. I didn't care for them."

"Ugly places of iron and stone sprouting out of the earth like sores, if I remember what you said before."

She smiled, not wanting the subject to go on any further. "You see why I don't like to talk about them. Horrible places."

"Yes."

"Where are we going, Dru?"

He sighed and squeezed her hand. "I want to show you another side of me. I want to show you the theater I built for my daughter . . . and my bride."

"Is it much farther?" She let the comment about Dru's mate pass, but he could see that it had touched her in some way.

"Not far. As a matter of fact, here it is *already!*" The theater *had* actually been farther away, but he had decided to risk using sorcery and have the castle realign itself. The sooner this was over, the better.

Dru had desired the chamber to appear to them in its simplest form . . . a soft dirt floor and blank curved walls. In some respects, it resembled a minia-ture version of the room of worlds minus the images covering the walls and ceiling.

"Is there more to it?"

"Much more." He waved his free hand and a marble floor of alternating black and white squares formed. "I can't say why we need a separate chamber to do what could be done anywhere, but Sharissa and I have preferred it this way."

He gestured to the left and the right. A slight tremor shook the room, but his spell still worked. Several figures, some human, some creatures of varying sorts, stood in what appeared to be random placement on the squares.

"Do your people have chess?" He briefly outlined the game.

She nodded, but her eyes were not on him. Rather, the figures themselves fascinated her more. "We have it, but not like this." Xiri started to walk toward one of the closest pieces on the giant board, a wide, armored figure holding a scepter and sporting a sadistic smile. "These playing pieces . . . is there something—"

Dru blinked and the board was now normal size. It rested on a glass table that was accompanied by two soft couches, one for each player.

"Why did you do that?" Xiri snapped. She immediately remembered herself and gave him an apologetic smile.

"You wouldn't like what you saw there. Shall we play a game?"

"A game? Now? When we still have to find Sharissa?"

Joining her, he reached out to run one of his hands in her long hair. "I thought you liked games."

Her face was stone. "You *know!*"

He tightened his grip on her hair. "You forget, Melenea, as much as you claim to understand me, I also understand you."

She laughed. Her form changed without warning and Dru found his hand holding nothing more than illusion. With daring quickness, Melenea took hold of him and kissed him long and hard. Dru finally succeeded in prying her away, his face deepening to a color akin to her hair.

"No, Melenea, not again. I won't be a part of your world. That's behind me."

"If you say so, sweet. Was it that question about those Seekers that told you? I wondered about that when you asked, though I thought you were suspicious before you mentioned them."

"They only verified that you weren't Xiri. You played a poor game. Tiny things that you knew that she couldn't. Rendel and Gerrod being brothers. The worst move yet, you couldn't even control your own personality. I gave you every chance. Sirvak wanted to tell me that it was under your sway. I guessed as much once I knew that you had gained entrance to the castle earlier, but Sirvak was unable to point you out as an imposter." Dru turned from her, nearly daring Melenea to do something, and walked over to the chess set. He fingered one of the pieces, the one that she had tried to study up close. "I sent it away knowing you, wherever you were, wouldn't stop me. Sirvak has suffered too much already and I know you're to blame."

"You know, Dru darling, you were always long-winded." She ran her hands along the contour of her clothing. "There is so much more we could be doing." Her hands stretched out toward him. "So many games to play." Melenea blew him a kiss.

A force like a maddened stallion struck Dru, throwing him over the table and spilling the chess set.

Dru rose and smiled. Melenea took a step back.

"Yes, I know that was supposed to be more than an ill wind. The difference between us, Melenea, is that I can talk while I cast protective spells. You merely talk." He picked up one of the chess pieces that had fallen to the floor. "I'll ask this only once. Do you have Sharissa?"

"Of course!" She folded her arms and looked at him in triumph. He would do nothing to her if it meant Sharissa's life.

Dru shook his head. "That was the wrong answer. I said I know you as well as you know me. If you had my daughter, you'd be more eloquent about it. You'd give me some of the fine points of what you'd planned for her."

Masterrr!

Yes, Sirvak?

Sirvak is yours again! She is Melenea! Beware!

I know that, my friend.

She took Mistress Sharissa to her home! Master Gerrod helped Sirvak to free her, though she fought us, but Sirvak could not get away! Mistress did, though!

Both pleasure and cold hatred colored the spellcaster's next words. *Thank you, Sirvak. Thank you for telling me all of that.*

Sirvak is forgiven? The beast feared that it would be punished for allowing itself to be taken over by the enchantress.

Of course. One more thing. Where is the one who came with me? The el—the female.

She wanders at the edge of home, seeking entrance. Masterrrr, her sorcery is strange.

Let her pass through, Sirvak. Guide her to me. I want her safe.

As you command, masterrr. The winged creature broke the link, its task clear to it.

He favored Melenea with a pleasant smile, satisfied to watch her react the way he had the day on the steps in the Vraad city. His silent conversation with the familiar had lasted all of a breath, perhaps two, at most. "You have nothing left to tempt me with, nothing left to threaten me with. Can you give me one reason why I should tolerate your presence here any longer, Melenea?"

His change had daunted her, but he knew that she was far from beaten. Melenea always had one more ploy, one more move.

She did not disappoint him. "Perhaps these?"

In her hand she held two gleaming crystals.

"Where did you get those?"

The enchantress had regained the upper hand and knew it. Dru had not expected to see the crystals he sought. They had, he supposed, been destroyed when Rendel had sprung her trap. "Dear Shari *gave* them to me, just before the trusting child left me by my lonesome. That was when I left my surprise and also made certain I could reenter your citadel . . . of course, that little mongrel creation of yours helped to a point. I should have known it would be unreliable in the end, however."

"Sirvak is very reliable. Your mistake was not realizing how independent its mind is . . . not like your other self, Cabal."

She allowed the crystals to balance precariously on the tips of her fingers. "Whatever. Well, darling? Have I met with your expectations? Do you want these little baubles? Should I let them fall?"

Her hand twitched and both stones tottered. At the last moment, she curled her fingers inward, restoring balance.

"You know, Dru, the trap was never meant for you. I was certain that faceless whelp, Gerrod, would gain entrance somehow, as tenacious as he is. I thought it would be a delicious trick on him. He's very much like you, you know. Were you ever intimate with the glorious Lady Alcia? It would certainly explain the differences between Gerrod and Reegan."

Dru did not dignify her with a response.

She tilted her head to one side. "No denial? No agreement? No thought at all?"

"Give me those crystals, Melenea." He kept his voice neutral. She would not play him like an emotional puppet.

"Certainly. Here." Melenea turned her hand palm down.

Reflex betrayed him. Hoping he did not have to fight Nimth as well as the enchantress, Dru snared the crystals with a minor spell. The action lowered his guard. It was a minuscule opening, to be sure, but the sorceress knew him as few others did. When she struck, it was more subtle, more emotional. Where an attack on his body would have likely been repulsed with little effort and most of those against the mind turned with even less, her spell touched on the least-defended part of Dru Zeree.

His memories.

"Cordalene!" he whispered. Her name had been *Cordalene*. Though his conscious mind had forgotten his bride's name, the subconscious could not. She had been, to his surprise, so very interested in the same things. What had begun as a casual joining no different from any other had become a drawn affair and then a sealing of bonds. Permanent mates were a scarce commodity among the Vraad, though there had been a few now and then. She was tall, slender, and with deep blue hair that tumbled to the ground, though dust never tarnished its beauty. They were both as other Vraad, still arrogant, still vindictive. Dru had beaten off two challenges by those interested in Cordalene. She had turned them down, but typically, neither had believed she meant what she said.

Cordalene stood before him, waiting for Dru to embrace her. He tried.

She collapsed into dust. Caught in the throes of the spell, he had summoned up a likeness of her, much the way Sharissa had called up the dancers.

Somewhere, Melenea was laughing at his stumbling, laughing at his futile attempt to recapture a cherished memory. Rage burned through the struggling sorcerer and his vision briefly cleared, revealing the mocking form of the enchantress. He tried to reach her.

Dru became lost in a second memory. Sharissa as an infant. The shock of discovering that their continued care for one another now extended toward the child. Most Vraad left the care of their offspring in the hands of their magical servants, golems and such. It might be that was why the hatred between young and old developed.

Sharissa cried and Dru took the infant in his arms. She dissipated into air. Another creation of the theater that his mind vaguely recalled existed in Nimth.

"This is *so* perfect!" Melenea purred from beyond his vision. "A wonderful place to end the game! I thought I would only be able to enjoy the torment on your face, but now I can watch you lose everything all over again!"

His hands almost found her throat. She backed quickly away, and before he could try again, the day of the duel confronted him.

"Serkadion Manee! No, please don't!" He could not stop it. Cordalene met with some nameless female counterpart, a Vraad who was also dead, the loser in another duel only three days after this one.

The combat itself was a swift blur; Dru had not been there to witness it. Despite his struggles, the inevitable conclusion confronted him. What remained of Cordalene was a curled ball unrecognizable as anything human. She had been turned in on herself. Dru remembered how he had secluded himself and Sharissa for months before he went seeking out his wife's killer. His need for vengeance was left unsated.

Then he had turned to Melenea.

"Melenea," he muttered.

She had brought back the memories and made him suffer them anew. The fog, the images—both those in his mind and the ones he had created with his sorcery—were swept away until only one figure remained. One that did not realize its mortality.

"Melenea . . ." His eyes impaled her.

The enchantress finally realized that her victim was no longer trapped in his delusions, but it was too late. There was no longer any means of escape. With his first coherent thought, Dru had sealed this room for the time.

"Melenea," he began for the third time. "You twisted me during a time when I was empty. You never knew me before Cordalene. You never really thought of how much of a Vraad I truly am, no matter how I might deny it now."

Her smile had died. Dru felt her mind tug at forces of Nimth, trying to create a path of freedom.

"You should have never made me relive all of that so realistically. You've reminded me of the danger you'll always be to Sharissa." He shook his head in true sadness, wishing she had not released the Vraad within him. "I can't allow that."

Unable to escape, she struck with another spell. It was less stylish, but very deadly.

Dru deflected it easily, the cold anger that Melenea herself had created fueling his will. He understood, however, that delay would eventually take its toll on him. This had to be finished before that happened.

She struck again and again, her spells taking on all forms and intensities that would have long destroyed any other foe who did not know her so well. When she had exhausted herself to a certain point, he took her and left her without the ability to move or even breathe. She would not die; the spell prevented that. He only wanted her to know exactly how helpless she would be.

"You like games, Melenea? I do, but more subtle, more ingenious ones. Chess, for example. I have just the place for you, a place where you can join some of my past adversaries, some of those who threatened what was mine and discovered that I am not so peaceful when it comes to defending my home."

He retrieved the chess piece again, tossing it to her as she stood frozen. At the last moment, he released her. Through sheer luck, the enchantress caught the object. She looked at it, not understanding, and then gazed once more at Dru, still defiant. She had always been able to play her way out of any circumstance. There had always been some weakness she had been able to exploit.

"Not this time," Dru whispered to her. He indicated the piece she held. "You thought you recognized the other. How about this one?"

An arrogant smile playing on her lips, Melenea held it up and stared at the tiny, detailed visage. Her eyes widened and the smile became a circle as she gasped. The chessman fell from her hand and bounced on the floor.

"You do recognize him? Some of them I allow to have the same form, though others often get a shape more representative of their personalities.

They'll live on long after I'm gone, always pawns where they were once players, much like yourself."

"Dru . . . you . . ." She was no longer desirable. Melenea had become a frightened creature.

He felt Sirvak's nearing presence. Xiri was with the familiar. Sirvak tried to make contact with him, but Dru refused. Not until he had finished.

"I should think this would thrill you, Melenea, my *sweet*. Haven't you always insisted that life is a game?"

Xiri could not be allowed to see him like this. Dru gestured quickly and the chess set re-formed on the glass table, the pieces all lined up in their starting positions. For the first time, it became obvious that the game was lacking one more figure. Dru smiled at that. He had not known he had been so close to completing the set.

Only a moment more. That was all he needed. A moment more of complete control of his powers. He faced Melenea, lover and nemesis, and pointed at the empty square.

"Your choice," he said slowly, drawing out her agony as she had drawn out his moments before. "What would you like to be?"

WHEN SIRVAK AND Xiri joined him, he had just finished admiring the board and was now putting it away. The chess set was one of the few things he had decided to bring with him to the other world. It would serve better than anything else to remind him of what he was leaving behind.

"Dru!" The elf held him tight, her body shaking. He stood frozen for the first few seconds, then clutched her with equal need.

"Do elves take on permanent mates?" he whispered after he had kissed the top of her head.

"They do." She pulled his head down so that he could kiss something other than her hair. When at last they broke, she looked around. "Sirvak spoke of danger, of this Melenea! What happened to her? Did you—?"

"I've introduced her to a new game. It will keep her attention for quite a long time." He carefully ignored her questioning expression and looked up at Sirvak, who eyed him with an understanding that no other, not even Xiri and Sharissa, could ever match.

"Masterrrr," the familiar finally dared. "The mistressss is nearr. Master Gerrod is with herr."

Master Gerrod?

Low, rolling thunder shook the walls of the pearl edifice.

"The storm is finally breaking." Deadly news for the Vraad race. They would have to risk the storm if they wanted to leave here. Still holding Xiri, Dru opened his hand and studied the crystals he had retrieved from the floor. They were, he knew, useless now. Melenea had apparently drained them of their contents. She was beyond asking questions and so whatever knowledge his former lover had possessed was now beyond them. Rendel might have aided them, what with his vast knowledge of the two realms, but his haste had made an end of him, unless . . .

He separated himself from Xiri. "Sirvak! Show me where Sharissa and Gerrod are."

An image of the two on the outskirts of his domain flashed before him. Still caught up in the aftermath of his fury, it would have been a minor task to bring them to him. Yet, knowing how much worse he and Melenea had probably made the situation already, he turned to Xiri.

"Guide me." The urge to demand more from Nimth was hard to suppress. "I want to bring them here."

His emotion and her care brought swift results. Gerrod, openmouthed, stared at the sorcerer and his companions. His eyes were shrouded by his hood, but it was very likely that they were almost as wide as his mouth. As for Sharissa, she took one moment to drink in her surroundings, focused on her father, and then ran to him, enveloping him in her arms.

"Father! I thought that you were dead! Melenea! Did you know that she—"

He covered her mouth with one hand. "Hush, Sharissa. We'll have time later. I'm sorry, but right now I need to speak to your friend."

"Me?" Gerrod's mouth, the only part of his face clear enough to judge, twisted in a guilty curve, though Dru had not accused him of anything and had never even intended on doing so. He made a mental note to ask the Tezerenee what there was to feel guilty for, but after they had dealt with the present crisis.

"You, Gerrod." He walked over to the motionless figure and put a companionable arm around the younger Vraad's shoulder. "We have to talk about things . . . like your brother, the shrouded realm, and why you are still here. Most important, we have to talk about getting out of here."

"Out of here? You mean—"

"Yes, I think you have information, or know where to get it, that I . . . that *all* of us are in need of." Dru paused and turned back to the others. "Sharissa. Xiri. Forgive my brusqueness. I think you can both understand. Talk to each other. I want you to know each other as much as possible."

The two women eyed each other in open curiosity.

"Sirvak!"

"Master?"

"Your wounds. Are they—"

"I will take care of them, Dru," Xiri volunteered. She looked at Sharissa. "With your help, if that is all right."

"Of course."

Dru gave Xiri a nod of approval. She was already working to make her relationship with his daughter a pleasant one. "Good. When you are healed, Sirvak, I have a task for you." He reached into a hidden pocket and removed something. "Here!"

The familiar sat back on its hind legs and caught the object with its remaining forepaw. It peered at the tiny figurine.

"What is it?" Sharissa leaned closer. Her face screwed up into a look of absolute disgust. "It looks like Cabal! Too much, in fact!"

Xiri had also studied it. Her eyes flickered to Dru, who saw that the elf observed more than surface details. "A work of art. It almost looks alive."

"Part of my chess set. The piece that was missing. I want Sirvak to gather the pieces together. I intend on taking it with me."

"But you never play with it!" Sharissa protested.

"It has memories I want to keep," he commented, already turning back to Gerrod. "Now, Tezerenee. We have to speak about your brother."

Their eyes on Dru's retreating figure, neither Sharissa nor the elf noted the pleased look in Sirvak's inhuman visage as the familiar dropped the tiny chess piece to the floor and watched it bounce until it lay among the rest.

XXI

THE SUN ROSE above Lord Barakas Tezerenee's Dragonrealm and the patriarch could only look at the burning sphere with bitter hatred.

The clan had barely survived. Nearly half were dead or dying, and another third were injured. Night, even with the aid of the two moons, had not been able to reveal the true cost to the Tezerenee.

Tezerenee tactics, he pondered as the light of the sun glittered off the armored corpses of his people. *They knew Tezerenee tactics.*

Rendel. It could only be Rendel. Among the missing, only he would have been so willing to part with the knowledge. Gerrod was, of course, lost in Nimth; he could not have been the source, regardless. Ephraim and his band, who had been the cause of the cross-over disaster, had come to mind, but this smelled too much of Rendel. Besides, Gerrod's description of the mad state of Ephraim was enough to convince Barakas that this world had claimed its first Tezerenee blood long before this battle. That left only Rendel among the living, but not if the patriarch was ever able to lay his hands upon him. The execution would be a slow, deliberate one.

"Father!" Lochivan, still garbed for battle (though the bird creatures had apparently abandoned the war with the coming of light), knelt by the patriarch's feet.

"How many, Lochivan?"

"Forty-two. Three more will die."

Not quite as terrible as he had thought, Barakas decided in sour humor. They still numbered over sixty. Not much for a conquering army, especially since he could not field all of those still functioning. It would do. They had survived the night of death from above and come out of it with the knowledge that for all their numbers, the avians had suffered worse casualties. More than twice their own number had perished. It was unfortunate that the Vraad were so outnumbered. Attrition was the one factor he could not compensate for.

If only our magic had worked. . . . The avians had used their talismans to good effect, mostly because the clan of the dragon had lacked reliable countermagic. Only when they summoned their strongest emotions were the Tezerenee able to trust that their spells would function as they should. Last night had been no exception. This world allowed the sorcery of Nimth to work, but only after a struggle.

We survived. We will prevail. The words, for the first time, sounded hollow even to the patriarch. *Would* they survive another assault in the night? How could they live if their days and nights were spent in constant struggle? He had no doubt that the clan had but a day to rest and repair. Had he been master of the bird people, Barakas would have divided his forces, created for himself two armies— one of the night and one of the day. Harass the foe so that they were never able to recover. Cut the weakest from the ranks until there was no one left to cut.

The Lord Tezerenee knew that the thing to do was abandon this place and find safety until he had the strength to return, but there was no place to go. The avians controlled this land, save for remnants of some other monstrous civilization. The elves survived because they respected the birds and caused no trouble. Under no stretch of the imagination could Barakas see the clan bowing to horrors like those who ruled here. He knew that the avians thought the same way. Permitting the Vraad race to establish itself would mean the end of their reign.

So this is how the Vraad race ends, he concluded, staring in the direction of the mountains where his enemies regrouped. *A last stand that will still leave its mark on those feathered misfits. They will not forget the dragon banner. It will haunt them for generations to come.*

The thought gave him morbid satisfaction, as if now the deaths would be worth it. Still, he could not help thinking that if their sorcery was more reliable or their numbers greater . . .

His eyes closed as something teased his senses. It was only a ripple, but there had been a disturbance in the nature of the Dragonrealm, as if it was no longer whole. A familiar feel, perhaps taste, had been his to savor in that brief moment. He recognized it as Nimth.

"Lochivan." His son, still kneeling, rose at the sound of his name. Reegan might be the heir apparent, but it was Lochivan to whom Barakas entrusted most of the tasks that he wanted completed. "Lochivan. Did you sense something to the east? Something of Nimth?"

"Sire, I felt some presence and it may have been as you say, but I could not swear to it."

"Spoken well. Could you find it?"

"I think it might be possible. What is it, Father?"

Barakas stroked his beard. He gazed thoughtfully at things only existing in his mind. "From bitter Nimth, it could be either our salvation or our death."

Recalling those left behind, Lochivan said nothing.

"Find out, but be wary. It may be that the avians' threat has become secondary. Go now!" The Lord Tezerenee chuckled to himself as his son departed to comply with his commands. The irony of what might be out there was not lost on the patriarch. It was possible that he had achieved what he had always dreamed of, uniting the Vraad race, making it one vast force with a common goal.

"How unfortunate," he finally muttered.

NIMTH RAGED, SHRIEKING its disapproval with thunder and accenting its fury with lightning. Whirlwinds spawned and died. The land shifted and shaped itself. A haze was slowly spreading, one that did not bode well. A few adventurous spellcasters had gone out to study it, the Vraad's belief in their individual immortality still dominant at the time. That belief, like so much else on Nimth, began to erode when it became evident that the explorers would not be returning.

Dru's domain gave the thousands some protection, but the storm was all around them, spreading the poisoned magic everywhere. The castle no longer obeyed commands without hesitation. One sorceress had already been lost, crushed between two walls that had closed on her with surprising speed. After that, no one *else* demanded the right to create for themselves private chambers. The Vraad had become, against their preferences, a socializing people. It was now the only way they felt secure while they waited their opportunity to cross to their new home.

From the top of the tallest tower, the lord of the domain and a figure nearly buried within a massive cloak watched over the proceedings. Just beyond the edges of the Zeree domain, the shrouded realm already intruded. It was a bit of a shock to both men. Their calculations had said the way would open again and it had. What they had not predicted was that it would spread to encompass a region twice as great as the castle of pearl. Dru wondered if the founders had had a hand in the stunning development.

"Dragon's blood!" the half-seen Gerrod muttered as he watched the latest band vanish. "This is unnerving!"

Dru agreed. His experience with the ghost lands had been from the inside. Seeing the change from without made him appreciate Sharissa's shock all the more. The group of Vraad riding through the phantom field had started out much the way he had, a living being surrounded by specters of another world. Solid flesh mingling with translucent unreality.

That was the way it began. The deeper and deeper they rode, the less distinct was the difference. Midway to the forest, the riders grew faded around the edges, as if the vision of those observing was failing them. Yet, it was not their vision, but those they watched who were lacking. By the time half the remaining distance was covered, the ruined landscape of Nimth was visible through the backs of the riders as nearly as much as it was through the forest and the field.

When the refugees entered the forest, they were already part of the other world.

"They're across," Gerrod said. He mentioned it every time, possibly because he still worried that the cross-over would fail before he had departed Nimth. The hooded Tezerenee had shocked Dru with his knowledge of the shrouded realm and its intrusion upon Nimth, not to mention the horrors racking the Vraad birthplace. Gerrod had not only looked over many of his brother's notes, but he had discussed Dru's work with Sharissa over their long trek to the Zeree domain. That, coupled with his own research, made him as capable as Dru in many things.

The Tezerenee was still nervous around his father's former ally. He had explained his fears, had explained why Sharissa had not received Dru's summoning, and, despite the assurances he had received in turn, still expected the elder Zeree to turn on him.

With the danger of misdirected sorcery, which they had experienced in the lands of Melenea, they had chosen to use it as little as possible. Food had been the one necessary use. The duo had walked most of the way, limiting teleportation and flight to those areas most stable.

Exhausted by their ordeal, they had finally dared to rest for a time. Sharissa had suffered most since her life had been more sheltered than his. Gerrod allowed her to sleep while he merely rested. It was during that time that Dru had reached out to the Vraad, telling them of Rendel.

"It was that which frightened me, Master Zeree," the young Tezerenee had said, his face buried deep in the folds of his hood. "I had aided your daughter, but being a Vraad, would you have seen that as sufficient cause to spare me if you, like the rest, were hunting the dragon lord's children?"

In the end, Gerrod had known he would have to face Dru, if only because the other sorcerer was the only one who knew some path out. Alone, he could never begin anew the recreation of the Tezerenee method. He had not been all that certain he wanted to, either. It had always left him feeling disturbed, as if the final fusion of Vraad mind with dragon-forged host bodies would be some monstrous hybrid.

"How many are across, now?" Gerrod asked, returning Dru to the present. "How much longer?"

"A third are through, maybe a little more." The immigrating Vraad were crossing in groups of about one hundred, an unmentioned but symbolic reference to the founders that he had decided on. The bands, bringing only what their animals and themselves could carry, were entering the border region as soon as those before them had vanished into the woods. It kept the pace consistent enough to prevent a mad rush by those still waiting. "A good thing we have never numbered more than several thousand. This would have never worked otherwise."

"Will it be the same over there?"

"I doubt it." Gerrod seemed to want more of an answer, but Dru had none. There were too many question marks.

"What *did* happen to Melenea?"

He had tried to put that behind him, but the younger Vraad would not let him. This was the third time he had skirted around the fate of the enchantress, possibly because he could not believe she was gone. Dru could understand that; even now, he sometimes felt as if her eyes were on him. "Are you afraid you might join her?"

His companion swallowed. Dru had meant it as a joke, but Gerrod was still nervous about his own fate. "No! No," the other replied quickly. "It's just that . . . that . . ." He looked directly at Dru, who tried his best to perceive eyes somewhere within the hood. "It's just that I still feel as if she's left some last treat for us. The way she left the one that killed Rendel."

Gerrod had taken his brother's death with little remorse. It was disconcerting, however, to note that the Tezerenee had felt the same as he had about the enchantress. What was there about Melenea that she could still haunt them after Dru had meted out justice to her?

Below, a commotion attracted their attention. A rider was approaching, one who had *returned* from the other realm and raced to the citadel as if a horde were closing in behind him.

"Tiel Bokalee," Gerrod said. "He is one of Silesti's new dogs." Silesti wanted to make an example of the young Tezerenee now that Rendel was beyond him. He had only grudgingly allowed that the hooded Vraad was nothing like his clan and had been as summarily abandoned by the patriarch as the rest.

The newcomer, an unremarkable example of Vraad perfection, was dismounting when the two of them arrived in the courtyard. His hand twitched as if something had bitten him. The latest of the storm's minor assaults; everyone in the courtyard had been struck with pains of varying degree that came and went without warning. It was perhaps not so minor an assault. One Vraad was comatose; the searing pain in his head having ravaged his brain. No one assumed he would recover, but Dru intended on bringing him anyway.

"Dru Zeree." Tiel Bokalee acknowledged him with a bow. Gerrod received a dark glance, but nothing more. "We have a visitor. One of the dragon clan."

Gerrod turned away even though it would have been impossible to read his emotions if he had not.

Dru considered the rampant possibilities before responding. This was not the time to begin a war with the Tezerenee. "And what has Silesti done?"

"He insists this is your task to perform. Your decision will be his decision." The choice did not sit well with the messenger.

"That means you need to cross-over." Gerrod's voice wavered. "They're my cursed kin. I'll go with you, make certain they haven't something else in mind."

The unspoken reason was that he, like Rendel, did not care for the idea of separating from the one person who preserved his existence. A Tezerenee was a Tezerenee to the other Vraad.

"There will be no one to watch this end."

"Sharissa can do it. The familiar will guide her and that—your elfin friend—will be here to aid her, also." Gerrod indicated the next group of Vraad, who were already departing. "It works on its own now that they understand cooperation. She won't have much to do. The bulk of the storm is still beyond us," he added, jerking in sharp, sudden pain. "*Thankfully.* We should be back before it reaches your land. We should be *finished* here before it grows too wild."

Dru's hands stung. "Then let's be done with it. Give me but a moment to contact my daughter."

"I'll retrieve a pair of mounts."

He nodded absently, his mind already reaching out. *Sharissa?*

Father?

Gerrod and I must be gone to the other side. The Tezerenee have arrived. I want you to watch things while I am gone. Xiri and Sirvak will aid you. I'm certain.

Her fear was evident, but she held it in check. *I understand. It won't be anything terrible?*

I don't think either side can afford a battle. If the Tezerenee have sent someone, it means they want to talk. Barakas would not talk if he held the advantage.

Good luck, then.

I leave it to you to tell Xiri and Sirvak. Watch the storm. What we've experienced is no more than a prelude. The worst is still coming. If it looks as if it will roll over the area before everyone is through . . . He held back for a breath, wondering what she would do if it depended on her. Even he would have been hard-pressed to come up with a solution. At last, he simply finished, *Send them all through, but not in a rout. A rush will kill more than the storm will.*

You'll be back before that, won't you?

I should be. He broke contact, hoping his own emotions had not influenced her. It was not possible to maintain complete confidence in the face of the storm and no contact whatsoever with the guardians, whom he had expected to see long before this. Were they waiting to see if the Vraad had enough sense to complete the task themselves? There was so much that made so little sense where the guardians and their enigmatic masters were concerned.

"Get down, damn you!"

Tiel Bokalee's steed, a black animal that reminded Dru of the missing Dark-horse—would the creature from the Void ever find his way back?—in both form and temperament, reared and kicked at the ground. Bokalee managed to bring the horse under control, cursing because he had to risk himself physically rather than simply use his sorcery. Any excess use strengthened the growing assaults of the storm, something no one wanted.

A tiny figure scurried over Dru's feet. He started to look down, but agony ripped his knees and he ended up half sprawled on the courtyard floor. Rats or magical imps became secondary to merely surviving the pain.

It turned out to be a mercifully short attack with no aftereffects save an uncontrollable fear that standing would bring about a relapse. Gerrod had just been returning with a pair of mounts, but he let them wander loose as he rushed to Dru's side.

"Are you all right? What happened? I heard a horse shrieking. . . ."

"He was spooked. Something tiny, but probably spawned by the storm, like my pain." Dru recalled the chaos of Melenea's citadel and realized that there must be less time than he had calculated earlier. "Forget it. Let's move on."

With Bokalee leading them, they departed the citadel grounds and, before long, entered the shadowy ghost lands.

I will not fear this, Dru repeated to himself over and over again. He could not forget his first encounter and the chaos that had precipitated. They had no idea if the path through would remain open indefinitely. He had been told that the intrusions had been instigated by the mind of the land, the thing that had once been the individuals of the founding race, but not once had the guardian really said that they still controlled it. The one had even admitted that they did not understand the faceless incarnations of their lords. If it was the whim of the masters to further test their potential successors, then Dru would not put it past them to seal off Nimth at any moment and see if those trapped within were intelligent enough to find another solution. He had a nagging suspicion that the founders had not been *that* different from the Vraad.

The sun gleamed bright, nearly blinding him with its abrupt appearance. Dru blinked and looked around. They had already crossed. He had been so entangled in his fears that he had missed the entire trek. It was a loss he could live with, the sorcerer decided.

Vraad were everywhere. It was the first thing Dru noticed. It was the first thing *anyone* would have noticed. The woods and the fields were filled with men and women who stood or sat or walked about. The one thing they shared in common was an aura of disbelief, disbelief that the sky was blue and the wind was only a gentle whisper. No one thought to build themselves vast fortresses—unless they had tried and failed already—and it seemed as if no one had even broken away and departed to find their own destiny. If anything, the Vraad were even more interested in the company of one another than they had back in Dru's domicile. There, it had been forced; here, it was done out of an increasing insecurity. So used to being the masters of all they surveyed, the spellcaster's people were having trouble coming to terms with a new and very defiant land.

The lone Tezerenee stood away from the rest, visibly nervous. He wore one of the face-concealing helms, but Gerrod had evidently recognized him, for he raised a hand and shouted out the other's name. "Lochivan!"

"Gerrod?" The armored figure relaxed a bit, likely thinking that if one of his own could ride among the outsiders, then *his* life was not in danger.

Silesti stood nearby, close enough so that the Tezerenee knew he was there because of him and far enough away so that the dragon warrior knew better than to try to deal with him. The somber Vraad greeted Dru but said nothing more, emphasizing with his silence that he would listen but not take part. The hour belonged to Dru.

Dismounting, the master mage and Gerrod met with Lochivan.

"How is dear father?" the faceless warlock asked his brother, the sarcasm in his tone deep and biting.

Within the narrow slits of his helm, Lochivan's eyes closed in weariness. "Insane with anger, or perhaps just insane. We were betrayed, Gerrod, betrayed by Rendel to a race of bird creatures!"

"How appropriate! Familial betrayals seem the norm with the clan of the dragon!"

Dru silenced his companion with a curt wave of one hand. "You said 'bird creatures'? Manlike?"

"Very. They used Tezerenee tactics and Father believed it must be Rendel . . ."

"Well, you needn't worry about punishing him for his crimes," Gerrod broke in. "Rendel is very, very dead."

Lochivan would have asked for details, but Dru did not have the patience. "We don't have the time for this! Why did Barakas send you?"

The other Tezerenee looked uncomfortable again, but for different reasons now. "He did not . . . not exactly. He . . . he sent me to find out what was happening here and whether we faced annihilation from our own kind as well as the birds. I . . . when I saw what was happening, I dared to make myself known." He gave Silesti a surreptitious glance. "*He* met with me and said that if I valued my existence, word would be sent to the true benefactor of the Vraad, meaning *you*, I suppose, who would decide my fate."

Dru turned and met Silesti's gaze. The other grimaced, already reading his decision. Dru avoided Gerrod altogether and studied Lochivan, trying to find the man, not the Tezerenee.

"What did you come here for?"

Lochivan revealed a brief smile. There had still been a few doubts. Not now. He knew this outsider would listen. The clan might still survive. "Help us. Help us to push back the avians and claim the land. You *have* to do it. This is your home, too. You need our skills; we need your numbers."

"Is this your offer or your father's?"

"Mine, of course."

Gerrod snorted, but did not otherwise interrupt.

"Your offer," Dru mused, taken by the Tezerenee persistence. "Your offer and any your father might have are rejected. We won't save this world for you."

Silesti was smiling now. Both Tezerenee were confused. Dru indicated the masses idle around them. "Do you think that even I could make them fight for the Tezerenee? Do you think they want to fight at all? Does it look as if they do?"

"We will *all* perish if we remain divided!"

"This is a new . . . no . . . this is the *true* world. It has laws of its own. Have you cast spells? Has your sorcery worked true? I can see by your eyes that it hasn't."

"Our numbers—"

"Will be insufficient. Most of this continent is controlled by the Seekers." Dru's use of the name raised eyebrows, but no one cut him off. "You've fought only one group. Even combined, we don't yet have the power to face them down. Our day will come, though, if it's meant to."

"We have to survive until then!" Lochivan protested, looking to his brother for support.

Gerrod shrugged, but tried. "I think he would be open to suggestions, Master Zeree. Anything to save the clan."

"If I knew what to do, I would suggest it. I'm still concerned about those I've helped to cross. If our survival can include the Tezerenee, I have no objections." *Too many ifs*, Dru thought. *If the guardians would help them this one time, it would be all he could ask.*

For you, it will be permitted, a familiar voice within his head suddenly replied. *For you and your efforts, not for such as those.*

Dru looked around. The other Vraad stood motionless, all of them watching him. They had also heard the voice, but knew that it had been directed at only one of them.

Why now? Why after I've had to do so much have you returned?

A sensation of worry and lack of direction touched him. The guardian was no longer certain of its place in the world. *Those who have returned speak less and less with us. Their purpose is much like that which we were created to serve, but they move in ways that we do not understand and, at times, have not cared for. They are our masters and something else. We do not know whether to obey them or not. At least one among us has broken away and others have suggested withdrawing from this plane and waiting to see what it is the faceless ones have planned.*

Did your . . . did the faceless ones send you here?

This is my doing. It breaks the old laws set upon us and when I have aided you I will depart with the rest. You, I felt, were owed something. You are the potential they must see in your race. That much still remains the same from those first days when the founders sought to raise their successors. Therefore, ultimately, I perform my duties.

What will you do? Dru had difficulty believing anything would turn the patriarch from his dreams of conquest.

I have seen in your mind this Lord Barakas of the Tezerenee. He might protest your decision, but he will not protest that of his god.

Is that what you are now? came the second voice from nowhere. *Is this how you perform your duties for them? Godhood does sound much more our forte.*

The Vraad around Dru stood petrified, listening to a potential argument between entities they could not see or sense, only hear in their minds. As for the master mage, his own imagination allowed him to form images where there were none. He could see the dragon facing off against the wolf, one that, unfortunately, looked too much like Cabal.

This is my doing, the mock dragon informed its counterpart.

I am only here to support you, the wolf said slyly. *This is the very thing I desired . . . to be master, not servant.*

I still serve in my way! This is for the completion of the original task set upon us when we still had masters we knew!

My desire, also. Their *desire, too, if you will permit.*

Though Dru could not sense them, he knew that the other guardians had joined the first two.

All of you are agreed, then? the dragon asked in tentative tones. *What was suggested once will be done?*

"Dru, what is happening?" Silesti shouted. Everywhere, Vraad were standing and staring into the sky as if that would allow them to see the creatures deciding their fate. They had thought they had come to their new homeland, only to wonder now if they had merely postponed their destruction.

"Be quiet, fool!" Gerrod returned, yet he, too, looked to his companion for answers.

While the Vraad had been talking, the other guardians gathered here had given their assent to whatever plan had been put forth. Dru could understand no other part of what was going on save that there had been a full revolt against the creatures who had once been the unquestioning masters.

Not a revolt, manling, though some would like to believe it so, said the guardian who favored Dru.

The darker one stirred, but it did not respond to its opposite.

The mock dragon continued. *Your people must make one last journey to a place where they can grow in strength and mind. Once you have been placed there, we will leave you be. It is not right that we interfere.*

Except when necessary, the wolf whispered in Dru's mind. *Only when necessary.* It sounded too much like Melenea in tone and personality. He wondered whether it was touching upon his own memories, forming for itself a personality. Only those guardians who had actually spoken with him seemed to radiate any image of self. The rest were like ants, identical in feeling and response despite earlier claims of individuality.

The guardians had made their decision. He would have to return to Nimth immediately and inform those still there, but if—

They know, his guardian interrupted. *All Vraad save the Tezerenee now know. Such was how it was decided.*

"What do you even need us for?" he shot back, unable to keep the helplessness and the bitterness from his voice. Why had he struggled so hard just for this?

Because if you had not, we would have chosen not to interfere and the Vraad race would have died out, a failure for the second and final time.

Founder law, the wolf chuckled.

"You'll need me for the Tezerenee," Dru suggested out loud, so that all could hear. "Barakas will trust me more than anyone else here, even his kin. He'll know that the Tezerenee can rejoin the Vraad race without fear of reprisal." *Hopefully,* he added to himself.

It may be that the guardians had caught the last, for the mock dragon's tone lightened a bit. *It could not be done without you . . . and this one as well.*

Gerrod stirred and what little of his face was visible was pale with fright. "Me?"

You, came the very final reply.

With that, the world blinked, sending Dru, who had almost expected this, and Gerrod, who had not, to a place of carnage . . . where they found themselves standing before the startled yet fearsome gaze of the Lord Barakas Tezerenee.

XXII

"Dru Zeree. Gerrod. I hardly thought to see either of you again."

"Yes, it's a pity, isn't it, Father?" the patriarch's son retorted.

"You'd do better than to speak that way to me."

Dru ignored the exchange, surveying the carnage that the surviving clan members had still not succeeded in clearing. Bodies dotted the area, both Vraad and Seeker. Not surprising, the Tezerenee had taken their toll on the attackers. They would not survive a second major assault, however, not as reduced in numbers as they were.

"Lochivan came to you, didn't he, Zeree?" the Lord Tezerenee asked, his eyes burning as he noted Dru's interest in his losses. "He has lost his nerve."

"He's regained his sanity, O conqueror father!"

"Gerrod, be quiet." Dru wondered why the guardian had chosen to include the hooded Vraad in the confrontation. For that matter, there was no sign of the guardian itself. He could sense its presence, but it had not yet made itself known to Barakas. Why?

The younger Tezerenee quieted. His father glared at the two, as if actually wondering why they had come. Having silenced, for the time being, the argument, the robed sorcerer chose to press on. "We've crossed, Barakas."

"Obviously." Several armored figures, now aware of the newcomers, had been drifting toward the trio. More than one pointed at Gerrod. Dru began to understand why the shrouded Vraad was with him. Gerrod was one of them, but had been abandoned back in Nimth. Now, he stood in their midst, facing his father. He served as a beacon, something they recognized from a distance that they knew should not be here.

"Not like you," Dru continued. "We found a true path, one that allowed us to cross physically. More are coming. The entire Vraad race will soon be across."

The patriarch's face was as pale as bone. "You have my congratulations and my growing impatience. Why don't you tell me why you're truly here? Terms for surrender? Is that what you want? Do you think we will turn our lives over to those who would love nothing less than our living hides stretched across racks where they could inflict us with whatever tortures suited their desires?"

As horrifying as the image might be, Dru could not deny that there were those who would have gladly done exactly as the patriarch had said. Yet he also knew that the Vraad were capable of other things.

"Let the past fade with Nimth, Tezerenee! The time has come for the Vraad race to meld itself into a people, not a vast collection of spoiled and sadistic individuals."

Dragon warriors, female and male, now surrounded them completely. Barakas glared at them, but did not order them back to their grisly tasks. "We need nothing. The clan will survive!"

"Is *this* survival?" another voice challenged. Heads turned in simultaneous fashion as the Lady Alcia strode into the center of the circle. She was still the warrior woman, beautiful, elegant, and deadly, but there were signs of exhaustion evident in her visage. "How many of the children you purport to love must die? Anrek and Hyria are among the bodies!" Her cool facade began to crumble away before their eyes.

Dru could not place the names and neither, it appeared, could the patriarch. He brushed them aside by turning back to the fate the Tezerenee would supposedly receive at the hands of their cousins. "We might live longer by returning to the fold, outsider, but what is life when pain is all that you offer?"

"I can't promise you that the clan will be accepted without conflict. If I did, I would not blame you for turning away and walking off. I'd do the same."

"Things have changed, Father," Gerrod offered. "Most of the people have changed, though I doubt forgetting will be possible."

"That was *Rendel's* doing! If I could . . ." Barakas clamped his mouth shut, the Lady Alcia's expression warning him of the potential for personal disaster if he carried his anger at his son further.

Dru glanced at Gerrod, who turned his way and shrugged, his shadow features an emotional mystery. Neither of them felt it was the time to discuss Rendel's demise.

"All this talk is nonsense!" Barakas straightened to his full height. His presence was nearly overwhelming. Everyone stepped back or froze save Dru. He had faced the bearlike Vraad before and would do it again. "Nonsense! We will all perish unless we combine! This is a land we must struggle to tame, a land we must take by force from the monstrosities that abound here! There is no other place for us to go!"

Do not tell him of me yet! the guardian's voice suddenly warned Dru, speaking only to him. *Tell him only that there is another place and it can be reached. The time is not yet right! Let him hear all before . . .*

Before what? Running a hand through the silver band of hair he had given himself what seemed a millennium ago, Dru told Barakas, "There is a land beyond the seas in the east. We have a way of reaching there and a way of ensuring that the Seekers—the avians—do not disturb us. There will be land we can tame and time for us to renew our strength. Relearn our sorcerous skills as well. This is a world where different paths must be taken than those that turned Nimth to the rotting shell it now is."

Hopeful gazes and encouraging whispers spread through the Tezerenee and the handful of outsiders who had come with them and survived the attack. Barakas seemed to weigh his words.

His answer will be the same, said the guardian to Dru. *He has set his own path and can find no way to turn from it without his pride and mastery suffering.* There was some hint of surprise in the guardian's tone. *He would rather they all die here, futilely battling to the end. It is a thing I have watched all too often. It is one of the reasons so many hopes failed over the endless aeons.*

What can we do?

Stall a few moments more, that is all. He will have his excuse to accept your terms.

What does that mean? the sorcerer asked. Dru received only silence as an answer. A chill ran through him. The guardian was planning a show of strength, so to speak, something more than his eruptive appearance from the earth. *That* should have been enough by itself. Certainly, it had impressed Dru. Yet he recalled that once he had known the wolf would not attack, he had lost much of his fear and wonder. This guardian planned a lesson of some kind, then . . . but what?

"You have betrayed your position, Zeree," the patriarch said, suddenly drawing strength from somewhere. The mood of his people sank as his own rose. They were so used to being controlled that no one even spoke out, even though it was their own future, their own lives, that were at risk. "The Vraad have always subsisted on their magic. All Vraad save the *Tezerenee!*" Barakas looked triumphant. "Even in a land without danger of foe, you would be unable to survive. None of you know how to exist long without the aid of sorcery! Sickness, hunger, accidents, weather . . . all factors that you do *not* understand! If anything, *you* need us! You need our knowledge, our skills at survival! It might be better asked that instead of we joining you, you join us!"

"Astounding!" Gerrod muttered. "Lochivan had the same arrogant offer! In the face of so much death, you can still be so damned demanding!"

Be ready! came the alert from the guardian. It would say nothing more of what it planned.

The air was filled with the now much too familiar sounds of great wings beating.

"They're back!" one of the Tezerenee shouted. His voice did not sound eager or determined, but rather almost terrified. For all their battles in Nimth, they had never faced a true foe in so great numbers.

"Barakas—" Dru started.

"This is the time to fight, not flap your mouth, Zeree! You'll find escape by teleportation impossible; they have some way of countering it with their blasted medallions!"

The Tezerenee were already doing their best to organize for battle. Two flying drakes were brought up. Weapons of every sort materialized in hands. Archers were already positioning themselves. A few confident souls were doing their best to work themselves into a will strong enough to cast competent spells.

Lady Alcia remained behind as her husband ran off to direct his people. "Master Zeree, if you have anything that will aid us, as you seem to indicate, this is the time! If not, you will surely die with us!"

Gerrod whirled on Dru. "What has that blasted bit of living magic put us into? Would it not have been sufficient to merely drop us from a great height and see if we can cast a spell before we splatter on the ground?"

"Just wait." It was easy to tell them to do that, but believing that they had not been abandoned was almost even impossible for Dru to believe now.

Such a pessimistic lot, the welcome voice said. *The time has come for my appearance.*

"What was that?" the Lady Tezerenee asked in shock, turning in a vain effort to see something that was not visible. "What is that I sense?"

The Seekers dove from the sky in numbers that boggled even the most hardy of the Vraad. Barakas himself hesitated, visibly overwhelmed. Death had surely come to the Tezerenee. Not even at their best could they hope to fight so many. Aeries from miles had likely added their numbers to the ranks. Seeker tactics did not apparently match those of the humans. The avians intended to destroy the invaders once and for all, not whittle away at their ranks.

The earth erupted. Only Dru knew what was coming. For everyone else, it was as if the world had chosen this particular moment to wipe from its surface

the annoying little creatures that sought to wreak such havoc on it. Even Gerrod, who should have had an inkling, looked to his feet, as if the ground beneath him would be the next to open.

Molten earth and rock from the bowels of Barakas's Dragonrealm—Dru
found that even he had fallen prey to the use of the term since there was no
other—rose in so furious a geyser that, in its initial explosion, it seemed likely
to shower every avian and Vraad in sight.

In the midst of so much chaos, with humans scurrying for cover and Seekers
frantically trying to keep themselves high enough above the danger, Dru found
himself wondering what the land itself thought of this. It was strangely silent
for being so abused. The mind of the land certainly had to know what occurred
and how one of its former servants was breaking the rules that it had once imposed when it had been the individual minds of the founding race.

Perhaps it *did* know. Perhaps the actions of the guardians were not so revo-
lutionary as they *thought*. From what he had seen, the ancients had been master
manipulators.

It was slowly becoming evident to the rest that there was something unique
and unnerving about this searing geyser. None of them had been burned; they
were just realizing that the storm of death had never taken place. Instead, the
vague shape that Dru already recognized was beginning to draw their attention.
Both sides were spellbound by the sight and each knew that the other was not
responsible for this.

A rainbow of colors danced about the nearly complete outline of the great
beast the guardian favored. It nearly made the form of the dragon itself look
mottled, as if it had sprouted from the rainbow.

There will *be no more war.*

It was said with only the barest inflection, as if the speaker were such a
power that this clash was only the least of annoyances. Dru allowed himself a
brief, hidden smile. The guardian had a sense of theatrics, a sense of the greatest moment when it could best deliver its message. He understood why it had
waited; it had known the Seekers would soon strike, perhaps even timed the
encounter with Dru and the others so that they would arrive just a few minutes
before. This drama was not merely being played for the Vraad. The guardian
was assuring that the avians would have no desire to cross the seas again in a
second quest for the secrets of the founders.

As if the last idea had already been transmitted to the Seekers, the avians tried
to retreat, hoping, evidently, to hide in their aeries until the danger was over.

The fiery head of the dragon turned its burning gaze in the direction of a
tall male avian who had to be the leader of the assault. *You know the power I am. I
will be heard or even the aeries will afford no comfort.*

As one, the Seekers froze in the air, hovering as best they could and trying to seem as harmless as doves. More familiar with the potential of what towered before them, the guardian and the artifacts of the cavern smelling of the same sorcery, they knew better than to disobey so direct a command.

It would almost be best if the lands were cleansed of all of you! The peace would be restored. The balance would be maintained.

Vraad and Seekers became allies in fear. There were shouts and squawks, none of which made any sense from where Dru stood.

The mock dragon looked down upon the insignificant humans. *There is little that redeems you, but a bargain has been made to preserve your existences, a bargain made by one who came among you.*

The eyes of several dozen Vraad turned to view Dru with new wonder. Even Barakas studied his former ally with uncertainty . . . and why not? Had he not made the dragon the totem of the clan and emphasized its might so much that over the centuries he had come to believe in his own words?

It is not yet your time here. Perhaps in the future, when you have adapted to the land . . . or it has made you adapt. You will be taken to that place with the rest of your kind.

Several Tezerenee nodded in vigorous fashion, taking the words of the guardian as god-given law. Beside Dru, Gerrod snorted.

"Serves them right to think that thing's their true lord," he whispered with malevolent pleasure.

As to you, the draconian head once more focused on the Seekers. *The future will decide your fate. Return to your aeries and work to make that fate one you will survive. These creatures are not for you, nor are the ways of the ancients. Do with this land. This will be the only warning you receive.*

Knowing that they had been dismissed, the avians fluttered off in a panicked rout. Dru doubted the creatures would learn. They would probably avoid the continent to the east, but changing their ways otherwise was likely too much for even a deity, albeit a false one, to demand.

Let the one marked by silver lead you to your people and your home, the mock dragon uttered, its words taking on an even more imperious tone, *and remember that there are those that watch over this land. You would do well to respect that.*

Barakas, despite his fears, was not set to abandon everything just yet. He dared to stalk toward the blazing form and look up into what passed for its eyes. "Blood has been lost here! Blood of the Tezerenee! It cannot go unavenged! This land is meant to be ours! You said as much! Why wait until later?"

There is a time for everything. Your time is not now. The blood you speak of should tell you that. There is no honor in a wasted death. The guardian then spoke words that were intended for Dru alone. *I fear you will have to watch this one after I and my kind have departed from your lives. Despite my efforts, I think he will not let the years pass in peace.*

I could have told you that, Dru replied.

The Lord Tezerenee had quieted down, brooding over the mock dragon's words. It was clear that the imposing presence before him was having its own effect, words or not. At last he nodded. "Yes. I bow to your wisdom." The huge figure took on an air of humility and knelt. "Praise be to the Dragon of the Depths, who will guide us to our destiny!"

Around him, Dru watched in stunned amazement as the Tezerenee slowly followed the patriarch's lead. The only two figures left standing were the sorcerer himself and Gerrod, who shook his head at his kin's actions.

Dru Zeree, you must bring the two groups together. Can you do so?

I can only try.

The draconian head acknowledged his response by dipping low. *Then, we move on.*

And they did.

One moment, they had been gathered in the site of the Tezerenee's near-last stand. In the next blink of an eye, Dru found himself standing amid the wooded area near the ghostly region leading to and from Nimth. On this side, the jagged landscape of Nimth penetrated the fields and forest, a spectral sore that the master mage hoped to soon never see again.

There were few other Vraad. Silesti and a handful of those he had designated his subordinates stood waiting. Lochivan was with them, looking quite harried. It was clear that they had been awaiting the return of Dru and Gerrod.

Gerrod had materialized a little behind Dru and behind the hooded Tezerenee were his assembled kin. Though they had been kneeling when the sudden transfer had taken place, the clan of the dragon now stood, save those injured too badly, of course. The instant he recognized his situation, Barakas stepped forward to stand beside his former ally.

Silesti noticed them and bristled at the sight of the patriarch. The other Vraad grouped around him. Lochivan stood as motionless as he could, not wanting something unpleasant to develop while he remained so near to the enemy.

It was up to Dru. He cut off both the patriarch and Silesti as each attempted to talk. "No more of this! Vengeance has never done us one bit of good! Silesti, we respect one another, but both of us have been responsible for things as terrible as what the Tezerenee have done! In their position, you might have acted as they did! True?"

He knew he had been correct when Silesti could not answer. Still, it was too soon to congratulate himself. They might yet be at one another's throat. "This is a new world, both of you! This is not Nimth. This world will not let you destroy it without it trying to destroy you beforehand." Dru played his final card, the one that would strike the two warring Vraad at the heart of what they believed in. "Look at the power of the guardians. They move us as easily as we might carry a handful of dirt. The peace is *their* one demand. Which of you is willing to disappoint them . . . and to explain yourself when they come to find out the reason why?"

Silesti's swallow was audible. He had watched time and again as Vraad after Vraad were taken away to the guardians' chosen destination. There was no denying the power of something that swept up groups of the sorcerous race without effort.

Across from him, Barakas, too, was having his second thoughts. As the one sentinel had said, the patriarch was one who would bear watching in the future. Now, however, he looked from Silesti to Dru and then back to where his people lay dead. He had seen how easily the dragon being had dealt with the avians and how simple it had been to take the surviving Tezerenee and displace them. Yet, the dream of conquest was not completely forgotten, not even now.

"I will not offer my friendship," the patriarch finally replied. "But I will offer my cooperation. Silesti, it was never my intention to leave the rest of the Vraad race behind. However, it was the fault of my own blood, so I must take ultimate responsibility."

It was as close to an apology as one might ever hear from the lips of the lord of the dragon clan. Silesti knew that. "I offer my cooperation, too . . . provided Dru Zeree is the final arbiter."

Though he had expected that something such as this would eventually develop, Dru wanted desperately to decline. He had performed more than his share in the name of the Vraad race. All he wanted now was to rest. Yet he knew that an uneasy triumvirate, which was what had apparently formed here, had more chance for stability than a simple alliance between two rivals left unchecked. It would be up to Dru to keep the peace, as he had so many times already.

Barakas was nodding, his eyes having flashed to Dru in time to note the sorcerer's reaction at being chosen for the unwanted position. "Agreed, if Master Dru also agrees."

He had no choice. "I agree."

No one even suggested they shake hands.

Dru exhaled slowly, relieved that this, at least, was over for the moment. There were other matters demanding his attention, matters that had twisted his gut throughout the Tezerenee recovery. "Silesti! My daughter and my . . . my bride. Did they cross safely?"

Silesti shifted his stance, looking more like a child caught at some mischief than a master sorcerer. "No one has emerged since the group that arrived immediately after you. I sent Bokalee back in to see what was the matter." The Vraad looked embarrassed. "He still has not come back."

"Not returned? And you left me unsuspecting?" Dru searched for the first available mount. A winged drake belonging to one of Silesti's new followers was the nearest. Without a word to the others, he raced off toward the animal.

"Master Dru!" Gerrod called. "Wait!"

"Zeree!" bellowed the patriarch.

They were nothing to him at the moment. His success in bringing the Vraad race to the true world and of binding, if not actually healing, the wounds between the Tezerenee and the rest would mean little if Sharissa and Xiri failed to cross before Nimth was sealed off by the guardians.

"Give me that!" he ordered. The stunned rider handed the reins over to him. Dru leaped onto the drake's back and urged the creature upward. It fought for a moment, uncertain as to what this stranger was doing riding it, but Dru's raging will overwhelmed it. Spreading its massive wings, the drake rose swiftly into the heavens.

The trip across was a blur, even more so than the last. Dru stared at the transposed landscapes without seeing them. Visions of Sharissa and Xiri, even of loyal Sirvak, were all he saw. The drake, which had begun to renew its struggles when it had first realized its new rider intended on reentering the ghost lands, flew as swiftly as it could, as much out of fear of the sorcerer as of the unsettling region around them.

Nimth welcomed Dru back with a storm that made his own rage a minuscule thing in comparison.

He had underestimated both the speed and the danger. Whirlwinds were everywhere. Lightning dotted the ground with craters. Dru made out what might have been the scorched remains of one or more Vraad, but he was too high up and the weather too fearsome to take the time to look closer. He only prayed that those he searched for were not among the dead.

The haze that represented the worst of the magical storm had not quite reached the castle, but it was closing fast. If what he had seen so far was only the precursor, Dru knew that no one would survive the maelstrom before it died.

Droplets splattered both rider and drake and the mage's first thought was that it was, against all odds, actually raining. That thought died as his mount roared in agony and Dru discovered that the liquid was burning holes in his clothing.

As he steered the injured animal down to the courtyard, he made out several Vraad trying their best to organize one final cross-over. There had to be several hundred. More than a few would die before the rest made it. He was gratified to see, however, that the remnants were working in as orderly a fashion as possible. They had evidently already suffered the effects of the acidic rain, for most of them resembled nothing more than walking piles of cloth and armor.

How could his estimates have been so off, he wondered. What could have pushed the storm to greater intensity?

Several Vraad spread out as he landed. He handed the shrieking beast to one of those who dared to wait despite the danger. "How long before you leave?"

"A few minutes! No longer!" said the muffled figure.

"My daughter?"

"No one has seen your whelp!"

Dru abandoned both his mount and the helpful Vraad and stumbled inside to the safety of the castle.

"Sharissa! Xiri! Sirvak!"

There was no response. He tried to reach them with his mind. Whether Xiri would respond was questionable since they had never tried to link, but he hoped that one of the others . . .

Masterrr?

Sirvak! Where are you?

In your work chamber. The mistressesss seek to hold back the worst of the storm! Something has upset the balance, Mistresss Sharissssa says!

Let them know I'm coming! he commanded, already moving toward that direction.

They know.

Dru broke the link, the better to think over the situation. What his daughter and Xiri tried to do was a losing cause, but if they could buy everyone a little more time, that would be sufficient. A few minutes for those outside to depart and a few more for the three—four counting Sirvak—to follow.

He was up a short flight of stairs before he realized the stairs should not have been there. The breathless spellcaster looked about. He was heading away from where he had intended on going. The castle's ability to shape itself to the whims of its master had gone beyond the boundaries he had set on it. It was now shifting nearly randomly. There was a chance that he might never reach the chamber where they worked.

Sirvak?

No answer. Something kept the link from forming. Something blocked his mind.

A *huge* something blocked his path. Dru had a momentary vision of teeth, blue-green fur, and eyes that reminded him too much of a lost enchantress before a massive paw struck him on the left side and sent him hurtling against a wall that seemed to form just for the purpose of stopping his flight. The Vraad slid to the floor, his bones vibrating from the shock and his head threatening to split in two. His eyes would not obey his needs and he could barely even make out the closing form of his attacker.

"Where is my *lady*, sweet one?" Cabal asked in a snarling parody of its mistress. "She must see what Cabal has done to please her!"

The massive wolf limped as it moved, one paw having suffered great damage from a bite that seemed just the size of Sirvak's beak.

"Cabal could play with you for long or short time, little one! Tell what you have done with lady and it will be short!"

Dru tried to stall, hoping his mind would clear enough for him to defend himself. "How did you get . . . get in here? Where have you been? We never saw you!"

As the spellcaster had suspected, Melenea's vanity was Cabal's as well. "Lady carried Cabal in her pouch! Let Cabal loose when she entered here and then ordered that havoc must be created!" The endless array of sharp teeth filled Dru's eyes. "Cabal has used own magic to encourage the storm! It obeys Cabal as Cabal obeys Lady Melenea!" That reminded the beast of what it had wanted from the figure sprawled at its feet. "Where *is* the lady?"

Now! Dru thought. *I have to strike now while its mind has turned to her!* He tried to concentrate, but Cabal instantly reached out and batted him with its injured paw. The familiar whined, but had it tried to use its other forepaw, it would have likely fallen forward. Unlike Dru, Melenea had not been concerned with healing her creature. Why bother? She could always summon another.

"*Mistake*, betrayer of lady. You do not answer, you must play with Cabal." The wolf opened its maw wide, intending to take the struggling Vraad by the legs and worry him.

Masterrr! Move!

A winged form darted toward the eyes of the unsuspecting monster. The rejuvenated Sirvak tore at Cabal with its long talons. The larger familiar howled in distress and pain as blood flowed over the top of its muzzle.

"Pain! Eyes!"

Cabal reacted wildly, but Sirvak, intent on giving Dru as much hope as possible, waited a moment too long. The wolf's good paw shot up like a fleet arrow, catching the smaller creature. Cabal brought the paw down with Sirvak beneath it.

Dru had dragged himself to the stairs, but when he saw what was happening, he tried to act. Even now, though, the pain that made his head throb refused to let him concentrate enough to do anything else but shout in vain.

"Sirvak!"

The black and gold familiar had only enough time to squawk once before Cabal crushed it.

"Sirvak, no!" came Sharissa's horrified voice. She stood behind the huge wolf, her face stretched in terror at the death of the one thing she had been able to call a friend during her childhood years.

Trying to turn and seize her, Melenea's legacy slipped. Cabal had tried to stand too long on its injured limb alone, and combined with the imbalance caused by Sirvak's mangled form, the blue-green monster's front half had little sure footing. It slid midway down the staircase, nearly taking Dru with it.

"Where are you?" Cabal cried out as it tried to right itself. "Come and play with Cabal!"

It was blind. Sirvak had done that much. Though it could still scent them, Cabal had no eyes whatsoever.

Sharissa did not care whether it could see or not. Dru looked up and saw both his daughter and Xiri moving to the stairway. Sharissa's visage was cold and deadly. For the first time, she looked like a true Vraad.

To the horror of both her father and the elf, she called to the killer stumbling to its feet on the steps. "I stand above you, Cabal! I am up here! Play with *me!*"

"Sharissa! Get away!" Dru shouted madly. He hoped that at the very least he would turn the wolf's attention to him. His head was nearly clear enough. If Cabal would just stumble around for a moment or two . . .

"Speak to me, *Shari darling!*" Cabal cried, again mimicking its mistress.

"I'll do more than speak!" Rage fueled her words and her will.

"Come—" That was as far as Cabal got before flames engulfed the familiar's entire body. The monster roared, both pain and accusation in its cry. Nothing else burned but the horrible creature. Even Dru, who lay nearly within arm's reach of the magical killer, felt no heat.

Cabal tried one pitiful spell in an attempt to save itself. The attempt failed and with it the wolf. Howling mournfully, the blazing beast collapsed. The fire did not go out until there was nothing left of Melenea's last ploy. Dru recognized the source of his earlier misgivings, the sense that Melenea still waited. He suspected that the tiny creature that had run over his foot might even have been the familiar. In its tiny size, it could move from place to place, wreaking the havoc its mistress had desired.

That was ended now.

Sharissa fell back, both exhausted and disgusted, but Xiri was there to catch her. The two Vraad looked at each other. Dru nodded and smiled, though he knew neither of them felt any happiness.

Outside, thunder announced the storm's intention to continue on with or without the helpful influence of Cabal. The harsh noise brought them all back to the reality and the peril of their present situation.

"We have to leave as soon as possible," Dru commanded, rising slowly and unsteadily from the floor. "Gather what you need and come with me!"

Sharissa could not speak, but she looked at Xiri. The elf was uncommonly solemn. "Sirvak . . . took care of all of that. The last of your horses wait for us below. We knew we could not stay much longer. When we tried to contact you to tell you to stay where you were, that we would be joining *you*, we could not find you." She indicated the few traces of ash that marked Cabal's fiery demise. "I suppose it was that one that blocked the link. Sirvak offered to fly ahead and find you. It already feared the worse."

Not desiring to sound cold, Dru replied, "Then there's no reason to remain. You two go to the horses."

"What will you do, Father?" Sharissa asked, finally able to stand on her own. Her eyes were wide and gave her a hollow appearance.

"Find something appropriate for a shroud," he said quietly, testing his own ability to stand unaided. He stared pointedly at the remains of his most loyal of servants. "Even if Sirvak died in Nimth, this place will not claim the body. I won't let it."

Sharissa smiled gratefully, then let Xiri lead her down the stairs and away from the tragic scene. Dru waited until he was alone. He knelt by the battered form and picked it up. As he carried it off, searching in his mind for something that would give the familiar's crushed body a proper sense of dignity and honor, Dru whispered to the limp form of the only one who had ever really known the pain in his mind and heart, because that one had been a part of him from its creation. "Time to go home, Sirvak. Time to rest . . . at last."

XXIII

THE FIFTH DAY of their new life found the Vraad still alive and whole. The Tezerenee, while unwelcome by most, had proved themselves most useful. Their well-honed talent for things unmagical made them teachers for the rest. They were, in turn, granted a grudging sort of respect that Dru hoped would blossom into greater acceptance. He had no plans of fasting until that time, however.

They lived in the remains of the ruined city of the ancients. It had already been agreed that instead of building a new home, they would repair the one left for them. Few spoke of journeying out to create their own domain, though the Tezerenee did tend to live on the opposite side of the city. There was more than enough room. The city ran deep as well as tall. Many of the buildings were connected by underground chambers and tunnels that would take months, perhaps years to explore. They seemed harmless places, though Dru was leery about descending into them. He shrugged it off as a Vraad trait. After so many centuries of having so great an expanse of land to himself, it was difficult to completely accept the new arrangements. He was not the only one who felt that way, but neither Dru nor the others would have traded their present situation for the past.

Silesti continued to organize the bulk of the Vraad race. The triumvirate still worked. Dru continued to wonder how long that would last. Sharissa had told him he was just being a pessimist.

She was popular among the immigrants. Sharissa now walked confident among the others and her understanding ways helped greatly during a time when most were trying to cope with the changes. Sorcery was still a touch and go thing. Dru was the most competent, having learned from his new wife.

He and his elfin bride now stood near the place where they had uncovered the final lair of the founders. Dru had come here every day, expecting to find the rift leading to that place. He was curious what future the faceless beings had planned for the Vraad or whether they just might leave the refugees alone. Unfortunately, his efforts had, until now, come to naught. There had been no trace of the rift. He had walked the region carefully. It had been sealed.

Today, however, was different. When he had woken that morning, a familiar voice crawling through his mind had quietly said, *Come to the place where we first met, manling. I will be there to greet you.*

Sharissa was mapping the city for the benefit of all and was already out. She had taken to this new place better than any other Vraad had and was already undisputed leader whenever talk of an expedition to some sector was mentioned. Dru was pleased that his daughter had found a place for herself after the shameless way he had kept her trapped all these years for what he had thought was her own good.

Gerrod was the only person other than his own bride to whom Dru might have talked. The hooded Vraad, however, lived far from the rest of his kind. Not completely trusted by those the Tezerenee had abandoned, he was no more welcome among his own kind, not while Barakas still commanded. Gerrod had become too independent for his father's tastes. The patriarch did not want his example to taint the clan. Dru had offered the young, shadowy Vraad a position as his second, but Gerrod had opted for his solitude. He also worked to redevelop the proper use of his abilities, but in ways that likely did not match those of the elves. Again, Dru knew that it, like so much else, was a problem not yet settled.

Only Xiri stood with him now, in the middle of the ruined square, but she was Xiri no longer. Her name was Ariela and the reason she had never told him her birth name was that in her clan tradition declared that the name be kept a secret, one which would be revealed first to the man she took as a mate. In a moment of truth after they had bound themselves to one another, the former Xiri had told Dru that she had let loose with the comment about her secret because she had been attracted to him from the first moment, despite his being a hated Vraad.

Dru sensed the presence of the guardian before it spoke to him.

The custom of mating was known to us through the ways of the founders. We congratulate you. We also give our sympathy, as best we understand the emotion, for the death of your trusted servant.

"Thank you." In the emptiness of this place, Dru felt more comfortable speaking out loud, even if it was to a being that had no form. He wished the guardian had not mentioned Sirvak; after five days, the pain had not grown any less. Dru could push it aside, but it was still there.

Your efforts with your people are also to be commended, manling.

This was leading up to something. Dru could feel that. He held on to Xiri—*Ariela*—as if he might be torn from her at any moment.

We are departing this plane now, Dru Zeree, but we will continue to observe. The question of how to deal with those who are and are no longer our masters remains unsettled and may never even be settled, something you might understand. This, however, we have decided. No one will interfere with them or attempt to harm them in any way. It is very likely that they will take the action themselves, but if that is beyond them now, we will act instead. All of your people will wake tomorrow with this knowledge in their heads.

"Then why summon me, if you plan to inform everyone?"

I come to that in a moment. The guardian hesitated, then pushed on more quickly. *Nimth is sealed off. It could not be destroyed without affecting this world. It, for all your sakes, should never be sought. Only trouble will come from the chaos that is now Nimth.*

That was easy enough to obey. Dru wondered why anyone would *want* to open a new path to the mad world.

Now we come to the answer to your question. It was not my idea to summon you here. I act only on their behalf and it may be that I have understood them wrong.

"Them?" Ariela asked, her tone indicating that she knew who it was the guardian spoke of.

The Gate materialized before them, tall and frightening. The dark, reptilian forms raced along its edges as usual, but their eyes were always focused on the two figures standing nearby.

From the Gate's maw emerged two of the faceless beings. There was still no telling them apart and Dru decided it was not worth the effort. The two blank-visaged figures stood across from the couple and waited.

It was the guardian who broke the silence. *They want to teach you. They want you to care for this land. Most of all, I believe they want your help in keeping the future alive.*

Dru could sense that it was true. Whether it was an attempt by the creatures before him to communicate their desires or simply something he read into their stance, Dru could not say. The sorcerer only knew that he understood them, to a point. He and others like him would be guardians of sorts, just like the mock dragon and its kind.

No, much more, added the entity. *You will still be a part of the future; you are too essential to be denied that. The others are not yet ready to be left to their own devices. In some ways, I will envy you. You have an ending, a destiny. You and yours will change and grow where we no longer can.*

The sorcerer turned to his wife. Dru knew what his decision would have been if he had never met her. This was a partnership, however. "One last journey?"

She smiled at him, as ready as he to take on this challenge providing they were together. "One last journey, *wicked Vraad.*"

The featureless figures stepped aside for them. Dru looked into the sky at the last moment, as if by doing so he would see the guardian. "What about Darkhorse? He's the one thing I still feel bad about. You had no right to send him back to that place, even if it was somewhere out there he came from."

If the dweller from the Void, as you have called that place, returns, we will not exile him again . . . and I think the one you call Darkhorse will most definitely return. It might even be that from where you go you will be able to aid him in his efforts.

"One more thing, then. Do you think our race will succeed? Do you truly hold any hope for us?"

I do now. The guardian's voice was fading. Its task was done. *More important, so do they.*

Dru gave the departing entity a grateful smile. When he could no longer sense its presence, the sorcerer turned to his wife, who indicated her readiness by squeezing his hand.

They walked through the portal and stepped into the room of worlds.

The chamber was filled with more of the faceless, cowled figures. To Dru's surprise, they bowed to the newcomers. One of them, possibly the closest they had for a leader, walked up to Dru and extended a partially formed hand in an unmistakable gesture.

Dru clasped it and nodded, for some reason at last truly feeling at home.

CHILDREN
OF THE DRAKE

I

WHAT DO YOU think?" Rayke asked, prodding at the feathered corpse at their feet. The body, nearly petrified, was that of one of the Sheekas, the lords of the land. It was manlike in form, had walked upright and had the usual limbs. It was winged as well and covered from head to clawed foot with feathers. The face was very avian, even down to the eye structure that forced a Sheeka to cock the head to the side so as to focus on a target, and the beak was designed for rending the toughest of flesh. Besides these natural weapons, the Sheekas had cunning minds, too, a formidable combination that had allowed them to rule for several thousand years.

Rayke seemed disappointed, as if someone had deprived him of some dark pleasure.

Seen together, the two elves who stood over the sprawled form might have appeared to be brothers. They were of a similar height and both were clad in the same forest-green outfit that consisted of a shirt, pants, shin-length boots, and hooded cloak. Both had light-brown hair that only barely covered their curved ears, and eyes that were the color of spring.

Physical appearance was where the similarity ended. Faunon, younger than Rayke by a hundred years though each looked as if he had seen no more than thirty summers, often thought that his companion was, by far, more blood-thirsty than even the old ones who clung so tightly to the ways of pomp and circumstance that they were always challenging one another to duels. It was for-tunate, then, that he and not Rayke had been put in charge of this expedition into the lands of the avians . . . or what had *once* been their lands. So far, they had only found those hapless victims like this one, Sheekas who had fallen prey to some spell they had unleashed in an attempt to rid themselves of their rivals, the more ancient, armadillolike Quel.

Unfortunately, it seemed that the spell had proven more detrimental to the spellcasters than to the intended targets. The Quel lived in the southwestern portion of the continent, so there was no telling for the time being what damage they had actually suffered. A party of elves was headed that way and, if they returned, their information would be pooled with that of this band.

"I think," Faunon finally replied, recalling Rayke's question at last. "I think that they must have made a terrible mess of trying to reverse their spell, whatever it was. This can't be the result they wanted," he concluded, stating the obvious because one had to do that sometimes with Rayke.

Faunon turned around and gazed at the massive peaks to the north. Somewhere in there was an aerie, that much they knew. It was still occupied . . . the elves had seen one or two Sheekas fluttering among the mountains . . . but by only a token flock, not the massive horde that had lived there only a decade before. The inhabitants there had suffered not one calamity but two in the past ten or so years. There was evidence of a third group that had come and gone like the wind . . . yet who had seemed to clean up after themselves so as to leave little trace for the elves. All that he had discovered was that this other race had fought the Sheekas, held their own against the large flock here, and then abandoned the place for somewhere else.

But where?

"Let's go back to the others," Rayke muttered. He looped his bow around his head and his left arm. The question of the third group meant nothing to him. The council had ordered them to discover the extent of the damage to the empire of the Sheekas, not an easy task since the birds did not have an empire as elves understood it but rather vast communities that controlled great regions of the continent. As far as Rayke and most of the others were concerned, their duties ended there.

That was one problem with his people, Faunon thought as he stepped back from the rock-hard corpse. They either had no inclination toward curiosity whatsoever or they were obsessed with finding out about everything under the sun. No moderation save in a few individuals such as himself.

"Just a minute more, Rayke," he returned, putting just enough emphasis in his voice to remind the other elf who was in charge here.

His companion said nothing, but the flat line of his mouth spoke volumes enough. Rayke had angular features that reminded Faunon of a starving man, and the look on his face only added to that effect. Angular features were not uncommon among the elves, but Rayke's were more severe than most. Faunon's own visage was a bit rounder, more pleasant, so some of the females of his tribe were apt to tell him time and time again until their lilting voices got too much on his nerves and he had to excuse himself from their company somehow. There was another problem with his people: when they saw something they wanted—or someone—they became very, very persistent. He sometimes wondered if he was really one of them.

"Well?"

Faunon started, realizing he had lost track of things. Doing so in front of Rayke made it doubly annoying. He pretended instead that his daydreaming was actually a collecting of his thoughts. "Notice anything wrong with this?"

"With what?"

"The bodies and the land."

"Only that there are a lot of the former scattered around the latter." Rayke smiled, pleased with his clever response.

Faunon kept his own face neutral, trying to hold back his anger. "And the land seems relatively untouched, doesn't it?"

The two of them scanned the area, though each had done so several times already. There were inclines where it was obvious that there had been none before, for trees and bushes jutted at angles no self-respecting plant would have chosen, almost as if something had dug up the ground and then only halfheartedly tried to repair the devastation. A few trees appeared to have withered and petrified much the way the avian dead had, but most of the wooded region seemed fairly healthy overall. Still, Faunon found it astonishing that he was the only one who had paid any note to the peculiarity of the landscape.

The other elf lost hold of his smile. "It *does*. We've come across some areas where the land was overturned, but, even there, the plants and smaller animals were thriving."

"As if they had been bypassed, protected . . . or perhaps *healed*," he added, suddenly feeling that the last was closer to the truth.

"Protected by what? Certainly not the Sheekas. They would have protected themselves first, I think."

"Perhaps by whoever fought the bird people and then vanished," Faunon suggested. Likely, they would never know. This land, which his own people could not claim as their birthplace, having fled to here, as legend put it, from the horrors of another world countless millennia ago, had an air of mystery about it that defied the efforts of the elves. Faunon himself knew that the Sheekas and the Quel had not been the first masters here; that, in fact, several other races had preceded them. This was an old world despite its vitality.

Rayke sighed. "Are you going to begin *that* again, Faunon?"

"If need be! It isn't enough to know that the Sheekas have suffered a calamity that may speak the end of their reign; we have to know if their disaster has the potential to reoccur! If we—"

Something huge went crashing through the trees, sounding as if it had fallen from the sky at a remarkable speed. Faunon, whirling, caught sight of a huge black shape moving in and out of the trees that finally registered in his mind as a horse . . . but *what* a horse! A stallion, to be sure. He stood taller than any that the elf had ever seen and ran with a swiftness that the wind would have been unable to match. If the steed was responsible for the din they had heard, he had changed his ways in swift fashion, for now the animal ran as silent as the shadows he so resembled.

"What *is* that?" Rayke whispered. He had turned pale. Faunon knew that his own visage matched in shading.

"Let's follow it!"

"*Follow* it? Do you see how fast it runs? We will never catch it!" The other elf sounded almost relieved at the last.

"I don't intend to catch it! I just want to see what it is! Follow me!" Faunon raced after the black beast, darting around and over obstacles as only one of his kind could. He did not hear Rayke, but he knew his companion had too much pride to stay behind. Not that it would have mattered to Faunon if he had. Catching a glimpse of this swift phantom was paramount in his mind, and he knew that it would require his best efforts to do that. Against many another creature, an elf's speed would have proven a match; not so, this animal. He had known that from the start. What he also knew, however, was that the mighty steed raced toward an open field. There, his quarry would be quite visible, though distant. Faunon was not too concerned with the distance. Elves had excellent vision. Besides, like Rayke, he did not want to get *too* close to anything as massive and powerful as the black horse. He only wanted to ascertain its existence and the path it was taking. By no means had he ever thought of trying to do anything more.

The horse, however, had apparently had other ideas.

He almost ran into it and wondered how he could have ever missed seeing so terrifying a figure. It loomed over him, having somehow managed to turn back and come upon them without making a sound. Faunon did a very unelf-like thing and slipped, collapsing to the earth less than an arm's length from the demonic stallion.

"I have come back, but this is not the place!" the fearsome figure bellowed down at him. It had long, narrow eyes of the coldest blue, eyes without pupils.

Faunon wished he had an answer that would please the ebony monster, but only air escaped his mouth. He could not even utter so much as a single sound.

"This is the place but it is *not* the place!" One hoof gouged a track in the ground. The elf was all too aware of what that hoof could do to his head if the steed decided to remove him.

The unnerving animal stared at him for a short time. Faunon held his breath throughout the study, wondering what the beast found so interesting. Then he felt the probe. It was surprisingly tentative for so powerful a creature, almost as if the ebony stallion were shamed by his own actions.

Mere moments later, the head of the beast snapped back. He scanned his surroundings in renewed fascination. "So that is it! Astonishing! So many things to learn!"

With an abruptness that left the elf's mouth hanging, the darksome steed backed up, turned, and raced back in the direction it had been heading earlier. Faunon's acute senses noted that there was no trail of any sort on the physical plane, though he did smell power of an unidentifiable sort. It was as if a ghost had come and gone, though that made no sense considering that he and Rayke had, in their initial encounter with the demon, heard the animal before they saw him.

"Are you all right?" Rayke asked from somewhere behind him.

"I'm . . . fine." He was actually surprised that he was. The shadowy steed had owned his life for the duration of their brief meeting. Faunon could think of a dozen different ways he could have been killed. He had been thinking of them throughout his trial despite his best efforts not to. Had the demonic stallion noted those fears at all during his probe?

The other elf's hands were around his torso as Rayke helped him to his feet. A quiver still ran through the former's voice. "What *is* that thing? No horse! Not even one of ours! Was it a shapeshifter?"

"Yes, no, and maybe. I was too at a loss to think much about it while he was here. I doubt that was one of us, though. The sorcery needed for that sort of change would kill most of us! No, there was something wrong with that horror, as if he came from some place other than this world. Somewhere very different."

The two stood staring at the spot the ghostly horse had abandoned. Finally, Rayke asked, "What did he want, Faunon? The way he spoke, he was looking for something. Do you know what?"

Rayke knew of the probe, perhaps had even been probed himself. Faunon shook his head. "I don't know, but he found something in my mind that satisfied him . . . he was *gentle* about it, Rayke! He could have plundered my mind; I could feel he had the will to do so, but he didn't!"

That part seemed not to concern his partner. Rayke continued to stare after their departed intruder. "Where do you suppose he went?"

"East. Straight east."

Rayke grimaced. "There's nothing that way."

"Maybe he plans to go on straight to the sea . . . or *beyond* it."

"Maybe." The other elf's eyes widened. "Do you suppose he had something to do with the death of these Sheekas?"

It was a thought that had not occurred to Faunon, and he had to credit Rayke for the concept. "I don't know. We may never know."

"I'd be happy with that. Let's get back to the others, Faunon. Let's get away from here before it decides to come back!"

There was no argument over that. They had discovered all that there was to discover—unless something *else* ran past them—and it would be dark before long. Faunon generally had no fear of the dark, but, after this encounter, he had a growing desire to be back among his fellows where there was the comfort of numbers.

As they hurried through the woods, moving nearly as silently as the shadow steed had, a nagging feeling grew in Faunon's head. He was not one for signs and omens, being one of the newer generation of more *practical* elves, but he could not shake the sensation that the creature he had faced was yet one more hint of something vast to come, a change in the land as he and his people knew it. If the Sheekas were truly nearing the end of their reign, as the Quel had before them, then someone would come to displace them. The land had seen such change time and again, though the elves had never been part of that cycle, merely onlookers.

Ducking under a low branch, Faunon grew more troubled as his thoughts progressed. The Sheekas and even the Quel had been predictable creatures; the elves knew where they stood with those two races. Who was to say that the same would hold with their successors? Who *would* their successors be? There were no other races that could claim dominance.

There was little to justify his fears, but he believed in them nonetheless. As they neared the spot where the others were to meet them, Faunon discovered that he was, for the first time, hoping for the continued survival of the arrogant avians. The elves knew how to coexist with them, if no more than that. The next masters might feel that there was no need for his race to continue on.

They had escaped such a fate once before, when, legend had it, they had discovered the path that freed them of the horrors of the twisted world of Nimth and its lords, the sorcerous race called the Vraad. At least that was one threat that the elves no longer had to fear, Faunon decided, drawing what little comfort he could from that.

Nothing the future held could ever match the cruelty of the Vraad.

II

THE COLONY HAD lasted for fifteen years now. This world did not bow to their will as the last had and, far more important, they no longer had the strength to back their arrogant desires. Now they were often forced to do things by hand that they once would have scoffed at performing so. It was a long, frustrating fall from godhood for the Vraad, for they had, back in dying Nimth, been born to their roles. They had escaped to this world from the one they had ruined with little more than their skins and had discovered too late that, for many, Vraad sorcery would not work here the way it had before . . . at least not without terrible effort and more than a little chance of the results being other than what they had sought.

Yet, for all they had succeeded in accomplishing during those fifteen long years, there were many who still could not accept that the godlike days of yesteryear were at an end. They had once moved mountains, quite *literally*, and some were determined that they would do so again—whatever the cost. Thus, those that had some success with their spells ignored the side effects and consequences.

Lord Barakas, patriarch of the Tezerenee, the clan of the dragon, was one. He had come to this world with the intention to rule it, not be ruled *by* it. Even now, as he and two of his sons sat in silent contemplation of the sight before them, the dreams of what might have been and what might still be filled his thoughts nigh on to overflowing.

He stared west, utilizing the tallest hill in the region so as to get a glimpse of not just the lands but the seas farther on as well. The riding drakes, great green creatures that more resembled massive but unprepossessing lizards rather than the dragons they were, had begun to grow restive. The patriarch's sons, Reegan the Heir and ever-obedient Lochivan, were also growing restive. Lochivan was the slightest of the three, which by no means meant that he was small. It was just that Reegan and Barakas were two of a kind, huge bears with majestic beards; two giants who looked ready to bite off the head of any who dared so much as cough in their direction. All three riders bore the same coarse features that were dominant throughout the clan, though Lochivan's were tempered a bit by some additions passed down to him by his mother, the Lady Alcia. He also had a mix of brown and gray in his hair. Barakas and his heir had darker locks, though a streak of silver had spread across the patriarch's head over the last few years. Other than that, Reegan was a fairly good physical copy of the dragonlord. Beyond the physical, however, the resemblance ceased. The heir lacked much in terms of the patriarch's vision.

The sun, directly above, continued to bathe them in heat. Lochivan shifted, trying to keep cool in the cloth padding and dark-green, dragon-scale armor that clan members fairly lived their lives out in these days. Long ago, when they had been lords of Nimth, it would have been less than nothing for him to utilize his skills to make the body-encompassing armor both cool and weightless.

Here, in what he considered a damnable land at best, such effort meant wasted energy and nothing more. The magic of this world still refused to obey him with regularity. Only a few had any true power, and even fewer had abilities comparable to the Vraad race of old.

None of the three were among them, though the patriarch came near. Near but not enough for what he desired.

That was why neither Reegan nor Lochivan dared to disturb their father. This period of contemplation was all that kept him from striking out at random at his own people.

"How far do you think it is?" Barakas suddenly asked. His voice was flat, nearly emotionless. That hardly meant he was in a quiet mood. Of late, the patriarch had become mercurial, going from indifference to rage at the blink of an eye. Many Tezerenee wore marks of his anger.

Lochivan answered the question, as he always did. Reegan might be heir apparent, but he lacked subtlety, something needed for times like this. Besides, Lochivan knew the answer that would suffice; it was the same one he had given his father for the past three weeks. "Not far enough to escape our grasp forever. Not by far."

"True." The Lord Tezerenee's eyes did not focus on the lush lands below, but at the glittering sea near the horizon. His prize lay not on this continent but across the stunning expanse of water in another land. He had even given it its name, one that had spread to this place though he himself could not think of it as anything but "the other continent." Across the seas lay his destiny, his *Dragonrealm*.

"Father." Reegan spoke quietly, but his unpredicted interruption could only mean that he had some news of importance to convey. Reegan would never dare speak to his father without a very good reason for doing so.

Barakas looked at his eldest son, who indicated with a curt nod that the others should turn their attention to their left. The dragonlord shifted so as to see what had caught Reegan's eye and gritted his teeth when he saw the reason.

One of the Faceless Ones. It was a parody of a man, having no features whatsoever, not even hair or ears. It was as tall as a normal man and wore a simple, cowled robe. It was also facing—if one could use the term—the three riders, watching them with its nonexistent eyes and unperturbed by the fact that the trio was now staring back.

"Let me cut it down, Father!" Reegan's voice pretended at disdain, but a barely noticeable quiver revealed the fear that the creature stirred within his breast. Lochivan, too, was discomforted by the sight of the harmless-looking being.

"It is forbidden to do so," Barakas reminded his son, his own voice taking on a steely edge. He, like his sons, would have desired nothing more than to crush the interfering horror beneath his mount's clawed feet or cut it to ribbons with his sword. Anything to wipe its existence from this world.

"But—"

"It was forbidden by the *Dragon of the Depths!*" the patriarch snapped, referring to a being he had, over the past decade, come to think of as the Tezerenee dragon totem come to life. When the Tezerenee had faced annihilation at the hands—talons—of the bird creatures in that other land, the god had burst forth from the ground wearing a body of stone and molten earth. It had scattered the Sheekas, or Seekers, as the Vraad preferred to call them, with only words. It had taken the surviving clan members and sent them to this continent to join their fellow Vraad, utilizing only the least of its power in the process.

Two things that the Dragon of the Depths—the Lord Tezerenee's own name for the entity—had commanded had remained with Barakas. One was that there might come a time when the Tezerenee would return to the Dragonrealm in triumph. Lord Barakas yearned for that day. The other thing touched him in the opposite manner. His god had ordered that the Faceless Ones be left unharmed. They were to be allowed to do what they desired or else.

For the Tezerenee, that was almost unthinkable. They shared more than a legacy with the unholy creatures; they shared a common origin, at least in the physical sense. It was one that kept them from ever truly feeling comfortable among their own people, even though most of the other animosities had died over time.

Barakas took up the reins of his mount. "Let us be gone from here! This place no longer soothes!"

Reegan and Lochivan acquiesced with great eagerness.

Steering their drakes around, the three urged their animals back in the direction of the city. They had some slight difficulty at first, for these animals were not mindbroke as had once been the way. Mindbreaking back in Nimth had been a simple process by which the Vraad had taken the will of their mounts and shattered it, leaving an emptiness that the master could fill as he deemed necessary. It had always made for very obedient steeds. Unfortunately, mindbreaking now had a high casualty rate and the Tezerenee could ill afford to lose many drakes. Unlike the western continent, where the Tezerenee had *intended* to go, drakes were fairly scarce on this continent.

Another fault among many that this place had, as far as Barakas was concerned.

The mounts finally gave in to their riders and, building up speed, raced up and over the winding landscape. The crimson cloaks that Barakas and Reegan wore, designating them as clan master and heir apparent, respectively, fluttered madly behind, looking almost like bloodred dragon wings. The refugees' city lay in a valley and so much of their trek was downhill, though smaller hills forced them to take a route that twisted back and forth often. Here, the drakes held an advantage over their equine counterparts. Their claws dug into the slope, preventing them from stumbling forward and throwing their riders to their death. Horses had their own advantages, true, many more than the reptilian mounts, but a riding drake was more than just a beast that carried a Tezerenee from one point to another. It was a killing machine. Few things could stand up to the onslaught of a dragon, even as simpleminded a one as the mount below the patriarch. The claws would slice a man to segments; the jaws could snap a victim in two without strain.

Most important, they were the symbol of the Tezerenee.

The city soon rose before them, from the distance looking like little more than one massive wall. The new inhabitants had rebuilt the encircling wall first, making it almost twice the height of its first incarnation because their overall loss of power had made them fear everything. The city itself had been a vast ruin when the Vraad had first come, an ageless relic of the race from whom they—and countless others, it appeared—had sprung. Those ancients had been far more godlike than the Vraad could have ever hoped to be, easily manipulating their descendants into a variety of forms. They had sought successors to their tired, dying race. In what could best be described as irony, their final hope lay in one of their earliest failures—the Vraad. The Lord Tezerenee's kind had been abandoned to their world, a *construct* of the ancients, where it was supposed they would kill themselves off. Instead, the Vraad had outlasted nearly everyone else. Only the Seekers still held on, but they were already in their decline, so the Dragon of the Depths had said.

To Lord Barakas, the rebuilding of the city was a waste of effort that he had only condoned while he bided his time.

"Dragon's blood!" Lochivan swore, pointing at the path ahead. "Another!"

Near the very gates of the city there stood a figure identical to the one that they had left behind no more than moments before. For all Barakas knew, it *was* the same being. *They* had the power to flaunt. The Faceless Ones were, after all, all that remained of the minds of the very ancients who had built the city. They still sought, in their own mysterious way, to manipulate the future of their world—meaning the Vraad. The Lord Tezerenee gritted his teeth; it was by his doing that they had been given physical forms through which to interfere further.

Of their own accord, the gates swung open in time for the returning Vraad. The Faceless One, like his predecessor, remained passive as they neared. Barakas could not help touching his own face as they rode past the still figure. The skin

Barakas touched felt like the skin he had always known, but it was of the same origin as the body that those ghosts now wore. Every Tezerenee, save one, wore a shell created by the now-lost combined magical might of the clan. Even a few non-clan members, outsiders whose loyalties had extended to the patriarch, had such bodies. It had seemed like the perfect solution when no way had been found to cross from Nimth to the Dragon-realm in a physical manner. Through the aid of one Dru Zeree, the only outsider Barakas respected, the Vraad had rediscovered the secret of ka, or spirit travel. The ka, guided by others, could cross the barrier that the bodies could not. There was only one major stumbling block: the spirits needed a suitable host.

It was Barakas himself who had come up with that solution. Though they could not cross, the Vraad could influence their future world through sorcerous means. It meant a dozen or more individuals acting in concert for even the slightest of spells. For the arrogant Vraad, that was an impossibility that only the Tezerenee, who were used to working with one another, could overcome. Under the patriarch's masterful guidance, they had created an army of golems whose ancestry could be traced to the larger, more majestic cousins of the very mounts he and his sons now rode. Those soulless husks were to have waited for the tide of Vraad immigrants, but things had gone wrong after only a few hundred had been molded. First, those to whom the task of manipulating the spell of formation had fallen vanished without a trace; Barakas suspected that the ancients had been at fault there, also. Then the damned ghosts had stolen most of the bodies for themselves.

The creature was lost from sight as the riders moved farther on into the confines of the city. The patriarch drew no comfort from that. As far as he knew, there were probably half a dozen more of the horrors observing him and his sons from less conspicuous posts. It was their way.

Dru Zeree had once explained to him that the last of the ancients had released their spirits into their world, giving the lands themselves a mind of sorts. The golem forms provided by the patriarch's plan had offered an opportunity for that mind to provide itself with hands to further its work, an apparent oversight the founders had not thought of until it was too late. Barakas had never known how much of that explanation to believe and did not really think it mattered. What mattered was that an army of ghosts had stolen not only his creations, but the empire he would have had if the rest of the Vraad had been forced to swear fealty to him in return for access to their new world. Worse yet, each of the walking monstrosities reminded him that a part of him lay rotting back in foul Nimth . . . unless some scavenger still living had already devoured him.

The gates closed behind them, the magic of Dru Zeree flaunting itself once more. As hard as he had strived, he could not match Zeree's abilities. Even his counterpart's daughter, Sharissa, was more capable. Yet another bitter pill he had been forced to swallow each day of each year.

A few Vraad wandered about, looking much more scruffy than they had back in Nimth. Without nearly limitless power to see to their every whim, they were being forced to maintain their appearances through more mundane means. Some were not proving adept at the process. They wore robes or shirts and pants, all fairly simplistic in design considering the extravagant and shocking garments most of them had once worn. Several Vraad were clearing rubble from another crumbling dwelling. They were sorting out the good pieces for use in either building the structure that would replace this one or for some other project, perhaps another useless tower. To Barakas the working Vraad looked more pathetic than industrious.

The gods have fallen, he thought. *I have fallen.*

Still, the city had regained bits of its ancient glory. Someday, it might be completely whole again. Children were becoming more numerous than they had back in Nimth, though that was not quite so impressive as it sounded when one considered there had rarely been more than a few dozen young at any time during the old days. Near-immortals with no taste for familial relationships did not tend to make ideal parents. Those few who chose to do so generally ended up fighting their offspring at some point. Barakas, in creating his clan, had turned that energy outside rather than inside. His people, the only true clan in Vraad society, now numbered over one hundred again, not including additional outsiders who had sworn loyalty to him during the past decade and a half. Children were rampant in the section of the city that he had taken over.

Some of the locals turned away at sight of the three Tezerenee. The patriarch ignored them, their anger being both misdirected and petty in his eyes. Faced with the loss of the majority of the golems, Barakas had sent his own people through, effectively abandoning his former allies for the most part. If they wanted to blame anyone, he had argued in the beginning, it should be the Faceless Ones themselves. He had acted as any of them would have acted. The clan came first.

At least they were no longer clamoring for the deaths of every Tezerenee. It had been the dragonlord's people who had helped them cope with their new, mundane lives, for the Tezerenee were adept at surviving with only their physical abilities. Barakas felt justified in thinking that this colony would have been dead if not for his folk. Even Dru Zeree and Silesti, the third member of their triumvirate, could not argue with that. There were not enough adept sorcerers to guarantee everything.

His thoughts were disturbed by the appearance of a tall, well-formed woman with flowing silver-blue hair that nearly fell to her waist. The white dress she wore clung to her form, marking its perfection. Her gait indicated a confidence she had never had before her arrival in this world. She was possibly one of the most accomplished spellcasters they had now, though, being less than four decades old, the newcomer was little more than a child by Vraad standards.

She was Sharissa, daughter of Dru Zeree.

Barakas pulled back on the reins, slowing his mount in gradual fashion so as not to appear overanxious. He glanced quickly at Reegan, whose eyes were wide as he followed every movement of the young woman. The patriarch had been encouraging his eldest to pursue the lone offspring of his rival for quite some time, and Reegan had been only too eager to do just that. While Barakas prized her for her status and sorcerous abilities, he knew that his son saw her in more coarse terms . . . not that the patriarch could deny her beauty. Sharissa had changed somewhat in the time since their coming. Her face was rounder, though the cheekbones were in evidence. Like other Vraad, she had crystalline eyes, aquamarine gemstones that grew brighter when they widened. Her brows were arched, giving her an inquisitive look. The expression on her face seemed to be one of mild amusement, but Barakas knew that it was actually because her mouth curled upward naturally.

"Lady Sharissa," he called out, nodding his head.

Her thin yet elegant lips parted in what he knew was a forced pleasantness. She did not care for many of the Tezerenee—save self-exiled Gerrod, came the unbidden thought. Barakas quickly smothered any further notions concerning that son. Gerrod had chosen his own way, and it had meant a hermetic life that defied everything Barakas had taught his people. As far as the patriarch was concerned, the relationship had ended there.

"Lord Barakas. Lochivan." She smiled at them, nodding in return, then finally added, "*Reegan*. How do you fare today?"

"Always well when I see you," Reegan blurted.

Barakas was almost as surprised as Sharissa at his eldest's words. The young Zeree colored a bit; she had not expected such complimentary bluntness from the hulking figure. The patriarch held back a smile. She could hardly claim that he had engineered that comment. It was too obvious that Reegan's stumbling words had been his own. For once, his son had taken the initiative. If there was one thing that Sharissa had no defense against, it was honesty.

"How is your father?" he asked, filling the silence that had started to grow too long for his tastes.

"He is well," Sharissa returned, looking a bit relieved. For all her skill and knowledge, she was still naive in the ways of relationships. Her father had kept her away from most of the other Vraad for the first twenty years of her life—and she was less than twenty years older now. A short time to the long-lived Vraad race.

"And his mate?"

"Mother is also well."

Barakas took note of her use of the term. The Lady Ariela Zeree was not Sharissa's mother; she was not even a Vraad, but an elf from this world. Dru's daughter had never really known her birth mother, though, and she had come to care for the elf so much that it seemed only natural to call her father's mate *mother*. Barakas hid the distaste he felt. The elf was a lesser creature, wife of Zeree or not. She did not belong among the Vraad.

He realized that Sharissa was waiting for him to say something more. It disturbed him that he found himself drifting off so much more of late. Had it something to do with the white hair he had discovered of late . . . or the wrinkles at the corners of his eyes?

"Lady Sharissa, you know a little about those *creatures*, don't you?" Lochivan suddenly asked. He did not have to elaborate as to what creatures he referred to. Everyone knew he meant the Faceless Ones.

The Lord Tezerenee glanced at his younger son, but held his peace.

"I know a bit." She was cautious. Like most of the Vraad, she was ever wary of their desire for domination. Barakas wanted very much to assure her that she need not have worried; there was already a place for her among them. Such vitality and power could not be wasted.

"Have they shown any purpose? Do their actions mean anything at all? All they do is stare . . . if you can call it that, since they have nothing with which to stare! I keep thinking they know something. Fifteen years of staring must have *some* purpose! It's gotten worse during this past year, too!"

She was interested; the patriarch could see that. Sharissa was interested in anything that had to do with her new world. "You noticed that? They seem more attentive of late; I thought that, too. I can't think it means us any harm, however. They want us to thrive."

Do they? Barakas wanted to ask. Again, as with so many other things, he held his tongue.

"What about your father? Dru works with them in their citadel. Surely, he knows more."

Sharissa shook her head, sending fine hair cascading back and forth. Reegan was having trouble keeping his interest in her from growing too obtrusive. He had always had that trouble.

"Father always says it's like working with a jigsaw puzzle with more than half the pieces missing. Somehow, they teach him things, but he never realizes it until afterward." She smiled at Lochivan, seeming to forget for the moment that he was a Tezerenee. "It frustrates him no end."

"I can imagine."

The two of them talked to each other with an ease that stirred Barakas. The patriarch was truly the father of his people, having cultivated no less than fifteen sons and several daughters over the centuries . . . likely many more that he had forgotten about, too. Of those he recognized, the two most intelligent had proven bitter failures to him. Rendel had betrayed the clan, seeking his own way in the Dragonrealm. He had died, thanks to his own foolishness. His shadow, younger Gerrod, was no better. It occurred to him now that here was one who could fill the gap of knowledge the other two had left. He had only thought of Lochivan as superbly obedient, never intelligent. Yet . . .

Sharissa was glancing his way, and he wondered when she had turned her attention to him. She was now all artificial politeness again. He had slipped and allowed his thoughts to show, something he would have never forgiven any of his people for doing.

"If you will excuse me, I must prepare for an excursion. Someone came across one of the founders' earlier settlements."

"Oh?" Lochivan leaned forward. "Where?"

"Northeast. I must be going now. Good day to you all." She nodded to the trio and departed at a pace that emphasized her sudden desire to be away from them.

Reegan's pained expression reminded Barakas of a sick drake. Lochivan turned to his father the moment Sharissa was a fair distance away, and the two of them exchanged glances. Northeast was where Gerrod had, of late, made his home. It might be coincidence, but, then again, it might not be.

"Shake yourself out of that stupor, Reegan," the Lord Tezerenee ordered at last. He then returned his attention to his other offspring. "Lochivan, I give you leave to depart. I know you, too, have things that you must attend to. Yes?"

It took only a moment for Lochivan, who had not had *any* duties to attend to, to understand what his progenitor was saying. He nodded. "I do. My thanks."

The younger Tezerenee twisted the reins and urged his mount away from the other two. Barakas turned one last time to his eldest, his heir.

"Dragon's blood, idiot! Snap out of it and come along! You can't very well sit there mooning all day!" He had miscalculated Reegan's desire for Sharissa. The last thing he needed was a lovesick hulk. When desire ruled, the mind became worthless—and with his eldest that was doubly so.

Reegan managed to stir himself, urging his mount to follow that of his father. Barakas hid his disgust under a mask of blandness. He should have known that Reegan's words to Sharissa had not been born of any cunning but of true infatuation for the young Zeree.

His mind awhirl with thoughts concerning the future of his clan and the potential that Sharissa Zeree promised that future—if the patriarch had his way—Lord Barakas could not be faulted for not noticing yet a third of the featureless entities he so loathed. It watched the backs of the two Tezerenee grow smaller and smaller as they rode away, then, evidently losing interest, it turned and started off in the direction that Sharissa—then Lochivan—had gone.

III

SHARISSA HAD NOT wanted to confront the Tezerenee, especially Barakas and Reegan. It was, she knew, impossible *not* to confront one or another member of the dragon clan. During the past five years they had become especially noticeable in this part of the city. The anger that many Vraad felt for them had faded with time and the knowledge that the Tezerenee had proven invaluable over and over almost since the beginning of the colony. The clan now held greater influence with their race than they ever had back in Nimth, although she doubted that the patriarch saw it that way. Though he had always pushed for physical prowess, the dwindling of their sorcery to near nothing meant that their lack of numbers would now hurt them in battle. Still, more than a few of those outside the clan now looked to Barakas for leadership. Emboldened, the Tezerenee were once more walking among their fellows, daring their rivals to do something.

So far, things were still in balance. Silesti still held the majority of the folk in his hand, and her father influenced both sides to work with one another and ignore gibes and covert glances. It was Dru Zeree more than anyone else who kept the triumvirate successful. Left to their own devices, Silesti and Barakas would have begun the final war among the Vraad the same day the refugees had arrived in this world.

Barakas hoped to swing the balance to his side, and one method involved Sharissa's marriage to Reegan.

"Not if I have anything to say about it," she muttered. Sharissa did not particularly hate Reegan, and his words had touched the romantic part of her, but he was not what she sought. She was uncertain what it was she *did* seek, but it could never be this younger, more coarse version of the patriarch himself. Reegan would become his father in all save cunning. The heir was a creature of strength and skill, but not knowledge. He needed Lochivan to guide him in subtle matters.

Lochivan. Sharissa wondered if the Lord Tezerenee knew that his other son was one of her closest friends. Never a lover, but more like the brother she did not have.

As she walked, her eyes absently marked the progress that had been made of late. The western and eastern portions of the city, which was actually more of a giant citadel, were almost completely rebuilt. Most of the ancient buildings had been found to be too untrustworthy and had been torn down as needs arose. Thanks partly to the powers of the few who had the necessary aptitude for sorcery here and the physical work of the many who did not, there were now several towers and flat-roofed buildings. They were a bit too utilitarian for her tastes, but she hoped that would change. Most of the structures were empty, optimistic thoughts of a growth trend in the Vraad population making the people continue working after they had re-created enough of a home for the present inhabitants. It was a good way to keep them busy, too. That was one thing all members of the triumvirate had agreed on from the first.

There were a few traces of Vraad taste that she did see. Some of the arches were a bit more extravagant than they should have been, even to the point of being decorated with fanciful creatures. A wolf's head over one doorway gave her pause, reminding her too much of memories of Nimth. She knew, however, that the carving was actually a symbol designating they who lived there as among Silesti's favorites. Unconsciously following in the footsteps of his enemy, the third member of the triumvirate had chosen to make the wolf one of the marks by which his authority was known.

Something stepped out of a shadowy alley, startling her. She kept from losing face by stifling the gasp before any of it escaped her lips.

A smooth, featureless visage stared back at her. She, like Barakas, referred to them as the Faceless Ones, but most Vraad called them the *not-people*, likely because they did not want to have to accept them as anything remotely akin to their own kind. There were traits the beings had that touched too close to those of her kind.

The Faceless One confronted her for only a moment. With an impatient movement, it shifted around her and kept going. Sharissa followed its departure until it was out of sight, then exhaled the breath she had forgotten to release in the shock of the encounter.

A stray yet disturbing thought edged its way to the forefront—had the Faceless One seemed nervous? Generally, they did not go darting around those they ran across, but either changed direction completely or circled around their victim with a slow, almost casual pace. They did not go scurrying along as this one had. It was almost as if something else were occupying the creature's thoughts.

What could so demand the attention of one of the beings that it would lose the reserve that its kind had become noted for over the years?

Then Sharissa felt the first stirrings of another presence—one so powerful and so *different* that it might as well have been purposely announcing its coming. Perhaps it was; she could not say for certain. All she knew so far was that this was no Vraad . . . save perhaps Gerrod, who was capable of many extraordinary changes.

A pall of silence wrapped itself over the area, as if others were sensing the same as she. Reaching out, she touched upon the strength of this world. Of the few who had adapted almost completely to their new home's ways, some now claimed they saw a spectrum when they sought the power. Others claimed that their vision was that of a field of crisscrossing lines going on into infinity, lines of force. Sharissa knew that neither group lied; she was the only one, evidently, who saw both, depending on the whims of her subconscious. It was the most probable reason why she had become, without exception, the most adept of the Vraad. Even her father, who had learned from both his bride and the Faceless Ones, could not match her. What did confuse Sharissa was that Ariela, who had been conceived and raised on the other continent, also could not match her adopted daughter. The elf claimed to know of no one among her people who touched upon the powers with the ease that the young Zeree did.

There were times when Sharissa felt proud of her unique position . . . and times when it became a heavy burden and a threat. Among the Vraad were those like Barakas who saw her as a tool or were merely jealous of her abilities. Everyone tried to manipulate her, but she had learned to handle most of them. In the final days of Nimth, one of her father's former lovers, an enchantress named Melenea, had used Sharissa's innocence in a ploy that had almost meant the death of both Zerees and Gerrod Tezerenee. It *had* meant the death of her father's familiar, Sharissa's childhood companion. Sirvak had died defending his master and mistress from Melenea's horrible pet, Cabal. That incident had steeled Sharissa's heart. No one would ever use her again, not if it endangered those she cared for.

The presence was growing stronger, as if whoever it was raced toward the city . . . from the *west*, she now saw. The nearer to the city it came, the more astonishing its power was . . . and the more inhuman it seemed to be. No Vraad could possibly claim such ability, such *otherness*.

Father, she recalled with a start. *I have to tell Father!* It might be that he knew already, but one could never tell. Sharissa reached out to him with her mind, trying to establish a link. Linking minds was more chancy than it had once been, possibly because few now had the ability to maintain it long. In the case of her father and her, the trouble was compounded by the fact that Dru Zeree was not quite in this world, but in a compact dimension where the founders had built their last citadel before they had chosen to give their souls to the land. While those within could observe or contact the outside, breaking through the barrier from the true world was something only their blank-visaged avatars could do with any consistency, or so she thought. There were only theories as to how they communicated among themselves.

Father? She held her breath for a time, awaiting his response. When the familiar touch of the elder Zeree's mind failed to manifest itself, Sharissa tried again. All the while, she felt the ever-closing presence of the outsider, the . . . *creature.* It made her wonder how the Tezerenee could have failed to notice such a being; Barakas might be a shadow of his former self, but he was still one to be reckoned with. How could he have failed to sense the coming intruder?

There was, as yet, no answer from her father. If he had noted her summons at all, he would have contacted Sharissa by now. That meant the only recourse was to go to him herself. Her expedition all but forgotten, she turned and headed in the general direction of the city square. It was there, in a bit of the city that by Dru's own command had been left untouched, where she would find the tiny, hidden rift that was the entrance to the pocket universe of the founders, the place where her parents now spent most of their time. The path would be open to her, she hoped. There had been occasions when Sharissa had been forced to wait until her father departed his private domain in order to talk to him.

A few Vraad, making their own way to whatever projects held their attention, stepped aside as she rushed past them without so much as a glance. Whether they felt anything, she neither knew nor cared. If anyone else was disturbed by the newcomer, then they could follow her or come on their own.

One body did *not* move aside for her, and she almost ran directly into it. Sharissa *would* have collided with the other figure, save that a pair of strong hands caught her and held her still.

"What is it? Something must be amiss for you to go running blindly into folk!"

"Lochivan! I can't talk! I have to find my father!"

The Tezerenee released her. "Then I will walk with you. You can tell me why you're so upset that you have not teleported instead of wasting so much time *walking*."

Sharissa colored. She stepped past Lochivan and resumed her journey. The Tezerenee fell in beside her, easily matching the pace. He had grown up on quick marches.

"I thought it would be best not to attempt such a spell," she finally replied. Sharissa had never told anyone, not even Dru, why she so rarely employed such timesaving spells. Teleportation had been a dangerous, foolhardy thing in the last days of the old world, and it had nearly cost her father his life.

The younger Zeree knew she was being ridiculous, but she had never gotten over her fear that one day a teleport spell would send her into some place from which she would never return. It was impossible to explain the feeling to anyone who could no longer perform the spell. They would have hardly felt sympathy for her plight.

"Why? What is it?" Lochivan asked, his brow furrowed. He was uneasy about something, perhaps several somethings. Sharissa wondered if he felt the oncoming stranger's presence.

"Something . . . someone . . . of a different . . . I can't explain it, but don't you feel the approach of a presence in the west?"

"Is that what that is?" He glanced in the direction of the gate through which he and the others had entered earlier. "But anything that close . . . we should have seen it during our ride. . . ."

"That's what I thought, too." A suspicion formed. "Did you, Lochivan? You are probably one of only two of your folk that I might expect a true, unmasked answer from. Did you see anything? Sense anything?"

"Nothing!" The vehemence with which he answered revealed his deepening worry. "There's nothing west but forest and plains . . . and the seas, of course. Dragon's blood! *Seekers?*"

He had come to the same conclusion she had. The magical guardians of the city, the founders' ancient servants, had been her only other choice. Formless save when they chose to dress themselves in the very earth and rock, as the one the Tezerenee called the Dragon of the Depths had, the guardians felt of this world, this ancient place. Not so the newcomer. There was only the slightest trace of this world on the intruder, as if it had briefly been a part of this place but had, as Sharissa noted again, come from somewhere beyond. Since Nimth was closed off, that left only the other continent and its masters. It *had* to be the Seekers, yet were they not part of this world, too?

Lochivan paused and removed one of his gauntlets. "Sword and shield! What a time for this!"

Despite the urgency of the situation, she paused. Her companion's presence was comforting, which soothed her enough to keep her thoughts from running too amok. It would be worth the time to wait for him, providing it was only for a few seconds. Besides, the frustration in his voice made her curious as to his difficulties. "What's wrong?"

He reached in between his dragonhelm and his armor and started scratching with such a fury she thought he would draw blood. "A damn rash! Nothing deadly, but it's spread around the clan quite a bit! The skin gets dry and stays that way! Sometimes it itches so badly that I'm forced to stop everything and scratch until . . . until it becomes tolerable again."

Lochivan pulled his hand away and replaced the gauntlet. He sighed. "As it finally has, thank the dragon. It's over. Get moving!"

A bit surprised that a warrior like Lochivan would succumb to a rash during a moment of crisis, Sharissa nonetheless said nothing to him and did her best to keep from revealing any of her thoughts. She would have to mention this plague of irritation to her father when there was time. It might only be a rash now, but who was to say what it might become in the future?

They had barely progressed more than a dozen steps before the sorceress nearly came to a halt herself.

Something was in the square they were trying to reach. Something that was the same presence she had noted outside only a few minutes ago! Now it was *inside* and *ahead* of them! Yet, it had just been *outside*—

"Serkadion Manee!" she uttered, stunned. The name of the ancient Vraad scholar was a favorite oath of her father, and she had picked it up over the years.

Lochivan did not have to ask what was wrong. As she turned and looked at him she could see that the Tezerenee felt what she did. . . . Who could not? Sharissa scanned those Vraad standing or walking nearby. They were all pausing in their present interests and twisting about to stare in the direction of the square. A silence had fallen upon everyone in sight. One or two had enough presence of mind to make note of the duo moving toward the source of the disruption. To the young Zeree, they looked almost frightened. In their hearts, many Vraad feared that, now mostly bereft of their fabulous abilities, they would become easy prey for some outside threat.

That might very well be the truth, Sharissa realized.

"I have to teleport," she announced, her words more to steel herself for the task at hand than to alert Lochivan.

"I'm coming with you."

"Hold on to my arm, then."

He did, holding her a bit tighter than he likely thought. The clan of the dragon, meaning the patriarch, frowned on any show of fear, regardless of the reasons. There were times when she felt pity for the sort of life that Gerrod and Lochivan had endured.

Grimacing, Sharissa transported them to the square.

Her first thought was that it had grown as dark as night even though there were still a few hours of sun left. Then she noted, with much chagrin, that her eyes were squeezed shut.

"Gods! Look at him, Sharissa! Have you ever seen something as grand and startling as that?"

She opened her eyes with care. There were other people around already and all of them were just as entranced by the great beast in the square.

"A horse!" she whispered. A glorious ebony steed! She had always loved her father's horses, magnificent mounts that he had bred without any use of magic—almost as a challenge to himself. Yet, no horse she had seen could measure up to this creature. . . .

It was this steed that her senses had noticed. It was this animal that emanated the unbelievable power that so disturbed the minds of nearly every Vraad, whatever their sorcerous abilities.

"Where is he? I will not be denied him! I will not again be thrust back into the cursed nothingness I was forced to endure for so long! Where is my friend, Dru Zeree?"

Sharissa knew then what and who this was. He was called Darkhorse and he had, for a time, aided and traveled with her father after the sorcerer had been lost in the ghost lands where Nimth and Barakas's Dragonrealm had intertwined like two cursed lovers, together yet unable to touch one another. The guardians, in obedience to the millennia-old instructions of their lost masters, had seen the shadow steed as an aberration that could not be allowed to exist here.

In deference to Dru, they had not destroyed him, but rather exiled him . . . supposedly forever.

They had underestimated the creature.

People shuffled nervously around the square, uncertain as to what the ebony stallion might do. Many of them had abandoned something or another. A few folk were even half-dressed. Even though most of them had not heard of Darkhorse, they recognized sorcery of a kind that was in some ways even greater than what they themselves had once wielded.

"You look like Dru Zeree!" the thundering voice accused the crowd. He pondered this for a moment, then asked, "You are Vraad?" An icy, blue eye focused on one unnerved person after another, finally fixing on the only Vraad there who did not turn away: Sharissa. "*Where* is my friend?"

"Sharissa!" Lochivan hissed, grabbing hold of her from the side.

She blinked, realizing she had been about to fall forward and wondering what it was about Darkhorse that brought on such a reaction. She had almost thought she was going to fall *into* him . . . but that was ridiculous, wasn't it? Yet the sensation had been strong, even demanding, until Lochivan had stepped in to rescue her.

The demonic stallion tossed his head, such an animallike action that it destroyed some of the uncertainty Sharissa felt. She took a deep breath and stepped up.

"I am Sharissa Zeree, Dru's daughter. I—"

"Aahh! Little Sharissa!" Darkhorse bellowed with pleasure. His change of manner was so abrupt that Sharissa forgot herself and stood there with her mouth open.

Darkhorse trotted toward her. "Friend Dru spoke of you during our travels! How delightful to see you! How wonderful to find you after an eternity of cursed searching for this place!"

"Careful, Sharissa!" Lochivan whispered. He had one hand on his sword, though she was uncertain as to what he imagined he could do with it. From what little the sorceress knew and what little she had seen, it would take more than a blade to stop this creature.

"Careful, *indeed!*" Darkhorse snorted in response. His hearing was remarkable. "I would not harm the appendage of my friend Dru!"

"Appendage?" Sharissa was not certain she had heard right.

"Shoot? You were part of him and are now separate, yes? What is that called for your kind?"

"Offspring. Child. Only I was not part of him, but actually the . . ." She trailed off, thinking how long it might take to explain the process of birth to an entity that did not understand the concept in even the most remote terms.

Several of the onlookers had turned to her, not because of her inability to explain something to Darkhorse, but because she was on speaking terms with the invader. Relief was spreading among them, however. The great sorceress was once more dealing with their problem. This incident would only add to her prestige, a good thing since it was already assumed that she would take her father's place on the triumvirate should something happen to him.

Darkhorse surveyed his surroundings. "You have altered much in the shape of this place, albeit not where I stand! I feared I might have come to the wrong place, but then I recalled this one area and opened a quicker path to it! There have been so many worlds, so many universes I have searched through!"

He had made no comment concerning the protective spells that the Vraad had enshrouded their city with over time, spells that would have given *her* pause but did not, it appeared, even deserve acknowledgment on his part.

The intruder sighed, a very human sound that he must have learned from his former companion. Sharissa sensed the longing and the weariness. "Fifteen years is a long time, I imagine," she said, trying to soothe him. "It can be an eternity."

He gave her a strange look. "Through your father I have some understanding of the term *years,* little Shari! Know that when I say I have spent an eternity searching for this place, I am not being facetious or exaggerating! In your fifteen years, I have crossed a thousand thousand lands in as many worlds! Time, I have discovered, does not move the same everywhere and moves not at all in the cursed place friend Dru so aptly called the Void!" Darkhorse twisted his head so that he stared at the heavens. "The sky is more cluttered than the Void could ever be, even if this place were thrown into it! How could I have ever survived such an existence before Dru came?"

The question was not one he expected an answer for. Sharissa waited until the huge creature had calmed before saying, "My father will be happy to see you again. I can take you to him if you want."

"Little one, that is exactly what I was attempting! Last I knew, friend Dru was in danger and I had been thrust back into a place I hoped never to see—or perhaps *not* see is closer, I cannot say—again! I thought he might be in the room of worlds in the castle of the old ones, but I could not find the opening to that small universe! I feared those beings who guarded it when last I was here had sealed it, but there is no trace of them . . . and I could hardly forget the smell of those cursed horrors!"

Lochivan joined Sharissa and leaned close. "Should you not do something about all these people? They look like little children asked to solve a complex thaumaturgical question that has baffled masters! Assure them that all is well."

She saw the sense of that. Raising her arms, the sorceress called out. "There is no need to worry! There's no danger, no threat! This one is a friend of my father, and I will vouch for his actions!"

It was a pathetic speech as far as Sharissa was concerned, for it went nowhere toward answering the many questions that must be flowing through the minds of the Vraad who had assembled here. She added, "You will hear more from my father when he has had time to speak with our guest. I promise you that."

That was still not satisfactory in her mind, but the others seemed willing to live with what she had told them, understanding, perhaps, that they were lucky to know what little they did. The other two members of the triumvirate would be more vocal. Sharissa glanced at Lochivan; Barakas would know soon enough. Whatever friendship she shared with this Tezerenee, he was loyal to his father.

"You'd best go, too. I don't think I am in any danger, not from everything my father told me about Darkhorse."

"I should say not!" bellowed the beast.

Looking very, very uncomfortable, Lochivan bowed to both of them. To the young Zeree, he said, "Best I be the one to tell my father. I'm truly sorry, Sharissa, but he *should* know about this." He stopped, his words sounding as pathetic to him, no doubt, as Sharissa's had to her. "Be prepared for him. Darkhorse changes the balance if he stays around. You and I both know that."

The Tezerenee turned and joined the many others who were slowly splintering away from the crowd. Sharissa mulled over his warning even as she smiled at the darksome steed. If he chose to stay for any length of time, he *would* change the balance. Those whose loyalty teetered even a little would flock to the support of her father. Darkhorse was a potent ally. If the members of the triumvirate ever came to blows with one another, the demonic stallion might easily prove the deciding factor. Dru Zeree had no ambitions other than keeping his people together, but the same could not be said of Barakas and Silesti. The latter was one of those who had more than one legitimate reason for despising the patriarch of the Tezerenee. Several years of working side by side had not lessened the tension between them.

Darkhorse was scuffing the rubble-strewn soil with the impatience of one who is at last within striking distance of his goal after an epic odyssey but cannot find the front gate. Sharissa quickly joined him. "It's this way. The Faceless Ones moved it."

"Faceless Ones?"

"'Not-people'?" she added, wondering if he knew them by that title.

"I know not these others. Are they Vraad, also?"

"No, they're—" The young Zeree broke off. Better to show him one than try to describe the living legacies of the founders. She scanned the square, looking for the inevitable form watching them. Her eyes narrowed as her search progressed. Darkhorse waited in silence, his chilling gaze following hers.

The area was devoid of the featureless beings. Sharissa, thinking back, could not recall seeing one since her encounter in the alley. That particular creature had rushed off, as if unsettled. None of its fellows had been among the crowd that had gathered at the coming of Darkhorse. That alone made her nervous. Why would the Faceless Ones, who studied most everything else around the Vraad, avoid the startling return of the Void dweller?

Was there something they feared about Darkhorse? Vengeance? Surely not! The guardians had dealt with the ebony stallion as they might have a tiny insect. Their masters, even though only reflections of what they once had been, were not without their skills.

"Well? What is it you want to show me? Come! I wish to see little Dru again!"

"Let me show you the way, then." Still at a loss concerning the absence of the not-people, Sharissa led the shadow steed to an area to his right. Several Vraad still looked on. It did not matter if they saw where the entrance to her parents' home was. Only those the sorcerer desired to allow in would be able to cross the rift. She had no idea if Darkhorse would be allowed to make the journey unimpeded or whether she would have to find her father first. They would discover that in a moment.

A ripple in the air was her first sighting of the hole. As she neared it, Darkhorse close behind, it seemed to widen for her. Within its boundaries, the sorceress could make out a huge wooded meadow. Flowers dotted the field, sentinels in a sea of high grass.

Sharissa put one foot into the tear in reality, then stepped through. The square, the entire city, had vanished. She turned around and saw the rip. A huge, jet-black form filled its dimensions.

"At *last!*" Darkhorse trotted through the magical entrance-way unimpeded. "At last I am here!"

She could not help smiling. "Not yet, but soon. We still have a short distance to go."

His disturbing eyes followed the lay of the land. He laughed. "Only this? After the journey I have suffered, this is scarcely more than a single step!"

"Then let's take that step." Sharissa could hardly wait to see the look on her father's face when he saw the surprise she was bringing.

FROM THE EDGE of the square, Lochivan observed the departure of Sharissa and the monster. He had hoped that it would be unable to cross, but that hope was shattered a second later when it vanished behind Zeree's daughter. Yet another piece of news that would interest the patriarch.

Abandoning his watchpost for where he had left his mount, the Tezerenee pondered the significance of the demon's arrival. Though he was not one to whom prescience had been gifted, Lochivan knew that this was a moment of destiny in the lives of the Vraad. The creature called Darkhorse altered everything, and he knew that the Lord Tezerenee would work to make the future one to his liking.

Lochivan wished there were someone else who could relay the tale to his father. There was not, however, and he was, after all, his sire's son. Even if it might someday mean the death of Sharissa's father, his duty was ever to the clan.

The last thought disturbed him most, but, as with so many in the past, he merely buried it in a secret place in his mind and hurried to perform his duties as a good son always did.

IV

IN THE EASTERN quarter of the city, behind a wall of belief that divided those who followed the dragonlord from those who did not, Lord Barakas held court. Sleek red dragon banners hung from the walls. Torches created a legion of flickering specters from those folk assembled. A young wyvern, hooded, stood perched on a ledge to one side of the dais that made up the far end of the chamber. The hall was, to be sure, a mere shadow of the grand, looming citadel that the Tezerenee had once occupied before the migration, but any lack of presence upon this structure's part was more than made up for by the numbers now kneeling in respect to the patriarch. Outsiders, meaning those not born to the clan, outnumbered the armored figures by a margin that made Barakas smile. He had dreamed of such a kingdom, though he now knew it to be tiny in comparison to the vast numbers the Seekers boasted. Still, it was progress. With so many now obedient to his will, his prestige had grown . . . and that, in turn, meant even more followers. One day, not too distant, he would be undisputed master of all.

Then he recalled the gray that was spreading in his hair and the wrinkles forming on his face and the smile died. He could not be growing old. Vraad did not grow old unless they chose to do so.

Guards clad in the dark-green dragon-scale armor and fierce dragonhelms of the clan lined the walls. Most of them were nephews, nieces, cousins, and offspring. There were both men and women, each of them skilled with the weapons they held. They were doubly deadly now; the near-disaster against the Seekers had given most of them a true taste of battle. In the eyes of their fellow Vraad, who had never more than dabbled with weapons, it made them ominous, fearsome sights to behold.

"Is something amiss, my loved one?" a throaty voice whispered in his ear.

Was she growing older, too? Lord Barakas turned to his bride, the Lady Alcia. She was still the warrior goddess, even in regal repose upon her throne, striking and commanding. Like her husband, she was clad in armor, though of a lighter, more form-fitting type. The patriarch took a moment to admire her lithe body. Tezerenee armor was designed with appearance as well as safety in mind . . . and the patriarch had always enjoyed the female body. This was not to say he did not respect his wife's abilities. When the Lord Tezerenee was away, it was the Lady Tezerenee who maintained control of the clan, who organized all major activities. She was, he would gladly admit, his other half.

"Barakas?"

The patriarch started, knowing that he had drifted off again. In any other person, it would have meant nothing; most people were prone to daydreaming. Not so Barakas. There had never been time for daydreaming. The formation and then growth of the clan had always demanded his total attention. "I'm fine," he finally muttered under his breath so that only she could hear him. "Only thinking."

She smiled, something that tended to eliminate the severe cast of her otherwise aristocratic features. The Lady Alcia was always most beautiful at these times.

Barakas straightened in his throne, gazing out at his people. "All may rise!"

The crowd stood as if his words had caused someone to pull up the strings of several hundred marionettes. Even most of the outsiders, who had not been raised from birth in the martial traditions the dragonlord had created and, therefore, could not have reacted to his command with the same precision, moved in fair form to their feet. They were learning. Soon, everyone would learn.

Reegan, standing by the right of his mother, stepped forward. "Is there anyone with a boon to ask of the lord of the clan?"

Two outsiders, already rehearsed by others for this moment, stepped forward into the empty area between the dais upon which the thrones stood and the main part of the great hall where the crowds waited. One was a man who had been stout at one time but had lost much weight now that he was forced to do physical work to survive. The other was a woman of rather plain face and form who wore a gown that had seen better days. She had tried her best to recapture the beauty that had once, no doubt, been hers in Nimth, but makeup could not perform sufficient magic for her sake. Both supplicants were nervous and wary.

"Your names," the heir asked without emotion.

The man started to open his mouth, but a form in the back of the chamber caught the patriarch's attention and he signaled for silence. Esad, another of his sons—by his bride, that is—indicated that there was a matter needing the patriarch's personal attention. Esad, like most of the Tezerenee, knew better than to interrupt court with anything trivial. The dragonlord's interest was piqued. He turned to his lady.

"Would you hold court for me, Alcia?"

"As you wish, husband." She was not surprised by his request. Over the centuries, the Lady Alcia had performed this function time and again. Her decisions were as final as his own. A supplicant who failed to gain her support would lose more if he tried to convince the patriarch to alter the decision. That supplicant might also lose his head.

"Kneel as the Lord Tezerenee departs the court!" Reegan cried out in the same emotionless voice.

The throngs obeyed without hesitation, though a few newcomers were openly curious at this sudden breach of form. Barakas ignored them; his eyes were still on Esad. Now he saw that Lochivan was with him. So much the better. Lochivan would not be back so soon unless he had something terribly important to report.

The two younger Tezerenee stepped back out of the main hall as their father met them. Both went down on one knee, as did several guards on duty in the corridor.

"Stand up, all of you! Lochivan. Is he your reason for summoning me, Esad, or do you have another matter?"

"None, father," the helmed figure replied, a bit of a quiver in his response. He had never been quite the same since the clan's crossover and the near-destruction of the Tezerenee by the Seekers had only added to the damage within his mind. Something inside had been broken. Esad had become a disappointment to the patriarch.

"You are dismissed, then."

Esad bowed and walked away in silence. Barakas put an arm around Lochivan's shoulders and led him down the corridor in the opposite direction. "What matter brings you back so soon? Something concerning the younger Zeree?"

"In a sense. Father, what mention has Dru Zeree made of a huge pitch-black stallion called Darkhorse?"

"Not a horse at all, but a creature from beyond. . . . One of our demons of legend, perhaps. Master Zeree is tight-lipped when it comes to his first journey here before we crossed." The patriarch paused in midstep, then backed up to look into his son's eyes. "Why do you want to know?"

Lochivan looked as if he was not certain his father would believe what he was about to say. "It . . . he's *here*. Today, mere minutes after we separated, he materialized in the city . . . in the square. Surely you *felt* his power!"

"I felt something as I dismounted. Your brothers Logan and Dagos have been ordered to discover what it was."

"They are on a wasted mission, then. I have seen all that anyone could see of this . . . this leviathan. He crossed all of our barriers and entered the city untouched, materializing, in all audacity, in our very midst."

"Seeking, no doubt, the rift to Zeree's private world, Sirvak Dragoth, as he calls it." The Lord Tezerenee's tone spoke volumes concerning his envy. To have a kingdom all your own . . . and to waste it on only two or three Vraad and a hundred or so cursed not-people. It had been a point of contention among the triumvirate. Dru Zeree passed on only whatever secrets he felt obliged to pass on. The rest remained to him and his family alone.

"Sharissa spoke to him—"

"He listened to her?"

"As if she were his tried-and-true friend! She is the daughter of his companion . . . his teacher, too, I suspect. For all his bluster . . ." Here Lochivan shifted a bit, uneasy about voicing his opinion on so unpredictable a subject. "For all his bluster and power, this Darkhorse sounds more like a child than an ageless demon."

Barakas considered that for a moment. "What finally happened?"

"She led him through the rift and into her father's domain."

"He was not *barred* from entering it?" More than once, Tezerenee, at their lord's command, had covertly tested the doorway to Zeree's pocket universe. In most cases, they had not even been able to locate it, much less try to enter. Those that *had* managed to discover the tear in reality walked through it as if the rift were only air and not a gate at all.

"He walked through with ease."

"Interesting." Barakas stalked down the hall, each element of information being turned over and over in his mind. Lochivan scurried along, knowing he had not been dismissed yet. As he had expected, his father's interest was piqued.

Sentries in the corridor snapped to attention as their lord walked past, unmindful of their presence. Lochivan, trailing, nodded to each and scanned them for any slack behavior. That many were related to him did not matter; if he failed to report or reprimand someone who was not performing their duties to their best, it would be he who suffered, son or not. After all, Barakas had offspring to spare; one son more or less would not touch the patriarch's heart.

"He will have to depart Zeree's bottled world at some point," Barakas announced.

"Yes, my lord."

"He is a creature of vast power. Not as vast as the Dragon of the Depths, of course, but still a creature to be wary of, I suppose."

"It would seem that way." Lochivan's visage, what could be seen of it behind the helm, had grown perturbed.

"And we have some little power to work with, especially if we work in concert." *To a point!* Barakas added to himself. It was becoming more and more difficult to do even that much, almost as if the land was seeking to wipe all vestiges of Vraad sorcery, which demanded and took rather than worked *with* the world, from existence.

Lochivan chose to remain silent, trying to decipher what it was his father intended.

The Lord Tezerenee turned down a side corridor. His eyes wandered briefly to a nearby window that overlooked the jagged, decaying courtyard of some ancient noble—so he imagined it to be, that is. Whether this had been the home of some noble was a matter of conjecture; the truth was lost to time. Barakas liked to think of it as such, however, just as he liked to think of the debris-covered yard as his personal training ground. Each day, Tezerenee fought on the treacherous surface, testing their skills against one another or some outsider seeking to learn from them. The ground was left purposely ruined; no true battle took place on a clear, flat surface. If they fell, they learned the hard way what could happen to a careless fool in combat.

Tearing his gaze from the window, Barakas made a decision. He smiled and continued down the corridor at a more brisk pace.

"Lochivan," he summoned.

"Father?" Lochivan stepped up his pace and managed to catch up to Barakas, though it was hard to maintain a place at his father's side. Barakas moved with a swiftness most of the younger Tezerenee could not match at their best.

"You are dismissed."

"Yes, sire." It was to his credit that the younger warrior did not question his abrupt dismissal. During the course of his life, he had come to know when his father was formulating some plan and needed to be alone. Lochivan turned around and returned the way he had come. Barakas took no note of his departure. Only the thoughts melding together within his mind interested him.

A patrol, making its rounds, quickly made a path for him. There were three warriors, one a female, and two drakes about the size of large dogs. The warriors, their faces obscured, stiffened like the newly dead. Barakas started past them, then paused when one of the drakes hissed at him, its darting, forked tongue seeming to have a life of its own.

Barakas reached down and petted the beast on the head. Reptilian eyes closed and the tail swept back and forth, slapping against the legs of its human partner. The Vraad tugged on the leash he held, pulling the drake's collar a bit tighter in the process. Studying beast and handler, the patriarch's smile widened.

To SHARISSA, IT was as if her father had become a small boy. He had greeted Darkhorse with an enthusiasm second only to that which he displayed for his own family. She understood his excitement. Friendship was rare among her kind. Only the circumstances of their escape from Nimth had forced the Vraad to treat one another in a civil manner. Many still held their neighbors in some suspicion, although that had lessened since the first turbulent year.

Watching him now, standing among the sculpted bushes of the courtyard and talking in animated fashion with the huge, soot-skinned Darkhorse, Sharissa realized how much her father himself had changed over the last few years. She had always marveled at the differences he made in this little world and the one outside, but never at the changes those endless tasks had performed on him. His hair was a dying brown, more white now save for the impressive silver streak running down the middle. He was still narrow and nearly seven feet tall, which somehow was short in comparison to the shadow steed, but his back was slightly stooped and he had lines in his hawkish visage. The trimmed beard he wore had thinned out, too.

Fifteen years had altered him, but, for a short time, he was again the majestic master sorcerer that she had grown up loving and adoring.

"He had always hoped the dweller from the Void would find his way back," a strong yet almost musical voice to Sharissa's side informed her.

Ariela was shorter than Sharissa, which made her *much* shorter than her husband, Dru. Her hair, like the younger Zeree's, was very pale and very long, though in a braid. Her arched brows and her tapered ears marked her as an elf, as did her emerald, almond-shaped eyes. She wore a robe akin to the dark-blue one worn by her mate, but this one somehow found the curves of her body with no trouble whatsoever. Ariela was trim, athletic in form, and skilled with a number of weapons, especially the knife. Her aid had proven as invaluable as that of the Tezerenee had in keeping the refugees alive until they could fend for themselves.

"I can't blame him. Darkhorse is unbelievable! What is he? I still don't understand!"

"Dru calls him a living hole, and I am inclined to believe that."

"He has flesh, though." It *looked* like flesh upon first glance. Sharissa had even touched it. She could not deny, however, that she had felt a pull, as if the ebony creature had been about to swallow her . . . body and soul.

Ariela laughed lightly. "Do not ask me to explain any further! Even your father admits that he only hazards guesses."

Nodding, Sharissa looked around. Other than the four of them, there was no one in sight. During every other visit she had made to Sirvak Dragoth, the Faceless Ones had been visible in abundance. Now, as it had been in the square, they had vanished. "Why are we alone?"

The elf frowned. "I have no idea, and Dru was too excited to notice. They were here until just before you announced yourselves." She studied her stepdaughter's eyes and whispered, "Is there something amiss?"

In a similar tone, Sharissa replied, "You know how they seem to be everywhere. Before Darkhorse materialized in the city, I came across one that I can only describe as agitated. It hurried away, and when I looked for it I couldn't find it. Then, when I reached the square, I found hundreds of Vraad but not one of them!"

"That is not normal . . . if I may use the term in regard to them." The not-people were watchful to the point of obsession. Any event of the least significance was liable to attract their unwanted attention. An event of such magnitude as Darkhorse's return should have attracted more than a score. Though only living memories of the founding race, the entities had continued to perform their ancient tasks without fail. That they would cease now was beyond comprehension.

"You *chose* to return to this place? Remarkable!" the fearsome steed roared. Both women turned and listened.

"My curiosity overcame my fear," Dru responded. He indicated the tall structure that was the bulk of the citadel. "So much our ancestors knew! So much that was lost when they passed beyond!"

"Not far enough for my tastes! I still desire another confrontation with their servants! They had no right!"

Dru had no answer for that. Sharissa had heard him say the same thing more than once. He had feared that his unearthly companion would be forever lost in the Void or some place even worse . . . if any place could be worse than a true *no*place like that.

Darkness was beginning to descend, and the shadows began to shroud the sorcerer. Neither Dru nor his daughter had ever found a plausible explanation for the heavens and the differences in time among the various realms created by the founders. How could there be suns and moons for each? Dru had explained once that the ancients had succeeded in separating slices of reality, so to speak, from the true world. Each realm was a reflection of the original, but altered drastically by both the founders and time. The spellcasting necessary for this was all but forgotten.

It was disturbing to understand that Nimth, too, had been but one more reflection, a terrarium where the Vraad had been raised up and then abandoned.

"I understand your feelings, Darkhorse," Dru was saying, "but Ariela and I have come to care for Sirvak Dragoth as much as anyone could care for their home."

"Sirvak Dragoth? Is that what this place is called?"

"I named it thus." The elder Zeree glanced at his daughter. Sharissa felt her eyes grow moist as he explained the origin of the name. "I had a familiar, a gold and black creature crafted with careful attention to its personality. Sirvak was loyal and as good a companion as any. It helped me raise Sharissa after her mother died. Sirvak perished saving her life just prior to our leaving Nimth. For what deeds it performed for both my daughter and myself, I saw no more fitting memorial than to give its name to this citadel." He paused, clearing his throat. "I'd rather have Sirvak back . . . but a new familiar could never be the same creature."

Darkhorse shook his mane in obvious discomfort. "I understand friendship, little Dru, but love is beyond me! That he was a good memory to you is all I can comprehend!"

The shadow steed laughed then, an abrupt thing that jolted all three of his companions. One eye twinkled at Sharissa. "But come! Let us speak of joy! Darkhorse has found his friend at last! This is a good thing! I have missed your guidance, friend Dru, your knowledge of the countless things abiding in this cluttered multiverse!"

"And I welcome the chance to talk with you, but I have other tasks that require my attention. My kind depend on me, Darkhorse. A decade and a half is not enough to ensure the future of the Vraad, especially as weak as we have become."

"Then what of your offspring . . . an interesting word. Did she truly leap from you?"

Sharissa chuckled and was joined by her parents. Darkhorse's random lapses in the understanding of language was one of the many things she recalled about the creature from her father's tales. The leviathan was, in many senses, the child that Dru had described. It only proved how different his mind-set was from those of humans and elves. So knowing and powerful, yet so naive and defenseless in other ways.

"I would be happy to spend time with you, Darkhorse, as long as you understand that I, too, have duties to perform."

"Duties! Tasks! How you must enjoy them, so important do they sound!"

No one tried to correct him. Besides, Sharissa realized, she *did* enjoy much of her work. There was still so much to learn about their new home. The deep maze of catacombs and chambers beneath the city had barely even been touched. Gerrod's discoveries, which she had completely forgotten about in all the excitement, now beckoned once again. It was still a welcome change, considering her first twenty years of life had been confined mainly to her father's domain.

"It's settled, then." Dru stifled a yawn. He and Ariela were early risers, often already active well before dawn. The couple always ceased what they were doing, however, when it came time to watch the sun rise over the horizon. Sharissa joined them now and again, but always kept to one side. Her parents lived in yet another world of their own when they watched the arrival of day together.

"You are weary," Darkhorse pointed out, ever ready to state the obvious. "I recall that you enter into the nothingness you call sleep when this happens. Is that not so?"

"Yes, but not immediately." The elder Zeree rose. "I know you don't sleep, Darkhorse, and you rest only on occasion, so is there some distraction I can offer you?"

The ebony stallion glanced at Sharissa. "Will you also be entering sleep?"

"Not for a while."

"Then I will join you for a time, if you do not mind?"

She looked from Darkhorse to her parents. "I was planning to return to my own chambers back in the city. Will that be all right?"

"The other Vraad are likely still leery of him, but if you stay together, there should be no problem." Dru smiled at his former companion. "Try not to frighten too many people . . . and keep your lone wanderings to a minimum until I've spoken to my counterparts in the triumvirate."

"I will be the image of discretion and insignificance! No one will take notice of me!"

"I doubt that." The master mage chuckled. "A few of those fine folk might even benefit from a jolt or two, now that I think about it!"

"Do not encourage him, Dru," Ariela warned, though she, too, laughed at the vision of still-arrogant Tezerenee running across the shadow steed in the dark of the moons.

Sharissa kissed both her father and her stepmother on the cheek. In Dru's ear, she whispered, "How are things progressing?"

"I pick up something here and there. I've expanded the dimensions of this little dreamland of mine . . . and I think the changes are making some sense at last. Have you talked to Gerrod?"

"He refuses to leave his dwelling and he's grown more distant, almost like a shadow." Sharissa paused. "Gerrod still insists the lands are trying to make us over again, that we'll become monsters like the Seekers or those earth diggers you mentioned, the Quel."

A bitter smile replaced the pleasant one Dru had maintained up to this point. "We were monsters before we ever crossed to this world. We only wore more attractive masks then."

"The people are changing. . . . I mean . . . not like Gerrod said, but becoming—"

"Will you two be whispering to one another all evening? If so, perhaps I might as well accompany Darkhorse back to the city." Ariela's arms were crossed, and she wore an expression of mock annoyance.

"I'm leaving," the sorceress said, dressing her words in a more pleasant tone. To Darkhorse, she asked, "Will you follow me?"

"Would you like to ride, instead?"

"Ride?" She had not thought of that. They had walked the entire way from the rift to the courtyard because she had not thought of Darkhorse as a mount, but rather a being much like herself. Ride a sentient creature such as this, one that her father termed a living *hole*?

"You need have no fear! Little Dru rode me quite often! I am stronger, more swift, than the fastest steed! I do not tire, and no terrain is my equal!"

His boasting eased her concerns. "How could I resist such superiority?"

"I only speak the truth!" The demonic horse somehow achieved a semblance of hurt.

"I believe you." She went to his side and, once he had knelt, mounted. There was no saddle, but the fantastic creature's back moved beneath her, shifting into a more comfortable form. If only all horses could make their own saddles!

"Take hold of my mane."

She did, noting that it felt like hair despite knowing that it was not.

"Take care, both of you," Dru said, waving.

"We're not going on any great journey, Father!"

"Take care, anyway."

Darkhorse roared with laughter, though Sharissa was not certain as to why, and reared.

They were racing through the gates of the citadel and down the grassy meadow below before she had time to realize it.

It may have been that Darkhorse felt her stiffen, for he shouted, "Have no fear, I said! I will not lose you!"

She wondered about that. When Darkhorse had mentioned he was swift, she had still pictured his speed in terms of an actual mount, not the creature who had raced toward the city from the western shore in a matter of minutes. Now, Sharissa flew. Literally flew. The ebony stallion's hooves did not touch the ground; she was certain of that. Her hair fluttered straight back, a pennon of silver-blue reflecting in the light of a moon that was not one of those existing outside of this domain.

They were through the rift and once more in the ruined square before Sharissa even thought to ask if Darkhorse knew where the tear was located. Now she understood her father's vivid yet unsatisfying telling of his rides with the black steed. One had to experience it to understand.

The days ahead, Sharissa decided, would be interesting indeed.

IN THE CITADEL that was and was not his, the sorcerer and his elfin bride walked arm in arm to their chambers, not even bothering to watch Sharissa and her fearsome companion depart, for Dru knew the Void dweller's ungodly speed well. Thus it was that neither noticed the return of the Faceless Ones, the not-people, at the exact moment that Darkhorse and his rider returned to the true world. They stood without the walls, all those who had chosen to return to flesh and blood, and stared with sightless gazes after the vanishing duo. If Sharissa could have seen them now, she would have noted a different emotion than the uneasiness she had observed in the one in the city.

V

THREE DAYS HAD passed. One day he might have understood, but not three. Sharissa Zeree did not ignore her promises. She had said she would come, and he had prepared for her—three days ago. Now he could sense her nearing presence, at *last*, but there was another with her, one who fit nothing in his experience. Sharissa had brought someone with her, but who it was defied his abilities. He knew only that the two of them would be within sight of his hut in little more than a minute.

Hardly enough time to prepare himself. The glamour cast three days past had faded.

What goes on here? Gerrod Tezerenee wondered as he pulled the hood of his cloak about his head, carefully assuring that his features would be shadowed. With so little time available, it was possible he might blunder and cast a spell of insufficient strength. It would not do for her to see what had become of him . . . though eventually *all* Vraad might suffer the same fate. How ironic that he should be one of the first.

His eyes on the window facing the southwest—and the city he avoided with a passion—the warlock tried to concentrate. He had to finish before she was too close, lest she notice his conjuring and wonder. Dru Zeree's daughter was far more knowing than she had been when they had first met. Then, she had been a woman in form but a child in mind. Now, Sharissa walked among the Vraad as one to whom those thousands of years her senior paid homage. She was *the* sorceress.

A tiny figure on horseback materialized at the horizon. Gerrod frowned and lost his concentration. A single rider. Sharissa. What she rode upon, however, was like no steed he had ever known. Even from here he could see it was taller than the tallest horse and stronger, the warlock suspected, than any drake.

It dawned on him then that what he felt was the ebony mount. *It* was the source of great power that he had sensed.

The pace the creature set ate swiftly at the distance separating Sharissa from the hut that Gerrod presently called his home. Cursing silently, he forced himself to concentrate again on the glamour. It would be a hurried, confused thing, but it would have to do.

A light wind tickled his face. Gerrod allowed himself a sigh of relief. It was no true wind that had touched him, but rather one that indicated his spell had held. He wore his mask once more.

"Gerrod?" Sharissa was still far away, but she knew that, at this distance, the Tezerenee could hear her with ease.

There was no time to locate a looking glass and inspect his work. He would just have to hope that he had not given himself some horrible disfigurement. That would be bitter irony, indeed.

It was late afternoon, which meant that the sun was more or less behind the newcomers. Gerrod knew he would have to work things so that it was Sharissa and her—*what?*—that had to suffer the sun. He dared not let the light shine too bright upon his visage.

"Gerrod?" The slim figure leaned forward and whispered something to the tall stallion, who *laughed* loud and merrily. Sharissa shook her head and whispered something else.

It was time for him to make his entrance . . . or exit, since he was presently within his hut.

Black cloak billowing around his somber, gray and blue clothing, Gerrod stepped out into the sun, his head bent downward to maximize the shadows he desired. His heavy boots on the rocky soil alerted Sharissa of his presence.

"Gerrod!" Her smile—a *true* smile, not the one formed by the natural curve of her mouth—caused a twinge within him that he pretended to ignore.

"You are late, Mistress Zeree." He had meant to say it as if her tardiness had hardly mattered, but instead it had come out as if he had felt betrayed. Gerrod was pleased that she could not see his face now, for it was surely crimson.

"I'm sorry about that." She dismounted with ease. "I brought you a visitor I think you'll be interested in meeting."

He studied the equine form before him, noting how it was somewhat disproportionate to a normal horse. After that, he nearly stumbled, for the longer he gazed at the beast the more Gerrod felt as if he were being drawn into it. In an effort to escape the sensation, the warlock looked into the creature's eyes—only to find he had made a mistake. The pupilless, ice-blue eyes snared him like a noose, nearly drawing him further to the brink of . . . of a nameless fate he had no desire to explore further.

Blinking, he withdrew deeper into his cloak. There was always safety there. A cloak had spared him the anger of his father more than once while he had still lived among his clan. It would protect him now.

"What is it?" he asked.

"*It?* I am no it! I am Darkhorse, of course!" The stallion pawed at the earth, digging gullies in the hard, rock-filled ground. "Talk to me, not *around* me!"

"Shhh!" Sharissa pleaded to the menacing form. "He was not being insulting, Darkhorse! You should know that by now! He can't be blamed for not understanding what you are, can he?"

"I suppose not." Mollified, the beast ceased his excavation. He trotted a few steps closer to the warlock, who dared to be defiant and not back away, though he desperately wanted to. What *was* this monstrosity?

"Easy," the sorceress suggested to her companion.

"I merely wanted to see him better!" Darkhorse studied Gerrod's darkened visage so thoroughly that the Tezerenee knew the stallion saw through his glamour. "Why do you hide in such shadow?"

"Darkhorse!"

"My own desire, nothing more," Gerrod returned, speaking a bit more sharply than he had wanted. This was not going the way he wanted it to; he had no control over the situation. Between Sharissa's belated appearance and her unbelievable companion, the warlock could not think quickly enough.

"Darkhorse!" The slim woman came between them, guiding her companion back to a more decent distance as she spoke. "What Gerrod chooses to do is up to him; I've warned you about how we Vraad are. We are very much individuals; I thought three days would have shown you that already."

This beast is responsible for her not coming sooner, Gerrod noted. He had assumed as much, but it was a part of his nature that he liked to have things verified for him. It also made Sharissa's absence more forgivable in his mind. What was he compared to the mighty Darkhorse?

As he wondered that, memories concerning the unsettling creature returned to the warlock. Master Zeree had spoken of his unusual companion during his temporary exile from Nimth, an accidental exile due to too much curiosity upon the sorcerer's part. Gerrod had taken some of the elder Zeree's tale as pure embellishment, finding that the concept of a being such as Darkhorse was beyond him at the time.

Not so now. The hooded Tezerenee knew now that, if anything, Dru's story had failed to fully emphasize the astonishing nature of the ebony stallion. Small wonder. He doubted that tale could do justice to what stood before him.

"You apologize to Gerrod," Sharissa was telling Darkhorse. The warlock found that amusing; she treated the leviathan as if he were no more than a child. Yet Darkhorse *did* look contrite.

This creature . . . a child? Gerrod could not believe his own notion.

"I apologize, one called Gerrod!"

"Accepted." It was fortunate that the hood and the glamour hid his expression; the smile on his face would have likely angered both newcomers. *A child!*

"I'd wondered what became of you, Sharissa," the warlock said, seizing control of the conversation now that he had a better idea of what it was he faced. According to Dru Zeree, Darkhorse was an eternal creature, but one that had, it seemed, a very limited experience with things. Gerrod knew how to handle such personalities. "I can see now why you might have forgotten."

She colored, a simple act that somehow pleased him. It was a becoming sight . . . not that *he* cared about such things. His work was all that mattered.

"I'm sorry, Gerrod. I had to make certain that people grew used to Darkhorse as soon as possible, since he intends to remain for some time. The best way was to let him be seen in my company as I moved about the city. Whenever I needed to talk to somebody, I would introduce him to them."

Excuse me, have you met Darkhorse yet? Gerrod found the scene in his mind almost too much for him to handle without laughing. "And how successful were you?"

Sharissa looked less pleased. "Too many of them are distrusting. They think my father will use him as a tool to reorganize the balance of power in our triumvirate."

Her last words darkened the Tezerenee's mood. "My father being one of the chief proponents of that fear?"

"Actually, he has not come to confront Darkhorse yet. Silesti has, however."

What Silesti did was of no concern to Gerrod, but what the warlock's father did was. *You've remained in the background, have you, Father? What, I wonder, are you up to?* The patriarch was not one to sit back during a potentially volatile situation.

"I find that interesting," he finally responded. "Have *any* of my clan made the acquaintance of your friend here?"

"Only Lochivan. The rest of the Tezerenee don't seem interested."

What Lochivan knows, Father knows, Gerrod wanted to say. He knew that Sharissa enjoyed his brother's company, but he also knew that Lochivan was an appendage of Lord Barakas. It would have been impossible to convince the younger Zeree of this fact, however. She saw Lochivan much as she saw Gerrod— Tezerenee by birth but with minds of their own. Not like Reegan or Logan or Esad or any of the others.

"If the rest of the clan shows no interest, it's because my dear sire is *very* interested." He shifted around them, forcing the two to turn in order to face him. Better and better. He nearly had the sun behind him now. Gerrod found himself able to relax a bit more. "Never trust a sleeping drake."

His meaning was clear, but he saw that Sharissa did not take it to heart. "Lord Barakas can scheme all he wants. What could be possibly do to Darkhorse?"

Many things, Gerrod wanted to say, but the ebony stallion cut him off.

"Who is this Lord Barakas? Why should he wish me trouble?"

"Lord Barakas Tezerenee is my father," the warlock explained, his eyes seeing memories. "He is cruel, ambitious, and as deadly as the monster that graces the clan banner."

"This is your parent?" Darkhorse shook his head, sending his pitch-black mane flying back and forth. It *looked* like real hair . . . "You speak of him with disgust, possibly even *hate*! I do not understand!"

"Gerrod and his father have had differences," Sharissa offered in a diplomatic manner. "Lord Barakas is ambitious, Darkhorse. It would be wise to be careful when you do meet him. I doubt that he can cause any true problem, however. Not one of his people has the skill to match you—or even come close, for that matter—in power."

"I *am* amazing, am I not?"

"I would rather not speak of my father anymore, if you do not mind." The subject had stirred the warlock's insides. He could taste the bile. To Sharissa, he said, "I assume you have finally come to see my discovery. It's hardly as magnificent as I first thought, but there are a few fascinating items you might be interested in studying. It is late to be starting, but we can still—"

The guilty look she flashed at him made Gerrod stop.

"I'm sorry, Gerrod. Actually, I mostly rode out to explain to you why I was gone and how I won't be able to come here for a while."

Anger and a sudden, unreasonable feeling of having been betrayed stirred the hooded Tezerenee's baser instincts. He came within a breath of reaching out with his mind to a source of power she could not know he controlled, one that would allow him to strike out at random with sufficient results to assuage his bitterness.

"Too much is happening right now," Sharissa went on, oblivious to his warring thoughts. "If Darkhorse is to stay among us, he has to be made a familiar sight to the others. There's talk among many of Silesti's faction that my father will use him to put an end to the triumvirate. They think he plans to rule from Sirvak Dragoth as some sort of despot, if you can believe that!"

"*Your* father?" The anger dissipated. How could anyone who knew Dru Zeree believe the sorcerer would ever desire to rule the Vraad? The elder Zeree was nearly as much a hermit as *he* was. He had only agreed to be part of the triumvirate in order to keep Silesti and Barakas from killing one another and the rest of the Vraad in the process.

"Would that be so bad?" the demonic steed asked, his voice booming. "Friend Dru is a remarkable creature! He would only do good for your kind!"

"It was toilsome enough to get them to live with one another, let alone follow another Vraad's commands. Master Zeree is admired by many, but, in the eyes of our folk, the triumvirate guarantees that no one Vraad's will can be law. We are a very suspicious, individualistic race."

Darkhorse shook his head again, a habit, Gerrod realized, that signaled the beast's confusion.

"I'll try to explain later," Sharissa said. She gave the warlock an apologetic smile. "I *will* be back . . . and you *could* come to see me once in a while."

"Perhaps," was all he said in reply. They both knew that he would never voluntarily return to the city. That would mean contact with his clan, possibly with his father.

Sighing, Sharissa stepped to the side of her inhuman companion. Darkhorse bent his legs in a manner that would have crippled a true steed and lowered himself so that she could mount. Gerrod saw the creature's back ripple and shape itself to conform to the rider.

"It won't be too long," the sorceress added, trying to make the best of things. "Father can only do so much. He needs my help in all this."

He said nothing, knowing that any words escaping his lips now would do nothing but weaken their friendship. That might make her decide *never* to return. Then he would be completely isolated from his kind.

"Good-bye, Gerrod." Her smile was a bit feeble, possibly because she could not read his shadowed face and, therefore, did not know if he was angry or merely hurt. Sharissa knew how much he looked forward to her visits, and the warlock had assumed that she also looked forward to them. At the moment, he was not so certain anymore.

"Watch yourself," the Tezerenee blurted. "Never trust a sleeping drake, remember?"

"She has nothing to fear while I am near!" roared Darkhorse. He laughed at his own unintentional rhyme.

"As you say."

The ebony stallion turned toward the direction of the city, reared, and was already off before Gerrod could even raise a hand in farewell. Sharissa waved back at him for a brief time, but the lightning speed with which the astonishing creature ran forced her to soon abandon that act in favor of further securing her grip on his mane. Within moments, the duo were dwindling dots in the distance. Gerrod had wondered why she had ridden all the way out to him merely to tell him she would not be able to stay, but now he saw that, to Darkhorse, the distance separating the city from his habitat was little more than a short jaunt. Their much slower arrival had been planned; a speeding Darkhorse might have been mistaken for some dire threat.

"So understanding about some things, yet still so naive about others." He hoped she was correct about his father. Barakas was hardly the type to sit calmly while a potential threat such as the ebony terror represented was allowed to roam among the Vraad at will.

Knowing he was now safe, Gerrod removed both the hood encompassing his head and the glamour masking his features. It was good that Sharissa was, to a point, predictable. She had the skill and power to teleport from the city to here, but she would not make use of that ability. Her uneasiness when it came to the spell was what kept his secrets safe from her. As long as Sharissa gave him the time, he could hide what he was becoming and what he had discovered.

She would have been shocked if she had seen his unprotected visage. Even his erstwhile parents would have likely felt some sympathy for his plight, especially as they would soon follow him . . . as *all* Vraad would.

His hair was turning gray, and there were lines gouged into his skin that only age could have wrought. The others had never thought about how their sorcery was what so extended their life spans, but he had found out the truth the hard way. His own experiments, which had taxed his lifeforce further, had turned him into a creature older in appearance than either Dru Zeree or the patriarch. He could have been his own grandfather, the warlock thought in sour humor.

Sharissa would have sought to aid him, but he wanted nothing of her sorcery. He would not give in to this world, become one of its creatures. Gerrod was certain that the Vraad faced either death from old age or, if they surrendered themselves completely to their new home, a worse fate. Dru had told him of how the Seekers and others like them had once had the same ancestors as he. The founders' experiment had altered them, made them monsters. He was no more willing to fall to that fate than he was willing to let the decay of his body take him. Somehow, someway, he would save himself.

Whatever or whoever the cost, he reminded himself as he stared at the empty horizon over which Sharissa and Darkhorse had disappeared.

"WHAT IS THE purpose of this?" Rayke wanted to know. He was tired, and when Rayke was tired he grew incredibly irritable. The other elves kept silent, knowing that this was between him and Faunon. It was yet another tiny stab at the latter's authority, which had grown a bit strained of late, what with Faunon's insistence on exploring every hole in the ground, no matter how small.

Faunon, contrary to their belief, would have welcomed interference. Rayke was making *him* irritable. Had they not been told to be thorough? With the bird people in disarray, this was the perfect opportunity to make a better study of the outlying cave systems dotting the southern edges of the mountain range. The one they now stood before had all the marks of once having been used on a regular basis by either the avians or someone else.

"Try to hold your voice down to a mild eruption," he whispered at Rayke. "Unless you are so eager for a fight you are purposely shouting loud enough for every Sheeka in the world to hear."

"At least that would be something more worthy than this poking around holes," the second elf muttered, nevertheless speaking in much quieter tones.

"This will not take long. If this one does not extend into the mountain deep enough, then the others will not, either. If they *do* go farther, then the council will want to know, just in case they decide the time has come to claim the cavern aerie."

Rayke grimaced. "The council would not sanction anything as energetic as a footrace, let alone an assault on even a near-abandoned aerie."

For once, they found common ground. "They would be fools not to take advantage of this. Think of what the birds must have stored in there. Look at what we found just lying scattered about the countryside!"

One of the other elves shook a sack he carried. It was about the size of his head and quite full. The sack represented the party's greatest treasures, the enchanted medallions that the avians generally carried or wore around their throats. The precision and power of such artifacts was legend even among the elves, but there had been few for the race to study, for the bird people guarded them jealously and most were designed to destroy themselves if their wearer perished. These had not. If Faunon was correct, they had simply been abandoned. Why, he did not know. That was for the council to decide; they enjoyed endless theoretical debate, especially when it meant they could ignore more pressing matters.

Let them play with these while others take up the gauntlet, Faunon thought. *We'll make this world something more than merely a place we ended up. We'll make a future for ourselves!* Deep inside, he knew that he was dreaming. The elves as a race would never organize themselves sufficiently to make a difference in the world they had found. Too many believed that simply existing alongside the animals and plants was all the meaning there was to life. It was simple and it was safe.

"Well? Are we going in, then?" Rayke, now that he had given in to Faunon again, was eager to get things over with.

"Not all of us have to go in. Two or three should be sufficient."

"The two of us, then." It was always Faunon and Rayke. Faunon went because, as leader, he felt he was responsible for everything they did. If he was leading his party into danger, it was only right that he act as the spearhead, so to speak. Rayke, of course, preferred to do anything but sit around and wait. The others, less inclined to act unless they were commanded to, were more than willing to let the duo take the risks. Traveling and exploring were fine for them, but they were now more than willing to head home.

"The two of us," Faunon agreed. Despite their constant arguing, both elves knew they were safest with each other. Each could depend on the other to be at his back if it came to a fight. The rest of the party tended to fight as elves always fought, as a collection of individuals, not a team.

"Give us an hour," he told the others. "If we are not back by then . . ." *If we are not back by then, we will be dead or, worse yet, prisoners of the birds,* he finished in his head. There was no need to tell the others what they already knew.

Rayke had already pulled out a small glow-crystal from one of the pouches on his belt. The tiny crystal worked better than a torch when it came to producing light. Each member of the party had one. Faunon retrieved his own, and the two elves started forward. Rayke already had his sword handy, and Faunon followed suit as they stepped into the cave.

It had definitely been hollowed out by other than natural means, he saw. The walls were too smooth, the floor too flat. That was both encouraging and worrisome. It meant the tunnel system probably did go where he believed it did, but it also meant that they were more likely to run into trouble if anyone or anything was still using the cave.

There were a few tracks on the ground, mostly those of animals. The spoors were all old, so he did not fear that they would surprise a bear or young drake at some point. If they had, it would have informed him of one fact, that searching the cave was of no use. The avians would never let a wild animal take up residence in one of their active passages.

"We are heading earthward," Rayke commented. The mouth of the cave was already an uncomfortable distance behind them.

Faunon held the glow-crystal before him and verified his companion's words. They *were* heading into the earth. He suspected he had been wrong after all. The birds tended to dig upward, toward the sky they loved so, rather than down. Why would . . . ? He smiled at his own stupidity. "This might not be the birds' work."

"Quel?" Rayke had evidently picked up on the notion at the same time as he had.

"They did control this domain at one time."

"Quel, then."

Both elves grew more relaxed. If this was indeed a Quel-made tunnel, they had little to fear from its builders. The only Quel still active were those existing in the region of the southwestern peninsula . . . *if* they had not suffered the same disaster as the birds had. For all Faunon knew, the Quel had finally passed the way of the previous masters of this world.

Again, he wondered who the new masters of the realm would be. Why could it *not* be the elves? Why did his people sit back and let others rule?

He knew he must have said something out loud, for Rayke turned to him and asked, "What was that?"

"Nothing."

"We are going to be out of sight of the entrance in a moment if we keep heading down and to the left like we are doing."

Faunon saw that it was true. He was tempted to turn back, but decided that they might as well go a little farther. A tiny feeling nagged at his mind, as if he were just sensing the fringe of something. When the elf tried to concentrate on it, however, it almost seemed to pull away to a place just beyond his ability to reach.

The tunnel, he decided, though the explanation did not suit him. *It is all this earth around us.* Tunnels were for dwarves, assuming any still existed, not elves. Elves enjoyed sunshine, trees, and—

"Water!" Rayke snarled, turning the word into an epithet. He had good reason to do so, Faunon thought as he, too, gazed at the sight before them.

The passage dipped farther down . . . but the rest of it was submerged beneath a vast pool of water as inky as a moonless, starless night. It almost looked as if someone had purposely filled the tunnel up at this point.

"That ends it, Faunon." The other elf started to turn.

"Wait." Faunon was all for departing as well, but he wanted to get a closer look at the pool. With the crystal before him, he stalked over to the edge and knelt. His face and form were reflected back at him, ghoulish parodies of the original. Even this close, he could see nothing beneath the surface. Faunon was tempted to drop the glow-crystal into the pool and watch its descent, but the unreasonable fear that he would disturb something best left not disturbed made him pause.

"You will not see anything! I can tell that from here. Why do you not just—"

Sleek, leathery hands rose from the pool and clawed at Faunon's throat.

"Get back!" Rayke rushed forward, his blade extended toward the water.

Faunon lost his grip on the glow-crystal and it plummeted through the water, momentarily illuminating the world beneath. He saw, for an instant, his attacker, a broad-jawed, amphibious creature built along the lines of an elf. It had round, almost froglike eyes and webbed hands and feet. Without thinking, he thrust with his sword at the water dweller and had some slight satisfaction when the blade bit into one of the creature's arms.

A second blade passed by Faunon's right. The point of Rayke's sword skewered the monstrosity through the neck. It let out a bubbling gasp and shuddered. By now, the crystal was far below. Faunon's attacker became little more than a stirring in the black depths of the pool. Occasionally, the ever-receding speck that was the gem was briefly covered by some part of the thrashing creature's limbs.

At last, the surface of the pool grew still. The body of the would-be attacker did not float to the top, yet another odd thing. The glow-crystal had sunk out of sight, revealing the incredible depth of the tunnel.

"Quel tunnel, definitely," Faunon said, rubbing his neck and thinking about the claws that had almost torn his throat. "But that was a Draka. They serve the birds."

Rayke cleaned the tip of his blade off. "Draka are not generally so blood-thirsty . . . and they are usually cowards more often than not. That one wanted to tear you apart."

Again, Faunon felt as if something was nearby. He knew better than to try to concentrate on identifying it. Better to leave now, before it grew too interested in them. The other elf apparently did not feel whatever it was he did, so per-haps, Faunon hoped, it was just a touch of paranoia or exhaustion.

"Can we go now?"

He nodded to Rayke and stood. A quick wipe cleaned his own blade well enough for now; he would do a more thorough job on it when they were away from here.

"Where to next?" his companion asked as they abandoned the submerged passage.

"South."

"South?" Rayke looked at him wide-eyed.

"That *is* the direction you want to go, is it not?"

"South. Yes, but I thought you . . ."

Faunon took the one last glance back at the pool just before their trek took them around the curve and blocked his view. He thought he saw bubbling at the surface, but he had no desire to go back and investigate further.

"I changed my mind. I think I would like to go home."

The other elf did not press further, which, to Faunon, was a good thing indeed. It meant he would not have to try to explain a growing fear that had no basis other than a simple, nagging sensation in the back of his mind . . . a sensa-tion that he somehow sensed was, like the fearsome stallion, only a precursor for things to come.

VI

As MUCH AS she disliked having to tear herself away from Darkhorse, there finally came a point when Sharissa had to return to some of her other duties. She had come to realize that the very night after her unsatisfying visit to Ger-rod when, returning to her domicile, the sorceress found petitioners. Their grievances were petty, as far as she could recall, but it had been her idea to take on some of her father's lesser roles in order that he might deal with more im-portant projects. In time, Sharissa hoped to convince him that it would be good if he took on subordinates. Unlike his counterparts, Dru tried to do everything for fear that, if he did not, the balance of power would shift too far to one side. It had almost been impossible to make him give her this much. Not that she had not had enough to do without taking some of *his* work in addition to her own roles.

Like father like daughter? she thought wryly.

The petitioners were dealt with accordingly, but Sharissa soon rediscovered her other projects. One of the few Vraad who worked with her brought up the subject of the system of subterranean chambers existing beneath the city. In some places, the surface level was proving treacherous, for time had weakened the earth here and there and one person had already died when the floor beneath him gave way and he fell to his death. At some point, Sharissa had started organizing a mapping campaign that would seek out the weak areas. It now became evident that those involved had no idea what they were doing when she was not there to supervise them. How, she wondered, had her kind ever survived the crossover? Sometimes the sorceress was amazed that they could even feed themselves.

Darkhorse was gone when she looked for him. The next day, she found he had returned to Sirvak Dragoth, but not before shocking several inhabitants by racing about the city perimeter in the dead of night.

"You can't do that," Sharissa scolded, pacing the length of the chamber where she did her research. It was part of an oval building that had once contained a library, although all the books had crumbled with time. The young Zeree was starting to fill the shelves with notebooks of her own, however, and, with the aid of others, hoped to one day gather a collection as vast as the multitude of mantels indicated the collection of the founders had been. She had once feared that Darkhorse would not be able to maneuver himself through the narrow, winding halls, but Sharissa had forgotten that he only *resembled* a horse. Watching him shift and shape himself accordingly had been a novel if stomach-wrenching experience. "Do you want to undermine what we've accomplished? If you go scaring folk needlessly, they'll fear you all the more! Have you any idea of the image you project?"

The massive, pitch-black steed laughed. His chilling orbs were all aglitter as he voiced his amusement. "A fearsome one, indeed! One fellow dropped to his knees and pledged his loyalty to friend Dru . . . and all I did was *wink* at him as I passed! Nothing more!"

"Do you want them to fear my father?"

He sobered. "It is not Dru that they fear; it is me!"

"And you represent him."

"I—" The sight of so menacing a creature suddenly struck still by understanding almost made the sorceress forget her annoyance with him. The feeling did not last long, however.

"You have much to learn about the pettiness and suspicious nature of the Vraad, Darkhorse."

He was slow in replying, but what he said surprised her at that moment, though, in retrospect, she would realize that she had seen it coming. "I do not care for the ways of the Vraad very much. They are not like Dru or you. They curse me behind my back, thinking I have ears as weak and foolish as theirs, and call me monster! They do not *try* to understand me, while I have willingly struggled to comprehend all things around me! Nothing I do lessens their fear and distrust! I have acted in all ways I can think of, yet they care no more for me than when I first appeared in the square!"

Darkhorse did something then that Sharissa had never seen him do. He turned his head to the left and blinked. In all the time the sorceress had spent with him, she had never seen the ebony stallion blink. That, however, was nothing compared with what occurred immediately after, for a brilliant glow materialized before the eternal, a glow that expanded in rapid order.

A portal! Darkhorse had not made use of this skill since his stunning arrival, and so it had taken Sharissa a moment to comprehend what it was the eternal was doing. His every movement reminiscent of a frustrated child—the young Zeree recalled herself—Darkhorse gave her no time to react. He was through the magical gateway and away within seconds. She had barely time to call his name before the portal shrank into nothing, leaving her standing alone in the middle of the chamber without a notion as to where he had gone or what he planned to do.

"Serkadion Manee!" Sharissa wanted to throw something against one of the walls, but forced herself to stay where she was until the desire died. Why was nothing easy? Why did everyone have to fight her, no matter how minuscule the reason?

Sharissa waited, but after several minutes passed and the shadow steed did not reappear, she knew it was futile to sit and worry any longer. Darkhorse was predictable in some ways. He would return to the square and then to Sirvak Dragoth. Either that or spend a few hours running wild through the woods and plains—hopefully without spooking anyone else. He had done this once before. Of one thing she was certain: the eternal would not abandon the city, not while his companion of old remained there. He had no one else to turn to and, unless she had misread him, which was possible but not likely, the dweller from the Void desperately craved friendship. It was as if Darkhorse had tasted a fruit long forbidden to him. Had he not, after all, searched world after world for her father after the guardians of the city had exiled him from this place?

Realizing that Darkhorse would return only when Darkhorse chose to, Sharissa returned to her work. There was always so much to do, so much to organize. Ever the first to admit she was very much a reflection of her elder, the sorceress knew that, before long, she would become so engrossed in what she was doing that the day—and, she hoped, the shadow steed's *tantrum*—would pass without her even realizing it.

First on her agenda was the mapping situation, something long overdue and growing even more so each week. That led her to a reconstruction phase recommended by one of the Vraad who assisted her. It had something to do with an expected need to increase food production through farming, she recalled. . . .

"LADY SHARISSA?"

She looked up, blinked several times in rapid succession when it occurred to her that it was getting dark in her chamber, and then frowned when the unsightly figure standing near the hall entrance moved closer. He carried an oil lamp that served more to add an appearance of ghoulishness to his features than it did to illuminate the room. That he had gotten this far meant he had bribed one of her aides. She would have to speak to them in the morning.

"Bethken, isn't it?"

He bowed, somehow keeping the lamp balanced at the same time. "It is, yes, lady. I know it grows late, great lady, but I wondered if I might—"

Trying to hide her disgust, Sharissa waved the robed figure forward. Bethken had once been a stout man—by choice—but fifteen years had taken their toll on his girth. For some reason, though, his skin had never taken a fancy to his new slimness and had, therefore, merely gathered in layer after layer of loose flesh about his person. Bethken looked very much like an old waterskin just emptied. As for his loyalties, he had none. Like many Vraad, he was technically under her father's banner, but that was mostly because the others had never had anything of sufficient value to sway him. No doubt, he had come in the hopes of gaining something of value from her. "What is it you want?"

"First, allow me to offer you light." He put the oil lamp down on one of Sharissa's note sheets, staining it in the process with oil.

The sorceress wanted to scream, but she knew that was bad form. For many Vraad, Bethken's way was as close as they could come to being congenial. It was not supposed to matter to Sharissa that what he seemed more like was a serpent sizing up a tasty field mouse.

In an effort to avoid further damage to her work, either from stains or, worse yet, a flash fire, she took the lamp, placed it on a stand nearby, and said, "My thanks to you, Bethken, but I can provide my own light."

The petitioner stumbled back as the chamber became brilliantly lit by a soft, glowing spot near the ceiling.

"Gods!" The other Vraad looked up, an envious expression blossoming as he admired her handiwork. "If only I could . . ."

"You came to see me for a reason?" She did not care for the way his eyes grew covetous when he turned his attention back to her. He could see her much better in this light, true, but it was not merely lust for her that she read. Bethken was one of those to whom a loss of power was like stealing the food from his mouth. He hungered for it, and the wonders it could give him. In Sharissa he saw much of what he hungered for.

"It is always glorious to see such skill in these dark times, lady." The man fairly fawned upon her. Any success he might have had, however, was countered by the constant shifting of his loose skin as he talked and moved. "Would that we could return to the days of our greatness."

"I doubt even you would want to return to Nimth now."

"Hardly!" He looked shocked, as if she were mad to even make mention of such a thing.

"Good." Sharissa nodded. "Now, what is it you *want*? I have many things to do."

"The demon; he is not about?"

"Darkhorse is no demon, Bethken, and, as far as your question . . . do you see him here?"

His laughter was forced. "Forgive me, Lady Sharissa. I meant him no insult. It's just that it would be better if he were not here; he might grow heated at some of what I wish to convey to you."

If you ever succeed in conveying it, the sorceress thought wryly. "Go on, please."

Bethken bowed again, sending his folds of skin into renewed jiggling. "You know that Silesti's faction has been vocal concerning their fear of the dem— your companion?"

"Of course."

"I have heard that Silesti thinks to go beyond mere words, that he desires to *remove* the creature."

He was obviously hoping for some sort of dramatic reaction, but Sharissa had no intention of satisfying him. She had heard the rumor already and knew it to be false. Silesti had admitted to Dru that the thought had crossed his mind, but he had decided that it would be a breach of faith to Sharissa's father, whom he respected and, though neither man would admit it, even liked. Silesti trusted Dru, and the elder Zeree trusted the somber, black-suited figure.

"Your news is hardly news to me."

The man looked crestfallen. It was interesting how so many people came to her with what they imagined was important information. Like Bethken, they wanted compensation, of course. To be owed a favor by any of the members of the triumvirate or even someone close to them was a coup indeed.

"He seeks to call a meeting of the triumvirate, at which point he will—" the unsightly man babbled.

"Strike. He'll kill my father and the Lord Tezerenee and chain Darkhorse." *As if chains could hold an entity such as the shadow steed.*

"I thought—"

"You do have my thanks for trying, Bethken. I'm sorry that you went to the trouble of coming all the way here for this. I hope you don't have far to walk."

Her less-than-subtle hint that he had overstayed his welcome mortified the wrinkled figure. He hemmed and hawed for a moment, then bowed once more.

"Perhaps another time, Lady Sharissa. It was no trouble, and I have the satisfaction of retaining a memory of your beauty. That is reward enough. Good night!"

Bethken remained bent over as he backed out of the chamber. It was not until he had vanished from sight that Sharissa recalled his oil lamp. She started to call after him, then decided that he knew by this time that he had forgotten it. Certainly walking about in the dark should have informed him of the fact. If Bethken returned for the lamp, Sharissa would give it back to the horrid man and turn him out again. If he did not, she would have someone return it in the morning.

Her research soon enveloped her in a cocoon of forgetfulness. More than once she had followed in her father's footsteps, sometimes finding the morning sun creeping across the table where she worked. Each time that happened, Sharissa swore she would not do it again.

She finished writing notes about another of her pet projects, a study of the effects on the various individuals who made up the population of the city. Of late, many Vraad had grown more weathered in appearance. She could not bring herself to think of them as old, because then she would have to think of her father dying at some point. Still, it was highly probable that, in abandoning Nimth, the Vraad had lost part of what made them near immortal. Something in the sorcery of Nimth that was missing in this world . . . unless this was some trick of the lands themselves.

Looking up, Sharissa thought, *Could what Gerrod said once be true? Could this world be changing us to suit its, the founders', desires? Is that what the Faceless Ones are doing among us?*

Almost as if conjured by her thoughts, a shape seemed to move across the entranceway. Sharissa squinted, but the figure, if it *had* been there, was now gone. Thinking of Bethken, she rose and walked carefully toward the outside corridor. At her command, the ball of light floated down from the ceiling and preceded her into the hall. Sharissa glanced left and right, but the corridor was empty.

She had no idea what the hour was, but knew it had to be very late. Returning to her notes, Sharissa started to straighten things away, fully intent on returning to them after a good sleep. Her task had barely begun, however, before her attention was caught by a flickering motion to her side.

It was the oil lamp. The sorceress smiled at the apprehension she had briefly felt touch her. Reaching over, she doused the flame.

Her hands succeeded in preventing her fall to the floor, but only just so.

If someone had asked Sharissa to describe the sensation she had just experienced, the young Zeree might have best put it as the lifting of a veil from her eyes. The night was the same, but it was now part of her existence, not merely a thing in the background.

. . . sa!

"Darkhorse?" She shook her head in order to clear her thoughts further. Had there been a voice in her head, one that reminded the sorceress of the ebony stallion? Sharissa waited, hoping to catch something more. The Vraad had some ability in mindtalk, but this had been no Vraad. She was not even certain there *had* been a voice. Perhaps it had been a stray thought of her overworked mind, but then, what had it concerned? *Sa* was no word she recalled, but it was the last syllable of her own name, and Sharissa had, at that instant, felt an urgency.

The nearest window gave her a view of the center of the city. She strode over to it and peered outside. One of the moons was visible—Hestia, if she recalled—but nothing out of the ordinary was revealed in the dim illumination the harsh mistress of the night offered.

"I'm a tired fool," she muttered, smiling at her own silliness. If Darkhorse had called to her, he would certainly have tried again after having failed to reach her the first time. The eternal was nothing if not persistent. In fact, it was more likely that he would have materialized before her rather than call to her using the less-than-trustworthy method of mindtalk. For one with the stallion's abilities, it was a simple thing. For the weakened Vraad, it was much, much more difficult. No, Darkhorse had not called her; she could not sense his presence anywhere—

Anywhere? Her mind snapped to full alertness at last.

Sharissa could not sense Darkhorse anywhere. He was in neither the city nor the surrounding countryside. When he had first come to the western shores of this continent, the sorceress had felt him almost at once. She had been the only one, as far as she recalled. If *she* could not find him, then it was certain that no one else could either.

Sirvak Dragoth! He has to be there! Though there was no reason to believe the eternal was in danger, Sharissa had a feeling of foreboding. She knew that he was *not* in Sirvak Dragoth. Even from there, Sharissa had always been able to vaguely detect his odd magical emanations, an apparently natural and ongoing process of the stallion's nebulous "body."

Nothing. It was as if Darkhorse had left the continent. While it was very possible he had, she could not see him leaving in so abrupt a manner, even after his petulant attitude earlier. He would have come to speak to her, to say good-bye. In many ways, the leviathan was very predictable. Sharissa knew him very well after only these past few days. His habits were ingrained to a degree that even the most predictable human could not match.

Her work completely abandoned now, Sharissa pondered what to do next. If her fears were without merit, then she was thrusting herself into a mad, futile chase. If there *was* merit, then what *had* happened to her father's old comrade . . . and did her father know?

The desire for sleep was beginning to nag at her, but it was still only an infant in strength. The longer she delayed, however, the more dominant the demand would become. Sharissa began plotting her move, knowing that her time limit was short; the sorceress had already taxed herself the night before.

It was a shame, Sharissa thought, that she had no hound to follow his trail— providing Darkhorse had even left one. He moved more like the wind, and the only way she had ever been able to keep track of him was by reports from fearful and angry colonists and her own higher senses. Gathering information would take too long, and she had already tried to detect his present position.

The whimsical notion of the hound intruded upon her thoughts again, but it took Sharissa time to understand what it was her subconscious was trying to tell her. What use was a hound when she had no trail, and what did it have to do with her now useless ability to sense where Darkhorse was at this moment?

A hound followed a trail left by its prey, but there was no trail . . . was there?

"Not *physical*, but maybe magical!" she hissed, frustrated at herself for not seeing it sooner. Darkhorse was unique, being a creature whose very substance was akin to pure power given sentience. Yet, both Vraad sorcery and that of this world left a residue of sorts.

Did Darkhorse leave such a trail wherever he went?

She searched with her mind, seeing first the prismatic view of the world, then the lines of force that crisscrossed through everything. That the others who held some degree of power saw only one or the other when they sought to use their abilities always bothered her, for she wondered why she had been singled out. In fifteen years, the sorceress had never been able to train anyone to see the lifeforce of the world as she did.

To her surprise, the trail was clear. So foreign a magic was Darkhorse that he was a blight upon the otherwise colorful and organized landscape Sharissa perceived. Even after nearly a day had passed since his frustrated retreat from her scolding, the memory was still strong.

I didn't see this? It was not so surprising, in retrospect. Did she study her shadow every day? What about the footprints she left in the soil when she went walking in the fields beyond the city? When one was astride so overwhelming a being as Darkhorse, even the world itself faded into the background.

"Sharissa?"

The voice startled her so, coming as it did after so many hours of solitude. Sharissa turned, already knowing who it was who had invaded her chambers. "Lochivan? What do you do here at *this* hour?"

The Tezerenee chuckled and stepped into the light. He carried his helm in the crook of one arm, allowing Sharissa to see the clan features he tended to hide more often than not. In truth, between Gerrod and his brother there was no comparison; Lochivan favored his father's ursine features far too much to be considered handsome. "I drew a late watch. The patriarch plays no favorites, especially where his own children are concerned. When my watch was over, I could not sleep. I thought the solitude of the city would help, so I walked." He shrugged. "I've known of your habit of staying up till all hours for years now, Sharissa. I thought you might be awake when you *should* be sleeping. When I saw the light and your figure outlined in the window at one point, I knew I was all too correct in my assumption."

She was chagrined; it was true that this was not the first time he had stopped by. It was only that his timing could not have been worse . . . and his presence reminded her of who in the city would most profit by Darkhorse's disappearance, though she found it hard to believe that the entire clan could muster the strength to threaten him.

"Is something wrong?" He had taken her silence to be, in part, an acceptance of his presence. Lochivan gazed around the vast room as he joined her, his eyes resting on Bethken's unwanted gift. His mouth crooked upward at the ends as he put his helm on the table and examined it.

"A present from someone trying to worm his way into my favor," she explained, then, realizing she had never answered his first question, added, "Nothing. Nothing's wrong. I was just about to retire for the evening."

"What's left of it." Lochivan put the lamp down. "I probably shouldn't bother you, then. I can come back during the day."

Despite herself, Sharissa could not help feeling that there was something amiss with the conversation. She knew what she was *not* telling Lochivan, but was there something else that he was not telling her?

"Lochivan, what do you know about Darkhorse?"

His eyes told her she had guessed correctly the reason for his being here. It had been too coincidental, even recalling his previous visits.

He said nothing, but there was now a tiny flame, a match or some minor use of power, at the tip of his index finger. The oil lamp flickered to life. . . .

SHARISSA REREAD THE notes she had taken on the subterranean mapping project. *Should take care of any worries, she thought. Now if they'd just do it the way I've described it and let me get on to something else!*

Looking up from the table, the sorceress had the oddest feeling that something had passed her by, some event she should recall. Considering the many duties she had usurped from her overworked parent, not to mention her own research, Sharissa was not surprised that she might have forgotten something. Her eyes wandered the room in a distracted manner while she tried to think of what it was.

Her gaze came to rest on the oil lamp, which blazed high even after hours of use. The slim sorceress studied it further, finding some doubt in the image before her but at a loss as to explain just exactly what was out of place.

Should she douse it? A part of her saw the needless waste of oil, yet it seemed so unimportant a task, hardly worth rising for. She could always douse it when her work for the night was finished. That was not that long, was it?

Still, when she turned back to her work, her mind refused to leave the lamp to its function. It was as if the simple object was becoming the focal point of her existence.

I'll just douse the flame and put it out of sight. It had to be getting very late if she was so concerned about a simple object. Sharissa started to rise, but then her attention wandered to a page of notes concerning a reconstruction phase that somehow involved future food production. The sorceress sat down and started to read. The plan had merit, but had she not read something similar to it? The more she perused the notes, the more the sorceress wondered at the familiarity of the recommendation.

The parchment fell from her hand. At the bottom of the recommendation was an analysis of the plan—in *her* handwriting and dated this *very* evening!

"Serkadion Manee!" she swore. Small wonder it sounded familiar to her; she recalled now reading it and making the suggestions at the bottom. How could she have forgotten it? Had the night drained her so much?

A shadow on the table flickered, as though living.

Sharissa turned and stared at the lamp—which she knew she had planned to dispose of at some point.

The sorceress rose from her chair with such fury that the glow she had cast to light the chamber grew momentarily into a miniature sunburst and the chair itself went tumbling backward as if seeking to escape her. Sharissa resisted an impulse to return to her work, to begin anew her research that she had abandoned earlier.

The closer she moved to the lamp, the stronger the flame became. The young sorceress found herself slowing more and more. She renewed her efforts instantly, knowing that if she continued to slow at the rate she had been, she would never even come within arm's reach of her goal.

She all but closed her eyes as her fingers neared the flame, for it not only blazed as bright as her own magical light had, but the movements of the fire had a hypnotic effect.

"You've fooled me before! Not again!" she snarled at the innocent-looking lamp.

The flame rose high, almost causing Sharissa to pull her fingers back lest they be burned. Instead, she remembered herself and reached forward to end the battle between the devious trap and herself. "Not good enough!"

Tongues of hungry flame washed over her hand, seeking to blacken and curl her slim fingers before finally reducing them to ash. So it would have been if Sharissa had been any other person. Reflex had made her pull back the first time, but thought had reminded her that she was, after all, one of the most powerful spellcasters among her people. This pathetic thing before her was a clever but not so potent toy whose greatest strength had been its anonymity. Now that she knew the enemy's choice of weapons, there was no difficulty. It had only been the lamp's hypnotic gleam that had stayed her so far.

Her hand came down on the source of the flame and she cupped the mouth, holding her hand over the opening until she was certain she had ended the threat. A simple probe verified that the lamp was once more just a lamp. As long as she did not light it, it could not assault her mind. That was how she had evaded its trickery last time, only to fall victim to it again when—

"Lochivan!"

She knew her anger and her growing exhaustion were making her reckless at a time she should be thinking clearly, but that did not seem to matter the more she thought of the betrayal. Lochivan had always been her good friend, almost as much as Gerrod . . . who *had* warned her that his brother's good company meant nothing when the patriarch gave a command.

"Lochivan, damn you!"

The Tezerenee *did* have Darkhorse. She remembered everything now, including the brief contact between the ebony stallion and herself. True, Sharissa could no longer sense the eternal, but she knew the trail would point to the drakes and their masters. "Lochivan, you and Barakas better pray to your Dragon of the Depths that Darkhorse escapes and gets you first!"

It would mean a spell of teleportation. She had cast such a spell only a few times over the years, her irrational fear that she would end up in some limbo similar to the Void keeping her from performing the spell on a regular basis. Darkhorse needed her aid, however. She could not know if her father had sensed his former companion's danger, and Sharissa did not have the time to seek him out—not in her distraught mind, that is. Each moment that passed, and too many had passed already while she hesitated, made rescuing the shadow steed more and more unlikely.

She raised her arms and took a deep breath. A moment to collect her thoughts and she would be gone.

A disturbing sensation brushed her mind. Something flashed around her neck, making it all but impossible to breathe.

Behind her, a voice, Lochivan's voice, calmly said to another unseen intruder, "Just in time. I told you not to doubt me."

Sharissa's world became a buzzing blur . . . then a shroud of silence and darkness.

VII

"Gerrod."

He looked up at his sudden guest, the enveloping hood masking any surprise he felt at the newcomer's intrusion.

"Master Dru."

In the light that did succeed in invading the hut, Dru Zeree was a fearful sight. Gerrod's eyes narrowed. The sorcerer's hair was going gray, and there were lines across his visage. He was worn out from something, yes, but Gerrod recognized something else, something that those who saw the elder Zeree every day would not pay so much attention to because they themselves were probably suffering a similar fate.

The sorcerer was aging. Not at so great a pace as the Tezerenee was, but aging nonetheless. Gerrod shivered. It was yet another confirmation of his fears about this land. *Still,* the warlock could not help thinking selfishly, *Master Zeree has at least had the luxury of enjoying a healthy life span of a few thousand years or so. Why is it I who is cheated?*

"I need your help, Tezerenee. You know him better than I, and I think you have the ingenuity that will enable you to follow him wherever he has taken her."

The warlock shifted, knowing he looked more like a bundle of cloth than a man. He did not care. The cloak and hood allowed him to withdraw from the world for a time. His few visitors also tended to believe that his appearance was designed to unsettle them. "You might explain a little what that statement is supposed to mean to me."

Dru sighed, trying to remain calm. "Barakas has Sharissa. I'm sure of it."

Despite his best efforts, Gerrod could not prevent himself from jerking to attention. "What do you mean? Does he think he can hold her in his private little kingdom? My sire has always been mad, but not stupid! What's happened? Is it civil war at last?"

His visitor waved him to silence. "Let me . . . let me explain better." Dru visibly collected his thoughts. "At some point probably three days ago, Sharissa and Darkhorse vanished. . . ." He shook his head. "You don't know of Darkhorse, do you? I suppose I have to explain him—"

"I know him. Continue on."

A puzzled look flashed across Dru's visage, vanishing the instant he resumed his tale. "They disappeared. No one noticed until the next day. I should have, but Sharissa often lost herself in projects lasting through the night. As for Darkhorse, the pocket universe supporting Sirvak Dragoth seems to dull my perceptions of his presence. It wasn't until I left the citadel and returned to this world that I noticed his absence. Soon after, people began asking about Sharissa. I found she had ridden out of the city in this direction—"

"She visited me. That was how I knew of your Darkhorse." Gerrod mouthed the words with care, not wanting Sharissa's father to know just how upset he was becoming. The sorcerer might then wonder why this Tezerenee would be so torn over his daughter's disappearance. They were known to be friends, of course, but still . . .

"She returned from that visit. I found that out later on. After questioning a few more trustworthy souls, I learned she was last known to be at work in her chambers. Someone said I should look for a man named Bethken, who had evidently sought Sharissa out for some reason, but I couldn't find him. His quarters were empty. Anything he could have carried was gone."

"You think he's under my father's protection."

Dru took a deep breath. Gerrod knew that the worst was yet to come, and he had to admire the elder Zeree's ability to remain coherent throughout what must surely be an ordeal of the greatest magnitude for him. "I journeyed to the eastern sector of the city, not wanting to believe the patriarch would do something so foolish, but rumors, substantial ones, kept insisting otherwise." The sorcerer shook his head. "I'll not go over what I discovered concerning Darkhorse, save that I think he fell to your clan also. His disappearance . . . *total* disappearance . . ."

He touched his temple, indicating that Darkhorse was beyond even his higher senses. Gerrod had already suspected that. He, too, had noted the absence of the creature upon waking that morning. Not knowing any better, he had merely assumed that Darkhorse had departed on some exploration with Sharissa. It would not have been at all surprising. She hated teleportation, and the phantom steed gave her a way of crossing distances in little time.

Gerrod looked up and saw Dru anxiously waiting for him to digest what had already been told. "And what did my father say about all this? I assume he gave you some imperious speech."

"The sector was empty. They were all gone."

"*What?*" In his shock, the warlock knocked over a sheaf of notes, spilling them on the stone floor he had so carefully constructed for this, his latest abode. He ignored the scattered sheets. "What do you mean? Gone? Preposterous!" Yet, despite his words, Gerrod recalled his own past and how swift the clan could be when it desired to move from one location to another. It was one of many aspects of his father's constant war games, the need to move while the enemy was distracted.

Move over a thousand people during the dead of night? The patriarch would hardly leave his followers behind, not if he was planning a new empire. "Where did they go? East seems likely."

"I can't say for certain. Darkhorse's presence could very well be shielded from me, I suppose." The elder Zeree was tired, so very tired. Gerrod could sympathize, being just as driven in his own way. If anyone knew of his research and the hope and fear some of it stirred inside him, they might be tempted to put an end to the warlock . . . or praise him as a hero to his folk. Gerrod had no desire for either destiny. He was not even comfortable with his great discoveries. They promised death as much as they promised life.

"They must have left *some* trail!" There was something amiss. Something more that the master mage had not yet revealed to him.

He was given the answer almost immediately. "There is a trail, a vague and possibly false one, but I lack the ability to follow it to its conclusion. I told you about my time in the Void and how I finally escaped, didn't I?"

"You are surely not suggesting . . ."

"Darkhorse can open . . . paths . . . into other realms. He did so for me that once." Dru's features relaxed for a moment as his memories surfaced, then, recalling his daughter's predicament, the sorcerer continued. "I may be crazy, but it explains why I can find no trace. I've searched east as far as I dare, but I've known from the start that they didn't head that way. No, I think that perhaps because they held Sharissa, Barakas was able to force Darkhorse to create a path for the Tezerenee to march through—a path I believe must extend, not to anywhere on this continent, but to a domain the patriarch hasn't been able to forget despite the last fifteen years."

"*The Dragonrealm.*" Gerrod said the name his companion could not, the cold tone in his voice much like the tone he might have used greeting his father, the clan master. It was almost too much to accept, but it was so very like the elder Tezerenee to plot such madness and make it work. Paths beyond this world that led to the Dragonrealm. His father, after years of bitter loss, at last having the means by which to build himself a grand empire. The magic of the creature called Darkhorse doing so easily what, to the warlock, was a feat even the Vraad at their most powerful would have had difficulty in performing.

Sharissa stolen.

"Will you help me?" Dru asked in expectation.

"What is it you want of me?"

"A way to follow them. I know you, of anybody, must have some theory. Silesti and I have more than enough volunteers. This time, the drake and his children will be made to pay!" The sorcerer's hands crackled with power.

Gerrod marveled at the power before him even as he was revolted by it. Each time Sharissa had come to visit him, he could not help thinking how this same power had, under the control of the founders, made creatures like the Seekers from men who had once resembled the Vraad.

"You seem far more capable than I in this matter," he pointed out. "If anyone has the ability, it's you."

The glow faded with an abruptness that made Gerrod blink. Dru put his face in his hands. "I *can't!* Nothing I know is sufficient!"

"Your blank-faced allies—"

"Walk about as if all is right in the world! If I had less faith, I might believe they were, in part, responsible for no one finding out until after it was too late! A thousand souls and who knows how many drakes and other animals . . . and they vanished *overnight!*"

Recalling how their sorcerous servants had acted toward the creature from the Void, in the end exiling him for what was supposed to be forever, the warlock did not doubt that, from the first, the not-people had seen Darkhorse as an agent of chance disturbing their carefully crafted experiment. It was not beyond his imagination to visualize their pleasure at the shadow steed's sudden departure. That Sharissa had also been taken was merely incidental.

Gerrod knew his belief in this was built on his own distaste for the featureless beings, but he cared not a whit. They were, in his eyes, the enemy. It was one of the few opinions he shared with his former clan.

He stared for a time at the one Vraad other than Sharissa he had truly come to admire. Dru ran his hands through his graying hair, the silver streak somehow remaining unmussed throughout the motion. Gerrod realized that Dru had probably not slept since discovering that Sharissa's disappearance coincided with the departure of the Tezerenee. There was even enough worry left over for the monster the mage called friend, although Gerrod was only mildly interested in the ebony stallion's fate. It was Sharissa who mattered.

The warlock came to a decision. It was not one Gerrod liked, but, he admitted, it was the *only* choice he could have ever made. "I may be able to do something. I need five days."

"Five days." There was no life in the master mage's voice when he spoke. Dru Zeree was no doubt thinking what could happen in five days. His daughter might be dead or, as far as Gerrod was secretly concerned, suffering a fate worse than death.

Becoming a Tezerenee through marriage to one of his siblings, likely Reegan.

It was no secret that the patriarch coveted her abilities. He was likely convinced that she would pass her powers down through her children—a possibility to be considered, the warlock admitted to himself. Dru saw Sharissa as only a hostage for Darkhorse's cooperation, which was just as likely. Given time to recover his reason, he would recall the second choice, too. By then, however, Gerrod hoped circumstances would change.

"Five days, yes. I want you to do something for me during that time."

"What?"

Gerrod leaned forward, whispering as if the two of them were being watched . . . and who could say for certain that they were not? "Keep a careful eye on the not-people. Note what they do and do not do. Observe what they observe."

"What is it you expect me to find?" Given a task, Dru Zeree was restored to life. His love for his daughter was a weakness, but Gerrod knew that it could also be strength. Yet, where he himself was concerned, the warlock thought love was fine, but not when it went so deep that it prevented one from thinking straight. He considered himself fortunate that he had never reached such an extreme. Those who cared too much, be it for one of their own blood or even a lover, tended to allow themselves to be drawn into foolhardy predicaments.

"It is too soon to say," he said, finally responding to the other's question. The warlock was sincerely thankful that his visage was more or less obscured from the other Vraad. It would not do for Dru to see his expression at this moment. "Trust me that it's necessary."

"All right."

"There is no more to say, then. Good day to you, Master Zeree." Gerrod turned away and pretended to reorganize his notes. He heard Dru shift for a moment, as if the latter was uncertain how to handle the curt dismissal. Gerrod continued to play with the sheets until the silence had stretched more than a minute. At last, with a casual air, he turned back to where Dru had stood. The sorcerer was nowhere to be seen. The warlock shook his head. For all his ability, Dru Zeree was helpless without Gerrod's aid. Under other circumstances, it might even have been comical.

Rising, he began to search among his few belongings for a box he had stolen, unbeknownst to either Zeree, from their citadel back in Nimth. Master Zeree might realize that the request for five days was a ploy, although the warlock doubted that. It was best to begin now, however, on the off chance that the sorcerer *might* return early for another reason. If so, Dru would find that Gerrod had exaggerated a bit about the time he needed for preparations. Not five days, but rather five *minutes*. Five minutes or not at all . . . if he succeeded in finding the box he sought.

Gerrod pulled aside a ragged bit of cloth that had once been a bag and stared down at his prize. He picked up the box gently and carried it over to the floor, opening it even as he knelt.

The warlock mouthed a few nonsensical syllables as he surveyed the contents, the sounds acting as a memory trigger that slowly began awakening the power that slumbered within him. From the box, he picked out a single perfect crystal, a prize from Dru Zeree's lost collection. *You will do for a focus, I think.* What, he wondered, would the other Vraad do if they knew that he had recaptured some of what they had lost in crossing over? What would they offer him for a return to at least a shadow of their glory days, their days of godhood?

What would they offer him for the chance to truly call upon Vraad sorcery without draining their own lifeforce?

Nothing he *wanted.*

His nose began to itch. Gerrod sniffed the air. If he closed his eyes, he could almost imagine he had returned to Nimth. The same sweet, decaying smell permeated everything. It was always so when he dared to awaken the link he had wrought. The seemingly impenetrable barrier that the founders' sorcerous servants had placed around Nimth had finally given in to his onslaught, albeit at great cost. Gerrod could now draw strength from the world of his birth and use it in this one rather than burn away his own lifeforce as his brethren did. However, there were limits. Even though he had breached the barrier, the warlock could not widen it. He had tried more than once, risking the contamination that Vraad sorcery spread in small doses over his new homeland . . . and himself. Perhaps it was even some subconscious hesitation on his own part that made him fail to open the breach further; he could not say.

Still, it was not enough. With time, he suspected he could extend his life span, but not truly give himself the immortality he had come to desire. There had to be another way.

What if one could bind the sorceries of the two realms together . . . ? Gerrod found himself abruptly wondering. He swore at himself and forced such dangerous notions from his mind. He would save Sharissa and the creature Darkhorse and that would be the end of it. His other goals, his dreams, would have to wait for a different solution. To touch upon the lifeforce of this domain would be tantamount to surrendering to it the way the others were, one by one. It would also open him to a fate worse than dying—becoming a monster like the Seekers.

The Tezerenee knew he was stalling, that he was, deep inside, afraid to take the final steps.

"Sharissa." His own blood held her prisoner. The lord drake and his children. His father. His father had Sharissa.

Gerrod slammed the crystal onto the floor, knowing it would take harsher treatment than that to crack the artifact. Afraid he might be, but he would hold back no longer. If nothing else, the warlock would go through with the rescue, not just for the sake of the woman, but to shatter the arrogant dreams of his former people . . . and especially his not-so-dear father.

He smiled as he thought the last.

"THAT WAS NOT there when we came this way," Rayke commented.

"Yes, I think I would have noticed it," Faunon retorted. He reprimanded himself immediately after, knowing that Rayke's statement was born of uncertainty, possibly even a little fear. Faunon could not blame him or any of the others for that fear; his own rash reply had sprung from the same emotion.

"Where did it come from?" one of the others asked. The elfin leader was certain each and every member of the party had asked the same question over the last hour.

Well? he asked himself. *Where* did *it come from?*

They peered through the woods at the huge stone citadel, a masterful yet oppressive piece of building. It looked massive enough to house a few thousand folk, and its principal tower rose so high into the air that Faunon almost wondered if it overlooked some of the lesser mountain peaks. He knew the last was only a trick of the eye, but still . . .

"No elf ever built something like that! No Seeker, either!" Rayke's hand squeezed the grip of his sword.

"Not in only a few days' time."

"Look there!" whispered a younger elf to Faunon's right.

A drake rose into the sky. The elves shunned the creatures out of principle; they were ill-tempered monsters who tended to try to take bites out of anything that moved. Drake meat was not all that tasty, either. It was not the beast that caught their attention, however, but what journeyed *with* the draconian horror.

"Someone *rides* it!" Rayke blurted. His eyes grew large. Faunon stared in wonder at the rider. It was roughly the size of an elf, though much more massive. The dark green armor it wore blended with the skin of the drake, making the two almost seem like one. A ferocious helm that mirrored the toothy visage of the mount obscured the rider's features. Faunon was not even certain the newcomer resembled anything approaching elf. While it appeared to be shaped akin to the members of the expedition, the same could have been said of the avians or the Quel.

"There is another one!" someone else whispered.

"More than one," Faunon corrected. Behind the second duo came a third and a fourth. "It is a patrol."

"We should leave here, Faunon!"

"They might find us any moment—"

"Be silent!" Rayke hissed. "Lest you help them find us all the sooner!" Faunon's second turned to him. "What do you say? Do we leave or do we risk it longer? This must certainly be of interest to the elders!"

"But not at the cost of our own lives. We should move farther back and to the west. We will find thicker cover there, but a much better view."

The party took heart from his rapid decision. Faunon hoped they felt calmer than he did. This was hardly what he had expected. When he had asked himself who would be the future rulers of this domain, he had hardly expected the answer so soon. It was very obvious that these newcomers had arrived with the intention of conquering themselves an empire. Sooner or later, they would cross paths with the elves. It behooved the party to discover what they could of these potential—*potential? . . . certain!*—adversaries.

Moving with a silence that would have done them proud even among their own kind, the elves abandoned their position. A good thing, too, Faunon saw. The route the flyers were taking would soon bring them too near the elves' former location. Had the group stayed where they were, the patrol would have seen them from the sky.

Against aerial combatants, Faunon knew his men had no chance. It would take more than a few arrows to pierce the hides of the drakes and, judging by the skill with which the armored figures controlled their beasts, trying for an eye or mouth would be nearly impossible. The newcomers did not wear their armor purely for show; they moved like warriors born.

Time passed far more quickly than the elfin leader would have preferred. He glanced back and saw that the drakes had not yet reached the abandoned position. That struck him as a little odd. Their pattern of flight should have brought them over the wooded area by this time. It was that danger that had made moving quickly so critical.

Rayke came up beside him, trying to make out whatever it was that disturbed his companion. "What is it? Have they seen us?"

"It could be nothing . . ."

They heard a faint crackling in the woods to the east. To Faunon, it sounded like a death knell . . . for all of them.

"Ready yourselves!" he whispered. "They are coming for us!"

More than a dozen toothy monstrosities, each carrying one of the armored figures, burst through the woods not more than a breath or two after his warning. That was time enough for the elves, however. Arrows flew from those who had carried bows, striking at the forerunners. Each struck a vital part of some rider's body, but, unfortunately, the armor proved too strong. Even tinged with elfin magic, the shafts only bounced off, save one lucky strike that went through one of the eye holes of the nearest rider. The figure fell backward, dead in that same instant, but his stirrups would not allow him to fall off and so he bobbed up and down like some macabre puppet while his mount kept pace with its brethren.

"Archers! Mounts first!" Faunon knew the riding drakes could not be maneuvered so well this close. The trees and bushes worked to his advantage for the moment, but soon the drakes would be close enough to make use of their talons and teeth. He wanted them dead before that.

Though the results were, for the moment, unseen and unfelt, a second battle had also progressed. Elfin magic met a sorcery that felt so vile, so self-destructive, that Faunon wondered what sort of creatures they fought. He had hoped his men would have an advantage there, but such was not to be. At the moment, the two warring magics were at a stalemate, though how long that would last was anybody's guess. Faunon suspected the tide would *not* be turning in the elves' favor. Already he could feel the strain on his mind, and he was only shielding, not attacking, with his somewhat lesser sorcerous ability.

The riders were being forced to spread their line because of the trees. An arrow burst the eye of one drake, causing the draconian horror to halt in its charge and seek in vain to remove the cause of its pain. The rider struggled for control.

We have a chance! Faunon thought as he readied himself for the first attacker.

He heard the beating of wings above him and knew they did not belong to the Sheekas.

The aerial patrol had known their position all the time. "We have been tricked!" With a sinking feeling, Faunon watched the drakes descend even as those on the ground continued to surge forward. Of the dozen who had burst through the trees, two were dead. Nine riders still lived, but four of them were on foot. Perhaps if his men broke for the thicker foliage, they might be able to regroup and make a better stand there—

"Faunon! Watch your back!"

The voice was Rayke's. Faunon rolled to one side and heard a *whoosh!* as one of the flying drakes soared upward again, its wicked claws thankfully empty.

Another elf was not so lucky. One of the archers, paying too much attention to the armored figures darting in and out of the trees, did not notice the diving horror until he was plucked from the ground. The hapless victim had only time for a short scream before the drake took his head in its massive maw and *bit* down.

Faunon turned away, wanting then to heave the contents of his stomach out. He fought the nauseating feeling, but only because he knew others might suffer while he was giving in to his lesser emotions. Better to turn those emotions to energy.

Watching the sky for any other threats, he moved into the trees to his right. The battle on the ground had been joined, with three of the attackers taking on their elfin counterparts in hand-to-hand. Riders on drakes rushed back and forth, chasing after elusive prey. Faunon's men knew what he also knew but could not acknowledge. They would *die* here. Outnumbered and outflanked, they would perish, but not before taking out as many of the newcomers as possible. That was what the elfin leader planned, also.

The drake riders above had forgotten him in the chaos, his one attacker perhaps thinking his mount had slashed the elf to death even though it had not succeeded in grasping him. Whatever the case, Faunon was going to use his anonymity to his best advantage. If he could get behind the armored foes, he could come up on them one at a time and take them down until someone finally noticed him. It was not the most admirable way to fight, but Faunon had always been a pragmatist.

A drake came bounding toward his hiding place, but its rider was nowhere to be seen. Faunon held his sword ready, hoping he would not have to waste himself on the leviathan. Providing it did not kill him, the noise would certainly alert the enemy.

Fortunately, the wind was Faunon's ally and the creature itself seemed more interested in flight than battle. Faunon saw why: one of its eyes was closed and bloody, and it was bleeding profusely from a neck wound. Part of the elfin blade that had performed what would be, in a matter of minutes, the killing stroke, still remained lodged in the wound. That meant its owner was probably dead. He hoped the unknown elf had at least killed the monster's master.

He followed the bleeding drake's path until it was safely away, started to turn his attention back to the task at hand, and then returned his gaze quickly to where the beast had vanished.

Barely visible among the trees was a trio of riders clad akin to the attacking force. These, however, sat and watched with a confidence that marked them as the leaders. One, as massive as any bear the elf had ever come across, even wore a crimson cloak. He and the others seemed to be watching the pitched battle with mild interest, nothing more.

Faunon decided to change his choice of targets.

The sounds of battle were beginning to die behind him as he made his way to the threesome. That meant the others were either dead or captured. Faunon was ashamed with himself for leaving them, even if it had been to try to inflict worse damage on their adversaries. Still, there was little he could have done once the airdrakes had joined the battle, and now he had a clear opportunity to deprive the invaders of hopefully one or more leaders. It was possible that these riders meant little in the hierarchy of their people, but it would make some of their kind a bit more wary of simply going out and slaughtering elves if they knew that they, too, were at risk.

"Get out of there!" someone barked.

Faunon jerked to a halt, thinking he had been discovered. A second later, a warrior on foot appeared, the sword in his left hand being used to prod the wounded drake ahead of him. They were moving in the same general direction as the elf. He held his breath and waited. Neither seemed particularly inclined to attentiveness, which was his only hope. It did lessen his chances of success, however. He wondered if there were more warriors lurking in the woods around him and if he could avoid them long enough to at least take one of the patrol leaders down.

The drake had stopped and was sniffing the air. The armored figure poked at it with his weapon. "Move or you'll rot right here! Dragon's blood, you're a stupid one!"

A chill ran down Faunon's spine as the drake turned and began to sniff the air in the elf's direction.

The wind had started to change.

Unmindful of its cursing warden, the wounded animal started back. The elf readied his sword and, as an afterthought, tried to prepare a spell. While his higher senses were acute, his practical abilities were less than most of his kind.

It was why he could only shield himself with sorcery during a battle. Some, like Rayke, could do battle on both the magical and physical planes, and at the same time.

Slowing, the drake sniffed again. It was only a few yards away now. The armored guide joined it and tapped the beast's side with the sword one more time. "Turn around!"

The drake swayed, its injuries draining more and more of its energy, but it would not turn. It hissed at the trees shielding Faunon from the sight of the warrior.

"Is there . . ." The armored figure grew silent, then studied the area that so interested the drake. Faunon knew his luck had run out.

"Lord Reegan! There's one of them he—" The warning was cut off as the elf burst from his hiding place and jumped his discoverer. Raising his sword, the warrior tried to defend himself, but, not apparently expecting the reflexes of an elf, moved too slowly. Faunon pushed the blade aside and thrust at the place where the helm and the breastplate met. Unlike Rayke's successful strike at the Draka, the elfin leader was unable to put the point of his weapon through his opponent's throat. The blade cut a crimson trail across the one side of the warrior's neck.

"Kill!" the armored figure shouted, his breath coming in gasps. He backed away, hands clutching at the wound and his helm, which had been shoved upward and was obscuring his vision.

Faunon had no time to finish him, for the drake, though dying, was still a deadly foe. It snapped at him, trying to avoid its handler as it shifted for better position. The elf jumped away, trying to keep close to the wounded warrior, who had, to the former's surprise, fallen to his knees.

Somewhere, he knew, the three riders were converging on him, but he dared not take his eyes from his present predicament. The drake clawed at him, but weakness made it come up just short. Faunon tried to impale its one good eye, but the drake, perhaps having learned from the loss of the other eye, shied.

No longer needing to fear discovery, the elf unleashed a spell. It was a haphazard one, his first having been lost at some point in the battle, but he thought it might give him the precious seconds he needed.

A voice, coming from an invisible source behind the drake, commanded, "Back! Away from him! Now!"

The reptilian menace halted and sniffed the air. It was puzzled and uncertain.

"Back, I said!" The voice was that of the warrior whom Faunon had wounded. The warrior himself lay sprawled on the ground, blood over half his armor. Confused, the drake hissed at the world in general and remained where it was. Its limited mind could not comprehend that the tiny creature before it was playing it for a fool. The mimic spell that Faunon had cast was one he had used on occasion in the past to success. He carefully raised his sword, ready to try one last strike should the drake disobey the voice, as it had before, and charge the elf.

Panting, the wounded beast started to turn. Faunon began to slip back into the woods, hoping he still had a moment or two before the others came for him.

He screamed as a mind-numbing pain shot through his right side. Looking down, he saw an arrow protruding from his thigh.

"Well?" asked a gruff, disappointed voice. "Why don't you finish it off?"

"The drake or the elf?" countered another. There was a convivial tone to this one's voice, as if he might be as willing to offer Faunon a drink as he might be to kill him.

"What do we need the elf for?"

"Father will want him. You know he said he wanted a captive."

Faunon's entire body throbbed. He heard the sound of drakes trotting and looked up at his captors. It was, of course, the trio that he had been trying for before the wounded beast had given him away. The massive figure with the crimson cape was looking at a thinner warrior to his right who carried in one hand a bow. Behind both of them came the third. He evidently had a lesser place in the hierarchy, for his posture was that of one who is among his betters only by sufferance. All three still wore their helms. With all that had happened, Faunon still did not know what they looked like.

"We have that other one," rumbled the bear.

"He will be dead before long, Reegan. I only wounded this one so he could not run. He should satisfy Father."

The one called Reegan turned to the third member of their party and pointed at the limp, armored form by the weary drake. "See to him."

Faunon was beginning to feel neglected. Had they forgotten he still had a sword? He held it before him, daring the one who had dismounted to come closer.

The calm rider shook his head. "Put that down. It will not do you any good."

"Come to me and see!"

"I think . . . *damn!*" Reaching up, the armored figure took hold of his drag-oncrested helm and removed it. Faunon saw a pale visage that, if it struggled, might be called handsome in a poorly lit chamber. He studied the ears. Unlike an elf's, they were rounded.

The eyes were the most disturbing feature. They were crystalline. He had never heard of such a thing. Beautiful but cold. Round where the elfin orbs were almond-shaped.

Could they be . . .

"Bothering you again, Lochivan?" the ursine rider asked. For the first time, Faunon noticed how that one's helm had been designed so as to allow the heavy beard to flow free.

Lochivan was scratching at his neck. "I must be allergic to something here! It's been worse since we crossed!"

The third rider, who had been inspecting the warrior sprawled in the grass, called out, "He's dead. Blade severed the artery in his neck."

"A good strike," Reegan complimented. "Let me see your weapon."

"You don't think—" A force that nearly tore his fingers off yanked the long, narrow sword from his grasp. It went spiraling through the air, at last landing perfectly in the left hand of the massive warrior. Reegan turned and nodded to his companion, as if proud of what he had just accomplished.

"I told you. The power has returned to us. I don't know how or why, but it has." Lochivan had ceased his scratching. A vivid red mark covered his neck. He smiled slightly at the wounded elf, who was starting to sink to the ground from a combination of exhaustion, pain, and simple frustration. "Reegan is very fond of weapons," he explained companionably. "More so than most Tezerenee."

"Is that what you are . . . Tezerenee?" It was not a name familiar to Faunon, yet it filled him with relief. Their bearing, their arrogance, had reminded him of something else, some fearsome demon from stories that his mother had told him.

"We were born to the Tezerenee, the clan of the dragon," Lochivan offered. He replaced his helm, and Faunon, studying it, could not help but be drawn by the eyes of the dragon. They matched those of the man who wore the helm. Lochivan indicated Reegan. "My brother and I. These others, they are Tezerenee by adoption; that is why they fight with less skill. All of us, however, are known together as the *Vraad*." The warrior cocked his head in what might have been actual curiosity. "Being an elf, I thought you might have heard of us."

Faunon pressed himself against the tree that was still, at least in theory, supporting him. He stared without hope at the two mounted riders.

"I think we can take that for a positive response," Lochivan finally said. He glanced at the warrior standing ready by the corpse of his fellow.

"Bind him and drag him back to the citadel."

VIII

"YOU SEE, DEMON? I keep my promises. You've done what I've asked and I've woken her. I hardly need to have done that, you know."

Sharissa's soul swam in a sea of emptiness. The voices were all she had to latch on to, and they had, until now, seemed so very, very far away. Now, however, she found herself moving toward them with ease.

"I see that you like to give freely what is not yours to give, what actually belongs to the one you claim to give it to! That is what I see!"

They were familiar voices and, though she did not care for one of them, they promised light where she could only recall darkness.

"Do not bestir yourself, demon. The bonds that hold you have not weakened in the slightest. I would rather have your willing cooperation than this need for pain."

Closer. Sharissa knew she had almost found the light.

One of the voices shrieked in unbridled agony. Her flight slowed as she sought some way to give solace to the one in pain. There was nothing Sharissa could do, however. She knew she would have to wait until she was back in the light.

The shriek died down into silence. Then, just as she feared she would become lost again, the first voice spoke. Its tone was smooth and, despite the sympathetic words, mocking. "You force me to do things I would rather not do, demon. *You* are the one causing yourself pain."

"Darkhorse?" Sharissa could not yet see, could not even sense her very body, but memory, at least, was returning. At the moment, it seemed the most precious thing she possessed.

"That should be enough to satisfy you. Now, back where you belong."

"The Void swallow you, Lord Bara—"

"Darkhorse?" Sharissa struggled to open her eyes. Memories of the attack returned. She had been a fool. Something in the spell of the lamp had alerted the Tezerenee to the fact that she had freed herself a second time. It was a simple spell, one well within the ability of many Vraad, and she had not thought of it.

Why the lamp, though? Why cloud her perceptions if they planned to take her?

"Are you feeling ill at all?" Barakas Tezerenee asked from the darkness.

A dim crack of light sliced its way through the endless black void. As the sorceress struggled, it grew into a band of murky shapes and movements. "Darkhorse, where—"

"Shh! Take it slow, Lady Sharissa. You've been asleep for over three days. That deep a slumber turns the body numb. It takes time for the blood to regain momentum."

"Barakas." She turned the name into a curse. "What have you done to Darkhorse? To me?" Sharissa regained a vague sense of her body. She tried to move her hands, but was unable to tell if there were any positive results.

"You will come to understand, my lady. Before long, you will even stand in the forefront of our destiny."

"The Faceless Ones take your speechmaking!" she shouted, putting all her renewed energy into her response. To her dismay, she almost found herself sinking back into the darkness because of her anger.

"I *warned* you to take it slow. You'll likely have a rampaging headache because of your tirade."

Sharissa tried to draw upon the lifeforce of the world, only to find a wall within herself that would not permit even the least of spells. It was a mental block, as if each time she sought to do something, her concentration slipped just enough to make her attempt fail.

Something wrapping around her throat . . .

"What did you do to me, Barakas?"

His form—it could only be *his* form—grew larger, nearly filling her limited field of vision. He could be no more than a yard away, yet the patriarch would still not come into focus. "Merely something to keep you from reacting without thought. This is something that should be talked out after you've had an opportunity to see what we've accomplished, what we intend."

"My father won't stand for this, Barakas! Neither will Silesti! Between the two of them, they have the numbers to overwhelm your pathetic little army."

Her body was nearly her own again, though, at the moment, that seemed no great victory. Every muscle screamed agony, not surprising since she had not moved in three days. With an effort, the sorceress reached for her throat.

"It won't come off unless I wish it."

"You expect me to follow you in anything when you treat me like this? What have you done to Darkhorse? I thought I heard—"

"He will recover. He left me no choice. Perhaps *you* will be able to convince him of the correct way of things once you've had a chance to taste our harvest."

The huge armored figure was slowly coalescing into something with distinct features. Sharissa, struggling, was able to raise herself enough so that she could rest on her elbows. It allowed her to focus her gaze better on the patriarch's own crystalline eyes. "You are waxing poetic, Lord Tezerenee, but all the pretty words and familiar speech won't convince me of anything other than the fact that you are not to be trusted." She gritted her teeth, knowing how her next words would probably affect him. "You, patriarch, have no concept of honor whatsoever. I'd rather believe that the smile of a drake has nothing to do with its hunger than believe one promise of yours."

The back of his hand caught her squarely on the right side of her face. Sharissa rolled onto her side, panting and bleeding, but also satisfied with the reaction. She was also thankful the patriarch had not been wearing his gauntlets.

Turning back to her "host," she displayed the marks of his anger. "As I said, no concept of honor."

Barakas was gazing at his hand, as if it had betrayed him. He looked up, studied her damaged face, and frowned.

"My deepest apologies, Lady Zeree. I have not slept since you forced yourself upon us. I will have someone take care of your injury and, at the same time, bring you something to eat. Tomorrow, after we have both rested, I will show you my world." With no more farewell than that, the patriarch turned quickly and stalked toward a doorway that was only now visible to the recovering sorceress.

"Barakas! If you think I plan on merely waiting here . . ." Sharissa rose, her legs unsteady, and took a step after the dragonlord, who was already in the outer corridor.

One hand on the door, Barakas took one last look at the young Zeree . . . and slammed the thick wooden door shut. Sharissa heard the sound of a key turning in a lock and swore under her breath. "Barakas!"

She put a tentative hand on the door and pushed. It would not give. Sharissa had known it would not, but had felt compelled to try anyway.

"Damn you, Tezerenee!" Her legs began to buckle. Utilizing what strength she had left to her, the sorceress stumbled back over to the simple bed that was, she now saw, the only piece of furniture in the chamber aside from a single chair in one corner. Her legs gave out just as she crawled onto the bed.

Sharissa rolled onto her back and scanned her surroundings. A narrow slit near the ceiling allowed only minimal sunlight in. One torch provided the rest of the illumination, not that the gray, spartan chamber offered any visual attractions.

Three days! Where was her father? Where were the other Vraad? Barakas had at last broken the tenuous peace that had existed since the creation of the triumvirate. Was there an army even now surrounding the eastern sector of the Vraad city? If so, why could she not hear anything?

Memories of the impassioned voice of the dark eternal returned to her. Barakas Tezerenee had forced him to aid the clan's cause. In what way? Her heart beat faster. Had Darkhorse turned the others away? Was her father dead? Did Barakas rule now?

Her questions, her very thoughts, began to fragment as the beating of her heart was echoed in her head. Sharissa put a hand to her temple and tried in vain to ease the pounding. Nothing helped. The sorceress did not even have power enough to rid herself of the headache. For that, too, she cursed the Lord Barakas Tezerenee.

When sleep at last claimed her again, she welcomed it with open arms.

"SHARISSA?"

It was a female voice that tore her from the bliss of true, unforced slumber, and at first she thought it was someone else. "Mother?"

"No, Sharissa, only Lady Alcia."

Her eyes snapped open. The striking warrior queen sat beside her, a bowl of food in one hand. Behind the matriarch stood two female Tezerenee in full battle readiness. Whether they were daughters of the lady or merely clan sisters, Sharissa neither knew nor cared. Only one woman truly held importance in the clan of the dragon, and that was the patriarch's bride. "He fears to face me again?"

Alcia smiled, a surprisingly soft expression for so commanding a visage. "He still sleeps. I thought it would be better if I spent some time with you first and tried to answer some of your questions."

"Good! Where is my father? Where is this place? What do you think—"

Her visitor held up a warning hand. "Not yet. I will answer questions, but only after you have eaten, young one. And do not try to ask me questions while you eat, either. You will get nothing more from me until this bowl is empty. Do you understand?"

Mention of food and the relentless smell rising from the bowl forced Sharissa into surrender. She gratefully took the bowl and spoon from the Lady Tezerenee and started in on the contents. It was a stew of some sort, filled with meat and vegetables and seasoned to perfection.

Watching her eat, Lady Alcia looked almost like a doting mother. "I am so *very* glad you enjoy it. I made it myself, but I've rarely had someone from outside who could tell me if I've succeeded with it. Tezerenee make terrible critics. They will eat anything, even if only to prove they could live off moss, if necessary."

The last brought a brief smile from Sharissa. She often forgot that the ruling mistress of the clan had been born an outsider and that much of the blood of the clan could be traced to her. "It is good. Thank you."

"Not at all. Please keep eating. You will find it will strengthen you."

It was true. Though this was not enough to satiate her, Sharissa at least felt well enough to move. Her headache had also receded, though enough of it remained to remind her of what she had experienced earlier.

"How long did I sleep this time?" she dared to ask after swallowing her latest mouthful.

"Only a few hours. It was just after dawn when you were disturbed the first time. The sun is now directly overhead. No more questions until you finish. I mean that."

The remaining contents of the bowl vanished in quick fashion. Though she had gulped much of it down in order to ask some of the many questions that burned within her, Sharissa could not help feeling disappointed, too. She wanted more—at least another bowl.

"That is all." Alcia took the bowl and spoon from her and put it aside. "You have to ease your hunger gradually, or else you are liable to make yourself sick. You can eat in a little while, after your stomach has settled again."

Now that the time had come, Sharissa's anger rekindled itself. She recalled again the patriarch's temper and the voice of Darkhorse. The voice and the *pain.* "Where's Darkhorse?"

"He's been put away for now." Lady Alcia's tone reminded Sharissa of Lochivan's friendly manner of speech. The young sorceress was suddenly reminded of the fact that, while it was true the woman before her had been born an outsider, she had spent countless centuries as the bride of the dragonlord and the mother of most of his arrogant children. Sharissa could no more trust her visitor than she could Lochivan.

"What does that mean?"

Rising, the Lady Tezerenee took hold of Sharissa's arm and guided her up. Rest and food were already working their wonders. The sorceress found she could walk with only the slightest difficulty. *Something else in the food besides meat and vegetables,* she decided.

Sharissa had not forgotten her question. She repeated it the moment she was certain her legs would not collapse.

The matriarch sighed. "That is something Barakas or Lochivan could explain better—"

"Lochivan!" Sharissa spat on the floor. "If he comes within sight of me—"

"He lives to serve his father," Alcia said, taking her charge by the shoulders and massaging some of the muscles. "Would *you* do any different?"

"My father is a good man!"

"By your standards. Tezerenee have different standards. Most Vraad have different standards. You look fit enough for a walk, I think." As she said the last, the Lady Tezerenee snapped her fingers. One of her shadows stepped to the door and opened it. The other moved until she stood behind her mistress and the outsider. Sharissa was reminded of lithe hunting wyverns as she observed their movements. These were women born to the clan, not adopted like many newer Tezerenee. Barakas had allowed newcomers to swell his ranks over the last decade and a half, but evidently still reserved the most vital roles for those of his blood. Guarding his mate was likely a position open only to the most skilled.

"What about my questions? You said you'd answer them."

"Some of them will answer themselves when we get outside. At the very least, showing you what my husband has achieved will aid any explanation. You *should* get some walking in, too. Judging by your back, I would have to say that every muscle in your body needs to be loosened. Come along."

With Lady Alcia guiding her, Sharissa made her way to the corridor. Each step seemed easier than the last. "You seem to have a *magical* touch when it comes to cooking, my lady."

Her regal companion smiled politely. "It is a wonder what one can do with the proper ingredients and skills."

They spoke no more for quite some time, Sharissa, knowing she would receive no useful answers from her host, being satisfied with inspecting the domicile of the clan. She found the endless gray corridors and windowless chambers disturbing, their appearance more reminiscent of the unsightly citadel the Tezerenee had abandoned back in Nimth. Yet, these had to be some of the deeper levels in the eastern sector, didn't they? Where else could Barakas bring her? Had he spent the last fifteen years so greatly redesigning his tiny domain into a miniature version of the one he had lost? It seemed a futile and outrageous project even for the patriarch.

More and more she felt as if she were back in mad Nimth. The dragon banner hung on every wall. Armored warriors, male and female, stood guard everywhere. A drake patrol, the two beasts straining at their leashes, passed them just before they reached a staircase leading *downward*. Sharissa lost all interest in the toothy hunters as she paused to stare at the steps. The sorceress had come to assume that she was in some lower level, possibly beneath the surface, but this staircase spiraled down at what first appeared to be forever.

"We have five levels to descend to the surface. Is that too much for you? Do you feel weak?" Alcia put a hand on her shoulder, but Sharissa was not taken in by the concern. If the matriarch had thought it would serve her people's interests, she would have been just as willing to *push* her down the steps.

"I can make it." There was no attempt to hide the edge in her voice. It was best to remind the Tezerenee that she did not consider herself the guest they wanted her to believe she was.

"Do not let your defiance make you foolish. You could hardly plot any escapes if you collapsed on the staircase and fell to your death, could you?"

Sharissa looked up at the Lady Tezerenee, but the latter's visage was unreadable. Unfortunate as it was, Sharissa saw much in what Lady Alcia had said. While the food had aided greatly in restoring her strength, her control over her body was still a bit tenuous. Who was to say that she might not miss a step?

"Perhaps it would be best if you held my arm."

"Of course."

As they started down, Sharissa's legs quivering a bit, the sorceress remembered the collar around her throat. *Very odd that I could forget this,* she decided. Subtle magic? If she grew complacent about the collar, it might not be long before she *did* find herself listening to the words of Barakas. More than ever, Sharissa knew she had to struggle to keep her concentration on her predicament. She could not be sidetracked by anything that did not directly deal with the situation.

Tezerenee sentries saluted smartly as her royal guide passed them. After a moment, it occurred to her that they were also saluting *her,* as if she were a visiting dignitary and not a prisoner.

"This honor isn't necessary." She made no attempt to hide the sarcasm.

"You are the daughter of Dru Zeree and a capable sorceress in your own right. Your status is high among our folk. It may be that, before long, your status will be even higher."

"If you mean will I marry Reegan and add my power to your people, you've—"

"Here we are," Alcia interrupted, acting as if she had not even noted her charge's retort. They had reached the bottom of the staircase.

To each side, massive corridors extended into eternity. Turning around, Sharissa saw yet another corridor, this one even greater than the others.

The great hall, she decided. The Tezerenee would reveal it to her before long; Barakas loved to hold court. Considering the high marble columns and the polished stone floors that made up what was basically a walkway, she suspected the great hall itself would be more sumptuous than past Tezerenee courts.

Where is this place? Nothing in the eastern sector matched this place. There were places more splendid, but they were in the styles favored by the founders, not the more deliberate tastes of the dragon men.

"Sharissa?" Lady Alcia stood with one arm extended toward two huge, iron doors, each with the symbol of the clan worked into the very metal. Only two guards stood at the doors, but they were possibly the largest Tezerenee she had ever seen other than the patriarch and his heir. If they were not Alcia's sons, then they were the products of the Lord Tezerenee's occasional outside liaison. Love his bride he might, but Barakas saw part of his duty as clan leader to include the relentless task of increasing their numbers in whatever way necessary.

Thinking of the differences between Gerrod and Reegan, the young Zeree wondered if the Lady Alcia had secretly formed a few liaisons of her own. They might be Tezerenee, but they were also Vraad.

She rejoined her guide. As they and their bodyguards approached the doors, the two sentries opened the way for them, visibly straining as they pulled the doors open.

Sunlight flooded into the corridor, blinding an unsuspecting Sharissa. She gasped and put her hands over her eyes. Her companion took hold of her.

"I'm so sorry! I should have realized that your eyes would be sensitive after three days of darkness or dim light. You had no trouble with the torchlight in the halls and on the stairs, so I merely assumed—"

"I'll be fine." The sorceress removed herself from the matriarch's grip. "I can see well enough already to continue." She blinked in rapid succession. A myriad pattern of spots made it impossible to focus on anything, but she could make out general shapes enough to walk without stumbling. "Lead on."

"Very well."

A cool breeze, very welcome after the stifling air of her cell, caressed her cheeks. The air smelled of life unspoiled by human intrusion. It smelled . . . *different.*

Even before her eyesight had cleared, she knew she was no longer in the city.

The Tezerenee led her out into the world. Like a blind person newly granted sight, the sorceress tried to see everything. The tall, menacing tower of the citadel, the utilitarian buildings that flanked it on each side and held, she knew, the riding drakes. A massive protective wall that surrounded the patriarch's private domain. Sentries walked the wall, each warrior ready for the worst. Airdrakes carried patrols over the walls. Following the route of one such patrol, her eyes were suddenly attracted by a chain of mountains in the distance. They were unfamiliar to her, yet she felt she should know them.

In what could only have been three days, the Tezerenee had evidently built themselves a stronghold. It was as ugly in its own way as their own, with their typical jagged towers and harsh lines. The clear blue sky, the light breeze, and the birds singing in the distance seemed, when forced to endure along-side the citadel, mere parodies of their once-glorious selves. Nothing remained beautiful around the Tezerenee.

Sharissa turned on the Lady Tezerenee. Her bodyguards readied their blades, but the warrior queen waved the two back. "How did you do all this? Where did you get such power? The effort to create all of this—"

"Was beyond us, yes. Even now, though our power now is greater than it was these last years, this still would have required months of effort. Fortunately, there was one who *did* have the strength."

The young Zeree's eyes narrowed dangerously. "You made Darkhorse do this! You made him do this with my life as the key to his cooperation!"

"We never threatened your life." Lady Alcia scratched her neck as she spoke. Like Lochivan's, it was red and dry. Sharissa recalled his mentioning some rash or minor disease spreading through the Tezerenee and wondered if she would suffer that along with everything else.

"Why don't you quit acting as if I'm a guest?" The sorceress tugged at her collar. It grew surprisingly tight, making her choke. The Matriarch reached forward and pulled Sharissa's hands away from her throat.

The collar became bearable again.

"Perhaps we should go back inside."

Sharissa slapped her hand away, which made the bodyguards bristle again. "Why don't you—What is that?"

Two Tezerenee were dragging a limp figure between them. He was slighter than either and his clothing reminded her of her stepmother's clothing.

"It would really be best if you . . . Sharissa! Stop!"

Too late. Sharissa darted past one of her companion's watchdogs and raced toward the two warriors dragging the still form. "You there! Stop! Now!"

Still holding their captive, the Tezerenee turned to see who was shouting. They looked at the ungraceful figure in white and then at each other. One reached for a blade, but the second shook his head and said something that she could not make out.

Lady Alcia's people were no doubt right behind her, but Sharissa did not care. She had to see who it was they had and whether the poor soul was still alive. Most of all, she had to see if he was what she thought he was.

As she neared them, the guards looked past her and nodded. When she sought to lift their prize's head so that she could see his features, no one stopped her. The sound of heavy footfalls grew louder behind her.

There was no denying the visage. There were differences, of course, but his race was not in question. He was an elf.

Judging by the blood and bruises, he had resisted their questioning. Sharissa glanced up at the two guards, but they were untouched by her smoldering eyes.

The elf began to cough. His eyes opened, handsome almond-shaped tears. It took him a moment to focus and, when he did, he seemed surprised.

"Eve—even among the living death there—there is beauty. Impossible to—to believe you have such a heart of stone."

He had taken her for one of them. "I'm not—"

"You must come back with us now, Lady Sharissa," a cold female voice said. The Lady Alcia's bodyguards stood directly on each side of her. Coughing once more, the elf forced his gaze upward, despite the fact that it obviously hurt him to move so much. He eyed the two with interest, then returned his gaze to Sharissa.

"My lady," the bodyguard urged. "This is not something to concern yourself with."

As if on cue, the two warriors holding the elf turned their prize away and once more began to drag him away. Sharissa started after them, but the bodyguards held her back.

"He was part of a force of elves that sought to come upon us through stealth and kill us. With the demon's aid, we detected them and caught *them* by surprise."

"You made Darkhorse aid you in killing them?" The sorceress doubted that the story was as Lady Tezerenee had told it. More than likely, the elves had been scouting the citadel, wondering what it was. Still, what was a party of elves doing on the eastern continent when—

"I see by your eyes that you've finally come to the realization. I wondered for a time whether or not your mind was functioning well." Lady Alcia nodded, the smile on her face much akin to the one the patriarch wore when he was pleased with results. "Yes, this is indeed the Dragonrealm, Sharissa."

"How could you . . . Darkhorse again! Everything you've accomplished is because of him! You still haven't brought me to him! Is he dead? Injured?"

At a signal from the matriarch, the bodyguards politely but firmly began to guide a struggling Sharissa back toward the citadel. Lady Alcia walked before them, still acting as if she and Sharissa were amiable companions. "How do you kill a thing that does not, by any standards we know, live? He's been disciplined, but no more than any other disobedient subject has. When he performs well, he is rewarded as well."

"*Rewarded?*" Other than freedom, the Tezerenee could have nothing the shadow steed wanted.

"We want him to be a part of the clan's destiny as much as we want you to be."

"You want him to save you from the Seekers! Even Darkhorse won't be enough to hold them back! He'll probably laugh while the bird people tear your empire down around you!"

"The avians no longer represent a threat . . . at least, not one that we cannot deal with ourselves."

Sharissa stretched forward, trying to come alongside the Lady Tezerenee. "What do you mean?"

Alcia considered the question for a time before finally replying, "It might be better to show you."

"Show me?"

"We brought a few of them in for study. So far, we have not found a cause for their fate." The matriarch had altered direction. The two bodyguards steered the helpless Sharissa after her. She did not struggle, for once truly wanting to follow. If what Lady Alcia had said was true, then there remained no force capable of withstanding the Tezerenee, especially if Darkhorse was their tool.

"You know," her host remarked, stopping and turning around so that the two faced one another. "I think this would be an excellent opportunity to show you the true depth of our strength!"

"What do you . . ." Sharissa began, but Lady Alcia merely snapped her fingers . . .

. . . and they were standing in another chamber, a dark, dank place lit by torches. A Tezerenee leaning over a table looked up. Sharissa, still in shock from the unexpected teleport, did not immediately recognize his shadowed visage.

"You did that as if it were nothing! All four of us! But I thought that you—"

"The old ways are returning. It is as if Nimth is part of us again." A smile, a Tezerenee smile, slowly spread across the striking face. "We are not the near gods of our past, but we are again a sorcerous power to be respected."

"It's as if our destiny is being drawn for us by the hands of the founders themselves," added the figure by the table. "The day promised to us by the Dragon of the Depths has come."

Sharissa struggled with her captors. "Lochivan!"

"I hope you will find it in your heart to forgive me, Sharissa." Lochivan wore no helm; he seemed actually sad, though she was not so willing to believe him after his betrayal. "I truly think it would have been best if—"

"That will be *all*, my son."

"*Forgive* you, Lochivan? I wouldn't—"

He vanished before she could finish. Sharissa ended with a scream of frustration instead.

"When you are more willing, the two of you should talk," the Lady Tezerenee said in a calm voice. She pointed at the table. "For now, this is what should concern you. This is what you wanted to see."

Sharissa blinked and glanced without care at the thing on the table. An artifact. A statue carved to resemble a Seeker. Of what interest . . .

"She does not understand. Bring her closer."

In silent obedience, the two bodyguards brought Sharissa within an arm's length of the table and its contents.

She gave it another glance . . . and could not pull herself away from the thing's contorted form. The careful detail of horror, the avian eyes staring at death. The mouth open in futile rejection of fate. The awkward sprawl of the body.

It appeared the consistency of marble, this thing before her, but Sharissa knew that if she touched the long, sleek wing or the muscular torso, she would not feel stone, but rather feather and flesh.

"The Dragonrealm is ours, and without even a fight," Lady Alcia said with satisfaction. Sharissa looked up, unable to think of anything sufficient to say. The matriarch added, "My husband is disappointed. He so much looked forward to a good battle . . . with us winning, of course."

As she spoke the last, one hand absently scratched at the reddish area on her neck.

IX

FROM THE TOWER in which his private chambers lay, Barakas Tezerenee watched the vanishing of his wife and the others. Sharissa Zeree would be suitably impressed with the way of things by the time Alcia was finished. Her encounter with the elfin prisoner had been perfectly orchestrated, as he had expected. There lay potential in that meeting; unless he missed his guess, she would try her best to speak to the prisoner in private . . . although it would not be so private as she believed.

All things come together, the patriarch thought in satisfaction. He patted a square container upon which the mark of the Tezerenee had been emblazoned.

"Father?"

Barakas turned and faced Lochivan, who had materialized, as was proper, on one knee with his head bent downward. "All goes well, my son?"

"Yes, my lord. Sharissa is in the chamber even now. By this time, she is aware of the nature of the corpse."

"Perhaps she can tell us what happened. That would be an added prize."

"Does it matter so?"

"We must strive to further ourselves. If the legacy of the avians can aid us, so be it." The patriarch looked down at his son. "You are a few minutes early."

Lochivan did not look up. "I deemed it more beneficial to our goals that I depart the chamber. Sharissa is not comfortable in my presence."

"She will have to learn if she is to marry your brother."

This time, the younger Tezerenee *did* look up. His helm hid much of his visage from his parent, but Barakas knew his son's mind. "Is that necessary, Father?"

Barakas started to scratch his wrist, but fought down the urge. "I listened to you. I allowed you to use that sycophant to drop off your little gimmick. You had raised good points. Now, I see that we no longer have to worry about Dru Zeree following us . . . not, at least, for quite some time."

The kneeling figure did not speak, knowing there was more to come.

"Your toy failed. She fought it, proving she has a will worthy of the Tezerenee. The cross-over had not yet commenced, and her interference might have brought the rest of the Vraad down on us, something I did not wish at the time." Something caught the corner of his eye. He turned, but all he saw was the box sitting on a table. A simple magical test of the barriers proved they still held, so he knew that it was not an escape attempt he had noted.

Lochivan made the mistake of looking up. Barakas returned his attention to his son. "I find I am more than satisfied that taking her was the correct maneuver after all. Reegan needs a strong hand to guide him. She will be that guiding hand once I have molded her properly." He folded his arms. "Now, do you still have qualms?"

"No, sire."

It was a lie and they both knew it, but the Lord Tezerenee also knew that he could rely on Lochivan to obey him in all things. "Very well. You are dismissed. . . . Wait."

"Sire?"

"Tomorrow, I want a force ready to ride to the mountains, ground and air forces."

"Yes, Father."

"Go."

Lochivan vanished without even rising. It was an act that attested to the rejuvenation of the Tezerenees' power. They were not yet the masters they had once been in Nimth, but that day could not help but be drawing near, the patriarch believed.

He started to turn back to the window once more, when, for the second time, something caught his eye. It was gone before he could do any more than register its existence, but the Lord Tezerenee froze where he was, for there was something familiar about the shape, a shrouded, possibly human shape.

Quickly moving to the box, he touched the seal. There had been no trickery; the box was, indeed, still protected against assault from both without and within. He felt the presence trapped inside stir to renewed fury.

"Struggle all you like, demon," Barakas whispered to the one imprisoned within. "You *will* bow to my control, or else I'll leave you in there and lose you somewhere in the deepest cavern I can find."

The struggling subsided. Fear was gaining ground. Barakas had introduced

Dru Zeree's deadly companion to a place even worse than the emptiness of the Void. It had not been difficult to uncover the shadow steed's principal weakness. He feared to be alone.

In the box, there was not even the nothingness of the Void to share Darkhorse's fate, only the ebony creature himself.

"That's better. If you behave yourself, I will even let you see Lady Sharissa again." It would serve as a lesson to both. He would see that she was helpless despite being free to move about, and she would note that even a might as great as he was little challenge to the Tezerenee.

It was the next step in breaking their will.

Removing his hand from the box, Darkhorse's ungodly prison, Barakas scratched at his throat. He still wondered about the image. Was it a trick of his eyes, eyes that had, of late, not seen as well as they should have? Was it just his imagination? If so, why pick *that* one image to conjure to life?

Why would he imagine the startled vision of his traitorous son, *Gerrod*?

SOMETHING HAD GONE wrong terribly wrong and he didn't know what to do and he didn't know where he was and how he had ended up here but the last thing he remembered was *almost* reaching his goal but his father had been there, *hadn't* he?

"Stop it!" Gerrod screamed at himself, not caring a whit at the moment how mad he must look. He put his hands to his ears as if by doing so he could silence his own inner voice. Yet, the insane thoughts rambled on for several breaths before the warlock was finally able to bring himself under control.

In perverse fashion, it was his *father's* words that provided the willpower.

We are the Tezerenee. The name Tezerenee is power. Nothing is greater than our will.

Until this moment, those words had always struck him as contradictory and simplistic. For all his father's speeches, only *one* will really mattered among the clan of the dragon—the patriarch's, of course. Now the words reminded Gerrod that his father would not allow madness to rule him so easily. The Lord Tezerenee would fight it with as much strength as he would a physical foe. It all depended on how you focused that strength.

Gerrod would not allow himself to fail where he knew his father would succeed.

Through silent contemplation, he brought order to his thoughts and quelled, if not cast out, the fear. It occurred to him then that he had closed his eyes upon losing his hold on his destination and had not opened them again.

From the darkness of his inner self, Gerrod found himself thrust in the light of . . . *nothing?*

For lack of a better term, he was willing to call his surroundings white, though white implied something, if only light and color, and this was neither. It was simply a vast nothingness.

"Dragon's blood!" he hissed, momentarily slipping to a favorite Tezerenee oath.

He was floating helplessly in what could only be the emptiness that Dru Zeree had tried so desperately to describe, but always in so very inadequate terms. Gerrod could see why. Nothing, no words, could match the truth. There was no description that could do justice to the Void.

Calm. He had to remain calm. Master Zeree had escaped this place, and so would he.

What had happened? Gerrod recalled his brief intrusion into the real world and the sudden vagueness of his destination, as if the teleport spell no longer had a certain path to fix upon. His father had been there, a risk the warlock had been willing to face, but not the dweller from the Void. Why? The spell should have brought Gerrod to Darkhorse, unless there was some unforeseen barrier. . . .

A box. He recalled a box. There was something about it that had drawn him, something—

"You are not other I."

"What?" Gerrod looked around, trying to find the source of the voice.

"Other I was becoming boring. Maybe you will be entertaining."

"Who is that? Where are you?" the warlock shouted. He tried to turn around, but in the Void it was impossible to say whether he had achieved any result or not. Certainly, nothing but emptiness spanned his field of vision. It might have been a different nothing than the moment before, but how would he know?

"I am here."

A vast hole opened up before the floating Vraad. Gerrod's stomach began to turn. This was sounding too familiar to him. The hole quivered. Gerrod wondered how one could have a hole in the middle of emptiness. This was a part of the Void's tendencies that he had never come to terms with even after mulling over the story for years. The natural laws that he was accustomed to had no meaning here. If the Void felt a hole could exist in the midst of what was basically a *bigger* hole, then so be it.

"You're real!" Gerrod's blurted remark was superfluous at best, but staring at this creature, even after having faced Darkhorse, he could not help but want to deny the sight before him.

"You have a funny inside voice. It makes all sorts of funny noises."

It was reading his thoughts, the surface ones, at least. Dru Zeree had mentioned that Darkhorse had done the same—

"Darkhorse? What is a Darkhorse?" The black, bottomless hole grew larger, its borders coming within a few yards of the nervous Tezerenee.

The warlock kept a careful rein on his thoughts. Any loose notion would be easy prey for the creature . . . and there was no promise that it was as friendly as Darkhorse had been.

"Darkhorse is like you."

"There is nothing like me." The blot was proud of that fact. "There was other I, but other I is gone."

"Darkhorse is other I. It . . . he has a new name."

"A name?"

What sort of mind did this creature have, Gerrod wondered, that it could read his thoughts well enough to learn his speech but not understand various terms and ideas? Master Zeree had described a similar situation with Darkhorse, but not how irritating it could be. There were already too many emotions vying for mastery over the warlock without one more addition.

"What . . . is . . . a . . . name?" With each word, the hole grew larger. Gerrod now found himself truly having to worry that he would be devoured, swallowed, or whatever the case might be if the creature continued its growth.

"A name is what you call something. I am Gerrod. If you talk to me, you might mention my name so that I will know that you are speaking to me."

"Gerrod, you are amusing, Gerrod. Gerrod, what else do you know, Gerrod? Gerrod, come and Gerrod entertain me further, Gerrod!"

"That's not what I meant." He wondered if it mattered that his visage was still covered by his hood. Would his annoyance and fear register to this bizarre horror?

The hole chose that moment to swell further. Gerrod tried to wave himself away.

"Why do you do that? Why do you wiggle your appendages so?"

"You . . . your *body* would swallow me! If you get any closer, I'll die—" It could hardly understand that term. Gerrod hurriedly sought another. "I'll be no more. I won't be able to entertain you again!"

The blot paused, but its tone did not encourage the young Tezerenee. "You . . . fear . . . me."

He could not deny it. "I do."

"I like its taste." The dweller from the Void seemed to consider things. At the very least, it was both still and silent for several breaths. "You are more entertaining than the other things I have met!"

"Others?"

"I absorbed them! It was fun, but this is more fun! I think I shall play with you!"

"Play?" Try as he might, Gerrod could not keep the quiver from his voice.

Could it be that the spell, unable to fix upon one creature, had brought him instead to one akin to what he sought? How else to explain his meeting this brother of Darkhorse's so soon after his debacle?

Was it that soon? Had not Dru Zeree said that time was not a consideration in the Void? How long had he actually been there?

I will not allow panic to rule me! he thought, teeth gritted. *I have to get away from this thing before it loses interest in me and decides to . . . to . . .* The warlock found he could not bring himself to complete his thought.

"Do something else for me!" the hole demanded.

What did he know about Darkhorse that he could use to divert the creature's attention? "Can you make yourself take up less area?" He indicated with his hands what he meant. "Can you make yourself this big, for instance?"

The blot was suddenly the very size he had indicated. Gerrod blinked in astonishment at the speed with which the dweller reacted to his suggestion. He had known that the shadow steed was swift to react to things; Zeree had made that clear. What had not been clear was *how* swift those reactions were. He would have to be careful about what he did. Gerrod could not allow the monstrosity to know what was happening.

"Now what?" bellowed the blot, its voice still reverberating with harsh consistency in the human's ears.

Now what? indeed! Have it become a horse like its brother? No, that would likely rely on the dweller's searching through the warlock's thoughts for an image of a horse. Gerrod had no desire to allow this entity to go rooting around his mind. It might not leave him the same.

A shock tore through his system, so abrupt that Gerrod had no time to brace himself for it. He screamed loud and full and could not say when he at last was able to stop.

"Entertain me, I said." The cold tone left no doubt as to where the agony had originated.

"You—"

"The other little things like yourself, they were entertaining for a time! I found they did interesting things when I touched them like that! I learned much from them! I learn much from you! I even have a *name* now!" It giggled, a disquieting sound. "I fooled you I did! A good game, wasn't it? Here you explain to me what a name is and I *had* one all the time!"

Mad . . . inhuman, utter madness! It babbles like an idiot, but an idiot who could easily erase my existence whenever it chooses, the Tezerenee thought, his panic, despite his efforts, gaining too great a foothold. How could he divert the insane creature long enough to find a way out of this emptiness? There had to be something in what Dru Zeree had told him about Darkhorse!

"You were very clever," he finally told the hole. "You had me tricked completely. You were almost as clever as Dark—the other I you mentioned. He was very, very clever."

The blot stirred, swelling in size again. Gerrod wondered if he had gone too far. A notion had formed, but Gerrod was not certain whether it had any merit yet. Much of his success would lie in the dweller's arrogant yet childlike ignorance.

"I *formed* other I! Was that not most clever of all? How could other I, this Darkhorse creature, be more clever?"

The warlock's ears pounded. He clapped his hands over them and shouted back, "There are many ways to be clever! Some are more wondrous than others! Let me tell you the story!"

As if understanding his pain, the eternal's voice grew soft, almost subdued in tone. More and more, Gerrod was coming to respect Darkhorse for what he had become. *This* horror, on the other hand . . . "What is a 'story'?"

Gerrod hesitated. "Are you playing with me again? If you are, I won't bother telling you what a story is!"

"I am not playing with you! What is a story? Is it fun? I want fun! I understand fun!"

"It can be very fun." He would have liked to debate its concept of fun, but, being Vraad, Gerrod knew that his own folk, when ruling Nimth, had often acted just as sadistic, just as mad, while "enjoying" themselves. "A story is a . . . Suppose I told you about other I's clever trick and how I know of it. That would be a story of sorts." It would also be the opening he needed. There *was* something in Master Zeree's tale that could help him . . . and he had nearly let it pass!

"Your other voice hides! Why?"

He stiffened. The creature had almost caught his thoughts, his "other voice." "It has to hide before I can tell you a story. That . . . that is the way I am!"

The blot shrank again, evidently satisfied with the explanation. Gerrod felt as if he teetered on the edge of the proverbial precipice; his adversary was an unpredictable quantity. Any move, any wrong word, could spell the warlock's end.

"Do you want to hear my story?"

"It might prove amusing! I like to be amused, you know! How does a story begin?"

Gerrod breathed a sigh of relief. "Sometimes they begin with words like 'Once there was . . . ' or 'Long ago . . . '. This one begins 'There was a man named Dru Zeree . . . '."

He went into the story, editing, as best he could under the circumstances, any mention of how the outsider Zeree had found himself here or how the sorcerer and his newfound companion had left this place. While he told the tale,

Gerrod tried to mull over his own manner of escape. Vraad sorcery had not worked for Zeree. Might—he hesitated to even consider it—might the magic of the founders' world work here? He was capable of it, Gerrod knew that much, but to finally give in to it. . . .

His unnerving companion remained quiet throughout the story. The hooded Vraad put aside his other worries and concentrated again on the creature, for the tale was nearly complete. It was being entertained, that much was obvious. Would it follow through on his suggestion? Did it suspect what he had in mind and was simply playing with him?

". . . and when the other I burst forth, he was a new creature, a wonderful, huge beast who called himself Darkhorse!" What would his father think of him, floating in limbo telling stories in order to preserve his life?

"*I* have a name! Do you want to know what it is?" The blot sounded so much like an anxious child that Gerrod almost laughed despite the danger to him.

"What is it?"

"I am *Yereel!*" The hole swelled to mammoth proportions. Gerrod waved his arms and legs back and forth, but he felt himself being drawn into the gaping mouth that was his unwanted companion.

"Y-Yereel! Stop! Please!"

Yereel shrank down to a tiny blot little bigger than the warlock's hand. It—*he* seemed more appropriate now—giggled again. "I frightened you! Good! The taste stirs me as nothing else does!"

A decidedly different path of development than Zeree's creature took, the Tezerenee thought again. *How very unfortunate for me.* He decided to make no comment about the creature's—Yereel's—choice of names. If the dweller was happy, it was to Gerrod's advantage. In the meantime, the warlock had to press on. "Did you enjoy the tale?"

"Very much! Can I make one?"

"If you like. I have something better to entertain you with . . . and a way to prove yourself more clever than Darkhorse."

Though it was impossible to read any emotion in a hole, Gerrod was certain Yereel was intrigued.

"What is this way?" the blot finally asked.

"Change yourself as he did."

Hesitation . . . then, "I have never done such before."

"Neither had Darkhorse."

"I do not have this 'horse' to shape myself like."

The Tezerenee allowed himself a quick smile, hoping such a facial movement was beyond the dweller's comprehension. "That would only prove yourself *as* clever as him. If you want to prove yourself *most* clever, then you need a new form, one that Darkhorse did not do."

Yereel almost whimpered. "I *have* no other form to copy! There is only you and I!"

Gerrod pretended to consider that problem. "Well, then you could shape yourself into something like me! Darkhorse never did *that*! That would prove you more clever!"

"Wonderful!"

"It might be too difficult for you, though. . . ."

"Not so! Watch!"

Still the same tiny hole in the midst of nothing, Yereel began to turn in on himself. He continued to turn in on himself, never seeming to lose any more self. The warlock thought upon Dru Zeree's description of the metamorphosis. There were similarities and differences in what Yereel attempted now, but all that mattered to Gerrod were the final results.

The change in the dweller's appearance became more noticeable. Now, instead of a hole, he began to resemble a shell. Gerrod was not inclined to touch him and see if what he observed was true. During the course of their trek, Darkhorse had more than once absorbed adversaries like the Seekers, even though he had sported a more substantial form.

The shell toughened. Now was the time to test his theory. The hooded warlock leaned forward and asked, "How are you succeeding?"

From Yereel there was no response.

"Can you answer me? Can you hear me?"

Still nothing.

Darkhorse had entered what Master Zeree had believed was the equivalent of a pupa stage in insects. He had literally readjusted his essence in order to exist more comfortably in the real world. That transformation had lasted a day or more, if Gerrod recalled. He had no idea how long Yereel's would last, especially since time was not a known quantity in the Void, but he hoped it would prove sufficient for his purposes.

Gerrod exhaled. As simple as his triumph seemed now, it had taken a great deal out of him. Yereel was unpredictable; victory still might only prove to be a false dream if the dweller chose to burst free of his cocoon before the warlock was away.

"My spell brought me to this point. Vraad sorcery *must* work in this place!" Zeree had claimed it did *not* or, at the very least, did to no worthwhile effect. Despite those pessimistic thoughts, Gerrod was determined to attempt Vraad sorcery first.

He tried to pinpoint his destination. As it had been just prior to his accident, Darkhorse's presence could be felt somewhere beyond the emptiness of the Void, but not strong enough that he could latch on to it. Worse yet, Yereel's nearby form distracted him to the point where he finally gave up in disgust. Whether or not Vraad sorcery would work for him—and considering the link he had forged, he still believed it might—his current location made it impossible to be effective.

He could not return home. The shadow steed's position had been his sole point of concentration. The founders' world was lost to him—unless he attempted Sharissa's way.

"You're a fool, Gerrod!" Every breath he wasted meant that much more chance of still being here when the spherical shell floating before him hatched. He would have to give in, but only this once.

How had Sharissa described it? Relax and give himself over to the magic? There was supposed to be a spectrum or lines of force.

He saw neither, but he did feel a strange tingling in his body, as if some living force had permeated his entire form. A new wave of panic threatened to drown him, but he fought it off. This outworld magic would not twist him to its own interests! It was he who commanded!

Something briefly shimmered before his eyes. Not a spectrum. Not a field of lines crisscrossing into infinity. More like a path floating in the nothingness.

A path? Mention had been made of paths utilized by Darkhorse when he and the sorcerer had made their escape from the infernal nonplace. Reacting out of habit, he tried to snare it as he might a rabbit for food. Only when it proved impossible to find again did he think about what he was doing. Vraad methods did work with the sorcery of the founders' world, but not without great effort and a high level of chance.

"All right, damn you! Take me! Only this once!"

He relaxed his body, if not his mind, and let the power flow into him. It was more than a tingle now; he itched, but from *within*.

Paths, the warlock thought. *There are paths. I just have to open my will to them.*

It reappeared, a long, winding path running through the emptiness into a distant glow far beyond. Gerrod smiled. With the same presence of mind, he made himself drift toward the inviting trail. There was probably a better way to do what he had succeeded in doing so far, but he would leave that, as he had left so many things already, to more contemplative times. All that the warlock cared about now was reaching the path that would lead him to the Dragonrealm.

Another gleaming path crisscrossed the first.

His eyes narrowed. Even as the second brightened into view, a third and a fourth, one unconnected to the others, materialized. Gerrod swore under his breath, then openly as a horde of trails shooting this way and that formed before his eyes.

The Void was not so empty. In fact, it was cluttered beyond imagination, but by things so insubstantial that even a creature like Yereel had apparently never noted them.

Which one was the correct path?

He tentatively reached out with his mind, working as best he could *with* his newfound might, not against it. As a Vraad sorcerer, he would have been able to sense some of the differences between the paths. Hopefully, it would be the same now.

The first trail he stared at vanished a breath later. It was not one he wanted, that much he knew. Encouraged, Gerrod touched others and watched them fade away as his mind discarded them as possible choices. Most simply felt wrong, as if he knew without actually knowing that they went to a place the warlock was not interested in visiting. A few disturbed him greatly . . . and one was so chilling, so disquieting, that he abandoned it in near panic. Yet, wiping his brow, he was encouraged. Only a few dozen paths remained where there had been an endless array. Many had disappeared without his even studying them; it was possible his subconscious was now aiding his efforts.

Several more dwindled away to nothing, but then Gerrod recalled his companion. He felt an intense need to turn and reassure himself. It was more than merely sudden worry; he was absolutely *certain* that he had to turn around.

He did.

The cocoon was pulsating.

Yereel would soon emerge . . . and then what would Gerrod do?

He whirled around and scanned the paths remaining to him. Still too many to be certain.

"You're a fool!" he muttered.

All paths but one vanished as he made his choice. He knew it would take him to the land of the Dragonrealm, but no more. That, at this point, was all that mattered.

As if discouraged by final decision, his body was suddenly standing on the very trail. Gerrod took an anxious step forward. As thin as it appeared, it held him quite readily. It was narrower than he had thought, and Gerrod tried not to imagine what might happen if he took a misstep.

The same inner alarm that had warned him to look back now fairly shook his body with its intensity.

The Tezerenee needed no more encouragement. He raced down the glimmering, ethereal path and did not hesitate in the least, not even when the expanding glow before him suddenly flared and swallowed him up.

❊ ❊ ❊

BLUE SKY AND rocky hills greeted him. Gerrod, caught up in the welcome change of scenery around him, ran blindly for several steps before stumbling and falling.

Every oath learned under the tutelage of his father came back to him as he struck the hard soil and tumbled over and over again. Soft and comforting plant life was unheard of here. At the very least, none of it existed to ease his collisions. Only when he found a rock too large to roll over did the unfortunate warlock come to a halt.

How long he lay there Gerrod could not say. The outside world was only a blurred image when the Tezerenee forced his eyes open for a moment. He tasted blood and was surprised he was not drowning in the stuff. His body was bruised from top to bottom. Gerrod did not even want to know if he had broken anything, so he merely continued to lie where he was, hoping the pain would go away or that unconsciousness would claim him.

Someone prodded him with a heavy, blunt object, stirring him. Gerrod was aware that he had dozed, but not how long. The pain had lessened, though it was by no means insignificant. The prodding began again, this time at some of the more sensitive points of his body. Yelping, Gerrod scurried back as best he could and forced his eyes to open. At first, the same blurriness affected his vision. Gradually, however, things began to come back into focus.

Gerrod found sight did not improve his situation any.

The creature was taller than he would be if he could stand. It was also about twice as wide and none of that was soft. It was dull brown in color, although there were hints of orange. Parts of it glittered, as if someone had sprinkled it with diamonds. The blunt object turned out to be the top of a massive battle-ax.

He saw that there were at least five of the beasts, all of whom chose that moment to start hooting at one another as if discussing his fate. Gazing around at them, Gerrod could not help feeling he had been captured by some overgrown but quite vicious armadillos who had learned to walk on their hind legs just for this very purpose.

They were Quel.

X

THE WEEKS THAT passed were tense and dismal for Sharissa. She could find no way of removing the collar; twice she had almost suffocated, although no one else was aware of that fact. Barakas Tezerenee, who had spoken to her only thrice in that time, had promised to let her speak to Darkhorse . . . but the promises proved insubstantial. Most of her waking hours were spent with Lady Alcia or one of the other women of the clan. Sharissa found the patriarch's daughters as alike as most of his sons. She could not recall any of their names, and most of them even seemed to look alike. At least among the sons there was a little disparity.

Only Reegan and Lochivan seemed to matter now. Esad was also around, but his purpose in life was to carry information to his father and then scurry from sight. The rest were as identical as their sisters, cousins, and even those outsiders who had lived among the Tezerenee for a time.

He makes them all in his own image, she decided wryly when observing the Lord Tezerenee giving orders to the military expedition to the mountains. *Reegan most of all is his reflection.*

Three times she had been subjected to the advances of Reegan. He was pathetic in some ways, actually adoring her while he also lusted after her. His confusion kept him harmless for the most part, although he had tried to take more than her hand during the second encounter.

Lochivan, whom she had wanted never to see again, had been the one to interrupt what might have proven to be something worse. As if standing in the shadows and waiting for just such an occasion, he had come stalking toward them, two guards flanking him, and informed his brother that they were wanted. It was only after they had departed, leaving the two sentries to lead her away, that she had recalled her bitterness toward the amiable but treacherous Tezerenee.

She presently sat in her chambers, far more attractive ones than she had first received. Something was going on outside, something that had the Tezerenee stirred up. Her new chambers were on the uppermost floor of the citadel, barring the tower. This allowed her to view the courtyard and grounds and the mountains in the distance, a splendid view if not for the dragon men.

Rising and moving to the window, Sharissa peered outside. The gates were opening, and several riders were coming through. Those riding the airdrakes flew over the walls to join their brethren. To her disappointment, the expedition seemed fairly intact; the sorceress had hoped they might be decimated by some hitherto unsuspected force of Seekers.

Her eyes began to wander across the courtyard . . . until they focused on a figure she had been trying to see again. The elf, as usual, was accompanied by unwanted companions who dragged more than led the prisoner to a small, rather insignificant building to the left of her window. This was the first time he had been removed from the lower-level cell that had been his home since being captured. Did that mean he had finally told them what they wanted, or were the Tezerenee merely bored with him?

Suddenly she wanted out of her room. She had that much say, if little else. Sharissa departed the window, heading now for the door. It was not locked, but she had no intention of trying it. There were certain ways things were done around here, and she had come to accept them.

"Guard!"

A moment passed, a moment that seemed an eternity, before someone opened the door. One of her nameless female bodyguards stepped in, weapon ready. Sharissa had not even attempted to remember her bodyguards' names; the guard changed so often that it was impossible to keep one name or another straight.

"You wished something, Lady Sharissa?"

"I *wish* to go outside and get a little air."

"You do not need my permission to do that. I am here for your safety and to see to your needs."

The tall, slim sorceress put her hands on her hips, her only rebuttal to the claim that the Tezerenee had just made. "I know the courtyard is open to me, but I also know that you will be watching me . . . for my own good. I merely thought I would inform you first."

The guard stood there as if not sure she understood the mind of this outsider. That was as Sharissa wanted it. A touch of arrogance with a touch of confusion. Act both cooperative and defiant. She found, with few exceptions, that the clan had trouble coping with her.

Her only true threats lay in Lochivan, Lady Alcia, and, of course, Barakas himself.

THE COURTYARD WAS abuzz with Tezerenee crowding around the returning force. Sharissa, wandering on the outskirts of the assembled throng, noted the positive aura of the Tezerenee. The news the expedition brought was favorable. That could only mean that they had faced no true opposition and that the aerie of the Seekers was either abandoned or so pitifully defended that nothing stood in the clan's way of claiming it.

She caught a glimpse of Lochivan, who had, at the last moment, not led the expeditionary force. That honor had instead gone to his younger sibling, Dagos, whom she knew little about and, therefore, did not want to risk making suspicious by asking too many questions just yet. Dagos was almost a nonentity, automatically obedient to his lord and sire and having little personality to call his own. Why he had been chosen to lead was a decision she questioned, but trying to second-guess the patriarch was impossible.

As she surveyed the crowd, she kept an eye on her guard. The woman was caught between her duties and her interest. That was as Sharissa wanted it. She moved nearer the crowd, always walking away from her shadow. The guard also moved nearer, which only made her curiosity grow. The Tezerenee's eyes lingered on Lochivan and Dagos, who were discussing something animatedly.

Sharissa, the chaos shielding her, slipped away toward the elfin prisoner.

She felt no great victory for outfoxing the sentry; the woman would find her. What the sorceress wanted, however, was a few moments of private conversation so that she might take the measure of her fellow captive. If he still had any will left, there was a chance he could aid her in truly escaping. If not, he might still be able to give her some idea about the surrounding territory and where she might go.

Another reason, and one she would not admit to herself, was that, like her father and Gerrod Tezerenee, she had an overactive curiosity about new things . . . or people.

She entered the building where he was held. There were no guards. They had joined the others, an indication of how important the purpose of the expedition had been to the clan. Sharissa made her way down a short corridor and peered through the first cell door she found. Being the sole prisoner incarcerated there, Sharissa was not surprised to find him on the first attempt.

It was doubtful that the elf even needed guards; after more than one thorough questioning and little food or water, he was more of a shell than a living creature. His wrists and ankles were chained, and the chains resembled her collar, which explained why he had tried no magic. His head hung forward, as if he slept, but the moment she put a hand to the bars of the cell, he looked up.

The fire was still in his eyes. They had beaten his body, but not his will.

"I remember you." Though a bit hoarse, his voice was smooth and correct. "You look so innocent compared to the others. I suppose it works to your advantage."

"I am not one of them."

"You . . . you look like one of them, although you dress more like a woodland spirit than living death. You also walk around freely."

She leaned forward, inspecting him with a different perspective now. "You don't sound as beaten as you appear."

He laughed, but it turned into more of a croak. "I am very well beaten, mistress!"

"No, I think you're holding out better than you pretend."

"You think I *want* this to go on and on? You think I enjoy this pain?"

His lips were chapped, and it was clear he was suffering from dehydration.

Sharissa searched the area, but she could not find any water. Nor did there seem to be a key to his cell. She would have to talk to him from here.

"Listen to me! I'm not one of them! We're part of the same people—"

"Which makes you a *Vraad*." He took no pains to hide his distaste.

"We are *not* all the same! Look at this!" She nearly put her hands on the collar, but restrained herself at the last moment. Sharissa hoped he would recognize her predicament, else she would be forced to prove herself to him in a more painful manner.

He stared at her neck, but said nothing. She waited, always fearing that someone would, in the next breath, enter the building and deprive her of a chance for private conversation. After a time, the elf closed his eyes. The sorceress tried to ready herself for a demonstration that would, she hoped, convince him before it killed her.

"You *could* be a trickster," he commented without opening his eyes. "The collar could be nothing more than display for my benefit."

"I can prove it to you easily enough." Sharissa began to tremble. It would not be an easy thing. She was brave, but no one liked the thought of accidentally choking themselves to death.

The elf's almond-tear eyes opened, burning into her own. He shook his head as best his bonds would allow him to do. "That will not be necessary. I think . . . I think I will trust you on this."

A sigh of relief escaped her. "Thank you. I was willing to prove myself, but this is hardly an experience I've come to enjoy."

"I know the feeling." He rattled his chains and pointed at his own collar. "My name, mistress—the one I give you, that is—is Faunon."

"I am Sharissa Zeree. Definitely a prisoner like yourself."

"I've seen how they treat you, mistress, and I wish they would treat all their prisoners so!"

She reddened. "I didn't mean to downgrade what they've done to you! It's true I've been pampered, but only because they think I will become one of them."

His smile unnerved her. "Perish such a horrible notion! That would be like turning a flower into a weed!"

Time had to be running out. "Listen, I only came to see if you still have the will to escape. I know only tales about this region, and I'll need your help!"

"How fortunate for me."

"I would help you regardless of whether I needed you or not!" Ariela had never been this difficult to talk to! Still, she could not blame the elf for his rather cynical attitude. "Are you interested?"

He managed to give her a dry chuckle. "Do you think I would prefer to stay here?"

"I don't know when I'll be back yet. There's . . . there's another who has to come with us, but I have to find where they've hidden him."

The elf gave her a quizzical look, but she had no time to explain about Darkhorse. "Never mind! I promise I'll be back soon!"

"I am in your hands. Thank you for giving me something to think about."

For some reason, his last statement, coupled with his expression then, made her redden. The sorceress rushed to the door leading out of the building and quickly listened for any sound of movement. It had long ago occurred to her that she had been extremely fortunate so far. Was it possible that they had *wanted* her to meet with Faunon? It was the sort of devious plot that Barakas appreciated.

So much the better. If they were willing to give her the opportunity, she would find a way to make them regret it.

There were a few Tezerenee in sight, but none of them was facing her direction. Sharissa slipped out the door and hurried away, trying to put as much distance between her and the elf as possible. They might be watching her at this very moment, but she could play the game. If it turned out that she was incorrect and that no one knew where she was, then her precautions were appropriate.

Sharissa had a sudden desire to return to the days of her childhood, when things had been much, much more simple and straightforward.

LORD BARAKAS SUMMONED her later that day. It was a formal audience, meaning she would stand and listen, speaking only when required. Her bodyguard informed her of this latter part as they walked to the audience. Sharissa hardly paid her any attention. She would not change. The patriarch expected her to be defiant, and she had no plans to disappoint him.

They were nearly there when a tall, dragonhelmed warrior stepped out of a side corridor and blocked their path. "I will escort the Lady Sharissa from this point on. You may retire for a time."

"Yes, my Lord Lochivan."

Neither said anything until the other Tezerenee had departed. Then, before the sorceress could build her bitterness up for a sufficient verbal volley, Lochivan removed his helm and said, "I apologize for bringing you to this place. I tried my best to leave you out of all of this, but you were too willful."

"You mean I saw through your treachery!"

"Too late, if you recall. It was not treachery, either. You know my first loyalty is to the clan. I did succeed in convincing my father that, if you were left behind, there would be less support for Master Zeree if he chose to follow us. For you, the other Vraad would rally; for Darkhorse, they would be less inclined. You and your father were the only danger to the success of our plan."

His manner was companionable, as usual, but Sharissa had no faith in appearances. "Whether you tried to help me or not hardly excuses what you helped to do to Darkhorse! Where is he? Again and again, I've asked the patriarch about him! He promised to let me see Darkhorse, then *refused* later!"

Lochivan scratched his throat with his free hand. The young Zeree saw that the rash had spread; the Tezerenee's skin was red and dry, almost scaly. She almost felt a compulsion to touch her own throat, but she knew that it was not a rash that afflicted her. Only a collar.

"Matters came up." The warrior would not elaborate on the subject, but continued, "Tonight is intended to make up for that. You will see Darkhorse at the audience."

"Will I be able to talk to him?"

"*That* I cannot say." Replacing his helm, Lochivan reached for her arm. She gave it to him with great reluctance and only because she now desired the audience. He smiled through his helm, but Sharissa turned away, choosing instead to look forward. Her companion grunted and began to escort her to the Lord Tezerenee's court.

The two of them had barely started when another warrior came down the hall. Lochivan stiffened, and Sharissa instinctively clutched his arm tighter. The Tezerenee coming toward them weaved about as if either drunk or wounded. No blood decorated his breastplate or his dragon-scale armor, but neither did he appear to be inebriated.

Lochivan was furious. He released Sharissa and stopped before the newcomer. "What is the *matter* with you?"

"Painnnn . . ." the Tezerenee rasped. He refused to look up. One arm wrapped across his torso, while the other helped him guide himself along the corridor. Sharissa's fear turned to sympathy. Now that he was closer, she could see that he was wracked by pain. Tezerenee or not, he needed help. The concerned sorceress reached for him, but Lochivan barred her with one arm.

"Leave him be." To the bent-over figure he commanded, "Stand up! Remember that you are Tezerenee! Pain is *not* a consideration!"

Sharissa glanced at her companion, who had, while he talked, almost become his father.

"Yesss . . . yes, my lord!" The warrior straightened, but his body quivered. He did not look at the two, however, and Lochivan did not seem inclined to press the suffering warrior for any more.

"That is better! Have someone look at you! You may go!" Lochivan turned away with an imperious air about him, as if the warrior no longer existed in his eyes.

"By your leave," the trembling figure managed to get out. He marched away, stumbling now and then.

Sharissa watched him vanish down another hall. She whirled on Lochivan.

"That man was practically dying! He could have found someone to look at him by now if you had not insisted on appearances!"

"I held him for only a short time. He is a Tezerenee; he is trained to live with pain." He took her arm. "Now, come! The Lord Barakas Tezerenee awaits you!"

She allowed him to take her arm, but made it clear with her tentative touch that she loathed his very existence. Since his treachery, the sorceress had seen Lochivan in a new light. Many of his mannerisms now appeared forced, as if the true Lochivan was some creature hidden within the body that walked beside her, a creature that only played at humanity. He might as well have been a drake instead of a man.

They had walked little farther when they arrived at their destination. Two iron doors, again flaunting the dragon or drake that was the symbol of the Tezerenee, stood before them. Even as they neared the doors, guards reached out and opened the way for them. Within the chamber, someone who evidently had remained alert announced their coming.

"Lady Sharissa Zeree! Lord Lochivan!"

Sharissa was just wondering whether all the Tezerenee went by "Lord" or "Lady"—all of the patriarch's *children* did—when the sheer immensity of the grand court finally struck her.

The chamber almost seemed designed to hold the entire clan, plus every outsider loyal to the patriarch. The ceiling floated so high above her head that, had it been colored the same as the sky, she would have been willing to believe that they were outside. Banners hung everywhere, almost as many as there were Tezerenee. Fully armed guards lined the walls from the entrance to the marble dais on the far end. Wary handlers kept leashed young drakes under control. On the shoulders of several of the assembled figures, both armored and not, were perched hunting wyverns.

"Come along," Lochivan whispered. She had been so over awed by the assembled throng and the massive dimensions of the chamber that she had paused.

Ahead of them, seated on tall thrones that were, in turn, located on the uppermost level of the dais, were the lord and lady of the Tezerenee. Lady Alcia sat in regal splendor, calmly observing the two newcomers. Lord Barakas, on the other hand, leaned on an elbow and brooded over some thought. From his expression, it was clear he barely noticed Sharissa or his son.

Between and a step behind the thrones stood Reegan. His hands were behind his back, and he stood as if inspecting his legions . . . which, in a sense, he was doing. For the first time, she saw him as the power he would become should Barakas die. He only needed more tempering, something the patriarch wanted her to take a part in.

I might as well marry a drake!

Lochivan continued to walk her down the long, carpeted path that led to the clan master and his bride. When they were nearly halfway there, Barakas finally looked up. By the time they had reached the end of their journey, an open area just before and below the dais, his eyes had become fixed on her.

"Lady Sharissa," Lochivan announced, at the same time falling to one knee in deference to his parents. Sharissa made no move to follow his example; she was no Tezerenee, and kneeling would be seen only as a weakening of her will. Instead, the captive sorceress nodded to her hosts, beginning with Lady Alcia.

Barakas gave her a patient smile. "My Lady Sharissa Zeree. Welcome."

She said nothing. Beside her, Lochivan rose.

"Your reluctance to be here is understandable, and your will is admirable. You have been very patient—"

"I've had no choice!" the sorceress snapped.

"—and I hope that soon you will be able to dispense with that uncomfortable collar." The patriarch went on without pause. He straightened, and turned to the rest of those assembled. "Loyalty is utmost. Obedience is rewarded and defiance is punished."

On an unspoken signal, a Tezerenee brought forth a large box. It was elaborate in design and, although Sharissa's senses were dulled, very likely magical in some respect. The warrior knelt before Barakas and presented it to him. Nodding, the patriarch took the object and dismissed the newcomer. Barakas turned back to Sharissa and her unwanted companion.

"Please be so kind as to step back."

Lochivan took her arm and pulled her gently but firmly to the front row of the assembled followers. As he did, he whispered, "Say nothing! Watch first!"

Sharissa, who *had* been on the verge of speaking, clamped her mouth shut. She had wanted to ask again where Darkhorse was and when she would be able to see him. She had even planned on mentioning how the patriarch had *promised* her and then apparently broken his promise. Despite the absolute power he wielded among his clan, Barakas was a slave to his pride.

"We have come into our own once again!" the Lord Tezerenee uttered. His hand ran along the side of the box, as if he were caressing it. The young Zeree realized he was performing some sort of spell as he spoke. "Our powers are still far from their glory, but they *have* increased, almost as if we are linked to Nimth once more!"

The last statement made Sharissa frown. There was something in it she felt she should know about, but what that was she could not say. What concerned her more at the moment was the box and its purpose in all of this.

"I now demonstrate for our guest some of the extent of our might!"

He opened the box.

"Freeeee! By the Void! Freeee!" The near-mad voice bellowed in relief. Sharissa felt the floor vibrate as the prisoner of the box burst forth, still screaming its happiness at being released.

A thick black substance poured from the box to the floor below the dais. As it flowed, it took on shape, becoming more and more one distinct form. Sharissa needed no one to tell her who it was; his voice alone had sufficed.

"The emptiness! All alone! Curse you, Barakas Tezerenee! Only you could make a place more horrifying than the Void!"

Darkhorse stood before the patriarch and his mate, pupilless, ice-blue orbs glittering in swelling anger. His hooves tore at the stone floor, gouging valley after valley.

The sorceress could hold back no longer. She pulled free of Lochivan, who was somewhat dazed by the shadow steed's remarkable entrance. "Darkhorse!"

"Who calls?" The ebony stallion swung around and glared her way, not immediately recognizing her. When he finally did, he was so overjoyed he laughed. Most of those in the chamber put their hands to their ears. Barakas remained unmoving. "Sharissa Zeree! At last!"

He started toward her running figure. They were almost within reach when Sharissa felt the familiar but frightening touch of her collar. She could no longer breathe. Darkhorse halted at the same time she did, but not, it appeared, because of her predicament. Rather, he was trembling, as if he, too, suffered from pain.

On her knees, she tried to imagine what to do. Her collar was choking her, but she had made no attempt to touch it. Strong hands took her under the arms. As the slim woman fought for breath, she was dragged back from her one friend.

The collar grew loose.

"You . . . you call *me* demon, Lord of the Tezerenee! You are the monster!" Darkhorse trotted a few steps farther away from the sorceress. "I might have survived, but you would have *killed* her!"

"She will be fine," the patriarch responded. He remained calm, almost uninterested in events.

Leaning against Lochivan, who was the one who had pulled her away, Sharissa realized that Barakas had once more planned well. He had allowed both of them to learn in the most deadly way that they could not come within a certain range of each other, lest one or both suffer. More than likely it would be her, although the patriarch had evidently discovered many of the eternal's weaknesses.

"Can you stand?" Lochivan asked quietly. He sounded both unnerved and ashamed. "I had no idea what he planned. I would have warned you about your friend if I had."

She did not reply, choosing instead to break free of his grip and rise on her own. Once certain her legs were sturdy enough, she looked first at Darkhorse, who still looked to be in pain, and finally at the patriarch.

"I must apologize, Lady Sharissa. A necessary measure. The demon has been of great value, doing by himself what we cannot—as yet—do en masse."

"I always—" She coughed, her lungs still not fully satiated. "I always thought you believed in as little sorcery as possible. Was it not you who preached of the true strength being that of the body?"

"A good warrior utilizes the best of weapons for each situation. Your demon friend gave us access to our rightful empire. While we experimented with the powers we found reemerging within us, he built this citadel with his own skills. Through his efforts, we were able to secure ourselves while we developed."

"And this is how you reward him!" She indicated the box. "What sort of horrible trap is *that*?"

"This? This is merely a box." He held it up for her to see. Across from her, Darkhorse cringed like one whipped again and again who must now stare at the very tool that had done the evil work. "There are a few minor additions, spells that make it impossible to hear all but my voice and prevent something within from speaking to any but myself. It is proof against his sorcerous being and only I can open it, but it is, in the end, still only a box. It inflicts no pain upon him."

"It is *agony incarnate!*" roared Darkhorse. "I cannot move! I cannot speak! He becomes my only contact! I have been so *alone!*"

Careful to avoid stepping too near Darkhorse, Sharissa moved toward the patriarch's throne. Sentries instantly appeared before their lord, their weapons ready for the sorceress.

"Away!" Barakas rose and pushed them aside with his free hand. He put the open box in the crook of his arm and surveyed the defiant Zeree. "You had something to say?"

What *could* she say that would not be empty bitterness? Barakas held the upper hand. He had given her this audience just to humiliate her, to show how hopeless her cause was. "Would anything I say make a difference to you, dragonlord?"

"Very much, in fact," he said, reseating himself. Though he now wore an apologetic expression, as if he regretted his earlier actions, Sharissa knew better.

"The collar is a great travesty that you should not have to endure. Your place should be beside us!" At those words, Reegan, who had been standing quietly behind his parents, suddenly grew attentive. Feeling his eyes upon her, Sharissa forced herself to keep her own attention focused on the patriarch. She would not acknowledge the heir, her intended mate if Barakas had his way.

"I have no desire to even stand *near* you, Lord Tezerenee. I never will."

The assembly broke into a fearful murmur. Others had likely died for saying less to the very face of Barakas Tezerenee. Yet, despite the implications, the patriarch seemed unconcerned about the remark. Instead, he stroked the lid of the box once, then gently closed it. Darkhorse shuffled back a few steps out of what could only be fear. Energy crackled around the subdued stallion, and he seemed to freeze. Some bond tied him to the box.

"Remove the collar."

Renewed whispers spread through the clan. Lochivan marched up to Sharissa, who stood as lifeless as stone. What could the patriarch be planning? Did he think she would simply stand there once her abilities were hers to utilize again? She could—

As Lochivan reached up to her neck and touched the collar, Sharissa realized she could do *nothing*. Fight? Even if she were the greatest power among these Vraad, she could hardly expect to take them all on and win. Barakas would be the most well-protected target of all. Flee? Where would she go? What would happen to Darkhorse . . . or even Faunon, whom she had made a pact with? She could hardly escape without them, especially with both so helpless. Who was to say how much Darkhorse in particular would suffer?

Lochivan slipped the magical collar from her throat, but Sharissa felt no eagerness. Another collar now threatened to suffocate her. It was a collar forged from her fear for the others, notably Darkhorse. She saw now why Barakas had not taken her insult to heart; he knew she would follow him, if only because she could not abandon a friend. He might not even know about her visit to Faunon, but he certainly knew how much the ebony eternal had come to mean to the sorceress.

"Sharissa . . ." Darkhorse muttered, his tone indicating he also knew why she did nothing now that her powers had been restored.

She was once more alone before the clan master, Lochivan having stepped back with the deadly manacle. One hand slowly went to her throat, where she absently rubbed the skin. The act unexpectedly recalled to her the constant scratching many of the Tezerenee did during the course of the day. Sharissa let her hand drop.

"Good," Barakas said, nodding at the same time. "You see? Your welfare means much to us, Sharissa Zeree. I want you to work *with* us."

Cooperation? Work *with* the Tezerenee? Was there something more to this audience besides her humiliation? Had the patriarch found himself in need of her abilities?

Barakas leaned forward, as if speaking to the sorceress as a fellow conspirator in some plot. His voice, however, was loud enough for all to hear.

"There is to be a second expedition, a larger one, to the mountain aerie abandoned by the bird people. It will be led by myself and leaves in the morning." He shot a glance at Darkhorse. Though the shadow steed moved his head and glared back, it was evident that he could still do little else. Whatever spell bound him to the box made his ability to move subject to the will of the patriarch. He might as well have been a puppet on strings.

Pretending to forget the eternal, Barakas looked at the cautious spellcaster before him and continued, "Your knowledge and skills would be invaluable to our effort, Lady Sharissa. We would like you to join us."

Or Darkhorse will suffer? she wondered. Had the patriarch passed on to her a silent, veiled threat or had he so turned her that she now saw imaginary plots in each movement, each *breath* he took?

"Of what use would I be to you? Even now, shorn of your trinket and in full use of my powers, there's nothing I can do that you cannot do." Now it was her turn to glance at Darkhorse. "Through fair means or foul."

Again there was stirring among the Tezerenee. A normal court under the patriarch no doubt consisted of Barakas preaching and his followers nodding in silent obedience. Even Sharissa's rebuffs, as futile as they probably were, were jarring to the Tezerenee and their loyal outsiders.

Barakas leaned back in his throne. The time had come for the fatal thrust. She steadied herself, wondering what he could throw at her that would bring about her willing cooperation in a Tezerenee effort.

"Are not the founders a particular interest of yours?"

She said nothing, afraid what might come out.

He read her expression and nodded. "The avians are merely the latest of a continuing chain of squatters. The first and true lords, if the word brought back is true, were the *founders*—our *accursed* godlike ancestors!"

"The founders . . ." she whispered. Her strength began to abandon her as she realized he knew exactly how to play on her desires.

"It is one of their places of power."

Sharissa could not, would not face Darkhorse as she bent her head earthward and replied in a quieter, resigned voice, "I'll go with you."

The Lord Barakas Tezerenee nodded imperiously and, looking up at his people, announced, "This audience is at an end."

A legion of silent specters, the throng began departing the court. A hand fell softly onto the young Zeree's shoulder. She looked up at Lochivan, but did not really see him. Her mind was back to a time, fifteen years before, when she had been manipulated time and again, mostly because of her lack of experience in dealing with her kind. Now, it appeared as if a decade and a half had never been. Once more, she was being turned this way and that like a small child. Frustration and anger smoldered within her as it never had before.

Her expression must have altered, because Lochivan quickly took his hand from her shoulder.

I will not *be manipulated again!* Last time it resulted in the death of a friend.

The sorceress whirled and followed the other out, not even bowing to the lord and lady of the Tezerenee as was probably proper. Lochivan, reacting late, was forced to follow behind her. She *would* journey with the Tezerenee to the cavern. She *would* do her best to unravel whatever legacies the founders and their successors had left there. She *would* find a way to free Darkhorse . . . and Faunon, too.

Most of all, she would ensure, in some way, that the Tezerenee, *especially* their master, would never make use of those legacies.

XI

TWO DAYS AMONG the Quel had answered no questions for Gerrod. He still had no idea how long he had been adrift in the Void. To his own way of thinking, it had been a mere handful of hours, but he knew from his talks with Dru that time played tricks where the domain of nothingness was concerned. What might seem hours might prove to be months. For all he knew, his people were dead or, worse yet, Sharissa was a valued member of the clan, bride to the heir and mother of his children.

A heavy thump against his back sent him flailing to the ground. Around him, the Quel unleashed a chorus of hooting. From earlier confrontations, he had come to the conclusion that this was the bulky creatures' equivalent of laughter.

Rising with as much dignity as he could muster, the Vraad scanned his surroundings once more. They were traveling southwest and, while Gerrod was not yet certain, he suspected he was far from where he wanted to be. In the distance, there appeared to be a vast body of water, possibly a great sea, but trying to focus on it was impossible. For the last day, he had been forced to shield his eyes from everything, even his inhuman companions.

The problem lay in the fact that *everything* around him *glittered* like so much perfect crystal. The Quel themselves were not excluded; being so close, they were sometimes blinding. Looking down helped a bit, but even the rocky ground beneath his feet sparkled.

He knew the cause. This region was laden with crystalline fragments of all shapes and sizes, scattered about as if at some point there had been a great up-heaval, perhaps the shaping of this land by the world itself.

The glitter of the Quel was not natural but camouflage. Their shells consisted of a series of folds that, at birth, must have been much more open. In each fold were countless gems that the shell had eventually grown over, albeit not completely. Any Seeker in the sky would be half blinded by the landscape already, and the crystals on the Quel would make them blend into all that glitter.

How well that protection worked outside of this region was debatable.

The crystals had one more use that was no doubt planned by their users. They had a dizzying effect on those unused to them. Somehow, the Quel had identified him as a spellcaster; it might be that they had even spotted him coming into the Dragonrealm. Upon deciding to let him live, which had turned out to be the point of an unintelligible argument that had lasted more than a quarter hour, one of the armadillolike creatures had dragged him forward and thrust a particularly bright gem before his eyes. The blindness caused by the bright sunlight reflecting off of the gem had been temporary, but it had been accompanied by what he had taken at the time to be simple heat reflection. It had given him a headache, which he had thought of as a minor nuisance until he tried to clear his head. The concentration he needed was not there. Had he tried any serious escape attempt utilizing his abilities, it was just as likely he would have included himself in any attack on his captors.

The headache had vanished, but only so that the dizziness could replace it.

Another hour passed. The sun was on its downward arc, which, unfortunately, put it before the travelers. *Am I to go permanently blind?* he wondered. His companions were indifferent to his situation; they appeared to have a series of eyelids, all but the outermost one transparent to a certain point. The brighter it became, the darker their eyes appeared to grow as another lid slid into place. He wondered whether it was a natural ability or whether they had altered themselves much the way the Vraad had once.

A heavy hand—*paw*, as far as the disheveled Tezerenee was concerned—took hold of Gerrod's arm and dragged him to a halt.

"What is it?" he snarled, both frightened and angry. He wanted to teach these overgrown beasts their place, but, to his misfortune, they already knew it. To them, *he* was the animal.

The one who had stopped him raised its battle-ax and pointed to one of the minor hills that had just cropped up to their right. Gerrod spent more time staring at the weapon than at yet another of the land's unremarkable features. He had felt its weight more than once, usually when he was swatted with the flat of it, and knew that no human could have lifted it from the ground, much less used it in so casual a manner.

The Quel beside him hooted and pointed at the hill again. The Vraad started toward it, but was pulled back as if he weighed less than nothing. The Quel hooted again.

Gerrod shook his head, hoping that they understood by now that this was his way of saying he did not understand. The warlock had been shaking his head quite a bit in the past two days.

Frustrated, the massive creature prodded the earth and made his prisoner look down

Something was burrowing through the ground toward them.

He tried to back away, but the Quel held him. The burrowing form moved closer. Gerrod tried to formulate a spell, but the dizziness prevented him. His captors had brought him here to be sacrificed to some horror they worshiped. It had to be. Whether it killed him or not, he would have to try a spell . . . *any* spell!

A swat on the head put an end to that thought. His head pounded and his ears rang, all in addition to his ever-present impediment.

It burst forth, claws ready . . . and proved to be nothing more than another Quel, only larger than the others.

The warlock found himself falling before the newcomer, propelled there by the one who had taken his arm.

A snouted visage looked down upon him, contempt for his pathetic little form more than apparent. One head-sized paw reached toward him, claws bared, and Gerrod was almost certain he was about to breathe his last. Instead of crushing the warlock's skull, an act that would certainly have required little exertion on the Quel's part, the earth-digger took him by the collar and dragged him closer.

"Dragon's blood!" he gasped. His shirt and cloak collars were pulled so tight that it was nearly impossible to draw air.

His new captor hooted several times to the other, who returned his noises with some of their own and then turned away. They were departing.

What now? the bedraggled Vraad wanted to know. Only one thing came to mind, but surely the armored monstrosity would not—

Gerrod in one hand, the Quel effortlessly began to burrow in the ground.

"No! I can't! Stop!" He struggled to free himself, but his horrific keeper took no notice of his weak efforts. Visions of being buried alive shook Gerrod's very being. The earth grew nearer and nearer; he might have been sinking in quicksand. Already, most of the Quel's unsightly form was covered with dirt. Only the wrist and hand that held his captive were still visible.

The warlock took a deep breath and barely had time to hold it before his face met the ground. He shut his eyes and prayed that death would be quick.

Loose dirt tried to enter his nostrils. Gerrod could not move his hands forward and was forced to exhale through his nose in order to clear it. He began struggling for more air.

The Quel and he broke into a vast tunnel.

Light of a limited source allowed him some inspection of his surroundings. The dim glow came from several crystals lined along the tunnel wall. Those nearest were brightest. Gerrod tested the air—having no other choice by this time—and found it dry but breathable.

He was aware that this could hardly be the same tunnel that his present guardian had come from. Most likely, it stood some distance beneath or to the side of the one the Quel itself had burrowed. Why it had chosen to make a path of its own rather than take this one in the first place was a question Gerrod doubted the Quel would answer even if the two of them could understand one another's language. Like Zeree's Seekers, the earth dwellers had mind-sets much different than those of the Vraad. Perhaps this tunnel was specifically reserved for the transportation of surface creatures like himself.

Satisfied that his charge was in fair shape, the Quel pulled the Tezerenee to his feet. From somewhere a long, needlelike spear materialized. Gerrod could not recall seeing it before, but there had been no time for such unimportant observations until now.

The Quel pushed him ahead and leveled the spear. Gerrod understood his meaning and hastened to comply.

He had walked only a few yards when he began to sense the intense aura of sorcery all about him. Some feature about this place seemed to draw from the natural forces of the land. Gerrod was near a place of power, a well of magic of sorts. It was not merely the crystals in the walls; their only purpose seemed to be to light the portion of the tunnel where travelers happened to be. Still, Gerrod had enough knowledge of crystal sorcery to realize that the Quel might have other gemstones that gathered the raw energy of the world for their later manipulation. There were many things that could be achieved through that particular magic that normal Vraad sorcery—and possibly even Dragonrealm sorcery—could only struggle in vain to achieve.

If I can find those gemstones . . . There might yet be a way out of all of this, Gerrod decided.

It occurred to him than that he had not felt any dizziness since being brought to the tunnel.

He turned on the Quel, who froze and readied the spear, and cast a crude but deadly missile of fire at the creature.

The armadillolike horror hooted in derision.

Gerrod's mouth hung open as he desperately tried another gambit. He could *sense* the power around him; why could he not cast even the simplest of spells?

Sufficiently amused, the Quel ceased hooting and jabbed at him with the spear, clearly desiring that the tiny, weak thing before it stop playing and keep walking. Gerrod did so, his resistance all but dead. Whatever caused power to gather here was drawing what he attempted to summon even before he could make use of it. The warlock was as helpless as ever. His only consolation lay in the fact that he no longer suffered from any dizziness.

It did nothing to soothe his weary mind.

The Quel proceeded to steer him down tunnel after tunnel after tunnel. It was not long before Gerrod gave up trying to memorize his path; the tunnel system consisted almost entirely of one winding trail crossing another. There were at least two points where he was almost certain they had backtracked. His guard, however, continued to steer him along with purpose.

Claustrophobia began to set in. They were on a downward route—at least *that* much Gerrod had been able to tell, little good it did him. The tunnels were growing narrower. He pictured the many tons of earth above him and what would happen to the tunnel should a slight tremor occur. It was with great relief that he finally noticed the brilliant illumination far down the opposite end of the latest tunnel. So certain was the tired warlock that they had somehow reached the surface again that he almost started running. Only a reminding hoot from the Quel behind him kept him from doing so. For the rest of the trek Gerrod struggled to maintain his composure. A spear in his back—*through* his entire torso, more likely—would make his return to the outside world a short one, indeed.

It was not until he was mere yards from the mouth of the tunnel that it became clear that this was *not* the sun that glowed so bright.

Gerrod stepped out into the last domain of the Quel.

To call it a city was perhaps to use a misnomer. There were no streets, no buildings as a Vraad would know them, and the Quel he saw moving around were not going about the mundane daily activities that made up city life. Gerrod had spent a few days in the Vraad colony during its first years, mostly at the request of Dru Zeree or his daughter when they needed his assistance with some project, and he recalled some of the things he had seen his people doing in order to get through yet another day. The creatures before him, some so distant they were little more than shapes, moved with purpose. Whether they climbed the walls of the massive cavern, burrowed from one tunnel to another, or simply walked across the smooth floor, they traveled as if their existence depended on it.

He looked up and found what he had taken for the sun. The ceiling of the cavern was dotted with thousands of crystals, but, unlike the gems in the tunnels, they were not the actual source of the light. Instead, he saw that the light came from elsewhere, perhaps even the surface, and was reflected again and again by the array spread throughout the ceiling. It was a masterful manipulation of the crystals' natural abilities and required no sorcery—something that would have been impossible under present circumstances anyway.

The Quel who guarded him had come to his side and was also staring out at the city, but not for the same reason. It located another of its kind, who looked more or less exactly like every other Quel that Gerrod had seen, and signaled to it. The other monster hooted a short reply and climbed along the wall toward the duo.

Both fascinated and horrified, the warlock could only watch. That such huge beasts could move about so nimbly down here and climb from one precarious position to another was astounding. He hoped they did not plan on having him attempt to mimic their skill; if so, it would be a short climb—and a fatal fall.

"Sharissa Zeree," he whispered. "What have you gotten me into?"

Gerrod soon found that he had once more been turned over to another guard. The newcomer looked him over, reached out with a speed remarkable for its size, and wrapped the helpless Tezerenee in a one-armed bear hug. While Gerrod struggled to keep from being cracked into small pieces, the massive, armadillolike creature managed a handhold on the wall and pulled itself out of the tunnel and into the huge cavern. One-armed, the Quel somehow scurried across the wall for some distance before diving into yet another tunnel. Even as it landed on its feet, it released its prisoner. The warlock fell to the floor an ungainly sight.

More tunnels followed. Gerrod was convinced that this *was* to be the rest of his life. He pictured himself going from tunnel to tunnel—with occasional panic-filled rides in the arms of leaping Quel—until he came out of the other side of the world. Would that be the other continent? he wondered. Likely not. With his luck it would be the bottom of the middle of the sea.

He tried another spell at one point, a spell whose results would be for his eyes only if it did succeed, but the strange power that the Quel race controlled still held sway. Sorcery would not save him here; he would have to rely upon his mind and body.

When they came at last to yet another lit cavern, the warlock gave it only a cursory glance at first. It held only a few Quel, who darted this way and that or stood conversing near the center, and not much else. A few tunnels dotted the sides of this chamber.

There was a pause that dragged out much too long for Gerrod. He turned to his captor and, though he knew the creature understood him as well as the warlock understood a drake, asked, "Well? Which way?"

He nearly lost his composure when the guard looked down at him as if listening and then abruptly pointed toward the group clustered around the center of the chamber. It was pure coincidence, the Tezerenee told himself. The Quel could not possibly understand him; that had already been proven . . . hadn't it?

A deep grunt from his companion warned him that he had a very short time limit within which to respond to its command. The needle spear that this one also carried emphasized more than that particular point.

As Gerrod stepped into the cavern chamber, the Quel within looked up from whatever they were doing and stared at him. Unlike those he had met so far, these eyed him more with an open curiosity than with contempt or hatred. Gerrod met the studious gaze of one and noted an intelligence there that was far above those who had brought him here.

The Quel conversed for several seconds, the sounds emitted by the sentry indicating the respect in which it held the others. When that was done, the one who had matched gazes with Gerrod stepped forward. It waved a paw at the warlock, who walked in cautious fashion toward it, his eyes constantly returning to the guard. Quite suddenly, Gerrod wanted to leave this place and return to the monotony of the tunnels or even the blood-coursing fear of a cavern crossing. He knew now that he had at last reached his destination.

As ever, the Quel seemed to take his responses with a touch of amusement. Dru Zeree's short experience with the monsters had told the warlock little; most of the Quel the sorcerer had encountered had died shortly after in combat with a party of Seekers.

Would that I could trade places with you now, Master Zeree, Gerrod thought sourly.

Behind him, he heard the guard depart.

A host of Quel descended upon him before he was halfway to the one who had summoned him forward. The hooded Tezerenee buried himself in the confines of his cloak and cursed his inability to defend himself. Even a sword or ax would have been nice. It would have at least given him some comfort in his final moments.

They hovered about him, gesturing and hooting to one another like a parliament of owls. Several of them spoke to him, their unintelligible comments often ending on a questioning note.

One outshouted the rest, possibly the same one who had first waved to him.

It indicated he should follow it. Glad of anything that would free him of the imposing circle of figures, Gerrod obeyed.

There was a platform in the center of the room, a low one, which was why he had not seen it behind the Quel when he had first arrived. On it were arrayed several rows of crystals, some in patterns and some not. Many individual stones had been purposely cut to create new shapes. The Quel leader—Gerrod was willing to *assume* that this was the leader—picked one up and held it out to the Vraad.

Fascination momentarily overwhelming caution, he took the crystal from the outstretched paw.

Understanding—cooperation—question?

Caught unaware by the immediate influx of images and impressions, the Vraad dropped the gem. The chaos in his mind evaporated like so much early-morning dew. "Manee's madness!" he swore, eyeing the jewel as if it were alive.

"What was that you . . . did you . . ."

The Quel who had given him the crystal pointed to it again. With so many fearsome faces around him, Gerrod could do nothing but obey, yet he moved with as much caution as he felt they would allow him. He had a fair idea of what purpose the crystal served, but the sensations that had invaded his thoughts had frightened him.

His hand snared the gem . . . and the impressions returned to torment his mind.

Weak . . . elf . . . question? . . . Quel . . . enemy . . . question?

"Not so fast!" The images became jumbled. The warlock saw distended versions of himself and the Quel. There was also what must have been an elf.

The crystal served as a way of communication, but it was limited when dealing with two such diverse minds. A Quel obviously did not think in the same terms as a Vraad. Still, it was better than no communication at all. Gerrod simply had to puzzle out the images.

He wondered why his captors needed no such gems, but then recalled all of the crystals embedded in their armored hides. Why not include one of these among the rest? They would never be without a means of understanding an outsider. The guards *had* understood him after all; it was just that *he* had been without a means of translating *their* words and thoughts.

Elf . . . question?

Did they think he was an elf? "No, not an elf. I'm a Vraad. Vraad."

Vraad . . . question? . . . nest . . . question?

What did they mean . . . "Do you want to know where I come from?"

He felt an impression of approval. The Quel, long experienced in this method of communication, were having an easier time understanding him.

Though he did not have to speak, Gerrod felt more comfortable doing so. "I come from—" Should he tell them about Nimth? The colony? "I come from across the seas to the east."

No other land . . . statement! . . . arrival here . . . question?

They refused to believe in the other continent. Could this be the work of the guardians, the founders' magical servants? "I came from across the seas. I didn't mean to come here. It was an accident."

Land is dying . . . statement! . . . Sheekas . . . Seekers . . . same . . . question? . . . loosen living death . . . horror . . . statement! . . . Lost . . . statement! . . . winged ones triumphant . . . statement!

"Wait! Please wait!" Too much at once! "The land is dying? Which land?"

He saw the very terrain he had walked through for the last two days. For the first time, he felt the despair of the armadillolike race. Why had he not noticed the bleakness of the landscape the first time? There was some plant life, but it was widely scattered and barely able to sustain itself. "This land? This land is dying?"

The Seekers—his host had picked up the Vraad name for the avians—had unleashed some living death upon their foes. Gerrod felt a chill when the Quel thought about what had happened. Whatever the avians had loosed had sucked the life from this domain.

"I understand . . . I think."

He was buffeted by more. Now that he had been told of the disaster that had befallen them, the Quel showed him the dead, petrified corpses that were cold to the touch. Gerrod watched wave after wave of Seekers dive from the sky to finish the task, not an actual event, he discovered, but simply the way the Quel visualized their slaughter by their avian foes. They had not actually seen any of the bird people since the last desperate gamble that had saved a portion of their race. It was a certainty among the Quel that the Seekers would soon be on their way.

Their mortal foes would find this domain bereft of survivors. The earth dwellers had planned for this eventuality.

Cities abandoned . . . statement! . . . the dead left behind, a trick on the birds . . . statement! . . . survivors gathered in this cavern, a place unknown to the Seekers . . . statement!

It was becoming a little easier to understand them. Each time the Quel told him of something, the crystal indicated whether it was a query or a comment. He admired the skill with which the artifact had been crafted, but wondered how the gems could work so close to whatever it was that made sorcery impossible here.

It occurred to him that he had not tested his powers in the last few minutes. Perhaps he was no longer bereft of his abilities. It might be interesting to—

The same images and impressions struck him again, only with more force. This time, he paid more attention to them; realizing that there must be a reason they were telling him all of this. What he had taken for a city, for instance, had not been such, at least not compared to what the images revealed to him. Though underground, what the Quel passed on to him was more like what he would have recognized as normal. There were buildings and roads, yet all of it was still deep beneath the earth. The huge cavern that he had passed through had been dug out as a precaution, a place for the Quel to flee should their cities be assaulted.

And so they had been.

More and more was impressed upon him until Gerrod had finally had enough. He put up a halting hand—hoping the Quel understood its meaning—and said, "You want something of me. What is it?"

You elf/not elf . . . statement!/question?

He nodded slowly. "Yes, I am not an elf, but there are similarities." Had he gotten the meaning correct? Should he tell them that they and the elves shared with him a common heritage? Should he mention to them that the Seekers as well were related? Gerrod covertly scanned his companions and decided that it would not be an intelligent move to introduce such radical notions to creatures who could tear him apart without exerting themselves. "You had your patrols searching for elves, didn't you? One of them just lucked onto me instead."

Several Quel broke into muted conversations. The warlock knew he had guessed correctly; they had sought out an elf, and the patrol, not familiar with the Vraad race, had taken him for one of the woodland dwellers. In their eyes, the physical differences between elf and Vraad were fairly nonexistent.

Short path of travel . . . statement! The Quel leader took Gerrod by the arm, its grip surprisingly gentle. The ravaging claws were carefully turned so as to not rip into his arm. He marveled at the difference between this group and the various guards that had dragged him across half this region. Here he had been treated with a grudging sort of respect, as if these Quel understood that, while he was different, he was capable in his own right.

Could they aid him in his own quest? If he assisted them in whatever their endeavor was, they might be willing to do the same. He chuckled at the thought of legions of the creatures bursting forth from the ground beneath his father's feet. So concerned with the sky and the surface, the Tezerenee would never expect an invasion from under the earth. The patriarch knew of the Quel, but, to him, they were only a story retold by his respected rival, Zeree. The Tezerenee had actually faced the Seekers; they were a recognized threat.

The Quel who held him glanced his way when the warlock started chuckling, perhaps trying to understand what the sounds meant. The crystals might translate the sense of amusement, but Gerrod had no idea of their limitations. He had picked up emotions here and there during their peculiar conversation, but they were always associated with impressions directly transmitted to him. Nothing that did not matter to the situation at hand had been conveyed to him. He hoped his mastery of the astonishing crystals was sufficient to prevent his own random thoughts from being sent out. Until he became more proficient, the Tezerenee decided again to continue speaking out loud in order to keep his thoughts focused.

More proficient? How long, he wondered for the first time, would he be here? Despite their politeness, the hulking creatures had not once indicated that the Tezerenee would be allowed to leave even if he *did* perform whatever task they needed him for. Like many Vraad, the Quel might be capable of smiling, or however they expressed themselves, while at the same time burying their spears or axes in one's back.

To Gerrod, the tunnel he was led into suddenly grew very oppressive, reminding him of the path to a crypt. His, perhaps.

It grew cold, the first time Gerrod had felt cold since coming here. Even the Quel seemed touched by it, for they slowed their pace and a few looked around in what a Vraad would have been growing anxiety touching upon fear. Only the leader seemed nearly the same; its peculiar eyes blinked constantly, but it alone kept the steady pace. The warlock was not reassured, however. He had met enough madmen and fools. For all he knew, the worst of them now dragged him by the arm toward chaos incarnate.

They came to the mouth of yet another cavern, but unlike the others, this one was as black as Darkhorse. Gerrod could see nothing within even after allowing his eyes to adjust. As he turned to his guide, the warlock saw the rest of the band back away a few steps.

The leader's eyes surveyed him from head to toe. Was he being measured? Had the Quel begun to wonder about Gerrod's ability to survive whatever lurked within?

"What is in there?" he asked.

You/we . . . yourself/ourselves . . . statement!/question?

What could *that* mean? He asked the question again, but received only the same response. It made no sense no matter how he turned it. The impressions were jumbled, uncertain. Gerrod came to the conclusion that the Quel could not explain, might not even know. Maybe that was why they needed an outsider like an elf. Whatever lay waiting within the darkness could very well be beyond their comprehension. Once more, he was reminded of how different their minds were from those of his people. It might be that there was nothing for him to worry about.

Gerrod did not believe that for a moment.

As it turned out, his choice was made for him. The Quel leader gripped his arm tight enough to make the Vraad gasp . . . and dragged him inside. The others hung back and waited.

Somehow Gerrod found himself in front of the Quel leader, though he could only tell that by touch. The creature's grip was now the only thing he could be certain about; his eyes could make out nothing in the darkness, and all sound appeared to have ceased the moment they entered.

The Quel released its grip and vanished into the darkness.

"Wait! Where are you?" The warlock turned around, but he could not find the path back even though it should have been visible. "Dragon's blood! Don't leave me in here! I cannot see a thing!" He feared to move, uncertain as to whether his next step would take him over some unseen brink or into the waiting arms of . . . of what?

When, however, it became apparent that no one would be coming to retrieve him, the warlock finally dared a tentative step forward.

A thousand blinding suns brilliantly illuminated the chamber. Gerrod put an arm before his eyes and drew the hood of his cloak over his face. After such complete darkness, the light was doubly harsh. He would have stayed as he was, wrapped tight in his cloak, but for the whispering. He could not make out what they said, but there was a familiarity to their voices, almost as if they were all the same voice, but speaking of different things. None of them heeded the others in the slightest.

They have thrown me to a legion of madmen or demons! he decided. *Monsters who, no doubt, I will soon join in madness!*

What *was* it about the voices that sounded so familiar to him? There were differences, to be sure, but the tones and inflections were the same regardless of that. He knew those voices, knew them to be only *one* voice.

One voice . . .

"Cursed Nimth," the Tezerenee whispered. "What sort of mockery is this?"

He slid the hood back a little and found the light more tolerable now. The discovery disappointed him, for Gerrod had hoped for an excuse to keep from looking. Now, the only thing holding him back was his own cowardice.

The mocking laughter of his father assailed his ears, but Gerrod understood that out of all the voices he heard, his sire's was the only one solely of his imagination. The rest were very real.

He looked up and saw them—the faces in crystal.

They were everywhere, the faces, because, unlike the other chambers, there was nothing here *but* crystal. The floor, the ceiling, the walls—from tiny, indistinct specks to huge, horrifying demons, the faces were all about. They babbled on in a frantic manner, as if their very lives depended on his understanding them. Try as he might, Gerrod could not make out one true word. He strained to hear the whisperings of an ancient, balding seer and the harsh mutterings of a hooded fiend whose face refused to focus for him. Another, a young, amiable figure with a shock of silver hair amidst a field of brown, talked to him as if they were close friends. Even still, the warlock could not make out what the other was trying to convey, despite desperately wanting to understand *one, any one,* of the phantoms trapped in the crystals. He knew them now, knew them as well as he knew himself.

That was who they were. No matter how changed—and some were very, very changed—they were *all* Gerrod.

XII

SHARISSA HATED THE riding drakes. She hated their appearance, their attitude, and their smell. They could not compare to a horse. Yet, she had been forced to ride one these past two days. The beast was stupid, and it often grew sidetracked. Once it had even snapped at her for no reason whatsoever.

The patriarch listened to her complaints with the air of one tolerating a whining child. It made no difference whether or not she was having trouble with her mount; Tezerenee used drakes for riding, especially when it was always possible that they might be engaged in combat at any moment.

The force that journeyed to the mountains moved with caution. Teleportation was still a spell beyond most of the Tezerenee, and so they were forced to travel in a more mundane manner. The patriarch also distrusted the absence of the Seekers. Barakas might claim that the aerie was abandoned, but he apparently believed that there was risk enough that rushing into things might result in chaos. He had even brought along a very submissive Darkhorse, who turned his head every time Sharissa attempted to speak with the eternal. Darkhorse was ashamed of his actions, despite the fact that much of what he had done had been for her sake. The captive sorceress did not blame him for anything, but trying to tell him that was proving impossible.

Evening came at last. Barakas gave Reegan permission to give the signal to halt. The heir did so in a sullen mood; he still burned over his father's decision to leave his mother in control of the burgeoning empire. Reegan had assumed that the patriarch's being absent would allow him to exercise his long-overdue desire to rule. The heir had even argued with Barakas at some length, but the end had been inevitable. All that Reegan could do was sulk afterward, and he had done so with a determination almost admirable.

Sharissa was just descending from her troublesome steed when a familiar and unwanted voice rose behind her.

"Allow me to help you, Sharissa."

"I can do without your help *or* your friendship, Lochivan!" she retorted, dismounting as she spoke.

He aided her nonetheless. "I understand your bitterness and I know that nothing I can do will make up for the wrongs you believe of me, but we will be together for quite some time—all our lives, in fact."

"I thought is was Reegan the patriarch wanted me to marry, not you."

A brief chuckle escaped him. "I might admit to having had some thoughts on the subject; I like to think that you might find me a bit more entertaining than my bullish brother. That was not what I meant, however. I merely refer to a fact that you must come to face before very long—that you are now and shall ever be a part of us. There is no going back."

She tried to take her pack from the drake's back, but Lochivan moved around her and took it before she could even touch it. "Only a body of water separates me from my father and the other Vraad. Either they will come for me or I will go to them."

Lochivan signaled to another Tezerenee, who rushed over and took charge of the riding drake. That detail taken care of, the patriarch's son started walking, Sharissa's pack still under one arm. The slim woman followed, if only because she knew that he would keep walking regardless of whether she followed. As long as he had her pack, Sharissa knew she would have to listen to him.

"The crossing is deadly; the elf your father took as a mate must have told you that."

"She survived, didn't she?"

"Others perished. Besides, do you think you can sail there all by yourself?"

"I have the use of my abilities back—no thanks to you and yours, Tezerenee."

He paused before a clear, smooth location that would leave her near the very middle of the camp. Coincidentally, several Tezerenee stood patrol nearby. "The elves, I understand, are not without their own measure of power. We may be mighty, but the elements must always be respected."

Reaching out, she tore the pack from his hands. "When have the Vraad ever respected the elements? Have you so easily forgotten Nimth?"

"Hardly. I have learned more than you think, Sharissa. I respect this world. That will *not* keep me from doing my duty to the clan, though. The Dragonrealm must be brought under control. This idiocy of one race after another passing beyond must end. Already it seems to have claimed the Seekers. We are, if you recall, the founders' last hope for a successor. We cannot disappoint their memory."

While he had been talking, Sharissa had knelt down and opened the pack. Each of the food items she removed could have been conjured instead of carried, but Barakas wanted sorcery kept to a minimum. Unlike the millennia of excess that Nimth had suffered under the Vraad, this world was more grudging. The Tezerenee might be able to use the old world's sorcery, but it still drained them physically. Even Sharissa had bodily limitations. Barakas claimed he wanted everyone at their best should an attack occur. It was also possible that the Seekers might not yet know that they were coming. An excessive use of magic might alert the avians and destroy any advantage of surprise the expedition had.

Sharissa doubted that these were the foremost reasons. She suspected that the patriarch wanted his men to take the aerie without the aid of sorcery; it would serve to bolster morale and add credence to the belief that an empire in this land *was* their true destiny.

"Listen to me!" Lochivan hissed as he came down on one knee next to Sharissa. His voice was very low and very anxious. "I *am* your friend whether you believe me or not. I am thinking of you!"

"As long as it doesn't interfere with your noble thoughts concerning your clan. I'm tired, Lochivan. Go talk to one of your brothers or sisters or cousins or anyone, but stop talking to *me*."

He rose, a dark shadow outlined by the last dim rays of the sunken sun. "You and that elf . . . two of a kind!"

"What about the elf?" Sharissa tried her best not to look too interested.

Lochivan took her interest as an opening. "I have to spend another fruitless evening trying to convince him of the futility of holding back any longer. With his companions dead and his people far away, he should be reasonable. Instead, he merely grits his teeth and stares into space."

She barely heard most of what he said. "What have you done to him *this* time?"

The edge in her voice did not go unnoticed. "Only what must be done. We have been careful; damaged, he is no good to anyone. He knows this land better than we. His knowledge must be added to our own."

Could she possibly——? The thought was so outrageous that she nearly discarded it immediately. Sharissa looked up at the dark figure of Lochivan. "*I* could speak to him if you would only let me."

"Why would you want to do that?"

His disbelief was expected. Why would she help the Tezerenee? The sorceress hoped her answer would soothe his suspicions. "I want to save him from any more of the hospitality of Barakas—him *and* Darkhorse. Let me see what I can do. If I succeed, I expect to be able to spend a bit of time with Darkhorse, too."

"You *expect*—"

She raised a hand. "Does not the patriarch say that those who serve shall be rewarded? Have I asked that much?"

Lochivan was silent for so long that Sharissa feared he had rejected her suggestion out of hand and was merely marveling at her gall. Then he laughed.

"I will ask for permission. It may amuse him as much as it does me." He began to depart, then turned back and, in a quiet voice, added, "It may come as no surprise to you that you are being watched."

"I hardly thought Lord Barakas *wouldn't* safeguard against my good intentions. I think I know what might happen should I desire to test my abilities."

That produced another good-natured laugh. "You would be wasted on Reegan, Sharissa."

She busied herself with her blanket and did not reply.

"I am dismissed, I see. Should I gain permission for you to speak to the elf, I will send word. Until then, good evening to you." His heavy boots crushed fallen twigs and leaves as he moved off. Sharissa waited until the sounds grew faint before turning around to watch his departure.

"I would rather marry Reegan," she whispered. "At least *he* I can trust to be consistent."

"LADY SHARISSA?"

The sorceress blinked sleep from her eyes. Night still shrouded the land, but that did not tell her anything of import. "Is it near morning?"

"No, my lady." A female warrior was bent over her, helm in one arm. Dressed in something finer than armor, she probably would have been attractive. Tezerenee had in general done without magical alterations to their face and form, preferring to live with what nature had chosen for them. For many Tezerenee, that meant less-than-pleasant features. A few of the patriarch's offspring, such as Gerrod or his late brother Rendel, had been fortunate enough to gain more from their mother than their father.

"What hour is it?"

"We are barely past midnight, Lady Sharissa."

The warrior was scratching her cheek. In the light of the partial moons the sorceress could see that the same dryness that many Tezerenee suffered had spread to this one's cheek, ruining what beauty she did have.

Sleep made the sorceress slow. There was a reason why a Tezerenee might have come to her now, but she could not think of what it was. "Then why have I been disturbed?"

"The Lord Barakas Tezerenee has given you permission to speak with the elf."

"Alone, of course."

"Of course, my lady."

They both knew this was far from the truth, but arguing about it would avail Sharissa naught. She would merely have to be careful how she spoke with Faunon. He would understand why. The elf was no one's fool.

Sharissa rose. "Give me a moment." She picked up some of the food, including some of the Tezerenee wine Reegan had given her. That the clan of the dragon could make such excellent wine was their only saving grace in her eyes.

When she was ready, the Tezerenee led her to the wagon where Faunon was kept. Two sentries stood ready to receive them. Sharissa expected to see Lochivan nearby, but could not find him. It did not break her heart.

Her guide spoke to the others and indicated Sharissa. One of the guards nodded and both stepped aside. Nodding as if their obedience was to be expected, the sorceress strode past them and over to the wagon door. The Tezerenee preferred a wagon that was more of a room on wheels, including windows and a door. There was no real need for such an elaborate structure where a simple cloth-covered wagon would have sufficed; the wagon was merely a result of the clan's tastes. In some ways, it resembled a tiny citadel. Sharissa knew that it was even protected to some extent by defensive spells.

A light from within blinded her when she opened the door. Her eyes, accustomed to the darkness, took a moment to recuperate. Sharissa saw that a lamp illuminated the interior and wondered if it had been left specifically for her use. The lamp hung on a hook in the ceiling. Beyond it were several mysterious sacks from which emanated a slight magical aura, but nothing that made her worry. Supplies of some sort; she had seen their like often.

Other than the sacks and the lamp, only one other item decorated the wagon's interior.

Faunon.

He was chained so that he could sit on the floor with his legs outstretched, but there were other chains above those, an indication that sometimes he was forced to stand, probably during questioning. Physically, Faunon looked no worse than he had the last time the tall sorceress had spoken to him. Vraad torture, however, did not necessarily leave its marks on the skin.

She closed the door behind her, even though that did not mean that they could not hear her. It would give them a sense of privacy at least. "Faunon?"

The worn figure did not respond.

"Faunon?" Sharissa's voice quivered. Had they killed him and left the corpse there for her to see? Was this Lochivan's mad jest on her?

His chest rose and fell. Sharissa breathed a sigh of relief, more horrified at the thought of his death than she would have believed. The elf was the only being other than Darkhorse that she could think of as a friend.

He looked up. His handsome features were marred by dark circles under his eyes and very, very pale skin. Despite the excessive anguish he had gone through since last they met, the fire was still alive in his eyes. As they focused on her, the flames burned brighter, as if her presence heartened him.

"Lady Sharissa." He coughed. "I was told you would be coming. I thought their words just another torture. I thought I would never see you again."

"I couldn't get to you." It would do no harm to speak a little about their last encounter. She knew by now that they *had* at least known of it, if not what the two had actually said during that encounter. "Then, I found you had been moved."

"These Tezerenee like to play games. One . . . one of those games is to move me from one place to another, with each . . . each progressive accommodation worse than the last."

Sharissa moved close enough to touch him. "I'm sorry. I should have tried harder . . . for both you and Darkhorse."

"And what could you have done? There is a saying among us elves,"—he gave her a weak smile—"one of our *many* sayings, that more . . . more or less means one should wait for the proper time, for eagerness and overconfidence have brought down many an empire. In this land, we have seen much truth to that."

His ability to still find strength despite the situation encouraged her.

"I asked them to let me talk to you, Faunon. I told them I might be able to gain your cooperation."

"You will always have my cooperation. It is only these Tezerenee who will not."

"There must be something you can tell me, something that will save you from further questioning for the time being. Something about the land or about the caverns in the mountains." She was almost to the point of pleading. If she failed, the Tezerenee would only redouble their efforts in regard to the elf. Sharissa's heart beat madly when she thought of that.

Faunon shook his head. "I told them about the caverns. What little I know. I warned them to stay away, that even the Seekers no longer trusted the place."

"Why is that?"

He laughed, but it was a bitter sound. "I told them that something *evil* lives in the lower depths. They, of course, thought I was trying to pass on some ancient legend, but this thing is a recent horror. My people have spied upon the aeries before, including the caverns, and no one has ever spoken of any monster."

"Are you certain?" Unlike Lochivan or Barakas, Sharissa was willing to believe what the captive elf was saying. She could see the truth of what he said in his eyes. She could see many things in his eyes.

"As certain as I am of anything," he replied, but his voice was distant, as if his mind were elsewhere. Sharissa blinked and turned away until she was certain she could face him without reddening.

"Is there anything else you could tell them? Are there many Seekers left here? Have you seen the upper caverns?"

"I saw a huge, unearthly stallion race to the east. It was weeks ago, but they might—"

She shook her head. "That was Darkhorse."

"Darkhorse?" He gave her an appraising look. "I thought the name only fanciful. There are many such names among us elves. When you used this Dark-horse's name, I did not think it was meant to be so literal. For a Vraad, you make interesting friends. First an ebony demon and then myself. I thought your race rather arrogant toward outsiders."

"Are all elves the same? You hardly seem as formal I was always told."

"I take your point." Since the start of her visit, or perhaps even *because* of it, Faunon had grown stronger and more coherent. Sharissa was pleased, but realized that it all meant nothing so long as they were prisoners of the Tezerenee.

"This Darkhorse," interrupted Faunon. "You mentioned him as a fellow prisoner. Is the dragonlord so powerful that he could bind this stallion to his will?"

Outside, something thumped against the side of the wagon. The sorceress listened for a moment, but when it was not repeated she decided it was nothing. "He wasn't before. They're growing stronger, Faunon. Soon, they'll rape this land as they did the last . . . and I can do nothing to stop them!"

"Nimth. That's what it was called, wasn't it? The world we fled from? The world the Vraad ravaged?"

She nodded.

His mouth was a grim line. "I doubt they will find this domain so pliable. It has faced others before your people. There were many who wanted to adapt the land to them instead of working with it. Whenever that happened, the land seemed to make *them* adapt."

"What do you mean?"

"Have you felt any different since coming to this world? Any change at all?"

"I felt more at home than I ever had on Nimth. It was a glorious change for me." For the first time, she recalled the wine and food in her hands. The young Vraad showed it to Faunon, who momentarily dropped his question and smiled at the sight. "Is that wine? Could I have a bit of that before I continue? Our friends have given me nothing but brackish water, albeit all I could drink."

"Let me help you." She brought the wine to his mouth and tilted it. Faunon, his eyes on her, swallowed twice and then indicated she should stop.

"Thank you . . . gods! What sweet honey!"

"The Tezerenee make it."

"Proving that they have at least one good quality, I suppose." While she broke apart some bread and cheese for him, he returned to his subject. "Having spent these few wonderful moments with you, I can see that you and the land would have no quarrel. The same cannot be said for the dragon men, however. The land will not tolerate them."

Sharissa thought to ask him if he knew of the founders and how their kas, their spirits, *were* a part of the land now, but the telling of that would take her much too long.

A heavy weight fell against the wagon, striking so hard that the entire structure shook.

"Are we under attack?" Faunon asked, frustration at being chained during a time of danger taking over. The sorceress had thought of trying to remove the chains, but, recalling that they were like her collar, knew it would be an exercise in futility.

She rose. "I'll see what it is."

"You could be killed!"

"I'll not wait for whatever it is to come to us!"

With great caution, she reached for the door handle. Sharissa raised her other hand, ready to cast a spell the moment she opened the door.

A hulking figure from without burst through the door as if it were dry kindling.

"Lllaaady Zzzzzerrreeeee," it hissed.

It wore what looked like the remnants of armor, not that it needed any, for it had a natural scale armor of its own that went from head to foot. The fiend was almost human in form, but bent awkwardly, as if it was trying to move as a man but not built for the purpose. The hands were more like the paws of the riding drakes and ended in equally sharp talons.

Worst of all was the visage. As the body could only mock that of a human, so too did the face, only more so. The eyes, though crystalline like a Vraad's, were long and narrow. The horror's nose was virtually nonexistent, two mere slits in the center. Its mouth was full of teeth that were pointed and made for tearing flesh from a kill.

It was coming for her.

"Lllaaady Sharisssssssa!" It reached out for her, but she jumped back just in time. The creature was like some legacy of mad Nimth. She tried to concentrate, knowing that only seconds separated her from death. Physically, the frightened sorceress was no match, but her powers might save her if she could only think.

If only it would stop flashing those teeth! she kept thinking.

"Sharissa!" Faunon called from behind her. That snapped her out of it. It would not only be she that perished if she failed to act, but also Faunon, who could not even defend himself.

"Lllaaady, I—"

Whatever it sought to say, Sharissa would never know. A spell formed in her mind and was completed accordingly. Brilliant, scarlet bands swarmed around the reptilian terror, who fought them with the savagery of an animal cornered. The bands began to tighten around its arms and legs. Sharissa breathed easier.

A yellow aura originating from the creature evaporated the bands just as it seemed the battle had been won.

"Yooou mussst—" the creature started to say, forked tongue lashing in and out of its mouth.

Before her eyes, it twitched once—and fell forward, already dead.

There was an arrow in the back of its neck. The shot had been so perfectly aimed that death had been instantaneous.

"Inside!" a voice shouted.

Two Tezerenee in full armor came rushing in. One of them bent down and inspected the sprawling figure while the other kept his sword ready should it turn out that, impossible as it was, the monster still lived.

"Well?" roared the same voice that had ordered the two inside. Lochivan peered in, his bow ready.

"Dead, milord."

"Roll it over."

The warrior who bent by the corpse removed the arrow and did as Lochivan commanded. Everyone stared at the horrible features.

"This is the armor of one of our own, milord."

"I can see *that*." Lochivan looked up at Sharissa. "Are you injured at all?"

"No." For the first time in weeks, she was actually happy to see him. "I held it back, but it had sorcery of its own."

"Yes, I know. It killed one of the sentries outside by sorcery. Quietly, too. The other sentry did not notice until the first fell to the ground. By that time, it was too late for him to save himself, much less the first man."

"Milord!" The Tezerenee who had studied the dead monstrosity stumbled back, unable to hide his shock. "This is one of us!"

"What? Impossible!" Handing his bow to the other man, Lochivan knelt and inspected his kill. His hand roved over what remained of the armor and then to the face. He stared hard and long, trying to make sense of what lay before him.

Sharissa, too, was staring long and hard. Unbidden came the memory of the

warrior she and Lochivan had confronted in the corridor just before her public
humiliation by Barakas.

"Lochivan," she started. "Do you recall the man we met in the hall? The one
doubled over from illness?"

He looked up. "I recall him." Unlike his father, the sorceress was aware that
he could name every Tezerenee in the clan, be they born by those of the founding blood or outsiders who had joined the ranks at one time or another. It was
even a point of pride with him. "That would make this . . ." Lochivan turned to
one of his men. "See if Ivor can be found! He was among the chosen for this
expedition since he was a part of the first."

Hearing this, Sharissa's brow furrowed. Was it pure coincidence? "Is Ivor a
relation?"

"A cousin. Obedient, little else. He was one of the earliest to cross over from
Nimth."

As the one warrior departed to fulfill his desires, others arrived. One saluted
Lochivan, who stood. "Well?"

"There are three dead. We found another man gutted a short distance from
here."

"Nothing more?"

"Nothing."

"Dispose of this . . . this . . . dispose of him in a discreet manner. Is that
understood?"

"Yes, milord."

While the others began dragging the body out, Lochivan noticed Faunon for
the first time. Ignoring Sharissa, he marched over to the elf and knelt by him.

"What trick was that, elf? Are your fellows out there now?" He gripped Faunon's jaw in one hand. "Have I been too lenient with you?"

Sharissa's relief at seeing Lochivan faded. He had no right to treat Faunon
so. "What could he know? What part could he have played, Lochivan? Look at
him. You've reduced him to little more than a shell!"

"It . . . it . . . is all r-right, my l-lady." With the return of the Tezerenee, Faunon was exaggerating his condition. Sharissa tried not to react, understanding
that Faunon wanted them to believe he was weaker than he was. To Lochivan,
the captive replied, "I know . . . nothing, friend. That I swear t-to you. Do you
think I w-would have invited such . . . such a menace into this p-place when I
cannot even defend myself? I w-would rather you slit . . . slit my throat than
for . . . for me t-to be torn apart by so grisly a beast."

"Do you claim that the elves did not do this?"

"Your man was ill before this, Lochivan," Sharissa reminded him again. It had not been proven that this was indeed the one called Ivor, but she suspected such evidence would be forthcoming. "It could have been something else."

He sighed. Standing, the Tezerenee removed his helm and scratched at his throat, where the dry patches of skin had spread. It had become so familiar a habit with him that he no longer even complained when it itched. "Perhaps you are correct. The Seekers have been conspicuously absent."

She did not understand. "I thought the aerie we travel to had been abandoned and the Seekers were dead."

"There are a few to weed out. Survivors, nothing more."

A change in the expression on the elf's visage made the young sorceress's eyes dart to Faunon and quickly back again. At mention of the caverns, he had become lost in thought, as if making some connection that she could not. Once Lochivan left, perhaps she could—

"I am afraid that I must terminate your conversation with the prisoner," the armored figure said at that moment. "You will be given another chance to speak with him, I think. For now, I would prefer that you be where I can guard you better."

"Me? It was one of your people that suffered—"

"And he came for you. It may be that you are seen as a risk to whoever is responsible. I want nothing to happen to you, Sharissa." Lochivan's tone softened toward the end.

She wanted to argue, but the outcome would be the same regardless. Behind the Tezerenee, Faunon indicated that she should agree. Too much protest and they might change their minds about allowing her to talk to him again.

"Very well." It was doubtful that sleep would be so easily forthcoming.

"Let me escort you back."

"That will not be necessary." She did not want him touching her.

"You will be safer. This may not be an isolated incident."

As before, there could be only one outcome. Conceding defeat, she nodded and gave him her hand.

"You have . . . have my gratitude as . . . as well," Faunon commented as the Tezerenee was about to lead her out. "How fortunate that you were so nearby."

Meaning that Lochivan had either been spying on them or had been waiting for Sharissa to leave the wagon. The Tezerenee glanced her way, but did not return the elf's comment. He did, however, lead the slim woman out of the wagon much more swiftly than necessary.

Outside, several Tezerenee were still moving about. Two moved to clean the debris that had once been the door. Sharissa looked for signs of the sentries' bodies, but they had already been cleared away. She felt some pity for them, but not quite as much as she would have for the elves their kind had slaughtered weeks ago. Much of what the Tezerenee suffered they had brought upon themselves.

Only two days from the citadel and this had occurred. As she and Lochivan walked away from the carnage in silence, Sharissa wondered what the coming days had planned.

Somehow, she felt it would only be worse.

XIII

"She sleeps, sire."

"Good." They stood in his tent, the three of them. He used the tent as his base of operations, which was why he felt justified in having it when the rest of his warriors slept outside. The patriarch was only partly clad in armor, it having taken him longer than normal to dress. He found it a bit disturbing, but laid aside that minor annoyance in the face of the outrageous incident with the abomination.

Reegan, fully clad and more than a little angry at the loss of sleep, asked, "What did you do with its carcass, Lochivan?"

His brother, still kneeling, replied, "It is being buried discreetly. Father, the monster is none other than one of our own. Reegan, you know of Ivor?"

"It was *Ivor*?"

One of our own, the Lord Tezerenee wondered. *They have struck down one of our own in the very midst of my camp and despite my precautions!* The entire area had been carefully laced with defensive spells. He had always eschewed such things in the past, preferring to rely on the readiness of him and his people, but of late he had not moved as swiftly as before and his clan appeared more hesitant than they had during their first days here.

"Three other men died. All adopted outsiders."

A small loss, but a loss nonetheless. Some of the other Vraad who had joined his clan would be growing nervous. The patriarch needed things to stay on course in order to assuage their fears. The expedition would have to be more alert than they had been.

"What happened to him? What sort of change?"

Lochivan bowed his head. "I do not know. It was suggested that the Seekers might have done this."

"Suggested by whom? The elf?" Reegan sneered. "Of course he'd blame them! He's covering for his—"

"Reegan, be silent!" The patriarch tugged at his beard and mulled over the possibilities. "If it was the elf or his friends, I imagine they could do just as well if he were rescued. They would not leave him to our mercy. Tell me, Lochivan, does he seem like the suicidal sort?"

"He's a warrior, father, and willing to risk himself, but I think this would be asking too much from him. His death would serve no purpose."

From out of the corner of his eye, Barakas saw his eldest building himself up for another tirade. The patriarch turned in time to stall the outburst. Reegan frowned, but remained silent.

"Ask those who knew Ivor better if he has acted differently of late." A thought occurred to the Lord Tezerenee. "He was a member of the first expedition?"

"Yes, sire."

Could it be that Ivor had discovered or touched something he should not have? Did some trap lie in wait for the Tezerenee? Barakas thought of the box and its unwilling occupant. He had been wise to bring along the dweller from that emptiness that Dru Zeree had called the Void. Taking the caverns might not be so simple after all.

"What do you intend, Father?" Reegan dared to ask.

"We will continue on at the same pace. Losses are always to be expected. More may fall before this is ended. Even one of you may succumb."

Reegan and Lochivan shared an expression of anxiety. It did not occur to the patriarch that he himself might succumb. He *was* the clan, after all.

"Let it be known tomorrow that Ivor and the others died honorably. Ivor especially. You are both dismissed."

His sons bowed and quickly departed, no doubt first intending to alert their siblings as to what had been discussed before obeying his other commands. Barakas, meanwhile, forewent removing his half-worn armor for a time, instead continuing to ponder the incident that had claimed the lives of the warriors and almost that of Sharissa Zeree, too. In a sense, he almost envied Ivor one thing. The hapless warrior had come closer than anyone to truly knowing the glory of the dragon that was the clan's totem. His only trouble was that he had not had the will to master whatever spell had affected him.

Had it been himself, the patriarch decided, he would have turned the transformation to his own desires. He had the will that Ivor had lacked. He, lord of the Tezerenee, would have become the living symbol of the clan.

Barakas started to scratch himself, but, realizing what he was doing, forced his hand down. In the past few days, the rash and dry skin had begun to recede. Soon, he would be rid of the irritation. The more it was fought, the less it became.

It was, as he had preached so often, merely a matter of will.

* * *

THEY TALKED AND talked, yet what they struggled to say escaped his ears. Most were difficult to focus upon after a time, as if the more he tried to define their features the more murky they became.

Gerrod could only stare at them, caught up in some inexplicable spell of fascination that would not allow him to turn from them and search for the way out of this madhouse. Every move that the warlock succeeded in making toward that effort only brought him to new and equally disturbing visages.

"Dragon's blood!" he whispered for what was either the first or the hundredth time—Gerrod could no longer keep track. He barely knew himself anymore, much less what happened around him. A drake could have stalked him at its leisure, taking him as he stood there like a fool. Yet, it was impossible to pull away.

With a mixture of fear and childlike awe, Gerrod stretched a tentative hand forward and touched one that most resembled him.

A difference he could sense but not see spread throughout the room. Something began to tug on his cloak, but, caught up in his dreaming, the warlock barely even noted it. He heard a faint sound that might have been a summons or merely the wind, an insignificant noise that Gerrod quickly forgot.

The hood of his cloak was pulled down over his eyes.

Gerrod struggled, seeking to return to his gazing even though a part of him knew the danger of that. He could not remove the blinding hood, however, for powerful arms caught him as a pincer might have, preventing him from even raising a hand in his defense.

The siren whispering of the faces in the crystal was overwhelmed by excited hooting in his ears. He was dragged backward by one or more powerful forms.

The whispering ceased. The compulsion to stare at his twisted reflections dwindled away to near nothing.

His captor released him. Gerrod fought for breath that had been denied him for some time, although he had not realized it until now. The warlock turned around and faced the one who had dragged him free.

It was the apparent leader of the Quel. The armadillolike creature looked at the Vraad with what seemed to be open concern.

"I . . . I will be fine in a moment," Gerrod told it, reacting to what he thought was a question. He hoped the crystal translated his words and thoughts properly.

The Quel hooted in an unintelligible manner and pointed at the human before it, ending the gesture with a shake of one clawed paw. Gerrod looked at himself and frowned in confusion until he recalled that he could no longer understand the Quel's hoots. What had happened to the crystal was beyond him; he could not recall dropping it in the chamber or, for that matter, leaving it anywhere.

Gerrod cursed, utilizing his father's name as part of the bitter epithet. Now of all times was a situation demanding explanation, and he had lost track of his only means of communication. He wanted to know what the purpose of the chamber was and who had built it. The warlock could hardly recall the events just prior to his reluctant entrance into the mad cavern. Had the Quel built it, or had they found it? From the way they acted, he thought the latter might be a better choice, but his mind was too fogged to be trusted.

Despite the ordeal he had suffered, Gerrod wanted to go back. Not in a haphazard fashion, as his first journey had entailed, but carefully, with full respect and preparation for the power within.

He was about to indicate with his hands that he desired to return to the crystal cavern when the world spun around him. Gerrod watched the ground rush toward his face, only to have the collision halted by the ready arms of his armored companion, who seemed to be expecting just such an incident. The warlock had no time to think why that might be so, for he passed out the next instant.

WHEN HE AWOKE, the Quel were huddled around him, passive in their interest in his condition until they saw that he was conscious. Then, like players donning masks, the earth dwellers grew excited at his recovery. Gerrod frowned, hoping they would take his expression for concern over his own condition—which it was in part—and not because he was suddenly suspicious of their interest in him.

They had brought him to another chamber, one that barely passed human standards for survival. He was on a mat of some sort that smelled too much of his hosts and cold earth. The warlock slowly rose, fending off assistance by the Quel with a shake of his head. The massive creatures backed away far enough to give him room. It was impossible to say whether they once more played at emotions, but Gerrod thought they seemed a bit surprised at the speed of his recovery. No doubt their own kind had entered the chamber of crystal before him, but what had happened to those unfortunates was something they had not revealed to the Vraad so far.

Far worse than me, he decided. *Far worse if their fear of that place is real.* He was certain it was; the Quel, whatever their purpose was, would have been better served if they had pretended confidence rather than fear, which added to Gerrod's supposition that they *were* frightened of what they had discovered.

What did they see in that place?

"I need—" The warlock stopped as the leader gave him a crystal, either the same one or one identical to it; Gerrod had no idea.

Mind intact . . . the fear not eaten . . . question?

So that was it. Those who had preceded him had lost their minds to some sort of fear. Whatever the Quel saw, it was too much for them. Yet, someone had pulled him free. How?

While he pondered that, the armadillolike being repeated its question.

"I'm fine." Not quite the truth, but good enough for them. Gerrod had no intention of telling them about the voices—his voice—that still whispered inside his head. The voices wanted him to return to the chamber, to come back and listen once more to what they had to say.

He would. Of that he was certain. Even if the Quel decided otherwise, the warlock would return to the chamber.

Food consumed . . . time passing . . . question?

The alteration in the course of the conversation took him by surprise, but it took him only a moment to puzzle out the meaning. He was being asked if he required food; how much time had passed since his fainting spell?

"How long have I been unconscious?"

The answer was nothing monumental; he had been unconscious for what was, if he had Quel time standards figured out, no more than two hours, maybe three. The blackout had actually done him more good than bad; Gerrod had not been given a chance to recover from the trek earlier in the day. He still coveted a full night's slumber, but crumbs were always better than nothing at all. For once, life as a Tezerenee paid off. Under his father's rule, each clan member had learned to work at his optimum with only the least bit of sleep.

His stomach argued that food was another commodity that he had, of late, dealt little with. Gerrod wondered whether the food here would be as unappetizing as the mash the patrols had carried. Perhaps, but he would eat it nonetheless. For the task lying before him, a task he was not even certain he understood, the Tezerenee would need his strength.

As if already sensing his acknowledgment, a newcomer, smaller than the rest but still almost the human's height, brought him a bowl of some soupy substance. Gerrod, his eyes on the tinier Quel, sniffed the contents . . . and shivered. He broke his gaze and looked down at the bowl.

The mash would seem a delicacy in comparison.

When he looked back up, the tiny Quel was gone. He wondered if he had finally met a female. None of the other Quel were inclined to respond to his casual thought, but Gerrod was certain he was correct in his assumption. If so, then those with him were almost certainly males—unless, of course, the newcomer had merely been a juvenile. The Vraad could not accept that, however, and reinforced his newfound belief by thinking of his present companions in male terms as much as possible, despite their otherwise identical appearance to the smaller Quel.

Under the unblinking observation of the inhuman assembly, Gerrod ate. The meal went down quickly, partly because they had given him no spoon, thus forcing him to tip the bowl and gulp down mouthfuls of the disgusting muck. He swallowed faster after the next wave of noxious scents fluttered up his nostrils during the first taste.

"No seconds, please," Gerrod muttered as he handed the nearly empty bowl to one of the other creatures, who promptly threw it aside as if no one would ever wish to use it now that the human had. That reminded the warlock of his true situation. For all their act of friendliness, these Quel were no more companionable than the sentries who had brought him here. They had thrust him willingly into a situation that had broken the minds of one, possibly more, of their own kind. If not him, an elf or the representative of some other race would have done just as well. The Quel did not care; it was more important to find out about their discovery.

The leader chose that moment to hoot deep and long to his fellows. Without protest, the others began to shuffle out of the chamber. No one paid any more attention to the lone Vraad, not even the commanding Quel, who stood by in silence while the others departed. Only when the two of them were alone did the massive beastman turn to his guest.

The mask slipped then, revealing some of the true mind behind the inhuman visage. A savage yet calculating mind as deadly in its way as those of the Tezerenee's own folk. Had not Gerrod been able to remind himself that he was, as far as he could see, the Quel's only key to the crystal cavern, the warlock would have feared for himself right there and then. They needed him, else they would not have taken care of him while he recovered. Despite the physical danger that the Quel before him represented, the warlock was able to smile.

Perceptions of the chamber . . . statement!

The odd voice/images in his head jarred him, but he quickly recovered. "You want to know what I saw, is that it? You want to know why I still have my mind?"

Agreement . . . statement!

Would there be any harm in telling the truth? Gerrod doubted it and so he told the creature everything he had observed, heard, and felt. It seemed perfectly acceptable to do so, despite his present status. Throughout it all, the Quel leader remained motionless, as though hypnotized by his tale. Occasionally, he would project a question, mostly about some minor detail. The Vraad learned little from the questions save that there had to have been more than one victim of the chamber. How many Quel had tried to conquer the fear within and failed? More than once he sensed the very edges of what the Quel had discovered, but each time his captor buried the images and emotions before too much slipped by.

All too soon, the story ended. Gerrod was struck by sudden anxiety. Was he wrong? Had he given them what they needed? Was he no longer of use?

The sole remaining Quel leaned forward, his breath more fetid than the haunting aroma cast by Gerrod's recent repast. *Cooperation . . . continued existence . . . statement!*

The warlock nodded, trying to ignore the rapid beating of his heart. "I like living. I'll cooperate."

Purpose of crystals . . . weapon against enemy/foe bird folk . . . statement!/question?

"What? Oh." Gerrod nodded, yawning. "It might be a weapon you could use against the Seekers." He had no idea *how* it might be used as such, but Gerrod was certain it could be turned into a weapon. By that time, he hoped to turn it on his captors instead.

A neglected part of his mind summoned up the fate of Sharissa, recalling to him his original purpose. He fought it down, convincing himself that this crystal chamber would aid him in that respect, if only by giving him time to plot his escape. That he would have been drawn to the cavern regardless was a point he tried not to dwell upon. Forsaking Sharissa for his own interests, even for a time, was something he would have expected of his father.

Period of rest . . . statement!

"I . . ." Gerrod could not recall what it was he had wanted to say. He yawned—long and hard this time. A sleeping potion in his food. Why had he not thought of that? The warlock laid his head back and yawned again. Did it really matter? He could begin his escape plans when he woke. Yes, that sounded better. He would be well-rested after this, and any plan required his utmost strength and concentration.

Agreeable . . . passive be . . . statement! came the projection from the Quel beside him. Gerrod nodded. Whatever his host wanted, so long as it meant sleep. Come the morrow—or *whenever* he finally woke—the Tezerenee would begin his plotting.

As he began to drift off, Gerrod thought he heard someone chuckle. It was not a sound that Quel were capable of imitating properly, and he knew it was not his own voice he heard. For a time, the warlock struggled to stay awake, waiting for the sound to reoccur. He was still straining to hear it again when he finally lost the struggle with the god of sleep and faded away.

* * *

ESCAPE, HE FOUND later, would not be so simple. Two days—estimated, since he could not see the sun—passed. It was not merely the efforts of his companions that kept him in the underground world, but his own overwhelming sense of discovery. There was too much that beckoned him in a way akin to the chamber of crystal, albeit not with such consistent attraction. Though they were by no means the masters of crystal sorcery that the builders of the chamber had been, the Quel were not without skill. Gerrod had yet to see, much less inspect, the thing that they called the "gatherer," but he imagined it to be a gem of astonishing proportions if what the lender conveyed to him was true. How it was able to absorb and distribute the magical forces for use by the Quel was a thing beyond him. It was, besides the ancient cavern, the only place they would not allow him to roam.

Walking with the leader, who *was* male after all, the warlock fingered some of the small gemstones in his belt pouch. They were akin to the one that allowed him to speak with the Quel and probably could be turned to that use, but he had other ideas concerning them. It was surprisingly easy to obtain them; they were mined in such vast quantities that he had been stunned when first shown. Each young Quel was brought here soon after birth. They were identical in almost every way to the parents, save for the soft almost unfurrowed shells that would change and harden over the years. The crystals of understanding, which was as close as Gerrod could comprehend the title, were among the first and foremost received by the young when the shells grew ridged. The hard skin would eventually grow to cover most of each crystal, forever making it a part of the creature and ensuring that, at least from the Quel side, communication of a sort would always be maintained.

Stealing three from a hill of thousands had been childishly easy. So easy, in fact, that Gerrod wondered from time to time whether his companion had *wanted* him to take the gems. No matter. They represented the first inklings of a plan of escape, a plan that would only take place once he had returned to the cavern and confronted the truth behind the faces—not to mention whatever other secrets lay within.

Let us not forget Sharissa! he chided himself. It was becoming too easy to lose track of his situation. Not just Dru Zeree's daughter, either. It was also too easy to forget what his true visage resembled—an aging, doddering fool of a Vraad. That was what Gerrod saw every time his reflection caught his eye.

A nervous Quel rushed up to the leader and the two began a series of rapid responses to one another. Even with the crystal, the warlock could make no sense of what they said. The images he received were murky, almost as if the Quel were making an effort to prevent him from understanding. It did not surprise him; he knew that his time with them was limited to his usefulness. He also knew what they would do when the secrets of the crystal cavern were theirs.

The leader whirled on him, dark eyes narrowed. He hooted low and quick, a sign of anger and worry as Gerrod read it. *The surface . . . spy in the sky . . . observation of intention . . . statement!*

The Tezerenee was dragged along while he was still attempting to decipher the message. Something was happening on the surface, a scout or someone . . . in the sky?

A Seeker?

The three of them entered yet another chamber that Gerrod had not come across before. How extensive was the domain of the Quel? He had been given to believe that they held only a remnant of their former power. If so, then their empire had rivaled that of the Seekers in scope.

A handful of Quel surrounded an image. The warlock, peering over tall, rounded shoulders, watched as a tiny figure fluttered over a miniature land no larger than Gerrod's forearm. The entire scene was being projected through a crystal that stood on a tripod in the middle of the room.

It was indeed a Seeker. Gerrod did not recognize the landscape, but from its rocky and nearly barren appearance, he felt safe in assuming it was part of the peninsula that was the Quel's home.

The Seeker paused in midflight, its wings beating rapidly to keep it in the air. The image was too small to identify it as male or female; as with the Quel, the two sexes were too similar to identify readily.

One of the watchers grunted and touched a side of the crystal. The scene magnified. It was a female, the Tezerenee saw, though the information made no difference. He still did not know why a lone Seeker would risk death to come to the land of its hereditary enemies.

Reaching to her neck, the avian tugged at a chain. Gerrod squinted and saw the medallion hanging by a chain around her throat. The medallion was almost the Seeker equivalent of the crystals the Quel utilized; it generally protected its wearer and contained some vicious spell. Not a few of his clan had died facing weapons such as this. The Tezerenee moved as close as he could to the image. Beside him, the Quel leader glanced his way, but ignored him further when he saw what the tiny human was about.

The Seeker removed her medallion—and promptly dropped it into the dirt far below her.

Among the Quel, there was a stirring of confusion.

The leader gave a command, again something that Gerrod could not make out. He knew by now that he was being purposely blocked out.

Some of the Quel turned to their superior with a sense of confusion evident in their movements. One bleated, the questioning note undeniable.

Shoving the hapless Vraad to one side—and almost against the far wall—the leader faced his questioner and repeated his command.

Dipping his head, the questioner returned to the crystal and, under the watchful gaze of all present, including the recovered Gerrod, touched another face of the crystal.

During the brief encounter, the Seeker had remained where she was, still hovering. Only as the one Quel touched the gemstone did the Vraad realize that the avian had been offering a truce. She would have to know that the Quel controlled this region. Her life had been offered in exchange for a meeting.

The Quel leader chose to decline that offer.

Blinding brilliance filled the image, forcing many of the huge, armadillolike creatures to shield their eyes and momentarily stunning the unprepared human. Gerrod blinked time and time again until at last some semblance of vision returned to him. He looked up, trying to see around the swimming spots that dotted everything in sight. The image, too, had cleared, and the warlock was able to make out glittering hills and the occasional tough plant. Of the Seeker, he saw no sign.

The same Quel who had controlled the crystal before now touched it again. Gerrod watched the scene shift, abandoning the sky view for one that observed more of the surface. The leader hooted, his tone and stance smug.

When he saw what remained of the ambassador of the Seekers, the Tezerenee was relieved that he could not smell it as well.

The Quel were well-defended. The lone avian never had hope. In what reminded Gerrod of a horrible parody of many a fine meal he had eaten, her charred corpse lay sprawled on the hard ground. The female's face, what was left of it, was buried in the soil, saving the warlock from seeing her accusing eyes. She had come in peace—unless his captors knew otherwise—and they had burned her to death.

Their weapon had been the land itself. Many of those gleaming fragments seemingly scattered about the countryside actually served another purpose. Like the array of gems that brought light to this world beneath the surface, these had been arranged just so. With their knowledge, the Quel merely manipulated a few at a time to create a beam of intense light. It was a horrific application of the childhood habit of burning bugs with a simple lens.

Our people are truly related, he thought in disgust. Such a trick would have appealed greatly to many of his fellow Vraad. His father would have found it a marvelous toy to add to his arsenal.

Around him, the various Quel began to lose interest now that the crisis was past. Only Gerrod seemed concerned over what the Seeker had wanted in the first place. It was not likely she would sacrifice herself. Something had concerned her and her kind enough for them to take this chance. He wished he had studied her closer. What condition had the avian been in before her death? Was it only his imagination or had she seemed worn, defeated in purpose?

Madness . . . bird people . . . death . . . statement!

The Quel who always accompanied him had returned to his side. The message was garbled, but at least they were communicating with their "guest" again. Gerrod understood enough; his host thought the Seeker had to have been insane to do what she had done. As for whose "death" the huge creature referred to, Gerrod could not say. There were too many interpretations that made sense considering the enmity between the two races.

Certain that he and his companions would be departing, Gerrod turned toward the chamber's mouth and took a step. A heavy hand belayed that thought by catching at the shoulder and twirling him about until he came to face the leader again.

The Quel leaned close—too close, as far as the warlock was concerned. He covered his nose.

Tomorrow . . . cavern of crystal . . . Gerrod/elf/Vraad searching . . . Seekers dying . . . statement!

The hooded figure could only nod wordlessly as his eyes met and broke away from those of the Quel master. Something had come of this after all. He would finally be returned to the cavern. At last, he could study the ancient wonder and find the reason for its existence, for those damnable faces. In the process, he would turn it to his own needs, not those of the armored monstrosities who held him.

Yesss . . .

The short, sibilant response was not Quel in origin, yet neither did it seem human. Gerrod hesitated, not certain whether he had imagined it or not. The Quel moved about as if nothing were amiss. Beside him, the leader indicated that it was *now* time to depart. Gerrod obeyed without question, but his mind still searched for a repeat of the brief yet chilling statement.

Nothing. A figment of his imagination, most likely. He could come up with no other satisfactory explanation, yet even that one felt weak. What else *could* it be, though?

Gerrod was quietly but soundly urged toward the corridor by the same massive paw that had halted his progress a moment before. Just as he reached the mouth of the cavern chamber, however, he paused again, unable to relieve his mind of this peculiar burden. If only a figment, why did it seem so real, so familiar? Why could he not dismiss it, a simple one-word phantasm of his mind?

And why did he now, without warning, fear to enter the very cavern he had so desired to return to for the last two days?

The Quel urged him on again. As he walked, the warlock could not help wondering once more just what it was the Seeker had wanted and what possible threat ignorance of her message would bring down upon his captors . . . not to mention *himself?*

XIV

BARAKAS GAZED UP at the mountains towering before them and smiled. "Magnificent! Truly worthy!"

Even Sharissa, whose mind continued to dwell upon that terrifying yet sad incident of a few nights before, had to agree with him. The mountains *were* majestic, more so because they were natural formations, not something that had been conjured up, as in the old days of Nimth.

"No one can long look at the Tybers and not feel their power," Faunon whispered to her. He had, in the last day, been given leave to ride at the head of the expedition alongside Sharissa. The elf had finally agreed to guide them, mostly out of concern for the young sorceress. She found his interest in her both pleasant and embarrassing, and matters were not helped by his occasional glances and reassuring smiles.

Merely fellow prisoners, she told herself. *Our only common interest is escape from here.* That he was a welcome change from most of her kind she was not yet willing to admit to, not even to herself.

Escape was still out of the question so long as the patriarch controlled or contained Darkhorse. Sharissa tore her eyes from the grand scenery and studied the box that was slung near the Lord Tezerenee's leg, ready for quick use, if necessary. It was never far from his side, and she already knew that the spells were specifically tied to him, making the chance of someone else opening it slim—at least without injuring or even killing the occupant within the box. Darkhorse could be destroyed; that was something she knew to be very true by now. He was not the invincible, godlike being from beyond that her father's tales had once indicated to her. Rather, he was very, very vulnerable to many things. *Too* many things.

"This would be a good place to strike," Faunon whispered to her, meaning the Seekers, who had yet to make an appearance during this entire journey. Even though they had at last reached the mountains, which still meant another day's journey to the base of the one they sought, the Tezerenee were not acting overconfident. Many of those born to the clan were undoubtedly replaying their near massacre by the avians some fifteen years before over and over again in their thoughts. Everyone talked of the incident with the unfortunate Ivor, a victim, it was decided, of some twisted avian spell.

Faunon had tried to convince them otherwise, but his voice went unheard in this matter. He was convinced that Ivor had been transformed into that monstrosity by another power he claimed lay deep beneath the caverns the Seekers had used as an aerie. Only Sharissa believed him, and she had to admit that part of her belief was based on growing emotions for Faunon.

Up ahead of the column, scouts on airdrakes were flying back to the column. Lochivan rode the lead beast, his own request. The expedition halted at the patriarch's command and waited for the scouts to land.

"Father." Sharissa noted that his voice had grown hoarse. Lochivan leaped off his mount and knelt before Barakas. He gave his elder brother a cursory nod and said, "We ride amidst a region soaking in untapped power."

"I told you that," Faunon could not help pointing out. So much of what he said went through the ears of his captors and out into the heavens. The elf turned to Sharissa and, with a wry smile, asked, "Why did they bother to bring me along if they won't believe anything I say?"

Reegan twisted around in his saddle. "Be silent!"

The sorceress knew that Faunon was taking risks every time he spoke out, especially when he was near Reegan. Perhaps because he desired her so much, the heir apparent was the first one to take note of the link between Sharissa and the prisoner. The huge Tezerenee was jealous.

Lochivan continued. "We saw little sign of recent avian activity, but we found several Seekers who had died at one point or another. It appears that they were *fighting* among themselves."

"Indeed?" Barakas stroked his beard and sank into deep thought. Lochivan, waiting for the sign to continue, absently scratched at his throat.

"We can ride right in and take over," Reegan suggested with his usual lack of timing and thought. Sharissa almost felt sympathy for him.

The patriarch only shook his head. "Do not be absurd again. There *have* to be Seekers about. Not all of them would be so obliging as to flee or die for our sakes. If we had charged in, swords ready and magic flying, we would probably be dead now. This is still *their* domain for a time. They will defend it to their utmost."

"We cannot stay here until we've rooted them all out of the rocks," the heir protested. "That might take years."

"*That* I agree with." The Lord Tezerenee tapped the side of the shadow steed's horrible prison as he pondered a decision. He ceased the tapping and eyed the box with new interest. "Perhaps there is a more efficient way."

Sharissa urged her mount closer to the patriarch, her heart sinking as what Barakas might be plotting occurred to her. "Haven't you put him through enough? Isn't that box pain enough for him to endure?"

"This should be relatively painless, I think."

"You know what I mean!"

"More lives will be saved by this in the long run, my dear Sharissa," Barakas replied, his smile as false as his words. "At least . . . *Tezerenee* lives."

He lifted the box so that it rested in one arm and ran his hand over it, repeating the same pattern he had earlier, albeit in such a manner that it could be performed with a single hand, not two. Sharissa could sense the bond that tied the Tezerenee lord to the spell and thus Darkhorse to him. She still had no idea how to free the ebony stallion from it, and that was what held her back from escape. Barakas was by no means an opponent she could hope to overcome by direct action. Only by biding her time would she have a chance—but when would that be? The sorceress had no intention of waiting until she was married and bearing the children of Reegan. The very thought stirred her to renewed determination. Perhaps at some point on this very expedition Sharissa would find a means of solving her troubles.

She could only hope.

Barakas lifted the lid.

A wave of darkness rushed forth, almost as if the patriarch had unleashed night upon day. Yet, this darkness screamed its pleasure and fear, screamed wordlessly as it slowly coalesced into the familiar form of Sharissa's tormented friend.

"Movement! Sound! Sight! By the ungodly Void, I am free of it again! Free!"

A few of the Tezerenee shifted in nervousness, fully aware of what the overwhelming creature before them could do if allowed full will. Barakas and those of his sons who rode with the column sat in relaxed silence, fully confident in the patriarch's hold on the eternal.

His initial thrill at being released from the torturous container abating, Darkhorse glared at his armored keeper. Even Lochivan, who now stood beside the drake his father rode, and Reegan found other things to contemplate rather than meet those cold eyes. Barakas, on the other hand, met them with the same commanding indifference that he met most other things with. He knew very well who held sway here, and all of the eternal's staring would not lessen the truth of that.

"*What* do you *want* of me?" the shadow steed bellowed. His front hooves tore at the earth below. Sharissa did not doubt that he wished it was the clan master beneath those heavy hooves.

"I have a task for you, one that should prove simple considering your abilities."

"Barakas, please don't *do* this to him!" the sorceress called, her pride a forgotten thing in the importance of the moment.

The patriarch turned and studied her briefly. Although the dragonhelm hid most of his features, she could hear the disdain in his words. "Do not demean yourself, Lady Sharissa. A good warrior makes use of all weapons available to him, and I would be remiss if I did not use one of my greatest. He will ensure that no harm comes to you."

"To her?" Darkhorse paused in his kicking. He looked from the patriarch to Sharissa. "What threatens her?"

"Nothing, Darkhorse! He—"

A gauntleted hand touched the lid of the box, causing the demon steed to freeze and Sharissa to quiet almost instantly. "*She* rides with us into the interior of this mountainous region. I cannot guarantee her safety should we be attacked. You know the strength of the creatures who control this domain. Terrible it is, wouldn't you say?"

Darkhorse laughed, but there was little defiance left in him. He had been nearly broken by the periods of imprisonment in the box. "I served you in such a way earlier, monstrous one! I . . . I told you of those creatures, the elves"—he indicated an alert Faunon—"and where they could be found. Your sorcery, then, was not sufficient for the task! I *gave* you lives I had no right to give!"

A nod was the only acknowledgment he received from the lord of the Tezerenee. "This should prove much easier and more fulfilling, then. These are Seekers, creatures of the kind who attacked and captured your old companion, Dru Zeree. These are the creatures who would do harm to his daughter. They make no exceptions; her life means as little to them as my own does. If we were attacked, it will be difficult to keep an eye on her."

"I have my *own* power with which to battle them," she reminded the two. "If it comes to a struggle, I will fight them. I do *not* want needless deaths."

Despite her assurances, the ebony stallion wavered more. "You have not seen them as I have. They mean little to my power, but you . . . you lack my resilience."

"So she does," Lochivan agreed, aiding his parent in the Tezerenee effort. Barakas gave a slight shake of his head that Sharissa noticed. He needed no aid in this matter, she knew. The patriarch held all the trumps.

"I gave you the elves because I feared for her . . . and I feared that cursed creation of yours! Do not ask me to add to my sins! If they come for you, *then* I will take them!"

"There was a time when you would have taken Dru Zeree. Do you remember that?" The Lord Tezerenee's hand toyed with the lid.

"I did not know better then!" Darkhorse's head was bowed. Sharissa knew what he was recalling. A simple yet powerful being existing in the regions of the Void, the eternal had no concept of life and death. Absorbing the few outsiders he came across in the endless limbo had meant nothing. Only after his time with her father did Darkhorse begin to comprehend the value of one's existence. If he or those he cared for were attacked, the stallion would fight. To kill those who did not even know of him, however . . .

"You have your choice, of course. I would be minded to let you remain out if you perform well, but if I cannot trust you to even protect one you profess to care for, I see no reason to leave you free. Who knows what havoc you might cause. Yes, perhaps returning you to the box until the day comes when I might find a task worth the trouble of summoning you again—"

Barakas began to tilt the open box in the direction of Darkhorse. To Sharissa's shock and dismay, she saw that her father's old companion was quivering with fear. He had even grown a bit distorted, as if his fright were so great it even interfered with his ability to hold shape.

"There is no need for that."

His voice, for all its deep rumble, was meek and abashed. Darkhorse stared at the ground beneath him, unwilling to look at those before—especially her. Sharissa shook her head, and tears ran down her cheeks.

"I will find these Seekers for you . . . and eliminate their threat."

A beatific smile crossed the patriarch's half-hidden visage. "Thank you. I see no reason why you cannot begin now. Do you?" He pointed at the mountains far ahead. "I want you to search there, near our destination. Search the northern region until I summon you back."

Darkhorse shook his head, sending his mane flying. He seemed taken aback by something. "But that leaves—"

"I have *given* you your task. I want it performed as I said. No rebellion. Nothing will happen to *anyone* here if you obey me to the letter. I *promise* you that."

The demon steed snorted. "You are more foul than anything spawned among the endless realms I crossed during my now-regretted search for this accursed world."

"Yes, we must talk of those places when *this* realm is secured. Now, *go!*"

Darkhorse dipped his head in a mocking salute. "I am your servant, dragonlord."

Rearing, the ebony stallion turned and raced off. Sharissa watched the receding figure, then turned to Faunon for support. The elf wore a dour look. He did not seem that sympathetic to Darkhorse's plight.

"Faunon, I—"

"They died because of him. That is what he said."

"It was *his* doing!" She pointed an accusing finger at Barakas, who was turning to watch their antics with mild amusement. Many of the other Tezerenee were watching, too, but Sharissa did not care. She would say what she had to say. If Faunon abandoned her because he could not accept Darkhorse's earlier actions, then the sorceress would be alone in her efforts. That might be an obstacle she could overcome, but his absence would create an even worse problem for her.

You are too romantic to be a Vraad, her father had once told her. Perhaps so, but she felt no reason to change, even if it meant hurt.

"There will be time for discussion later," Barakas interrupted, evidently deciding there were better things to do.

Sharissa quieted, hoping that Faunon would see things clearer if he had time to let his emotions cool. He might then see what fear could do to even the bravest of creatures. The elf did not know Darkhorse; he could not see the child that the eternal was. Recalling her own youth, not that distant in the past, Sharissa knew the limits of a child, even as strong a one as the dweller from the Void.

Ahead of them and high in the sky, the dark form soared out of sight.

Securing the box, Barakas told Reegan, "We move out now. The confusion will be to our advantage."

"Yes, Father." The heir turned and signaled to the column.

The Tezerenee readied their weapons and spells. Lochivan rejoined the scouts, who, once he was settled on his steed, urged their mounts into the air. Lochivan's band circled the column twice and then spread out ahead of it.

"We are in the company of madness," Faunon whispered.

Tilting her head just enough to see him, Sharissa once more tried to explain Darkhorse's apparent weakness of spirit to the elf. He cut her off with a look and whispered, "The anger was more for their benefit. I understand all too well the limits one faces. If not for your suggestion, I would have likely broken soon, anyway. These dragon men are very skilled at what they do, especially the pleasant one."

She glanced up at the tiny figures of Lochivan and his airdrake. "I once thought I knew the true man."

Faunon grimaced. "You probably do. His pleasant attitude is no game, so far as I saw. He would probably smile while he cut your throat if something amused him."

"That's—" The Vraad was about to say that the elf's words were cruel, but then she recalled her most recent encounters with Lochivan. If it benefited the clan and his father, Lochivan would have indeed cut her throat, all the while explaining that he hated to do it but there was no choice in the matter. His lord and master had ordered him to do it, and thus there was no room for argument.

An invisible wave struck Sharissa. She moaned and nearly lost her grip on the reins. Her mind was on fire, and she had a great urge to unleash her power at random if only because it was what burned her.

To her side, Faunon shouted, but she could not understand his words. Several Tezerenee were also shouting, one of them the patriarch himself. The pain-riddled enchantress put a hand to her head, but the pressure within was too much. She started to slide to her right. Part of her knew that if she fell from her drake she would be trampled by one of the others, for the reptilian mounts had grown skittish, but Sharissa lacked the concentration to maintain her grip.

An arm caught her before the sorceress could slip very far. At first she thought it was Faunon, and so she smiled. Only when things came into focus did she see that it was *Reegan* who had saved her. He had backed up his mount and put himself between the two captives. Over his shoulder Sharissa could see Faunon burning a hole with his eyes through the Tezerenee's wide back.

"Are you well?" he asked, genuine concern tempering his otherwise gruff voice.

"Yes . . . I am." She disengaged herself from his grip as quickly as she was able, but not before his hand slid down her side a bit. Her smoldering expression made him release her that much quicker, and he immediately urged his drake forward. Reegan did not look back even when he was once more near his father.

"I tried to get to you," Faunon informed her, their mounts once more side by side. Bound to his animal by the magical chains, his mobility was limited. "But he was over here as soon as it hit us. I was lucky he did not *push* me off my animal! His eyes carried that intention!"

"What . . . what happened to us?"

"The demon has met the enemy," Barakas declared. He gazed back at the young Zeree with excitement radiating in his every movement, every breath. "The first blow has been struck, I think."

A second later, a blue light flashed in the distance. It was bright but brief.

The patriarch turned back to see what startled his people so, but missed the light. Reegan informed him of what had happened. Barakas nodded.

"We can expect more such waves and probably worse before this is over."

"They might *kill* him!" Sharissa raged. "You were able to capture him! What happens if they kill or capture him?"

A shrug. "Then it will amount to the same thing. If he's captured, I can hardly let him be turned on us, especially you. I think your black friend would agree with me on that."

She pulled back in shock at his response. "You'll kill him?"

"Eliminate the threat to our security, yes. Darkhorse would never want to bring harm to you. He would prefer my way, rest assured."

From another point nearer to the column but to the left of the previous location, a rumble and minor explosion brought renewed silence to the Tezerenee. Sharissa was both relieved and dismayed by the second blast; it meant that Darkhorse still survived, but it also meant that he had probably killed for her. If the Seekers lived in such a weakened state as the sorceress had been led to believe from the evidence, then it was possible that they might have left the expedition alone. Not so now. Now, there would most definitely be an attack. The avians would know that Darkhorse was controlled by the Tezerenee, and if they could not destroy the weapon, they might be able to destroy the one who unleashed it instead.

It was apparent that Barakas thought the same. He ordered his men to even greater caution, if that was possible. As swift and accurate as the shadow steed was, he would not find all of the Seekers. They were too skilled, too crafty for that, even if they were mere reflections of their former might.

The column renewed its steady crawl toward the caverns. According to Lochivan, the late Rendel's notes had indicated that his brother had titled the mountain Kivan Grath. That had brought a harsh laugh from Faunon, who understood the meaning of the name.

"Kivan Grath," he had announced in grandiose tones. " 'The Seeker of Gods'! How very, terribly true!"

Asked to explain, the captive elf returned to his tale of ancient sorcery and some dark thing now lurking in the depths of the underground caverns perforating the mountain.

The selfsame mountain had been in sight for the past few days, looming over even its taller neighbors by quite some height, but now it was nearly the only thing they could see before them. Regardless of whatever else lay in sight, Kivan Grath overwhelmed the scene. It was still hours away, but a casual glance might lead one to believe that no more than a single hour would be needed to reach it. The leviathan's size wreaked havoc on perspective. Everyone had trouble believing it could be so tall; they were more willing to believe that it *must* be closer than the patriarch had estimated.

A second wave of random magical force washed over the riders, but this time they were at least prepared for its coming if not its intensity. It was terrible enough that the land here radiated a power of its own; the forces unleashed by both the Seekers and Darkhorse added a new dimension of fear. So far, the only effect was a twisting, churning sensation that touched every spellcaster— and that included most of those assembled for the expedition. The longer they were forced to endure it, the more chance it might affect them in other, more horrifying ways. No one had forgotten Ivor.

"We should turn back!" Sharissa argued as the second wave passed.

No one but Faunon paid heed to her words, and he was not in any condition to follow through on her suggestion. The Lord Tezerenee acknowledged her comments, but replied, "It will be over soon. The first expedition found only a few scattered flocks."

She was not satisfied with his response. "What if they hid the bulk of their strength for when you returned with greater numbers? How much better to snare many rather than a few! We could be attacked from all sides at any time!"

To her surprise, the patriarch nodded. "I *expect* to be attacked—and at any moment!"

"But . . . you can't be serious . . . Darkhorse is . . ."

"He *is*," Faunon said, the elf shocked nearly as much as Sharissa was. "Look at him. He has ridden us into the tearing beak of the bird folk . . . and performed the deed willingly!"

Turning away from the two stunned captives, Barakas laughed. The sorceress scanned the high ground on either side of them. Some of the Tezerenee had airdrakes, but most had only the swift but ground-locked variety. Granted the Vraad had massive sorceries at their beck and call, much of it the vile but deadly Nimthian sort, but that might end up bringing death to them just as readily as the medallions of the Seekers. As with their former home, this world did not deal well with the old sorcery. The greater the spell, the worse the backlash.

It was interesting—and worrisome, Sharissa had to admit—to see many of the armored figures around her turning to one another with apprehension. Had the patriarch neglected to inform his people that he *knew* they would be riding into a trap? Had they been led to believe that Darkhorse would clear much of the danger away?

Beside his father, Reegan suddenly straightened and pointed at something in the distance. It was Lochivan and the scouts . . . but were there fewer of them than there had been before?

"It's about to start," Barakas commented needlessly. He looked around in expectation.

The sky darkened as manlike forms filled the air above them.

"To your duties!" Reegan shouted. Tezerenee were already raising their bows or some other weapon. If it came to a physical assault, those with swords and lances would defend against any attackers who tried to kill the archers while they reloaded. Several Tezerenee were grouping together in what was obviously the beginnings of a major spell. Others were attempting personal conjurations. Barakas sat on his drake and waited. Sharissa wondered at his sanity, but forgot him when she realized Faunon was completely defenseless. A well-placed rock would put an end to him.

The avians had the advantage. They controlled the sky and the high ground around the column. They knew the land. While there was room for the drakes to maneuver, it was all open to the Seekers.

She wondered why the Seekers did not just bury the entire Tezerenee expedition under tons of rock. Perhaps they no longer had that ability, considering the numbers who had perished because of some prior spell.

"Why does he not summon the demon back?" Faunon wanted to know. "We would stand a better chance!"

"I don't know!"

A warrior behind them reached for his throat and gasped. That was all. He fell from his steed and was lost under the milling forms of the drakes.

Archers were already firing. Two Seekers plummeted to the ground, already dead, but most of the others had moved out of range.

Sharissa's mind was tugged in all directions as the two sides warred on the sorcerous plane. Men screamed around her, but she could not afford to aid them. Instead, she pulled Faunon to her and cast her best defensive spells.

"You should be fighting them," Faunon counseled. "The avians will not ignore us for long merely because we behave. They will save us for when the true threats have been eliminated."

A huge form fell in front of them, sending the drakes into a fearful rage. The sorceress was forced to contend with both beasts, but she still managed to bring them under control. The missile proved to be the corpse of one of the bird folk. It had hit the ground with such intensity that much of it was no longer recognizable. Whether sorcery or arrow had killed the Seeker was a moot point, but it raised another danger. With the avians directly above the column, it was possible that even in death a Seeker might take a foe with him. Sharissa craned her neck and gazed into the heavens. It seemed to her that the greatest concentration of Seekers was over their present location.

Lowering her head, the exasperated sorceress again saw Barakas sitting calm amidst chaos. He was doing little more than surveying the scene and shouting out the occasional order. He *was* waiting for something.

His eyes met hers and she was certain that he smiled, although the helm, of course, made it difficult to be certain. As if responding to her anger and confusion, the patriarch pointed into the sky behind her. Sharissa spun around on her saddle, fearing that even more Seekers were winging their way toward the doomed column, cutting them off from any retreat.

There was indeed a mass of winged terrors racing toward the battle, but they were not Seekers.

They were Tezerenee. Not one band, but two. They converged from the east and west, coming together just as they reached the mountains. While their numbers were not as great as those of the avian attackers, they had height and mass to their advantage. They also had the confusion of battle to count upon. Several of the Seekers noted them, but that knowledge did them little good. Engaged in combat, both magical and physical, with the column, they could not break away without opening themselves up to a rain of death from below.

Many tried just that, regardless of the risk. Seeker magic was evidently more limited, at least as far as this particular group was concerned. Those who turned to flee proved inviting targets for the archers, who brought down many before the spellcasters could take their own turn. A few Tezerenee still fell; not all of the avians were abandoning the struggle. The bird people seemed to radiate a quiet desperation as they fought the humans, as if they knew that they were fighting to preserve what was already lost to them. Yet as their arrogance and miscalculations had evidently unleashed some horrifying spell back upon their own—as Faunon and the petrified corpses had suggested to her—so now did those same faults thrust the Seekers into a trap from which there was little hope of escape.

Barakas had expected a trap and laid one of his own. This was why the expedition had moved as slowly as it had. The patriarch had sent out two smaller forces composed of airdrake riders and hidden them somewhere in the wooded lands southwest and southeast of here. Somehow, they had come just in time, though Sharissa could not recall any signal. She had certainly sensed nothing.

The patriarch, she knew, would be more than pleased to explain later. What mattered now was surviving until the newcomers were able to finish the task at hand.

"Beware!" Faunon shouted. "One has his sights upon us, Sharissa!"

That much was true, but the young Zeree felt no assault. Instead, faint images swirled about her imagination, images she vaguely recognized as Seekers.

"Sharissa?" The elf bounced against her, the only thing he could do to stir her since he was bound.

"No! Stop that!" she warned. "It's trying to tell me something!"

Above, the Seeker dodged two arrows. It increased its mental assault, strengthening the images Sharissa perceived.

Seekers in a cavern . . . the cavern the Tezerenee sought.

Her father had told her of the fashion by which the avians communicated with outsiders, but he had indicated touch was necessary for the best understanding. That was not possible, but there *were* barriers that *could* be brought down.

"Sharissa! You are dropping your defensive spells!"

"I know! Trust me!" She hoped he would not press her, for her own resolve in this was wavering. What if she were playing into the talons of the Seeker?

The last barrier fell . . . and the Vraad sorceress was deluged with vivid images of what had been and what might be. The vision of Seekers hard at work on a master spell through which they hoped to rid themselves of the last of the Quel, the massive armadillolike race that had preceded them as masters of this continent. Sharissa gasped at the sight of the horrifying beast, although deep down she knew she was absorbing some of the avian's own fear and hatred of the elder race.

The spell was not totally of their own fabrication. Another had influenced them in its making. Something made the image blur, and she found herself now seeing the effects of that spell. It had not been a sorcerous backlash that had killed so many of the avians, but a successful but costly full reversal of the very spell. They had realized that what they unleashed would not stop with merely the Quel, and if they allowed it to go unchecked until their old enemies were no more, then it would be too strong to ever stop.

It had taken the greater part of their population to force the—Sharissa saw a vision of fur, teeth, and huge claws digging through earth, but received no name for the monstrosities—into the lands north, where they could be made to sleep until it was possible to destroy them all.

The image blurred again and she was back in the cavern, but her view kept shifting, as if she were traveling through the system of passages leading deep into the earth. The Seeker's fear touched her; he did not want to have to show her what lay below, but it was necessary for her understanding.

Faunon was shouting in her ear, trying to stir her, she supposed, but his words were so long and drawn out that they sounded like moans. Everything around her had slowed. Her mind had become attuned to the swift thoughts of the avian, who was desperately trying to communicate as much as possible before—

Pain and then total emptiness rocked her. The baffled sorceress screamed, knowing that what she had felt was *death*. With great effort, she forced the chilling sensation down and opened her eyes.

The patriarch's second force had engaged the avians, who were trying to both retreat and fight. Lochivan's mount flew by, though she only got a glimpse of the Tezerenee himself. Of the Seeker who had been trying to communicate with her, she could see nothing.

"He fell among the drakes yonder," Faunon informed her, knowing who she sought. "There probably is not too much of him left."

His cold tone received a vicious glare from her. He stared back at her in defiance. "I saw that he was about to die. I have seen what has happened to those caught up in a linking of minds when one dies. Sometimes the survivor goes mad . . . or simply drops dead. That was why I was shouting at you!"

"He was telling me . . . telling me . . ." Sharissa's head swam.

"Were you injured?" another voice asked, disturbing her recollection of what the avian had tried to warn her about.

"*No*, Reegan, I was *not*."

"They're trying to retreat," the heir apparent informed her. Even though there was still combat going on, he no longer seemed to care. Sharissa was more important. Had it been Faunon or Gerrod, she would have been pleased by the attention. Not from this one, though. Never from Reegan.

"They're being slaughtered," she corrected him with grimness.

The attack had been, in the long run, a pathetic last gasp by the bird folk, and now they were paying dearly for it. Darkhorse was still out there, either killing them or—and she felt guilty for hoping it was the former and not the latter—dead from one of their spells. She did not care for what the Seekers were, but her brief contact with them had at least made them worthy of some respect. Knowing they could not hold back the invaders, one of them had tried to at least warn them of some threat.

But *what* threat?

Mountainsides were no longer safe for the avians. The airdrakes ferreted them out and, in many cases, tore them apart without any command issued by the rider. Some Seekers proved more fatalistic; Sharissa saw one female throw herself upon the nearest warrior, even though it meant exposing her undefended back to the other. She died from a drake's slash, but not before her own talons took out the throat of her opponent.

Barakas was coordinating the reorganization of the column, leaving the bulk of the fighting to those in the air.

"They must have been desperate to pull such a stupid stunt as this," Reegan added. "I expected more from them." He laughed for no reason that Sharissa found humorous.

Faunon shook his head. "They were desperate, yes, but never stupid. Not the bird folk. If they did this for any reason,"—he looked at Sharissa—"we will know about it before long."

"What's that?" The patriarch was riding over to them. There was blood on his armor from some encounter. He was in a jovial mood, as if something he had feared lost had been found again. Sharissa noted he was breathing heavier than she would have thought. The battle, as short as it had been, had taken more out of Lord Barakas than she suspected he thought.

This was her chance. As much as she yearned to study the treasures left behind by the founders and those who had followed them, the desire was far outweighed by the knowledge that the caverns also held an apparent evil that frightened even the once-mighty Seekers. It had, if she understood the images thrust upon her by the dead avian, brought about the downfall of their empire.

"Barakas, this is our last chance to turn back. If you would just listen—"

"Turn *back?*" The clan master was flush with enthusiasm now, which possibly meant that he had not been as confident as he had pretended to be prior to the attack. "I should say not! We've eliminated what little threat remained to us! There will be no more Ivors now, no more hidden threats!"

"But there's something in the caverns that—"

"The *elf's* tale again? I thought better of you, believing nonsense like that . . . or perhaps you don't. Perhaps you're just trying to spread fear, as he tried."

"I saw one of the damned birds try to attack her, Father," Reegan offered. "It's likely shock or some nightmare cast by the beast before it was skewered."

Barakas found that acceptable, stilling any further argument from Sharissa with a wave of his hand. "I'll hear no more of it, then."

The two captives looked at one another. Faunon gave her a brief, bittersweet smile. The sorceress bit her lip, but knew the cause was lost for now, if not forever.

The Lord Tezerenee had already forgotten her. He turned his eyes skyward, where two drakes were descending upon the group. One was the creature Lochivan utilized, a mottled monster larger than any of the rest by almost half. The other likely belonged to whoever had been placed in charge of the secondary force.

"Ahh, here they are!"

Remaining seated, Lochivan saluted his sire. "Was it satisfactory, Father?"

"Most." Barakas scanned the region once more, as if afraid he had missed something important the previous times he had looked around. "And still plenty of daylight with which to work."

The newcomer to the expedition scratched at his neck until a glare from his lord made him pause. "As you predicted, Father, the demon made a perfect signal. We could hear and see his battles from where we waited."

"Did you doubt it, Wensel?" One hand touched the box. "It might be a good time to call him back, I think."

Lochivan was squirming in his saddle. Sharissa was certain that he, like Wensel, wanted desperately to scratch, but knew better than to do so in the presence of Barakas. Possibly because he sought to keep his mind off the itching, Lochivan asked, "What are your orders, sire?"

The box was forgotten for the moment. "I want the entire force ready in a quarter hour, save for those needed to flush out the few surviving birds. I want us moving on immediately after that time limit has expired! Do you understand me?"

Once more Sharissa would have liked to attempt to convince Barakas of the danger awaiting them, but once more she knew that he would not listen, that her warnings would only *fuel* his desire to be there sooner.

Faunon whispered, "Courage. This is something we *must* go through now. If they are going, it is better that we do, too."

"Separate those two," the patriarch commanded, pointing at Sharissa and the elf. "His words have been twisting her resolve. Until I say otherwise, they will *remain* separated. Lochivan, I give you charge of the elf. Reegan, you protect the Lady Sharissa."

"Yes, Father!" The heir smiled at Sharissa, who turned away only to find her eyes resting on Kivan Grath.

Barakas followed her gaze. "Yes, there it is. So very near now." He turned his mount toward the north and the mountain, but not before adding, "With any luck, my lady, we will be camping at the foot of that mountain this very evening! Maybe even the outermost caverns, if the sun holds true!"

"Why not fly there now?" Reegan asked. "There's nothing to fear."

"And no more reason to hurry. This is *our* world now, Reegan. We have all the time we could ask for in which to explore its treasures and shape it to our tastes." Barakas studied the sun. "Which does not mean we shall dawdle here any longer. You have your tasks; be about them. Reegan, you and the Lady Sharissa will come with me."

"My lady?" As the heir apparent urged his mount next to hers, Sharissa could not help thinking of the Seekers, who had once ruled this domain and were, in so many ways Barakas could not see, similar to the Tezerenee. They, like the patriarch, had probably once thought that time was their servant, not their enemy.

The avians' empire had lasted centuries, perhaps even millennia. Now, riding again toward the towering Kivan Grath, the place of the Seekers' folly, Sharissa wondered if Barakas' empire would even last out tomorrow.

XV

LIKE THE TOOTHY *maw of some great petrified beast*, Sharissa thought as she stood near the base of Kivan Grath and stared up into the cavern mouth that was their goal. To some, like Reegan, it still seemed foolish to camp at the foot of the mountain when they could be exploring the cavern. To the captive sorceress, it was foolish to be anywhere near here in the first place. That she had even for a time looked forward to exploring this ancient place and the artifacts within, shamed her. If nothing else, it had detracted from the goal she *should* have been striving for—namely, escape for herself and her companions.

They had returned Faunon to his wagon prison. As for Darkhorse, he was still free of the box—a promise Sharissa had been surprised to see Barakas keep—but he was carefully monitored by the Tezerenee. The patriarch had allowed her to speak with the shadow steed for a few minutes after their arrival here, but no more. Darkhorse, usually vocal, had become more and more reticent. He did not like being used, especially for the tasks set for him by Lord Barakas.

The eternal's assault in the northern mountains had been the signal by which the other Tezerenee force had known when to attack. Barakas had not said so, but it was clear that, while he could have used Darkhorse in the battle— something that might have saved some of the lives of his own followers—he did not completely trust his hold on the ebony stallion. That in itself encouraged the young sorceress, for where there were uncertainties, there was the potential for exploitation.

But what? She had to be careful. Barakas was, in many ways, an unpredictable quantity. Much of what he did, as he had admitted, was for effect, not merely for success. If a plan of his own design meant a few more lives but misdirected the efforts of his adversaries, the Lord Tezerenee was willing to live with those extra costs.

And, for some horrible, inexplicable reason, so were his people, the very ones he was willing to sacrifice.

To her right, the warrior whose task it was to watch her this evening straightened to attention. Sharissa did not even have to turn to know who it was. Barakas would have summoned her to him, not come to speak to her. Reegan had already been to see her, evidently in a pitiful attempt to renew his bid for her hand—as if they needed her approval for that. Of the remaining Tezerenee, only one other bothered with her.

"Is there a specific reason you wanted to see me, Lochivan?"

He chuckled, and his voice rasped as he spoke. "You always amuse me, Sharissa."

She did not look at him, preferring now the haunting image of the darkened caverns above. They were little more than dark patches in areas not quite as dark, but it was enough. Anything, so long as it and not Lochivan occupied her eyes. "Did you want something?"

"Only a few moments of your time." The tall Tezerenee was directly behind her now. For some reason, she found his nearby presence even more chilling than of late. It was not merely because of his betrayal, but some growing change in the patriarch's son himself. "First, your elf is well. I saw no reason to press him on any questions tonight. Thanks to you, he has been very cooperative."

"I'm glad . . . for *his* sake . . . but I wish you'd stop referring to him as *my* elf."

Lochivan shifted so that he now stood near her right shoulder. She could hear his breathing, a slow, scratchy sound that made her wonder if he was suffering from the altitude a little. Even ignoring the mountains, the land itself was well above sea level. One or two Tezerenee were already suffering some altitude sickness. Overall, however, it was not proving to be a problem; most of the dragon clan had grown accustomed to altitude from countless time spent riding airdrakes.

"He *is* your elf. I see it, and I know Reegan sees it. In fact, he wanted to speak to the elf a short time ago. Did he speak to you, by any chance?"

"Reegan was here."

"And by your tone, he was rejected again. Tread carefully, Sharissa. Each day of life for your friend is a bonus at this point. My brother would be willing to risk father's ire if it meant disposing of a rival . . . even if it's one who has no hope, anyway."

She did not know which part of his comment troubled her more, the threat to Faunon's life or the fact that Lochivan saw how close the two captives were growing to one another. Perhaps it was even the personal interest he had in the situation. His tone was not that of an outsider looking in but rather someone who had a personal stake in the results and not merely because Reegan was his brother. Sharissa recalled his earlier words.

"And would you be willing to risk the patriarch's ire, too? Does Faunon have something to fear from you?"

His hand briefly stroked her arm, causing her to tremble. The guard, of course, would be blind to all this, or else Lochivan would have never dared touch someone his father had chosen for the heir. "I am his—*your*—only hope."

"What do you *mean?*"

His breathing had been gradually growing worse, more harsh and rasping. "It isss . . . is growing late. Good night, Sharissssa."

"Lochivan?" She turned, but he was already walking away. Any thought that his departure was due to what he had hinted to her vanished as the sorceress saw him clutch his sides. His breathing had worsened even more in the few seconds since. Sharissa took a step toward him, wanting to help the Tezerenee lord despite her personal feelings.

The guard blocked her path. "Lord Lochivan desires privacy, my lady."

"He's ill!"

"A passing fever, Lady Sharissa." The guard, a woman, stared through the young Zeree.

"Did he tell you that? I don't recall him having the chance to do so."

"No, my lady. I make my own judgments. I've seen similar of late. Besides, if the Lord Lochivan wanted aid, he would have requested it." The Tezerenee sentry's voice was mechanical; she had been trained well by her masters. If they chose not to speak of their ills, she would defend that decision to her utmost.

Lochivan was already lost in the darkness. Sharissa sighed at yet another example of clan obstinance and infuriation. If she lived among them for the rest of her days—a horrid thought *that!*—she would never understand them.

"It's getting late, my lady. You should be rested for tomorrow," the guard suggested pointedly.

She nodded, knowing that sleep would be something long in coming under the watchful eyes of Kivan Grath. Taking one last look at the leviathan that both invited and repelled her, Sharissa gave the warrior woman leave to lead her back to the rest of the camp.

The wind was picking up. To her ears, it began to sound like a mournful wail—possibly a lament for those foolish enough to believe they were going to be able to make the mountain's secrets their own without a greater cost.

THE MORNING CAME both too soon and yet not soon enough. The light of day lessened some of the uneasiness that Sharissa felt, but, as she had expected, her night had been one of tossing and turning. From the looks of the Tezerenee, who had already preceded her in rising, she was not the only one who had slept troubled. A surliness had spread throughout the camp. Many of the Tezerenee were also scratching at their throats, chests, and limbs, a sign that the rash was still running rampant. The sorceress was thankful that what with her close involvement with the dragon clan she had not contracted whatever it was that affected them. How long would her luck last, however?

Her latest guard, yet another woman, brought her some food. Simple fare even by Tezerenee standards. Food was the least of the expedition's interests this morning; most of the Tezerenee were visibly impatient to be about the task of invading the ancients' lair and seeing just what it was they had been fighting for. By the time she was finished, the Tezerenee were already organizing themselves for the short climb and what they hoped would be a treasure trove of power and riches.

Riches. For all he sought greater and greater power, Barakas was not one to turn down any jewels and such that might have accumulated over the millennia.

A warrior arrived shortly after her meal. He knelt as if her rank actually meant anything to his masters and said, "Mistress, your presence is requested by our lord ruler. Now, if possible."

If possible? she thought wryly. If Barakas was requesting her presence, he expected her to comply, not dawdle, and everyone knew that. Still, Sharissa decided she would set her own pace this time. Rising slowly, she asked the kneeling warrior, "Does he say what it is he wants me for? Is it urgent?"

"He indicated that you would be among those beside him when he entered the caverns in glorious triumph."

Of course. It would be a gesture of his so-called respect for her and a strictly symbolic gesture. The sorceress smoothed her clothing, taking special care to draw out the simple action for twice as long as necessary. By the time she was finished, the warrior had dared to look up, wondering, no doubt, what was taking this outsider so long to obey the patriarch. Sharissa gave him a regal smile and indicated he had permission to rise. He did so, but with jerking movements that revealed some of his annoyance. Like so many Tezerenee, he and her guards were never certain how she was supposed to be treated. A prisoner this one might be, but she was also a respected guest of the clan master.

It was a predicament that probably required more thought than they were used to. Sharissa kept her amusement hidden as she followed the newcomer and her own guard to the patriarch.

From a distance, she located both Darkhorse and Faunon. The latter, spellbound, sat atop a winged drake. His visage was that of one who is resigned to death and merely wishes to know the time it will occur. When he turned and saw Sharissa, however, he was able to give her a brief, tired smile. She smiled back, but her heart grew heavy.

Darkhorse was more of a distant blot, but she sensed as well as saw the eternal. The huge, ebony stallion paced back and forth as if confined to a corral, although the eagle-eyed sorceress could perceive nothing. Sharissa tried to contact him through subtle manipulation of her power, but a wall of blankness stopped her efforts each time. *She* might be free from her magical bonds, but the other two were not. As long as they were slaves to the clan's power, she would be unable to contact much less help them through sorcerous means. The patriarch had planned well, completely separating the three most troublesome elements of his band from one another.

Barakas and a small group, likely his sons judging by their stances, awaited her near the northern edge of the camp. From that location, they had an excellent view of the cavern mouth.

Reegan noticed her first and whispered to his father, who had been in the midst of explaining something involving a parchment he held in one hand. The sinister box lay at his feet, a tantalizing treasure the woman knew she would never get near if she tried to take it. The patriarch turned and greeted her as if she were a prized daughter. "Aaah! Lady Sharissa! Good! Ready for this momentous day?" To one of the helmed figures, he suddenly said, "We may begin now! Ready the expedition! Those remaining behind here are to be alert and not to fear! They will share equally in what we find within! Assure them of that!"

The Tezerenee he had spoken to saluted and vanished to obey.

Walking to meet her, Reegan offered his hand. Sharissa reluctantly took it, but only because Faunon's visage formed in her mind. If she allowed the heir small victories, he might not be so inclined to murder. Reegan smiled as if she had just granted him her love and tightened his grip on her hand. The warrior who had brought her and her personal guard both departed in silence, no longer needed. Besides so many of the ruling family of the Tezerenee, there were a number of ready sentries within sight. Only a madman would attempt something among so many deadly, skilled fighters.

Her attention drifted as she watched Barakas turn away from her, pick up the devilish box that bound Darkhorse to the Tezerenee clan master, and hand it to an expectant Lochivan. Though her eyes were on the box, she also noted how the latter stood as if pain still taunted him. He was too far away for her to tell if his breathing was still impaired.

"The demon goes first," the Lord Tezerenee said. Lochivan nodded, glanced her way, and walked off, the artifact tucked under one arm. His pace was much quicker than she would have thought necessary, as if he wanted to be away from his father before Barakas noticed something was amiss.

"Your airdrake awaits, my lady," Reegan whispered. Sharissa followed the wave of his other hand and saw the beasts. The sorceress had not given much thought as to how they would reach the cavern mouth, assuming that the clan had at least a dozen different methods. Riding yet another drake was not among those she would have chosen, but it was probably safer, relatively speaking. Materializing at the entrance of the cave system would, as Barakas had once pointed out, be an act of folly. The Seekers might be gone, but it was almost a certainty that they had left gifts of an unpleasant nature behind. There might even be more of them hidden in the caverns, although Lochivan's surprisingly easy entrance during the first expedition seemed to indicate otherwise. Still, Sharissa could not help thinking that so much good luck *must* be a trap. It could hardly be *this* easy to take the aerie.

She found herself thinking that last statement again when the drakes began to land and nothing had touched them. Several warriors had landed before them and set up a line of defense, but they had nothing to show for their efforts. Not so much as one trap had been found—and the Tezerenee were nothing if not thorough when it came to their search. Ahead of them and pacing back and forth like an officer inspecting his troops, was Darkhorse. He glared at the coming Tezerenee, but would not even blink in Sharissa's direction. Whether he was still ashamed to be in her presence or whether he was merely bitter about the offhand way his hated master was utilizing him was impossible to say at this point. Knowing Darkhorse as she did, it could have been both.

"I like this not," Reegan muttered, but no one paid him heed save for the captives.

They dismounted and stood before their goal. Several guards rushed over to take their mounts. Only the initial party would fly up here. Other Tezerenee were already making their way up the winding, treacherous paths that had been cut into the rock long ago by some forgotten race but had fallen into disuse with time.

"Do we take the elf?" one of the figures nearest to Barakas asked, his every word and movement showing deference. Sharissa could not recall which of his offspring had come on the journey, but this *had* to be one of them.

"Of course, fool! Why bring his carcass along if not to make use of it!" Reegan growled.

The patriarch nodded, allowing his eldest's outburst to go by without reprimand—this time. "Undo his feet, but see that his arms remain bound behind him." Barakas smiled as he admired the height of the cavern maw. "I see no reason why we cannot proceed."

He marched forward without any other preamble, catching many of his people by surprise. Lochivan snapped his fingers in Darkhorse's direction, and the shadow steed, evidently knowing what was required of him, trotted close but not too close to the patriarch's left side, matching his pace. Reegan and Lochivan followed and were in turn succeeded by the rest. The heir apparent paused only to signal two guards to lead Sharissa up to where he was. Faunon was also steered toward the front of the party, but closer to Barakas, which prevented the sorceress and the elf from even looking one another in the eye.

"Light," Barakas requested with the tone of one who knows he will receive whatever he desires.

One of his faceless sons raised a hand palm upward. From his palm, tiny spheres of flame leaped to life. One after the other, they departed their birthplace and took up residence in the air above the party.

When a full dozen of the dancing elementals floated around their heads, the patriarch ordered a halt to their creation. The light bearer closed his hand, smothering a tiny sphere just bursting into being. Sharissa knew the balls were not alive, but could not help thinking of the act as akin to a nasty child crushing a butterfly in his hands. Tezerenee, like many Vraad, cared little for the tiny things in life. Such deaths were inconsequential.

"Dragon's blood!" The stunned oath, considering what lay before them, would have seemed insufficient save that it came from the patriarch, the one among them least inclined to such shock. As for the rest of them, Sharissa herself included, they could only marvel at what the light revealed.

The cavern radiated history. It was not so much something to be seen as felt. The incredible age of the place could not be denied. Perhaps the ruined city and pocket-universe citadel of the founders held more specific knowledge, but those places dealt more with the original race itself. This citadel within a cavern, on the other hand, was a tapestry of sorts outlining the successive yet failing races of the lands now called the Dragonrealm.

While there were traces of those who had preceded them, it was the handiwork of the last inhabitants, the avian Seekers, that was most dominant. Other than a few broken medallions, she had never seen any products of their civilization. The paintings covering one smoothed wall, however, could only be Seeker in creation. Each spoke of freedom of the sky and conquests, many of them against the creatures called the Quel. There *were* scenes of aerie life, such as the raising of young and what appeared to be a festival. Some of the paintings were life-size, and all of them were oddly colored, as if the bird folk perceived colors differently. Angles were also askew, and Sharissa recalled how truly birdlike the avians' eyes were.

They were, she had to admit, beautiful. Beautiful and sad, in retrospect of what had happened.

Sculptures and reliefs, mostly of Seekers in flight, also dotted the chamber. One was simply that of a head more than twenty feet in height. The subtle differences in each figure made her wonder if they represented specific folk in the avians' history. She would probably never know. If the Tezerenee worked true to form, most of this would be replaced. The Seekers had likely acted the same centuries ago when they had taken this cavern over from the previous tenants.

So many other things drew the eyes, but what demanded the most attention in the end were the rows of towering effigies made to resemble creatures both true and fanciful. It was possible, Sharissa thought, that they even represented some of the races that had preceded the Seekers. Like a swarm of ants, the Tezerenee began to spread out as they approached the huge figures. Reegan and Sharissa followed the patriarch. Lochivan was one of the few who seemed little interested in what he saw. He seemed satisfied to stand back while the others wandered over to the massive, lifelike statues. Sharissa, noticing his reluctance, saw him touch the box. Darkhorse, still pacing Barakas, suddenly froze in midstep. She was certain that the ebony stallion was still conscious, but the spells of the patriarch prevented her from discovering whether or not that was true. The young Zeree lost her interest in the marvels around her and tried to go to him. Reegan, seeing the object of her change of heart, refused to release his grip, however.

"Nothing'll happen to the demon," he muttered, trying not to disturb his father, who was lost in study of the statues. "Lochivan will just keep him out of the way."

There was a crash from behind them. Sharissa, the patriarch, and the rest whirled around, fully expecting that a trap had been sprung at last. Instead, a fearful warrior stood beside a platform that he had bumped into. A crystal and parts of the platform itself had shattered. The fragments glowed briefly with escaping power.

Barakas stared the man down, then turned to the rest of those in the cavern. "The next man who breaks something will find *himself* in as many pieces! Explore, but do so with care!"

He turned his attention back to the statues. Some of them were damaged, and a few had been tipped in what had nearly been a domino effect. Barakas touched one of those standing, a figure that was tall, gaunt, and resembled one of the walking dead.

"Gods!" he shouted, pulling his hand free almost the instant after he had touched the effigy.

"What is it, Father?" Reegan asked, not so much concerned as fascinated by his father's surprise.

"It . . . there's . . . forget it! No one touches these until I say so! Do you all *understand* me?" His eyes focused on Sharissa. "Not until more is known about them."

"We should be away from this place," Faunon suggested, both unnerved and frustrated at being here.

"Nonsense." Almost in defiance of the elf's words, Barakas pointed to a series of tunnels to the left of the cavern entrance. "I want those traced for a good thousand paces. If they go further, mark your place and return here. The same with those behind this,"—the patriarch surveyed what stood behind the effigies. It was a ruined set of steps that rose for some distance and ended nowhere in particular—"this dais. Yessss, a throne must have stood here once."

Soldiers rushed to obey, their places instantly filled by newcomers. Barakas removed his helm and watched them for a moment. The dragonlord then smiled at Faunon as if he had proved to the elf that there was nothing to fear, that he, the patriarch, had the situation under his complete control.

The Tezerenee were everywhere now, each warrior trying his or her best to please their lord and master. They skirted around artifacts and broken relics as they scoured the tall cavern chamber for anything of interest. Now and then, one of them would find something of sufficient importance that the patriarch would deign to investigate himself. Several times he vanished from sight, even daring short excursions into various subchambers.

Like a plague of thieves! Sharissa gritted her teeth. How much would be lost despite Barakas's warning to be careful? This was a search that should have required months of careful work, not a few hours of haphazard running around.

While the Tezerenee searched, the three captives waited. Darkhorse was still frozen in place, and Lochivan, who still made no move to aid in the search, appeared to be disinclined to release him. Two guards watched over the anxious elf. Faunon flinched every time a warrior touched something or passed within arm's length of the massive statues. As for Sharissa . . . she was forced to endure Reegan's nearness and the fact that she was not being allowed to even participate, despite Barakas's offer back in the citadel.

The latter problem became less significant as Reegan held her closer. With no one paying attention, the heir apparent was growing more and more familiar with her. He leaned near and whispered, "This will be the throne room of *my* kingdom, Sharissa. Did you know that?"

Rather than turn her face to his—and risk his suddenly desiring a kiss or some such foolishness—she stared at the statues. They were so very lifelike, Sharissa almost thought they *breathed.* . . .

"The elf gave us a rough idea of what this continent is like. One of his fellows had a map, although we didn't tell your friend that until we could see if he was lying—which he wasn't, lucky for him. Father's got the land divided between my brothers and me. Thirteen kingdoms now that Rendel's dead and Gerrod's as good as the same. We lost Zorain in the fight yesterday, or else there'd be fourteen."

She had no idea who Zorain was save that he had obviously been yet another offspring of the patriarch. More to keep him babbling about something other than their would-be relationship than because she was interested, the sorceress asked, "What about your sisters and your cousins?"

He shrugged. "There'll be dukedoms and such, not that it matters. Father has it all worked out."

Were the eyes of the catman figure she now stared at staring *back* at her? Impossible . . . *wasn't* it? "Where does he plan to rule? What kingdom will your father rule?"

His stiffening body made her glance at him despite her resolve. "He never says."

The statues called her eyes to them once more. They had an almost hypnotic way about them, one that *demanded* her attention. "That doesn't sound like the Lord Barakas Tezerenee."

Reegan said nothing more, but another short glance showed his brow furrowed in thought. He was also scratching at his throat where the dry skin caused by the rash had spread all over his neck and probably down his chest. His unsightly appearance only made the effigies that much more inviting to gaze at.

"Lochivan! Reegan!" The patriarch's voice echoed again and again throughout the cavern passages. Small, hideous creatures, disturbed by the loud noise, fluttered from their darkened places, realized they were in light of some sort, and scurried back to the sanctuary of the cool shadows.

"You'll have to come with me," the bearlike Tezerenee needlessly informed his prize. Sharissa did not argue; it would have been useless and, besides, standing around only frustrated her more. At least now she might learn something of value to her own goals.

The two of them passed close to Darkhorse. Though his cold blue eyes had no pupils, Sharissa knew that he watched her. Thinking of his predicament, she looked over to where Lochivan still stood, apparently trying to decide what to do about the eternal. In the end, he left the hapless creature the way he was, something that infuriated the sorceress further. It seemed that Darkhorse was to spend the rest of his existence trapped in one infernal torture or another and only because the Tezerenee found it useful.

Before this day was over, she would have another talk with Barakas. If it meant sacrificing some of her own liberty—small as that was—then so be it.

Lochivan joined the two, his eyes never veering from the path before him. He walked as if he wanted little to do with his brother or the woman to whom he had hinted deep affection for. This close, Sharissa could hear his rasping breath again. His gait was off as well, though not in any one way she could fix upon. It was almost as if he had broken some bones and had them reset by someone with no knowledge of what they were doing.

She noted the present location of the box, for all the good it did her. Lochivan kept it away from her, one arm cradling it much the way an infant would have been—not that she could imagine any of the Tezerenee holding a child.

"Where are you, Father?" Reegan called. The voice had come from somewhere behind the crumbling dais, but the back wall seemed pockmarked with passages, any one of which might be the tunnel the patriarch had chosen.

A warrior stumbled out of a passage and, realizing who stood before her, quickly saluted. "You were seeking the clan master?"

"Yes, is he in there?"

She nodded, stepping aside as quickly as possible. "He is several hundred paces below. The tunnel dips and finally ends in another chamber. You will find him there."

Reegan nodded his satisfaction with her report. "Be about your duties, then."

When the soldier was gone, Lochivan turned to his brother. He sounded no better than the last time. "Take the Lady Sharissa and go on ahead. I . . . I will be along in a moment."

The other Tezerenee studied his younger brother for a moment, then nodded. "May it pass quickly."

"It will. It is only a matter of *will*. As he has always said."

It took no great thinking to understand that they spoke of the rash or disease that had afflicted so many of them. Lochivan seemed to be suffering more than the others, although she had hardly been among the Tezerenee long enough to know that for certain. Sharissa tried to take one last peek at Lochivan, but Reegan purposely steered her so that she would have to look through him to see what was happening to his brother.

Someone had lit the dry, ancient torches that stuck out from the sides of the passage. The Seekers, she recalled, were also creatures of the light, which made the torches no great surprise. What she still marveled at was why they had lived in such a place as this when they so obviously reveled in flight.

They were near the end of their trek when a figure came walking up the passage from the opposite direction, virtually blocking their path. The patriarch and his eldest blinked at one another. Sharissa, studying the clan master, was puzzled by the equally puzzled look dominating his features.

"Lochivan is following us, Father. He should be here in a few moments."

Sharissa tried to make herself as small as possible in the hopes that Barakas would pay her no mind. A suspicion was dawning that she was uncertain as to whether to reveal or not to the Tezerenee.

"And what has he discovered?" the patriarch asked. Behind him, two warriors appeared. They seemed a bit confused about why the passage was blocked by their masters.

The question left Reegan at a loss for a moment. He finally sputtered, "N-nothing! It was *you* who summoned *us*! You called to Lochivan and me. I brought the Lady Sharissa because—"

"Never mind." A grim expression settled onto the Lord Tezerenee's face. "Turn around this instant. We are heading back to the main cavern."

"But why—"

"I did *not* summon you at all!" the patriarch growled in exasperation.

Swallowing hard, Reegan fairly spun Sharissa around. She allowed herself to be led ungently back up the way they had just come, her mind racing. Her suspicions had been correct, but was she in error for not saying anything? If this were some avian trap, would not she suffer as well?

They burst out of the side passage, almost catching Lochivan by surprise. His back to them, he slammed his helm down over his head and turned to see what the trouble was. The sorceress glimpsed the box lying to one side, so close but impossible to touch with so many dragon men nearby. Besides, there was still the danger of trying to destroy it without affecting Darkhorse.

"You!" Barakas shouted at his other son. "You heard me, too, then?"

"Yesss, Fath—"

"Damnable birds! What are they up to?"

Was there a hint of fear, Sharissa wondered, amidst the patriarch's blustery anger?

They followed Barakas around the ancient dais and out into the center of the cavern. Tezerenee were filling the chamber, weapons drawn from sheer habit even though many now were more able with sorcery. The patriarch paused and searched for the enemy. Sharissa tried to join him, fearing for her companions, but Reegan pulled her back. She found his concern commendable, albeit unwanted.

Barakas turned in a complete circle, searching for some attack, some reason for the trickery played on his sons. It was clear he noticed nothing out of the ordinary, however, for the sorceress heard him swear.

She tried again to see her companions. Her view of Faunon was completely blocked by the milling, armored bodies of dozens of Tezerenee soldiers. Darkhorse, however, was another matter. Tall as he was, the top of his head was still visible despite the waves of high-helmed warriors still pouring into the cavern chamber.

As if drawn to the eternal by Sharissa's own interest, Lord Barakas strode toward the petrified steed, his followers parting like a living sea before his wrathful form. "You!"

The shifting of the crowd bettered her view. Darkhorse, of course, did not respond to the patriarch's angry and accusative call. He could not as long as Lochivan held him that way.

"This is *your* doing somehow!" he shouted. Without turning around, the clan master added, "Lochivan! Release him so he can answer my questions!"

"What nonsense are you bellowing, dragonlord?" the ebony stallion roared without preamble. His hooves scarred the floor as he vented his own frustration and anger in the only way allowed him.

Barakas faced him without fear. "What trickery do you play here, demon? Should I return you to the box?"

The physical change in Darkhorse's manner shook Sharissa to the bone. He cringed and shook his head in an almost human manner. "I do not *know* what you mean! I have done nothing! I *saw* nothing!"

"Do you deny the summons in my name that brought my sons to me?"

Darkhorse eyed the human as if he were mad. "I do not deny it! I heard it, but it was none of *my* doing! You of all people should know how thoroughly tied I am to you!" He shook his head again, this time in what the sorceress recognized as disgust in himself and his captor. "I heard the call and watched them as they passed my field of vision! Ask any others here if they heard the call and then ask yourself if I could have even performed that little magic?"

"I've no need of asking my own what they heard!" the patriarch's tone was as intense as Sharissa had ever heard it. He almost seemed close to a fit. She could not recall his ever acting thus in the fifteen years since the crossover from Nimth.

Barakas was losing control of himself.

He clamped his mouth shut and stared at Darkhorse for a moment longer before turning and facing his people. "None of you heard or saw anything other than my voice? No one is missing who should not be?" There were murmurs among the throng that indicated negative responses to both questions.

They'll be turning to Faunon next, she thought. He should be safe, she knew, considering that the chains and bonds kept him from performing any sorcery as much as the box and spell did the same for Darkhorse. Still, being one more familiar with this land, the elf might be in for some very deadly questioning.

The crowd shifted again, partially revealing the area where the Tezerenee had kept the elf. Sharissa tried to find him, to at least make eye contact with him.

Where *was* he?

She tried to squirm around, but Reegan, his mind on what his father was about, held her tighter without even realizing it. In frustration, she leaned by his ear and whispered harshly, "You can let me be! I won't run anywhere, you know!"

It proved to be the wrong thing to do. His attention on her now, the heir realized that she was trying to locate the elf. His jealousy apparent even through the helm, he turned to glare at his supposed rival.

He, too, failed to see any sign of Faunon.

"The elf!" Reegan roared, pulling all eyes to him. Sharissa grew numb, understanding now why she could not find Faunon.

Lochivan, one of the first to follow his brother's gaze, completed what Reegan had been trying to relate to the others. He spoke in sibilant but clear words, his breathing growing heavier with each syllable. "The elf isss gone! He hasss essscaped!"

Her silver-blue hair cascading down into her face, Sharissa shook her head at their misunderstanding. She doubted very much that it was by choice the elf had vanished. He had been in no condition to make any escape. That meant that either someone or something had helped him to flee . . . or taken both Faunon and the guards for much darker, deadlier reasons.

XVI

THE QUEL DID not always think in terms of night and day, a fact that turned Gerrod about more than once. His companionable captors kept track of the passage of days for many general purposes, but sleep evidently was something one did when one was tired and not because the sun had set. Even at night, the caverns were generally lit, some of the energy of the sun having been stored away in crystals whose function mimicked that of the gatherer crystal. This excess energy allowed the earth dwellers to work at their project on a full-day basis, newcomers spelling those whose period of work was at an end.

Now Gerrod stood before the pitch-black entranceway to the cavern of crystals—or cavern of *faces*, as he had come to think of it. This was his third time at this place, the second having occurred approximately yesterday by his calculations. He felt as if he had hardly recovered from *that* farce. Five minutes trying to combat the whispering visages, to conquer them, had left him drained, helpless. Only the fact that he had prearranged with the Quel leader a time limit had saved him. It had also, unfortunately, proved to him that he could not succeed in there without performing one particular spell first.

The Gerrod Tezerenee who stood before the fearsome chamber was a different Gerrod than the one the Quel had first captured. Sharissa would have known him. She would have seen the face she was so very used to, the one that, until now, had been a mask only for the last year or more.

He was young again, full of a great vitality that was more than what rest and food alone could bring. Utilizing the chamber demanded physical strength and endurance of the supplicant. Gerrod, loathing every moment required of the spell, had summoned the old Vraad sorcery again, uncertain as to what damage it might cause but knowing he had to be at his physical best for the chamber. Those who had designed the chamber had been more, so *much* more than the lone Tezerenee. Even now, temporarily young again, he risked overtaxing his mind and heart.

A Quel beside him hooted in impatience. The creature's call did not translate, which meant that it was merely a hint, not some statement berating his hesitation. Nonetheless, Gerrod knew he had to begin. The longer he waited, the less patient his inhuman companions would grow.

He stepped inside . . . and back into the world of madness.

The faces began their urgent whispering again. He still had no idea what they were trying to tell him, and this time the warlock did not care. Only one task was of any importance now.

His head started to swim. "Not *this* time!"

Long, forced strides took him across the chamber. His last two visits were jumbled memories, but he thought he recalled a set of crystals in the wall that differed from the others. At the very least, faces had not stared back at him from there.

Might they be the key to controlling this place?

He was already tiring. Even his renewed youth was not sufficient. A new, wild fear arose within him, that his spell was wearing away. He had wanted to save the rejuvenation spell until death was nearly calling for him; there was no telling how many times he could extend his life span this way. Binding himself to the magic of this world held no promise, either. Extend his life he might, but as what sort of creature? A part of him whispered that his fears were all panic and nothing more, but the warlock paid as little heed to that whispering as he did the rest.

A little further. His goal lay before him, almost within arm's reach. The whispering grew more intense and he almost paused, hearing for the first time a snatch or two of coherent speech.

"—not bow to me! If they will not, I will raze the city and all its—"

"—and that I should have started all this! Would that I could have turned time back, warned my—"

No! He would *not* listen! With a deep breath, Gerrod lunged at the wall where the faceless crystals were fixed.

The chamber was flooded with intense light.

The hood protected his eyes for the most part, although annoying sprites danced about for several seconds before his constant blinking dispersed them. Gerrod blinked one last time and turned to see what changes he had wrought. He knew without having to look that the whisperers had vanished. Certainly they had at least stopped their infernal murmur.

For a short time, he could only stand there, wondering if perhaps he had transported himself somehow to another chamber.

There was a world beyond the walls. No matter which direction he looked, save for where the controlling crystals were, Gerrod gained the impression that he was now inside a glass room of sorts. The many facets of the crystalline walls distorted the images, but the warlock could easily make out hills to one side and a smattering of trees near them. If he turned halfway around, he saw more hills and a grassy field in which a small herd of what appeared to be wild horses grazed.

"Where is this place?" he muttered. "Where *am* I?"

As if in response, the world vanished, to be replaced by a view that—he narrowed his eyes and studied the landscape before him—that could only be his father's Dragonrealm as seen from one of the *moons!*

"Serkadion Manee's bones!" he whispered in awe. The ancient Vraad would have relished this sight. Gerrod had read some of the elder Zeree's tomes, including one by the long-lost Manee himself. A vain soul, he had shared one thing with the sorcerer and Gerrod. A love of discovery, especially when it concerned knowledge.

"Sharissa!" he whispered to himself, so used to talking out loud for the mere sake of hearing another human voice. "I can use this to find her!"

And small good that will do you! the warlock thought in the next instant. *How will knowing where she is help when you yourself are a prisoner here!*

Where *was* here? He studied the vast display, taking into account the slight deviations due to the multitude of crystal faces that made up the image, and finally found what he sought. A tiny mark much like a dragon glowed near the outermost tip of the continent. It was a peninsula, as he had thought.

"And Sharissa Zeree?" It was a wild hope, but that was the only kind Gerrod knew of late.

As he feared, nothing happened.

"Perhaps if I picture her." He thought it would be an impossible task, so rarely had he seen her in the past few years, but her face and form proved quite distinct from the moment Gerrod concentrated. Her flowing silver-blue hair, the perpetual smile that was caused by the peculiar yet haunting curve at each end of her mouth, the bright, inquisitive eyes that glittered so much more than those of other Vraad . . .

"Dragon's blood!" The poetic touches to his thoughts were ousted before the truth of them became too much. He succeeded in keeping his imagination to the more mundane, picturing her as best he could and thinking *location . . . location . . .* in so adamant a way that the other, more private thoughts could not gain a foothold again.

The panoramic display before him clouded . . . and became a dark cavern so overwhelming that Gerrod forgot for a moment that he was *not* standing within it, but only viewing it from afar.

Better . . .

The cavern scene vanished as Gerrod's sudden panic at the ghostly whisper in his mind made him think of escape. No new image replaced the old; the crystalline walls remained cloud-filled.

"Who is that?" he shouted.

There was no response; he had hardly expected one, but had tried nonetheless. He shook his head, thinking of the whisperers and how they still intruded in his thoughts even though they had vanished. His imagination was plaguing him, nothing more. Gerrod kept expecting to hear their voices, so it was not surprising that he should conjure one up now and then.

Satisfied that the voice was no more than his own musings, the warlock returned to the task at hand. Soon, the Quel would work themselves up enough to send one of their own in to retrieve him. He wanted progress before that time, either something to give to them to prove he was aiding their cause or enough knowledge that he could utilize this massive artifact to find and flee to Sharissa.

He returned to the controlling crystals and, with great respect, touched them. His thoughts on the young Zeree, Gerrod was not surprised when the clouds dwindled away and he found himself staring at the mouth of a cavern.

"Better," Gerrod whispered, unconsciously mimicking the fanciful voice. The basic manipulations were surprisingly easy to understand once you knew about the controls, the hooded Vraad noted. *Why should they make it too complicated? It would only make using it frustrating. And here I was a moment ago fearing I might never learn anything!*

Gerrod was not overwhelmed by his success. Anyone with even a basic knowledge of the workings of crystal sorcery would have been able to accomplish what he had. Still, better that *he* had found it rather than his father or one of his brethren . . . or just about any other Vraad other than the Zerees, for that matter.

"This is a cavern, yes, but show me where . . ." He smiled as the map returned, indicating that the place in question was . . . was *far* to the northeast! "Only two-thirds of a continent away! A good thing I didn't end up in the sea with such accuracy as that!"

Mountains. A vast northerly chain of mountains. His brother, Rendel, had made some notes about these mountains, especially one in particular. Rendel, as secretive as any Vraad, had never written why the one mountain, Kivan Grath it had been named, was so important to him. Anyone who knew him, however, such as Gerrod or his father, understood that even the slight references indicated something of great import. That there were also mentions of Seekers and history in that same passage, albeit in seemingly unconnected paragraphs, was enough for the warlock.

"Your *treasure trove*," he muttered. "The place you abandoned your clan for!" It had to be . . . but if Sharissa was there, then that meant that the Tezerenee were there also. That, of course, meant his father.

Now, more than ever, he had to find a way to reach Sharissa. The secrets of the founders were not something to be left to the imaginative if single-purposed mind of his progenitor.

Another, simple touch of the controls . . .

Where had *that* thought come from? His hands moving as if directed by another, Gerrod slowly reached for the master crystals. *Was* there a way to travel from one location to the other? Nothing in the chamber seemed affected by the devices of the Quel, but he had been afraid to attempt any sorcery of his own, for fear it would touch him more than he desired. He still distrusted utilizing the magic of either torn Nimth or this world, but using the crystal chamber's power would not, the warlock believed, affect him since it did not require any part of him save simple thought.

There were other considerations that might have contradicted his suppositions, but desperation made him ignore them as he touched the first of the gemstones.

The familiar hooting of a Quel made him pull his hands back.

At the mouth of the chamber, the Quel leader, the only one willing to risk himself, stood staring at the sight before him. His animal features were partly covered by a metal helm that covered both ears completely and left only narrow slits for the eyes. A thick coil of rope was bound about the waist of the behemoth and stretched beyond the entranceway, enabling those without to pull their ruler to safety once he had his prize—Gerrod himself.

"Not yet," he called, trying to act calm, even disgusted. If the Quel could be convinced to leave him be for a bit longer.

With great effort, the massive beastman turned and peered at him. Gerrod still did not know what it was that affected the Quel so, but the lead helm was the only way they could even tolerate the cavern for more than a few moments. Unfortunately for them, even the helm had only limited protection.

From what he had learned to read in the posture of his underground acquaintances, the Quel was in shock. What the newcomer saw was hardly what he had expected to see. There was no sending by the Quel ruler; he might have seemed literally dead on his feet if Gerrod had not been able to make out his breathing.

Act!

The thought was overwhelming, not that the frantic Tezerenee needed much urging. He was already thinking that the chamber itself was a certain sign of the progress he had made—progress that should have been immediately brought to the attention of his hosts. Turning back to the controlling crystals, Gerrod fumbled with them.

He heard the Quel stir behind him, hooting a warning that the Vraad paid no attention to. Gerrod fought desperately for domination of his hands; they strived to move in unfamiliar patterns, as if they, not he, knew what was best.

The Quel was not armed, which gave Gerrod a few more precious seconds, but the moment the huge, armadillolike beast was within arm's reach, the warlock was dead and both of them were quite aware of that notion.

Hearing the heavy footfalls, the snarling Vraad relinquished his claim on his own hands and let them play across the pulsating gems.

The chamber grew blindingly brilliant again. Gerrod, prepared for either this or death from the neck-shattering blow caused by a Quel arm, closed his eyes.

A shrill, jagged shriek tore at his eardrums.

When the light faded and he still found himself among the living, the Vraad cautiously opened his eyes.

He was in a cavern, but not the crystalline one.

Stunned, he spun in a circle and scanned his surroundings with fish eyes. This was no image conveyed by a fantastic magical array of crystals; this was a very real and very familiar cavern. The one, in fact, where Sharissa awaited rescue.

Where is she, then? he asked himself, knowing better than to speak out or make any other sort of noise that would attract his former clan. *And what do I do when I find her? Fight the combined talents of my father, brothers, sisters, cousins, and every gifted outsider they've dragged along?*

It had, Gerrod discovered in horror, never *truly* occurred to him that he might actually arrive at this point. To be certain, he had *assumed* he would, but other than materializing, grabbing Sharissa Zeree from those who guarded her, and whisking the slim, beautiful sorceress away, the warlock had never given any consideration to a workable plan. Now, this close, he needed one desperately.

A dim light from a crack in the cavern ceiling kept him from standing in total darkness, but Gerrod decided to risk things further by supplying himself with illumination of his own. A spell of such insignificance, even though it was of Vraad sorcery in origin, could hardly affect him, could it?

He refused to consider the matter and flicked his fingers. A tiny blue flame burst into life in his palm. Despite its size, its light spread far enough to let him see more clearly what might lurk nearby. Gerrod took in his surroundings again, grateful that there appeared to be no horrific change. The cavern walls were still filled with shadows, but nothing capable of hiding some monstrous subterranean creature. The satisfied Vraad began walking around searching for a direction in which to travel.

What he found first was the Quel leader—what remained of him.

A rise had hidden him from view, but, now revealed, he was a ghastly reminder to Gerrod of what sorcery could do to those careless or accidentally caught at the fringe.

Even in the tiny blue light, the back of the Quel glittered, a tiny celestial map of twinkling stars. The shell was the only part of the earth dweller that had not been brutally ravaged by the ruler's unexpected passage. Gerrod turned away briefly at the sight of the head, a spreading wreckage of metal and flesh.

One of the Quel's arms had been torn off and scattered somewhere out of sight. The legs were twisted over the shell as those of a rag doll might have been but not any way in which a creature with bones would have liked to experience.

Bits of rope still remained, causing the warlock to wonder what the other Quel might be thinking.

"I'd like to say I'm sorry about the sudden departure and its cost to you," he muttered at the tattered corpse. "But the truth is that I'm *not*." The pale Vraad contemplated the remains before him and added, "It could have been quicker and less disgusting, I suppose."

Seeing the Quel had altered something within Gerrod. He had been re-minded of his own mortality once too often in the past fifteen years. Not only did he face death from his present course of action, but every use of Vraad power tore at both him and the land within which he was forced to abide. Why exactly the Quel had suffered such a fate and he had not only added to his fears. How could he hope to save Sharissa when he did not even know how to save himself?

The hooded Tezerenee tried to convince himself it was only nervousness that played on his emotions, but the attempt to calm himself failed.

I can show you the way to safety . . . for yourself and those you care for . . . I can give you . . . life . . . forever . . .

"But—"

I brought you forth from the underworld of the Quel and guided your hands when the critical moment came. I urged you forward when you might have slipped back and failed. Yessss . . . I am your savior more than thrice over.

The voice in his mind, with its impelling, hypnotic tone, could not be de-nied this time. It was not a remnant from the legions of the whisperers, whose tale he still did not understand, nor was it his overtaxed imagination. No, this was someone who spoke to his innermost self, who sought to offer guidance that he only now realized he needed in order to preserve himself.

If you would have these things I offer you, then follow my path downward.

"Path?" he asked, though it was a certainty that his newfound companion hardly needed to hear him to know his mind.

My path . . . the invisible being said.

A cavern passage that Gerrod could not recall seeing earlier stood before him—no more than fifty feet from him, in fact. The tunnel was illuminated, but not by gemstones in the wall or ceiling, as the Quel had designed them, but from a narrow path in the very center of the passage floor. The warlock peered down the cavern tunnel and saw that it continued on out of sight . . . but not before the passage itself sank downward.

"What about Sharissa? What about the one I came for?"

All will be yours . . . if you follow *my path . . .*

Was there a hint of childlike eagerness in the voice's tone? Gerrod found he did not care. The offer was too inviting, too perfect in its timing, for him to resist very much. He stepped toward the tunnel.

Extinguish the light.

"The light?" He glanced at the blue flame floating before him. "My light?"

Your light . . . yesss . . . only then . . . yesss, that is the way of things . . . only then can you follow my path.

It seemed such a small, insignificant thing to ask that Gerrod merely shrugged acquiescence and closed his hand into a fist. The blue light winked away.

Now . . . follow.

He did, not noticing the time as he moved deeper and deeper into the depths of the cavern system. The path was always there before him, glowing with willingness to guide him. Sharissa always remained in his mind, but as something he more and more came to believe he could only achieve with the aid of that which awaited him at the end of his journey. That the notion grew the more he listened to the smooth words of the voice did not occur to him.

Time at last seemed to pull at him, slow him down. Gerrod had lost track of how many turns he had made and whether they had been to the left or the right. That he was ever descending was the only certainty he knew.

A little more . . . just a little more.

He came at last to the mouth of a cavern. The glimmering path faded to nothing just beyond. From where Gerrod paused, no more than five paces from that maw, he could see nothing but darkness. Pure darkness, as if light had no place being here.

You came across such darkness before, the voice, so very confident now, reminded him. *Beyond that darkness was the light of the chamber that brought your release from your captors. You recall that, don't you?*

The parallels between this cavern and the crystal one were not lost upon Gerrod. Steeling himself, he walked the last few steps and passed through into the cavern.

It was still as black as Darkhorse's body—and almost as unnerving.

"Where are you?"

Here.

Ahead of him, the warlock caught a glimmer of something moving, something that glowed in flashes, as if not all there. It had a vague shape, somewhat animalistic in nature, but which animal Gerrod found it impossible to say. More than one, perhaps.

"Who . . . what are you?"

I am . . . your guidance.

Not quite the answer that the Tezerenee was looking for, but he certainly could not argue with his peculiar benefactor, especially whenever the comforting tones of the creature washed away his uncertainties.

As they were now. *Your kin will not find you here. Their senses will not reach. You are safe.*

"Shar—"

She is well. They are confused. I have played a game with them. Your friend has been very useful in that, for the ideas come from her memories.

Again, there was shifting in the darkness. Two burning coals that might have been eyes flared at the cloaked and hooded human, then vanished again.

"This would be the time to strike, to—"

Soon. Things have not yet been played to their completion. Very soon, now, however.

Gerrod hoped so. As much as he appreciated the assistance of this fantastic being, something kept nagging at him, pushing him toward flight. Why? Here, he was safe from his father.

Yesss . . . safe here from everyone.

The warlock shifted. He disliked having his thoughts so easily taken. It reminded him too much of the Quel.

No! roared the voice. *Let your mind stay open! Do not shield it!* The sheer force that struck the Vraad nearly toppled him. He stumbled back, wrapping his protective cloak tighter around his body.

Possibly realizing that it had overstepped itself, the creature in the dark returned to the smoother, calming tones with which Gerrod was more comfortable. *It is essential for your protection that you do not block me from your thoughts. I will not be able to aid you should you be assaulted unless I can be with you at all times. You understand that, don't you?*

It should not have made that much sense, but, for some reason, it did. Nodding, the warlock relaxed a bit. He was still concerned over many things, however.

"What will we do? How do you plan to rescue Sharissa?"

When the time comes, she herself will aid us. There will be confusion and fear among the armored ones. Trust that they will have too many other things to consider to keep their full attention on your female.

Sharissa Zeree was not his woman, but he could not bring himself to argue the fact, not when there were so many more immediate considerations with which to deal. "The Tezerenee are not weak; their combined might allowed them to cross a vast sea by magic alone. The dragon totem might be only a symbol, but it very well represents my father. He *is* the dragon, in many respects."

His words only brought low, mocking laughter from the darksome dweller.

Once more, there was a flash of burning eyes and the barely visible outline of some great beast. Each time, the being looked different, as if it experimented with its appearance, seeking the most fearful and imposing.

He is the dragon, as you say . . . and more so than either you or he or any of his people think! The laughter rose briefly again. *Much more so!*

Standing alone in the pitch-black chamber, his spectral companion still chuckling, a spark of reason pushed Gerrod to wondering if perhaps he had been better off with the Quel after all.

XVII

"WATCH HER!" BARAKAS roared to Reegan, his temper, for the moment, completely out of control. The patriarch turned on his own people. "Why do you stand around? Find the elf! Tezerenee blood is on his hands!" Nothing was mentioned concerning the elven blood on the clan's hands, which might have given Faunon a good reason for anything he did to the dragon men.

"Do you want him alive?" Lochivan, his head turned away from his father, asked in his peculiar voice. To Sharissa, it seemed he was finding great interest in the stalactites or anything else other than the Lord Tezerenee.

The patriarch, too, did not even look at his son. The two of them might have been talking to other people. "Not necessarily."

Sharissa leaned forward, her anger held back only by Reegan's strong hands and the ever-present box that Lochivan presently carried. "Barakas! Don't do—"

"Take this." Lord Barakas pulled out a small object from a belt pouch. It looked like a small crystal to the struggling sorceress, but one that had been *constructed*, not formed by natural means. "Use it if you trap him in a chamber with no exit other than where you stand. Make certain that there is *nothing* of value in there first."

Bowing his head, Lochivan took the sinister artifact. Barakas retrieved the box at the same time, securing it in one arm. He looked thoughtfully at the still form of Darkhorse, who met the gaze of the patriarch with his own baleful eyes. Sharissa still could not see how anyone, even the patriarch, could meet those ice-blue orbs and not turn away.

"And do you want me to deal with yet another irritation to you, dragon-lord?" Darkhorse dared to bellow. "It appears I must do all the work here! Of what use, then, are all these toy soldiers of yours?"

The barb struck as true as if a mortal blow from a sword. Barakas jerked back and quickly glared away any rebellious thoughts by his people. He was perspiring, something that Sharissa had rarely noticed him doing. Each time an event went awry, a little part of him seemed to vanish. The gray that she had noticed in his hair seemed to be spreading, too, now that she took a closer look.

The others are suffering from some rash, but he suffers from aging! the Vraad sorceress marveled. *He fears he's losing control!*

Many of the Tezerenee had already departed, and the patriarch's last look had sent most of the rest running. Lochivan had been one of the quickest to depart. Only a handful of warriors, Reegan included, remained.

"You must be taught respect again, I see," the clan master whispered, his voice cold. He reached for the box.

Darkhorse shivered at first, then his eyes narrowed as he steeled himself for the patriarch's worst. "The one who truly needs to learn respect is *you*, lord drake!"

"You've not tasted all that this can do, demon. I think the time has come to truly reprimand you!"

"No, you won't!" Sharissa focused on the patriarch and willed her power to the forefront.

The skin and armor of Lord Barakas crackled and wrinkled, but only a moment. He looked down at what she was doing to his form and took a deep breath. As he exhaled, the devastation to his body dwindled. The cracked skin healed itself and the armor resealed. His eyes were death as he looked up at her.

"Dragon's oath, Sharissa!" Reegan muttered in her ear. He attached something cold and numbing to her throat. Sharissa felt as if a part of her had been torn away and knew that she had wasted her one chance to utilize her abilities. The Tezerenee had again nullified her. "You shouldn't have done that, not at all! He let you wander loose only because he had other spells handy to keep you under control! Didn't you ever wonder?"

She had not, and that might be proving fatal now.

"*After* I have punished this errant monstrosity, Lady Sharissa, I fear I will have to teach you your manners, also! I will regret that, but it will be necessary."

He touched the box and turned expectantly to Darkhorse.

The shadow steed quivered, awaiting the pain. When he realized that nothing had happened, that he was apparently free of the box, he laughed loud. "Ohh, I have *waited* for *this*, dragonlord!"

He leaped at the startled patriarch.

For all his speed, the eternal could not reach the patriarch in time. Sharissa, struggling anew with a distraught Reegan, watched as Darkhorse slowed more and more the nearer he tried to get to his adversary. Barakas continued to draw swift patterns over the box, trying to regain some sort of control. At that moment, the best either could do was a stalemate.

A voice that sounded like Lochivan's shouted, "Reegan, you half-wit! Forget her and help Father!"

The heir apparent obeyed instantly, the Tezerenee code of serving the clan master—set down by Barakas himself, of course—enough impetus to sway him. He shoved Sharissa back toward a pair of guards standing near the ancient effigies and started forward. The sorceress doubted he even had any idea what he could do.

One of her new watchdogs reached out to take hold of her, but another armored figure caught her arm first. Both Sharissa and the warrior looked up into the helmed countenance of Lochivan.

"I'll take the Lady Sharissa. Help get aid. We may need my brothers and sisters."

The two guards obeyed without question, as they had been trained to do, but the young woman eyed her companion with growing suspicion. Lochivan was moving without the pain of a few minutes before and his voice was smooth, much the way it had always been before recent events. It was almost like standing next to a ghost image from the past.

"This way," he urged.

"What are you—"

"Do not argue."

They were walking into the midst of the towering statues, Lochivan looking as if he wanted no one to follow them. Sharissa wanted to ask where they were going, but then she lost all interest in that as something new demanded her attention.

The statues were pulsating. Not randomly, but like a massive heartbeat. The sorceress glanced at the human and inhuman visages, fully expecting to see the mouths open and the eyes blink. They did nothing of the kind, yet she knew that life did indeed reside within those forms and that it had been stirred to action by someone.

"This will be good enough." Lochivan came to a halt in a region that Sharissa saw was approximately the center of the area surrounded by the effigies. He seemed to be waiting anxiously for something to happen.

Something *was* happening, but not what he wanted. The magics of the two combatants were illuminating the cavern chamber like flashing lights at a festival. Darkhorse and Barakas were still trapped in their stalemate, both powers aglow. Tezerenee surrounded them, all afraid that anything they did might accidentally throw the balance against their lord. Reegan wandered at the outer edge of the circle that had formed out of tense, armored bodies, and Lochivan, standing opposite him, was—

Lochivan?

"It happens! Hold tight!" her companion warned her just as she looked up, realizing now that he was not the son of the patriarch but . . . but *what*?

Her question vanished as instantly as the cavern itself did. One moment they were standing in the center of a growing field of power, the next they were standing in darkness.

Doppelganger or not, she held tight to him. There was a coldness about the dark that she cared little for. It reminded her of a tomb or some other place where death was dominant. Even noting that her ability to utilize her powers had returned did not ease her mind.

Come to me, my children. Enter my court and be safe from those above.

They did, Sharissa almost without choice. Her body moved forward before she had even come to a decision. The false Lochivan was beside her, matching her pace. She could not see him clearly enough, but the sorceress was certain he was almost as confused and frightened as she was, a peculiar thing since it was he who had brought her to this place.

There is no need to fear. I will protect you. I have given my oath on that.

She could, of course, question the fact that she did not know how trustworthy their unseen protector was; if Sharissa was correct in her assumptions, then this *was* the evil that Faunon had spoken about so often in the past.

Evil is . . . evil is sometimes power misunderstood. Yesss, that is the way of it.

It was reading her mind too well. Sharissa strengthened her mental shields.

It chuckled. *Allow me to relieve your fears. Elf, your lady is here.*

"Sharissa?" Faunon's voice cut through the darkness. A dim glow, reddish in color, formed an aura around a figure moving toward her. When it was nearly within arm's reach, she could see that it *was* Faunon. Sharissa almost leaped into his arms when she recalled that the Lochivan beside her was a copy. How did she know that this one was not?

Tell her who you are, elf. Prove to her that she is among friends.

From the expression on Faunon's face—if it *was* Faunon—he did not completely share the unseen speaker's opinion. Nonetheless, he tried to convince her. "Touch my hand, Vraad. Carefully if you like."

Separating from the false Tezerenee, she reached out a tentative hand. Her fingertips grazed the top of his left hand. As she started to pull away, he grabbed hold of her wrist. His grip was gentle but firm. The sorceress felt a tingle run through her.

"Faunon!" She started to reach for him, then recalled her other companion. "But who is this, if not Lochivan? I know you! I could tell that much the way I could tell this was Faunon."

"You do know me, Sharissa." The armored figure also wore a dim, red aura, something she had not noticed before. Sharissa gazed down at her hands and saw no such thing surrounding her, yet it should have been impossible to see her fingers in this darkness.

What magic was afoot in this place . . . wherever it was?

Lochivan's treacherous form faded into a cloaked figure whose face was half-buried in the confines of a deep hood.

"Gerrod?" She was more ready to believe it was just another trick. Gerrod was across the seas to the east.

"It is me, Sharissa. Master Zeree came to me, suspecting that I could follow you where he could not." The warlock spread his hands in a gesture of embarrassment. "I went astray for a time, but I've found you at last."

"Gerrod!" She hugged him tight, so pleased to see *someone* with a link to home. The hooded Tezerenee stood with his arms open, uncertain as to whether to return the hug or not.

All is well now. Friends are together at last, came the voice.

Her initial euphoria died as Sharissa recalled the present. She stepped back and looked up into Gerrod's countenance. "Where are we? What is this place?"

"As near as I can tell, we are deep below the mountain my late and unlamented brother Rendel called Kivan Grath."

"Then the dragonlord and his people are *above* us!" Faunon blurted out.

They will not come here. I have seen to that.

"Who is this, Sharissa?" the warlock asked, indicating the elf. She could sense a growing tension between the two and feared that it was she who was the root of it. Never before had she suspected Gerrod of such jealousy, but it was evident in his words and his stance. How long had he loved her? She cared for him, yes, but . . . did she care for Faunon more?

"This is Faunon. An elf. A prisoner of your father."

"*This* is a Tezerenee?" Faunon searched himself fruitlessly for a weapon. Someone, likely their unseen savior, had released him from his bonds. Seeming to recall this, the elf steadied himself in a manner of someone summoning up the will to cast a major spell.

She quickly intervened, for it appeared Gerrod was about to counter Faunon's attack with one of his own. "No! Stop it, you two! Faunon! Gerrod despises his clan almost as much as you do!"

"Almost?" the warlock snorted.

"How does he come to be here?"

"Simple enough to tell." Only meeting Sharissa's eyes, Gerrod related his experiences, including his confrontation with Darkhorse's counterpart, the Quel city, and the crystal cavern. Faunon took much of it in with skepticism, but the unseen entity, who remained silent during the actual telling, finally acknowledged the truth of it.

Even as I took you and your guards, elf, so too did I bring this one . . . and your lady. There was no mistaking the pride it carried.

"And what *are* you?" the elf demanded, turning to face where he believed the unseen being must be.

The laughter that assailed their minds was a bit too uncontrolled for Sharissa's tastes. Yet, there was something familiar about the creature . . . something . . .

She recalled what it was. "I know you! I know what you are!"

Do you?

"I do!" She looked at Gerrod, who would understand what she was about to say. "He—it—is one of the servants of the founders, one of the *guardians!*"

Gerrod was skeptical. "They abandoned this plane. There was argument over whether they should obey the dictates of the Faceless Ones or even if the founders' experiment should be continued. There was apparently one that—"

"That broke from their ranks!" Sharissa peered into the darkness, searching for something to focus on. She thought she saw two glittering specks, eyes, perhaps, but could not be certain. "You're the outcast, the renegade!"

Faunon was about to ask what she spoke of, but her last words had struck a nerve—if it had nerves—of the being.

I am outcast and renegade because I see the future as it must be! I will not be servant to dusty memories! I will be the future!

"And lo, a god was born . . ." muttered the elf.

Yesss, I like that! I will be a god as they were!

It was time, Sharissa decided, to turn the conversation to another direction. The guardian was building itself up to a megalomaniacal outburst of truly godlike proportions and had to be brought down. "And what about us? Why are the three of us here? Why bother rescuing us?"

Hesitation. Then, *I remember Dru Zeree. I remember his knowledge. You are his offspring. You possess the same traits. When I sensed you among the Tezerenee, I knew that I must take you. Use you.*

"He told me something of the same sort," whispered Gerrod.

"And me?" asked Faunon, not at all sounding as if he really wanted to know.

You are here because of her, but I'm certain you will make yourself useful.

Sharissa was drawing conclusions from what had been said, but she needed more. The sorceress hoped her thoughts were sufficiently obscured, else she was playing directly into the mad guardian's hands—not that it had any. "What about Darkhorse? Why not bring him here?"

This time she was positive she felt the entity stir in growing anxiety. *He has no place here.*

"But he, like Faunon, is a friend. A *good* friend!"

Twin coals, fully ablaze, burst forth from the darkness. They glared at the trio, the eyes of a would-be god, but Sharissa, at least, felt more like a child was trying to make a scary face at her than that she was being menaced by a fearsome being with the power to do anything it wished. How godlike *was* the guardian? Was it bluffing?

He has no place here. Not in my world.

"What are you going to do with us?" Gerrod wanted to know. He looked weary and disgusted with himself.

Do? Nothing! I am your friend. I am friend to you all. You will witness my experiment and the culmination of my vision. I have succeeded where the founders failed! I will bring to this world the successors they failed to create! There will be so much to do—

"And you want us to *guide* you!" At last Sharissa understood their place in the outcast's vision. It had broken away from the others after countless millennia of absolute loyalty. "The Vraad manipulated their world for generations, but you, for all the time you've existed, have little or no experience at this! All your existence you have served the founders' wishes!"

Faunon found this incredible. "He *wants* us to help him control the lands!"

You will help me . . . or I will let you leave.

The trio stood there for several seconds, waiting for some clarification, but the guardian was silent. Finally, her patience already thin, Sharissa took it upon herself to ask the fatal question. "What sort of threat is that? What waits for us out there?"

The eyes were joined by the vague outline of a tremendous beast—possibly a wolf. From the way it winked in and out of existence, it was obvious that the outcast was testing forms, trying to find one that pleased it. *While we have talked—for longer than you think—the new kings of the land are being born.*

Her eyes widened. She had thought that their conversation had been delaying the work of the guardian.

Your thoughts, Sharissa Zeree, and those of your companions, are mine as well. It chuckled again, taking amusement in their confusion and realization.

"What's happening above?" Gerrod demanded. "What's happening to my people?"

Concern? For them? I am merely bringing out their true nature—both here and in the splendid citadel they have built. They were worthy of rule before, but now their success is guaranteed!

While Gerrod stared without seeing, his mind on his brethren and the fate the renegade had cast for them, Sharissa sought some way to turn back what had been set in motion. "Your own kind will not permit this, guardian! The land itself, the legacy of your masters, will stir at this affront! You've broken the most sacred of laws set down by the founders!"

She had hoped to stir uneasiness, but the entity was *gloating*, not fearful. *The land sleeps for as long as I will it and those others like me have left this plane. They will not know what occurs until after it is done and I have proved myself!*

The warlock, meanwhile, had stirred himself to life once more. He took a step toward the barely seen outline in the dark and shouted, "Damn you! I'm asking again! What have you done to them?"

The laughter again. *We will see how well they truly follow the totem of the drake.*

Gerrod turned around, seeking the entrance to this cavern. "I've got to go to them! Warn them!"

"You hate them!" Faunon quickly reminded him. Nonetheless, the elf, too, looked as if he wanted to find any path leading away.

The hooded Tezerenee did not deign to reply, but Sharissa understood. Gerrod cared for his clan, for individuals within it. His hatred was for those who ruled it—his father, Reegan, Lochivan—and he was not even willing to consign those three to whatever fate the guardian had in mind.

There is no way out of here, came the triumphant voice in their heads. *And you would only suffer the same fate as they.*

"It's *true,*" Faunon whispered to Sharissa. "I cannot find a passage anywhere!"

A living fury came among them. Gerrod, looking all too much like the drake that his people looked to as their symbol, confronted the elemental. There was a stirring of power like none that the sorceress had felt in fifteen years. In fact, it reminded her of only one thing, but the intensity of it was beyond what should have been available to the warlock.

Vraad sorcery. *Oh, Gerrod!* She shook her head in disbelief and reached out with her senses to verify the horror before her. *You've broken the barrier between worlds! You've let the foulness that we created seep into our midst!*

She understood some of why he had performed the unthinkable, but that did not forgive him—even if this proved to be enough to aid them in escaping.

A quake rocked the cavern as the warlock unleashed a tangle of glowing, scarlet tendrils at where the guardian supposedly was.

"The curse of the Vraad!" Faunon snarled, emotions in turmoil. He had told her that his legends spoke of the way of the Vraad race, yet she knew that while he loathed what Gerrod represented, he, like her, hoped it would at least do some good.

Gerrod's spell did not stop. He continued to feed the lifeforce of Nimth into it, twisting that world a little further and doing untold damage to the Dragonrealm at the same time. Even with all of that, there was still no reaction from the target of his wrath save that the dim image had vanished. It was still there, however. All three of them could feel its overwhelming presence.

By now, the tendrils filled the space before the threesome, illuminating the chamber as it had never been illuminated since their arrival. Sharissa silently verified that there was, indeed, no passage out. This cavern was a bubble in the mountain rock.

Gerrod screamed as his body finally gave in to the rigors of his sorcery. He collapsed to the floor.

The tendrils pulsated with such intensity that the sorceress and the elf had to cover their eyes.

Silence lingered for more than a minute, by Sharissa's reckoning.

Slowly and so quietly that they at first thought that they had imagined it, the laughter of the mad guardian rose and reverberated around them.

The tendrils winked out of existence.

Gerrod looked up, his face drawn and far older than his father's. The toll of unleashing so much destructive sorcery had drained more than his strength; it had drained a part of his life from him, too.

A fitting position to be in, it said, and they all knew it referred to Gerrod's sprawled form. He had only risen to his knees by the time it added, *Fitting for one who faces his new deity!*

Faunon was shaking his head in dismay, but Sharissa was not satisfied with the outcome. Was it her imagination, or did the presence of the outcast seem just a little bit less oppressing than it had been before the attack?

It did not reprimand her for the traitorous thought, another interesting note.

Still, the guardian was enjoying its latest victory. The two fiery eyes returned, focusing on the trio as a whole. *I think perhaps I would like you two to join your poor companion!* Sharissa felt an unstoppable urge to kneel. Despite the uselessness of doing so, she fought it all the way to the ground. *I think it is time to give your god the dues deserved!*

Her head was just being forced downward—mortals were not *supposed* to look up in the presence of gods, of course—when another voice entered her head and commented, *Rest assured, outcast, you will receive all that is due to you.*

The cavern exploded into turmoil. The two humans and the elf fell flat in the hopes of avoiding what seemed like the world itself at war. Even the tremors caused by Gerrod's spell had not rocked the cavern like this. Sharissa glanced up and saw that the ceiling was cracking in places. She hoped that none of the pieces that chose to fall would be above them. With no passage out, they were trapped. Trying to teleport out during such madness would have a greater chance of making them part of the mountain than sending them to safety. That their best odds lay in lying still and hoping for the best was not something the younger Zeree cared to contemplate.

A bolt of purple lightning flashed across the cavern. Something roared in the dark. The floor cracked next to Faunon, who quickly rolled over to Sharissa when it became apparent the fault would continue right underneath his original position. Large chunks of rock and earth broke free of the ceiling and plum-meted downward, one landing within a few yards of the frozen sorceress. She muttered ancient Serkadion Manee's name and tried not to think about where the next fall would land.

As quickly and violently as it had begun, the tempest died. The three were plunged into darkness, not even their auras remaining to give them some sense of light.

"Sharissa?" Faunon's voice was like a beacon. "Are you hurt?"

She coughed, clearing some of the floating dust from her lungs, and, in the same quiet tones, replied, "I think so. I won't trust that until I can see myself. Gerrod?"

There was no answer. His last image burned into her thoughts, Sharissa stirred herself to movement.

"Where are you going?" the elf asked.

"I need to find out what happened to Gerrod."

Would light aid you in this?

She froze at the return of a voice to her mind. "I don't need your mockery now. If he's dead, it's your doing! What happened?"

The voice was almost indifferent, a great contrast to earlier conversations. *I think you mistake me for the other. Is that so?*

"What do you mean?"

I am not the outcast, the one who would be a god. I have been called such by others of your kind, but I have never yearned for that which was not my calling.

"You're another guardian?" She wished there was light, even though she still would have seen nothing. Unless they willed it, the guardians were always invis-ible.

The chamber lit up so bright that Sharissa was blinded. An angry curse from behind her told the Vraad that Faunon, too, had not been prepared.

Gerrod was not affected by the light; he lay on his stomach, his cloak and hood obscuring most of his body. She quickly moved to his side.

I am.

"What?" Her question came back to her. "Oh. I see. Are you . . . you must be . . ." She could not think, being busy in checking the Tezerenee's condi-tion. Sharissa gasped when she pulled back the hood. Gerrod was an old man, wrinkled and dying. "No!"

It is his own doing. He should have never sought what we had barred from this world.

"I don't *care* about that! Can you help him?"

I could. Guardians, it seemed, shared many of the same faults.

She looked up at the ceiling, ignoring the loose rocks as she shouted, "Please!"

For the daughter of Dru Zeree.

Gerrod groaned. His eyes opened. Sharissa, looking down, saw that he was as she had always known him. His strength had been returned to him with as much effort as she would have used in taking a single breath. "Thank you."

"For what?" the warlock asked, thinking she talked to him.

I have spared you where I should have punished your impudence, Gerrod of the Tezerenee.

"You!" The warlock rolled to his feet, ready to take on what he imagined was his opponent of before.

Your link to the dead world is no more. I have reconstructed the barriers, made them far stronger than you could ever be. Also, as I told Sharissa Zeree, I am not the renegade. If you prefer, your own people gave me a name, however irrelevant it is. Let me appear to you as I did to them.

The cavern was tested by yet another tremor, albeit a much more subdued one than those prior. Where the ground had split open, gas drifted skyward. The cavern grew warmer and, to their dismay, molten earth began to spew forth.

Have no fear for your lives.

Rock, loosened by the series of quakes, broke from the ceiling. Sharissa looked up, saw one above Faunon's head slip free, and started to shout a warning. Before she could do so, however, the fragment, as if moving of its own accord, ceased its downward motion and *flew* toward the growing eruption, where it was joined by more of its kind.

More rock and molten earth gathered. A shape formed, only a vague parody at first, but more and more distinct with each passing second. Sharissa was thankful the cavern was so huge; the thing before them nearly touched the ceiling itself. Fragments kept breaking off as it expanded, but nothing came within even a few feet of the trio, much less the ground itself. The fragments would return to the leviathan and merely help strengthen some other portion of its body.

When the great wings stretched, impossible wings of stone and magma that refused to obey gravity's dictates, Sharissa was almost certain that she knew who and what stood before them.

They were all on their feet now, worn but unharmed. The sorceress frowned at the massive unliving creature, trying to keep in mind that this was merely a shell the guardian had made and nothing more. "The Dragon of the Depths?"

That is it.

Faunon was beside her. It felt good to have him near, especially after facing such chaos. He leaned close, as if whispering would not be heard by a thing that could read their minds at will, and asked, "You know *this* one, too?"

"He—it—can be trusted." *I hope so,* she added to herself. To the new guardian, she asked, "How did you come to be here? The other one was certain it had protected itself from the danger of discovery."

The mock dragon dipped its head. The indifference gave way to a touch of embarrassment. Most of the guardians, the great familiars of the ancients, had little in the way of separate personalities. Only a few, such as the two they had met this day, could be called individuals. *It was not the outcast we sought. What drew us here was the warlock here.*

"Me?" Gerrod withdrew to the confines of his cloak, giving him the appearance of a living shroud.

Somehow, the guardian made the eyes narrow, though they were only bits of stone surrounding glowing balls of fiery earth. *We did not sense the renegade, for it had shielded itself well, but, with so much of its power already in demand, it could not sufficiently shield the presence of so much Nimthian sorcery.*

"Then Gerrod actually did you a service," Sharissa interjected, fearing that the warlock might still face some punishment.

The dragon head withdrew. *Not by choice . . . but because of the magnitude of the outcast's crime, the warlock is forgiven . . . for now.*

Glancing at Gerrod, the sorceress's relief gave way to renewed worry. From what she could read in his stance and his shadowed features, the patriarch's son was not defeated. He would attempt, someday, to reestablish his link.

My time grows short, and there is much to do. I will take you from here and place you where you must be.

She was not certain she understood what the guardian meant, but decided to trust its judgment. It had befriended her father, after all. Instead, she asked, "What became of the outcast?"

That one has evaded us for the moment . . . but it will eventually be taught the folly of its ways.

Knowing how time meant little to these virtually immortal creatures, Sharissa wondered what damage the renegade would cause before that. She decided not to ask.

"And my clan? What about them?" The warlock walked closer, defying the entity who had stripped him of so much power. "What about the insanity your counterpart plotted for them?"

The long hesitation stirred the curiosity of all three. The Dragon of the Depths seemed to be considering its response carefully, as if even it was uncertain it cared for the answer. Sharissa walked over to where Gerrod stood and put a comforting hand on his shoulder. He shrugged it off, not even looking her way. More hurt than she cared to consider, the young woman returned to Faunon, who tried to smile in sympathy but failed.

The land will do what it chooses to do, and I will abide by that decision.

"That is no answer!" the angry Tezerenee shouted.

It is the only answer. It is the sum of my existence. If the land finds some use in the renegade's actions, which will still not excuse that one, then the experiment will follow that new path. If not, the land, not I, will choose to reverse what was done.

"But the renegade interfered with the experiment! If what it said was true, it even dared to subdue the mind of the land!"

All true and all irrelevant now. Before their eyes, the mock dragon began to crumble. A wing collapsed and the lower jaw dropped to the cavern floor and shattered. Despite the din, the voice was still very clear in their minds. *The land will decide . . . but you have a choice in the matter. I tell this to you, Sharissa Zeree, because of the respect with which I hold your progenitor. Whatever changes are wrought upon your kind, those who fight them will only succumb that much more harshly. You have a choice in how you are adapted to this world. The elf is proof of that. His kind have remained more or less untouched.*

The three stumbled back as the body collapsed and the magma receded down the hole it had spewed forth from.

And now, I will take you to where you must be.

"What do you mean 'must be'?" Faunon, who had stayed silent most of the time, shouted at the last moment. Understanding his sudden worry, Sharissa would have lent her voice to his—but the cavern and the guardian had vanished and they were now *elsewhere.*

"Well," came a familiar voice, one that hinted at no sleep for days and terrible stress suffered during those waking hours. Any arrogance was little more than mockery now. "Welcome back . . . and you, too, my son."

Elsewhere was the main cavern that Sharissa and Faunon had been plucked away from by the mad guardian. The voice belonged to the patriarch, who sat upon a high-backed throne now standing atop the dais and looked down at the three stunned gifts that had been placed before him.

XVIII

"I must admit that I had not thought to see you—any of you—again since your escape, what is it, five days ago?"

"Five days?" Faunon leaned his head toward Sharissa's. "We were not down there more than an hour!"

"So we thought, but the first guardian hinted that we might have been talking longer than it appeared. Who can say what they're capable of? That means the damage could only be worse if—"

"I would *appreciate* it," the patriarch interrupted. He straightened. His armor was covered in dust and——she squinted——blood? "Yes, I would appreciate it if you would recall who it is you face. I am, after all, lord of this domain."

"This sounds very familiar," Gerrod muttered. His father, possibly under-standing what he said, focused on him. The warlock retreated into his cloak.

"You. For all that you have disappointed me, I am pleased to see you. I sus-pect, however, that you have not come here because you seek admittance into the clan again."

Gerrod shook his head. Some of the Tezerenee present stirred at that. Sha-rissa, scanning the cavern, thought that there were less of them than she recalled from last time. Many of them were wounded, too. *What had happened since her untimely departure?*

"Reegan." At Lord Barakas's summons, the heir separated from the others and hurried up the steps. The patriarch gave him a hand. Reegan took hold and aided his father in rising. "Nonetheless, I am still pleased to see you, if only because I might require your intuitive skills."

"What happened here, Father? Is everyone . . . is everyone the same?"

"An interesting way to put it. I might find it even more interesting to find out where you have been that you would ask such a thing." With Reegan's aid, he traversed the steps, stopping when he was at the bottom. "For now, however, I think it would be best if I told you what has happened. We've been busy of late."

As the patriarch began, Sharissa looked around for Lochivan. There was no sign of him, and she wondered whether it was his blood that stained the Lord Tezerenee. Also missing was the infernal box prison. "Where's——"

Barakas snapped his fingers. Guards belatedly surrounded the trio. Gaunt-leted hands stumbled to attach small collars to the necks of each. There was a bit of a struggle as Gerrod fought to keep his hood on. When it was at last down, he looked at the others as if expecting horror. Sharissa realized he did not know what the Dragon of the Depths had done for him. Knowing that de-spite his status he was still one of their lord's offspring, the guards replaced the hood when they were finished.

The patriarch shook his head at the warrior's obvious inefficiency. "Things are falling apart . . . and if you speak before I allow it, I will have them silence you. You don't want that, Lady Sharissa. None of us is in a very pleasant mood." To his clan in general, he commanded, "Bring forth one of the changelings!"

There was some scurrying, and a pause in which Barakas took time to steady himself. He became aware of Sharissa's questing eyes and quietly said, "All in good time, my lady. All in good time."

At that moment, the ranks of disheveled warriors gave way to four oth-ers carrying a bundle the size of a body. Gerrod took a step forward, but the patriarch shook his head. The newcomers waited, fascinated to be sure, but also prepared for the worst.

They were not disappointed. Sharissa had been waiting for this and was not surprised at what rolled out of the blanket that the Tezerenee lowered to the floor before them. Faunon nodded his head; he had also expected this. Only Gerrod was truly taken aback.

"What sort of abomination is that?"

"It was a cousin of yours once," the clan master informed him. "There were seven others besides this one. It took us all this time to hunt them down, and more than twice as many warriors to kill them."

The corpse was of a creature resembling the unfortunate Ivor as he had been those few moments Sharissa had confronted him, only this one was even more reptilian than that hapless soul. The shape was not even quite humanoid anymore, but almost truly like that of a drake.

"It looks like a Draka," Faunon commented.

"Draka?" Reegan asked.

"They have many names, many of which sound similar. Some think they ruled here long before the avians and the Quel. They serve—*served*—the bird folk. Of late, they've grown far more savage than they should be."

"I've seen them. Unimportant." Pulling himself free, the patriarch limped over to the disconcerting body. "*This* was one of my people, not some monster! I want to know what happened and who was responsible!" He gave the elf a long, appraising look. "Perhaps I should have had Lochivan question you more thoroughly."

Sharissa could not hold back. "Where is Lochivan now?"

"He is ill . . . and it is he who watches the demon's prison." That was all he would say on the subject, although she was certain there was more he was not telling.

Gerrod pulled free of his guards and, despite his father's warning, moved closer to examine his former cousin. He touched the leathery skin and removed some of the tattered bits of armor that still hung to the corpse. From what Sharissa could see from her vantage point, the shapeshifting Tezerenee had torn part of his armor off and literally burst through the rest. How much pain had that entailed? How much pain did the transformation itself entail?

The guards moved to bring the warlock under control, but Lord Barakas suddenly waved them back. To his estranged son, he said, "I will want to know how you come to be on this continent later, but for now I would appreciate whatever you can read from this . . . this horror."

He received no response, but that was Gerrod's way. The hooded Tezerenee probed for a moment or two longer and then looked up in the direction of, but not exactly at, his progenitor. "I'd like Sharissa to see this."

Reegan whispered something to his father, but Barakas shook his head. He looked at the waiting Zeree. "Go to him, but be careful about what you say or do. There will be no second escape. Especially for your elf."

In response to an unspoken command, one of Faunon's guards put a knife to the elf's throat. Sharissa gritted her teeth in order to keep from saying something that her captor would hardly appreciate. Escape was hardly one of her concerns at this time; she lacked the strength for anything so strenuous as that.

Joining Gerrod, she inspected the corpse. As she expected, he wanted to do the talking.

"This is what I've feared all these years—this and the fact that we are aging far more quickly than we were prone to back in Nimth."

"What are you mumbling?" Reegan asked, suspicious of anyone, it seemed, who was on better terms with Sharissa than he was. That included a vast number of people, as far as she was concerned.

Gerrod stared at his elder sibling with disdain. "I was wondering when the first of these appeared."

"There was one during the journey here," Sharissa offered. That first one had likely been one of the more magically sensitive Tezerenee. Or perhaps he had been a test for the outcast guardian, a way of assuring that what it sought to do was possible without killing the victim.

"There wasss another," announced a hissing voice. From one of the passages, an armored figure that could only be Lochivan stumbled forward. Despite the patriarch's claim that his son was ill, Lochivan wore full armor, even a full helm. He also carried the box, which was evidently making it difficult for him to maintain his balance, but he refused the aid of two warriors who came to his side.

"You are not supposed to be here," Barakas told him. Nonetheless, he was visibly proud of the fact that Lochivan would not give in to whatever was affecting him. "You should be resting."

"In thissss place? I heard the voicessss and came to sssee. Gerrod's question, however, desservess asss complete an answer as possible if we are to deal with thisss matter."

"When was the first one?" Gerrod acted as if he had never left the clan.

"During the first expedition. He killed another man before we could ssstop him. That wasss why I wasss ready for Ivor. I recognized the sssigns."

Barakas looked a bit troubled. "You told me they died when one of the drakes went wild."

Lochivan laughed, harsh and almost inhuman in his manner. He was now at the edge of the circle of nervous bodies surrounding the prisoners, the patriarch, and the poor, twisted form on the floor. "I thought the sssituation under control, even with Ivor'sss appearance. I thought I had made a pact that would sssave usss!"

"What are you talking about? You must be feverish!"

"He's not." Sharissa understood. Lochivan had known what was going to happen to her. That was what he had meant that one evening. He had made a pact that included her safety . . . so he supposed. In a sense he had been correct. Unfortunately, Lochivan had also been dealing with a being that chose to interpret the pact in whatever way suited it.

The patriarch turned on her. "What's that you say?"

"Tell him, Sharissa!" Gerrod urged. "Tell him, or by the claws of the drake I'll do so!"

She nodded. It would be best for them if the Tezerenee knew. It might even make them abandon this place as the Seekers had chosen to do. "We've met the one you made the pact with, Lochivan." She paused to let that sink in. "I think what you've seen is its way of fulfilling that pact."

"Impossible! I worked for the sssurvival of the clan! These horrorsss are not what I desssired!"

"Ivor and the others were how the guardian thought your clan would best survive this land."

"Stop right there!" Barakas roared. He pointed an accusing finger at the unsteady figure. "You will tell your tale later, and the truth had best be spoken!" The patriarch kicked at the rubble as he strode toward Sharissa and Gerrod, both of whom rose at his coming. "First, we will hear *your* story!"

Sharissa willingly related it. Gerrod and even Faunon also contributed, recalling as much as they could. All three were in unspoken agreement that if the Dragon of the Depths had dropped them here, it was to their interest to convince their captors of the urgency of their plight.

The Lord Tezerenee listened in silence, his only reaction to glance on occasion from one of his prisoners to another. The time difference interested him enough to provoke a question or two, but the rest was heard unhindered.

When Sharissa concluded with the second guardian's decision to send the three here, Lochivan spoke up despite the threat of punishment from his father. "Their tale tells most of it . . . but I thought the scourge was the land's doing, not this outcast abomination."

"I am still not certain on that," the patriarch said. "But that is neither here nor there."

"We've told you the truth about everything, Father!" Gerrod insisted.

To the surprise of all, Lord Barakas smiled. "And I am certain that you have! If so, then the danger is past! You said yourself that the renegade fled from the Dragon of the Depths! He has saved us again!"

Sharissa grimaced. This was not going the way it should. "Have you forgotten what the Dragon of the Depths said? There is no guarantee that this is over or that something worse is not yet to come!"

He indicated the corpse. "The first of those appeared the day you vanished; the last, three days later. There have been none since, and I would say there will *be* none again!" Looking down at the remains of what had once been one of his subjects, the patriarch added, "Someone drag that away and bury it. Let him and the others be remembered with honor, victims of a foe now fled!"

"Typical!"

"What was that, Gerrod?"

"Nothing, Father! Only that you've not changed! I prayed that, at least for mother's sake, you might have!"

"Alcia!" All triumph faded from the clan master's rough-hewn visage. "The citadel!"

"Citadel?" Gerrod looked at Sharissa for clarification.

"Your father forced Darkhorse to help him build a glorious citadel to the south of here." She pointed at the box that Lochivan carried. The bitterness could not be held back. "That is Darkhorse's reward for his efforts, his prison!"

"My mother and the others are not here?"

"Alcia." Barakas raised his hands above his head. "I sent a message announcing our imminent entrance into the caverns, but . . . nothing since then! They won't have known! I must go to her and see!"

He stood there for several seconds, his eyes closed. The room was filled with a sense of expectation. Sharissa was the first to wonder why the patriarch still stood where he was when it was obvious he had intended to teleport to his lady.

That thought had also occurred to Barakas, for he lowered his hands and stared at her in wonder. "The power! I had it! Now . . . there is still some, but I cannot summon sufficient for the task!"

"You won't find that power at your beck and call anymore!" It was Faunon who spoke, to the surprise of Sharissa. At a nod from Barakas, the guards released their hold. He purposely joined Sharissa and put an arm around her waist. She was a bit shocked at first, but found almost immediately afterward that she wanted him there.

"We are the only spellcasters here now, and our strength is not sufficient at this time to be of any aid."

"Step away from her!" Reegan bellowed. He drew his sword and started toward the couple.

"Reegan!" The voice born to command froze the heir in place. Barakas then added, "Continue, elf! What great revelation have you to make?"

"Sharissa probably knows," Faunon said, "but I spoke up without thinking, so it's my duty to tell you."

"Then be on with it, before I decide to let my eldest further denigrate himself!"

"Father—"

"Silence!"

Sharissa caught the barest hint of a smile on the elf's lips before he spoke. "The tales of our ancestors speak enough about the way of Vraad sorcery for me to recognize it. The sorcerous stench is enough to make me wish I had no ability to sense its presence. She also spoke of it during our time together— how it had suddenly returned to you."

"My link!" Gerrod looked at Faunon with a mixture of surprise and respect.

"When one makes a hole, things tend to leak out."

"The Dragon of the Depths resealed the barrier, made it stronger," Sharissa finished. "You're back to the way it was before."

Crystalline eyes narrowed. "You will take me there! One or both of you!"

Faunon snorted. "Even if I desired to, Vraad, neither of us has the strength, not after what we've been through. I am not even certain if it is safe to do so. My folk have lived here for far longer than you, and we have stories—"

"More blasted tales!"

"We have *stories*," he continued, relishing his role even though Sharissa could see that he understood the risks of pushing the patriarch too far, "about the times when the land is woken . . . as it has been by the renegade guardian."

"And what do thossse ssstoriesss sssay?" Lochivan asked. He had the box in both hands now, as if he intended to present it to Sharissa. Had Darkhorse known the Tezerenee was manipulating him? Had the eternal nearly sacrificed himself in order that Sharissa might be free? She hoped there would come time for the answers. She hoped there would come time for Darkhorse.

"That those who bring notice to themselves in such turbulent times may find they will soon not know themselves. That is what they say."

"Reegan," Barakas began, a fierce anger spreading across his features. "If the elf will not speak plainly on his next attempt, you have my permission to put him to the sword."

"Faunon," Sharissa warned.

He took her hand with his free one. "You remember what the second guardian said, that we could control the change. It's been so in the past. When the land is awake, there is wild sorcery. Those who make too much use of their power become more malleable, more sensitive to . . . change."

Barakas studied the ancient cavern. In a quieter voice he said, "I had decided to make this the citadel from where I would coordinate the rule of this land, a fitting choice since it would have been within the domain of my heir." Sharissa was interested to see that Reegan did not seem too pleased with that decision. He had hoped for a kingdom of his own, not one in which he would have little more status than before. The patriarch did not seem to care. "It seems it will have to wait a while, but it *will* be mine! Reegan! Attend me!"

Erasing the bitter cast, the heir apparent came to his father's side. "Sire?"

"You will remain here and continue efforts to ready this place. Be alert."

"Yes, Father."

"I also want the swiftest drakes readied for travel. Two dozen—no, one dozen! No more than necessary!" The patriarch turned to the trio. "*You* three will accompany me!" He waved off all protests, including one from Reegan, who hardly cared for the thought of Sharissa being taken away from him. Focusing on the sorceress, Barakas continued, "If I thought I could trust you, I would have those bands removed. As it is, they will remain around your throats. Do not think to remove them without my permission; you will find that they can bite!"

Sharissa started to speak, to say that this was something they all had to be concerned about, but she knew that the clan master would never believe she would ride willingly with him.

Lord Barakas Tezerenee looked around at his people. "Well? What are you standing around here for? There is much to do!"

The dragon warriors scattered, save for those few whose task it was to either protect their master or await further commands that might arise. Reegan remained, although Lochivan and the box, much to Sharissa's distress, had vanished. The hurried expedition to the Tezerenee citadel would only take her farther from the eternal.

"We will leave within the hour," the lord of the Tezerenee announced to his prisoners, "and ride until the drakes can run no more. We will sleep until they are sufficiently rested and then ride until exhaustion takes them again."

"And what of us?" Gerrod asked. "We are already worn out . . . as you must be."

"We are Tezerenee, Gerrod. The name Tezerenee *is* power, in case you have forgotten. We will endure what we must for the sake of the others! These two"—he indicated Sharissa and Faunon—"will just have to struggle along."

The warlock snorted, muttering something about speeches and beliefs, but his father had already turned away.

ALTHOUGH THEY WERE not given much opportunity for rest, the patriarch was true to his word when he had said that they would be leaving within the hour, the three did receive some food. Their lost days had wreaked havoc with their inner clocks, though, so the meal was first eaten in hesitation. Only when food began to warm her did Sharissa feel the pangs of hunger. From then on, she ate in eagerness, noting that her companions did the same.

Sentries watched them to make certain no one fiddled with the collars. Barakas had warned them of the danger of doing so, but evidently knew that here were three who could most definitely be trusted to try escape at some point. They would need their full abilities to do so.

They sat where they had been standing earlier, no one apparently having thought seats a necessity in this place. Only the patriarch's throne—where they had gotten that monstrosity, she could not guess—resembled anything designed for sitting, and that looked much too uncomfortable for most people. It was the type of throne she would expect from Barakas, a thing that required patience and stubbornness to endure.

For the brief time remaining, the sorceress concentrated on the stone leviathans mere yards away. Even with her powers muted again, something that seemed to be a habit of late, she could sense the life stirring within them. Why no one else did was beyond her. Faunon did look up now and then as he ate, almost as if he noticed something from time to time but could not place it. Was she that much more in tune with this world than they were? Sharissa had accepted her new home without question, marveling in the natural beauty that she, too young, had never known in Nimth. Perhaps that was one reason that she had learned to manipulate the binding forces of the world as none of the others had yet.

That did not explain why the powers within the effigies were growing greater in intensity with each passing minute.

What would happen when the land truly awoke? Was this the first sign?

Her thoughts died as Barakas returned to the central chamber. He still limped, but concern for his bride and his fledgling empire was making him ignore all but the worst pain. Reegan trailed behind him, looking like a hatchling drake that had been reprimanded by its mother. No doubt he had been trying, without success, to convince his father to either leave her here or let *him* journey with them.

The patriarch nodded to her. "You have been properly fed, Lady Sharissa?"

He seemed to use a title only when he wanted something, she realized. Steadying herself, she replied, "Fair enough for now. We could still use some rest."

"When you are with us long enough you will learn to sleep while your steed keeps going."

"I hope not to be with you long enough for that."

Barakas gave her a thin-lipped smile. "Honesty. It is a commendable trait, albeit a useless one right now."

"Father—"

"Silence, Reegan. You have duties, if I recall. Perform them as is fit for the future clan master . . . the future emperor."

The hulking Tezerenee glanced longingly at Sharissa, who made a point of *not* looking his way. Dejected, Reegan saluted his father and departed.

For one of the few times in her recent memory, the patriarch removed his helm. Sharissa was shocked to see that the gray in his hair was spreading. There were grooves in his face that only time and weariness could have carved. It reminded her somewhat of Gerrod's visage after his near catastrophe with Vraad sorcery down in the mad guardian's cavern.

Lord Barakas Tezerenee was not getting old; he *was* old.

"He *will* be emperor before long," the patriarch assured them. He met his estranged son's gaze and saw the emotion in there. "Yes, I am growing old at last. The dragonlord is nearing his end. Probably a few more decades and nothing else."

"At least you have lived all those millennia," the warlock returned. He indicated his own face. "There will be lines on this face soon enough. This world likes to kill those who will not bow to it."

The armored monarch cocked his head to one side as he studied Gerrod. Then, smiling a mocking smile, he shook his head and turned his attention back to Sharissa. "I have something I want of you."

"I'm hardly surprised."

"Hear me out. If you aid me, I will no longer pressure for a marriage between you and my eldest. You and the elf can go off wherever you please."

"Everyone always wants to throw us together," Faunon commented. Food, even this food, had done much to restore his humor, even if he and the others were still prisoners.

He was ignored by the clan elder. "Well?"

"You haven't told me what you want of me."

Gerrod leaned forward before his father could speak and warned, "Be careful of any promise made! Even oaths can be broken!"

"There will be no breaking of oaths!" Barakas seemed ready to kick his son back in place, but possibly knew how it would make him look to the sorceress. "This concerns your family, especially your mother and siblings!"

The warlock tried to pretend he did not care, but Sharissa already knew that, despite his abandoning the ways of his father, Gerrod had no desire to see his former folk come to harm.

"What is it you want?" she asked, in part trying to turn the patriarch's focus away from his son. Each time it turned there, the chamber grew noticeably colder.

He scratched his throat, but, unlike so many of the other Tezerenee, Barakas no longer suffered from the rash. "I want your cooperation—and theirs—for the time needed to ascertain what may or may not have befallen those at the citadel—and especially the Lady Alcia."

It was a bit of a rambling answer, but the thrust of it moved her as she thought not possible. Barakas might be her adversary, but his concern for his bride outweighed even his drive for power.

"I will swear by the spirit of the drake that you will gain your releases when I am satisfied that we face no threat. Well?"

"All of us?"

"All of you."

She studied him for several seconds, organizing her thoughts. There was one more thing Sharissa wanted of him, and now was the only moment she had a chance of getting it. If she let this pass . . . "Darkhorse must be included."

His altering expression almost made her regret her demand, but she could not leave the shadow steed under his control.

"You want the demon?" He struggled to regain composure and succeeded—in part. "Take him! Even with our sorcery reduced, we will prevail!"

"Then you have my cooperation." Her words were said in a simple and straightforward fashion.

Her quiet response made him halt his tirade. Barakas took a deep breath before saying, "My gratitude, Lady Sharissa. You will find I will keep my word in this, despite my sons and their opinions otherwise."

Meaning Gerrod and Reegan, she thought.

"Now that it is settled," the patriarch continued, "I may tell you that the drakes are ready for us. Guards!"

In quick order, they were brought to their feet and marched through the cavern until they came to the entrance that Sharissa and the Tezerenee had entered by almost a week ago. To her surprise, the patriarch bypassed several powerful flying drakes and started down the side of the mountain to where the wingless riding drakes awaited.

"We're not going by air?"

Gerrod, who understood the workings of his clan better than did his companions, explained. "It is Father's evident opinion that we would be too conspicuous from the sky. Besides, for the speed of this journey, travel by land will be swifter. An airdrake must rest more often, especially if it is carrying someone."

"That explains our relatively slow pace coming here," Faunon suggested. "He wanted time for his second force to reach here and be rested."

Aside from their guards, a handful of other Tezerenee were supposed to accompany them. Sharissa was surprised but relieved to see that Lochivan was one of them and that he still carried the box with him.

Barakas noticed his ill offspring. "Who told you to be here?"

"I mussst redeem myssself."

The patriarch looked uncomfortable, as if he wanted all the eyes around him to be looking anywhere else but at him and Lochivan. "Your *illness* . . ."

"I will keep it under control," the tall figure said in his strange voice. He did his best to allow no one else to see his face, possibly because he was so ravaged it would have disgusted some of his folk.

"I wonder . . ." Gerrod muttered.

"You wonder what?" she asked.

He turned, not having realized that he had spoken out loud. "Nothing. Just a thought."

The conversation between the patriarch and Lochivan grew muted. After a short exchange, Barakas finally nodded. It was difficult to read Lochivan by his movements, but he seemed very relieved.

"We've lost much of the day already," Barakas said to the others. "Please mount up."

They obeyed. When everyone was ready, the patriarch turned in his saddle and faced those of his people who would remain here. One of the Tezerenee held high a staff upon which the banner of the clan waved in the wind. Under the fluttering flag, the rest of the warriors, Reegan included, knelt.

"I shall return shortly. We have defeated threats both physical and magical, and this cavern, this natural citadel, will be the base from which an empire spanning this entire continent will be ruled. I have designated kingdoms for each of my most loyal sons,"—Barakas did not even glance in Lochivan's direction—"and my eldest, Reegan, will co-rule here until my death, when he becomes emperor. Thirteen kingdoms and, within those, twenty-five dukedoms for those deserving!"

"Another grand and glorious speech," Gerrod whispered in sour humor to Sharissa.

The patriarch did not hear him—or chose not to. "We have been separated from our people, and there is concern for their safety! In my mind, there is little to fear, but it behooves me to ride there in person! Once I have satisfied myself that things are in order, I shall return with more of our brethren and we shall began the *true* process of making this land ours!" He stared at Kivan Grath, as if it represented the entire continent. "We *will* shape this domain to *our* will!"

Barakas folded his arms, the signal that his speech was at an end. The Tezerenee rose and cheered as they were supposed to. Reegan unsheathed his sword and raised it in salute.

"Pomp and circumstance," Gerrod muttered.

"We *ride* now," the patriarch informed them, glaring at his unrepentant son.

Not completely willing to trust the outsiders, the patriarch left the managing of their drakes to the guards who rode beside them. One of those sentries took the guiding rope of Sharissa's mount and began to lead it, but slowly so as to allow the clan master's animal to move ahead. It was mandatory that the Lord Tezerenee lead, if only as a symbolic gesture.

The remnants of the expeditionary force continued to sound their approval and allegiance as the party moved out. Had she not been so exhausted already—and thinking about how tired she would be when they finally *stopped*— the sorceress would have admired their enthusiasm much more. As it was, she only hoped that they would still have such enthusiasm a month from now.

One of the Tezerenee standing nearest to where she was removed her helmet and began to scratch at an ugly patch of dry, red skin covering most of her throat and part of her chin. Sharissa stared at it briefly, but then the warrior guiding her drake pulled on the rope and the animal turned, putting the warrior woman and the others behind the young Zeree. Exhausted as she was, she did not bother turning around to get a second glance.

Besides, there were too many more important matters to consider. Far too many to worry about an annoying but evidently insignificant rash.

XIX

It was well after the midnight hour when the patriarch gave in to the urgings of his people to rest the drakes before they collapsed in midrun. By that time, Sharissa was nearly asleep in the saddle. Despite the clan master's assurance that she would come to learn how to truly rest while riding, the sorceress was more than happy to crawl off the unruly beast and drag herself to a safe and secure spot where she could try to regain at least a tiny portion of her strength. Gerrod and Faunon were not much better, nor were the Tezerenee themselves, even though they had actually had some rest at one point or another.

Only the patriarch seemed energetic, but it was the energy of the anxious, the worried. If he kept it up too long, it would drain him.

Sharissa's sleep proved little more relaxing. She dreamed as she never had before, but there was little in those dreams to give her comfort. In one, a hand rose from the earth and seized her, twisting her like clay and reshaping her in a hundred myriad forms, all horrific. In another, Faunon and she were embracing. It was a pleasant scene, and she knew that she was about to be kissed. Then his face had become some reptilian parody, but he had still tried to kiss her. That one had woken her up and kept her awake for more than half an hour, so real had that close visage been.

There were others, but they by and by were only shadowy memories, too vague to bother her much. Only one thing about them remained with her, and that one thing was enough to make her shiver.

Throughout several of the nightmares, she could hear the sound of the insane guardian's mocking laughter. It seemed to cross from one dream to the next. It was still ringing in her ears when a tap on her shoulder woke her again.

Sunlight burned her eyes. Faunon smiled down at her. He seemed fresher, but there were still marks of exhaustion on him. Sharissa did not care to think what she must look like. It amazed her that anyone could still find her attractive. At present, it would not have surprised her to look into a mirror and see a visage that would make a drake beautiful in comparison.

The elf extended a hand, which she took. As he pulled her to her feet, Faunon said, "It was a choice of one of them waking you or me taking on that task. I knew you were still exhausted, but I thought you might like to see my pale face a bit more than you would their metal masks."

"Very much so." She enjoyed the contact between them and let it linger a bit before releasing his hand. "Is there food?"

"I would not have disturbed you if there had not been." He waved a hand at two bowls by their feet. A stew, much like the one that the Lady Alcia had once fed to her so long ago and smelling almost as good. She recalled that incident because it had seemed so out of place when dealing with one of the Tezerenee. Sometimes it was troublesome to remember that the clan's mistress had been born an outsider, that there had been no clan until Barakas had pulled together his disjointed group of relations and welded them into the only true family among the Vraad. Not known for being familial, the concept of a clan was something known only from the early days of the race. Barakas, however, had assured that it would never be dismissed lightly—and his bride had been his other half in the struggle. She, almost as much as the patriarch, had helped to make the Tezerenee the force they were.

Sharissa found herself hoping that nothing had happened to her.

"Where's Gerrod?" she asked, trying to put the Lady Alcia from her thoughts.

Faunon handed her one of the bowls. He hesitated, then answered, "I saw him last with his brother. They journeyed away from the camp."

Trying to do something for Lochivan's illness? It was the only reason she could think of. Not all of their past differences had been ironed out, but a common concern for their own people had, at least, brought them temporarily together. Had it been any other family, the young woman would have been happy for Gerrod. As it was, she hoped he was not becoming one of them again.

A shadow fell upon them. The two looked up into the dragonhelm of a Tezerenee. "My lord bids tell you that we leave shortly. Prepare yourselves."

Her companion groaned as the warrior marched off. "I have seldom ridden so much. To think I once thought a horse a terrible animal to cope with. Merely sitting astride one of these monstrosities is worse."

"What are you expecting to find?" she asked abruptly. Sharissa felt a need to know as much as she could, and Faunon was her only source of information. Of all of them, only he had been born to this land.

The humor of a moment before slipped away, revealing the serious soul beneath. "I do not know, my beauteous Vraad. The only thing predictable about the land's ways is its unpredictability. I regret to say that the two of us have just as likely a chance of being correct." He took her hand. "I am sorry I cannot help you."

She squeezed the hand and, on impulse, leaned forward and kissed him. While he was still staring at her in open shock, the sorceress smiled and said, "But you do."

FOR THE SECOND time, they rode as if the renegade guardian itself was snapping at the tails of their mounts. Gerrod and Lochivan, who had come back just before preparations for the day's mad journey were complete, separated as if things had not changed between them. Sharissa had looked at the warlock for some sort of explanation, but Gerrod had merely pulled his hood over his head and buried himself in the all-encompassing cloak. The only thing she could tell was that he was even more worried than yesterday.

The sun was high in the sky when they departed. Again it was a mad race, everyone seeking to maintain the pace that the patriarch had set. This day's was worse than the first, and Sharissa had a suspicion why. She was certain he had tried again to teleport to the citadel and, of course, failed. That only made it more essential that they cover as much ground as possible each day.

It was impossible to speak, but she did glance at Faunon whenever possible. He returned her looks with a tight-lipped smile. Until the coming of the Tezerenee, he would have never thought riding a drake possible. He probably still did not.

On her other side, beyond the Tezerenee guard who paced her, Gerrod stared straight ahead. Only once did he turn his eyes to Sharissa, but the hood shadowed them so well that it was as if she stared into the sightless face of a dead man. She turned away and regretted it a moment later, but, when she sought to apologize, his attention had already returned to the path ahead.

To find Lochivan, she had to crane her neck and look back, a dangerous trick to attempt for very long, which meant that she was forced to do it more than once just to get a good glimpse of him. He was riding at the back end of the column, his head down so that even if he had not been wearing a helm, she would have been unable to see his face. At the side of his saddle bounced Dark-horse's insidious prison, apparently in Lochivan's permanent keeping despite his betrayal. Angry at herself for not demanding the eternal's release from the box, Sharissa swore she would bring that up with Barakas the moment they stopped. If she could convince him that Darkhorse would listen to her and not seek ven-geance, then he might prove willing to allow the ebony stallion freedom. Per-haps if she mentioned the aid that Darkhorse could give them . . . though that depended on how strong the eternal was. He had, she recalled with bitterness, been punished hard for his attack upon the lord of the Tezerenee.

It was night again when they finally halted. Drakes were good for long bursts of speed, but then they had to rest much longer than horses. They also had to be fed, and that meant meat. For this journey, the Tezerenee had packed as much as they could carry of the special feed that they added to the beasts' meals. Mixed in with the meat, it would greatly supplement their needs and prevent any chance, however slim, that the drakes might snap at their masters in their search for fresh food.

As she had sworn, Sharissa sought out the patriarch as soon as she had dis-mounted. Behind her trailed her latest silent shadow. Barakas she found speak-ing to one of the other guards, evidently setting the watch for the night. Barakas could delegate everything if he chose, but that was not his way. A leader, she had heard him say long ago, did not sit back and grow fat and lazy. He worked with his subjects, reminding them of *why* he was their lord.

Barakas dismissed the warrior just as she walked up to him. In the back-ground, she caught the vague image of Lochivan spending an overlong period of time busying himself with his steed. He seemed to be watching his father closely, as if wanting something.

"What is it you wish, Lady Sharissa?" the patriarch asked. He sounded as worn out as she felt.

"I have a request of you, my Lord Barakas."

"Formal, is it? Tell me something first, my lady. Are you rested enough to make good use of your abilities?"

Somehow this encounter had been turned around and he was now asking a favor of her. She kept her peace, thinking it would be best to hear him out. It might help her own cause. "I'm hardly rested, if that is what you mean. If you

want to know if I can teleport to the citadel, I doubt it. All I remember with
any confidence is the interior; you wouldn't let me journey outside the walls
very much, if you recall."

"Something I think I am about to regret, yes?"

"I'm sorry." The sorceress was. It seemed there was never anything she could
do, but, in this case, it was the patriarch's fault. "And if it is all the same to you,
I would prefer not to materialize inside . . . just in case."

"I understand. I was attempting to appear outside the gates myself." Barakas
tugged at his graying beard. "And sorcery might not be safe yet. When I tried
just before the day's ride, I sensed something—immense, is the only way I can
describe it—spreading throughout the region of the citadel."

She thought of the land awakening and the outcast laughing, all still fresh in
her mind from the dreams. "Do you think that—"

"I do not know what to think." He dismissed the subject. "You had a request
you wished to make of me."

"It concerns Darkhorse."

"Does it now?" In the deepening dark, she could not see his eyes now, but
she knew they were narrowed, suspicious. "And *how* does it concern him?"

She took a deep breath. "I've given you my word that I will help you, and
you've given your word that you will release all of us. Until the latter happens,
however, I was hoping that you would let Darkhorse out—"

"He is my assurance that you will abide by your side, Lady Sharissa."

The young Zeree nodded. "I understand how you feel after the attack, but
he will listen to me. If I ask him to abide by my decision, he will do so, I'm certain. If not . . ." She hesitated, wondering what the eternal would think of this
offer. "If not, you can trap him inside once more and I won't make a protest."

There was silence for a time, then; "I will consider it over my meal."

"You've bound him to the box again. He can't do you any harm now!"

"Never underestimate an opponent, especially a wounded one. They are
often the deadliest." The patriarch nodded to her. "You will hear from me. I
promise."

He walked off without another word. Sharissa frowned and looked for Lochivan again, but the patriarch's son had vanished.

She wondered why the lord of the Tezerenee had left his other children behind. Even Lochivan would have remained at the caverns had he not defied his
father. Was it that Barakas worried about what they might face? Was Lochivan
only here because he had confronted his father with the Tezerenee need for
honor and redemption? Gerrod did not count; he was almost an outsider as far
as his sire was concerned.

"My lady," her shadow suddenly said, jarring her back to the here and now.

"You should get food and rest. My Lord Barakas will be demanding us to be ready when he is."

"Very well." She wondered when she would receive her answer. Tonight? Tomorrow?

Whenever he chooses to give it, Sharissa finally decided with a frown. She turned and wandered back to where Faunon would already be waiting with food for the two of them.

"WHENEVER" ACTUALLY PROVED to be just before she lay down to sleep. Most of the others were already resting, but she had located a stream and, despite the protest of the bodyguard, washed her clothing and cleaned herself. The warrior, to her surprise, respected her privacy and kept his eyes as much as possible on the nearby foliage. As tired as she was, Sharissa would have hardly cared if he *had* looked. She was only happy to be clean. Amongst the items packed for her were traveling gowns much like the one she wore. Where they had come from she could only guess, but they fit her perfectly and prevented her from having to put on the wet outfit once she was finished. They accented her form quite well, and she wondered if perhaps they had been brought along on the journey from the citadel, where Lady Alcia might have had them made for her.

Heavy footfalls warned her of the approach of a Tezerenee unconcerned with silence. Faunon and Gerrod, both sleeping within a few yards of her, either did not hear the newcomer or thought best not to interfere in what they knew nothing about.

"Lady Sharissa."

As was the way of the Tezerenee, only the patriarch had a tent. The sorceress and her companions slept in travel blankets provided by the clan, their heads resting on small mats provided with the blankets. To Sharissa, long used to expeditions exploring the ruins of founder settlements, this was heaven compared to riding a drake for hour upon hour. She was almost sorry she had to talk to Barakas now, but reminded herself it was for Darkhorse's sake.

"I was hoping you would make use of the creek. Refreshing, was it?"

"I would have appreciated your telling my watchdog that. I had to argue with him."

"My apologies."

"Have you made a decision about Darkhorse?"

"I have. I will not release him. You I may trust, but not the demon."

She felt anger stirring. "He won't—"

He silenced her. "That is my decision. I am, however, willing to do something for you and your elf."

"What?"

"Tomorrow, his weapons, and any you and Gerrod had, will be returned to you. Though I do not trust enough to remove your collars, I allow that you need some defense. We may need you three. You'll also be allowed to ride with your hands unhindered."

It was not what she had wanted, but it was better than having her request rejected and receiving nothing else. Still, she could not help comment. "You have me confused, Lord Barakas. I'm not certain whether we are prisoners or partners."

He laughed, but it was forced. "I find many things confusing of late, my lady. Good night."

Sharissa watched him walk off, still limping a bit. At times like this, she could feel pity for the aging dragonlord. Unfortunately, all that Sharissa had to do to wipe away the pity was recall what he did to those who failed or defied him.

Like Darkhorse or Gerrod.

TRUE TO HIS word, Barakas returned their weapons. Faunon took his sword back with no argument, but the look on his face made Sharissa smile for a brief time. Gerrod was far more cynical about things. As he pointed out, the odds were greatly against them if they attempted to escape. Either Barakas or Lochivan alone could take the three of them on and probably win.

Thinking of Lochivan, Sharissa searched for him in the hopes of speaking to him before the patriarch called for them to mount up. She found him already in the saddle, dragonhelm on, but bent over a bit as if his stomach pained him. The box was no longer attached to the saddle, which meant that Barakas had likely retrieved it. That did not concern her so much now as what might be wrong with her former friend.

"Lochivan? Are you all right?"

"My sssstomach turnsss, nothing more!" He refused to look at her.

"Lochivan—"

Her daily shadow rushed to her. "My lady, the patriarch bids you to mount your beast! We leave now!"

"You heard him," growled Lochivan. "It isss time to ride!"

She allowed herself to be led away, but the sorceress kept her eyes on the ill Tezerenee for as long as possible. Lochivan was worse than he had ever been. He should have never joined them. The trek was proving too harsh for his system to endure, even despite his admirable willpower.

Gerrod and Faunon, seated on their drakes, were waiting for her. The warlock glanced back at his brother and down at her, his expression a mixture of many conflicting thoughts. When she tried to ask him what he was concerned about, the hooded Tezerenee shook his head and found other things with which to busy himself.

"Follow!" Lord Barakas called, urging his mount forward. At the rate he was pushing them, they would see the citadel late tomorrow and reach it the following morning. Not as fast as he wanted, but swift enough for the rest of the band.

Hour upon hour they rode, pausing only to move around obstacles and break for a short meal. Sharissa still found herself unable to get used to the awkward, reptilian gait of the drakes and began to wish for more padding for her saddle. Faunon, she noticed, rode almost as tight-lipped as she did. Gerrod, on the other hand, being a Tezerenee, rode with the skill and ease only one trained early on could show. He seemed lost in thought, something not uncommon with him.

With the control of her mount mostly in the hands of her Tezerenee escort, the young Zeree spent much of her time looking around, seeking anything out of the ordinary that might spell peril for their party. She also took an occasional glance back at Lochivan, who was having more and more trouble controlling his own beast. That by itself was disturbing; it might mean that Lochivan was far more ill than he was pretending to be to the others.

It was no more than an hour before sunset when she noticed him lagging behind.

Her first glimpse showed him more than a dozen lengths behind the others. The second glimpse revealed a bent-over Lochivan trying to maintain control of his drake, who was starting to run off to the side.

She signaled to the Tezerenee next to her that he should look back. Sharissa watched him stiffen when he saw the trouble the patriarch's son was having with a simple task. The Tezerenee turned back to his charge and handed the guide rope to her. Then, urging his monstrous steed forward, he pulled up to the front of the party.

A handful of seconds later, Barakas was calling the party to a halt. By this time, Lochivan was probably at least a hundred lengths behind. His drake, in fact, had turned around and started back the way they had come.

"Lochivan!" the patriarch roared.

His son did not respond. Lochivan might have been unconscious for all he moved. Still, the patriarch tried again.

Sharissa had no patience for this. She turned her reluctant mount toward the distant figure. "If he does not come when you call, it might be because he has not the power to do so! He might be too ill to do anything for himself!"

With that, she urged her drake on, breaking through the unsuspecting Tezerenee and racing for Lochivan.

"No, Sharissa! Wait!" Gerrod cried.

Taking advantage of the confusion of the moment, Faunon ripped the guide rope from the hands of his own escort and rode off after the fearful sorceress. She gave him a look of thanks as he broke through after her, then concerned herself with trying to catch the other drake before it decided to take its helpless rider on a mad run into the wilderness.

"Lochivan!"

She saw him stir. He was still hunched over in a way that to her looked excruciating, but now he was at least acting. More than half the distance separating the party and the straggler were now behind her. She no longer had any idea if anyone was following her save Faunon. For all she knew, it went against the ways of the clan to aid someone who could not control his own illness. It would be just the draconian type of thought that the clan would choose to follow.

When only a third of the distance still remained, Lochivan suddenly straightened and glanced back. He kept most of his back to her, craning his neck just enough to see her. Even had he not worn the helm, it would have been impossible not to see his features, to read the pain that was likely near to crippling him.

She had no idea what to expect from him, but his reaction, when it finally came, so startled her that she almost reined the riding drake to a halt.

Keeping his back turned to her, Lochivan waved her away. Sharissa blinked, wondering why he would turn back the aid he so obviously needed. She had no intention of turning back anyway. Even if the Tezerenee thought he did not need help, the sorceress *knew* he did.

From behind her, Sharissa heard Gerrod's straining voice. He, like his brother, wanted her to turn *away*.

"Lochivan!" she called. "You need help! You're ill, Lochivan!"

"Turn away and *flee!*" he shouted. His voice sent shivers through her, for it was far, far worse than anytime prior. He sounded more like an animal struggling to free itself from a trap than a man.

The Tezerenee's drake began to buck, completely confused as to what its rider wanted of it. Lochivan kept waving the reins as he sought to discourage Sharissa from coming any closer. "Leave me be! Ssssave yoursssself, you little fool! Lissssten to my brother!"

He was hunched up again, as if straining against his armor, of all things. Sharissa tried to get close enough to reach him, but her mount suddenly balked. She kicked its sides and swore at it as she had seen so many Tezerenee do, but the creature refused to go any closer, instead skittering back and forth where it was, much to her growing annoyance.

Lochivan was practically folded in two, and his pain was now so terrible that he did not even try to hold back. His shriek only made the situation that much worse, for it renewed the frenzied back-and-forth movements of the drakes. Sharissa had to hang on for dear life—and then wondered why she was bothering with the drake. It would be easier at this point to abandon the mount and run to Lochivan.

Trying not to think about what a confused creature such as the ill Tezerenee's drake might do when she moved too close, Sharissa leaped off her own mount. From the edge of her field of vision, she saw Faunon pull up nearby and immediately abandon his own animal. To her horror, he ran directly toward the menacing jaws of the frightened drake.

"Deal with him!" the elf shouted. "I will bring the monster under control!"

She nodded, saving her gratitude for when this task was done, and cautiously made her way to Lochivan's side.

He was shivering, his visage still turned away from her, and his armor seemed not to match the shape of his body. The leg that she could see from where she stood looked to be broken, judging by the angle at which it was bent. How that had happened on the back of a riding drake was a question Sharissa could find no answer for. When she finally pulled him to safety, she could concern herself with questions.

"Lochivan! Dismount! That monster could throw you off!" In his condition, that might prove fatal. She moved a few steps closer. Now he was only just out of arm's reach. To her right, the sorceress saw that Faunon had caught hold of the reins, which Lochivan, in his pain, had finally lost. So far, he was keeping the drake from running amok, and that was all Sharissa could hope for.

"Get away from me!" He growled, waving one gauntleted hand at her while still trying to look away. Had the disease ravaged him so, or . . . could it be?

She lost hold of the frightening thought as his hand came within reach. Lunging, Sharissa took hold.

"Nooo!" With a turn of his wrist, Lochivan's gauntlet came loose—revealing a *twisted, clawed hand covered in dark, grayish scales!*

He turned toward her then, his other hand reaching for the helm that seemed to no longer fit him and was, in fact, straining to *burst*. "I warned you, Sharissa! I wanted you to not sssssee thisss! I wanted no one to ssssee this!"

The rest of the party had arrived. Barakas was already off his mount and running toward his son when Lochivan reached up with his clawed hand and, voicing his agony again, pulled the helm back so that his visage was no longer obscured.

"Serkadion Manee! Oh, Lochivan, no!"

"Yessss, Sharissa!"

A scaled monstrosity stared back at her, toothy smile mocking the wearer himself. It was small wonder the helm had seemed tight. The nose and mouth had molded into one and were expanding even as she watched. Despite its strength, she could see that the armor was tearing apart in many places as every part of the body went through the transformation at the same time.

Lochivan had not only become what poor Ivor or those at the cavern had become, but he was already progressing beyond them.

Their true nature . . . The mad guardian had said something like that when speaking of what the Tezerenee would become. She could hear the elemental laughing even now. The Tezerenee had not crossed from Nimth to the Dragonrealm by physical means; their spirits had entered flesh-and-blood golems that magic had created in this world. Those bodies, however, had not been formed from flesh taken from anything human. No, in his infinite wisdom and a desire to make the drake even more a symbol of his clan, Barakas had dictated that the source of those new bodies would be the dragons discovered on this world.

And now those bodies were becoming what they should have been in the first place.

"Lochivan!" The patriarch came up beside Sharissa and reached out a hand toward his son. The other Tezerenee, save Gerrod, who kept as far away as possible, were circling drake and rider.

"I wassssn't ssstrong enough, Father! I failed! I could not redeem mysssself!"

"Forget that! I can help you!"

"No one can! I . . . I have trouble even thinking of myssself assss ever being human! It . . . it issss . . . almost as if my mind changessss assss my body doessss!"

Barakas, ignoring the wild look in the reptilian eyes of his son, moved within arm's reach. His tone was smooth but commanding. "You are Tezerenee, Lochivan! Our very name is power! There is nothing that can withstand our will! You have only to let me help you fight it! You have only to let me—"

He broke off as a hissing Lochivan sprang from the back of the drake and launched himself at the patriarch.

"Lochivan!" Sharissa started to reach for him, to pull him from his father, but Faunon, abandoning the riding drake, reached her first and pulled her away.

"Are you mad?"

"Let me go!" She struggled unsuccessfully in his grip.

"They will help their master!" He indicated the Tezerenee.

The warriors scurried toward the two struggling figures. Afraid of accidentally wounding their master, they sheathed their swords. Three pulled knives out.

Lochivan, still hissing, looked up as the closest man tried to grab his left arm. With astonishing speed and savageness, the patriarch's son slashed out, ripping through armor and taking with it several layers of flesh. The warrior screamed and stumbled back, wounded but not out of it. Two more took hold of the abomination that had once been one of their lords and dragged him off of his father. Barakas quickly scrambled back. There was blood on him, but it was that of the unfortunate warrior.

"Secure him!" Gerrod, still maintaining his distance, called out. "He's growing stronger by the—"

Lochivan tore one arm free and, before anyone could react, reached over and took hold of the man gripping his other arm. He swung the warrior around, knocking one of his other attackers to the ground, and then *threw* his victim to the ground headfirst. Sharissa turned away as she saw the Tezerenee's neck snap backward as he struck the earth.

Two of the warriors tried to drag the unconscious one away, but Lochivan, never hesitating, turned and leaped at them. One who had his knife ready lunged and caught the misshapen figure on the shoulder where the armor had ripped apart. The blade dug into flesh, then snapped as it struck bone. Hissing, the bleeding Lochivan reached out and caught the man by the neck. When he pulled his taloned hand away a breath later, Lochivan carried part of the man's throat. The Tezerenee was dead before his mutilated corpse even fell atop his unconscious fellow.

"We should leave!" Faunon whispered. "That thing is liable to kill us all at this rate! At the very least, you should leave! I can help fend it off for a time!"

Sharissa shook her head. She knew that Faunon meant well, that he was worried for her, not for him. "I have a better idea. Let me go."

"So you can try to reason with him again? He is beyond listening now!"

"But Barakas isn't!"

He frowned, but, seeing the look in her eyes, nodded. As soon as his grip lessened, Sharissa made her way to the patriarch, Faunon close at her heels. The elf, likely very thankful now that Barakas had given him a sword, kept himself between his Vraad and the beast in the circle.

"Barakas!" Sharissa reached the patriarch, who stood staring at his lost son and not moving at all. "Barakas! I can help you!"

That brought him back to the present. "What can *you* do, Lady Sharissa?"

She pointed at the collar. "There are only three here who have power enough to stop Lochivan! I know him! Let it be me!"

"Release you? You have no care for Lochivan, Sharissa! He betrayed you, remember?"

"That doesn't mean I want him ending up like this! He may even kill all of us if you don't!"

Barakas glanced at his son, who was trying to catch one of the four remaining adversaries unwary. The circle had moved so that the unconscious warrior was now safe, but not for long if even one more man fell.

"Very well."

To her surprise, he simply reached over and gently removed the tiny band. "As simple as that?"

"Of course, but only I can do it."

She whirled and faced Lochivan. In her mind's sight, she saw the rainbow and the lines as only she of all the Vraad could see them. They were one and the same, only a matter of perceptions, but they represented the lifeforce, the power of this world. A force only she could, so far, manipulate to the necessary intensity.

Let my spell work! Let him not be too strong!

The battle had kicked up clouds of dust, and that was what she chose to use as the base of her containment spell. Faunon might think she would choose to kill the monster, but Sharissa could not do that. She was not a Tezerenee; she would imprison Lochivan if she could.

Lochivan, bloodlust evidently blocking all thought, did not notice how the dust settled thicker and thicker on his body. The Tezerenee did, however, and sought to take advantage. They were using their swords now that the clan master was safe. One of them thrust and caught Lochivan on the arm. He tried to grab the blade but missed.

"Stop! Kill only if you have to!" Barakas called. The decision was not likely to be popular, but the warriors would obey.

By now, Lochivan realized that something was wrong. The draconian visage curled up in animalistic anger, and he shot a deadly glance at the only one his mind recalled could be the source.

"Sharisssssa!"

She almost lost concentration at his call. Had she not been so worn from riding, the spell would have been completed by now. As it was, the sorceress had to struggle the nearer she came to the finish, and each second meant Lochivan was still a threat.

"Sharisssssa!" He struggled toward her, moving almost in slow motion. At first she thought her eyes were playing tricks, but then she realized that he *was* glowing. Lochivan was fighting the spell.

"No!" She threw all that she had left into it.

The misshapen form froze, an earthy statue of a beast enraged because it could not claim at least one last victim.

"The Dragon of the Depths be praised!" Barakas whispered.

"You might thank Sharissa, too!" Faunon muttered.

Sharissa smiled in relief and nearly fell into the elf's arms. "That was too close!"

One warrior went to check his unconscious comrade. The others waited by the encrusted figure, their swords raised and their helmed visages turned toward their liege.

"What do we do, Father?" Gerrod, still atop his beast, asked.

Barakas glanced at his remaining son, at Lochivan, and then at Sharissa. His voice shook at first, but he quickly corrected the shameful error. "Mount up. Everyone. Now."

"The dead, my lord?" one of the warriors asked.

"There is no time for them. Remember their names and that will be sufficient for their immortality."

Sharissa separated from Faunon and moved close enough so that she could whisper privately to the patriarch. "The spell won't hold him forever. He's growing stronger and stronger . . . and his body's growing, too."

"Will it hold long enough for us to be far from here?"

"It should, but—"

The lord of the Tezerenee turned from her, walking slowly toward his own beast. "Then that is all I need to know."

Gerrod rode over to Sharissa and Faunon, two riderless drakes sandwiching his own. He handed the reins to the elf and smiled grimly at Sharissa. "Do not ask me to explain his decision. I think I am just as surprised as you."

The wounded Tezerenee was helped atop his drake. He would see to his arm as they traveled. The other warrior, now conscious, needed help in the guidance of his mount from one of his brethren, but seemed all right otherwise. By the time Sharissa had mounted, the remnants of the party were ready to ride. Barakas took one last lingering look back at the still figure, then signaled the advance.

Beyond the horizon, the citadel and its own mysteries awaited them.

XX

IT SEEMED MUCH too soon and far too late when they arrived at the outskirts of the walled citadel of the Tezerenee.

"The gates are open," Faunon informed them while they were still a distance away. His eyes were much better than theirs. Once it would have been next to nothing for the Vraad to alter their eyes to their needs, but none of those with the elf even voiced the thought, not with the unpredictability of sorcery.

"I hear nothing but the birds in the trees," Gerrod added. "The citadel is silent."

Sharissa glanced at the patriarch and saw that his hands gripped so tightly around the reins that it was a wonder the reins did not snap. She could see that he wanted desperately to ride as swiftly as he could through the gates and see what had befallen his empire, but the training that he himself had imparted upon the clan held him back. No warrior went riding madly into danger unless he had something in mind.

The sun of a new day was barely over the horizon. No one spoke of Lochivan's tragic struggle, for fear of the look that crossed the patriarch's countenance when that event was even hinted at. Besides, now was the time to worry about what lay before them—and whether or not it might be better to turn and ride away.

"Stay together," Barakas finally muttered. He started to urge his mount forward, but Sharissa reached over and put a hand on his arm. He looked at her with nearly dead eyes.

"A suggestion . . . and a request."

"What?"

"Darkhorse. He'll help us here, especially when he knows I mean to enter regardless of his protests. It would be the best for all our sakes."

"Very well."

She blinked in surprise, watching as he lifted the box so that it rested on his lap. The ease with which she had convinced him worried her at the same time that it cheered her. Much of the patriarch's indomitable spirit had died over the past days. There was no predicting what he might do in his present state, and the sorceress had no desire to become part of some death wish. Still, she had sworn to help him for the time being, and she would not break that promise.

To herself Sharissa admitted again that she *wanted* to know what had happened—provided she survived that knowledge, too.

The Darkhorse who fled from the box this time was a greatly subdued creature. He did not shout, nor did he stamp and gouge the earth to show his fury. Instead . . . he wavered.

"What . . . what is it now, dragonlord?"

"Darkhorse!" Sharissa was stunned by the tentative tone of his voice. He had almost as little spirit as the patriarch. Her sympathy for the clan master dwindled to a shadow of itself as she wondered what sort of punishments he had meted out to the eternal.

"Sharissa." Darkhorse bowed his head low and would not look her in the eye. The ice-blue orbs seemed dimmer than she recalled.

"Will he be all right?" Faunon quietly asked her. "It almost seems that we might have to protect *him*."

"Even if he cannot, he will be better off free of that horrible device!"

The patriarch stirred himself. "Demon, your friend has requested we seek your assistance. The citadel of my people may now be a deadly trap to all those who enter. We might have need of your considerable power."

"My power is not so considerable now," the shadow steed muttered. "I have trouble keeping my form even. Why ask, anyway? You have my life in your hands. Merely command me as you have before."

Barakas looked down at the box in his hands. He looked at Sharissa. A spark of life still remained in his eyes. To the ebony stallion, he replied, "I made a pact with the Lady Sharissa. A pact of freedom if she will do this thing for me. That pact includes you."

He threw the box to the ground with as much strength as he could muster.

Darkhorse's horrific prison shattered with such ease that Sharissa and the others could only stare at it for several seconds.

"Hurrah," murmured a sardonic Gerrod in the background.

Life, or something akin to it, returned to the Void dweller. Darkhorse laughed, relief from the strain of so agonizing a captivity vying for dominance. He was still very weak, but now he at least had spirit. Sharissa smiled.

"I owe you much, patriarch, for what you did to me, but I will abide by my friend's pact. When this is done, however, we depart and, should your path and mine cross again, there will be a reckoning."

The warriors reached for their weapons, but Barakas waved them off. "I expected no less."

The shadow steed, still wavering in form, turned to face the party's objective. "Then let us be on with this task. I yearn for an end to this."

Grimacing, the young sorceress urged her mount forward. She, too, yearned for an end, but wished he had phrased things differently.

Gerrod rode up to where she and Faunon were and pressed his animal between theirs. The elf frowned in his direction, but kept silent because of the warlock's friendship with her.

"I have something for the two of you . . . small tokens of luck, nothing more." He reached out and handed each of them a small crystal. "Humor me and keep them with you." Before they could ask what he intended, the warlock was behind them again. No one else had paid particular attention to the exchange, so concerned was the rest of the party with their kin who had remained in the citadel.

Darkhorse trotted several paces ahead of them as they neared the Tezerenee settlement, he being the one least likely to face injury if surprised. Sharissa's eyes narrowed as she studied the open gate. It was not merely open, but almost off its hinge and very battered, as if something had sought to break through— but from the *inside.*

The riding drakes stirred and began sniffing the air.

"They smell blood," Faunon said, his eyes not leaving the battered gate.

"How do you know?" she asked. She could see no sign of blood, but that did not mean there was none.

"I can smell it, too. An acrid, coppery smell it is."

"Silence!" hissed the patriarch.

Maintaining careful hold of the reins of their animals, the party reached the open entranceway. The broken gate left more than enough room for a massive drake to pass through. Darkhorse paused and turned to the humans.

"Do I enter?"

"What do you sense?" Sharissa asked in a quiet voice.

"Everything and nothing!" He glared at Barakas. "I can no longer trust my senses."

"Enter, then," muttered the lord of the Tezerenee. "Enter, scan the area, and return to us."

"I live to *serve* you," mocked the unsteady stallion. He turned back to the huge arch and trotted inside.

Sharissa nearly held her breath the entire length of his absence. She recalled how it had felt to combat Lochivan and Ivor, both of whom had displayed astonishing potential in sorcery. In being transformed into these abominations, it seemed that the Tezerenee were also being adapted to the powers of the land itself. Why not, if the renegade had wanted them to be the new masters? Certainly with foes like the Seekers and the Quel still living, the new kings would need all the skills they could acquire.

Darkhorse returned. He was puzzled. "There is nothing that I can see or sense in any other way. This place is a chaotic maelstrom of force. If there is anyone here, I cannot tell you."

"No bodies?" Gerrod asked, much to the shock and anger of his former clansmen.

"There is blood, but no bodies, not even bits." The ebony stallion smiled humorlessly at the patriarch.

"We enter, then," was all Barakas had to say in turn.

The citadel was in ruins. Many of the smaller buildings had been completely leveled; others missed walls or parts of the ceiling. Rubble was strewn everywhere. One of the towers had collapsed, crushing the building below it. Even part of the surrounding wall had been battered.

"Random violence," the elf commented. "There seems no purpose in any of the destruction. Some of it looks as if the attacker ceased in midstream and departed."

"There is one consistency," Sharissa remarked. Lord Barakas turned at the sound of her voice. She pointed at one of the battered walls of a building that still at least partly stood. "Most of the rubble, save for the damage to the protective wall, lies in the courtyards and open areas."

"Meaning?" the clan master asked, not caring for her delay in stating the point.

"Meaning that the destruction came from within the buildings for the most part, then spread out here." She defied him to counter her claim with any of his own.

His only reply was "We will move on and see how the rest of the place fares. Only then will we investigate inside."

He was stalling and everyone knew it, but no one wanted to be the first inside the buildings—where the true carnage might be awaiting them.

A short time later, they noticed the prints in the earth. They had come across drake prints throughout their search, even before they had entered the citadel, but not so many as this. There were prints *everywhere*, many of them bloodstained. Sharissa was intrigued despite herself by the thoroughness with which the drakes appeared to have scoured this area.

At the clan master's command, two of the remaining warriors rode forward for a piece and vanished around some buildings.

"Where did you send them?" Sharissa asked, not liking anything that lessened the strength of their party.

"To verify something for me. They will be in no danger. The other gateway is not far from here."

"And us, Father?" Gerrod asked, his eyes darting here and there as if he expected a hundred Lochivans to leap out at them.

"We dismount. I need see no more of the yard. It is time to investigate the buildings."

Knowing the futility of arguing, Sharissa and her companions dismounted in silence. Two Tezerenee took charge of the steeds. As the sorceress smoothed her clothing, she happened to glance up at Darkhorse.

She could see *through* him!

"Darkhorse!" All thought of the ghostly citadel pushed aside for the time being, Sharissa ran over to the eternal and tried to touch him. His eyes were closed, and his form seemed wracked with pain.

"I . . . I am weaker than I supposed, Sharissa! I fear that I will be very ineffective for quite some time!"

"But you *will* be all right?"

"I . . . believe so." Darkhorse opened wide his eyes and glared at his former captor. "My apologies . . . for . . . any inconvenience, dragonlord! I do not know what could be the matter . . . with me!"

What remark the patriarch was to make would remain lost, for the two Tezerenee given the unenviable task appeared around the corner. They seemed anxious but not frightened, a good sign as far as the sorceress was concerned. Anything that frightened the Tezerenee was not something she had any desire to face.

The two dismounted the instant they reached the party. Both knelt before their lord.

"Speak."

One warrior, taller and thinner than his companion, said, "It is as you supposed, Lord Barakas. There is a great trail formed by the gathering of many drakes and leading out of the other gateway. The gateway itself is far more battered than the one we entered by. I would have to say a great exodus occurred here."

Barakas looked around to make certain the others had heard. His gaze fell for an extended time upon Sharissa.

"How long ago was this exodus?" Gerrod asked.

The second Tezerenee looked at his master, who nodded permission to him to reply to Gerrod's question. "A week, we decided. A few traces are older, a few younger."

"It started so soon . . ." Barakas studied the two scouts. "You saw no life."

"More blood and the remains of a riding drake, my lord," the first one responded. "It still wore part of a bridle. One of its own had killed it."

One of its own or something just as savage? Sharissa wondered if the same thought was going through the mind of Barakas. Why would two riding drakes struggle? They were trained to work beside each other. It would take fear or bloodlust of unbelievable proportions to make them turn on each other.

"We have our answer, then," the patriarch announced, turning so that he looked at everyone. "There was danger and people died, but the many trails indicate that the bulk of the clan has abandoned the citadel, choosing to go south, I suppose."

"Why would they abandon this place?" Gerrod asked, ever, it seemed, seeking to estrange himself further from his progenitor. "Something must have made them. Where is it, Father? Where did it go? Not after them, I think. There is still something here. Can you not feel it?"

"I feel nothing."

"So I have noticed."

Barakas reached for his son, but the warlock was too swift. Sharissa came between them.

"Stop it! Lord Barakas, if the others rode off, we should follow them, not remain here and risk encountering trouble that might prove too great for us to handle!"

The patriarch cooled down. "Perhaps you are correct. Perhaps we should—" He broke off. "Alcia!"

"What about her?"

He looked at the sorceress as if perplexed she would ask such a thing. "She's in the great hall!"

The rest of the party stirred, wondering how the lord of the Tezerenee could know that. Sharissa hesitated, then asked, "What makes you say that?"

"I heard her voice, of course!" Barakas looked at his companions as if they had all turned deaf. "She just called to us! She needs our assistance!"

Sharissa and the others stared at him.

"Bah! My ears are still good even if yours aren't!" He turned away and started toward the building in which the great hall lay. Though they had not heard anything, three of his warriors followed close behind. The other two remained with the riding drakes. Sharissa's companions looked to her, knowing that her oath bound them here.

"We could leave now," suggested the elf. "There seems nothing to accomplish here, and I do not like the thought of following someone who imagines voices."

Gerrod turned and stared after his father. "I *thought* I heard a sound like a voice . . ."

Sharissa frowned. "Why didn't you say anything?"

"Because I made out nothing distinct. Certainly not my mother calling us! I think I'd recognize that!"

"I wish I could *feel* anything that made sense!" she muttered. Sighing, the spellcaster started after the vanished Tezerenee. "I think we'd better follow him."

Something large hissed. Sharissa ignored it, thinking it merely one of their mounts, when Faunon put a hand on her shoulder and hurriedly whispered, "Sharissa! To your left!"

Staring out from the broken doorway of one of the nearby buildings, a savage-looking drake blinked at them. It was more than twice the size of the steeds, a true dragon. From the way it moved, it had just woken up. Reptilian eyes glared at the tiny figures and then at the suddenly apprehensive mounts. The two Tezerenee struggled to maintain control over the simple beasts.

"We rode right by that thing!" whispered Gerrod. "My father seems to have grown lax in his abilities as a warrior and a leader. He should have never—"

"Never mind that now!" Faunon touched the hilt of his sword, but then thought better of it. He glanced at the riding drakes, and Sharissa realized he was looking for a bow and quiver. There were at least three, but reaching them meant attracting the further attention of the waking horror.

With a hopeful smile on his face, the elf winked at her and took a step toward the mounts.

The dragon focused on him, growing more alert with each second.

"Go, elf!" urged Gerrod. "It will come for us soon enough! If the bow increases our odds, it will be worth it!"

As if the hooded Tezerenee's words were its signal, the dragon broke through the wall, hissing as it struggled to drag its entire body through the gap it had made. Faunon rushed to the nearest bow and started removing it and the quiver from the shifting drake.

Sharissa knew that he would get only one shot off. She also knew that Faunon could have used his sorcerous abilities but feared that the repercussions, as he had hinted, might be worse than the attack. The sorceress, on the other hand, had no such qualms.

She raised her hand and repeated the spell she had cast on Lochivan.

Dust rose around the dragon. It roared, snapped at the particles flying about, and then shook its head.

A wild force struck Sharissa and sent her falling back. Gerrod only partly succeeded in stopping her fall. The hard earth jarred her and made it impossible to focus.

"It's moving faster!" Gerrod roared. Through blurred eyes, she noticed his face strain with concentration, as if he sought to unleash a spell of his own despite his acknowledged aversion to the magic of this world. Behind them, the two sentries were shouting loudly, but she could not turn her head enough to see either them or Faunon.

A large, dark shape burst into her field of vision and raced to meet the charging leviathan head-on. Even with her vision watery, Sharissa recognized Darkhorse. "No!"

Weak from the teachings of Lord Barakas, the shadow steed was nearly little more than a true shadow. Yet, his presence could not be denied by the dragon, who moved to deal with this sudden rival.

"He will hold it, but for how long?" the warlock asked as he pulled Sharissa to her feet. "That thing struck back at you with power far greater than Lochivan's, did it not?"

"Yes . . . that's right."

"As I feared." She felt him stiffen and looked to see what bothered him so.

Another dragon, identical to the first, was climbing out of the ruins of another building behind the party.

"It is as if they were waiting for us to come!" Faunon, the quiver looped over him and the arrow already nocked, drew a bead on Darkhorse's adversary. He let loose instantly, but the dragon, as if sensing the new assault, somehow twisted enough so that the arrow, destined for one of its eyes, bounced off thick scale. "Rheena!"

The riding drakes were beyond control. Several hissed at the coming monstrosities, making Sharissa wonder if it might not be better to let them loose. Surely a dozen of them could easily dispatch these two.

A third hiss told them that things might not be so simple after all.

They're coming from everywhere! she realized.

There was a scream from where the Tezerenee had been struggling with their steeds. Gerrod suddenly pulled her to the side, toward the steps where Barakas had gone. Faunon followed almost instantly, nearly falling on her. A huge brown-green form dashed past her.

"The riding drakes have broken free!" she warned her companions needlessly.

"Much to the regret of all, especially the two poor fools my father left to hold them!" Gerrod rose, pulling the other two up with him. "One was trampled. I don't know what happened to the other, but I know that was his scream!"

Around them, chaos was coming to full bloom. The freed drakes scattered, some running and some turning to fight the intruders.

More dragons were creeping out of the ruins.

"This is mad!" Gerrod coughed as the dust raised by one of the drakes floated about the trio. "How could we not even sense so many? Where did they come from?"

"Don't you realize, Vraad?" Faunon snarled, waving an arm in the general direction of the creatures. "These are your loving relations!"

"Impossible!"

A familiar laugh echoed in their heads.

A new race of kings . . . it said, the voice dwindling in intensity with each word, as if the renegade guardian were fleeing now that its work was done.

"So much for the vaunted power of the other guardians and their masters!" the warlock muttered. "That thing has been waiting for us! It probably kept them silent so it could teach us a fatal lesson for not obeying it before!"

So it seemed, although Sharissa could not see how the outcast could have known they would come when they did. Still, that was a worry for another time. Right now their lives were all at stake. The rampaging monsters were all around them, cutting off any hope of escape through the gateways. It was doubtful that they could have outrun the horrors anyway.

"This way!" Faunon called, pointing in the direction the patriarch and the others had gone. There was still the question of what was happening to them. If the outcast guardian was responsible for the voice the patriarch had though was his bride's, then it could be nothing good.

They started up the steps and were halfway when she recalled Darkhorse. He was still engaged with the one dragon, dancing about and entrancing it much the way a snake might entrance its victim. The eternal, however, had little strength now, and against a creature that had already proven its natural magical abilities, the shadow steed stood a good chance of being defeated. Whether he could die or not was something Sharissa had no desire to discover.

"Darkhorse! This way!"

He seemed not to hear her. She began retracing her steps, but Faunon and Gerrod pulled her back up.

"Look before you run!" Faunon reprimanded her. He turned her head so that she could see the dragon making its way toward them. Unlike the others, who seemed more a mix of browns and greens like the riding drakes, it had a silverish cast to it and eyes that gleamed with more intelligence. It avoided the battling drakes and stalked the tiny figures with true purpose.

"But *Darkhorse* . . ."

"You know he only stays because you do! He'll leave when you are safe! Take her, Tezerenee!"

Gerrod did, securing a hold while the elf readied his bow. With the elf backing them up, they continued to climb the steps. Faunon released an arrow once he was at the top, but it hit just before the dragon's forepaws. The shot brought them a few seconds, but little more.

"And I used to pride myself on my shooting!"

"I think the dragon might have had something to do with it!" Gerrod suggested as he pushed Sharissa on. "I felt a tug, as if it made use of sorcery in its defense!"

"Rheena pray for us if it did!"

The doors of the building were open and, to their surprise, undamaged. Once through, Sharissa and Gerrod closed them while Faunon stood back and kept watch just in case. When the doors were finally bolted, they took a moment to catch their breaths.

"Where . . . where can my father be with all this commotion?" the young Tezerenee asked between gulps of air.

"The great . . . the great hall is where he said he would be," Sharissa suggested. "It's our best bet!"

"And then what? Sharissa, do you think your sorcery can teleport us out of here?"

She had already wondered about that and suspected that the answer was no.

Even if the guardian was truly gone, the wild magic inherent in the dragons outside was wreaking havoc upon her own abilities. There was also Faunon's warning about utilizing their powers during this time.

If it came to life or death, however, she would do what she could and damn the consequences.

They jumped away from the door as a massive weight pushed against it, causing the hinges to creak dangerously.

"*Gerrod!*" a voice without called.

"Dragon's blood!" the warlock nearly choked as he stepped farther and farther back from the doors. His pale visage was the color of bone. "I know that voice, but which one? Esad? Logan?"

"It hardly matters! I think the time has come to retreat from the doors!" Faunon suggested. "Sharissa! Do you know the way we have to take?"

He had only had limited access to this building. Gerrod had never even been inside here. Sharissa was the only one familiar with the building's design, not that the path was that difficult. Time was, however, of the essence.

She nodded. "Just follow me!"

Ignoring the severity of their predicament, the elf asked, "Do you think we'd rather wait around here?"

They could hear the dragon trying to break its way in as they ran, and it was obvious that the doors would not hold too long. Sharissa hoped to find the patriarch and then lead the party to the upper floors, where it would be impossible for the dragons to reach them. So far, they had seen none with wings, but that might not remain so. If these dragons were what she thought they were, then wings might be merely the next step in their evolution.

Together we can do something, she kept telling herself. *With my power, Faunon's, and what the rest can contribute, we should be able to teleport us all to safety.*

Should was the optimum word.

So engrossed was she in the planning of their escape that she nearly fell across the body lying across the closed doors of their destination.

"Careful!" Faunon caught her. It seemed that someone was always catching her. Sharissa felt brief pangs of frustration, but forgot her aggravation with herself when she saw who—or rather, *what*—she had nearly tripped over.

It was one of the Tezerenee. His head had been nearly severed from his body, but with good reason. With his helm off to one side, the trio could see that he, like Lochivan, had progressed through a part of the transformation.

"He was perfectly normal when we last saw him!" Gerrod objected.

"But he isn't now!" Sharissa forgot about the body and rushed to the doors. "Help me get these open . . . and pray we don't find another like him waiting for us!"

They heard yet another hiss down one of the corridors. Heavy thuds warned them in advance that this part of the citadel was not empty.

The doors proved not to be bolted, but something had been placed behind them that made it difficult at first to push them open. The combined efforts of the three, not to mention the knowledge that another dragon was only minutes from discovering them, proved superior to whatever held back the doors.

Sharissa peeked in as the doors spread apart and barely held back a gasp.

Lord Barakas stood with his sword out before him, as still as a marble statue. The great hall was in ruins, and she saw part of the mangled corpse of one of the patriarch's remaining two men. The other was nowhere to be seen, although it was almost a certainty that he, like the first, was dead.

Facing the clan master from where the thrones had once stood was the largest of the dragons that any of them had yet seen in the citadel.

"Now what do we do?" Gerrod asked.

The hissing in the corridors had multiplied. Sharissa did not think they had any choice, especially since it sounded as if the outer doors were beginning to give. She gritted her teeth and replied, "One dragon is always better than two or three!"

They stepped inside, and Faunon and the warlock quickly closed and bolted the doors behind them.

Barakas and the dragon before him had still not moved. It was as if they were waiting to see who would look away first. The dragon, a huge, emerald and black beast, bled from a number of cuts around its eyes and throat. Part of the patriarch's armor was in tatters, and he looked to be bleeding, although it was hard to say since his back was turned to them. Sharissa wondered why the dragon looked so familiar and then realized the monster resembled the ancient dragonlord in the ruins of the founders' settlements. Was this what the renegade had wanted the Tezerenee to become?

Reptilian eyes glanced the trio's way, but Barakas, oddly enough, did not choose to strike. The dragon, turning its attention back to the patriarch, almost appeared *disappointed* in his lack of effort.

Barakas, never taking his eyes from the dragon, called back, "Get out of here! I command you! Go on without me!"

"We would like to, Father," Gerrod responded with a touch of sarcasm in his tone, "but the family insists we stay for dinner!"

Outside the great hall, they could hear the hissing of more than one drake.

"Gerrrrod?" The dragon leaned forward, completely ignoring the armed Tezerenee, yet Barakas still made no move. "Gerrrod."

"Gods!" The warlock stumbled back as the jaws opened, and they stared into the beast's huge maw.

The behemoth suddenly recoiled. Sharissa thought it looked *ashamed* and horrified by Gerrod's reaction. The mighty head turned and reptilian eyes stared down at the patriarch. "Let it be donnne!"

Before their eyes, the dragon struck at Lord Barakas, but in so clumsy a manner that its lower jaw missed the top of the clan master's helm by several inches. The attack also left the dragon's throat completely open, but even then, Barakas hesitated before striking. When he finally attacked, it was as if his draconian adversary had purposely left itself open, for it delayed in withdrawing its head.

The patriarch's sword, propelled by his tremendous strength, went up through the throat, the back of the jaws, and directly into the brain of the beast.

The silence of the tableau lent an eerie feel to it. Making no sound despite the horrible pain it felt, the dragon pulled back. Barakas remained where he had been since the threesome had entered, defying almost certain death if the thrashings of the dying creature proved very violent.

Yet, the dragon did not thrash. It twitched as it moved, and the blood, a trail that began on the chest and hands of the clan master and continued back to the dais, continued to pour from the wound like some hideous river. With so much pain evident, it was surprising to all of them that the dragon seemed almost at peace.

Heavy thuds against the doors reminded Sharissa and her companions of their own danger. They moved closer to the center of the great hall. Barakas still had no eyes for them; he only seemed interested in the death of the leviathan. As it began to settle into the final moments of life, the patriarch walked slowly toward the dragon's head. The eyes, already glazing, watched him with what interest the dying beast could muster. It made no attempt to snap at him. Barakas knelt beside it and, removing his gauntlets, began *caressing* his adversary on the neck.

"Lord Barakas," Sharissa dared call out. "We need to leave this place! The others will be through those doors before long!"

He looked up at them. There was no life in his voice as he said, "I killed her."

"You cannot kill them all, though, Father!" the warlock argued, evidently thinking that the patriarch was intending to take on each and every beast as it came.

Sharissa understood what Gerrod did not and tried to keep him from saying anything more. "Lord Barakas! Is there another way out of here that might lead us to a safer place?"

"I killed her because she asked me," he replied, rising and staring at his son.

"It was a struggle for her to keep her own mind, but she was always the stron-gest besides myself. I almost thought she might have fought back the foul magic as I had done."

Gerrod's eyes jerked from his father to the dead beast. "Dragon's blood, Fa-ther! that . . . that *cannot* be—"

"Yes, Gerrod. That is my Alcia."

"That *thing* is—was mother?" The younger Tezerenee, Sharissa realized, had never taken the transformations and followed them to their logical conclusions. If one Tezerenee was affected, they all were, even the lord and lady who ruled. Barakas had survived through his incredible will. The Tezerenee still back at the caverns had probably survived in part because of his very presence. Of course, there was also the possibility that the renegade guardian had acted more cau-tiously in the caverns, considering that the region was a former stronghold of its creators.

A downpour of heavy thuds left cracks in the walls and ceiling of the cham-ber. Sharissa stood directly in front of Barakas and forced him to look at her. "Barakas! *Is* there a place we can go from here where the dragons won't be able to reach us?"

Behind the helm, his face screwed up in thought. He almost looked pained by the effort. She pitied him for what he had been forced to do, but there was no helping Lady Alcia anymore. Now was the time to worry about those still living.

He finally shook his head. "No. Nothing. The other entrances lead out into the main corridors."

"Which we know to be filled with our friends," Faunon remarked. He had the bow ready. The first drake through would have little room to navigate, mak-ing it a perfect target for one of his skill.

"We're trapped, then," she said. "Unless we teleport from here."

"Very risky!"

She indicated the buckling doors. "Compared to that?"

"A communal effort will be needed. I doubt I have the power to either tele-port us or open a gate long enough for us to go through. Do you think you could do it?"

"No." That had been one of her first considerations. A communal effort was the only choice she had discovered. Sharissa had hoped the elf might suggest another. "We'd best get to it, then! Gerrod! Are you up to it?"

The warlock slowly nodded. "Yes. Anything to be away from this damna-tion! What about my erstwhile father?"

The clan master had retreated into his other world again. His dreams had been shattered, and one of the strongest driving forces behind that dream, the Lady Alcia, was dead at his own hands. If anything could have broken the powerful Vraad's will, this could . . . and *had*.

"Hold on to him. We'll take him along. I can't leave him in here like this."

Hinges creaked as the dragons pounded away. Sharissa felt weak probes searching for them. The drakes were going through a change that entailed more than physical transformation. They were being adapted, as the guardians had said, and part of that adaptation was an affinity for the sorcery of this world. Sharissa hoped that the remnants of her party would be gone before the dragons became too skilled.

They stood in a small circle, holding each other's hands. Sharissa acted as the focus, drawing strength from her companions, even the somnambulant lord of the Tezerenee. Faunon suggested drawing an image from his mind and sending them there, but she lacked the concentration to do so. That left only a blind teleport, risky but their only hope.

"Wait!" Gerrod released her hand and dug into his clothing. He removed a crystal identical to the ones he had given to his companions earlier. "Take this and concentrate on the elf's thoughts!"

"What will happen?"

"I gave you the other ones because the Quel use them for reading and translating thoughts! They work from a distance, and I thought it would be a good way for me to find you if we got separated. I should have told you, but that's not important now! If you concentrate on your elf, what he thinks will be transmitted to you!"

She took the crystal and did as he described, finding with joy that Faunon's thought image was so clear that it was almost as if they were already there. She focused on the location.

The dragons' probes grew stronger. Inhuman emotions began to seep through, biting at her concentration.

The chamber faded.

The chamber reappeared.

"No!" They fell in a heap, shaken by the reversal. Sharissa felt a mind that she knew to be draconian laugh at them. *Do not leave ussss, Sharisssssa Zereeee! Do not take our lordssss from ussss!*

From the way Gerrod jerked, she knew he had heard the dragon, also. It was the same one that he had identified as one of his brothers.

The doors burst open, swinging back so hard they crashed into the walls and sent bits of rock flying.

The dragons swarmed toward them, the silver one in the front.

XXI

A DARK, FLEET phantom burst forth from the ground before the silver dragon.

"Back, lizard! Back or I shall stamp your pretty face into the rock!"

Out of surprise more than anything else, the huge monsters stopped. The silver dragon hissed at Darkhorse and roared, "Awaaaay from ourrr frrriendsss, demon! Awaaay from our tenderrr little frrriends!"

"I think not!" The eternal struck the floor with his front hooves, sending lightning sparks at the foremost drakes. The silver one hissed again and backed away.

"Sharissa! Come to me! You and your companions! Hurry now!"

Their eyes on the leader of the horde, Sharissa and the others rushed to Darkhorse's side. Gerrod had to lead his father, who simply stared at the dragons and muttered something that sounded like "Tezree" to Sharissa's ears.

"Be ready!" the shadow steed whispered when they were by him. "If I cannot—"

He never finished. The silver dragon, eyes on the party, caught sight of the great form lying limp across the farmost part of the hall.

"Motherrr!" The outraged roar echoed throughout the citadel.

The silver dragon charged.

"Too late, my friend!" Darkhorse bellowed.

The great hall and its foul inhabitants winked out of existence—to be replaced by a lightly wooded land.

"Praise Dru!" The eternal sank to his knees in the high grass. Sharissa quickly looked around and saw that everyone else was accounted for. She exhaled and hugged Faunon, so relieved was she to find they were safe.

With some reluctance, the two of them finally separated. Gerrod, still guiding his oblivious father around, curtly asked, "And where are we now?"

The area they stood in the midst of was part of a fairly flat region. Far, far to the north, the sorceress thought she could make out a mountain chain, although whether it was the same mountains in which lay the caverns was impossible to tell from this distance. At the moment, she only cared to know if they were safe or not.

"I think I recognize this," Faunon said, scanning the area again. "I think we may be south of the citadel."

"Far south?" she asked.

"Far enough."

"Unless they have the ability to track our magical trail," the warlock interjected, eyeing the elf in a way that Sharissa did not like. "It was how I ended up in all this madness, tracking the trail he left behind."

Looking at Darkhorse, Sharissa was horrified to see that he was becoming *transparent.* "Darkhorse! What's happening to you?"

"I . . . fear that I have almost exhausted my . . . myself. My being. The dragonlord . . . was . . . not lacking in his . . . his enthusiasm when he punished me!" He eyed Barakas, who stared at the trees without seeing them. "I cannot say I regret his present circumstances! I would wish him worse, but I know you would not care for such hate!"

"I can understand your bitterness, Darkhorse. Don't think I can't."

"Perhaps. That does not matter now. Give me but a moment and I will send you on the final leg of your journey." The ebony stallion slowly rose, and his form solidified a bit.

She was not certain she understood. "Where are you sending us?"

He snorted. "Where else? Home to your father and his mate!"

"But . . ." Her eyes met Faunon's. "But what about you?"

"What about me?" the elf asked, moving closer. In the background, she saw Gerrod turn in open disgust.

"Can you make it back to your people?"

"If I was going there." He gave her a weary smile. "I thought I was going with you."

It was what she wanted to hear, but she still could not accept his decision. "You probably won't be able to return here! The ocean voyage is deadly!"

"I have no reason to return, Sharissa. The elders were hardly even interested in my expedition. As far as they were concerned, this was the latest in a series of new masters of the land, nothing unusual. They agreed to our going more because they knew we would go anyway than because they really cared." He cut off any further objections with a long kiss.

Sharissa reluctantly broke away. "Then there's nothing holding us back. Darkhorse can—"

Gerrod, buried so deep in his cloak that his features were almost indistinguishable, interrupted. "I have a boon to ask of you, Sharissa."

"What?" Now that it had been decided that they were all leaving, she wanted to be done with the spell. To see her father and stepmother . . . to live a peaceful existence, at least for a time . . .

"Take care of my father. In his present state, he is useless to all, even himself. Someone needs to watch over him."

"And what about you, Vraad?" Faunon asked, turning a critical eye on the warlock. "Where will *you* be that you cannot care for him?"

"Here. I am not going with you."

Even the elf was stunned by the answer. Sharissa took a step toward Gerrod, but he retreated a like distance. Finally, she was able to ask, "But *why*? Why would you want to stay here?"

The sorceress had no way of knowing if he looked her in the eye or not, so dark were the shadows summoned up by the deep hood. "My interests lie here. My studies and such. Besides, my presence will only be a further strain on the powers of the demon horse." He shrugged, trying to be nonchalant where Sharissa could see by his very posture he was the opposite. "I have nothing I need return to."

Knowing Gerrod as she did, Sharissa understood the futility of trying to argue him out of his decision. Yet, she tried to come to him again, wanting to at least bid him a proper farewell and thank him for all he had suffered for her sake. The warlock would have none of her thanks, though. When she took another step, he shook his head.

"No time! He grows weaker and weaker, and all of us should be gone before the dragons or something else finds us."

At mention of him, Darkhorse steadied himself. He did not look at the hooded Tezerenee, but rather at those who *were* going.

"Where will you go, Gerrod?" Sharissa asked, wanting, at the very least, that much from him.

He would not give her that satisfaction, only saying to her, "I have an idea." The warlock raised a hand in farewell. "Good luck to you, Sharissa. I shall always remember you and your father."

"The time has come!" the eternal announced. "This will be our only chance, so prepare yourselves!"

Sharissa slipped her hand into Faunon's and drew the silent Barakas to them with her other. She met the elf's smile with one of her own, but then turned to stare at Gerrod one last time.

The warlock was already gone.

"Ger—" she started.

The world winked out of existence—and winked back in the next moment.

"We are here," announced a very weary voice. "I'm sorry. This is the best I can do."

"Where are we?" Sharissa did not recognize the region, but there were many parts of the other continent, too many parts, that she had no knowledge of.

Faunon looked up. "The sun has shifted greatly. More than a third of a day." His tone spoke of his admiration for the eternal's efforts. "We have traveled quite a distance!"

"This . . . this is the continent on which . . . on which your folk make their colony, Sharissa. I regret that I . . . I could not bring you there, but it is probably for the best. I have no desire to see them again." He rose, his very form wavering in the light wind. "Now it is time for *me* to take my leave."

"Not you too!" Was she to lose everyone now that she was almost home?

"I am sorry to leave you in these straits, but I am at my end. I *must* go, Sharissa." The shadow steed dipped his head in his equivalent of a bow. "I must replenish myself, and that cannot be done in your world."

"When will you be back?"

He almost did not answer, but, seeing her face, the eternal gave in. "Not, I think, in your lifetime. Not even in the lifetimes of your grandchildren, I suspect."

Suddenly, the woods seemed a very dismal and dark place. "Father will be upset with you. You only just came back into his life."

A stentorian sigh. "I will miss both of you. Give him my gratitude for his teaching and his friendship. I will treasure them both as I mend myself."

"*Will* you return?"

"Someday. Good-bye."

Sharissa blinked. Darkhorse was no longer there. She felt a sudden urgency and quickly reached for Faunon. "You won't leave me now, will you?"

"Hardly. They would have to drag me away fighting."

The Vraad sorceress restudied the lands around them, frowning. "I still don't know where we are." The wind blew her hair in her face. She pushed it aside and added, "We could be on the far side of the continent."

Faunon squinted to the west. "There is a hill that stands out among the others in that direction. If we climb it, we should be able to see for mile upon mile."

"Climb it?" Sharissa did not feel up to breathing, much less climbing.

"Walk to it and climb it. Both a must, I regret to say, my Vraad, unless *you* have the will and strength to teleport us there. I think my own reserves a little doubtful at the moment."

Her heart was willing, but that was hardly sufficient. Sharissa shielded her eyes and studied the descending sun. As much as she wanted to be home, there were other things to consider—their helpless companion, for one. Barakas was even now simply standing and staring at his gauntleted hands—which were still *covered* in the blood of the transformed Lady Alcia.

That settled it for her. "I have a better idea. I think it best if perhaps we stayed here, rested the night, and proceeded in the morning. We can't be very close to the colony or else I would have sensed something. Tomorrow, we'll both be better. Besides,"—she indicated the patriarch. As he stared at his bloody fists, he continued to mumble his nearly incomprehensible litany. The sorceress wondered how long he would remain that way—"I've got to help him wash away that blood, if only for *my* sanity!"

Faunon accepted her judgment and volunteered to find wood for a fire and food for their much-abused stomachs. He pulled out the crystal that Gerrod had given to him. "Do you still have yours?"

"I do. I cupped it when the spell failed. I couldn't bear facing Gerrod if I lost a second one." Now she would never have to worry about that. The somber warlock was far, far away and would likely never return. She considered their present location. "There must be water around somewhere. That's what we should look for first."

They were in luck. A small stream lay only a short distance from where Darkhorse had brought them. It was little more than a thin trickle, but even that seemed overwhelming to the suddenly thirsty duo. Even Barakas found interest in drinking. Sharissa had hoped that the cool water would snap the patriarch back to his senses, but he merely wiped his mouth and sat down by the stream. The former clan master had not even removed his gloves, so detached was he from everything.

Some sun still remained. Faunon disappeared into the forest, moving with the speed and quiet Sharissa had always imagined his kind capable of. She, meanwhile, started the task of helping Lord Barakas clean his armor. Had anyone told her that she would someday be doing this, the tall woman would have laughed. Now, it seemed like the correct thing to do. The patriarch was little more than a baby at present.

Her efforts were more or less wasted. The blood had already stained and dried on his clothing. She was, at best, able to lessen the horrifying effect of his appearance, but anyone taking a closer look would see the telltale stain on the armor. Tomorrow, when her will was stronger, she would use sorcery to eliminate what remained.

Barakas noted her efforts in an almost casual manner, occasionally breaking from his mutterings, which now sounded like "Prrr . . ." and "Tze . . . ," and telling her, "They won't come out. The blood's seeped to my skin. It will never come out."

After she had given up, he returned to his same somnambulant state. Sharissa finally brought him over to a tree and let him sit there with his back against the trunk. She then turned to attending to her own needs.

Darkness was now fast approaching, and Faunon was still not back. Sharissa understood how difficult his task might be, but she still began to worry. Even knowing she was here on the other continent, the sorceress feared that the night would somehow separate her from her last and most important companion. Barakas, in his present state, did not even count. She was alone, for all it mattered. Trying not to think of that, the Vraad began picking up fallen branches with which she could start a fire. Sharissa thought of creating one without wood, but even that effort seemed too much. Besides, she had always prided herself on not depending on her abilities when simple physical work was sufficient. To be any other way went against what her father had taught her.

At sundown, Faunon returned. He had wood to add to that which Sharissa had gathered from the nearby area and, most important, berries and a rabbit. She was thankful that he knew how to prepare it; the thought of having to cope with that after trying to wash the blood from Barakas almost made her ill.

The meal was sparse, but sufficient for their present needs. Sharissa gave the patriarch an equal share, which disappeared into his mouth in quick time. She had removed his helm, and so during the meal it proved impossible not to keep searching his face for some response, but the only thing he did when not muttering was screw his face up in thought again. She wondered what it was he was thinking about. There was a desperation in his eyes, that much she could see.

After the meal, they chose to retire. Faunon volunteered the first watch, assuring her that, as an elf, he could rest while still remaining conscious of what was around them. When she gave him a threatening look, he promised that he *would* wake her when her time came. Sharissa did not want him trying to take on the entire task by himself. Faunon was as worn as she was.

Sharissa fell asleep almost before her head even touched the ground. The dream began in that same instant. It was a chaotic chase of sorts, with the weary sorceress trying to keep ahead of a dark, loathsome thing of mist that stared at her with a thousand eyes. She escaped her horrific pursuer only to walk into the open maw of a great dragon with Gerrod's head upon it. Sharissa turned and fled from this monstrosity, only to hear the vicious laughter of the renegade guardian.

The chase went on and on, monsters and memories mixing in haphazard fashion.

When she jerked away, her first thoughts were of the relief of being freed of the endless cycle. Then she realized what had woken her and wondered whether or not the dreams might have been preferable.

"Nooooo! I am Tezerenee! Tezerenee is power!"

Faunon was already up and running toward the patriarch, who knelt against the tree and held himself so tight that Sharissa wondered if he thought he was going to come apart. His shouts became less and less coherent, reducing to the clan name and "power."

Sharissa moved to his side and tried to get through to him. "Barakas! Listen to me! There's nothing wrong! You're safe here!" It occurred to her that he might be physically injured, but in the chaos no one had looked beyond his outward appearance. "Lord Barakas! What ails you? Tell me and I might be able to help!"

"Tezerenee . . . Powerrr . . ."

"I think he might be calming," suggested Faunon. Barakas seemed to be slipping back into his catatonic state. She hated to see that, but it was better than his wild manner. The patriarch was strong enough to injure both of them.

The worried sorceress leaned closer. "Barakas?"

His movements were lightning, even against those of Faunon. Barakas shoved the two of them aside and, with an animalistic roar, ran for the deepest part of the forest.

"Stop him!" Sharissa cried.

"Too late," her companion muttered, but he tried regardless. The two of them followed the dragonlord's trail, trying to listen for the heavy footfalls that should have been so evident in the silence of night. Yet, the patriarch was as silent as a specter and faster, it seemed, than even the elf.

They gave up the chase only a few minutes later, forced to admit they could not even find his trail. For the elf, a creature of the woods, this was especially exasperating.

"It's as if he floated off or simply vanished! I should be able find *some* trace!"

"Could he . . . could he have become like Lochivan?"

"Could we have missed a dragon?" he responded. "Better yet, could a dragon have missed us?"

She tried to scan the area, but the trees blocked what little light the moons were willing to give them. "He seemed frightened of something!"

"Likely he was reliving his disasters. That would be enough to shake anyone. He might even have been dreaming of the death of his mate."

Tzee . . .

"Did you hear something?" she asked.

"Nothing. I am too worn to even listen. I am sorry, Sharissa, I truly am. If I could find his trail, I would keep going. The only thing I can say is that we could come back here in the morning and see if a trail reveals its secrets to us."

Where might Barakas be by then? Faunon was correct, though. They stood no chance of finding the patriarch. She doubted the light would change things. Barakas was gone. Gone forever, the final victim, Sharissa hoped, of his ambition to create an empire.

The irony was, his legacy *was* an empire—and of the very creature he had raised up as the symbol of his clan.

They returned to their encampment and settled down again. Sleep was not so soon in coming this time, but when it did, Sharissa was thankful to find it deep and dreamless.

Tzee . . .

It was difficult to breathe. Sharissa rolled over, trying to ease the constriction in her lungs.

Tzee . . .

She thought it was a dream at first, but then it occurred to her that if it was, she should not have been thinking so. She should have been enmeshed in it.

Tzee . . .

Rolling onto her back, Sharissa opened her eyes.

Her nightmare stared back at her.

She screamed, and was not ashamed that she did. Anyone would have screamed at the dark, cloudy mass atop her, a mass from which countless eyes peered at her. A sound kept echoing in her head, a sound that originated, the terrified sorceress was certain, from the horror above her.

It was the scream that sent it fleeing. She heard Faunon's voice as he shouted to her and watched in fear and amazement as the unnerving mass rose swiftly and fled into the deep woods. The elf chased after it, but it moved with the grace and daring of the fastest hawks and was gone even before he took a dozen steps.

All the while, Sharissa heard the same nonsensical sound in her head. *Tzee . . . Tzee . . .* The sound did not die away until long after the nightmare was over.

"Sharissa! Rheena, I will never forgive myself for being so stubborn! I broke my vow and tried to take the entire night's watch! It . . . that thing . . . must have come just after I dozed off!"

The sun was just rising, but the Vraad barely noticed it. Though the creature, whatever it was, had fled, she could not help feeling that they were still not alone, that someone else was still watching them.

"I have never seen anything like that!" the elf exclaimed, holding her as much for his comfort as he was for hers. "It made a sound in my head—"

"'Tzee,'" she said. "It kept repeating 'Tzee.'"

"That was it!"

"Tezerenee?" Sharissa whispered to herself.

"What?"

"Nothing." She cared not to think about it any longer. The possibility unnerved her more than the dragons had. She rose from the ground, allowing Faunon to aid her. There was still something not right. "Faunon, do you sense anything?"

His eyes narrowed, and he glanced about the area. "I had not given it much thought, not with that thing around, but . . . could it be it has not left after all?"

That might be the answer, but Sharissa could not accept it. This was something she had felt before, a familiar presence or presences. Not the guardians, but . . .

Stepping away from Faunon, the sorceress faced the seemingly empty woods. "Very well! You've been polite! You've not shocked me! I know you're there now, so you might as well come out!"

"Who are you—" The elf forgot his question as several figures slowly emerged from the trees. There was no place they could have been hiding. One moment they had not been there, the next they were. A dozen at least, all wearing the same long, cowled robes and moving with the symmetry that only they could accomplish. One might have thought they were all of one single mind.

The not-people, the Faceless Ones as others had called them, circled the Vraad and her companion.

"Sharissa! Do they mean us any harm?"

"One never knows," she answered truthfully. "I hope not."

A wan smile touched his face. "Since I have met you, my Vraad, I have been in one constant state of disarray. I never know what to expect!"

"I've fared no better," she admitted. One of the blank-visaged beings separated from the rest and stopped before her. "You're here." The sorceress tried to act as brave as she sounded. "What now? Why have you come?"

In answer, the long figure raised its left hand and pointed. They looked.

Like the Faceless Ones, it was standing where it could not have been standing a breath or two earlier. It was wide enough to admit both of them, though that was not what first drew their attention. As ever, it was the artifact itself that commanded the viewer's gazes. Standing there was an ancient stone archway upon which scurried a multitude of tiny, black, reptilian creatures in one seemingly endless race. The gray, stone archway covered with ivy was only one of many shapes this thing had, but each one radiated a feeling of incredible age and the notion that this structure was more than the portal it appeared to be. This was a thing *alive*.

"My father calls it the Gate," she informed Faunon. "A capital on the noun. He always felt it was more of a name, not a description."

"Is it truly alive?"

A shrug. "Was that thing that attacked us alive? I'm beginning to think that this is a world as insane as Nimth."

The leader pointed again.

"It wants us to enter, I think, Sharissa. What do you suggest?"

She did not trust the Faceless Ones completely anymore. They had an agenda of their own, and she was certain it did not always match that of her folk. Still, she could think of no reason to refuse—and wondered then if the cowled beings would even let her. "I think we should go through. I think it might be for the best."

He squeezed her hand. "We go through together. I have no desire to be left behind."

That thought frightened her. Would the not-people do that to her? Did Faunon have no place in their plans? Sharissa tightened her grip and nodded to the one before them. "Together, then."

Acting as if it wanted to assuage their fears, the leader led the way to the living portal. The featureless figure did not even pause. As it walked through the arch, they saw a flash and then the image of a building that the sorceress had no trouble recognizing.

Her face lit up. "Follow it! Now!"

They fairly leaped through.

On the other side, she paused and took a deep breath. Faunon caught the smile on her face and relaxed. "Are we there?"

She indicated the magnificent citadel on the top of the hill. Between the two and the grand structure was a well-groomed field of high grass and blossoming flowers. Sharissa could not recall a sight that had ever filled her with such relief and happiness. She started to run, pulling Faunon along and shouting to him, "This is home!"

So thrilled was Sharissa that she would later have trouble recalling the trek from where they had materialized to the gates where her father and stepmother had been waiting.

"THEY WANTED US outside," Ariela told her stepdaughter. "We wondered why. I often wish they would at least create mouths with which to talk."

"They might have to explain too much, then," Sharissa returned. "I don't think they would like that."

The foursome stood in the courtyard of the citadel that was the main point of Dru Zeree's pocket universe. They had spent the last two hours sitting and talking, learning what they could from one another about events here and overseas. Her father had offered them food and drink immediately, recognizing their need for both. Sharissa cast the simple spell herself, wanting to taste the pleasure of having her concentration and strength at more reasonable levels. She noted that it also seemed easier in general to complete a spell here than it had on the other continent. She pondered the theory that the land or the guardians might have had something to do with that, but decided not to mention it to her father for now.

Dru Zeree gave his daughter another long hug. "I thought I'd never see you again! When Gerrod vanished, I wasn't certain whether he would find you! He was my only hope." The master mage looked a bit uncomfortable as he added, "I'm sorry he didn't come back."

Ariela saved Sharissa the trouble of responding by turning attention to Faunon. "I thought I had seen the last of my own kind. I hope that Sharissa will allow you a minute now and then that I can usurp! It would be pleasant to discuss elfin life once in a while."

"To be sure. You can tell me what it will be like living among the legendary,

cursed Vraad. So far, the experience has been mixed." Faunon smiled quickly so
that no one would think he was having regrets.

"Perhaps you can start that now," Dru suggested, putting an arm around
Sharissa. "I would like to talk to my daughter for a few moments. Not long, I
promise you. Both of you still need rest."

"I'd like to sleep for a month or so," the younger Zeree admitted.

"Only a short conversation, then."

Faunon gave his thanks to the sorcerer for all the latter had done for him
and allowed himself to be led away by the Lady Zeree, who knew that her
husband would relate to her the essentials of the conversation when they were
alone later.

Dru turned and admired some of the fantastic, sculptured bushes in the
courtyard. So skillfully shaped, the animals they represented seemed ready to
frolic. Such frivolity, however, was far from the spellcaster's mind.

"So the clan of the dragon is no more."

She walked beside him. "In a sense, the clan of the dragon now lives up to
its name."

His smile held little humor. "I suppose so. I don't know whether to feel
sorry for them or fear for us. We will have to make some changes, and I don't
think everyone will agree to them. Since the departure of Barakas, Silesti's been
talking of taking his followers and establishing a second colony."

"That would be foolish!"

Dru shrugged. "It would be their choice. The triumvirate no longer has a
purpose in his eyes."

"But, if there does one day come trouble from the dragons . . ."

"By that time, Sharissa, we will hopefully be prepared. Let us not also forget
that trouble might come from unseen directions, too. The children of the drake
might prove our allies some day."

She looked at him in disbelief. "Those things? Never! Father, if you had
been there, seen Lochivan change and heard the voice of the silver dragon . . .
you'd never say what you just did!"

He steered the two of them toward the direction that the Lady Zeree and
Faunon had gone. "The Dragon of the Depths was here for a brief time. It
left a simple message, but until you arrived and told us of events, I had no idea
what the guardian was talking about."

Sharissa waited, knowing her father would continue.

"The guardian said that I should take heart, that each race of kings began as
tyrants and monsters but only this one can be taught to go beyond that. I asked
what that meant and where you, Sharissa, were. The guardian ignored my pleas,

though, and simply finished by saying that change *never* ends and we, more than anyone else, can shape our own future."

Her father frowned, still mulling over the possible meanings of the statements. Sharissa, knowing that the colonists also faced the founders' adaptations, understood better, but decided that explaining could wait until things had calmed again.

"That was all?" she asked.

"No, before that the sentinel warned that I should watch the Faceless Ones. Nothing more. I'd almost forgotten that."

"And where are they?" She had not seen one since crossing. Even the one who had preceded them had not been in the field when they crossed.

"Around. They appear totally uninterested in your arrival."

"They hide their true feelings well." She paused and, while he waited with fatherly patience, admired the peace and serenity of the moment. So much had happened and so much was still to happen. The changes wrought upon the Tezerenee might look minor in comparison. Her own experiences had changed her forever, giving her an even wider realization of the importance of the colony's survival and the place she might make for herself and her family. Burying herself in her work was fine, but it meant she missed some of the more subtle alterations. That would change. It *had* to change.

The children of the drake have their future, the determined woman thought. *Now it's time to ensure that we do, too.*

Tomorrow would be soon enough, Sharissa decided. At the very least, she deserved *one* day of relaxation, one day to rebuild her strength for the coming onslaughts of change. She hoped Faunon would not regret coming with her.

Sharissa hoped *she* would not regret coming back.

"Shall we find the others?" her father asked, perhaps thinking that she was so tired that she was beginning to drift off in his arms.

"Let us do that," the sorceress said, stirring herself and smiling at the elder Zeree. "And promise me that today we will all do nothing! Absolutely nothing!"

"If that's what you wish. Now that you're home, however, you will have all the time you want to relax and recover."

Her response was to kiss her father on the cheek. As they departed the courtyard in search of the two elves, Sharissa thought that between family and the future, she would hardly have time to relax and do nothing after this day was over.

For some reason, it did not bother her that much.

XXII

IN THE GREAT Tyber Mountains, the golden dragon roared. Frustrated and angry at himself, he again took out his anger upon the tattered remnants of a banner and other bits abandoned weeks ago by the few frightened little creatures who had escaped him and his kind. They had fled to the south, but he had chosen not to follow them once they departed the mountains. The Tybers, his struggling memory recalled, had been given to him. *He* was lord here.

So many things strained to burst forth from the fog in his mind. He knew of the sorcery that was his to control, but actually doing so was still beyond him. It was beyond all of his clan. Each day, however, the dragon king knew he grew a little closer to understanding the magic. It was the same with the wings. They had only started growing out of his back in the last few days. Pathetic little things, they would someday aid him in claiming the heavens.

Wings and magic were things he desired; many of the other bits straining to be recognized only confused him. A name, something he, as monarch of this drake clan, did not need. All knew who he was. He had killed two others to establish that claim.

Reegan. Why did it seem so familiar? What were *Tezerenee*? And who was the tiny two-leg that dared be where no other of his kind did? The little creature wrapped itself in a cocoon of sorts and stared at the dragon king as if they knew each other. For reasons his mind could not cope with, the dragon found himself unwilling to chase this little morsel. Since it kept a respectable distance, he let it be. It was a sign of his greatness that he allowed it to live, of course.

The dragon tore at the banner again. There was not much left of it, but he was always careful to leave something. He found he enjoyed mauling the tiny piece of cloth, though why was beyond him. Being what he was, it did not seem important.

Sharp, reptilian eyes noted the shadows that suddenly covered the ground before him. The dragon that had been Reegan looked up and, seeing the winged ones he knew to be mortal enemies, he roared his challenge. Within the vast confines of the mountains, other drakes responded to his summons. The winged ones had taken some of their brethren for slaves, and that was something he could not tolerate even though the bird folk's days were numbered. They might hold a thin advantage now, but the more time that passed, the sooner it would be to the day when the *drakes* ruled all.

The avians were descending around him. They meant to take *him* this time, it seemed. He roared yet again, calling his people and challenging the birds at the same time. When they were close enough for his tastes, the huge dragon charged.

As with the future itself, he would not be denied his place in this land.

SKINS
(A Tale of the Dragonrealm)

Life is only skin deep . . .

I

KALENA'S NOSE TWITCHED. Perhaps it had only to do with the constant smell of decay around them, but the tawny cat woman somehow felt otherwise. She pulled her cloak tight. This place disturbed her, set the very fur on her neck standing on end.

"There's an old keep up on that hill," the bearded human Brom pointed out. "Be as good a place as any to stay."

The third of their party, the hulking, beaked Gnor, simply grunted. Like all Gnor, this seeming cross between an avian and a bear spoke little. Gnor were hired for their brute strength. They had no individual names and did not accept any nicknames from their associates. A Gnor was a Gnor and that was it.

But even the presence of the mountainous creature did nothing to assuage the slim feline. She tugged at her short, black mane, then cursed herself for such a childish action. She, Brom, and the Gnor had spent three years together as successful smugglers and had faced adversity in many shapes and sizes. They had slept in far less appealing locations than an old, abandoned keep.

"We'll have to walk the animals the rest of the way, though," Brom continued, already dismounting. The old breastplate he wore over his shirt rattled. On the front could still be seen the scratched-out shape of a wolf's head. When Brom had relieved the Aramite's corpse of it, the first thing he had done was to remove the hated symbol. No one, not even a smuggler, wanted to be mistaken for something as foul as a wolf raider.

Once they had ruled the continent, but now only a handful of lands still suffered under their command. Centuries of tyranny had been broken by a visitor from beyond the western sea—a magical, shapechanging warrior called the

Gryphon. Under his leadership, the stricken realms had risen up and swarmed over the black-armored Aramites, sending most fleeing to their ships.

Neither Kalena nor her companions had played any role in the war, but they felt great gratitude to this Gryphon. After all, the downfall of the empire made business much easier and more profitable for those like herself. The Aramite had only had one simple rule for dealing with smugglers—if they were not sanctioned, they were hanged on the spot.

The Gnor dismounted from his own beast, a six-legged, broad-muzzled creature that passed for a horse among his kind. Kalena grudgingly followed suit, still wary. The overcast sky had already darkened the dank landscape and now the night promised to be completely black. Even her own exceptional vision would only be able to make out objects a short distance away. She wanted to suggest they move on, but knew that Brom and the Gnor would simply look at her as if she had turned coward.

What life remained in this region looked as sinister as the ruined keep. The trees resembled grasping fingers and the weeds teeth. The only sounds of animal life were the calls of the carrion crows. As they neared the stone edifice, Kalena again had the desire to turn around and ride off as quickly as she could. The animals, too, seemed anxious to go elsewhere, for they struggled against their masters.

Swearing, Brom finally tied his own mount to a hideous tree just beyond the wall. The Gnor did the same, then removed a huge ax from his animal's saddle. The sight of the seven-foot-plus behemoth wielding the sturdy weapon erased some of the cat woman's concerns. What in its right mind would face up to a Gnor?

"Light some torches," Brom ordered her.

Happy to be busy, Kalena obeyed. She had the fire going quickly and soon handed the others their torches. Seizing the last, the cat woman gazed around at the entrance. A somber-looking gargoyle, one wing broken off, stared down at the intruders. Moss filled most of the cracks between the stones. The wooden door had fallen off long ago and what had not been eaten by termites and worms lay off to one side.

"Looks to be pretty empty," the bearded smuggler commented. He eyed the interior. "A stairway and some back rooms. We should check those out. Gnor, you take the downstairs"—Brom did not mention that the Gnor's weight might make the stairway collapse—"we'll go up."

With a grunt, the hirsute giant headed to the back. Kalena and the human cautiously walked up the stairs. The wooden-frame structure protested, but did not give way.

At the top, Brom indicated that he would take the left, she the right. Each had two rooms to check. Kalena took some comfort in knowing that Brom would be within easy earshot, but she still drew her short sword. Unlike him, she wore only a thin, cloth hunting outfit under her voluminous travel cloak. Among her own kind, Kalena would have been barely clothed, but humans insisted on cumbersome garments, so she had made the best compromise. Even still, the low-cut top and slitted pant legs garnered the attention of many males.

The darkness seemed to close in around her as she stepped away from Brom. Forcing herself to focus ahead, Kalena reluctantly entered the first room.

A rueful smile spread across her full mouth. The torch immediately revealed nothing more than a dust-filled, cobweb-covered room bare of even a stick of furniture. No ghosts, no goblins. Holding the torch before her, she peered at the corners, but found absolutely nothing.

Feeling more and more foolish about her earlier misgivings, Kalena stepped out of the first room. Just one more to check and then she could rejoin Brom.

But whereas the previous chamber had been full of webs, the second was oddly clear, almost as if it had been constantly swept. It also contained the first furniture that the cat woman had seen in the entire keep. A tall, antique dress cabinet stood at the far end of the room. Scrollwork framed the polished images of rearing horses and handles made of what looked like gold.

The gold enticed her forward, as did the prospect that something of greater value might wait inside. Brom had regaled her with tales of smugglers and treasure hunters who had found valuables in the oddest of places. Why not here? At the very least, perhaps some antique object worth selling remained.

The gold handle moved readily when she turned it. The condition of the cabinet almost made her pause, but anticipation of what she might find inside made Kalena forge ahead.

But when she eyed the contents, her hand shook so much that she dropped the torch on the stone floor.

Kalena could not scream. All she could do was step back, her eyes unable at first to tear away from the monstrous sight dangling before her.

The faces . . .

Born of a race of hunters, Kalena nonetheless turned and fled. She raced down the broken staircase without thinking. At the bottom, some of her sense returned and she looked around for the Gnor. Even more than Brom, the Gnor would keep her safe now.

Only one of the two downstairs doors was open and from within came a flicker of torchlight. With a relieved gasp, Kalena rushed inside. Guilt that she had chosen the Gnor before Brom washed over her, but the cat woman knew that in this case Brom would understand.

But barely within the chamber, Kalena screamed.

The Gnor—or what remained of him—lay sprawled in the middle of the chamber. She knew it to be the Gnor only because of the general shape and the ax that lay nearby. The blood-soaked body itself was almost unrecognizable, for something had, with utter precision, completely *skinned* the giant.

"Not possible . . ." she muttered. "Not possible . . ."

She backed out of the chamber . . . and into a pair of arms.

Before Kalena could speak, she heard a voice whisper, "Don't scream. It's only me."

Although neither held a torch, her superior vision enabled her to make out Brom's welcome face. The bearded human gazed solemnly at his companion.

"Brom! Brom . . . the Gnor! He's . . . he's . . ."

"It's all right. I'm here."

She felt some comfort in his arms, but still the image of the goliath's corpse remained burnt in her memory. "Brom, let's get away from here! Whatever killed the Gnor must still be here! We can't stay!"

Despite his cool demeanor, he must have been almost as worried as her, for his body was covered in sweat, so much so that Kalena's hands came away wet and sticky where she had touched him near the throat and shoulders.

A sound from the direction of the room where the Gnor had perished made them both pause. Kalena could not be certain, but she thought it a faint moan. Could it be possible that after suffering such horror their companion might still be alive? Gnor were said to be hard to kill, but still . . .

Disengaging himself from her, Brom headed toward the other room. "Stay here," he ordered, drawing his sword. "I'll see to it."

As he vanished inside, the cat woman wiped her brow. As she did, for the first time Kalena noted a lingering scent. It smelled of Brom, but of something else. She sniffed her hands where she had touched him, then anxiously touched her tongue to one palm.

Blood. She knew the taste well. Her kind practically ate their meals raw.

Staring at her open hands, Kalena shook. What she had taken for sweat was instead blood . . . so much of it that her hands were covered. Her panic had made her not notice it earlier.

Brom's had been covered in blood . . . but with such a wound, he could hardly have stood, much less be so calm.

Then Kalena thought of the Gnor and what she had discovered upstairs.

"By the Dream Lands!" she gasped.

Whirling, she fled out of the keep and into the starless night. The branches of the trees nearby seemed to clutch at her, hold her. From her fingers erupted sharp claws, which she used to slash her way through. The region was silent save her own frantic breathing. Kalena did not look back, fearful that what had taken the Gnor was right behind her.

Fearful that it would still wear the face of Brom.

II

"THIS PLACE GIVES me a chill," Leonin grumbled. The wiry human rubbed his runny nose on his sleeve. "The battlefield was more inviting."

"Always complaints, complaints always," returned the red-feathered avian warrior riding beside him. Wide, pupilless eyes took in the dour landscape. "But this time agree."

Ahead of them, Morgis hissed, his forked tongue darting in and out between sharp teeth. "You both had the chance to turn back. I told you I'd go alone."

"And miss the reward for a live keeper?" sniffed Leonin.

Morgis hissed again, this time under his breath. He did not like being reminded of their quarry, one he felt responsible for letting pass. The Gryphon would have never made such an error. The Gryphon had been more than just a warrior . . . he had been a tactician and leader, the reason for the downfall of the Aramites.

And Morgis had ever been by his side. They had journeyed to this subjugated continent in secret, one a creature of myth—part man, part lion, part bird—and the other a drake warrior of the Blue clan, the son of the Dragon King who ruled from Irillian By the Sea. They had come as wary allies on a mission of discovery for the Gryphon and had become, through crisis and battle, comrades and friends.

But the Gryphon, his task nearly complete, had returned home to deal with other matters. Morgis, on the other hand, had found a purpose here among people and creatures who saw him as a savior.

To all appearances, he resembled a towering knight in green scale armor tinted with sea blue. The armor covered him from toe to shoulder, even down to gauntlets. Upon his head he wore a huge helm atop which a very lifelike dragon's visage acted as crest. Through the curved opening of the helm a visage both reptilian and human could be glimpsed. Like his armor, Morgis's skin was green in scale with hints of blue. His eyes were fiery red orbs and for a nose he had two meager slits.

Yet, all this was illusion, magic. The armor, the face, everything was false. What passed for mail was in truth skin, the skin of a *dragon*. The terrifying visage atop the helm was the true face of Morgis in his birth form. As a drake warrior, he wore two shapes. One was the almost-but-not-quite human one he now used . . . the other that of an immense, fire-breathing dragon.

The inherent magic of the drake race enabled them to go through such transformations almost from birth on. But despite the obvious impressiveness of a dragon's size, most of Morgis's kind not only preferred the smaller, more versatile humanoid form, but rarely ever changed back once they reached adulthood. Morgis himself had only transformed five times in the years since his arrival and only because of dire need. Ever he preferred good steel in his hand. It had reached the point that even the thought of resuming his birth shape proved painful.

Against the renegade keeper—the Aramite sorcerer—Morgis was aware that he might have to become a dragon. However, that would only happen if and when they confronted the wolf raider. Even when hunting such quarry, the drake found his present body more suitable. True, a dragon could see much from the sky, but the ground also presented many hiding places and minute clues. The sight of a dragon soaring among the clouds would also give the keeper much more warning.

Sniffing the foul air, Morgis did not wonder that the wolf raider had chosen this sorry path for escape. His power much diminished by the loss of the talisman that had bound him to his god, the lupine Ravager, the sorcerer was fortunate to have any spellwork available to him. Many of the keepers had perished from madness when the Gryphon had helped cut off their link. The few survivors had adapted in whatever way they could, but their resources were meager. Better to lose oneself in a blighted land such as this until some other magical source could be discovered.

They could not allow the sorcerer that time. Even one powerful keeper could mean the deaths of many innocents.

"It'll be nightfall in an hour," Leonin pointed out. "And with this overcast we can barely see as it is. Why don't we stop?"

The avian—who reminded Morgis of the hawklike Seeker race of his own native land—nodded agreement. "Night is falling, falling it is. Better to face the quarry in light."

"See? Even Awrak agrees."

Morgis shook his head. "If the two of you can agree on something twice in one day, truly it mussst be a portent." He gazed ahead, saw in the distance a structure atop a hill. "Perhaps we can find shelter there."

"Looks abandoned."

"A likely idea, consssidering our location."

Leonin tugged on his short beard. "Maybe there's some treasure left over."

"We have come in search of the Aramite, not fool's gold."

"No harm in looking, looking is no harm," commented Awrak with a tilt of his head. "We sleep there, anyway, yes?"

Yes, the bird man definitely reminded Morgis more of a Seeker than he did the Gryphon. Awrak was an opportunist just like the former. His people had fought their Aramite conquerors not so much out of a desire to be free, but because they had seen that the rebels already had the upper hand. Under the yoke of the wolf raiders, Awrak's kind had supposedly not suffered as much as most.

He had not wanted to be saddled with any companions, but the Master Guardians, the only true form of leadership in the freed lands, had insisted. Leonin, for all his sniffling, was a skilled swordsman, while Awrak's kind were immune to the magical mind tricks this keeper might still be able to use, something the drake could not claim. In fact, it was supposedly because Morgis had been magically distracted that the Aramite had managed his desperate flight out of the city of Luperion.

Everyone, from the simple forest dwellers to the Master Guardians, had come to depend upon him for so much after the Gryphon's departure that this failure ate at Morgis. He had led armies, seized cities, freed realms. Several times his father had sent missives demanding his return, but Morgis had ignored them. He had no desire to become a Dragon King, no matter the power his father wielded. The drakes were losing their control over that part of the world. Here . . . here he could carve out a new destiny for himself.

Here he could avoid certain matters.

The keeper could not be far ahead of them and, in truth, even Morgis felt fatigued. Besides, something about this land made him uneasy. Better to traverse it in what laughingly passed for day than to go wandering into some Aramite trap in the dark.

It was nearly night by the time they reached the old building, a once-formidable keep. Judging by what little he could see, the drake guessed that it even preceded the wolf raiders' empire. A good portion of it had collapsed, but the central building was in surprisingly excellent shape, even with an intact stairway.

The main chamber was clearly empty, but two closed doors at the rear piqued the curiosity of the newcomers. While Awrak and Leonin went to check the one on the right, Morgis investigated the other.

Sword in one hand and torch in the other, the drake kicked open the half-rotted door. A new gust of decay enveloped him. Hissing, Morgis strode in, ready for an ambush.

He found no wolf raiders, but an unsettling sight on the floor set every nerve taut.

Splatters of dried blood decorated the center of the floor, almost as if someone had just died there. Sniffing, Morgis noticed the blood was still fresh enough to have a scent. The battle had been a recent one, anywhere from a week or two to even the previous night.

"Where are you, keeper?" he muttered to the air. Had he found the Aramite's most recent lair? Some of the other sorcerers' attempts to regain what they had lost had to do with sacrifices, both animal and otherwise.

A raucous noise above made Morgis look up. Something dropped to the floor just before his face.

The blood-soaked leg of a large rat.

Two cat-sized carrion crows perched atop the rafters, ripping apart the unlucky rodent. A bit of fur wafted its way to the floor, following by a couple of crimson drops.

Sheathing his weapon, the drake grimaced. All he had found was the birds' feeding place. A life of war had made him almost miss the obvious. He was thankful neither of his companions had seen his reaction. Awrak and Leonin would not have let him hear the end of it.

"The great warrior," Morgis hissed. "The great *fool*."

The Gryphon would have made no such mistake. The Gryphon would have immediately recognized the situation for what it was, not what he expected it to be.

Small wonder that *she* had fallen for him so completely. How could a monstrous, scaled creature such as himself compare with the ultimate champion?

Retreating from the room, the reptilian knight sought out the rest of his party. To his dismay, however, they were not where they were suppose to be.

With a snarl, Morgis drew his blade again, then stepped to the center of the main chamber. "Leonin! Awrak!"

His shout echoed throughout the keep. He almost called out again, when suddenly he heard movement above and caught a glimpse of torchlight.

Awrak stood atop the stairway, his curved sword ready. From such a view, Morgis could make out the avian's backward-bending legs and taloned feet, yet another similarity to the Gryphon or the Seekers.

"Will bring down the roof, dragon, the roof you will bring down."

"What are you doing up there? Isss Leonin there, too?"

The slim form of his other comrade materialized next to the bird man. "No need to shout, Morgis. We and every critter for miles around can hear your booming voice."

"If you were where you were meant to be, I would not have to shout out your namesss!" He glared at the duo. "Find your treasssure?"

The human's sour expression gave Morgis some satisfaction. "Just a dress cabinet too big for us to drag along. Nothin' in it."

"Then come and help ssset up camp. Can I trussst you pair to deal with the horsesss while I gather wood?"

Leonin nodded. Satisfied, the drake sheathed his sword once more and went

outside. He hooked the torch into a hole in the outside wall, then started rum-
maging around the overgrown foliage nearby.

Whatever else one could say for this misbegotten land, it certainly offered up
enough firewood. All Morgis had to do was walk along, tearing off branch after
branch. All the trees near the keep had died, some of them long, long ago. After
only a few minutes, he had an armful, nearly enough for the entire night.

But as he reached for another branch, something amidst the foliage caught
his eye. Squinting in the dark, Morgis thought he made out a rather large shape.
It almost looked like—

Then a gasp from further down the hilly path made him forget all about
wood and sinister shapes. Morgis threw the firewood aside and peered in the
direction of the sound.

A cloaked form ducked into the woods nearby.

Weapon unsheathed, the drake darted to where he had last seen the figure.
He found no sign at first, but then the rustling of leaves and branches to the
west alerted him. Again he noted the dark outline of someone in a travel cloak.

"Halt! Ssstop where you are!"

The figure hesitated, then hurried on. Slashing his way through the woods,
Morgis gave pursuit. The dry limbs readily fell to his massive blade while ahead
of him the figure seemed caught by every twig. Nearer and nearer Morgis drew.

As another gasp escaped his quarry, he realized that he pursued a female.
She stood as tall as a human, but moved more lithely even despite being slowed
constantly by the trees.

But then Morgis had troubles of his own. Catching his foot on an exposed
root, the drake found himself falling forward, his blade flying from his grip. He
struck the harsh ground with a grunt.

Rather than make use of his blunder, the figure hesitated again. To Morgis's
surprise, she turned back, slowly making her way to him.

Distrustful of this change of heart, he pushed himself up as best he could.
His blade lay out of reach, but Morgis had other skills. Not as adept at magic
as his sire, he nonetheless could cast a defensive spell in an emergency. It was a
secret very few of those he battled beside knew.

But instead of attacking, the cloaked female carefully took his sword up by
the point and reached the weapon back to him. Morgis cautiously accepted it,
then waited.

"You—you're real, then," the shadowed figure uttered.

"Do I ssseem like some figment of your imagination?"

She shook her head. "No. That's not what I mean. What I mean to say is—
is that you're *you*. You're . . . alive."

"A trait we share in common." He held back from any other retorts, though, seeing the fear in her expression. She bundled the cloak tight around her. "You are one of the cat people. One of Troia'sss kind."

Her large, feline eyes blinked. Of course she did not know Troia, who had become mate to the Gryphon and mother to his children. Troia had stayed in the background, but she had been every bit as much a part of the downfall of the empire as the Gryphon had. With the grace and swiftness of her people, she had leapt into every battle, a true warrior queen in the eyes of many.

And so much more in the eyes of one drake.

"Never mind. Who are you? Why are you here? Thisss is certainly not a place for you."

She glanced back at the distant keep. "I had nowhere to go. I ran and got lost. I seemed to be running in circles during the day. I feared I wouldn't survive a second night . . . and then I saw you three come—"

Morgis was not the patient sort. He held up a hand to quiet her. "Let usss begin again. This time with more order. Who are you?"

"My name . . . my name is Kalena."

"Kalena. Your kind do not live in these lands. I must assume you have a reassson to be here where few would find you. A thief, perhaps?"

He saw that he had struck true. "Not a thief," she murmured. "A smuggler . . . at least I was."

"Not alone?"

"No. There was Brom," Kalena said his name with a fondness that informed the drake that the two had been more than business partners. "And, of course, the Gnor."

The Gnor. Morgis had fought alongside the ursine creatures during the height of the rebellion. Fearsome warriors, as worthy as any drake in battle. "Where are your companionsss now?"

She drew the cloak closer, leaving only her face open to the night. Morgis had to squint to see her worsening expression. "Dead. Both of them. In the keep."

Thinking of Awrak and Leonin, the drake looked back at the ancient edifice. "When? How long? We sssaw no bodiesss!"

"Last—last night. It took their—their—" Kalena suddenly threw herself into his chest, sobbing.

Unaccustomed to such emotion focused on him, Morgis initially stood frozen. Then, recalling how others reacted, he put one tentative arm around the cat woman, patting her gently but awkwardly near the shoulder.

But as he comforted her, his mind raced. He recalled the blood stain and how fresh it had seemed. It would have taken many rats to make such a mark.

What a fool he had been!

Kalena looked up, her eyes wider yet. "Your friends! You need to warn them! Brom and the Gnor, they didn't know to expect anything—"

"I cannot leave you out here," he hissed. "You mussst come."

"I can't—" Kalena started to pull away, then apparently thought better of it. "But—I've nowhere to go."

Morgis straightened. His full height put him on a level akin to the Gnor and he had abilities the other fighter had lacked. "Remain with me and you will be safe. I promissse you that on my honor as a drake warrior. . . ."

She said nothing, only nodding. Keeping her close to his free arm, he steered her toward the structure. They moved at a quick pace—Kalena with some lingering reluctance—but not quick enough to suit Morgis. He still did not understand what had killed the smuggler's comrades, but it had done so in the very place his own companions now awaited him.

He hoped he was not already too late.

AND FROM THE woods beyond where Morgis had found Kalena, several dark forms separated from the shadows . . . then slowly moved toward the keep.

III

"LEONIN! AWRAK!"

The drake's shouts echoed throughout the hollow building as he and the cat woman entered. The initial lack of response filled him with dread, but then he heard movement above and Leonin appeared on the upper level.

"You tryin' to wake the dead—" His gaze fixed on the figure next to Morgis. Although her form was all but obscured by the cloak, enough light from the torches existed to enable the human to see what his comrade had found. "Well! A lady in our midst . . . and fine, fine lady at that!"

Morgis looked at Kalena in the light. He had earlier compared her vague visage to that of Troia, but now he saw the marked differences. Kalena was younger, but her face had a maturity about it that hinted of a harder life than even the Gryphon's mate. Her fur was also lighter and a small scar ran down one cheek. Like Troia, however, she was overall very beautiful.

And immediately reminded the drake of the rare emotions he had felt whenever near his old comrade's female.

"Awrak!" Leonin called down the hall. "Get your feathered self out here and meet our guest!" With that, the slim fighter lithely descended the worn stairway, arriving before the cloaked Kalena with a flourish. He reached up to take her half-hidden hand.

Temper suddenly flaring, Morgis stepped between them. "Enough foolish-nessss! We are in danger here, human!"

"Danger? What danger?"

"Tell usss, Kalena . . . tell usss the *whole* ssstory . . ."

And as she did, Leonin's expression went from lusty to wary almost imme-diately.

Even Morgis listened with growing dismay as the cat woman told them of her search and how she had come across the cabinet. Like Leonin, she had thought that there might be riches within . . . but instead she had come across a horror the likes of which Kalena could never have imagined.

There were *faces* in the cabinet, a row of faces dangling from hooks like clothes. Most were human, but she recalled a few other races as well. At first glance, the startled smuggler had assumed them lifelike masks . . . until her acute sense of smell had indicated them to be much, much more.

"They were . . . they were *real*. They were real faces . . . but only the skin! And when I looked closer . . . I saw that it wasn't just the faces, not even just the en-tire head . . . but the rest of the *body* as well!"

That was when she had fled downstairs without thinking. Only at the bot-tom of the steps had Kalena realized that she needed to find the others. Brom was her lover as well as her partner, but at that moment the Gnor had seemed a much more desirable presence.

That is, until she had discovered his body.

Awrak descended just as she described finding the Gnor's grisly remains, but he had clearly heard more. The avian bristled and his clawed hands tightened on his weapon.

"A horrid thing, a thing so very horrid," he muttered.

"They say a lot of things awoke when the raiders' god was put away," com-mented Leonin. "They say those things've been waiting for centuries to play their own mischief . . ."

Morgis hissed agreement, then asked, "And neither of you sssaw anything?"

"There's that cabinet she mentioned, but it was empty. You didn't find no body, either, right?"

"None. Only tracesss of blood . . . which I was simple enough to think came from the mealsss of crows."

They looked around the empty chamber, studying each shadowed corner. Veterans all, they were used to foes wielding blades, not monstrous powers and bloody tastes.

"It is too late to go anywhere else. We will remain together, in thisss room, with a fire set in the center." Morgis recalled the wood he had gathered. "There isss fuel outside the entrance, only a few yards away. I will get it—"

But Kalena suddenly clutched his arm, her eyes wide. "No! Please don't leave me!"

Leonin snickered and Awrak let out a quiet, cooing sound, his equivalent of mirth. The drake's eyes flashed at the two.

"You can't turn down a damsel in distress, Morgis! She needs you! I'll go get it . . ."

Awrak followed. "Will bring in the horses."

Left alone with Kalena, Morgis was at a loss. He had brought her to safety, but now had nothing to offer her. Worse, she did not seem at all prepared to release his arm.

"I've never seen anything like you," she whispered. "Where do you come from?"

"From across the watersss. I am a drake warrior, ssson of the Blue Dragon, who rulesss Irillian By the Sssea."

Her enchanting eyes grew wider yet. "You—you're one of the dragon men?"

"Yesss." Morgis's clan had traded with smugglers and coastal towns for some generations, so their presence on this continent, while rare, was not unheard of. Still, Kalena stared at him as if seeing the most wondrous jewel in the world.

Her hand ran across his chest. "This scale. This is you, not armor."

"It isss ssstronger than mosssst armor . . ."

Leonin chose that moment to return, his arms full of dry wood. He chuckled at Morgis's obvious discomfort, then cheerfully carried the fuel to the center. "No need to disturb yourselves! I'll be lightin' the fire as usual."

A moment later, Awrak, too, returned. "Horses nervous, very nervous. Didn't want to come in, not come in at all."

In truth, he had to nearly drag the animals to the far side of the chamber. Morgis would have preferred the horses in a stable, but not this night.

The bird man eyed Leonin's efforts with disdain. "Be all night making that, all night." He made a squawking sound. "Not nearly enough wood, too, wood not nearly enough."

"My arms aren't as big as our scaly friend's here," the human said with a wink. "There's still some more just outside the entrance."

While Awrak went to retrieve the remainder of Morgis's load, Kalena finally disengaged herself and went to the small fire Leonin had managed. He looked up at her, grinning. The cat woman, her cloak still clutched protectively around her, knelt, taking in the warmth.

Grateful to be free yet oddly disappointed at the same time, Morgis kept watch. One hand remained on the sword at his side. It, the sheath, and the belt that held them—all gifts from the Master Guardians—were the only items on his person that were not actually a part of his skin. If he needed to transform, the belt would simply break, a necessary loss.

"So warm," he heard Kalena murmur pleasantly. His red orbs shifted to her, taking in her shrouded form and her young face. Again he recalled another feline face and the burgeoning emotions he had been forced to keep in check. More than in the Dragonrealm, it was not uncommon to find pairings of different races. Some, like the Gryphon and Troia, had even been blessed with offspring. Others had no such hope, but love bound them together.

There were times when he wished that he had sailed home . . . and other times he was glad that he had not.

A slight scraping noise arose from the open window to his right.

The sword came out. Morgis poised for attack. Leonin leapt from the fire, his own blade ready to back up the drake.

Nothing.

"Just a branch rubbin' against the stone," suggested the human.

"Maybe." Morgis glanced to the entrance. "Awrak hasss been gone for quite a long time, don't you think?"

"He has, hasn't he?"

Kalena slipped around the campfire and clutched Leonin's free arm. Morgis tried to ignore the thoughts that briefly raced through his mind upon seeing this.

"I shall go investigate," the drake finally declared.

"Want I should go, too?"

"No. Ssstay with her."

The cat woman rewarded his concern with a grateful smile, which Morgis pretended to ignore. Sword before him, he stepped out to where Awrak should have been gathering the wood.

But the avian was nowhere to be seen. The wood lay in a small stack, as if Awrak had prepared it, then wandered off.

Morgis sincerely doubted that his companion had done so foolhardy a thing.

Taking a risk, he called out the bird man's name, but the harsh wind swallowed his attempt. Morgis hissed. Bending low, he seized an armful of wood and quickly retreated inside.

Leonin frowned when he saw the drake. "By that armload you've got there, I take it our friend is gone."

"There was no sssssign of him. No *sign* of any *struggle*, either." Morgis forced out the two words, fighting the sibilation common among drakes when they grew excited or upset. This was not the time to fall into bad and very careless habits . . . especially in front of Kalena.

"Maybe this time we should all go out there together," suggested the bearded human. "That way we can keep Kalena safe and still watch for Awrak." Despite their many differences, Leonin clearly did not like the thought of something having happened to his verbal sparring partner.

But Kalena pulled back, shaking her head and drawing her cloak yet tighter around her body. "No! I won't go out there! We need to stay in here!"

"Easy, girl! No real fear! Morgis here'll turn into a full-fledged dragon if need be! Let's see any monster take *that* on!"

A tingle coursed through the drake. It bothered him more than it should have that Leonin had reminded her that Morgis was, in essence, a beast parading as an almost-man. Yet, his partner had a point. To save their lives, Morgis was prepared to transform and light the landscape afire. It shamed him that the human's offhand suggestion should have already been a done thing, that he should be out there even now, flying over the countryside in search of Awrak.

"You shall stay here, Kalena," he responded as soothingly as possible. "And Leonin will be your guard. I will search for Awrak alone."

"What are you going to do?" she asked, eyes so wide he thought he might willingly fall into them.

"What Leonin just sssuggested."

He undid his belt, handing the sheath and sword to the human. For all its size, the chamber had an entrance too low and narrow for him to fit through once he changed. Morgis would have to step outside, likely halfway down the ruined path. Even among dragons, he was considered a giant.

"Please take care!" Kalena called after him.

Her concerned heartened him as he stepped out into the ungodly night. Morgis kept a sharp eye out as he wended his way down, still hoping to find some trail leading to Awrak. Curiously, without a sword, he felt somewhat naked. The drake had little desire to change to his birth form, but that choice had been taken from him.

When he felt he had moved far enough away from the keep, Morgis took a deep breath and readied himself. Almost two years had passed since his last transformation.

But as he drew upon his innate magic, willed his body to both shift in shape and grow in size, a familiar tingling touched every nerve.

The transformation faltered.

"What'sss thissss?" he muttered, body shaking and head suddenly throbbing.

From out of the dead forest burst several armored forms.

The Aramites moved like shadows come to life, their ebony armor adding to their eerie and shocking appearance. Most wielded long, narrow swords.

Morgis's eyes registered at least six of the wolf raiders, three on each side of him. He instinctively went for his sword, then cursed his folly for having left the weapon behind.

But with or without a sword and although trapped in a mortal form, the drake was hardly defenseless. As the first Aramite came at him, Morgis twisted to the side, letting the blade's edge pass within inches of his chest. He then seized hold of the raider's wrist and pulled the Aramite forward using a strength far superior to any one human.

With a cry, his first foe went flying into the air, colliding with a satisfying crash into two of those attacking from the opposite direction.

Seizing the weapon of one of the fallen raiders, Morgis turned to confront the remaining trio.

"Slithering out of the shadows, eh? You are not the sons of the wolf! More like the get of a serpent!"

He met the arcing blades of two of the Aramites, first deflecting them, then swinging with such brute force that the raiders retreated. The third attacker thrust as Morgis completed his swing, nearly catching the drake under the sword arm.

As Morgis fell back, one of raiders he had bowled over started to rise. Seizing the still-stunned figure by the collar, the scaled knight pulled the hapless villain in front just as three swords sought the drake's heart.

Two of the points buried themselves in the Aramite's neck and shoulder. With a quiet grunt, Morgis's human shield slumped forward, momentarily blocking the other raiders.

But even as one opponent fell, more spilled out of the woods. One leapt at Morgis too eagerly and for his zealousness received a thrust through the unprotected throat. The drake managed to punch another, sending him sprawling, then jumped over the body.

Twice more he deflected their attacks, managing to wound one foe in the sword arm, but Morgis knew the odds were against him. One-to-one or even three-to-one, he had little doubt as to his victory, but against so many . . .

And then the tingling he had felt earlier returned, but with a painful vengeance. Roaring, Morgis fell to one knee, his grip on his weapon all but lost.

The Aramites fell on him then, trying to bury him under their combined mass. The mob assault actually took his mind from the agony within and the drake threw himself into the fight. With some pleasure, he heard bone crack as he hit one adversary. Seizing another, Morgis pushed to his feet and threw the struggling figure as hard as he could.

But his respite did not last. The pain returned, forcing him to the earth. Now the wolf raiders took distinct pleasure in pummeling him. They beat at the drake again and again, cursing him with a hundred names and venting their frustration over the loss of the grand empire on one of those most responsible.

Finally, a voice cut through the din, saying, "That will be enough. I want the beast alive . . . for now."

It was the last thing Morgis heard before the culmination of his injuries made him faint.

IV

HE WAS *DROWNING*. Water filled his lungs, making him choke. Morgis tried to breathe, but all he did was inhale more liquid. The black sea surrounded him and the drake could not find the surface. His heart pounded as the lack of air took its toll.

"Once more," commanded a voice filled with disdain.

A new wave washed over the drowning drake. He coughed again. Rough hands turned him over and he finally managed to spit up some of the water.

Slowly it registered to him that he rested his forehead against stone.

"Curious. I thought the blue dragons of an aquatic nature. This one looks as capable of life in the sea as a sand rat."

The comment received several gruff sniggers from various points surrounding Morgis. Spitting out more water, he managed to reply, "We are—are like the whalesss and—ssseals, fool! We hold air inssside—when we are given the chance t-to take it first!"

For his reply Morgis was rewarded with a harsh kick to the side.

"He seems recovered enough," said the voice that appeared to be in command. "Bind his arms behind him."

Several pairs of rough hands pulled the drake from the floor. Through bleary orbs, Morgis gradually recognized the interior of the old keep. Worse, he also recognized the guarded form of Leonin, but Kalena was nowhere in sight.

A sudden rage at what the wolf raiders might have done with her enabled Morgis to stand of his own accord. He pulled free of the soldiers, but then the tingling began and once more the drake slipped to one knee.

"There will be none of that."

To his left, he noted the source of his pain. Although for the most part clad like the other armored figures, the tall, broad-shouldered leader wore not the closed helms of his underlings but rather an open one with an elaborate wolf's head crest. The savage, lupine head looked nearly alive, a tribute to the dark god in whose image it had been cast. A small ridge of gray fur rode down the back of the helm, the tip just touching the figure's flowing cloak, also made of fur.

The face within the helm well-matched the savage crest. If this Aramite did not have the blood of the Ravager flowing through his veins, Morgis would have been surprised. Under a thick, curving brow, narrow black eyes glittered dangerously. The nose was long, narrow, almost canine, and the mouth was wide and almost lipless.

"I am Keeper D'Kairn . . ." he remarked with a politeness belied by his wolf-ish visage. ". . . and you are the drake, Morgis, son of the Dragon King, Blue."

The last was said with more than a hint of satisfaction and even more than a hint of teeth. D'Kairn's teeth were not pointed, as Morgis had half-expected, but they looked as capable of biting through flesh and bone as any predator's.

This was the keeper, the Aramite sorcerer he and the others had been hunting. Unfortunately, no one had told them that not only did D'Kairn have an entourage—some eight scruffy soldiers that Morgis could count—but he also had access to magic strong enough to prevent the drake from assuming his natural form.

"To answer an unspoken question, for days we knew that we were being pursued by fools. But we are far more appropriate in the roles of hunters and so you were allowed to pass, and we kept watch on you instead, waiting for the proper moment." He stared into the crimson eyes of the beaten drake. "You were no match at all for a keeper."

"You are a keeper without teeth," Morgis uttered to his captor. "Or should I say without a single *tooth.*"

He had the pleasure of seeing D'Kairn's dark eyes flash before the guards threw him back against the wall. Already softened by their earlier blows, Morgis felt the collision in every bone.

The gloved keeper removed a tiny item from his belt pouch, holding it up for Morgis to see. The pale crystal, perhaps three inches in length, had been shaped to resemble a fang. When Morgis had first seen such an artifact, it had glowed brightly in its wielder's palm. This one, however, had no life in it whatsoever.

"I still bear the gift of my Lord Ravager," snapped the sorcerer. "And one day it shall glow fiery again with his blessing . . ." He reluctantly put the crystal away. ". . . but until that glorious day comes again, I have learned to make due with a different and, admittedly, interesting method of spellwork."

Morgis hardly cared about what sort of magic the keeper had picked up, but D'Kairn's prattling garnered the drake warrior time to surreptitiously study the odds . . . and also try to determine what had happened to Kalena. "And what sort of spellwork have you turned to?"

"Blood magic."

All thought of escape vanished as the two words sank in. *Blood magic.* Morgis suddenly recalled Kalena's horrific tale of the skinned Gnor and the macabre appearance of her human partner. To the drake, it all fit somehow. Both had become part of some monstrous spell created by the fiendish figure before him.

"Blood, you sssay? Didn't spill enough in the name of your dog god?"

Face an emotionless mask, D'Kairn reached up and pulled from beneath his breastplate a small necklace, the end of which was an ivory-colored stone encased in a silver band. The keeper gently stroked the stone.

The tingling struck Morgis stronger this time. It was all he could do to keep from screaming. He tried to double over, but his guards refused to allow him even that minuscule relief.

"You will refrain from further blasphemous expressions, dragon," the lupine human commanded. "I want you alive—if not well—for the time being. You have some value to me."

"H-how fortunate."

"Not so much as you think. I have utilized the blood of men, of the cat people, of almost every race on this continent. Each offers power of a varying degree for a varying period of time."

"A Gnor w-would give you much, I sssuspect."

D'Kairn replaced the necklace within his breast plate, frowning. "Not as much as I would have imagined. The Syrryn actually provide much more."

Now it was Leonin who tried to reach the sorcerer. "You damned filth! I'll—"

The Aramite nearest Leonin struck him on the back of his head with a gauntleted hand. Morgis's partner tumbled forward, groaning.

Morgis hissed harshly, both in response to Leonin's injury and D'Kairn's horrific revelation. The Syrryn were bird folk.

Awrak had been a Syrryn.

"You will pay for that . . ." he muttered to the keeper.

This brought a chuckle from D'Kairn, not a pretty sound or sight. "No, dragon . . . *you* will pay. You will pay for all that you did, all that the Gryphon did, all that brought forth the ruination of our empire and severed from those like me the wondrous link to our god! You will pay . . . and in the process you will help me restore what was ours!"

Morgis had wondered how D'Kairn's mind had survived so intact after so many of his brethren had lost theirs when the Gryphon had somehow broken their sorcerous ties to the Ravager. Now he understood that his captor's sanity had *not* been spared. D'Kairn's madness was of a different, more deadly sort.

"All the magical power you can gather won't help you regain your empire, Aramite," the drake retorted. He indicated the handful of soldiers with the keeper. "And thessse will hardly be enough to police it for you."

"There will be more of them, dragon, and more keepers again! What I have

learned is sufficient to spread to those of my brethren still surviving and each
of us will then take on promising apprentices. The blood magic is fairly simple,
once you know how best to draw it. I've had much time and many subjects, you
know."

Kalena's visage flashed before Morgis's eyes, but he said nothing this time.
He swore, though, that if D'Kairn had done to her as he had Awrak and the
Gnor, the drake would see to it that the keeper met a like fate.

Of course, first he had to escape.

They were interrupted by two more raiders. Morgis's anger deflated as he
realized the odds were even more against him and Leonin. That made ten, in
addition to D'Kairn. Even if they somehow managed to overcome the soldiers,
the keeper still had some power left in his amulet, enough to keep Morgis from
shapeshifting.

"Well?" asked D'Kairn of the newcomers.

"The bird's disposed of, my lord," one of them replied. "No sign of the cat,
though."

The keeper shrugged. "No matter. Who will she run to?" He looked directly
at Morgis. "We have what we want."

But the drake paid little mind to the danger to himself. The guards had given
him some relief. Kalena had escaped D'Kairn's foul work.

The keeper snapped his fingers and the guards dragged Morgis over to Leonin. As they did, a husky Aramite with strands of graying hair thrusting out of
the bottom of his helm went up to the lupine sorcerer.

"I've got three men keeping watch out there now, my lord, but I'd be more
comfortable with three more. Just in case there are more following these."

"As you wish, Captain D'Falc. Your attention to proper duty is commendable and will be recalled when we have taken back that which is ours."

As the burly captain picked out the three, D'Kairn stepped to an open area
near one of the back rooms. The keeper crouched, then with a piece of chalk
taken from a belt pouch, began drawing on the stone floor.

"What's he doin'?" whispered Leonin.

"Preparing to take our blood . . ."

Leonin spat to the side. "I'll take his before I let him take mine."

Morgis felt the same, but neither were truly in a position to do anything. He
watched with growing trepidation as D'Kairn worked on his pattern. The drake
knew enough about magic and sorcery to understand that the keeper would
draw their life forces from their dead bodies, transforming those forces into dark
magic. The blood itself was simply the transport, the carrier of those forces.

But what part did the skinning play?

One of the soldiers that Morgis had earlier wounded approached the bound pair with bowls. The contents stank, but nonetheless the stomachs of Morgis and Leonin rumbled for lack of any recent meal.

"Keep your mouth open and keep swallowing," commanded the wolfhelmed figure.

The hot, coarse contents flowed down Morgis's gullet. The soup had the consistency of mud and nearly made him choke, but at the same time it strengthened the drake and cleared his weary mind.

After they had both been fed, the soldier gave them each a swig of water, then returned to the campfire. Around them, the other Aramites ate their own meals.

"I thought they were going to kill us," Leonin remarked. "Why feed us? Makes no sense."

"The ssstronger we are, the ssstronger our blood. D'Kairn wishes usss to be in prime shape when he sssacrifices usss."

And it appeared that it would not be long before that happened. The sorcerer now had a complex array of patterns before him and looked quite satisfied. He put the chalk away, then pulled out the necklace.

But at that moment, Captain D'Falc came rushing inside.

"My lord! None of the three guards are at their posts and there's no sign as to where they might've gone!"

"What of those you led out?"

"Just outside, guarding the entrance in case of attack!"

D'Kairn nodded, satisfied with the measure, then eyed Morgis and Leonin. "I thought we had verified that these two and the Syrryn were the only ones."

"Them and the cat, my lord."

"Yes . . . her. Her kind are born predators, aren't they? She may have decided to stay around after all. No doubt took the men one-by-one from behind. I appear to have underestimated the little vixen."

"I'll lead a patrol . . ." The captain's fist squeezed tight, as if already holding Kalena by the throat.

"No, I will lead the patrol. I have no time for any more petty interruptions. We shall track down the cat promptly and add her to the collection." He gave the two prisoners a savage smile. "The more the merrier, eh?"

D'Falc chose six men to come with them, leaving the remaining three to watch Morgis and Leonin. The hunting pack seized torches, then followed the keeper and the captain out.

Leonin immediately began struggling at his bonds, which rewarded him with a slap to the cheek by one of the guards.

"Don't move again!" snapped the Aramite. "And no talking, either!"

Although they obeyed the latter, Morgis and his companion shared eye contact. The disappearance of the three sentries gave them hope, but how long could Kalena remain hidden from D'Kairn's sorcery? Morgis was glad that she lived and admired her attempt to save them, but he feared that she would yet share her partners' fate unless she abandoned her rescue mission.

The minutes dragged by. The howling wind added to the tension. Occasionally, unidentifiable noises would stir up both the prisoners and their captors.

Then, a slight scraping caught Morgis's attention. Making certain that the guards did not notice his true reason, he stretched his neck as if trying to work the tightened muscles.

Above him, peering over the upstairs rail, a cloaked Kalena studied the tableau below her.

She noticed him watching her in turn and smiled. Morgis tipped his head to the side, a signal for her to depart the keep before the Aramites noticed her. Kalena, though, ignored his silent command, instead eyeing the movements of the three guards.

Fool of a girl! the drake wanted to shout. *Run! Save yourself!*

It was one thing to use her feline hunting skills to sneak up on individual sentries, but another to try to take three armed and armored men—never mind that one was wounded—in a place like this. The Aramites had not conquered a continent and become the fearsome legend that they were because of ineptitude. Even the Dragon Kings, separated from the wolf raiders by an ocean, had given them much respect, even dealing with them as they had no other humans.

The guards remained oblivious to her presence. One watched the front entrance while another stood near the prisoners. The injured one cleared away the remnants of the meal.

Kalena stepped to her right, apparently seeking a better venue in which to study all three. As she moved, however, her feet, all but hidden by the cloak, stirred up a small bit of dirt and dust.

The trickle of falling sediment made the injured soldier glance up in mild curiosity.

"There!" he roared. "Up there!"

The other pair instinctively reacted, rushing the stairway with weapons drawn. Eyes wide, Kalena hesitated, clearly stunned by what she had done.

"Run!" Morgis shouted. "Run!"

His cries stirred her to action. She fled down the hall and out of sight. The wolf raiders, however, were already more than halfway up and closing.

Brandishing his sword, the remaining Aramite angrily approached the drake. "Be silent you! I'll—"

But as he neared, Leonin, who had remained subdued all this time, pushed himself up on his feet and charged into the guard.

They collided with a heavy thud and despite Leonin's tied hands, he managed to bowl over their captor. The two fell in a desperate jumble, the guard's helmet rolling away.

Morgis was right behind him. Also unable to use his arms, he came around the Aramite and kicked at the other's now-unprotected head.

With a groan, the Aramite stilled.

"Can you reach his sword or dagger?" the drake asked of his comrade.

"The dagger would be better! And if I can't, nobody—aah! You see? Turn around!"

Turning away from Leonin, Morgis waited tensely. Behind him, he could picture the human, his own back to that of the larger drake, trying to sever Morgis's bonds with the procured blade. With Leonin's own wrists still tied, the work was difficult. Morgis expected the other guards to return before the deed was done, but at last the bonds loosened, finally falling to the floor.

Spinning around, the towering drake dealth with Leonin's ropes, then seized the sword dropped by the Aramite. His companion hurried to where the wolf raiders had deposited the captured weapons, locating his own beloved blade.

"We go after Kalena?" Leonin asked.

In response, Morgis simply headed toward the stairway. The cat woman had risked herself for them when escape had already been hers; they could do no less.

He had no doubt that with her claws she had climbed up the back of the crumbling structure and in through a window, but doing so in secret was a lot easier than trying to descend safely while being pursued. At the very least, if they chose not to follow her, the Aramites would drop whatever they could on top of Kalena, more than likely ensuring her death.

He and Leonin paused at the top of the steps. "I don't hear anything," the human declared anxiously. "Do you think—"

"We can only hope not."

They entered the room where they had last seen the Aramites heading. The chamber was so dark that even Morgis, who could see better at night than Leonin, could not even make out the back of his own hand.

"We need light, Morgis. I'd better grab a torch."

"It would not be good to separate—"

The bearded fighter backed out of the darkened chamber. "They're still out searching the landscape. I won't be a moment."

The drake hissed. "Just flee, Leonin. Take your horssse and ride fassst! Alert others to what we found!"

"And leave the reward for our friend D'Kairn all for you? I'll be right back! You do what you can, all right?"

Nodding wordlessly, Morgis watched his partner hurry down the hall, then turned to confront the darkness again. Kalena and her captors had to have gone this way. But where were they then?

As he stepped cautiously into the room, it seemed to get even murkier. A chill wind coming from well ahead wrapped around him, making the drake hiss again. An uneasy feeling crept over him.

His foot struck something solid.

Morgis bent down and felt for the obstruction with his free hand—then pulled the hand away when it immediately touched a hard yet ominously-moist surface.

A body.

V

HIS FIRST REACTION was to think of Kalena, but then common sense reminded him of the hard shell he had felt. His estimation of the cat woman grew by leaps and bounds. Now she had managed to slay yet another of their foes.

But that still did not answer the question of where she was now.

Wiping his hand as best he could, Morgis stepped beyond the body, seeking the source of the wind. He found it a few seconds later, a wide, shaded window opening into the pitch-black night. Again it struck him that the room was uncommonly dark, for the window, despite the decrepit shade, should have been obvious.

Pushing it open, the drake peered down, seeking some sign of Kalena.

Only then did he hear movement behind him.

"Leoni—"

"Die, monster!" roared a voice on the edge of insanity. "Die, damn you!"

An armored body struck Morgis with such force that the scaled knight tumbled out the window. As he fell, though, he reached back to grab something, *anything*—and took his attacker with him.

Morgis's sense of direction vanished utterly. He heard the Aramite cry out. One arm struck stone and with what strength he could muster, Morgis seized a jutting piece and held on.

He swung back and forth like some mad pendulum, the strain on his shoulder almost too much. Desperately he reached with his other hand, trying to find some hold there. In his present form, he was subject to many of the risks of humans. A fall from this height might not kill him, but it would certainly shatter his bones.

From below came a harsh thud.

Spurred on by the wolf raider's fate, Morgis finally located something for his other hand to grab. Still dangling, he tried to judge whether he had better hopes of climbing up or down.

The stone he had first seized made his decision for him, abruptly crumbling. Caught offguard, Morgis nearly plunged to his death. Instead, what remaining grip he had with his other hand gave him just enough time to locate another hold lower down.

Brute strength and luck had saved him so far, but the drake had no intention of trusting either to last much longer. Finding some stable if still precarious footing, he lowered his other hand and, with a force no human could have mustered, *dug* his fingers into the aged wall of the structure.

Repeating this risky act, Morgis managed to climb down more than half the distance to the ground. Each moment he expected either Leonin or the Aramites to find him, but the area was eerily silent.

When at last he could find no more handholds or footing, Morgis peered down again, trying to make out what lay below. Outside, he could see a little better, enough to at least let him judge the gap. The fall could still kill or maim him, but if he managed to position himself right, he might survive with only a few bruised bones.

Not satisfied, he scanned the darkness for a better landing place. Just beyond the rocky area where the Aramite had fallen, Morgis noted what looked like a softer, shrub-covered region. If he pushed himself hard, then tightened for impact, it might save him from any shattered limbs.

Might.

Little choice remained. The fact that neither Leonin nor Kalena had come in search of him worried Morgis. The sooner he rescued himself, the sooner he could do what he could for them.

"I ssswear I *will* make you pay for thisss, keeper!" the drake hissed. If not for D'Kairn's spell, he would not have had to suffer this indignity.

Bracing himself, Morgis pushed off the stone wall.

He fell much faster than he had expected, the black ground rushing up to greet him. Barely had the drake folded himself into survival position when he collided.

Despite his best efforts, Morgis could not keep a cry from escaping him. Every nerve, every bone, vibrated with such intensity that he was certain that he had broken all of the latter.

Then a shrieking pain in his right shoulder and a savage cracking sound left him bereft of any conscious thought. Morgis rolled and rolled, unable to stop himself. He struck rocks, dead shrubs, and rotting trees. Each renewed the agony.

He came to rest at the bottom of a gully, where he lay for several moments.

His head pounded mercilessly and when Morgis tried to move the one shoulder, he had to bite down to avoid shouting out.

Only with strenuous effort was he at last able to attempt to rise and even then the drake had to shut his eyes and grimace as he moved. He put his good hand down in order to brace himself, then managed to reach a sitting position.

At that point, he saw the skeletons.

The darkness could not hide what they were, nor the fact that there were many of them. They lay scattered, in different stages of decay, but most were old, picked clean long ago by the carrion crows.

But amongst them lay two large forms not yet bereft of their flesh if already missing the skin that covered them.

Kalena's ill-fated partners.

The Gnor was recognizable by his girth, if nothing else. The man by his general shape and skull. The sight of them, even in the dimness of night, was nearly enough to make the drake, who had seen many horrid things, throw up in disgust. Not a stitch of clothes remained on the human and not an inch of skin had been left on either. From head to toe, everything had been perfectly removed, almost like a peeled fruit.

Curiously, they did not stink. Morgis dared inhale harder, but only caught a slight hint of some musky scent. Only magic could have managed such a feat. Apparently D'Kairn did not like his sensibilities offended while he performed his monstrous spells.

And that thought brought him back around to Kalena and Leonin.

Hissing quietly, Morgis looked around for a blade. He could not find his own, but by the Aramite's body he located a dagger. Less than he had hoped but more than he had expected.

Pausing to gaze at the sprawled form, Morgis pondered the raider's manic shout. The desperate tone in the man's voice puzzled him. The drake had a reputation that preceded him—As D'Kairn had revealed—but in a land that produced such creatures as the Gnor, certainly Morgis was no more a monster than the Aramites' own hideous god.

Then again, the wolf raiders had never been known for their respect for any nonhuman race.

Testing his shoulder again, Morgis determined that it was not actually broken, but rather dislocated. With effort, he could clutch things or even raise it some, but not much more. Given time, he could remedy the situation, but for now he would have to get along with only the left limb. Even with one arm, Morgis was a match for any Aramite save the keeper and if he could catch D'Kairn by surprise . . .

Slowly he wended his way around the ancient structure. Foliage snagged him and his footing often gave way. More than one quiet curse escaped Morgis as his frustration mounted. Each moment of delay meant the possibility of his friends falling back into the keeper diabolical hands.

As he came around the front of the building, Morgis noted the lack of torchlight outside. Had the wolf raiders returned to the keep? If so, it made the drake's task that much harder. Out in the dark, the advantage became his.

Clutching the dagger, he approached the entrance. Lights flickered from inside, but whether they were from the Aramites' torches or the fire already set by Leonin, Morgis could not say.

In answer to his question, two armored figures suddenly stepped out, each brandishing a torch and sword. Although he could not see their faces, he could sense the anxiety in their movements.

"Nothing . . ." growled one with the voice of Captain D'Falc. "Back inside! Quick!"

That even the veteran officer acted nervous intrigued Morgis. Gaze still upon the entrance, the drake shifted to the right, trying to catch some glimpse of the interior.

Instead, he found another body.

Awrak's.

The bird man stared sightlessly up at the black heavens, his beak seemingly open in protest. His throat had been slashed open and another deep, dark ravine had been dug in his chest, dried blood still matting the feathers there. From what Morgis could make out of the angle of the body, the Syrryn had been tossed aside like an old, abused rag doll after his use to D'Kairn had been at an end.

Sharp teeth bared in growing anger, Morgis searched for the Syrryn's weapon, but could not find it. Closing Awrak's eyes, Morgis continued his slow but steady advance. He got within a few yards of the entrance, only to see that one nervous Aramite guarded it cautiously from within. Even if Morgis managed to slay the sentry, it would alert the rest of those inside.

From within he heard voices.

Keeper D'Kairn was in no pleasant frame of mind. ". . . be certain that I will take the cost of everything out on you and your friends before I finally grant you the relief of death!"

There was a moment of silence . . . then a harsh slap. Morgis had to restrain himself from rushing in. He would do no one any good committing to a suicidal charge.

"We should just kill her and be done with it, my lord," Captain D'Falc barked.

The drake hissed. At the very least, they had *Kalena*, whose only crimes had been first to warn Morgis and his comrades of the danger near the keep and then to try to rescue the drake and Leonin from D'Kairn.

He had to go in. Surveying the crumbling building, Morgis estimated his chances of reaching one of the open windows above. Unlike Kalena's people, his were not known for their ability to climb while in their mortal forms. He had been fortunate once . . .

But even as he considered his other options, a slight rustling from his left alerted the drake as to company. Gripping the dagger, he listened as the newcomer slipped closer.

At the last moment, Morgis spun about—

"It's me!" gasped Leonin. "Watch yourself with that thing!"

Morgis lowered the dagger. "I thought you were a prisssoner! How did you escape?"

Leonin peered at the entrance before answering the question. "I was just grabbin' a torch when I heard them approaching. Slipped into one of the back rooms, hoping for a window, but while I was feelin' along the wall, I stumbled into a hidden passage! This place is honeycombed with 'em, drake! Anyway, it finally led down the hill to the northeast of this place. Been circling ever since."

"I found Awrak a short distance from here, Leonin. Hisss throat and chessst had been cut deep."

"We knew that was likely what'd happened," remarked the man. Yet, his tone hinted of barely-concealed anger.

"They have Kalena a prisssoner, Leonin."

"Well, if she's still alive, it's because they want us runnin' in after her, isn't it? Of course, we'll come, but not the way they want, right?"

"As you sssay. Tell me, isss this passage still unknown to them? Were you forced to leave it open?"

The bearded fighter thought for a moment. "No, I shut behind me. They shouldn't be able to find it. We going to sneak in on them from behind?"

"Firssst tell me whether or not you think you can enter through the other end."

Not only did Leonin think it possible to do so, but he gave Morgis an estimate on how long it would take to reach the room. The drake did some calculations of his own, then said, "The timing must be just right. I will count to myssself until I think you are ready."

"And just what are you goin' to do, then?"

"It is what we both must do, Leonin. When I believe that you are in position, I will come from the front, asss they expect. I will make certain that they focus on me while you ssslip in and grab Kalena."

His partner snorted. "You're goin' to charge right in, draw them away, and let me be able to save the girl? You'd have to fall in among them to do that. The odds of you gettin' out—"

"My concern is sssaving her, Leonin. You understand me?"

There was a momentary silence. "Yeah, I understand you just right, Morgis."

"I am not foolhardy," the drake continued, failing to mention his nearly-useless limb. "Once Kalena is safe, I will abandon the struggle."

"Sure you will."

Morgis did have a plan, though, albeit a risky one. He was skilled with the dagger, able to toss it with accuracy that even Leonin could not match. All Morgis needed was a few seconds of surprise, enough time to manage one focused throw.

A throw that would end with the dagger deep in D'Kairn's unprotected throat.

Not only would that prevent any magical attack by the keeper, but it would also likely put an end to the spell D'Kairn had cast upon the drake. Then Morgis would not only be able to use his own magic, he would also be able to transform—assuming his friends had escaped already—*within* the old ruin.

That last alone would put an end to the rest of the wolf raiders.

He told none of this to Leonin, simply assuring the human once more that he would flee the moment they had escaped. Leonin did not entirely believe him, but with one final nod, the human darted off.

The time Morgis estimated it would take Leonin to reach his goal seemed to stretch to an eternity. In that time, the Aramites grew fairly silent, the only evidence of their wariness a sentry peering outside once. The quiet both encouraged and unnerved the drake; it might have meant that D'Kairn's men were growing weary, off guard, but it also might have indicated that the keeper had grown tired of waiting and had decided to use his lone prisoner to increase his vampiric powers.

At last it was time to act. Morgis crept up to the side of the keep, wondering why D'Kairn had left it so unguarded. The Aramites appeared confined strictly to the chamber inside, not the most competent strategy. What did they have in mind?

Morgis hefted the dagger. He would find out in a moment. If he could barrel into the lone guard, then throw, he felt certain that he would succeed. At the very least, his appearance at the entrance would make most of the raiders, especially the sorcerer and his captain, look only in that direction.

Knowing Leonin as he did, that would be all the time the human would need.

He took a deep breath—then rushed around the corner and inside the building.

But instead of one guard, there were suddenly two, one of them Captain D'Falc. Both charged Morgis, forcing a decision.

Hissing in frustration, the drake threw the dagger.

He had lost no sense of aim despite the abrupt alteration of his plans. The blade caught the more deadly D'Falc—who had purposely let the guard take the forefront—just under the chin, burying itself up to the hilt.

The Aramite captain tumbled forward, already dead. His sword dropped from his limp hand and skidded toward Morgis.

The sentry ran as fast as he could, preventing the drake from seizing the lost weapon. Two more Aramites hurried to reach him and in the back Morgis could see D'Kairn stroking the stone on the necklace as he watched the battle. Why he had not used it yet, Morgis could not say, but every extra second gave the drake some hope.

Curiously, besides the captain and the three who faced him, Morgis did not see the rest of the raiders. There should have been more . . .

He had no more time to think about it, for then the first foe reached him. Unarmed, Morgis dodged the initial swing, then the second. He could not see past his opponents or D'Kairn, leaving him unable to guess as to whether Leonin had managed to sneak inside. With three blades already facing him, Morgis chose to step back to the entrance. The longer he could draw their attention, the better.

The Aramites seemed perfectly willing to let him do just that. They kept their blades pointed at his chest, but did not lunge. Each matched him step for step. It was almost as if they waited for some signal—

Only too late did Morgis realize his mistake.

To the right and left of him, the walls suddenly reached out with arms of stone. Figures pulled out from the walls, snaring him on each side.

The images of rock and mortar dissipated, revealing to the drake that those who now held him were a pair of Aramites disguised by illusion. He quickly glanced D'Kairn's way and saw the keeper's mocking expression. Now Morgis understood why the sorcerer had seemingly done nothing.

He had already laid his trap.

VI

A TWIST OF his injured arm made Morgis cry out. The Aramite holding it twisted harder, clearly relishing the reaction.

"An absurd maneuver, dragon," commented the keeper, striding toward his captive. "And very predictable. You accomplished only your own destruction."

But as D'Kairn neared him, Morgis at last caught a glimpse behind the sorcerer and saw that Leonin had more than done his part. Gone was Kalena, a few cut ropes the only trace of her . . . and lying near where she had been prisoner, the slumped, still corpse of a guard. All done without the other Aramites' knowledge.

He allowed himself a mocking smile in turn. "I accomplished more than you imagine, human."

D'Kairn frowned, then quickly looked over his shoulder. The composure vanished, replaced by a barely-checked animalistic fury.

"You!" he snapped at two of the soldiers holding blades on the drake. "The back rooms! Quickly!"

"Your incompetence amazesss me, D'Kairn," Morgis continued, trying to keep his captor off guard. The longer he did so, the better the chances of his friends. "And you are the hope of these jackalsss? You will ressstore their devil-ish empire?"

For his remarks he was rewarded with more painful twisting. If only he had managed to slay the sorcerer . . .

D'Kairn came up to face him. Never had Morgis looked so close into the eyes of a human and read such evil.

"You call us jackals, devils. You are no better than us, dragon. You are a beast parading as a man!" He glanced down at the dead captain. "You will regret every one of the deaths you caused. First you will be tortured to within an inch of your miserable life in every manner prescribed and every manner we can de-vise . . . and then, when you have worn your voice hoarse pleading for mercy . . . I shall skin you alive the way you did my men. Your blood will be the foundation of my power and the losses here will be recouped a thousand times over—"

But Morgis was no longer listening to the other's tirade. "*What* did you sssay?"

Before D'Kairn could answer, one of the men he had sent to hunt for Kalena and Leonin rushed back. "My lord! There's a passage open in one of the walls!"

"So that was how you worked your plan . . ." The keeper pointed at all but one guard. "Take torches! Bring back their heads as proof to me!"

As the Aramites obeyed his order, Morgis struggled to be heard. "You fool! D'Kairn, you'll be sssending them to their deathsss!"

"Against your two friends? Hardly! Your trickery is at an end!"

"There'sss something elssse out there! The thing that ssskinned your men—"

D'Kairn touched the stone, sending pain through the drake. "You and your friends are the ones who skinned my men."

"Go out back! You'll find ssscores of bonesss and even some bodiesss! I thought you resssponsible, but now I sssee I was wrong!"

"Bind his mouth." The keeper turned from his prisoner.

Weakened, Morgis could not keep the lone guard from obeying the order. Muzzled, arms tightly tied, he could only watch and wait.

Despite his previous display of confidence, Keeper D'Kairn paced the floor in clear impatience as the seconds passed. Next to Morgis, the single guard fidgeted, hand constantly stroking the hilt of his sword. Morgis was aware of the fact that if he made one false move, he risked being slain simply due to the Aramite's anxiety.

As for the drake, he also worried about his friends and not because of their pursuers. He should have seen it sooner. D'Kairn had said that he had circled behind Morgis and the others, following instead of being followed. Therefore, the keeper had never had the opportunity to perform his insidious spellwork here. In addition, when D'Kairn had slain Awrak and used the Syrryn's blood to increase his power, he had left the body otherwise intact.

It had not been skinned.

And the more Morgis thought of the scant details of Kalena's story, the more he realized that what had stalked her and her partners had been something else entirely, something that had *long* made its home in the keep and knew all the hidden passages.

Something that had found more than a dozen armed and armored soldiers only a tempting target.

Before, the drake had thought that once Leonin had Kalena, it would be simple for them to lose the wolf raiders. Now, though, they might be running right into the waiting talons of the keep's foul denizen.

With the spell on him, Morgis was all but helpless. D'Kairn had the only potential weapon against whatever ghoulish creature lurked in the ruins, but the sorcerer was too focused on revenge against mortal foes.

D'Kairn kept most of his attention on the doorway to the one back room, no doubt assuming that the guard would be watching the prisoner. However, the guard's gaze also eventually drifted more to the doorway than to his charge. Both Aramites were clearly growing disturbed at the lengthening absence of their cohorts.

Morgis braced himself, waiting for what would undoubtedly be his last chance. They had bound his arms, but, as before, they had left his legs free.

The cloaked keeper paused, completely facing the doorway. Out of the corner of his eye, the drake noted that the guard's attention was fixed on that direction. One hand remained on the sword hilt, but the weapon was still sheathed.

It was the moment for which Morgis had been hoping.

Pushing forward with all his might, he leapt toward D'Kairn's back.

The guard shouted and tried to stop him, but his hand came away empty. Running as hard as he could, the drake lowered his head like a battering ram.

D'Kairn started to turn . . . but too late.

The much larger Morgis barreled into the keeper with such force that D'Kairn went flying. The sorcerer lost his hold on the necklace, which wrapped itself around his neck.

Stumbling on, Morgis made for the doorway.

He heard the guard in hot pursuit. Morgis prayed that the Aramites had done the obvious and left the entrance to the hidden passage open. If not, then he had just signed his own death warrant.

At first, all Morgis could see was darkness. A frustrated hiss escaped him just before he noticed that part of the wall to the left leaned out. Without hesitation, the drake threw himself into the passage.

Almost immediately, he collided with an inner wall. Bouncing off of it, Morgis staggered his way along, certain that the remaining guard was hot on his heels.

The clank of metal assured him of that fact. He swore under his breath. If at least he could free himself, then he could face the Aramite on equal terms. A drake with one good arm was certainly equal to a wolf raider with two.

Now he could hear the soldier's harsh breathing, a sign that the Aramite was gaining rapidly. Morgis knew that he would never make it to the end of the passage and even if he did, it might be to run into the other soldiers. The darkness of the tunnel did give him some advantage, though. The guard would have to almost be right on top of Morgis to see him.

The drake hesitated as a desperate plan suddenly came to mind. On *top* of him?

It was worth the risk. Even with the armor, he outweighed the wolf raider.

Morgis dropped to the floor, rolling immediately onto his back. He braced his legs and tried to ignore the throbbing pain in his shoulder.

A second later, a shadowed form came running toward him. Despite being only a few yards from the drake, the guard still ran at full speed.

Morgis's feet caught the Aramite full in the stomach. The armor prevented the drake from driving the breath from the wolf raider, but that was not what Morgis intended.

The Aramite fell forward.

Rocking back, Morgis used the human's momentum to help him throw the raider over his head. Caught unaware, unable to see well in the dark, the Aramite let out a startled gasp as he tumbled over the drake.

He landed with a hard crash, striking at least one wall before rolling onto the passage floor.

Unwilling to lose his advantage, Morgis quickly rolled over and fell upon the Aramite. He strained at his bonds as he dropped on his foe, but even his prodigious strength did not avail him.

Unfortunately, his adversary was not quite as stunned as Morgis had hoped. The raider grappled with the drake, quickly realizing that the prisoner could not seize him in turn.

But the Aramite failed to recall one basic fact. He faced a dragon in mortal form, but still a creature of legend born with fang.

And although it revolted Morgis greatly, he used what all his magic could never erase.

Opening his mouth wide, the drake sank his sharp teeth into the wolf raider's throat and tore it out.

There were those among his kind who still savored the freshness of blood, the freshness of the kill. Morgis, though, had been raised near Irillian by the Sea, where drakes were almost—but not quite—human. He found no sweetness in the taste, only a nausea, a regret. He was thankful that neither Leonin nor, especially, Kalena could see him now.

The Aramite let out one last gurgle before falling limp. Morgis waited a moment more—then spat out the foul life fluids as quickly as he could. Shame overwhelmed him. It was one thing to meet a foe in combat, but this . . .

Forcing his regrets aside, Morgis felt for the guard's dagger. That found, he worked at his bonds as swiftly as he could. All he needed was a bit of slack, a single piece of cut rope.

There! Morgis felt it give ever so slightly. He cut a bit more, then, dropping the blade, strained. His shoulder ached, demanding he cease, but Morgis refused. A little more . . .

The ropes gave way, tumbling to the floor. Morgis quickly exercised sore muscles, then checked his shoulder. The entire arm felt all but useless.

Nonetheless, he located the guard's sword and headed on, hoping he could yet catch up to Leonin and the cat woman. Morgis had heard nothing so far, which made him hope that clever Leonin and feline Kalena had combined their natural skills to easily evade their pursuers.

The passage wended its down, curving madly. Swearing silently as he ran, Morgis peered ahead for some subtle difference in the darkness that would indicate he had reached the end.

At last, a hint of wind caressed his face. Hissing, Morgis increased his pace. Ahead, a sliver of darkness lighter than that around it beckoned him.

The outer door of the passage had been left ajar, but not enough for the towering drake to slip through. He pushed at the false stone wall, finding it a harder trial than he had expected. Putting his good shoulder to it, Morgis shoved.

The door gave way—and the drake discovered the obstacle that had make his task so difficult.

What was left of a wolf raider lay almost jammed into the false wall. His breastplate had been torn apart as if made of silk and most of his face had been take along with it.

Kneeling close, Morgis could see that the skin had been expertly flayed.

Every muscle in his body taut, the drake surveyed the scene.

More bodies.

They lay scattered about, each in some varying stage of horror. Armor had done nothing for them, nor had their weapons evidently. Some were devoid of almost everything, including their outer flesh. Others looked as if the creature had paused in mid-work, intending to return.

A quick count verified that the entire pursuit party lay before him.

What can kill ssso swiftly? Morgis wondered. *Kill so ssswiftly that I heard no sssound even so near?*

There was no sign of his friends. From the evidence he had seen so far of the monster's work, it would have made more sense for their bodies to lie here among the others. That meant that they still might be alive.

But where?

Crippling pain sent him crashing among the corpses, the sword flying from his hand. He did not have to see behind him to know the cause.

"This is what it means not to have the order, the control, perpetuated by the empire!" D'Kairn's voice had an edge to it that Morgis had never heard before. The keeper sounded strained. "You curse us, call us *fiends*, but I see before me a thing more monstrous than anything we are accused of!"

Morgis could have argued that point quite well, having witnessed the atrocities performed by the Aramites in the name of their savage god, but another flash of bone-numbing pain coursed through him, preventing him from thinking at all, much less disagreeing with the sorcerer.

"This is not a triumph for you and your friends," D'Kairn continued, his voice nearer now. "These men have but sacrificed for the cause. I will still bear my research to others like me and we shall combine our efforts. We *will* bring this continent in line again!"

"If they are all asss you," the drake finally managed. "Then your empire isss dead and buried, keeper! A leader who sendsss all hisss men to their deathsss ssso carelessly does not ssstir much confidence in thossse others he would think to command!"

"Insolent lizard!"

The pain nearly crushed Morgis into the earth. How strong was D'Kairn's stone? Surely all this spellwork had to be draining it? The keeper had not had any chance to draw more from the dead.

As if reading his foe's thoughts, D'Kairn said, "I will drain every bit of life

force from your blood, track down your friends, and do the same to them . . .
after they have tasted what my wrath shall make of the power you grant me."

"Aren't you forgetting ssssomething? Your patternsss?"

Now the keeper's voice came from right beside Morgis. "There will be some
necessary loss, but you are a dragon, after all. However much is lost, there shall
be more than enough to satisfy me . . . you have my word on that."

You are a dragon, after all. . . . Yet here he was, face in the dirt, about to be
slain by a lone Aramite. A pitiful end. He could not even raise a finger to
help himself.

"D'Kairn . . . I am not resssponsssible for the deaths of mossst of your
men . . . there isss a creature loose in thisss ancient place—"

"Spare me your pathetic drivel. I—"

But whatever the keeper sought to say ended in a horrified gurgle. Something
clattered next to Morgis and the pain D'Kairn had inflicted on him vanished.
Movement was once more his.

Immediately he rolled away from the direction of the keeper, only to land
atop yet another flayed body. The same musky scent that he had noticed emanating from the Gnor filled his nostrils. He instinctively pushed away from the
slim corpse, certain that whatever fate had befallen D'Kairn would strike next
at him.

Only—neither the keeper nor whatever had attacked the him were anywhere
to be seen.

No! Something moved toward the ruins. A shape. That was all Morgis could
make of it. It vanished into the passage with an incredible swiftness.

Morgis tried to transform, but nothing happened. Despite the fact that
D'Kairn was no more, the spell remained active. Morgis looked around for the
necklace and the stone, but could not find them. Whatever had taken the keeper
had taken the talisman as well.

As he retrieved his sword from near the slim corpse, he noticed for the first
time that the body was feminine. At first he feared that he had found Kalena,
but then he noticed that the body had lain there for some time, for it was dry to
the touch, not moist and fresh like those of the slain Aramites.

But how much longer did Kalena and Leonin have? The wolf raiders were all
dead, which mean that the only victims remaining for the monster were Morgis,
his partner, and the cat woman.

Eyes narrowed, the drake hurried toward the ruins, hoping he would not be
too late to save the others and yet not at all certain he was not simply adding
himself to the rapidly-growing list of its victims.

VII

MORGIS DID NOT follow the beast into the passage, as it might have expected. Instead, he circled the keep, each step taken with a wariness he had not felt since the height of the war. Of his friends or his quarry he saw no sign. He still clung to the hope that he would find the former alive and well, but with each passing breath that hope sank more and more.

As he neared the entrance, the drake saw that the fire still burned within the building. However, Morgis did not take that as an invitation to enter freely. He also heard the anxious sounds of the horses and wondered why the monster had not taken them already. Bait, perhaps.

Trying to be ready for anything, the drake entered.

"Morgis!"

The hooded figure leapt up from its position near the fire and raced toward him. He hesitated for a moment until he saw Kalena's face under the vast hood.

She threw herself against his chest, her hands pressed close to his heart. The discomfort caused by her closeness was negated by his relief at finding her alive.

"I was afraid you'd run off or been killed!" She ran her fingers over his chest. "Are you cut?"

"My shoulder is dislocated, but there are no outer woundsss."

"No cuts," she murmured, planting her hooded head against him again. "That's good."

He gently pushed her back and asked, "Where isss Leonin?"

She looked behind her. "You only just missed him. He said he was going to search for you."

The drake hissed. "The passssage?"

"Yes, but—"

"Damn!!" Morgis felt like he was trapped in a maze, constantly running around the same places as he tried in vain to reach a conclusion. "Come! We may be in time yet!"

With effort, he moved the injured arm and seized a torch. Keeping Kalena behind him, he led the way through the back room and into the narrow corridor hidden within.

The passage was as silent as the grave, not an auspicious sign. Morgis wanted to shout to Leonin, but knew that would only alert their unholy adversary to their approaching presence.

They passed the body of the guard Morgis had killed. Although much of the blood had dried, a few moist drops still glittered in the torchlight. The drake tried to shield Kalena from the truth, but her feline eyes saw quickly how the man had perished.

"I am . . . sssorry," he murmured.

"It had to be done, I suppose." She looked slightly disappointed, but the expression vanished as she eyed him. "With so many so quickly it couldn't be avoided." She reached up and caressed his cheek. "It's forgotten."

He wanted to hold her hand there, but instead turned away. "Leonin needsss usss . . ."

Deeper and deeper they descended. Morgis frowned. Soon they would be at the end of the passage and still he had found no trace of his partner. Did the bearded fighter even now wander around the keep, intending to return by the entrance just as the drake had? What *folly* in the face of horror . . .

Then, bits of dark moisture on the floor caught his attention. He knelt down, using the torch to study them.

"What is it?" Kalena asked, leaning over his shoulder.

"More blood." He almost dismissed it, having seen so much already, but then noticed how it left a trail that started from in the wall on his left and headed further ahead down the passage.

Morgis jumped to his feet, holding the torch high and peering as far ahead as he could. The trail of moist, crimson drops led his gaze on . . .

Another body lay slumped in the narrow corridor.

Forgetting Kalena for the moment, Morgis hurried to the second form. None of the other soldiers had died in the passage, which meant that the body ahead could be only one of two missing men.

And but a moment later, Morgis's torch revealed a corpse too short and slim to be the remains of Keeper D'Kairn.

Leonin.

Drying blood gave the body a speckled appearance. Morgis set down his sword and gently touched what was left of his companion. For all the faults of both Leonin and Awrak, they had done their tasks well and had never abandoned a comrade.

The drake hissed savagely. He looked past the corpse, but saw only more moist droplets. The fiendish beast had made good its escape.

Suddenly, Morgis frowned. Continually he thought of it as a beast, a monster. It was both, but it was also highly intelligent. Not only did it know how to hide from its prey, but Morgis believed that only an intelligent killer would ever dream of skinning its victims. He thought back to what Kalena had told him of her discoveries and tried to connect that with everything that had happened.

Surveying the scene, something else occurred to him. He looked at Leonin's grisly form and recalled all the other victims he had come across. His fist clenched tight, but he tried to hide it from the cat woman.

"Ssso . . ."

"I'm so sorry, Morgis . . . too late again." Kalena, cloak shielding her body, shut her eyes for a moment. "He was a strong, good fighter."

"And it availed him nothing." Retrieving the blade and rising, he glanced behind them. "Come! There's sssomething I want to sssee."

"What, Morgis?"

"I would rather not explain now sssince I am not certain what it meansss." The drake put his sword arm around Kalena. "I want you to ssstay bessside me at all timesss. Do not fall behind me, underssstood?"

Her expression indicated that she did not understand, at least not entirely, but she nodded.

The trail of blood still shone bright under the light of the torch as they followed it back. A few smears here and there testified to where Morgis had been unable to avoid stepping in some of the dark fluid.

When they reached the area where he had first discovered the trail, Morgis eyed the stone wall. He tapped it twice with the flat of the blade, then saw that for which he had been searching.

"Kalena, I will ssstand ready with the sword and torch, but I want you to touch that area up on the left. That jutting piece there."

She carefully stepped up to the wall and did as he requested. Nothing happened.

"Harder, pleassse."

The cat woman repeated her effort.

The wall suddenly slid open like a door. Kalena jumped back.

But Morgis was there to guide her forward with his sword arm. "It isss all right, Kalena. The danger is not within."

Together they stepped inside. Flickering light suddenly danced about the room and more than a dozen pairs of staring figures stood waiting for the newcomers.

Morgis and Kalena reflected in mirrors.

Most were full-length, but some hung on walls. The majority had cracks. They had once been masterfully-crafted and expensive pieces, for the drake recognized gold and silver in the frames and even several with jewels.

And behind the array of mirrors, set against the walls of this hidden chamber, were several high, wide, and sturdy antique cabinets of the type designed for clothes.

Again, Morgis recalled what he had been told about Kalena's horrific find.

"It displaysss itsssself here," he muttered, drawing the cat woman along with him. Morgis positioned the two of them before the most elegant of the

mirrors, a high, gilded pane with genuine diamonds inset along the surrounding edge. "Thisss would be itsss favorite, I think, where it preensss itssself in its
new coveringsss."

In the mirror, Kalena's eyes were wide and unblinking. She stepped from the
drake's grasp and in fascination touched the glass. "Each flayed with perfection,
not the slightest harsh cut to the skin. That would have ruined the effect . . ."

"And whenever it wasss finished, it placed its prize in one of the cabinetsss,
including one that it kept upsssstairs, although *why* it left those where they could
be so easily discovered—"

"Those are the favorites," the cat woman whispered. "The best ones." She
touched her cheek, watching her reflection mimic her. "The ones without blem-
ish, the ones young and full of life . . ."

Morgis glanced at the darkened cabinets. "Of course. Ssso simple. Alwaysss
keep the favoritesss more handy . . . until it became evident that they were
risked upsssstairs."

He stepped toward the nearest of the closets and with the tip of his sword
prodded it open.

Hanging from hooks were seven skins so perfectly taken that Morgis could
almost imagine himself being able to put one on. Humans, elves, another
Syrryn, some canine-looking creature . . . the drake suspected that the variety he
would find if he opened all of the closets would stagger him. Then he noticed
that one looked slightly less than perfect at the edges and something else occurred to him.

"They don't lassst. Eventually, they decompossse, but it can preserve them for
a time." He sniffed. "And whatever it pressserves it with smellsss like musssk."

When Kalena did not answer him, Morgis turned to find her still staring
into the mirror. Closing the cabinet again, the drake returned to his companion.

"One more thing. It took me a moment to find it, but I've ssspotted the late
and unlamented D'Kairn's body over in the corner, behind the first mirrors.
Not quite finished with it—were you?"

He thrust the torch into the cat woman's voluminous cloak.

The cloth garment burst into flames. Kalena opened her mouth, but out
of it came no mortal scream of fear and agony. Instead, a monstrous keening,
an angry sound, shook the chamber and sent even Morgis back a few steps in
astonishment.

"My pretty one!" the cat woman's mouth said, moving irregularly. "My
pretty one!"

The fiery cloak opened up—and beneath the charring flesh that had once
housed Kalena, a spider-black form moved in a manner not possible for any
normal, living creature, with multi-jointed limbs that seemed everywhere.

Already most of the skin below the head had caught fire, but that did not appear to physically bother the horrid form beneath. It stalked toward the drake, growing taller and wider as it neared. Halfway to Morgis, it already looked down on him.

The twisted face of Kalena smiled at the drake. "My pretty one is gone, so my best one I will wear . . . a *dragon's* skin, a rare thing here! I have never been a dragon before!"

"I will keep my own ssskin, thank you . . ." Morgis slashed with the blade, but the creature looked unimpressed by the threat, so he waved the torch instead. Unfortunately, the pain in his shoulder nearly made him drop it.

The cat woman's expression changed to a frown. "Be careful! You might scar it more! I've been very careful, sacrificing all those lesser but pretty skins so they wouldn't interfere . . . and so I could keep yours so clean, so unmarred . . ."

The thing had purposely saved Morgis for last, literally trying to protect his scaled hide from the Aramites so it could later claim the skin for itself. It had acted as protector, using Kalena's feminine form to put both Morgis and the others off their guard. Even when D'Kairn had thought Kalena responsible for the deaths of the sentries, he had still seen her as more of a nuisance than a danger, using her as bait rather than slaying her when he finally had the chance.

"I will be most cautious when I remove it, I promise you," the macabre horror remarked cheerfully, its voice growing higher-pitched as the last vestiges of the cat woman burned away.

From what remained of the cloak emerged four long, razor-edged appendages. Each curved blade had a fine point, perfect for precision cutting. They were made of something that to the drake resembled dark bone or shell and moved with such swiftness that they were little more than blurs.

He had no doubt that they would cut through even his tough, scaly hide with ease.

Morgis cursed. He had expected the fire to deal with the threat. The false Kalena had not suspected that he had discovered the truth, discovered the horrific lies.

For supposedly the most vulnerable of all of them, the cat woman had survived quite well. Even that would have not been enough, but in the end, the fake Kalena had made one misjudgment. Leonin had not perished quite so recently as it had looked. The blood had been drier than that on the floor. Based on that, he had died at least before D'Kairn, whose blood trail it had been that Morgis had mistaken at first for his partner's. Yet, the cat woman had said that Leonin had just departed. Instead, his corpse had been dragged back to the passage.

All so that the monster could take Morgis when it thought it could do the least damage to the skin it so coveted.

Her reaction to the mirrors had but verified his suspicions, not that the knowledge did him any good now. Trapped, unable to transform, he had as good as given himself up to be flayed.

Like lightning bolts, the dark blades flashed back and forth. Below them, a pair of oddly-feminine human hands opened and closed eagerly. The monster would have had him already if not for the mirrors. It did not want to break the mirrors. It lived for gazing into them once it wore one of its stolen hides. Morgis watched as it moved gingerly past one, going out of its way when it could have tried to reach him.

More and more it resembled some upright combination of a skeletal arachnid and praying mantis, but with hints of human still in it. That it had probably once been human or of some similar race did not surprise him, not with the vanity it radiated.

He stumbled over something on the floor, nearly losing his footing. Immediately, one of the blades darted out to take his head, perhaps even pierce his skull and brain so as to minimize the damage to the skin. The drake barely deflected the attack as he fought to right himself. He crashed against one of the cabinets, which brought a furious keening from the demonic figure.

Smiling grimly, Morgis twisted around and brought the flames to the wooden piece.

The fire eagerly devoured the antique cabinet. The fragmenting visage of Kalena contorted further and the keening became a wail.

"My skins! My beautiful, wonderful skins!"

Almost unmindful of its prey, the creature moved toward the cabinet. Morgis leapt to the side, letting it focus on the piece. He glanced at the entrance, wondering if he could make it before the monster noticed.

But as he moved, another swordlike appendage shot to the side, almost skewering the drake. Morgis ducked back, trapped in the far portion of the secret chamber.

Kalena's mouth widened, widened further . . . then ripped apart. An ebony skull with strands of gray hair still attached to the scalp materialized as the burnt tatters fell away. The mouth opened to impossible dimensions.

A gray, viscous substance spewed from the mouth, washing over the burning cabinet. Wherever it touched, the thick liquid instantly doused the fire. A heavy, musky smell arose.

With rising fury, the monster whirled on the drake.

He did the only thing he could think of, setting another cabinet afire, then doing the same to a third. As the scuttling horror moved to douse them, he tried once more to reach freedom, only to be cut off by a pair of lethal limbs, one of which slashed at the arm that held the torch.

The torch fell, rolling away but causing scant damage on the stone floor. Morgis hissed. Evidently his monstrous foe had reached the point where it considered a little damage to his scaled hide a necessity.

"Nasty dragon!" it hissed in turn, the second closet already covered in the gray, preserving soup it likely also used to keep the skins fresh longer. "The wolf soldiers, they made it so hard for so long to gather good skins, always marching past and scaring off others, but when they stopped coming, others returned! So large and joyous my collection became! So much better than the dresses I once kept, the faces I once wore when mine grew old!" The eyes, which had become black pits, again studied Morgis covetously. "But you'll make up for it, yes, you will . . ."

Morgis rolled away again as the blades came down. One caught his injured shoulder, making him cry out. Again, the only thing that saved him was the creature's desire not to damage its surroundings. This was the one place it could not attack to its full potential.

Which did Morgis little good otherwise. Sooner or later, unless he escaped, the thing would corner him—and if he did escape it would have an even easier time of hunting him down outside.

Somehow he had to destroy it here.

As it moved in on him again, the drake snagged one of the elaborate mirrors and twisted the piece so that it faced its monstrous owner. The skeletal creature gasped and backed up. As Morgis had guessed, it cared little for its own horrible reflection.

He tried to take advantage of the distraction, but pain made him instead stumble to the side—where his feet became tangled in the limp form of the late, unlamented D'Kairn.

A single sharp hole half an inch wide had been made in the keeper's helmet—and skull. Despite the fact that part of the skin around the face had already been expertly peeled back, Morgis could still make out the Aramite's expression, a combination of arrogance and confusion. D'Kairn had never quite realized he was dying, the victim of a thing of sorcery even darker than his own.

The creature had missed a chance by not taking the drake immediately after, but Morgis had already determined that its judgment was based on its ancient vanities and its desire for the perfection of its skins. Trying to slay Morgis on the harsh landscape would have not only ruined D'Kairn's hide—clearly also a favorite—but risked damaging the dragon's.

You should have listened, keeper! If you'd turned a moment sooner, you could have used that foul trinket of yours and maybe saved us both! Of course, then D'Kairn would have killed *him.*

Thinking of the Aramite's stone, Morgis quickly searched the body. At first he could not find the amulet, but then realized it was buried under the head. He seized the chain—

Instinct made him move his head just before the razor tip of a blade would have caught him at the base of the neck. Instead, the monstrous appendage buried itself in the dead keeper's throat.

"More cuts! More damage!" The black horror howled at him. "No more!"

Morgis moved too slow. Another blade sank into his dislocated shoulder. He screamed as the creature lifted him up by the wound.

The macabre faced filled his view.

"A cloak . . . a small covering . . . that's all that's needed," it babbled gleefully. "Still a very, very precious skin! I will walk well with it, walk long with it!" It chortled. "I may even *fly* with it!"

As it had done with Kalena, the monster would take on the properties of the one whose identity it had stolen, make use of their abilities. Whether it could actually do what Morgis could not do—revert to a true dragon form—he could not say, but that would hardly matter to the drake once he was dead.

The blades drew nearer.

"Must be careful . . ." it murmured clinically, eyeing his head. "Must be precise, always precise . . ."

Morgis swung his good arm up, shoving D'Kairn's stone into the unholy face.

Nothing happened.

His grotesque captor laughed at his antics and one pointed blade went up to brush aside the hand obscuring its view.

Dropping the amulet, Morgis quickly seized the appendage, twisted it around, and, with a force no human could muster—*shoved* it into the monster's throat.

A gagging hiss escaped the creature as it struggled to remove the limb. Thick, dark red ichor escaped from the edges of the wound.

It convulsed. Morgis suddenly found himself slipping free without any hope of grabbing some other support.

The stone had only been a decoy. He had understood just enough of the Aramite's sorcery to know he would not be able to figure out how to use the talisman in time. However, it had drawn the creature's attention and elicited the overconfident reaction he had needed.

And there and then Morgis had used the only weapon he suspected could readily pierce the hard hide of the monster—the thing's own bladelike appendages.

He hit the floor hard and was at first unable to move. Fortunately, surprise and his inhuman strength had enabled him to shove the appendage in so deep that a good portion of it also thrust out of the back of the neck, leaving him the least of the creature's concerns.

A slight gleam shook him from his stupor. He blinked. The keeper's stone. Morgis seized it—only to have it break into several pieces. The drop had cracked it open, ruining it. Worse, despite its destruction, the drake could still sense that D'Kairn's treacherous spell remained intact.

A hacking sound reminded him that his ability to transform would be a nil point if he did not move fast. Morgis dragged himself forward, expecting each moment to be skewered.

He reached the area of the mirrors and glanced in one. Behind him he saw the monster—now turned away from him—still struggling, the floor around it covered with its foul fluids. The remaining limbs sought to pull the one free and looked to be finally managing some success.

Knowing he could not allow that, Morgis pushed himself up. He braced himself as best he could, watched the creature's back—and then leapt.

Weakness made his jump less than what he had hoped, but momentum was on his side. With a mass almost twice that of most beings his size, the drake struck the hellish beast.

They fell forward.

The skin walker hit the floor face down, driving the blade all the way through. It convulsed again, throwing Morgis aside, Choking harshly, the monster rolled to the side, colliding with one of the standing mirrors. The mirror tipped over, hitting a second . . . which in turn hit a third.

Glass shattered everywhere. Morgis collapsed against a cabinet.

A silence settled over the chamber.

When at last the battered drake could move, he saw by the light of the fallen torch that the monster lay dead. Driving the blade completely through had sealed its fate.

Its own mad desires had led to its destruction. Had it simply slain him early on instead of putting so much value in the pristine quality of his scaled skin, Morgis knew that his face would be hanging in a cabinet even now.

And that thought settled for him what he needed to do next.

DRAGON FLAME WOULD have made the keep burn well, but dragon flame was beyond him. He found what kindling and oil he could and, though it took him a full day, dragged everything—and every body—to the chamber of mirrors. Then, using a fresh torch, Morgis lit the huge bonfire.

He waited and waited while it burned, leaving the door open so that lack of air would not smother it. A being of flame, the smoke did not bother him as much as it would have most other races. That enabled the drake to make certain that *everything* was destroyed.

And while he watched, he pictured those who had died, especially one in particular. Likely that had indeed been her body that he had found near that of the Gnor. Had she done as the creature had described? Had Kalena run, praying that she would escape—and failing in the end?

Morgis still did not know the origin of the keep's cursed resident, but he could guess some of it. Vanity, obsession, and yet, some strange lack of self identity. The drake really did not care. What mattered was that the evil was dead and would no longer make a mockery of its victims' lives.

When it was done, Morgis closed the hidden chamber. He would have sealed the room or, better yet, razed the ruins to the ground if his powers had been his, but so long as D'Kairn's spell held, hiding the secrets so was all he could do.

The animals were still waiting for him, both those of his party and the Aramites' own dark steeds. He still found it interesting that the monstrosity had let them live, but of course they were harmless and could have been slain at any time later once they were no longer useful as bait.

That . . . and their skins had been worth nothing to it.

Injured as he was, Morgis could not control the small herd. He released all but four of the animals into the wild, keeping his, those of his comrades, and the one he was certain had been ridden by D'Kairn. Both D'Kairn and the captain had carried documents with them that hinted of other enclaves of Aramite resistance. The Master Guardians would appreciate those papers. They would also see to the honoring of Awrak and Leonin, fallen warriors in the struggle to free the lands. Likely the Guardians would also have the wherewithal to remove the spell on him—at least, so he hoped.

Of the keeper's research into blood sorcery, Morgis made certain that every shred had burned with the bodies.

The day had nearly vanished by the time he rode off, the ever-present cloud cover promising an early darkness. Perhaps it might have been more prudent to stay one more night in the now-safe keep, but the drake wanted to be far away from the place.

And as he rode off, his memories drifted to a time when *he* had wanted to wear another's skin, when *he* had wished he could have been the right one. A beautiful, feline face that he had pictured many times before formed in his mind, but this time another face, also beautiful and feline, overlapped it, blurring both.

Unable to separate them, Morgis finally dismissed both, concentrating instead on the present. There was still a war on and he had a part to play. There were foes to fight and lands to explore. Tomorrow he might find himself doing battle with an Aramite patrol or hunting another sorcerer . . .

Anything to keep him from ever again wishing to walk in someone else's skin.

ABOUT THE AUTHOR

Richard A. Knaak is a *New York Times* and *USA Today* bestselling author of over forty novels and numerous short stories, including works in such series as Warcraft, Diablo, Dragonlance, Age of Conan, and his own Dragonrealm. He has scripted a number of Warcraft manga with Tokyopop, including the top-selling Sunwell trilogy, and has also written background material for games. His works have been published worldwide in many languages.

In addition to this second volume of *Legends of the Dragonrealm*, recent releases include the bestselling World of Warcraft hardcover, *Stormrage*, *The Gargoyle King*—the third in his Ogre Titans trilogy for Dragonlance—and the Shadow Wing saga and Mage standalone for the World of Warcraft manga series. He is presently at work on several other projects.

Currently splitting his time between Chicago and Arkansas, he can be reached through his website: www.RichardAKnaak.com. While he is unable to respond to every email, he does read them. Join his mailing list for e-announcements of upcoming releases and appearances.